# HIGHGATE

# HIGHGATE

## THE LAST KNIGHT OF ST. JOHN

A NOVEL

Stephen Edward Paper

For my brothers, Richard and Thomas Paper, my mother Bernice and my father Charles, who had nightmares after reading the first draft.

# ACKNOWLEDGEMENTS

I would like to thank all the people who helped and encouraged me with the ideas and writing of Highgate: Matt Adler, Lewis Anten, Rajeev Datt, Wes Cookler, Chris Finnegan, Dahlia Greer, Rob Raymond, Ricki Sawyer, Cary Schwartz, Shahar Stroh and especially Nicholas Blurton-Jones and Steve Sobel, who with some very insightful ideas, helped me turn the book in a better direction; and Ann Fisher and Gerald Paul Lewis who helped with the editing, and Muzammil Waheed for the map design.

Many thanks to Chaslyn Solomon for the cover design and Dahlia Greer for the cover concept.

Please visit my website at www.stephenedwardpaper.com.

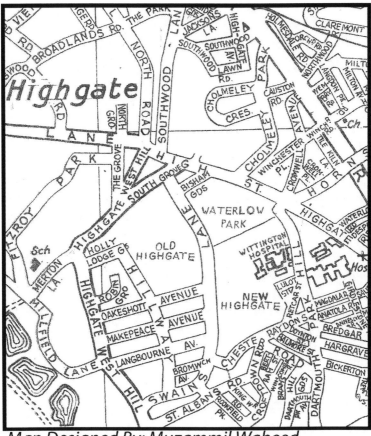

Map Designed By: Muzammil Waheed

PROLOGUE

# AHNENERBE

W hy had they summoned her? A faint, grim smile flitted across the leathery face of the Gypsy. What good were her so-called powers if she could not even divine the answer to this one question? Sniffing the cool air, Madame Dashevski studied the gray mountains in the distance, as if they might provide a clue. It was most troubling.

Sullen clouds darkened the skies to the east, casting shadows over the coffin-shaped wagons, with their roughly hewn wooden wheels and dull cloth coverings. A storm was in the offing.

Fields through which they passed looked singularly quiet and desolate, more remarkable for what they lacked: birds or flowers or signs of human habitation. She knew there must be people living in the vicinity, but where were they? It was as though the Germans had cleared a path for her of every sentient being. Yellowing grasses and the brown dying remnants of vegetation spread out over the valley as far as she could see. The rutted dirt path itself was untended and barren—impassable if the rain started. It was all unlike anything Madame Dashevski had ever seen, and invoked in her a feeling of dread.

Though a good many hours on their sojourn, the jagged peaks of the *Paderborner Hochfläche* seemed no closer than they had at first light. Looming like giant sentinels over the lonely plains of the Alme

Valley, they seemed to overwhelm the slow moving Gypsy wagons. But the mountains were nearer and this strange meeting was becoming that much more imminent.

Pulling hard on the reins, the old lady stopped her roan colored pair and stiffly climbed down from the buckboard. Fetching a boy, together they held buckets of water for the thirsty beasts, and patted their sweat soaked necks. The slow ascent toward the hill country was wearing, but there was the summons and it could not be ignored. The look of uneasiness remained on Madame Dashevski's withered features as she clambered back aboard the wagon.

Much later, as the first drops of rain began to fall, Madame Dashevski caught sight of the odd triangular shape and massive gray walls of Wewelsburg Castle, high on a sheer limestone rock southwest of the city of Paderborn. Evening was approaching by the time the path joined a paved black road turning away from the darkening valley and starting upward.

The ancient Gypsy woman was in the first of five horse-drawn carts now slowly wending their way along a narrow mountain switchback, one of many. From the moment they started up the steep road, which had many years ago been forcefully rent out of the limestone, and had originally been no more than a two-foot wide shepherd's path, the castle was lost from sight.

It could only be for a reading. They must have questions to ask her, but of what? Would she be helping them? Did these men not hate her own people? Should she avail herself to men she knew to be evil? Could she resist them if need be? There were so many uncertainties.

To the northwest, Madame Dashevski could see the shadowy dark green edges of the Teutoburg Forest. Almost two millennia ago, Germanic tribes had surprised and routed three of Quinctilius Varus's Legions, in one of the worst disasters in Roman history. Three whole Legions decimated, almost to the man, with the few survivors tortured to death or sold into slavery.

Now other Germans, Nazis, had alarmed her with their entreaty. Should the fingers of some dead Roman warrior pierce the ground and grasp upward at her, she could feel no less disconcerted.

The team of two horses trotted heavily, their breathing labored.

Alongside them walked the boy, reins in hand, whipping at them unmercifully, and swearing at them as they strained to pull the heavy cart. The ascent seemed almost vertical, and the horses were becoming more restless with each step. Suddenly the darker mare stopped, refusing to move another foot. Her mate neighed and reared. The boy saw fear in their eyes, but pulled at the reins, cursing loudly and lashing them more fiercely yet, until the pain from the bullwhip outweighed their terror, and the disconsolate beasts resumed the arduous climb.

Madame Dashevski started to hear the voices at a very young age, now some seventy years past, and, over all that time, she had what she considered, a remarkable inability to see into her own future. Those same voices warned her time and again not to try: it would not accrue to her any benefit. Furthermore, she was informed that it was impossible to change the future, and once a divination was given, it would most definitely fall true—it was only a question of the span of time in which the prophesy came to pass. Many times she wanted to renounce the powers, but it was her gift and she had been taught to believe it was a sin to forswear such a gift. And of course, she was human, and found it an impossibility to abandon her innate curiosity about the future. That morning she finally gave into temptation for the lone time in those seventy years, trying to outmaneuver the voices and thus gaze upon her own fate. Reasoning that it was intertwined with that of her tribe, she had looked into the hands of the tribal patriarch to see what would befall him at the behest of these new Germans.

The old man had his own superstitions: he would not bid the voices welcome in his tent. Two wooden barrels, one for each of them, were set up a small distance from the camp. He lit sticks of incense and with the same cinder lit his pipe. Sitting on the barrel he put out his hands.

Evil, horrendous images forced their way into her mind's eye quickly, almost as soon as she had taken his hands in hers. She saw visions of great howling black mastiffs, villages burning, smoldering ruins, buildings turned to rubble, men viciously tortured, women raped and children put to the sword. The intensity of the suffering bore down heavily upon her—sorrow so overwhelming, that she broke into tears while still in the trance. Her every attempt to drive these appalling sights away met with failure: they had only grown in intensity. A quavering, mournful voice spoke to her from the trance. "There is a great evil upon the land," it cried. "Those who were ignominiously damned and chastened so long ago, will once more seek to arise, throwing off their fetters and gleaning their sustenance from these new barbarians. Even as the great disquiet of man's inhumanity to man wakens this ancient evil, a new human conflagration has begun and renders unto it strength. The process has already begun. *There are three, and for humankind's salvation, they must remain forever unknown, forever separated!*" With a feeling of utter revulsion and helplessness, she dropped the patriarch's shrunken hands and emerged from the nightmarish vision.

An ancient evil? Brought back to life? What was this? And what meaning did the vision hold for her own people? Or for her visit to the castle? She had not recognized any person or place. A great evil? It was early May 1939. Madame Dashevski knew what kind of men these Germans were, and she knew she could not neglect their call. So, for the first time in her life, Madame Dashevski would see if she could change that future. If necessary, she would disobey every benevolent instruction that had been given her throughout the course of a long life. Perhaps she could alter the revelation if need be. There must be a way.

The rain pelted down fiercely as the wagons crested the last incline and Madame Dashevski saw the castle, set far back on a wooded field. A cool wind rushed its way through the pines, and caused the old crone to grab her sleeves and pull them tightly to her body.

Teams of workman—soldiers sweating in their uniforms—arduously dug in various places on the grounds outside the castle walls. The whole area was a warren of sinks, abrupt ridges, subterranean caverns and underground streams. In every direction she looked, she could see these uniformed men, and it gave her a premonition that they were digging graves for her and her people. But what was also strange, was that there were no peasants laboring, only soldiers. This must be a highly secret place.

As her wagon approached the castle's entrance, two guards, resplendent in black uniforms, with silver SS bars on their collars, death heads insignias emblazoned to the left side of their helmets, and submachine guns strapped over their shoulders, waved her wagon in, as though it was simply a matter of course. Although their expressions showed a degree of condescension at best, she was relieved. This was good. They were expecting her. They wanted to see her.

But soon after she passed through the heavy metal gate, the very next wagon was stopped and made to turn aside. All four remaining wagons were thus turned away and ordered to make camp on a flat, grassy piece of ground, some two acres in size.

Inside the castle walls she saw two large, black Mercedes sedans, one bearing the flag of a *Riechfuhrer* on a thin pole extending upward from the left front bumper of the automobile. A boyish-looking SS officer stepped up to the wagon and bowed.

"Heinrich Eber at your service, Madam," he said with the slightest hint of officiousness as he offered his hand. The *Obersturmbannfuhrer*, who greeted her in Romanian, her own tongue, helped her down from the wagon and motioned for her to follow. Madame Dashevski deferentially, but stiffly walked over the cobblestone steps to the entrance of the main tower.

The design of the castle's three towers was based on an isosceles triangle and built in the 16th Century by Prince Bishop Dietrich von Furstenburg, over an earlier 11th Century fortress used for defense against the Huns, and over yet another earlier stronghold from 930 A.D. Now, Nazi banners, with the swastika and the iron cross, were hung with precise conformity and distance throughout the inside of the gray stone walls. A large black flag, with the SS emblazoned in white, flew from the main tower. *Riechfuhrer* Himmler rented the castle in 1934 from the District of Buren for the symbolic fee of one Riechsmark per annum, to use as the headquarters of the *Ahnenerbe*, the Ancestral Heritage Society, which, among other esoteric tasks, sought to prove that the lost city of Atlantis was the original home of the pure Aryan race. Wewelsburg was Heinrich Himmler's personal domain.

The SS officer led her up three flights of stairs, until they were stopped before a great oak-paneled entrance, guarded by two more SS soldiers who pulled open two heavy doors and stepped aside for them to enter. A strong odor of frankincense and sandalwood emanated from the room, which was perfectly circular and lit by candle. In the center was a perfectly round table, much as King Arthur's knights might have gathered around. In her earlier vision, she had seen knights that she had guessed to be Teutonic. But around this table, some eight uniformed SS officers, including Himmler, milled about. A few others, in civilian clothing, were also in attendance.

There were white, purple and black candles on the table: three in the center, and the rest spread evenly about the table, eighteen in all. Divisible by three. It would be a séance. They had prepared themselves.

This was not good. A séance! For German Ministers and soldiers. What spirits would come to advise these men? Did they have such beliefs? Her attention was now drawn to the candles. There were black candles. A séance was much different from a reading. She would have much less control in a séance.

The soldiers and civilians were cavorting, joking with each other, conversing. They were eager in their demeanor, not nervous: quite unlike most people awaiting a séance.

She was led across the dark green and gray-bordered tiles covering the floor, each tile inlaid with its own unique symbol. There was a massive black flag with a red, black and white swastika hanging down from the domed ceiling.

"I will translate, Madam," said the young officer who had accompanied her from the wagon, as he pulled out the chair for her to sit.

The shriveled, bent-over woman took her place and waved her hand in a polite gesture of refusal. "*Nein.*" She was well acquainted with the language of the conqueror.

The other officers slowly took their respective seats at the table, nine in all, counting her. All others left the room.

The *Obersturmbannfuhrer* leaned over and spoke in German. "Please tell us if we have everything right. You are the master here. We are the pupils. You know how this is to be done."

"Only the candles," she replied in a raspy voice. "The black ones must go...they invite the evil." She was certain she noticed a wry smile come over the soft, porcine features of the *Riechfuhrer*. "All else is correct."

Eber hurriedly removed the black candles and then counted the rest making certain the number remained divisible by three.

"Who is it that you wish to contact?" Madam Dashevski asked.

"Arminius," *Obersturmbannfuhrer* Eber replied, a cynical expression on his lips. "Only him."

Arminius was the chief of the German Cherusci, and also a Roman citizen, who used his position to betray Varus's Legions.

Madam Dashevski looked about the room and slowly intoned, "All join hands and close your eyes." She allowed a few seconds for the officers to follow her bidding, then closed her own eyes and offered a prayer in earnest. "We ask the divine presence to watch over our proceeding, and protect us in all that we do."

The Gypsy once more surveyed the Germans. A thought that she should flee this place passed swiftly through her mind. "I ask all those sitting at the table to breathe in slowly through your nose, and exhale slowly out of your mouth." She listened for the sound of their breathing. "You must keep your minds blank," she advised.

The room was silent and dark. The powerful Germans obeyed her directions with an unexpected alacrity.

"Our beloved Arminius, we ask that you commune with us and move among us," the Gypsy woman began to softly chant. "Our beloved Arminius, we ask that you commune with us and move among us. Our beloved Arminius, we ask that you commune with us and move among us." She paused, then started the chant again, always in series of three. She would continue the chant until something happened: a sudden decrease in room temperature, a rapping sound, or possibly a slight ache in the same area of her body where the spirit had been wounded. Arminius was hacked to death in battle.

"Our beloved Arminius, we ask that you commune with us and move among us." Repeating this twice more, she paused, then began anew.

Some long minutes had passed, when an image of a man came into her mind's eye. "Are you Arminius?" she asked. The semblance appeared to be from a later era than that of the Cherusci. Now Madam Dashevski's voice became stronger as she commanded of the spirit, "Please rap once on the table if you are Arminius."

She could feel the tension in the hands of the officers that clenched her own. There was no rapping.

Again, in her mind's eye she saw a vision, this time a dark cave, with strange markings and images of gargoyles. Three names manifested themselves as though in a whisper. A voice, seemingly benign, bid her give these names and the locations of their final resting-places to the Germans. But she was confused. Something was wrong. Madame Dashevski sensed something dark, hidden, within its tone. Long minutes passed as the voice renewed its bidding.

The image abruptly vanished.

A chill moved through her fingers and toes and then spread through her body. Her hands began to tremble violently, her skin becoming clammy and a dull white. An iron vice seemed to have been placed around her skull. It was as if every evil in hell had somehow coalesced their malevolent presence in this one voice, a voice no longer gentle. She could not reveal this information to the Germans.

Once the trance began, the voices took over. She had never been able to control her mind in a séance. But how could she let a power such as this unite with men such as these? The earlier reading began to make sense, evil horrendous sense.

The two Germans on either side of her became alarmed and their eyes shot wide open. The old crone was crushing their hands.

"What?" the officer to her left asked.

And now Madam Dashevski felt something vile press in upon her jugular area. A foul sensation reeking of pure hatred penetrated throughout her flesh. "Tell them," a voice hissed in her mind. "The names and regions. TELL THEM!" She could feel her heart pounding in her throat and ears. She gasped for breath, and struggled to remain silent. Suddenly, her left shoulder burst from its socket with a loud pop as she cried out in agony. Another loud snap was heard and a gory rib protruded from the hag's side. The Germans stared on in horror.

Her eyes started to bulge. Blood poured from her nose and ears.

"TELL THEM!" the voice screamed in her head.

She heard her own voice as if wrenched out of her throat, "*Cristobal De la Guzman*. Seek him in the Levant. *Sinestre L'Anguedoc* in France. In England..." Through shear force of will she was able to stop, if only for seconds. Terror spread over her face as she remembered the divination: *"There are three, and for humankind's salvation, they must remain forever unknown, forever separated."* She knew she had to fight this demon with whatever means possible. Madam Dashevski might not change her own fate, but perhaps she could put an end to this heinous revelation. With an immense effort of will, she let go of the German's hands and clasped her mouth shut. The breaking of the chain of hands might weaken the hypnotic state. But even in so doing, she could feel her strength surely ebbing away. Revulsion and nausea grew in her, as the heinous, inhuman caress became more savage in its energy. The brutal convulsions would make her speak. It was only a matter of time. What could she do?

The candles flickered, then died, leaving an eerie orange glow and finally darkness.

She felt her mouth being forced open. Words were forming on her lips. With all her remaining strength, she thrust her right hand down to her boot, and withdrew a curved dagger. Swiftly bringing the blade back up to her throat, she drew it across. Dark red blood flowed down her neck and dripped to the floor, forming a ghastly pool, and Madam Dashevski slumped to the table, dead.

An officer began to relight the candles nearest him. Two others, visibly shaken, picked up the body of the hag as Himmler wiped sweat from his forehead. "Herr Eber," he said to the stoical, blond *Obersturmbannfuhrer.* "Was that Arminius that spoke through her?"

Eber shrugged his shoulders. "I have no idea, Herr *Riechfuhrer.*"

"Did it not sound as though she was about to name another?" Himmler asked.

"Yes it did, Herr *Riechfuhrer.*"

"Is there another fortune teller in the Gypsy camp?"

Eber stood up. "I will see, Herr *Riechfuhrer.*"

"And Herr Eber," a senior officer added. "This time make certain they carry no weapons."

"Yes Herr General."

As the soldiers carried Madame Dashevski's limp body to the door, it suddenly became rigid, standing of its own ghastly power and throwing them off as if they were no more than pesky gnats. Her eyes bulged out accusingly as she turned. Blood dripping from her thin lips and gurgling in her throat, the still warm corpse rendered a deep inhuman voice, barely intelligible, as it harshly intoned, "*Guillaume de Belfort*. Seek him in England."

The old hag's body fell to the floor.

# CHAPTER 1
# THE SAAR
# OFFENSIVE

It was a fine night for an invasion. All along the Caldenbronn Salient, a fifteen mile bulge in the line southwest of Saarbrucken, French skirmishers were preparing to advance into German territory. This would be the beginning of Gamelin's long-awaited Saar offensive that was meant to take pressure off the Polish army. At midnight, September 8th, 1939—seven days after the invasion of Poland, the French would be ready to strike.

Six floors underground in a musty, dimly lit barracks' adjunct, all metal and concrete and replete with cots, footlockers, walls covered with maps of the front, plus a few unopened boxes of grenades and rifle ammunition, an English lieutenant, Michael Hinton-Smith, sat on a cold metal bench silently checking his revolver, sliding the magazine in and out, peering through the muzzle, polishing the weapon from barrel to handle with a fine chamois cloth, then repeating the process.

Across the room, a sergeant stood bent over a large table map studying the border area. Briefly, he looked up at the lieutenant, a concerned expression on his face. "Are you all right, Michael?" Sergeant Major Cawkins asked. The constant fidgeting was beginning to worry him. "I thought you wanted to be here."

Hinton-Smith stared across the room at the sergeant for a few seconds before answering. "I want it to begin, Jack. That is all." The lieutenant flashed a cold smile. It was as if he knew exactly what the sergeant was thinking. Standing up, he holstered his revolver, walked over to Cawkins and looked intently at the map. "Here," the lieutenant said as he found their starting position. "Major D'Agapaeov told me we'll follow this path, some twelve to thirteen miles, a bit of it along this river, the Blies." A very thin blue line represented the river. "Mostly open country but it will be dark. No moon tonight." Hinton-Smith traced their path with his forefinger. "At Sarreguemines we'll meet up with another company. It'll be about a mile to the Saar from there." Hinton-Smith tapped the map with his finger. "D'Agapaeov intends to cross abreast of Auersmacher, garrison of 200." He took a pencil and marked the chart. "Lookout posts on fairly high bluffs here, here and here. There are three bunkers nearby the lookout posts. All face the narrowest part of the Saar and stretch for a good mile along the river. We should be far enough south to avoid being seen. Satisfied?"

Cawkins looked at him, almost frowning. "It's not a test."

"I know. Just letting you know I'm on point." The lieutenant looked at his watch. "It's almost 1900 hrs. Pretty soon, then. Right?"

"I certainly hope so," Cawkins said. Maybe he woke him up.

The lieutenant now started pacing the room.

Cawkins drew a long sigh as the lieutenant's steps made a perfect staccato on the barracks' floor. Maybe too much.

Seeing the look of consternation on Cawkins's face, Hinton-Smith once more sat down, still restless. Eventually, he pulled out a photograph of himself and a striking young blond girl and her younger sister standing in front of a black wrought-iron gate. The picture of Elizabeth and Kate managed to put him in a somewhat calmer state of mind.

Although he was smiling brightly in the photo, Lizzie was only forcing a smile, and when he looked carefully, he could detect the slightest look of apprehension on her face.

Oh Lizzie, he thought as he studied the weathered photo, you're still afraid of the North Gate. Her fear of the cemetery always amused him; how someone so grown up could still have a childlike fear of the unknown. In her defense, a lot of people were nervous around a cemetery and weird rumors abounded around Old Highgate.

Now Hinton-Smith smiled. He also liked the fact that when Cyrus Wilson took that picture of them, Lizzie held on to him so tightly he thought he would burst. He should scare her more often.

Kate was also smiling but there was something odd: her head was slightly turned toward him and her eyes seemed to subtly convey admiration. He never noticed that before and chalked it up to the sibling affection you would have for an older brother, even though they were not related: not yet anyway. He missed them, and Cyrus as well.

Should he have proposed to Elizabeth when he did, when he was fairly certain war was coming? Of course, he could not have known just how soon, but there it was. Elizabeth said yes and they were both elated and could hardly wait, but misgivings began to surface only weeks later when he received the opportunity to go to the Continent and observe the French Army. How could he turn it down? Thank God for Lizzie's support. Though it was not an order, Elizabeth encouraged him to go: it was his career after all. How many chances would he have like this? Would the war even last long enough for him to take part? They were still keen to get married, nothing had changed there, but the wedding had to be put off if he went to France. To choose between Lizzie and the French offensive had been the most agonizing decision he'd ever made, but now he'd made it, he was going to see it through as best he could.

Still, he could not help asking himself many questions: how long would the war go on? Was it fair for him to make her wait? What if this war lasted as long as the last one: four very long years? What if he didn't come back? That had never occurred to him. But he knew he could not stay out of this fight.

He had dealt with bullies before and that's what the Germans were. Just another bully picking on a weaker, smaller foe: this time Poland. He could not stand bullies.

Hinton-Smith now became aware of noise seeping into the room from his left. He tucked the photo away in his uniform jacket and walked up to a large plate glass window. In the adjoining quarters were soldiers. He had been so lost in his focus on Elizabeth he had not noticed them entering. He better start focusing on the coming event.

"Look over here," Hinton-Smith said, peering through the glass.

Cawkins looked up from the map. "I know."

In the barracks Frenchmen were stuffing cartridges into ammunition pouches, packing knapsacks with food, ammo, water and other necessities. Others stuffed extra cartridges into their pockets. A group of men loaded bullets into machine gun belts then layered them neatly into metallic boxes. An orderly placed bandages into a box with a large red cross emblazoned on its side.

Hinton-Smith pointed out a man greasing a musket that looked old enough to be left over from the last war. Many fixed their bayonets: some shaking them to make certain they were secure. A few rolled cigarettes, many smoked. Some looked ashen, others resolute, one man crossed himself, incessantly. It looked like he was saying Ave Marias.

"Well," the lieutenant said. "That lot looks nervous."

"You should be too. You're all neophytes," Cawkins said.

"Right. All yet to be bloodied."

Hinton-Smith kept staring. He could tell the officers by their kepis, white with gold braid. The other soldiers either wore steel helmets or had them hanging on their belts in back or at their sides. "I didn't admit anything, did I then?"

There was a brief knock on the barracks' door.

"Are you ready for the tour?" Major D'Agapaeov asked as he briskly entered the room. The major was lean and tall, in a crisp navy-blue uniform contrasting with a sallow complexion from spending so much time underground. Topped off by a white kepi of the Foreign Legion, the major was a striking, very erect, very martial figure though posted in this netherworld for months on end. "I can now take you to the observation domes."

"Good show, sir," Hinton-Smith said, walking up to the officer and giving him a formal salute. "Cannot wait to begin, sir." It would feel good to get back to the surface. This bunker was like a massive coffin. How had all these Frenchmen been able to stand it for so long? He had to admire their steadfastness.

The major laughed. "The young one is eager, no?"

"Too eager," Cawkins said, eyeing the boy.

"May all my men be as bold tonight," D'Agapaeov said.

Cawkins glanced up in time to see the lieutenant don a crisp new navy-blue kepi. He sighed. "Ready," he said laconically. An American ex-pat, he had been in the trenches in the First World War and knew the realities.

"Then let us go quickly," the major said, looking at his pocket watch. "While there is still enough light for you to see."

Hinton-Smith quickly glanced at his watch as well.

"After you, gentlemen," D'Agapaeov said. He opened the door for the two observers, recently seconded to his company from the British Army, and only arriving at the fortifications late that afternoon.

"Each casemate has two domes," D'Agapaeov explained as he led the men through a narrow steel corridor crowded with men in line slowly shuffling forward to scoop up grenades from a large stack of wooden boxes. There was a gray haze in the gallery from cigarette smoke.

"The NCO uses a powerful 21cm. periscope which extends out of the roof of the turret. The ground is constantly scanned from each dome. All the field you will see from there has been surveyed to the smallest detail so we can pinpoint accurate fire. When the enemy is spotted, the NCO sends the exact coordinates to the command post. They then send orders to the commander of artillery who in turn gives orders to the gunners in their turrets."

"Can the gunners see the targets?" Cawkins asked, trying to be polite. Fixed gun emplacements no longer impressed him after the news from Poland, the Blitzkrieg.

D'Agapaeov smiled. "No. The gunners can see nothing, much like the gunners in a ship. The orders to fire are given by repeater telegraphs, just as the orders from bridge to gun turret or to engine room are given in ships."

"How long does it take?" Hinton-Smith asked, focusing on every little detail. Though he'd spent hours studying the terrain and the various cities that were probable targets above the Saar River, though D'Agapaeov had given them access to the French plans in this sector, and though Cawkins had assured him he was as well prepared as possible, this was new to him. Adrenaline fired through his veins. Tonight would mark his literal baptism of fire.

The one thing he could not know, could not study until he was actually under fire, was how he would react when the bullets started flying.

Though he thought he'd managed to hide his nerves from the French, he knew Cawkins was not fooled. For all his bravado, Hinton-Smith could barely keep his last meal down. He knew he wasn't afraid of being killed or wounded, but that he would not measure up. Looking over at Cawkins, who ran his hand along the smooth bore of one of the huge guns, Hinton-Smith realized what he really wanted to do was impress him. Show him that he'd taught him well. Then he wondered if Cawkins was nervous. Cawkins? Nervous? No, not a chance. Then he smiled. Here was a man whom he greatly admired, aspired to be like. Yet he'd somehow become his trusted friend. That made him feel good, more confident.

Truth be told, Hinton-Smith hero-worshipped the sergeant, like one would an older brother.

"Each order to fire will take a minute or two to transmit, but from spotting the enemy to firing will be no longer than three minutes. Codes have to be given for which guns to use, type of ordinance, elevation, coordinates of the enemy, etc."

Three minutes seemed like a very long time to Hinton-Smith. One could not expect the enemy to stand still while they transmitted orders. Well-trained men could easily advance a couple of hundred yards or more in that amount of time, even at a walk. And then there was armor. The French were not stupid. They probably planned for that.

Hinton-Smith was a commissioned officer in the BEF, the British Expeditionary Force that would soon take its place alongside the French Army on the Franco-Belgian border. The lieutenant, whose tall and slender build reminded one of a long distance runner, was some hundred feet below ground level in the most formidable line of defensive works the world had ever seen.

The Maginot Line was a massive system of fortifications—the main line stretching from the Luxembourg border to the Rhine, defending the northeast corner of France from invasion. Heavy artillery protected by tons of steel and concrete, most of the world thought it was impregnable. There were two major fortresses in the Saar sector, Faulquemont and Haut Poirier. Cawkins and Hinton-Smith were in Faulquemont.

The major stopped in front of a massive room and put his hands on his hips. "This main gallery, we call the Caserne. Over there,"

D'Agapaeov said, pointing to their right, "is an infirmary, with showers for poison gas decontamination. To your left are the kitchen and storerooms. The command post, in the opposite direction, has its own telephone switchboard."

"An underground city," Cawkins observed. "What a racket from those generators. How do you sleep?"

"Yes." D'Agapaeov laughed. "Not easily, no? But hopefully neither does *Le Boche* as he contemplates the march into our guns." He gestured down a long dimly lit hallway. "This tunnel runs for over a mile, connecting with other local bunkers and gun emplacements. As you have seen, or heard, we have our own power plant. And here," he said, walking briskly to the wall directly in front of them and guarded by two tall soldiers, "is the elevator you will take."

"It's all quite an amazing feat of engineering, isn't it," said the lieutenant as the soldiers quickly slid open the wooden doors.

"Ride this to the top floor," D'Agapaeov said. "When you exit, you will see a metal door to your left. That is the observation cupola. From there you will be able to see the Front to the east. Is everything clear?"

"Yes. Thank you, major," Cawkins said.

"Thank you, sir," Hinton-Smith said.

"There is a single vertical hole through which the periscope is raised. We use a concentric counterweight, held on the largest bicycle chain you can imagine," D'Agapaeov advised. "You'll have to use a ladder to reach it." He looked at them to make certain they understood. They nodded.

"I will send someone for you when it is time. Adieu." D'Agapaeov turned and walked back down the dimly lit corridor.

"Why did I let you talk me into this?" Cawkins sighed as they entered the elevator.

"You were bored, mate."

"Did he give you that hat?" Cawkins asked, gesturing at the lieutenant's new kepi.

"That he did," answered Hinton-Smith.

"All you need now is a pencil-thin mustache and a goatee like the major. You'll be a real Frenchie."

"As much as you're a real Brit. But I'll start on it right away," the smooth-skinned youth replied with a grin, then rubbed his chin with his right hand in keeping with the jest. "Though I might need another year or two. I only just turned twenty, old man." He laughed as the elevator began to ascend. "Don't tell me you'd rather be lolling around in merry old England, letting the French have all the fun."

You've finally loosened up a bit, Cawkins thought. *Good.* He knew the lieutenant to become more aggressive when things got tight, when he was tense. He would rush, take risks. This might work well on a soccer field, but it could get him in a mess of trouble out here. They'd spent a good deal of time talking about it, but talk was easy. The more relaxed Hinton-Smith was, the more deliberate he'd be and that suited Cawkins just fine.

Dusk was falling quickly. Those who passed for meteorologists in the French army had forecast a dark clear night—no moon and not a cloud in the sky. A fine night for an invasion.

Cawkins was in very good shape for a man in his late thirties, and quite agile for one so large and muscular. The military life suited him well. "You look like you're calming down now," he observed. "Stay that way."

Hinton-Smith hurried up the ladder to the deck. Cawkins followed close behind. Looking around briefly at the maze of dials, switches, knobs and lights, the lieutenant put his hands on the periscope and started to look at the terrain. He smiled briefly then his expression and tone turned solemn. "I'm excited, Jack. I'll admit it. This is what I came here for. It might sound ridiculous, but I'm serious. Bugles blowing, regimental colors flying in the wind. I wish we were moving out in daylight and I could see the sun glinting off the standards. When the French Fourth moves forward, I'll be hearing the fife and drums. Even if it's only in my head, they'll be playing. I'll hear the sound of the armor as the knights ride into battle. Like every story I ever heard at the Regimental mess, or read in a book. Will it be glorious? I don't know, but this is why I came, Jack. Have a look." He turned the handles over to Cawkins and stepped aside.

Michael Hinton-Smith now unconsciously took out his revolver, stared at it for a second, then drew back and released the slide of the Browning automatic. The weapon felt cold in his hand and the impact of the slide against the barrel made a metallic clicking sound that echoed around the stale-smelling room.

Cawkins sighed. "How many times are you going to do that?" he asked. "Relax."

"Oh. I didn't even realize. Sorry. It's the adrenaline, isn't it," Hinton-Smith said with a quiet embarrassed laugh. He placed the revolver back in the holster.

Everything in Hinton-Smith's life had led him to this moment. He had played it over in his head a thousand times. He could not wait for the BEF to get into action. That was probably months down the line. As yet, only a few British soldiers were even on the Continent, but Hinton-Smith was presently attached to the French Army on the eve of Gamelin's attack.

"I have to see what it's all about, Jack. You told me yourself that you cannot simply know it, *battle* that is, intellectually. You have to go through it, hear the rounds whistling by your ears, smell the gunpowder, feel the rumble of the ground under your feet. Experience it."

Cawkins had come along for the ride. He looked through the scope at the dark countryside. "Let's hope it ain't all that exciting," he said.

"Besides, if Gamelin follows through to the Ruhr, the war's over."

Hinton-Smith was indeed feeling the strain of the moment, but he was good at keeping his emotions hidden. A solitary child, he learned early to keep his own counsel—it was a habit not easily discarded. Even with Cawkins he would be hard put to admit his stomach was churning, or his knees weak. For him, the waiting was the worst part. It was like the anticipation before a big football game, but in this game the stakes were quite a bit higher. He was tired of waiting in this cold, damp, steel-lined cavern that might as well have been a tomb. Still, Cawkins knew what he was feeling. Of that he was certain.

He wanted it to begin.

In less than an hour, they were leaving the safety of the tons of steel and concrete and the enormous 135mm howitzers and 47mm anti-tank guns of the fortifications to go into enemy territory. A scant ten minutes later, they would form up with the French company and press forward. They would reach the Saar by midnight.

"This is one more step in your real education, Michael," Cawkins said. "And if you can manage to not get yourself shot, it could prove quite valuable, but just don't let's go mistaking rashness for bravery. All that talk of glory is hogwash."

Hinton-Smith laughed as he looked at the broad-shouldered Cawkins. "You think I'm going to stand up straight, swagger stick in hand and go over the top. Is that it?"

"Well..."

"Hell no. I reckon I'll crouch and duck like crazy. And most of the time, I'll hide behind your enormous girth." The lieutenant grinned and looked at Cawkins.

"Right," the sergeant said in mock disbelief. They both started to laugh.

As the best of mates, rank had no barriers for them. Hinton-Smith and Cawkins were inseparable. The lieutenant had grown into manhood under the sergeant's tutelage. Even as a teenager, one could find him on the playing fields with Cawkins, with the sergeant demonstrating the finer points of kicking an American type football or on the shooting range firing an Enfield or pistol. Cawkins had even taught him how to throw a baseball. Cawkins soon went from mentor to friend.

They ate at the sergeant's mess together. They took leave together, Hinton-Smith often staying with Cawkins and his wife at their modest home in Surrey. They hunted quail on the moors in Scotland, and scaled the Cornwall cliffs, and went on archeological expeditions from the Orkneys to Pevansy Castle.

When Hinton-Smith was given a platoon, fresh out of Sandhurst, the British Military College, they conspired to get the sergeant seconded to his command. They took a great deal of pleasure in the fact their friendship was the subject of good-humored raillery back at Regiment. There were even rumors that Cawkins was almost an Englishman by then, though not just yet *that* refined.

Now the youngster had talked the oldster into coming to France.

Hinton-Smith stopped laughing and dropped his head. "All right, Jack," he admitted for the first time. "I'm nervous."

Sergeant Cawkins put his hand on the lieutenant's shoulder. "So am I, Mike. So am I."

"You!" the lieutenant said in real surprise.

"It's war, Michael. Men get killed."

"Yes," the lieutenant said with due solemnity. "But I wouldn't want to be anywhere else in the world tonight."

It was not long before a diminutive orderly in a navy-blue uniform entered the observation dome.

"Major D'Agapaeov presents his compliments, gentlemen. It is time."

An electric-powered tram transported Cawkins, Hinton-Smith and the orderly to Major Christian D'Agapaeov's small but elegant quarters. A brightly colored Persian rug covered most of the floor, and ornately carved bookcases, stuffed with well-worn copies of everything from Gibbon's histories to Diderot's poems, from Hume's treatises to Henryk Sienkiewicz's thick volumes, took up three of the walls. The major sat drinking a steaming cup of coffee from a mug in the shape of a Buddha. Two other oddly shaped mugs were sitting on the table waiting for them: one of a dragon, the other of Jeanne d'Arc on a rearing horse. There was also a bottle of champagne nestled between three long-stemmed crystal glasses.

"Welcome," said a solemn D'Agapaeov as he uncorked the Chateau de Rothschild '36 and started to fill the wineglasses. "We start it off right, no?"

"Well," said Cawkins. "This is just what I need." He put his hands around the cup to draw in its heat, hastily took a sip of coffee, then put down the mug and hoisted a glass to toast with the others.

"It is quite chilly this far below, isn't it?" the lieutenant said.

"About twelve degrees Centigrade," D'Agapaeov said. "Better for storage." The major held up his wine glass then looked at him with a wry grin. "To an auspicious beginning." He then tapped his glass with the glasses of Cawkins and Hinton-Smith.

"You French surely know how to start a war," Hinton-Smith said.

"May we finish it with as much alacrity as we begin it," Cawkins said soberly. For all the major's sanguinity, Cawkins was certain he detected an underlying sadness in his eyes. Once more having to fight the Germans. How many more times in his lifetime would they have to? The sergeant raised his glass again and said, "Let's drive the bastards back to hell. Here's mud in your eye."

D'Agapaeov stared at the two soldiers questioningly.

"Bloody Yanks," Hinton-Smith said, rolling his eyes upwards.

Cawkins had already lived a good deal of the life to which the lieutenant aspired. Born in the Oklahoma panhandle around the turn of the century, he was one of a long line of American cowboy-soldiers. He could count relatives who fought in every one of his country's wars. Cawkins's father was an itinerant Indian Agent who earlier rode with General George Crook and his Chiricahua scouts in the Apache wars. As a boy, young Jack grew up accompanying his father on horseback, touring the dusty, barren reservations of his home state. When the Great War broke out Cawkins felt the pull of his forebears. With a keenly felt American sense of fair play, and the additional attribute of a nose whetted for adventure, he left the States in 1915 to work his way over to England aboard a merchantman, while the United States was still isolationist. Once there, Cawkins immediately enlisted in the Imperial Army.

At first a private fighting in the trenches, by 1917 he was a lieutenant following Allenby to Jerusalem and Damascus. By the time he was ordered to go with the relief columns restoring order in Mesopotamia in 1920 he was a captain.

The army was now his vocation.

Cawkins married an English girl in 1925 and stayed in the British Army. He liked the feel of being one of these professionals, and would forgo the sometimes on, sometimes off army of his ancestors. Besides, he reasoned with some prescience, Britain's interests spread over so much of the globe, and encompassed so many different peoples, both with and without their consent, he was certain to be much more active than he would ever be in the United States Army. The United States had gone back to its isolationism almost as soon as the war ended, and in this, the British Army proved to be an additional advantage, for in times of peace, Cawkins's independent cowboy spirit often got the best of him, and he had been busted back to the ranks more times than he could count. Had he enlisted in the United States Army, he liked to tell his peers, by now he'd be on permanent latrine duty.

The major finished his drink and tossed the bottle to his orderly. Rubbing the side of his aquiline nose as if making a sign, he got up and said, "Let us begin," then threw his empty glass against the wall, shattering it. Hinton-Smith and Cawkins looked at each other, shrugging their shoulders in unison, then got up and followed his lead. Their glasses crashed against the wall simultaneously.

Hinton-Smith and Cawkins followed D'Agapaeov back to the underground tram. This time the cars were filled with soldiers. They glided down the rails through two hundred yards of tunnel until they came to another elevator. This ran another hundred feet to the surface where they went through a foot-thick armored door, emerged from the rear entrance of a massive gray concrete bunker, and crossed a steel bridge over a protective ditch, all on the reverse slope of a thickly wooded hill. After the last of the soldiers crossed the ditch, they formed up with D'Agapaeov's skirmishers. Two sentries then hauled the bridge back into the bunker.

The three hundred men of D'Agapaeov's rifle company were part of the 11th Division, 4th Army. They had only light mortars, light machine guns—no tanks or artillery—and a special allotment of rafts to cross the Saar. Their mission was to probe the enemy lines, take prisoners, move as far forward as possible, and stop if they met major resistance. The 11th Division would follow in their wake. This time, there was to be no "over the top."

D'Agapaeov led from the front as the men of the rifle company made their way around the casemate. Cawkins and Hinton-Smith, conspicuous in their khaki uniforms, which stood out in stark contrast to the dark blue worn by the French, stuck by the major.

Keeping in close order, the company passed through anti-personnel obstacles, and made their way around the man-made hill housing the casemate, until they faced east. Sappers had cleared a twenty-foot wide path through their own barbed wire and mines earlier in the evening, marking the boundaries with small yellow flags.

The soldiers filed through six rows of anti-tank barriers—upright rail sections embedded in concrete and also festooned with barbed wire—and then over two miles of open ground which had been cleared for fields of artillery fire. They trudged another ten miles through farmland and forests on the way to the frontier, then along the River Blies to Sarreguemines, where they rendezvoused with another rifle company a mile short of the Saar. Once there, D'Agapaeov directed his men to a small copse covering the better part of an acre. Here they found forty rafts hidden under olive green tarps and camouflaged with tree branches, shrubs and grass. Other soldiers had hauled the rafts down the previous night.

"Well. This is it," Cawkins said to the lieutenant as they shouldered a dark green raft with six others. "Hold on to that kepi."

"Righto, Sergeant Major," Hinton-Smith said. His nerves had quieted somewhat with the onset of the march. He was doing something. Much better than just sitting around waiting. The night was pleasant though a bit humid and he liked the feel of the cool sweat that dripped down the small of his back and beaded on his forehead: just like the feel of a good run. But, had he prepared enough, studied enough? Would there always be these doubts? The butterflies? He slapped his thigh in frustration. He determined to banish them from his mind.

Thirty minutes later, every platoon was assembled and ready. A thin mist had settled over the river reaching all the way to the far shore. No one saw the water till the lead scouts blundered into it.

Hinton-Smith and Cawkins, lumbering under the weight of the raft with the French soldiers, were scant seconds behind the scouts. Slowly wading out into the Saar to where the river was two-to-three feet deep, they lowered the raft to the water and clambered in.

Earlier, Major D'Agapaeov passed the word to his aide to have the men paddle on a thirty degree heading upstream to account for the force of the current, enabling it to bring them back to the chosen landing.

"First raft in the water," Hinton-Smith said to Cawkins. "We'll give old Fritz a bloody nose, I reckon." If he was going to fight his case of nerves he'd do it with a show of certainty. The show could often become the reality. "Let's go."

Cawkins could only shake his head. "Remember. We're here to observe. Nothing more."

When D'Agapaeov saw that his whole contingent was afloat, he swung himself aboard and gave the order to move out. The two soldiers holding the raft in place swung themselves in after the major, and everyone began to paddle for their lives—each man expecting a withering fire to emerge from the German side at any moment.

Strangely, nothing happened, not even desultory sniper fire. The only noise was from the splashing of oars and the labored breathing of the soldiers.

"I guess that's why you French picked this sector," said Cawkins. The sergeant appreciated a well thought out plan and D'Agapaeov graciously accepted the compliment with a simple nod and smile.

When they reached the other side, Hinton-Smith was the first man to jump out of a raft into the shallow water. "First on Jerries' soil," he yelled back at Cawkins, as he waded in to shore.

"Your lieutenant tries to win the war tonight, no?" said a bemused D'Agapaeov.

"Ain't that the truth," Cawkins admitted as he leapt out of the raft. "What did you slip in his drink? Some Bennies?"

Two soldiers in each raft remained behind while all the rest jumped into the water, then paddled back to the French side to pick up more *poilus*. Only a third of the soldiers made the first crossing. There were not enough rafts.

On the German side, the banks of the Saar were steep and broken with erosion. D'Agapaeov had the soldiers help boost each other up to the top of the embankment where a heavily wooded hillside, also quite steep, began. This third of the force would wait on a narrow strip of level ground as a covering force until two more groups had been transported across the Saar.

Hinton-Smith started up the slope by himself before most of the first wave of soldiers finished landing. Using both hands, he grabbed onto a sapling and pulled himself up. He was not thinking. He was acting, driven by the adrenaline. The French Army had a goal and as of now he was part of that army, the point of the spear, and so he would help them attain it: contact the enemy and take prisoners.

When he got waist high with the narrow trunk, he swung his left foot up and used it as a step. The first fifteen yards of the hill were slanted at a steep angle and the air was so heavily laden with moisture that the lieutenant found himself sweating profusely. The grass was too slippery to offer much purchase, and his boots slid as he tried to continue upwards. Wiping his brow he stopped and looked up the hill. The bank was so thick with trees, he seized the idea of using the trunks as though they were a living ladder, and began to climb them step by step up the bank. When he got to the top he would see the lay of the land and consider his next move.

"Where does he think he's going?" asked Medoc, a French corporal who was no less eager than Hinton-Smith, although his eagerness was only concerned with giving the Germans a good thrashing and then going home to his wife and three children. Most French soldiers were too cynical to care about the glory.

"Yes," said another enlisted man. "This English will beat us to *Le Boche*."

Now Medoc could not help himself. This was the French Army! An Englishman could not win this race. He cried out, "*Allez! Allez!*" and motioned for the other soldiers to follow him. Eleven Frenchmen started up the slope after Hinton-Smith.

Still standing knee-deep in the water, D'Agapaeov looked to the French side through his binoculars. He was concerned. The fog had cleared. Would the Germans see them? The boats were almost back across the Saar. Many soldiers were wading out to the rafts to hasten the crossing. The major looked at his watch. "We should have both companies here in another thirty to forty minutes. It will still be dark."

D'Agapaeov turned to his aide. "Send two platoons to secure the heights." Then he looked around as though he was missing something. "Where is your lieutenant?" he asked Cawkins.

Cawkins looked around as well. He had been absorbed by the river crossing, never an easy thing, maybe the hardest thing. Where is that kid? How could he lose track of him? Then he thought to look up the bluff leading to the top. There were soldiers climbing, already halfway up the hill. He could just make out the silhouettes. Cawkins squinted, his eyes trailing up the line of men. Yup. That would be him, leading the pack.

"I need a boost up top," Cawkins tersely replied as he motioned to the crest of the riverbank. "I'm going to kill that kid."

"I would call it an irrational exuberance," D'Agapaeov said evenly, a hint of amusement in his voice, then motioned to his aide. "Help the sergeant."

The aide called two soldiers who waded over and clasped hands to make a step for the sergeant. Cawkins then pulled himself to the top of the bank, saw the problem and solution in much the same manner as Hinton-Smith, and started to climb.

By the time Cawkins reached the crest, Hinton-Smith and the French soldiers had joined forces and already moved out towards Auersmacher, the nearest garrisoned city on the heights above the Saar. Cawkins, still breathing heavily from his climb, started jogging to catch up. His wet trousers, clinging to his legs as he ran slowed him down, making for an awkward lurching movement and a swooshing sound with each step.

The dirt road leading from Sitterswald became asphalt when it reached the outskirts of Auersmacher. Though only a scant sixty feet higher in elevation, this intersection of the roads enabled Hinton-Smith and his French compatriots a good look at the village. Street lamps were burning and Hinton-Smith could see that Auersmacher was a typical German city with a typical German orderliness. All the streets ran in a perfectly straight north-south or east-west direction. All the houses on a street had the same design, the same size, the same red-tile roofs, the same brick framing and cobblestone walls.

"There is a barracks near the center plaza," said Medoc, who had lived in Sarreguemines all his life, and who had visited Auersmacher a number of times; most recently in 1938 just after the Anschluss. "I have heard the garrison only numbers two hundred."

"You're right. It does," Hinton-Smith responded.

"It is very bright down there, no?" Medoc said cautiously. "Like daylight."

Before Hinton-Smith could comment, he felt a vice-like grip on his shoulder.

"Dammit. What the hell do you think you're doing?" Cawkins whispered.

"I was wondering what it's like to take a city," Hinton-Smith replied with a sheepish grin. "I thought I'd like to start small."

"I think we better wait for the major."

"*Toujours de l'audace,*" the lieutenant replied.

"That's pretty smart. Don't go quoting me Churchill!" Cawkins said, raising his voice. "Churchill be damned! You're pushing too hard. Attacking a fortified town with only a dozen men. That's just stupid." Cawkins glared at him. "You ain't even part of their damn army!"

"Don't be a rum chap," replied the lieutenant, unfazed as he started walking down the paved street with his new French mates. He had made up his mind and nothing would deter him. He knew it was tunnel vision but it quieted his mind. Set your goal and attack it in a straight line, no wavering. It was easier that way. "You're welcome to join us. Come on, then. Let's have a go." He thought Cawkins would have understood this about him by now.

"I never should have encouraged you to read," said the sergeant, but he unshouldered his rifle, took the safety off and started up the road after Hinton-Smith. "You're too damn stubborn. All you need now is the damn swagger stick." Cawkins had wanted one more dose of adventure, and he guessed he was going to get it sooner rather than later. It was either tie up the boy and end this campaign for him, and maybe his career, or go along to make sure he didn't get killed.

Hinton-Smith divided the men up into two groups; Medoc took half of them and led them cautiously up the west side of the road. Hinton-Smith, with Cawkins close by, led his group up the east side.

The night was dark and the air trailing in from the river was crisp. They were seemingly the only people on the streets, but they maintained order and proceeded as silently as possible, house by house, building by building, on their way to the center of the city.

An old gray mongrel limped across the street, briefly looking at the furtive soldiers, then paying them no more attention.

The road now opened up into the plaza, a perfect square, with a perfectly manicured lawn, about the size of a city block, bordered on every side by street lamps. Off to the sides of the square, there was a bank, a Protestant church, municipal buildings, two cafes, a market, a few hotels and a police station.

Hinton-Smith unfolded a crude map he'd drawn of the city. Quickly looking back and forth from the drawing to the actual buildings, he got his bearings, then drew Medoc's attention and pointed to a structure on the left that looked like a run down hotel. He mouthed the words "police station." Almost directly opposite was the garrison barracks.

Medoc quickly sent two men over to guard the station, then looked back at the lieutenant.

Hinton-Smith pointed to his watch, held up three fingers and motioned for the Frenchman to lead his men around to the back of the barracks. It was eight minutes to three. Medoc nodded his head in agreement and led his men around the side of the building.

Hinton-Smith refolded the map and placed it in his shirt pocket. Signaling his group forward to a small grassy area with benches, where they could spread out and enfilade the barracks if need be, he trotted across the cobblestone plaza towards the barracks by himself and was soon standing with his head and back flush to the wall next to the barracks' door. He was no longer smiling. This was it. He looked at his watch. Two minutes. Well, so far so good, but this place is lit up like we're on stage. What had he gotten himself into? Too impulsive. He should have listened to Jack. It was almost like he could not help himself. If there was a next time he vowed to be more cautious. But there was nothing for it. If Fritz didn't kill him Cawkins probably would. There was no turning back now. *Just don't muck it up.*

Nearby, Cawkins looked on in amazement. How had he let it come to this—letting the boy slip out of his hands? He had only agreed to come with him to France in order to avoid this type of recklessness. All he could do now was support the boy's rash plan. But Cawkins could feel the energy shooting through his arms and legs and he wanted it to begin as well. There was a rush being on edge like this. There was nothing like it and he had to admit he missed it. These were the times when he felt most alive.

Bringing his rifle up ready to shoot, he moved among the *poilus*, repositioning them further apart with three facing the barracks and two guarding the rear, and using the benches for cover. Cawkins's teeth were clenched tightly. This was not very many men.

At the same time, Medoc led his men down a narrow alley that led to the back of the west side buildings.

*   *   *

Not all the German soldiers were in the barracks. Sixteen were on the heights above the Saar, a mile west of Auersmacher. Another dozen or so had gotten leave and had gone to Saarbrucken, a much more cosmopolitan and larger city with a greater variety of entertainments: bistros, bands, taverns, beer and whores.

And one, a private, was about to be on his way to visit his girl-friend while her husband was away on business. All were completely oblivious to the amphibious assault south of them.

Fredrik Steuffel was supposed to be on guard duty on the eastern heights of the Saar, but this was a rare occasion and he wanted to take advantage. Besides, the French did not want war. And why would they waste their youth to help the Poles? Had they not learned their lesson the last time around?

A school teacher of French grammar, Fredrik Steuffel had only joined the reserves to earn a little extra money. He never believed the Allies would put up a fight. They had given up everything to the Germans before when circumstances were much more in their favor. Why should they fight now? His people had killed so many French in the last war that some said they had destroyed a generation. How could the French even assemble an attacking force? They were too far away from the Polish Front to make a difference in any case.

Steuffel truly believed the myth that if the German Army had not been stabbed in the back by their own politicians they would have won the last war and this new one would not have been necessary. This made Steuffel quite angry but he knew he better put it from his mind before meeting his lover. Elise never liked it when he talked politics and they would just get into a row and that was not what he wanted or needed on this rare night with her.

Steuffel was quite surprised when Hitler actually attacked the Polish and even more surprised when his reserve unit was called up and post-ed on the border. Now there was no teaching. Instead were days filled with marching, drilling, inspections, bad food, guard duty and more marching. Then there was the boredom of watching the river meander below the bluffs and the farmers on the other side going about their business, living a normal life. This made him angrier still. There was nothing of military interest in this sector though everyone knew the French line was only a few miles distant. The only good thing about it was he had met Elise.

On only his second day in Auersmacher, he saw her while shopping at the market for eggs to supplement his army rations. They arrived at the same shop and almost at the same time, each wanting to buy the last dozen eggs. He found them first and she came up to inquire just as the farmer started to wrap the package for Steuffel. As she let out a sigh of failure, Steuffel gallantly offered to split the dozen. Within a week, an affair began. Things move fast in such heightened circumstances.

So when she sent a note that evening, he sent a message in return. Then he tried to find a comrade who would trade watches with him. This failing, he decided to go anyway. The French would not attack. Not on the only night for three weeks when his lover was free.

As luck would have it, the day before he had bested his fellows in a marksman contest and won enough to purchase a bottle of good French champagne. It never hurt to get Elise in the mood.

He would wait until 4 A.M. If nothing happened in the meantime, he would leave his post and go. Though the night was quite dark, he had a clear view of the river. The fog had lifted and if they tried to cross, he would see them. Had he chanced to be another half-mile south, he would have been shocked. As it happened, from his position, just as expected, he saw nothing. At 3:30 A.M. he poured some cold water into his helmet, hung a small mirror on the wall of the guard shack, and shaved. Then he dabbed himself with just a touch of her favorite cologne. He jogged over to the bluff and took one last look across the river. There was nothing to be seen. At exactly 4 A.M. as planned, rifle in hand, he left for the village.

In fact, the French would not dare.

As Steuffel reached the place where the dirt road became asphalt, he noticed boot prints made of water, and decided to take the quickest route to Elise's house—right through the plaza in case of more rain. Everybody would be asleep at this hour.

This is odd, he thought after a few more minutes walk. Why are there only tracks of water? The rest of the road is dry. How could it rain like that? Walking more slowly and quite curious, he peered back and forth along the road, then stooped over to get a better look. There were a lot of tracks. That's why he thought it had rained. He stopped walking altogether and looked more closely at the road. There was not much light but he could see a trail of boot prints. Scratching his head and frowning, he turned around and retraced his steps to the dirt road. The tracks came from that direction and that direction led to the river. Either a group of people had been swimming or perhaps boating in the Saar. But why would they be swimming or boating so late at night. That was dangerous. One could not trust the current of the Saar. There were indeed a lot of tracks.

Now he was startled. His neck tightened and he reached for his rifle, bringing it down to the ready. What if it were the French? No. It could not be. It could not be soldiers. He would have seen them cross the river. He stood and thought. Ah. It was probably one of their own reconnaissance patrols returning from a scout on the French side. Steuffel laughed at his own silliness. He should be more concerned with getting caught absent without leave, or Elise's husband returning early.

Then he frowned, shaking his head. Why don't they inform us? Someone could get shot.

Perhaps he should head to the barracks first. He could see if lights were on and a patrol had just come in. They could not be that much ahead of him. If so, he could continue on to his tryst.

Steuffel slung his Mauser back over his shoulder. While he hurried forward, he looked for a place to stash the champagne. He should not be carrying the bottle if he had to go in and warn his commandant. Just in case. After all, he could always come back to retrieve it.

# CHAPTER 2

# AT ANOTHER TIME AND PLACE

## 1397 A.D.

Sir Charles Whyntowne ran his finger along the ancient Roman wall, now green with moss and lichen. Only three feet high and made of rocks held in place by a crude mortar, the wall stretched over most of the flat-topped hill, enclosing an area of some five acres of weeds and long grass. The ramparts of the abandoned castle loomed high above, and as he glanced upward, he could see one of his men waving a blue cloth. It was a signal: someone approached.

Sir Charles was tall and sinewy, with golden hair and beard that almost made him look saintly, and indeed, he now wore a monk's habiliment. His eyes were bright blue and seemingly, always burdened.

There was no hurry. The signal meant it was a man on foot, and if he just came into sight he was still a long way off. If he was one of theirs, he would then have to scale the mound before delivering any news.

Sir Charles walked toward the castle drawbridge. It had not been used in years. The moat was dry and full of long yellowing grass.

A slighter, younger man, also in the reddish-brown garb of a monk, came toward him from the grounds to the east of the castle. Peter Dillon had served Whyntowne as a page for three years, starting at the age of fourteen. Now he was a squire and would soon begin his training in earnest to become a knight.

"Sir Charles," Dillon addressed him as he approached. He was excited. "We enlarged the entrance to the escape tunnel as you asked, and the other work progresses."

"Good." He gestured upward toward the Keep. "Then it is time to start dismantling these walls. I do not want travelers to see them and come up here to satisfy their curiosity."

"Yes sir, but first you must come into the tunnel with me. It is as though it was made for us."

The squire took him by the arm and led him to the tunnel opening. The decrepit remains of a wooden hatch lay in the dirt off to the side and a lit torch had been stuck in the ground, still burning.

Bending over to grab the torch, Dillon proceeded to climb down a makeshift wooden ladder into the hole.

At the bottom, he held the torch up so Whyntowne could see.

"Follow me, my liege," Dillon said as he turned and started down a narrow circular shaft.

The pit was cold, damp and black as death itself. Sir Charles felt a chill creep throughout his limbs as he followed the squire into the bowels of the earth. It seemed unnaturally cold and smelled of mold and the detritus of a thousand years.

Edging slowly down the serpentine path, Sir Charles had the disquieting feeling that Dillon's torch was the only connection remaining between himself and humankind above, and it seemed very tenuous just then. They proceeded in single file, their hands bracing themselves on the damp walls. After some fifty yards, Sir Charles was sweating profusely despite the cold.

"Be careful here, sir," Dillon said as he stopped and pointed toward the ground. "They've laid a trap. See." He lowered the torch in front of him.

Whyntowne could see the path had widened a bit, but his stomach shuddered as he saw the gaping hole looming ahead.

"Nothing for it, sir," Dillon said. "We've laid two thick lengths of elm across. It's the only way forward."

"Let's get on with it, then."

"Yes. I'll cross first."

The squire bounded across the boards as if speed would see to it he reached the other side regardless of misstep. He then held the torch over his edge of the hole so Sir Charles could see.

"It is said there is a castle constructed in Germany, in the eastern countryside, to block a rent in the earth such as this," Whyntowne said as he peered down into the hole. "They say it is the exit from Hell, used by demons."

"Pray thee this is not the same my lord."

"Did any of our men...?"

"No. We proceeded with caution."

"Good," Whyntowne said as he started across the wood planks. "Have one of the men place a torch on either side." The coming task would be difficult enough without losing men before it began.

"Yes, my liege."

Sir Charles stepped off the makeshift bridge to the solid ground on the other side and breathed a sigh of relief. Many considered him to be a very brave man, but the journey across that bottomless black abyss came close to unnerving him.

They proceeded through the tunnel, soon going through a short, level passage, then down a switch-back stairway made of uneven wooden steps. The tunnel now angled more steeply. Sir Charles sensed it followed the slant of the mound. They had been underground for more than a half-hour.

"Look," Peter Dillon said. "This is what I wanted you to see." The squire moved his torch closer to the wall.

The torch's flame now unmasked stone tombs with faces and bodies carved into them, covering the tunnel wall as far as they could see, and both above them and under their feet.

"This place is a giant catacomb."

Sir Charles Whyntowne crouched down, his chin resting in his hands as if in thought.

"We must protect these souls from him," Sir Charles said. "Bring amulets and make carvings throughout the tunnel."

"Yes Sir Charles."

Sir Charles put his hands together before his face and bowed his head. "Thou unnumbered souls ensconced in this tomb, please forgive our treading upon thee. It is for a most holy cause. Amen."

The squire quickly knelt down and crossed himself.

"At the bottom, not far from here, the tunnel widens out for our purpose," Dillon said as he regained his feet. "The graves are almost dug. Everything is prepared as you ask."

"Then let us repair to the surface," "Whyntowne said. "I think a messenger arrives."

"One thing, my liege. We could cut a hole through the side of the mound, at ground level. We have made soundings. It is not too great a distance and would lessen our task. We could not find the escape hatch. It must have caved in."

"I have thought upon this," Whyntowne said. "I want no ingress where innocents or miscreants might wander into the crypt."

"Yes sir."

By the time they ascended, a messenger had indeed arrived and was at the surface to greet them.

"It is done," Brockingham said. "The bribes are given out to those who would take them."

"And the others?" Sir Charles asked. "How many?"

"Two."

"Will they give us away?" Whyntowne asked.

"I was advised to not approach them."

"Are they members of the Temple?"

"I don't think there were any other knights in the place."

"Then he is alone except for his retainers."

"Yes, and a few peasants, servants and women."

"Only two were loyal, Reginald?" Whyntowne was seeing the plan unfold in his mind.

"Only two. Either loyal or terrified. Shall we kill them?"

"Only if we must," Whyntowne said, his face showing a deep sadness. "Nothing must stand before us and our purpose."

Sir Reginald Brockingham, a bull-necked man, placed his left hand on the scabbard of his sword and nodded.

"Are you certain of the others?" Sir Charles asked. "Once inside we are at their mercy."

"I'm as certain as the amount of gold I bestowed."

"Good man," Whyntowne said, placing his hand on Brockingham's shoulder. They had been together on this hunt for a long time. "His resting place is almost prepared."

"It was made known to them that we are familiar with their families. An extra encouragement."

"This business doth fatigue me," Whyntowne sighed. "It makes me ill. Does the end ever justify the means?" He leaned on his great sword as though he would fall without it.

"Have stout heart, my Lord," the squire said, taking his arm.

"Thank you my friend. I am all right," Whyntowne said. The knight rested against his sword for some time before standing straight again. "When do we go?"

"It is a small manor. With a moat," Brockingham said. "We are better off, and quieter without our armor. A servant will open the small portcullis an hour past midnight. They sound the watch every hour on the hour. He will open it at the sounding of one A.M. and close it at the next. He assures me *L'Anguedoc* will be drunk and asleep by then. Only a man at a time will be able to enter this gate, but the drawbridge is too old and loud. He is afraid it could still wake him if lowered."

"The sound of the watch does not wake him?"

"The servants sound it among themselves. He will not hear it."

"He sleeps alone?"

"With his wench," Brockingham said. "One of the two not bought."

"Peter. Let me know when the burial site is ready."

"Yes, my liege," Dillon said.

"And remember the carvings. Place protections throughout the site."

Dillon nodded and jogged to the tunnel entrance, picked up the torch and disappeared into the ground.

"Do you really believe it is *L'Anguedoc*? This man goes by another name."

"I do not believe in coincidences," Whyntowne said. "We shall see tonight. Make certain everyone is at peace with himself and this deed. If anyone chooses to quit us, he has my permission and good wishes. It promises to be a long night."

"Longer for some, old friend."

"Yes. Longer for some."

They started down the hill a little before dusk, leading their horses along a narrow switchback. The men wore monk's cassocks, leaving all knightly accoutrements behind except for their swords and the instruments of their task. Two horses, though riderless, carried eighteen-foot logs with branches shorn. They would ride to within a mile of the castle-like manor, dismount and make the rest of the way on foot.

The same servant was to pull a cart into the manor that evening under the understandable pretext of supply, and this would be *L'Anguedoc's* manner of conveyance back to his tomb.

As they rode, Sir Charles Whyntowne thought of the many years they had been on this undertaking. From his first journey to Jerusalem, his Knighthood, his induction into the Hospitallers: had it all pointed to this? His selection, along with thirty others out of thousands. The passage to the East, the many years of study. He laughed as it occurred to him he was no longer a young man. None of them were save the squire. Hardly.

Then the long journey back with the knowledge to stop these men.

Once they learned they were the hunted they had disappeared.

Now, after many more years, they had found only one of them. He was certain it was *L'Anguedoc*. The others had voiced their hatred of France, of Louis. So had *L'Anguedoc*, but he had vowed to kill the king and so would come back. He was French and the others were not. No matter the man, there comes a time when he longs for home. After the king had died of old age instead, perhaps he would have stayed. They would see.

The night was dark but not unpleasant. Even as they rode Whyntowne could smell the scent of the first honeysuckle of spring. Stars were scattered across the heavens on a moonless night.

\*   \*   \*

It was a miracle they had found him at all.

The trail had gone cold when *L'Anguedoc* left Acre. The Crusades were as good as over by then. Acre was about to fall, and with it, the last Crusader garrison. They learned that *L'Anguedoc* had taken ship to Malta.

Whyntowne and his knights had scoured the countryside of Italy, Germany, France and the Low Countries, asking questions, looking for strange crimes, mysterious occurrences, anything out of the ordinary.

Silently, Sir Charles dismounted. Patting his horse on the neck, he handed the reins to his squire.

"Dominic and Heidel," Sir Charles said. "Stay with Peter. There is good pasture here for our horses."

"Yes," Dominic said, with a slight bow.

"Sir Charles," Peter Dillon said. "Please let me come with."

Whyntowne put his hand on the young man's shoulder. "You are our last line of defense. You understand this is important?"

"Yes, my liege," Dillon said, but he was upset. He wanted to be part of this dangerous endeavor.

"It is another stage in your training as a knight. You must be disciplined."

"Yes. I understand." Still, he lowered his head in disappointment.

When Brockingham slid off his mare, he got down on his knees and crossed himself. "May the Lord be with us. May we be strong."

It was a good time for prayer Sir Charles thought.

They would walk from here on in.

There was a small village nearby called St. Venant: only a few hovels, a tiny chapel and a tavern which also served as an inn. There was nothing else around for miles except for small farms belonging to a feudal estate a great distance away.

Some two months earlier, three of Whyntowne's men, dressed as merchants, stopped for a meal and hopefully a bed. They would head for Rouen in the morning. Up to that time, nothing had lifted their hopes in the search.

As they supped, they overheard low voices speaking of miracles and many odd things happening in a manor across the river from the town, and shielded from view by thick forests and two hills. They spoke of a man regaining his sight, how a family was cured of the plague and another young lady who had never walked a day in her life, got up off her bed, and though quite wobbly at first, began to walk like a normal person and had ever since.

They looked at each other intently, as all three had the same realization. What witchcraft was this?

The men paid their fare and sneaked out of the inn in the middle of the night when all around had become quiet. Fearing for their lives they rode straight to Versailles where they informed the new king.

Sir Charles Whyntowne was then summoned.

After a long and uneasy march through dark foreboding woods, the manor walls were seen rising out of the gloom. Though Brockingham had described it to him, Sir Charles was surprised at how small it was. Not something one would expect for a man of *L'Anguedoc's* dominion. Now he had his first doubts.

Perhaps it was to aid in his disappearance. These men knew they were being hunted, but there was a time when they were too formidable to be subdued. Their arrogance openly defied kings. Why had that changed? Was it because of us? Whyntowne knew he must not think in that way. It would lead to his own hubris and could spell doom to him and the men he commanded. Perhaps *L'Anguedoc* had grown tired. His was a very long life indeed. Men are not made for such a long life. He breathed in deeply. The smell of lilacs now permeated the night air. How wonderful.

*Could this be his last night on earth?*

"I think *L'Anguedoc* resides here to be less obtrusive, to not stand out," Sir Reginald Brockingham said. "Our design was to look at great castles or country houses. I never would have thought to look in such a lowly place."

"No one else I have ever heard of has these kinds of powers," Whyntowne said. "It must be him or one of the others." He watched as Brockingham checked a burlap bag containing amulets.

"One could argue whether or not we are fortunate," Brockingham said with a wry smile.

"Perhaps this time the Lord is on our side, for it is the very devil for whom we seek," Whyntowne said. "Why would he help these people? Because this is his last refuge? Or could he think to train other zealots, make an army like himself after first seducing them with kindness and good deeds?"

"In the end it is his arrogance that led us to him," Brockingham said. "He had to let others know of his powers. How great he is. This is his arrogance."

The other knights, twelve in number, were assembled around Sir Charles.

"Remember. When we are inside the servant will meet us and lead to *L'Anguedoc's* chamber. We will subdue any resistance. Be prepared for it. *L'Anguedoc* is not a fool."

"And those bought have half of their gold," Sir Reginald said. "It might be enough."

"Or they might think they will have all if we are dead," Whyntowne said. Pulling a dark gray helmet wrapped in cloth from his belt, he carefully took the covering off and showed it to the others. It was in two pieces, front and back that would be bolted together, and fully made of lead. The front was like a death mask, except the place for the eyes was covered in lead instead of open or covered with gold such as the death masks of ancient Mycenae. There was a hinge above where the mouth would be.

"The first task is to place the helmet on his face," Whyntowne said. "Thomas, Argive, Quentin and Lucien will hold him and I will secure the mask. This will protect us from his eyes. Here Reginald," he said, handing the back of the helmet to Brockingham. "We will bind the back of the helmet to the front until we return to the burial place. You others will secure his feet and arms with the ropes."

The ropes had been dipped in Holy Water and blessed. Holy amulets from the East were embedded in the ropes.

Many of the knights now knelt, bowing their heads and crossing themselves.

"Now we start," Sir Charles said. They began to head toward the castle and portcullis. Something he had not thought about in a very long time now came into his consciousness and caused a slight trembling in his limbs.

*Had not L'Anguedoc been slain before? A good hundred years earlier.*

## CHAPTER 3

# AUERSMACHER

xactly eight minutes after signaling the Frenchman, Hinton-Smith knocked on the barracks' wooden door. When a groggy, half-dressed German soldier came to the entrance, Hinton-Smith, holding his nerves in check, said in perfect German, "Good morning. I am here to tell you that the good city of Auersmacher has been captured by the French Army. I expect you to have your men assembled in the square in three minutes. Leave all weapons in the barracks."

The German, in the haze of sleep, scratched himself and shook his head as if to bring his mind fully awake. "Repeat, please."

"I am with the French Army," Hinton-Smith said. "You are my prisoners. Bring your men to the square. Leave all weapons."

The German bowed slightly. "Yes." Then he turned and shouted into the barracks, "Get up! Get up!"

Crouched down in the middle of the square, Cawkins could only shake his head. The lieutenant had not even bothered to unholster his revolver or unshoulder his rifle. The sergeant stood up and jogged over as the first of the Germans emerged, half-clothed and unshaven.

"Do you know what you're doing?" he whispered.

"Don't worry Jack," Hinton-Smith whispered back as the Germans filed out. "Most of the troops were sleeping. Besides, they're only second or third raters. All the first-line troops are in Poland."

"What do you do when your luck runs out?" Cawkins asked.

"Let's hope it doesn't," Hinton-Smith replied cheerfully.

You weren't born to luck, Cawkins wanted to say, but he thought better of it. He's young. He'll learn. "Just try not to push it," he said. Right now it was more important to tend to their new prisoners than lecture him. That would come later. Cawkins turned to start herding the Germans to the well-lit, well-kept, grassy center of the square.

\* \* \*

Indeed, Hinton-Smith was born to the life of an orphan. His parents had died in 1919 when he was only a three-month-old baby. There was no family to take him in, so his father's regiment, the Coldstream Guards, became his family. Kenneth Smith, his father, was a sergeant in the 2nd Battalion of the Guards, popular with men and officers alike. An only child of an only child, he had married Sarah Hinton, who was almost in the same circumstance. Her parents had died, leaving two young girls. The other had moved to the United States with her husband and only agreed to come over for the wedding, if Sarah and Kenneth hyphenated the names of any children so the family name of Hinton would not be lost forever, as her husband would not have any of that, what he called, "upper class nonsense," now that he was an American.

Kenneth Smith was certain he would live forever, having miraculously come through hellfires the likes of which a sane man would deny all existence: the Somme, Arras, Passchendaele; names that could live only in the collective nightmare of World War I. He had come through virtually unscathed, and so it was with little or no trepidation, that he and an old friend squeezed into a Fokker Biplane, captured at the end of the war and now rented to the odd pilot as something of a lark.

It was early on a bright Sunday morning in June, 1919, when they took off from a field near Arras and headed east to the old front, over some of the battlefields that had failed to claim them during the Great War. Tracing a great ellipse, they passed just north of Cambrai on the way to Maubeuge, headed north to Waterloo, and then came around west on the way back. The flight lasted less than an hour. The pilot, as much a daredevil as Kenneth Smith, spotted a farm near a village called St. Venant, and brought the plane into a dive.

"Watch this," he smiled, while leaning over to shout at his friend. "See the chickens? They'll think we're a giant hawk."

He laughed as he finally pulled up, after coming within twenty yards of what would have been a very abrupt stop. Down in the barnyard, the plane had caused general pandemonium as feathers flew, dogs barked, pigs snorted, cows bellowed, and everything ran and jumped in every possible direction.

"I wish it was a German farm," Smith yelled while turning back to see the quickly receding results of their prank.

The pilot laughed and gunned the engine, taking the plane down to tree level, and then, as they approached a large open field, even lower.

An old man who had seen some of the worst of the war and was still filled with hatred for *Le Boche*, or perhaps hallucinating that he was back in the middle of it, saw the unmistakable red and black Iron Cross glinting in the sunshine, and ran haltingly to his house on his game, war-injured leg. Throwing open the door, he hurried inside and grabbed an old Enfield, and ran back out to take up a position behind a thick oak wood table that he tipped on its side. He fired only three rounds as the Fokker lurched upward. One shot pierced the pilot through the heart, killing him instantly. Another cut a fuel line, which resulted in the engine sputtering, then shooting out smoke and flames and stopping all together. There were no para-chutes. Smith had never flown before, but as the plane went into a dive, he climbed out of his seat and tried to edge forward and squeeze into the pilot's bay. He knew he could not maneuver the plane with-out reaching the pedals at the pilot's feet and he could not reach them without pulling his mate free and tossing him out. There was little time but he could not bring himself to send his mate hurtling to the ground even if he was dead and he was not certain of that any-way. Grabbing for the controls he could reach, he tried to guide the plane toward a flat-topped hill, reasoning it was higher up and so they would not fall so far. There were some old gray structures on the hill, like walls. If he could keep the nose up and glide past them, he might be able to land on the flats beyond. Yanking vainly on the stick, Smith realized there was nothing he could do but say a prayer for his wife as the Fokker went into its final dive.

The plane exploded on impact. It was as though these ignoble fields of blood reached out beyond their time and reclaimed two who escaped the original slaughter.

Sarah went home to become one of the twenty million victims of the world wide influenza pandemic of 1919. The loss of her one true love so weakened her, spiritually and physically, that even the solace of her baby could not strengthen her will to resist.

No. Michael Hinton-Smith was not born to luck. But he was born with the impetuousness of his father, late of the Coldstream Guards.

Michael Hinton-Smith grew up the adopted son of his father's Regiment, and to an English soldier, the Regiment was everything. It was a clan, a family, with its own distinctive uniforms, insignias, customs, traditions, and history of glorious deeds. The Coldstream Guards, whose Regimental number signifying their status in the army was number one, had a particularly illustrious past.

Generations of fathers and sons, grandfathers and grandsons continued in service with the same Regiment. Having no parents to call his very own, Hinton-Smith considered every soldier and every wife as his parent, and they reciprocated, calling him son.

One older bachelor, Cyrus Wilson, had taken a special liking to young Hinton-Smith, and made it his mission in life to make sure his every need was taken care of, and more importantly, to provide an ethical structure and a focus to enable him to grow up straight and strong enough to join the Regiment, if he so chose.

Hinton-Smith's military upbringing taught him discipline and aggressiveness, which he put to great use on the playing field in soccer and cricket. This, and his many sponsors from the Guards, saw him accepted to Sandhurst, though it was quite an exception for someone his age, and even more so, class origins.

*   *   *

Steuffel moved forward cautiously, stopping as he edged up against the brick wall of Auersmacher's only bank, out of sight of the plaza. He could hear voices, some speaking in German, but he distinctly thought he also heard some French. What was going on? Was it a training exercise? He was caught for sure. He'd be court-martialed. Steuffel wished he still had the bottle of champagne. He would have opened it and drank it right there. At least the arrest would be more pleasant if he were drunk. As he pondered his alternatives, Steuffel listened more carefully. It sounded like the loudest German speaker had a foreign accent. That is strange. Slowly bringing his head around the corner, he saw a line of men coming out of the barracks and moving into the grassy center of the square to sit. None were in uniform or had weapons. Some were only in underwear. It seemed odd to him that the few men with rifles wore dark blue uniforms. Perhaps they were policemen. But why would they be ushering soldiers out of the barracks? Were they looking for him? Then he remembered the traces of water on the road. They were not police, they were soldiers! The French had crossed the Saar! "My God, it's the invasion!" he said in a whisper as he unslung his Mauser.

His shoulders pushed tensely against the building, he raised his rifle up close to his chest, and stole a second look. There were only a handful of the Frenchmen. He was an expert marksman though he had never aimed at a man before. If he could take out even a few, the others could have a chance to take the rest.

Steuffel took aim at the closest Frenchman and fired.

A soldier standing next to Cawkins crumpled and fell to the soft ground, as the retort of the Mauser rang through the still air. The other Frenchmen crouched down. As a few of the Germans got up on their hands and knees, others tried to stand to see what the commotion was about. Cawkins yelled, "Stay down or we shoot!" and moved his rifle in a wide arc over their heads, firing three quick shots to emphasize the point. Then he looked in the direction of the sound just as Steuffel popped around the corner and took a second shot. This time, his round caught another Frenchman in the shoulder. The man fell to one knee, but kept his weapon trained on the prisoners. Cawkins shouted to the lieutenant. "Damn it! We got a problem!"

"I'll take the sniper," Hinton-Smith said. "You see to the prisoners." Hinton-Smith motioned for one of the *poilus* to cross the plaza to flank the sniper. Then shouting in German, "Shoot anyone who moves," to the other Frenchmen so the Germans would understand, he turned and walked steadily towards the bank building, checking the clip of his service revolver as he walked. He kept his eye focused on the corner where the sniper had appeared.

As two more Germans shuffled out of the barracks, Cawkins ran over, and pushed them to the center with his rifle, yelling, "Move it! Move it!" No more Germans emerged.

From the back of the barracks, where he and his men had entered, Medoc also realized they were in trouble. He also fired his rifle, a garand. Then his group pushed the remaining Germans toward the front of the barracks at bayonet point.

As Cawkins reached the square, one of the Germans stood up as if to fight. The sergeant brought his rifle butt down hard into the man's face. Watching as the soldier fell to the ground holding his head in pain, Cawkins fired another round into the air to make sure the others understood.

Now some thirty feet from the bank, Hinton-Smith saw the muzzle of a rifle poking out from behind the brick wall. He stopped and raised his revolver. As the German's body appeared, the lieutenant fired one round, hitting him in the right forearm, just under the elbow. Steuffel involuntarily dropped his rifle and grabbed his wounded arm.

Hinton-Smith walked up to him. He had no animosity. This was war and there were rules. "Join the others," he said in German. "Your friends will see to your wound." He watched the German walk numbly to the plaza, then picked up the Mauser and walked back to the middle of the square as if he had performed the same cold-blooded operation hundreds of times.

Cawkins helped herd the remainder of the Germans to the plaza, then walked over to Hinton-Smith.

"That was goddamned stupid," Cawkins yelled at the lieutenant, not caring who heard him.

"What?" asked Hinton-Smith, somewhat taken aback.

"You don't walk straight at a man with a rifle. You don't shoot to wound. This isn't cricket on the schoolyard lawn."

"I ended the war for him," Hinton-Smith protested.

"How generous of you. What if you'd missed? He could have killed you. Then you would've left us with only a dozen men guarding two hundred. And they most likely would've followed his lead. I hate to tell you, but you can't count on leading a charmed life. This whole episode was goddamned stupid." Cawkins glared at the lieutenant for a few seconds then walked away.

Hinton-Smith, visibly shaken, stared after the sergeant. He had just captured an entire German garrison with only a platoon of Frenchmen, and he'd taken only two casualties, no deaths. He had performed coolly under pressure. The bullets had flown and he had measured up. He thought Cawkins would be proud.

By the time D'Agapaeov arrived with the two rifle companies, two hundred German soldiers and four policemen, all sulky, disheveled and sleepy, sat meekly and unarmed in the grassy square of the plaza.

*   *   *

Early the next morning, the two companies moved out again. By mid-morning the French were in the next village. From one village to the next, no German soldiers were seen, only bewildered peasants and townspeople, many of whom peered out from shuttered windows and avoided the streets. And so it went.

"Not a soldier among 'em," Cawkins said as they followed D'Agapaeov up the main street of Kleinblittersdorf at noon on September 8th. "Not even snipers," he added as he glanced warily up at the roofs and windows of the buildings, looking for the telltale glistening of sun off a rifle barrel.

The soldiers advanced in two single files, one on either side of the road. "The Germans seem to retreat at the least pressure," Hinton-Smith observed.

"All their troops are busy destroying Poland," Cawkins said. D'Agapaeov looked at Cawkins and laughed, but his laugh had no mirthfulness, it was melancholy. "I wager their covering troops are back at the Siegfried Line by now."

"At this pace, we will be in bloody Berlin in a month, won't we?" the lieutenant said cheerfully. In reality, he was trying to get up the courage to speak to Cawkins. He knew he had to apologize for his rashness, but it was hard for him to admit he was wrong.

The major proceeded with caution, signaling his men to spread out into plowed fields that stretched between villages. The lack of opposition was eerie, the men on edge. Better to stay off the roads: they were more likely to be sighted in. The men slogged over the damp furrows ever alert for mines. It was disquieting. There were not even minefields. Were they luring them in?

"They didn't expect us to do anything, Jack," Hinton-Smith said. "Did they? Did the Germans really think we'd give up Poland as easily as we surrendered Czechoslovakia?"

"Maybe," Cawkins replied.

"That would be bad form, wouldn't it," Hinton-Smith said. All right. Enough of this. He had shown a bit of bad form himself, earlier.

"Jack," Hinton-Smith said abruptly, "I was wrong back there. Really, I was pretty dim."

"Don't give yourself so much credit," Cawkins said gruffly.

"A complete, reckless unthinking arsehole," the lieutenant said.

"That's a little more like it. Let's hope you learned your lesson," Cawkins said. "As for me, it's forgotten."

The next city, Schonbach, was more of the same. From there, they advanced to Brebach, the outworks of the Siegfried Line, just southeast of Saarbrucken. Here they set up a command post in the local bank. They fortified the northern approaches to Brebach with temporary pillboxes made with sandbags. Light machine guns soon protruded from the pillboxes, with mortar emplacements to the rear. Cooks began to start fires and boil water. No one had eaten since the preceding night, and men's appetites were voracious.

And there they waited. Nothing happened for two weeks. No orders to advance came from Gamelin. There were no incidents with the Germans. The French did not shell the Siegfried Line for fear that the Germans would shell their cities.

By the tenth day, Cawkins was fed up. "I'm tired of this," he said to the lieutenant. "Let's go back to the Regiment."

"What about the offensive?" Hinton-Smith asked.

"It's over. I guarantee you. The French aren't going anywhere unless it's back to their own lines. This part is over."

Hinton-Smith was not sure. The Siegfried Line was only miles away. One quick thrust, and it would be theirs. But he realized something else.

"Jack," the lieutenant said, "I guess I'm still an amateur."

"You got that right," the sergeant replied. "Don't worry, Mikeyboy," Cawkins said, as he started packing his duffel bag. "There will be more of this to come. Probably too much."

Hinton-Smith took off his hat and scratched his head.

"Doesn't look like the French have enough stomach for it this time around."

Cawkins turned serious, grabbing the young lieutenant's arm and looking him straight in the eye. "Don't discount the Frenchies. In the Great War they were tough. They were just bled dry. I fought alongside some of them. It's still affecting them."

As Cawkins prophesied, on the 30th, the French were ordered to sneak away in the dead of night to the safety of the Maginot Line and this did more to sap the morale of the common French soldier than did any fear of the Germans.

D'Agapaeov was in a state of high dudgeon when he said goodbye to his two English friends. "I hate to say this about my commanding general, and I only do it because you are English and because you leave us. So disingenuous is Gamelin that, when pressured by the Polish envoy about living up to his commitments, he said a full forty divisions were involved, and they were chasing the Germans back although facing stiff opposition. I strongly demur. This offensive can only be labeled as a sham."

\*   \*   \*

In Arras, both Hinton-Smith and Cawkins were awarded the Croix de Guerre, presented by Gamelin himself. Not wanting to bring more notoriety to his feckless aborted offensive, the old general initially resisted the decoration. To have two Englishmen as the heroes of his fake invasion especially stuck in his craw. But D'Agapaeov would have nothing of it. He raised the issue with politicians grown disillusioned with the general and got his way. For his part, Gamelin made sure that a dozen *poilus* were decorated at the same time and the Englishmen were placed in the middle of the line to be less conspicuous; the ceremony took place in the early morning hours at a small countryside chateau.

Gamelin stoically pinned the medal on Hinton-Smith's chest, kissed him on both cheeks, then did the same to Cawkins and proceeded down the line of Frenchmen. Only the Englishman and American noticed the hint of a sour expression on the general's face.

"Well," Cawkins whispered. "Are you happy?"

Hinton-Smith grinned. "Yes. But I'm not sure it's enough."

"Oh boy," the sergeant sighed.

Still there was no real war. Hitler kept postponing his western offensive as the mild fall on the Continent turned into one of the coldest winters on record. Or perhaps the German thought he could pull off one last bluff.

Poland had been destroyed and neither the French nor the British had come to its aid. They had let their Ally down, but a rescue was both geographically and militarily impractical. The great armies sat around. Nobody went "over the top," or tried to thread their way through the barbed wire; no Stukas dove or tanks collided with the allied lines; and no artillery was fired upon either side. There were skirmishes at sea and battles in Norway, but for the most part of the next eight months, the French went underground and maintained the Maginot Line and the BEF, which had begun to stream in about the 4th of September, 1939, set up camps, trained, drank their tea and ate their scones on the Franco-Belgian border. The Germans called it "Sitzkrieg," the British called it the "Phony War." The French *poilus* were encouraged by German propaganda to think the British "Tommie" would leave him to fight it out alone, and the Tommies worried about their French Ally's ability on their right flank, but only one man thought, and this, only for a moment, that the French Army and Air Force would out and out collapse.

In London, this time around, there was no heroic rush to join the military machine. Men waited their turn to be called, but there was a rush to get married. August and September had the highest number of weddings ever recorded.

Hinton-Smith and Cawkins rejoined the battalion at the little French village of Bachy and spent the next months largely engaged in extensive drainage operations, constructing the defensive line, wallowing in mud, freezing, and, along with the men, learning to dig. The highlight of the winter was in December, when the battalion was visited by His Royal Majesty the King and lined the road to cheer. By January, the ground was covered with snow and ice, training was limited, and an influenza epidemic laid low some of the officers and men. After the first thaw in February, whereas the lieutenant kept busy organizing games to keep the soldiers fit, Cawkins bulldozed them into shape with marching, digging and calisthenics.

There was none of the excitement the lieutenant yearned for or expected. It was so boring that some officers sought permission to bring their polo mounts over to start a league, but were turned down by the French who frowned on such frivolity. After all, they were at war. So the Tommies trained, built pillboxes and tank traps to finish fortifying their sector of the Franco-Belgian border, and then trained some more to keep their morale high. They sweated in the cool morning sun digging miles of trenches out of the rock hard earth; they felled ancient oaks to create clear arcs of fire; they rolled out miles of thirty yards-deep barbed wire that shone brightly in the noon day sun like sharp metallic jewelry. And some, if not all, of their staff officers prayed that somehow the Belgians would relent before it was too late, and let them fortify the forward line of the Meuse-Antwerp.

In stark contrast was the laxity in training, boredom, draining of morale, and then, drift into alcoholism, which helped lead to the deterioration of the French Army.

Paris had, for all intents and purposes, the look of a city at peace and highly prosperous. There was no rationing of food, not even meat. There was no rationing of gasoline, even though all of it was imported. Theaters, operas, restaurants, and cinemas all were open, although there was a nightly blackout. The only air raids dropped propaganda leaflets on the French soldiers, telling them not to die for the British and the Poles.

And of course, Paris was the preference of most soldiers on leave.

*Au Lapin Agile* was Cawkins's favorite cabaret. Whenever he and Hinton-Smith secured passes they would head into Paris and camp out in the nightclub.

It was end of March and late in the day when the two soldiers disembarked at a crowded *Gare du Nord*. There were lines of people waiting to board, while many others of all stripes got down from the coaches. All along the tracks and platforms were hawkers calling out their wares and prices, everything from nylons to shirts and undergarments, to croissants, rolls, chocolate and cigarettes.

"Hard to believe we're at war, isn't it?" Hinton-Smith said as they made their way out of the station. "We can't get half of those things back in London." He looked at the bustle in the street and the many patrons enjoying themselves at outdoor cafes.

"Taxi?" Hinton-Smith asked.

"No," Cawkins said. "I'm tired of sitting. Let's walk." He had something to decide. Had the boy learned his lesson? Cawkins hoped a leisurely detour down the Boulevard de Rochechouart with its shops, coffee stands, fruit and vegetable vendors and ubiquitous newspaper kiosks would help clear his mind.

Uncharacteristically, the sergeant dawdled, keeping his thoughts to himself, and it took a long time before they were heading down Rue des Saules in Montmartre on the crisp spring afternoon. A few puddles still dotted the cobblestone street from an early morning rain. A pleasant breeze carried the scent of freshly baked pastries.

Soldiers walked past them in pairs or groups, some English, some French, and many civilians. Some were arm in arm with young ladies, who were very properly attired, though other ladies were quite scanty in their dress, especially for such a cool afternoon, but they were obviously getting ready for business. All seemed very carefree.

A pair of portly gendarmes stood on the corner beneath a street lamp, keeping tabs on the natives and foreigners.

"Thief!" someone yelled. Hinton-Smith spotted a scrawny young boy running away, purloined satchel in hand and managed a few steps before he heard a stern voice. "Will you settle down?" Cawkins said, shaking his head. "Look." The sergeant pointed to the policemen who were already sprinting after the crook, a good forty yards ahead of them. "It's their job."

"I'd catch him before that lot."

"Maybe. But not tonight, Michael," Cawkins said. Maybe he hadn't, but it was hard to blame him for trying to help some poor SOB. "I want a quiet evening." He also wanted a quiet conversation with the lieutenant.

As Cawkins and Hinton-Smith approached the club they could hear music and laughter coming from inside. Suddenly a half dozen gray pigeons bolted skyward as the door flung open and two young men in uniform came hurtling out, one after the other tumbling to the street and rolling over on the pavement like bungling acrobats.

"Looks like there's no end of excitement tonight," Cawkins said.

"They're two of ours," the lieutenant said as he spotted the insignia of the Coldstream Guards on their uniform sleeves, Walking over, he leaned down to lend a hand to the nearest one.

Not looking up or caring who it was, the private shook off the helping hand. "Watch it there, mate," Billy Graves said in a pugnacious tone. Then he got up on all fours, shaking his head to get his bearings. "I'll be right with you," he said as though preparing for a brawl. "Just give me a second."

"See what too much free time gets you?" Cawkins said. "There but for the grace of God…"

"I thought you had gone there, mate," Hinton-Smith said with a laugh.

"Maybe a couple of years ago," Cawkins said, clearing his throat. "Not now." He hoped he'd never looked that bad, but unfortunately knew he had at least come close.

The two soldiers both reeked of cheap liquor, cheaper perfume and tobacco smoke. Amos Parker, a corporal, grabbed onto a light pole and slowly pulled himself up and leaned against the pole till getting his balance. Finally standing on his own, he brushed himself off and noticed the sergeant and lieutenant standing in front of him.

"Billy. Billy," Parker whispered, using his foot to nudge Graves while at the same time trying to salute.

"Sir," Corporal Parker slurred as he swept a blond shock of hair back off his forehead and tried to come to attention.

"Billy! Get up."

"Huh!" Graves said. "Stop it, Amos. I'll get there." Graves looked up and saw the officer and sergeant. "Bollocks! Now we're in for it. I told you we shouldn't have come here, didn't I?"

"You did not," Parker said.

"Sir. Sergeant Major," Billy Graves said as he got up, straightened his tie and also tried his best to salute. "Sorry, sir."

The salutes were quite sloppy.

"Ah, sir. It wasn't you I pulled my arm away from, was it now?" Graves asked hopefully.

Hinton-Smith saluted back and laughed. "Are you lads all right?"

"Excuse us, sir. They tossed us out," Parker said. "Why in bloody hell would they do that? We're Allies."

"We only hit two blokes," Graves said.

"Don't forget the mug I broke over that Frenchie chap's head," Parker said.

"Oh," Graves said, placing his hand under his chin as if in deep thought. "That's true, sir. We only bonked three of the bastards." He scratched his head. "I forgot about that one."

"Right," Parker said. "Can you two gentlemen get us back in? There's a miss in there. I think she loves me."

"Right," Graves echoed. "Can you?" Turning to Parker, he said, "She's playing you for drinks, mate. She fancies that French bloke you bonked over the head."

"You broke a mug over a Frenchman's head?" Hinton-Smith asked in wonderment. It had taken a bit to register.

"That's what I said. He was wearing a beret and a silly mustache," Parker said.

"The bloke deserved it," Graves added, patting his mate on the shoulder. "You did good."

"Besides, she loves me." Then he pushed Graves and started to laugh. Graves put up his fists as though he was a bare-fisted prize fighter about to fight the corporal. Suddenly remembering his audience he dropped his fists and tried to come to attention.

"Can you get us back in there?" Parker asked. "There's some pretty girls."

Both were country boys, Graves the son of a farmer and Parker the son of sheep herder. It was their first time in Paris.

Leaving *Ferme d'Aigremont* on a train that afternoon, they arrived at the same *Gare du Nord* station a little before dusk and asked the first soldier they saw where the excitement was. Many sights and establishments were mentioned but the one that stuck in their minds was the cabaret *Au Lapin Agile*. Parker reckoned he overheard the sergeant talk about it and neither man wanted to go to a place where they might run into Cawkins: after all, what was the purpose of leave? But after two drinks apiece at a tavern near the station neither could remember any place else, so they hired a taxi to *Au Lapin Agile*.

These were men from their own company and right away Cawkins could see from the lieutenant's expression that he was going to help. He'd definitely have to put a stop to that.

"I believe you lads have had a bit too much," Cawkins said.

"Oh, Sergeant Major," Parker whined. "I only had me five ha'-pints. And it's still early, ain't it?"

Graves giggled. "I drank me some of that expensive French wine."

"Let me see what I can do, lads," Hinton-Smith said.

Graves put his right hand over his heart as if swearing an oath. "We'll behave, sir. I promise you."

"If none of them Frenchies give us guff," Parker added.

"I don't think so," Cawkins said. Then leaning over to the lieutenant he whispered, "You'd take in any stray puppy, wouldn't you? We passed an MP down the block. I'm going to get him before these two really get in trouble."

"You men stay here with the lieutenant," Cawkins said and then jogged off to find the policeman.

Graves and Parker watched the sergeant as he walked away. Even in his inebriated state it did not take Graves long to figure the lay of the land. The lieutenant was a softer touch.

"If those bastards won't let us back in, sir, can you take us to the Eiffel Tower?" Graves asked.

"Right," Parker said, quickly recognizing his mate's peasant cunning.

He'd run with it as well. "That would be a bit of all right, wouldn't it?"

"Do you think there are many women about, sir?" Graves asked. "At the Eiffel Tower, that is?"

"Let's wait till the Sergeant Major returns," Hinton-Smith said. Perhaps he could take them, he thought. They could sober up on the walk. Then he looked more carefully at the two. No. Better not. Cawkins was certainly right on this one.

After the two men were squared away in a make-shift gaol, Cawkins and Hinton-Smith entered the cabaret and took two seats near the stage.

The club was noisy and filled with smoke so thick one could hardly see the scantily clad dancers on stage. A six man group alternated from playing American "Big Band" music to French, and a pretty singer would occasionally accompany them.

Cawkins was silent as he quickly downed a mug of Guinness, room temperature to preserve the flavor. Ordering another, he cooled it down with ice cubes. He was bored out of his mind and knew that it would not take much to set him off in the same spiral as the two soldiers. He was even tired of looking at the gorgeous dancers, not something that happened very often. The sergeant had made up his mind. Now if it would only come to fruition. Cutting a piece of garlic crusted steak, he put it in his mouth and began to chew. After swallowing it, he washed it down with another large swig of ale and forcefully put his half-empty mug down on the table.

"Did they teach you anything to do with Intelligence at Sandhurst?" he asked the lieutenant.

Hinton-Smith stared at him intently before saying in a whisper, "Not enough intelligent NCOs or officers among the whole lot there." He laughed. "Or do you mean like spying?" He then shrugged his shoulders. "I'm game for anything right about now." His curiosity was quickly rising.

"What do you have in mind?"

"More like reconnaissance. Let's get down to cases before I drink any more or start thinking rationally. I ran into a buddy of mine at Staff two nights ago," Cawkins said, leaning over the table. "This is between you and me. Nobody else."

"I'll be discreet," Hinton-Smith said, placing his hand on his heart and smiling like it was Cawkins's liquor doing the talking. "Word of honor."

Cawkins looked around. The cabaret was crowded, many of the patrons drunk and boisterous. "Let's go upstairs. More private." The sergeant stood and motioned to a waiter, waving a few Francs for him to see and placing them near their empty plates. The two men threaded their way around the packed tables and started up a narrow flight of creaky wooden stairs. At the top they found an upright barrel with two benches. They sat. "I'm sober Mikey. And dead serious. He's recruiting for some kind of mission. Wouldn't tell me anything about it except to meet him tomorrow, early." Cawkins downed the rest of the semi-cool ale in one swallow. "I'm interested in what he has to say. If there's a part for you I'll bring you on. That's the best I can do." Cawkins began to fidget. He found it hard to say what was on his mind and drew it out slowly. "Michael. I have to know something." He paused to breathe in deeply. "Can you control yourself?"

Hinton-Smith looked at him, puzzled, but then he understood. "Yes."

"This could be important. I can't afford to have you running off half-cocked."

"Right. Got it."

"You sure?" He stared intently at the lieutenant.

"Yes."

"Then let's gather those boys and go back to headquarters."

"Right."

Early the next morning Cawkins sought out the friend. The mission was to be put in motion immediately and he pulled the sergeant into the intelligence unit at Bachy for a quick briefing. The sergeant, not having time to waste, tracked down Hinton-Smith in the officers' quarters.

Cawkins was never one to mince words. "You're in," he tersely announced. "Pack up your kit. We're leaving in less than an hour. You have thirty minutes to get ready."

Hinton-Smith looked at him, smiled and came to attention. He saluted and said, "Yes sir!"

Cawkins cleared his throat. "Come on now, Mikey. You're embarrassing me."

It was now the first week of May 1940. They did not know it, none on the Allied side did, but the invasion of France and the Low Countries would begin in less than ten days.

## CHAPTER 4

# ON THE HOME FRONT

I n London, at the time of the embarkation of the BEF, besides the anxiety attendant upon waiting for the "dogs of war" to loose, there was a fever pitch of excitement, and an awareness and edginess that does not come to people in their everyday lives.

Sitting alone at the window of a small, second-floor study in his two storied Victorian house, Cyrus Wilson watched some of his fellow Londoners walk up and down Swain's Lane. Some were couples walking arm in arm or holding hands, obviously in love; others were blokes probably headed toward the Hound's Tooth for a pint. A cobbler, his white smock smudged with bootblack, wheeled his wares home after a long day and he recognized a tobacconist also heading home.

Wilson observed that even though Londoners had been on the brink of war for what seemed like years, in a struggle which he had already divined was to be to the death, they still seemed to feel themselves alive, passionate, even happy (at least the young who did not remember the Great War).

Even as this unruffled London populace calmly awaited the Luftwaffe's bombs, they remained confident in their boys going to the Continent, knowing "the thin red line" would acquit itself admirably and send the Hun running.

There was, however, an ever growing irritation. They were suffering the pangs of a nation at war without the exhilaration of the actual fight: blackouts; rationing of food, gas, and other essentials; homes taken over (or given up) to be used as hospitals; the false bombing alarms; a million women and children waited to be dispersed throughout the countryside, not to mention the largest wartime dislocation of them all: mobilization. When war was finally declared, little changed. The boys in the BEF would soon feel it first hand, but here at home, only the previous dislocations were felt, except for a new anxiety for their loved ones and an urgent desire for any news. They could not really get the feeling of sinking their teeth into it, so the frustration remained.

Wilson's biggest frustration was one of age. He wanted to fight, to do something. Nearing seventy, he was still quite fit from his life in the Coldstream Guards and had volunteered for combat. The sergeant at the recruiting office had a different suggestion—the Home Guard.

\*     \*     \*

Elizabeth Hammond smiled at the young soldier who gave up his seat for her, and with a relieved look, settled into the seat and made herself comfortable. Elizabeth was of average height, with shoulder-length blond hair neatly parted on the left, slender arms, shapely legs and silky alabaster skin.

"You needn't have done this, lieutenant (she pronounced it leftenant). I'm getting down in three stops."

"Anytime, ma'am." Then with a bow bordering on the histrionic, he added, "Lieutenant Kenneth Roberts, at your service."

She smiled and blushed as she looked down and fiddled with her bag. It was not that she was relieved to get a seat; the ride on the Tube from Piccadilly to King's Cross-St. Pancras was only fifteen minutes, with stops.

Elizabeth was relieved to have finished the first day at her new work, coming through with flying colors. Everyone she knew wanted to help with the war effort and she secured a position with security clearance on merit alone. It must be rather important to need security clearance, she thought. Cyrus and Kate will certainly be proud. Perhaps a bit surprised as well. Of course she was only a secretary, but everyone was in uniform. She wondered if she would get a uniform as well. She would like that.

The steady thump, thump, thumping, of the car's wheels hitting each small seam of the rails and the rhythmic swaying of the car combined with her daydreaming to produce an almost soporific effect. Up all the previous night worrying whether or not she would secure the appointment, the excitement had by now worn off and she was exhausted. She had just dozed off when she felt a light touch on her shoulder.

"Ma'am." It was the lieutenant. Elizabeth knew what he wanted.

"I'm sorry, lieutenant. I have a boyfriend over in France, at the Front," she said with a great deal of pride, but also as nicely as she could, wanting to let the young man down easily. After all, he was a gentleman and soldier and she could not blame him. She was young, attractive and didn't she fill out her clothes quite nicely, thank you.

It was presently his turn to blush, but as in many embarrassing situations in this life, it would soon be hers again.

He gently whispered, "No ma'am. I'm off to the Front myself in a week, but that's not why I woke you. This is your stop, the third stop. King's Cross-St. Pancras. I thought you were sleeping. You had better hurry."

"Oh," was all she could muster as the smile quickly faded and a humiliated little grimace froze onto her pretty features. She bowed her eyes and avoided looking him in the face, then fleetingly glanced around to see if anyone else had heard their exchange. Rising quickly, she threaded her way through the other standing passengers on her way to the door. She was angry with herself. Why did she get so flustered? Kate would just laugh off something like this. It's such a bother.

Two minutes later, as she showed her two penny ticket, then queued up for the tube to Archway Station (she had to change trains from the Piccadilly Line to the Northern Line), she was still upset about speaking to that man.

She boarded the train for the fifteen-minute ride to Archway Station, and this time, with an abrupt chuckle to herself, determined she would grab a rail and remain standing for the short ride. When the train reached the station, she got down, walked across the platform and up the stairs to board a double-decker bus to St. Albans Road, where she lived in a third story flat with her younger sister.

"Kate! Where are you?" she yelled as she opened the door to the quaint, three room apartment with the dilapidated, off white wallpaper they had been meaning to redo. There was never enough time.

"Oh, what's this?" she said. On the floor were two letters. Picking them up, she saw one was a bill and put it on the counter as she looked at the other. No markings. It's from Michael. Elizabeth resisted the temptation to open it. She called into the bedroom, but her sister did not answer, so she looked in the pantry to see if there was anything edible to fix Cyrus. She had gotten into the habit of fixing something to eat at her flat, and then carrying it over to Cyrus Wilson's house. Kate might be there as well.

During the past several months of Hinton-Smith's absence, as they were drawn together by their common affection for the lieutenant, she and Kate had gotten to know Cyrus very well. At first they spent time with him because they were worried about him being alone and probably lonely, but by now he had become almost like a father to them and they could not wait to see him. She was very proud of her new work and could not wait to tell him every detail. And now, she had another reason to hurry; there was a letter from Michael only received today. She was so excited, and of course, relieved to hear from him, that it was very difficult for her to wait. She tried to sneak a look by holding the letter up to the light to see through the envelope, but stopped after a second. Have backbone my dear.

They had pledged to read his letters together. Dusk was coming fast, there was a new moon, and she did not want to be out on the street in the thick gloom of absolute pitch darkness that accompanied the "black out." She grabbed some scones and two apples and rushed out of the flat.

It was a little more than a half-mile to Cyrus's home on South Grove, and she was halfway there when it occurred to her that she had not eaten or drank anything all day, so intoxicating had been her new experience. She could almost taste the cup of tea that Cyrus was surely steeping at this very moment. Elizabeth hoped he had managed to get some milk. Things were getting harder to find every day.

She rushed down the street, almost seeming to break into a run, and was only a hundred yards from his house when she had to stop. The massive walls of Highgate Cemetery now loomed before her. Elizabeth's smile turned into a confused frown. A sense of disquiet, of foreboding took hold, accompanied by a barely discernable cold sweat and a shiver running down the length of her spine. Perhaps it was a premonition of the hundreds of thousands of young men who would soon be no more, and would populate similar quiet, dark, cold places in the earth, or that some day she herself would lie in rest in some similar dismal place. Irritated, she fumed, "Not again!" The sensation had gone away before, and would certainly go away in due time. But why did it keep happening? She laughed at herself for her childishness. Why not? Doesn't this happen to anyone who walks by a cemetery? Especially at night, and with this god-awful blackout? Every time she visited Cyrus, there was no way around it. She could avoid the New Highgate Cemetery, the one where Karl Marx and Herbert Spencer reposed, by simply walking up Highgate Hill, past Whittington Hospital and the statue, where she and Hinton-Smith had oftentimes stopped to look at the monument to Dick Whittington's cat and dream of their future together, and then past Waterlow Park to South Grove. However, when she turned down Swain's Lane, she could not avoid coming into proximity with Old Highgate, as Cyrus's house was located directly across from the north entrance. She had scrupulously cultivated the habit of walking on the opposite side of the street until reaching his house. Then she had to cross.

"I shouldn't come here at night by myself," she said out loud. Then shaking her head, she inadvertently squeezed her lips together in an expression that made light of her own foolishness. She started to walk, and through an uneasy force of will made it across the street, determined to listen to the sounds from the other side of the dark stone wall shielding the cemetery. The wall was too high for her to look inside, but listening proved she had nothing to fear, although, and this she also knew, she would be just as ill at ease the next time. "This cemetery's been here for one hundred years and you've never heard of anyone coming out to disturb the living," she very deliberately said to herself. "Nothing ever happens here. They go in, but they never come out!" With an afterthought, and a nervous giggle, she said, "You are silly. You're sounding like Kate."

\*     \*     \*

Elizabeth Hammond could not have known that in the past, over a span of some six centuries and less than a half dozen times, unfortunates had found their way onto the grounds where centuries later those foreboding breastwork-like walls would be erected to their present ten foot height, and into what was now Old Highgate. Or that hidden in the very recesses of the overgrown, jungle-like cemetery was another wall, enclosing a smaller, ancient cemetery. Those forlorned souls had wandered over that cursed, mildewed wall and never been seen again: a miscreant grave robber had tried to pry open a tomb in the thirteenth century; a pair of destitute young lovers had tried to hide from their parents in 1565; a child pickpocket had tried to escape his master, ironically only two years before the birth of Charles Dickens, whose family now reposed within. None were really missed. These ill-fated souls had but one thing in common; they had by chance wandered into the vicinity of that aforementioned ancient, forgotten cemetery.

Elizabeth sometimes heard sounds, and her imagination would run wild. She even told Cyrus that one time as she walked past, she was certain she heard a faint voice calling to her from within the cemetery walls. Try as she might, she had never been able to force herself to look into the cemetery through the bars of the harrowing North Gate.

This night, as Elizabeth stopped to listen, she leaned toward the walls as if that would help her to hear. Perceiving nothing, she began to walk again at a brisk pace, starkly conscious of the clatter of her own shoes breaking the silence of the night. Her courage did not last as she approached the iron bars of the North Gate: the gate Highgate legend deemed as evil. But this night, something unknowable drew her nearer. For once she would prove to herself that there was nothing malevolent about the gate, it was nothing more than hundred year old wrought iron. The worst you could do was cut yourself on it.

Her momentum seemed unstoppable. She could not turn away. Elizabeth had never before passed by the North Gate on this side of Swain's Lane. It was as if some inner force was trying to prove her bravery, or perhaps that there was, indeed, nothing to fear. She walked faster but continued on the west side of the narrow street. Why was she doing this, she asked herself? And then, as she passed the first iron pole, a grimy gnarled hand shot out through the bars and grabbed her wrist. Elizabeth turned a ghostly white; her heart leapt into her throat, her apples and scones came loose and fell, scattering on the cobblestone. She smelled something foul and felt herself being pulled nearer the gate. Why did she walk there? She was as good as dead. They do come out!!

Then there was a voice. They speak as well? But wait, she'd heard the distinctive gutter voice before. It laughed and smelled of rotten liquor. It was Jemmie Craven, the borough's unlovable sot and ne'er do well.

"Give us a few pence and I'll toast yer beauty," Craven said.

"Let go," Elizabeth said angrily. "How dare you?" She tried to pull her arm away.

"How do ye know I ain't no ghoul," he snarled. Then he said fawningly. "Just a few pence, me darlin'. Jemmie means no harm."

"Let go!" Elizabeth said, loudly this time, straining against his grip. "I'll report you."

"If you be a bit nicer, I might put in a few good words to me mates. Maybe they won't bother Cyrus no more."

Just then, another familiar voice offered relief.

"What's the commotion? Who are you goin' on with, ghosts? Hurry up, lass," Cyrus Wilson shouted from his doorstep. "Them in that place ain't in any hurry, but I'm about ready to starve!"

Jemmie's hand released her and withdrew beyond the gate. Elizabeth stepped back quickly, bent over to gather up the fruit and pastries, never taking her eyes off Craven, who stared at her with glee in his eyes. She then ran across the street to Cyrus, giving him a hug that almost squeezed the breath out of him.

"Either something's wrong or you want to suffocate me," Cyrus said.

Elizabeth did not want to cry but she could not help it. It was better not to bother Cyrus about that silly drunk. Cyrus Wilson had a temper, and there were more important things today, so she told a partial truth. "It's that cemetery wall. I can't walk by it without..." She then resumed her cry.

"Highgate Cemetery is an eerie but fascinating subject," Cyrus said, as though in that one sentence, pondering and summing up the whole of his knowledge of the grounds next to his house. "If you like your literary tales, some say that family members were inside the huge tomb of Sir Loftus Otway, paying their respects to his remains, when Bram Stoker happened to view them through the skylights, and envisioned the undead. And that became Dracula."

"Then there is the North Gate. The one you just came from, ain't it. I reckon the best stories concern it. People have sworn they've seen bodies rising from the ground through those bars, and a giant man, almost seven feet tall clad all in black. There was a young girl who insisted she'd seen a vampire there, then over a period of six months, she wasted away and died. It was only later, during her preparation at the funeral home, that the mortician noticed the two small puncture wounds on her neck."

"But me," Cyrus went on, now in a more soothing tone, "I reckon it's all a load of malarkey. I have lived across from that North Gate now these thirty odd years. I can even see down into the cemetery from my study...and I ain't never seen a thing but a stray cat or fox nor heard more than the hoot of an owl or the rustling through fallen leaves of a rat or some such."

He reached over to dry Elizabeth's tears with a clean, white handkerchief. Now she managed a smile and said, "I have a letter." She handed it to him.

"Well why didn't you say so?" Cyrus thundered, as he unfolded it, looked for an address, then ripped open the paper envelope.

"No post mark again?" Cyrus growled. "Who do those bloody fools think we are, German spies?" This happened to be what he said every time he received a letter from the front, even though he realized the necessity of not giving the Germans any information which could offer clues on the whereabouts of the various BEF units. Being an old soldier himself, he wanted to be privy to everything that was going on and took it as a personal affront to be left out, and even more of an insult to be tendered a commission in the Home Guard, which he regarded as a collection of amateurs, who had neither seen real service nor ever been under fire, and were probably, to his way of thinking, too cowardly to fight anyway.

Strangely, but in this instance peculiar to Cyrus, his stubbornness had got in the way of his divining the truth. He heard rumors about the group of Defense Volunteers, that Anthony Eden called for only days after the Germans had entered Poland, and immediately formed an incorrect opinion of them.

Cyrus could form an idea so strongly that it would become part of his very being, even when incontrovertible evidence was offered in dispute, and then, not even the force of a Krakatoa could dislodge it. Elizabeth could be equally stubborn. He had convinced her, and in a spirited collusion, they jokingly referred to them as the "defenseless volunteers."

He would have been greatly embarrassed to learn that most of the volunteers were former soldiers like himself. One company in Sussex alone boasted six former generals. Cyrus could be a stubborn man.

Elizabeth was now at ease and laughed, "Be happy you got anything." She grabbed his arm. "Hurry. Let's go in. If you're quick, you can read it before any of those Home Guard busybodies catch us."

Taking his eyes from the letter, he looked up at her and his expression changed from one of irritation to haste. "Bloody hell, Lizzie. You're right. Hurry. Your sister's inside brewing the tea." His eyes twinkled. "We managed to procure the milk," he added in the best upper class nasal voice he could contrive. "And a wee bit of sugar."

They rushed up the three steps to the house and entered. All the window shutters were already closed and taped flush to the windowpanes so as to emit no light from within. Cyrus Wilson quickly stuffed a towel underneath the bottom of the front door, then pulled tape down along the sides and across the top of the door just to make sure.

Kate appeared, holding a silver tray with a pot, three cups and a small pitcher filled with hot milk. There were three sugar cubes, one on each cup's saucer. No sooner had she put down the tray than she smiled. She saw the letter in Elizabeth's hand.

"You're so lucky," she said. She could not wait to hear from Hinton-Smith as well. Kate was tall and thin, with long dark curls that flowed freely down her back to her waist. Only sixteen when her sister had first started seeing the handsome young lieutenant, there was nothing at stake for the two of them, such as love or desire, so it was an easy step for them to become friends, and the best of friends they were. Although there was a touch of infatuation on her part, and the smallest bit of jealousy, she would not have admitted it, even to herself.

She placed one sugar cube in each cup, poured a thimble of the precious milk into each then finished by filling the three cups with black tea which turned a pleasant brown as it reached the milk.

Elizabeth beamed and affectionately rubbed her sister's shoulder. "Don't worry. One day you will find your own Michael. I'll be your maid of honor and Cyrus will walk you down the aisle. I'm certain of it."

Kate blushed. "I am certainly not worried," she said, somewhat annoyed that the insinuation was that the only thing she wanted in the world was to have a husband. It was condescending, especially coming from her sister.

Cyrus lit one solitary light bulb and they huddled close to read the letter together. It was nothing exceptional. Only that he had learned some French. Hinton-Smith was not one to boast about his deeds. "We heard the best part from that crank, the mayor."

Sergeant Cawkins, though not pleased with the lieutenant's actions in taking Auersmacher was not averse to giving accolades when due. The cause and ramifications were these: he described the action to a mate of his at Bachy Headquarters; the mate told a friend at the Coldstream Guards Regimental Headquarters in Aldershot, back across the Channel; the Mayor of the Borough of Highgate got wind of it at a Civil Defense meeting through a Guards colonel (Hinton-Smith had grown up as much in Highgate as he did with the Regiment, for his guardian, Cyrus Wilson, lived in the borough); and the mayor, a pudgy little man who always seemed to make his rounds in a black suit and brown derby, and a thoroughgoing glad-handed opportunist (or politician you might say), was convinced by his advisors that it would be an astute political decision to persuade some of the leading citizens of the area to have a parade through Highgate honoring Hinton-Smith. As more people jumped on the bandwagon, he went so far as to try to have the lieutenant brought home on leave to participate.

When turned down by the proper channels, the mayor with his usual prescience was heard to say, "We'll have the parade when the war is over and he returns. It will only be three or four months."

Hinton-Smith began to receive a great deal of publicity throughout London. His exploits grew so with each retelling, that some of the more cynical folks wondered whether there need be any other fight with the Germans at all, or if so, perhaps they could just send Hinton-Smith and that would be enough.

With all the attendant chatter concerning her love, Elizabeth's heart soared. She had chosen him, she persuaded herself, and it had turned out to be an excellent choice: he had become a bona fide hero and Elizabeth was certain she had known it would happen all the time. She and Kate had even gotten Cyrus in the bargain. And what was even better, out of all the women in London, and throughout England itself, Hinton-Smith had wanted only her. After all, they were engaged.

Quite often she envisioned her floor-length white dress and train, walking arm in arm with her lieutenant through a corridor of King's Guards, swords drawn and hoisted as if to form a canopy. Sometimes the daydream included a ceremony at Westminster, sometimes at Buckingham palace. Of course, the King would have to be in attendance for the great hero's wedding, hoisting drinks with Cyrus and Kate.

Except for the sometimes muddle, war could be grand.

# CHAPTER 5

# AT ANOTHER TIME AND PLACE II

As the servant had instructed, the hunters left the road where it crossed a small creek, and then followed the river's course through the forest till they came to an old sluice gate, once used to divert the creek to form a moat around the walls of *L'Anguedoc's* manor. Descending into the weed and brush filled channel, they continued on until the stone walls enclosing the manor once more came into view.

There were no men visible atop the walls.

"He has no guards," Brockingham said. "This is what I've been told."

"He is this confident," Whyntowne said.

"It appears so."

Circling around to the rear of the fortress, the men made their way to the moat.

The landing outside the rear gate was only wide enough for three grown men to stand at a time. This smaller drawbridge was always kept up unless there was an emergency.

Whyntowne and Brockingham crouched down to look into the dark moat, where water now lay stagnant below eight-foot walls of dirt and spanned some twelve feet across.

"It stinks of dead fish left to rot," Sir Charles said, turning his face away.

"Or dead bodies," Brockingham said. "It is well our man warned us of the moat. We'd never make it out of there."

Sir Charles stood up. "Did your man say anything of hazards?"

"No. He knows naught of *L'Anguedoc's* powers or history," Brockingham said. "But there are peasants hereabouts, and children. *L'Anguedoc* depends upon their good will. If anyone was hurt or killed in an unusual manner it could give him away."

"And cast a different light on his so-called benevolence," Sir Lucien Castillo said, before turning to go back to the packhorses.

Lucien and three others now unfastened the planks from the packhorses and brought them forward. Earlier, spikes had been pounded into one end of each log and a rope attached.

Argive Turnbull and Castillo then hoisted one of the planks upright on the edge of the moat. Sir Argive held the bottom to the ground while Sir Lucien took hold of the rope and slowly lowered the first piece of timber to the far side. Once it was in place, the other was lowered along side, together forming a narrow, sixteen-inch wide bridge.

Turnbull quickly bound the logs together and held them fast, while all except two removed their heavy boots to aid in their stealth.

Wind began to whistle through the nearby trees. The water in the moat was eerily roiled for being so far below. It almost seemed alive for a man with too much imagination.

Sir Reginald withdrew a golden amulet from his bag and held it out before the men. Threading a leather lace through a loop on the talisman, he placed it around his neck and tied it. The other men took amulets and did the same.

This was a protection they had been given in the Eastern lands.

"Let's see if your man was good to his word," Whyntowne said as he stepped up on the logs. He was not a man to send others into danger before him. Holding his hands out shoulder height to his sides for balance, he quickly made it across and tried the gate. His hands were sweating as he braced his feet and pushed the entry firmly. It moved, making a dull, grinding sound.

The portcullis was up and the postern unlocked as promised.

At another time and far away place, in the Crusades, Brockingham and Whyntowne had also bought their way inside more than one castle or garrisoned city, but that was in the Middle East and these fortresses were held by those of the Moslem faith. They learned there was always someone who could be bought though they never truly believed in them till they had successfully entered the stronghold with a host of men and taken it. Trust was a perilous luxury.

Now Sir Charles wondered if these people in this place were really bought. Betrayal was commonplace during the Crusades.

What would he find on the other side of these walls? Armed guards, *L'Anguedoc* himself?

Whyntowne signaled the other knights, bound the logs on his side and held up the rope for the others to grab onto while they crossed, one at a time.

When Brockingham and Castillo were on his side of the moat, Whyntowne slowly edged the gate wider and slipped inside, the two knights close behind and all with swords drawn. Within minutes, all of the knights were across the moat and gathered inside the shadows of the wall.

Two remained outside the walls as a lookout, gathering the boots and retiring to a copse some twenty yards away and facing the rear entry.

There was no one about, not even a dog. All was quiet. No fires burned and the manor was all darkness.

Now they had to find their way to *L'Anguedoc's* chamber.

"Where is our guide?" Whyntowne whispered.

"He was supposed to meet us here," Brockingham said, indicating the gate behind them. "If waylaid, he said he'd meet us at the stair-well to the left of the hall. Inside the manor."

These were fearless men. All knew the importance of their charge. All had prepared for this assignation for decades and all knew that they could die completing it: even that some of them must. But none faltered as they followed Sir Charles Whyntowne across a wide grassy area to the front of the building. Directly in the middle was a set of three steps leading into the manor. A thick wooden door was slightly ajar.

"There are winding staircases to the left and right of a large table at the far end of the main hall," Brockingham whispered. "*L'Anguedoc's* bedchamber is up and nearer the left."

"Thomas and Argive follow Reginald up the right hand staircase," Whyntowne said. "Quentin and Lucien follow me up the left."

"Donnell and Richard guard the door from here, and Herve and Sebastian will stand guard inside, just past the lintel."

Eight of the men went up the steps and entered the dark manor. There was a long rectangular hall, with three alcoves to each side, much like a church. Though they could not see far in the blackness, they knew the staircases started at the end of the hall. Inching forward they soon felt a soft carpet on the soles of their feet. As they crept down the long corridor, the carpet began to feel wet and sticky to the touch. Turnbull was much disconcerted by the feeling and sorely tempted to light a torch and ascertain the cause but he knew it was too dangerous. By the time they were halfway down the hall, it seemed as if there was more light, if still dim and some of them could make out a long wooden table. The stairways began to the sides of the table.

Whyntowne noticed a small pinprick of light to the left, as though a last spark shown in a fire before it died entirely. It drew his eyes upward.

Something was above them, barely swaying like empty sacks blown by a slight wind. Or slabs of red, blood red beef from a slaughterhouse.

Suddenly that spark burst into flame from a torch near the top of the stairs. On the other side of the table another torch burst into a small inferno. The manor was now alit. They could see.

Pools of blood covered a wide swath of the floor beyond the carpet and below their feet. That was the stickiness.

Seven bodies, still dripping blood, hung from ropes attached to a railing from the second floor.

Brockingham quickly jumped up upon the table to see.

"This one is the servant," he whispered. His eyes were cut out, his tongue and neck severed. The other bodies swung on either side of him, two women and four men, and all cut across the neck, all gutted like sheep.

The men stood in stunned silence until Whyntowne broke the spell.

"We are discovered!" he yelled. "To the stairs."

"Watch the door!" Brockingham shouted as he jumped down

from the table.

The two groups of knights now stormed up the stairs. Castillo and Brockingham seized the torches from their holders as they reached the top of the stairway.

Doors on the upper floor were thrown open or busted in, but every room was empty.

"Here!" Sir Lucien shouted as he ran along the upstairs railing. A door was open. Holding his torch in front of him, he cautiously entered a large chamber in the middle of the manor. A bloody dirk lay on the wooden floor along with dark prints the shape of boot soles. A window stood open. More blood lay upon the bottom windowpane. "At the window!"

Brockingham and Whyntowne hurried in. By the time they reached the window looking out onto the grounds, Castillo had already secured a rope and was repelling down the manor wall.

The others rushed down the stairs and circled to the back of the manor. The planks were stove in and useless. Castillo rushed to the front gate and began to lower the drawbridge. By the time the others reached the gate he had run to the rear of the castle and was following the tracks with his torch.

He was the first to find the dead bodies of the lookouts. They were in a death embrace, their hands around each other's necks. It seemed to Castillo as if they were forced to kill one another.

"How powerful is this fiend?" he asked as Whyntowne and Brockingham came up.

"Quite," Brockingham said with his usual manner of understatement. "We leave them here. We cannot let his trail grow cold once more."

"Go!" Sir Charles said. "Hurry. I will warn Peter."

As the knights donned their boots, Sir Charles sat down, his back against a large elm. His legs crossed and his hands resting upon his knees, he closed his eyes and began to concentrate. He pictured Peter Dillon's face in his mind's eye and chanted to himself over and over with an intensity that made the veins in his neck and arms quiver, "*L'Anguedoc* has escaped! Arm yourself! *L'Anguedoc* has escaped! Arm yourself!"

He continued in this manner for a full eight minutes, never breaking focus, banishing all other thoughts from his mind. Whyntowne had not tried this practice since he left the East, and never under such dire circumstances. His whole body trembled as he went on, "*L'Anguedoc* has escaped! Arm yourself! *L'Anguedoc* has escaped! Arm yourself!" until a warm sensation, almost repose, began to suffuse itself throughout his limbs, starting from his feet and moving upward through his calves and torso, finally reaching his head. He remembered this was as it happened before. Sir Charles got up in the knowledge his message had been received. He pulled on his boots and rushed into the forest following the others.

*    *    *

At the rendezvous, the horses had been hobbled in a pasture and were grazing peacefully.

Nearby, Peter Dillon lunged forward, thrusting his sword into an imaginary foe: sometimes he would picture a fierce dragon as the victim of his piercing blows, though now he conjured up a knight of the Order of the Temple.

"Look at the boy," Heidel said. "Were it only that easy to vanquish *L'Anguedoc*." He hoisted a large calfskin flask to his mouth and took a sustained drink of ale, then passed it to Dominic.

"No. Not tonight," Sir Dominic said but he chuckled in agreement. "He'll make a knight. I promise you."

"At least he's entertaining," Heidel said wiping his mouth.

After another thrust, Peter used the sword to fend off succeeding blows from his pretend opponent, then jumped up, flipping in the air and landing perfectly in back of the made-up enemy. "Touché!" he said, preparing to jab forward, when suddenly his hand flew open and he dropped the sword. He was paralyzed and scared. What was happening to him? Dillon could not even wiggle a finger or toe. His legs became wobbly, unconnected and gave way, dropping him to the ground.

As the others stared on in bewilderment, a horrendous image came into Dillon's mind along with Whyntowne's voice, and as abruptly as it started, the sensation left and the power returned to his limbs. He sprang to his feet and ran up to the knights.

"Sir Dominic," Dillon whispered. "*L'Anguedoc* escaped. We must prepare."

"Heidel," Sir Dominic said in turn. "He comes. Bring the pack horse."

"Are you serious? If he comes we are doomed!" Heidel said, even as he rushed to the horse. "We should flee. It is our only hope."

"We cannot," Dominic said. "We must at least delay him. It is our duty. We cannot lose his trail again."

Heidel brought the packs over to the others. "If twelve knights couldn't seize him how can we, two knights and a mere boy?" Heidel was sweating profusely. His nerve left him. He had never felt such fear and was ready to break away and run. Nothing else mattered. "*L'Anguedoc* is too powerful."

"I thought Germans liked to fight," Dominic said.

"When I have a chance," Heidel said, marching straight up to Dominic as if confronting him.

The squire walked up between the two knights. "Sir Knights. With all due respect, we must unite. I think I know how to use his powers against him."

"What, boy?" Sir Heidel challenged.

"Hear him out," Dominic said. "There's nothing to lose."

"Only time," Heidel said.

"He can read our minds, right?" Dillon said.

"Perhaps yours," Heidel said with due petulance.

"Right," Dillon said. "Mine. I know you are trained to withstand such sorcery. This is why Sir Charles used me as his conduit."

"What is your plan?" Dominic asked.

"We've hobbled the horses and I am their guard," Dillon said excitedly. "There are two other masks and many talismans in the packs. You two will take the masks and talismans and stay in the trees. You will keep your thoughts guarded, as if you were not here. I will think thoughts of betrayal."

"It is too risky for you," Sir Dominic said.

"From what Sir Charles has said, this *L'Anguedoc's* arrogance has no bounds," Peter Dillon said. "My guess is he would like nothing better than to turn Sir Charles' own squire against him."

"Or kill him," Heidel said. "We are better off taking the horses and retiring to Rouen to get more men."

"Perhaps he will kill me," the squire said. "But it is a chance worth taking."

"I'm not sure," Sir Dominic said.

"I will sit next to yonder oak," Dillon said, reaching into the bag and withdrawing two of the lead masks and three golden amulets with icons from the East. He put one talisman around his neck, tucking it inside his habit and handed the others to the two knights. "I will think thoughts of hatred for Sir Charles Whyntowne, the King, Our Holy Pope and my lowly position."

"What if your thoughts stray as is the wont of most men?" Heidel asked.

"They won't," Peter Dillon said, but without conceit of any kind. Reaching into one of the other packs, he withdrew a vial. "Give me your flask of ale, Sir Heidel."

"My drink?"

"Give it to the boy," Dominic said.

Heidel begrudgingly handed it over and immediately, Dillon took a mouthful, swallowing a little and swirling the rest in his mouth before spitting it out onto his hands. He then dabbed it on his clothes.

"What?" Heidel said.

"He needs the smell of alcohol about him." Dominic said, becoming more appreciative of Dillon's attention to detail.

Dillon then began to pour the contents of the vial into the liquor.

"Oh no!" Heidel said. "You've ruined it."

"You could still partake of it," Sir Dominic said. "It might give you more courage before you nodded off."

"If you question my courage once more…"

"It is known that *L'Anguedoc* is very fond of his ale," Peter Dillon said as he emptied the vial. "When he comes he will see me asleep with the flask between my legs. I am betting he will drink."

"Betting your life," Heidel said.

"When he is weakened from the poison, you will place the mask on his head and bind him with the Holy relics and amulets. Sir Charles cannot be far behind."

"Out of the mouth of a child," Sir Dominic said. "What courage. I am for it."

"More like foolhardiness," Heidel said, still unnerved. "How many survived?"

"I don't know," Dillon said. "I only know to prepare."

Dominic patted Peter on the shoulder. "We will tame the bastard."

"What if he doesn't drink?" Sir Heidel asked.

Peter Dillon held his broadsword up in front of his eyes, staring at it. "Then I will surprise him with a thrust through the heart."

Quickly taking the masks and holy instruments, the two knights hid nearby in thick undergrowth, while Peter sat down near the oak, his back leaning against the thick trunk, his sword under a cloak by his right hand, the calf-skin between his legs and his mind oddly calm. He now filled his thoughts with malice and betrayal.

"How will he do it?" Heidel asked. "It is impossible for one such as him."

"Shsh," Dominic whispered. "Mask your thoughts. Now."

Not far down the dark, rutted road, a man stopped moving. His ears keened forward like an animal's. He sniffed the air, then put his hands to his temples and concentrated. Nothing. He knew he should not have drunk so much that night, or any night, but he did love his libations. *L'Anguedoc* could not sense anything behind him, but he knew there were knights following him. He cursed himself for not being more careful. He had sworn the villagers to silence, but when in the history of man had that ever worked? They were only good for betrayal. The ministrations he bestowed were much too miraculous for them to stay hidden, for them to not speak of them. It was his own hubris that led to this. He laughed. Perhaps he had not learned as much as he should in the East. Even in those days before the teachings, he had been this way: a seeker of glory, renown. He always suspected it would ultimately be his undoing. Trying to remain anonymous in this backwater had succeeded only before he started to heal the villagers. In truth, he had done it in part as atonement for his many sins, but the outside world would never place the good on equal footing with the evil. They would kill him if they could.

Why could he not pierce their thoughts? For years he had come upon rumors that others had acquired the same powers as he and his fellows, but there was no tangible proof it was true. But if so, they could shield their minds from his.

How he had been found was of no importance. What he needed to know was how powerful these men were. If they were men such as he?

He quieted his mind and began to search for thoughts. Were there any of them near and unguarded? Quickly he got his answer. Not far from where he stood was a boy, seemingly asleep from drink. He could picture him dozing against a tree, but what was of more interest, he could sense hatred.

A name, Sir Charles Whyntowne, came into his mind. He could see him: a knight. A Hospitaller of the Knights of St. John. This was the order of knights rumored to have been sent to the East! To learn our secrets!

As if born of desperation, *L'Anguedoc* turned to the one hope presented to him. It was strange to him, but even though he had been invulnerable since the teachings, he still felt himself as human and mortal and susceptible to pain and injury as he had been before. Those memories of wounds and tortures when among the Moslems proved quite indelible. He would find this boy and ally himself. This Peter Dillon might know if Whyntowne and his knights are the ones or if they are mere men.

For the first time since he separated from *De la Guzman* and *de Belfort* he felt the necessity of aid.

The boy dreams of betraying his master, but *L'Anguedoc* knew he must be circumspect in his approach. He moved forward along the road with stealth.

Peter Dillon soon felt a presence nearing him. It was malefic and horrifying, and though he could feel his heart begin to pound, he went on with the chanting Sir Charles had taught him. He could not lapse for a second or he was done for. *"I hate Sir Charles Whyntowne! I hate the Pope! I hate King Charles!"* Over and over he chanted this mantra, even as he smelled a foul odor approach and equally foul breath. It was the stench of dried blood and stale wine. Had he not been strong of mind he would certainly have thrown up or bolted.

*"I hate Sir Charles Whyntowne! I hate the Pope! I hate King Charles!"* Even as he felt the flask pulled from between his legs he continued with a single mindedness. Even as he heard the liquid pour down the man's throat.

But then, as he heard the empty calfskin whip through the air and hit the ground, he allowed himself a small bit of hope that the tincture would do its work. His eyelids trembled and he felt himself roughly pulled off the ground, his sword out of reach.

"You dare to trick me!" *L'Anguedoc* bellowed.

"Why dost thou wake me so rudely, sir?" Peter Dillon said. "Are thee a knave? I have sword and will fight thee fairly if that is thy want."

*L'Anguedoc* looked at him, dropped him to the ground and laughed. "I will fight *thee* young sprout and tear out your eyes and stick them in your mouth and see you chew them as tasty morsels, or do you speak from the liquor?"

*L'Anguedoc* drew his sword and put the tip at Dillon's throat. Was this the boy whose mind he'd found? "I would know thy name before I slay thee, and I would know why you hate our good Pope and King, and a villain by the name of Whyntowne?"

"What, sir? Are thee a wizard that thou know this?"

Laughing once more, *L'Anguedoc* withdrew his weapon, resting the point on the ground. "Perhaps I will trade you your life if you answer me."

Even as he spoke, Dillon kept the chant up in his mind.

"It is mostly Whyntowne I hate," he said. "He uses me poorly, as his mule and servant. He beats me. See this." Rising slowly, Dillon got up and lifted his shirt. As he turned, *L'Anguedoc* could see stripes across his back, the scars from many whippings.

"What I want to know is this," *L'Anguedoc* said. "Has your master, this Whyntowne been to the Asian lands?"

Dillon dropped his blouse back down. "I have served the bastard for five years. Since I was young. He has not said so, but he has spoken of religions strange to my ear and he makes me wear talismans such as this." He pulled the golden talisman out from under his shirt and held it up. "Whither they come from I know not."

*L'Anguedoc* staggered back, repelled, but Dillon noticed something else.

"Thank you, good sir," *L'Anguedoc* said in a slurring manner. "But that is all I wish to know." He now hefted his sword and brought it back to land a killing blow.

As Peter Dillon quickly grabbed for his own sword to parry the thrust, *L'Anguedoc* stumbled and toppled over. The evil knight had barely hit the ground when Dominic and Heidel fell upon him, securing the mask to his face and binding his arms and legs with ropes and amulets.

"Methinks we need a stronger potion," Heidel said, staring closely at the empty vial then sniffing it.

Footsteps were heard as Whyntowne and Brockingham, swords drawn, ran up.

"You have him," Brockingham said.

"Yes," Heidel said. "We have him under control."

"That's why I left you here," Whyntowne said. "I knew you'd be resolute." He winked at Peter, more with relief than humor. "The crypt is ready. Let us go there now and finish with him."

*L'Anguedoc's* body was unceremoniously thrown over the saddle of a horse and tied to it like a large bundle of flour. He was strangely passive, Dillon thought. Perhaps the charms worked as well as the potion.

The knights mounted and set off for the burial ground.

## CHAPTER 6

# HOME GUARD

A certain member of the Home Guard Cyrus Wilson so ardently disapproved of was just now making his rounds of the neighborhood, though his being part of the Home Guard was not the only reason Bert Jones bore Cyrus's distaste. In fact, it had little or nothing to do with it. Cyrus did not like him before he joined the Guards, and he probably would not like him after he was no longer a part of the Guards.

Jones grew up around the cemetery and worked there for much of his adult life, bearing the stigma of an ungrateful populace and class system, until now, as a member of the Home Guard, according to many a vital cog in the defense of the realm, he had achieved a greater degree of respectability. Bert was a huge, vulgar type, who had made a career out of kowtowing to his betters (a great many) to the point of obsequiousness, and bullying his lessers to the point of near mayhem. He had rarely been caught out, though the local Bobbies were indeed familiar with his name, and now, with his sudden newfound appointment, he figured he had the right to bully a little higher class person.

Today, along with his mate, Will Baker, he buried two corpses, both elderly, and jealously coveted the gold jewelry those stuffy and wasteful rich folks buried with their stupid old aunt or uncle. Instead of crying for their souls, he knew they should be kicking themselves in the arse for abiding by the cadavers' wishes to be buried with their loot.

He was in very good mood as he approached Cyrus's house. He and his mate had already planned to sneak back to the cemetery after their rounds, dig up the fresh grave, and take the old folks' goods. "They ain't going to need them," he told Baker. "We ain't no damn Egyptians!" He chuckled. They both had the same idea. It was simply a matter of who spoke up first, or got there first. It was their game: they always split the loot.

Bert liked his cemetery work. He liked the idea of shoveling dirt on the high and mighty as well as the run-of-the-mill sod. He had a sort of pride of ownership, of place. Although obviously he did not own the cemetery, he felt he did. He belonged there. This was his, and this feeling was one of the reasons that put him in direct confrontation with Cyrus Wilson. Wilson was old, and Bert would almost salivate thinking about the time when he could throw his worn-out body into one of those holes. Cyrus owned the house that was perfect for Bert: a house that overlooked his ghastly dominions. Bert had done the appropriate brown nosing, had paid court to Cyrus and his house as one might court a fair maiden. He had offered to buy the house for an egregiously low price, then, begrudgingly, a more than fair price which he could not truly afford, but Cyrus Wilson had two unshakable reasons for not selling: he easily saw Bert for the scoundrel he was; and secondly and most importantly, he was set on giving the house to Elizabeth Hammond and Michael Hinton-Smith for a good start in their life together.

Now that Hinton-Smith was away on the Continent with no early prospect of return, Bert's latest stratagem was to bully Cyrus, but the old soldier merely laughed in his face. Bert, for his part, had nurtured hopes of vendettas for many of the real or imagined slights he had suffered at the hands of his "betters" over the years, and he was not above adding this latest to his accounts due.

*     *     *

"All Simla knows it. Ask there...and, Friend of the World, he is one to be obeyed to the last wink of his eyelashes. Men say he does magic, but that should not touch thee. Go up the hill and ask. Here begins the Great Game," Elizabeth Hammond read as she finished the eighth chapter of Kim. Cyrus truly loved his Kipling, but his eyesight was slowly failing and he liked listening to her soft voice. If she wanted to read it was fine with him: less eyestrain.

When Kate read to him she would do the British common soldier with a Cockney accent, the officers in an upper class snooty tone and Kim and all natives in a sing song Indian English and soon they would be laughing so hard he would have to beg her to stop before he collapsed.

"I will journey to India one fine day," he said.

"We'll all go. You and Michael and Kate and I." She smiled wistfully as she pictured the four of them in a howdah atop a massive elephant.

Dusk was fast approaching and she got up to take another tour of the room till she was satisfied that all the light was sealed in. Kate brought out a few more candles, lit them and returned to the kitchen.

"I'm tired of the blackout, Cyrus," Elizabeth sighed. "Do you really think they'll bomb us?" After waiting for a moment for an answer that was apparently not forthcoming, she retreated to the kitchen to help Kate ready their meager dinner. Cyrus smiled as he remembered the wording of the book: he loved Kipling and had read it himself at least half a dozen times.

But then he stood up, now intent on answering the question. Straightening himself to his full height he shouted, "I hope the bastards invade so I can shoot the lot of 'em," and then sat back down and went back to being irritated with the circumstance of having to live with all the inconveniences of wartime, without the actual event of war.

"Bring the bloody thing on," he said loudly, and he had said it for months, just like a great many of his countrymen. "And kick Chamberlain out with the first bomb."

"Bring back Winston," Kate shouted from the kitchen.

The infamous picture of Chamberlain waving the piece of paper from Munich, a treaty, with Hitler's signature, gnawed hourly at Wilson's gut. "Aye lass. Chamberlain's a national shame," he shouted back. "He was taken for a ride."

"They took us all for a ride," Elizabeth Hammond yelled.

"Winnie will come through," Kate Hammond added.

The front window suddenly burst into little pieces and a nice little round hole appeared in the covering shutter almost simultaneously with the crack of a rifle shot. The bullet continued on to shatter an old vase that Wilson had brought home from France after the Great War, before slamming into a brick wall. Elizabeth, instinctively, tackled her sister, driving both of them to the floor. She was incredulous. "Germans? How?" She looked for Cyrus on the floor, expecting him to take the same action. He was not there. Letting go of Kate and getting up on her elbows to get a better view, she was just in time to see him walking to the window that had been shattered.

Immediately she looked at his feet and was relieved to see he had his shoes on, as indeed he made a crunching sound as he walked over the myriad pieces of broken glass on the floor.

"What is it now," he asked, irritably, but almost absent mindedly, as he made his way to the window. Cyrus was not senile. He could laugh at a joke. Sad events might bring tears. He could reason, remember, and get angry, but with almost every word he spoke, and every action he took, there was now a nostalgic look in his eye. Someone meeting him for the first time might think there was something wrong, but in reality, as with many older people, one eye was on the present, and one eye was on the past, looking back on a long succession of events which could range from yesterday, all the way back to early childhood, for him some seventy years ago. Although this sometimes caused others to see him as a possible dullard, it seemed to pacify him and gave him the advantage of being able to compare or combine some present event, no matter how bad or frightening, with a worse or happier event from the past, and view it as if he was somehow outside the incident. In this circumstance, a potentially dangerous situation was, to him, only another aggravating inconvenience. "What bloody twit did this," he thundered. Examining the hole, he pulled off the tape and threw back the shutter.

Elizabeth jumped up, ran over and threw all of her eight stone into wrestling him to the floor, but careful to avoid the glass. Soon after this point, and a spirited resistance, he realized he better give in, until he could figure out a way to protect his girls, thus resuming his natural position as head of the household.

Kate crawled over next to them and whispered, "Well, you got us both quite nicely. Next time can you simply yell duck?"

"What is it, Cyrus?" Elizabeth asked breathlessly.

Cyrus was quite annoyed and embarrassed, more from his seeming surrender of authority to his, in essence, adopted daughter, than the disturbance. Of course, whom he was going to take it out on was a different matter. He looked at the front door.

A middle-aged, gravelly voice, with a distinct Cockney accent yelled at them from the street. "Hey! You in there! Cover up them cracks or turn off them lights or I'll fire again! There's a war on, and you know the rules!"

Elizabeth and Cyrus sat up at the same time, looked at each other, and simultaneously, with an enormous amount of disgust, said the words, "Home Guard!"

Kate looked at both of them, perplexed. She was not privy to their pet joke.

"I know that bloody twit," Wilson said.

Cyrus was by no means going to let this go. He jumped up as though he were a boy of sixteen and went charging round the room, turning on every light he could find, while Kate could not help breaking out in laughter at the sight. Then he gathered up pieces of the smashed vase and marched out the front door to confront the odious man. While Kate still laughed, Elizabeth put on a ferocious scowl in order to show the proper amount of disrespect to their persecutor then followed in close order.

"This is probably the first time you ever fired a gun and you're firing it at an Englishman," Cyrus yelled as he marched up and stood toe to toe with Bert, pointing his finger directly in the man's face. "Why do they even give you twits ammunition?"

"Bollocks, old man," Bert interjected before Cyrus could rail at him again.

"Do you see this vase?" exclaimed Cyrus, holding the shards up to within an inch of Bert's huge, misshapen nose.

Bert nodded gingerly to avoid a chance cut, and Elizabeth added, "See what you did, you oaf?" not wanting to miss putting in her penny's worth.

"Right, guv, but..."

"I brought this back from a real war, the likes of which you'll never see."

Elizabeth nodded haughtily in agreement. By now, Kate had made her way to the door and was trying as hard as she could to stifle her giggling, as she looked at Cyrus face down this enormous man who seemed almost three times his size.

"I was aiming for the light. I have a perfect right..."

"You have a right, a perfect right to fire on the house of a veteran," Cyrus screamed. "I'll report you to every authority in the country and you'll lose your bloody job..."

"And your precious defenseless volunteer's post," Elizabeth added.

"And then you'll be free to go to the Continent and do some real fighting instead of your usual pub habit."

Bert now spoke slowly and deliberately as he remembered how much bigger he was than this old man and how his position vis-à-vis all civilians had changed in the last few weeks.

"Mr. Wilson. I 'ave orders from the authorities and the Air Raid Warden to see the rules is obeyed. That includes the blackout. If you want to come to the nearest office wif me, that's fine. It's nothing to me, but it'll be the worse for you."

"Are you threatening me?" demanded Cyrus.

Bert very calmly put down his rifle, took hold of Cyrus by the collar, and lifted him one foot off the ground. Both girls stood with their mouths agape.

Elizabeth then rushed up and hit the brute as hard as she could, yelling, "Leave him alone!"

Bert, still holding Cyrus up with one hand, started to throw the back of his other hand across her face, thought better of it, and pushed her away into the bushes instead. Kate ran to her sister and yelled, "Let him down or I'll call the Bobbies."

By then, Bert had returned his attention to Cyrus.

"Listen here, old man," he sneered. "And you two, missies. You can tell anyone you like. I don't care. I'm doing me job. If you try to make things tough for me, there'll come another time when it's just us two...and maybe the little women." Then he dropped Cyrus and laughed and started to walk away. He turned back to them and asked, "Where's your little war hero?" After he felt he had let the words sink in for an appropriate amount of time, he sauntered off feeling very pleased with himself.

Just then, an air raid siren went off and all four of them looked towards the darkened sky. Bert turned back towards them, and with a sarcastic tone, sneered, "You better get to a shelter, folks. It could get dangerous."

Cyrus yelled back, "It's probably a false alarm, just like you're an imitation soldier." He calmed down as the brute disappeared from sight, turned to the two sisters, and said, "Our lads have been on the Continent for nine months now...people are speaking to each other, neighbors are friendlier. I know two people who actually forgave debts, one was pretty big, as well. I know a bloke who didn't speak to his brother for twelve years now, even though they only lived three blocks away—some kind of disagreement with the wives. He picked up his cane, walked over to his brother's house to see him, and they cried in each other's arms for twenty minutes."

"The war changes people, doesn't it," Elizabeth said. All thoughts of the bully were quickly forgotten. But how would the war change her or her relationship to Michael? What if he ended up crippled, or lost his mind, or didn't come back at all? What would she do? How strong would she be?

Kate put her arm around Elizabeth's shoulder as if she knew her innermost thoughts. She rubbed Elizabeth's arm. "Yes it does."

Cyrus nodded in the direction Bert had taken. "So why did that bloody fool get left behind?"

What the old soldier could not know, and indeed, this was only known to Bert Jones, was that this house, now owned by Cyrus Wilson for some thirty years, had at one time been owned by Bert Jones's grandfather. His father's father had been swindled out of the deed to the property and unceremoniously dumped out on the street with his wife and four-year-old son. Many were the times when Bert's father, also a gravedigger, and home for the night after a grueling day's work, would cry out in a drunken rage how that house, by all rights, should be his.

As his parents succumbed to disease and poverty, Bert promised them, that one way or another, a Jones would once again live on South Grove.

The humiliation of his grandfather was one thing, but as a small boy, witnessing the humiliation of his father and mother, sometimes having to live in a government shelter, even begging for food to feed their young ones, was too much for Jones and he vowed it would never happen to him. He would see to that with the loot he and Will Baker were accumulating from the cemetery and those rich old sods. On the day his fortune reached ten thousand bob—that was the figure he and Baker reckoned would classify them as rich—he would quit and show all those bastards, every last one of them that had ever made him or his father grovel. He truly hoped the older ones would still be alive.

He was not quite sure how he would do it, but certain he was it would happen. And Cyrus Wilson would be one of the first to feel his anger. In fact, he was not all that certain he would wait when it came to that old fool.

CHAPTER 7

# THE GAME'S AFOOT

he mission to Belgium had a sense of chaos, of unease about it from
the very beginning. To start with, Cawkins only received orders at
the eleventh hour. The colonel conducting the briefing said the mission would form the basis of a last appeal to the French to stay on the
Franco-Belgian border. A last appeal to reason: stay in the border fortifications. That was the pretext. He was to bring back incontrovertible
proof of the sorry state of the Meuse-Antwerp defenses. A circle of perhaps thirty people knew of the real particulars, and half of these would
soon be on their way to the continent. This was as much to conceal the
real objective from the French as from the Germans.

He was allowed to select Hinton-Smith as an aide. The lieutenant
would be duly briefed, but the hidden agenda of the assignment was
"for Cawkins's eyes only."

Then there began a frenzied dash to make connections. One minor
car accident on the way to a secret airfield, just south of Amiens, was suffered, before they were flown back to London on a fast Avro-Lancaster
bomber without markings, trading their uniforms for civilian gear during
the flight. The bomber captain had to feather an engine over the Channel
on the way back to England and the landing gear had to be manually
lowered as they made their descent. Met at the airport by another un-

marked vehicle, they were immediately whisked off to Victoria Station where they repacked their knapsacks with books, cameras, ropes and a tent, making a show of their tourist aspirations—there were known French agents, as well as Germans, watching the train stations as well as the channel ports. Barely catching the last Dover train, an hour and a half later they jumped down and sprinted to the docks to catch the last ferry to the continent. An unseasonable squall came up out of nowhere to threaten their ship as they approached the center of the Channel. By the time they checked into a humble, nondescript Ostend inn for the night, Cawkins could not help but wonder if someone or something either did not want them to go on the mission, or was trying to warn them.

Early the next morning, they shared some coffee and croissants, rented two bicycles from a tourist center, and leisurely started down the coast to Dunkirk, keeping their cameras busy, snapping pictures of locals, old cathedrals, indigenous species of birds and other flora and fauna to keep up the charade.

At Dunkirk, they headed almost due south along the road to Hazebrouck, taking more time as Cawkins made numerous sketches of the local fowl, and notes in code on the roads, rivers, bridges, hedgerows, and any other factors that could assume importance on a retreat. The following days, they were to continue southeast to Bethune, then east to Brussels and beyond to the Meuse-Antwerp. Other pairs of men were heading south from Dunkirk to St. Omer; others to Poperinge, Roeselare, and other points south of the Belgian and French coastal cities of Ostend, Calais, and Boulogne, although Cawkins and Hinton-Smith were the only ones heading east after the primary task was accomplished. The BEF was taking no chances. A very eminent general had an epiphany: what if the French line was rolled up and the BEF was caught between the Germans and the coast? Had it not almost happened in the last war? The highly secret objective was to scout the areas south of the channel cities in case the BEF was forced to withdraw. No one had previously thought on this; after all, the French Army was the most powerful in the world.

If the French found out, there would be hell to pay; an international incident with Britain's closest ally on the continent. The colonel ended on a note of finality. "You realize what it would mean if word of this got back to the French. I cannot overemphasize the importance of secrecy. Tell no one. Not your wife, not your lover, nor your mother. No one."

*　　*　　*

The second day back found them some five miles south of Hazebrouck, just north of the village of St. Venant, where they had rented a cottage for the night. The sky was overcast as they headed back to the village. Bits of clear blue peaked through the clouds and the air was quite brisk, and to the south, dark sinister clouds were a portent of rain. As they rode their bikes across a squat level-topped hill, Cawkins sighted a white-cheeked peregrine falcon. This was his alibi, and so he followed the bird with his binoculars as it floated over a hill. If he ever worked for counter-intelligence, he'd arrest every birdwatcher he found.

"Look at that," he said pointing out the falcon.

"Well," Hinton-Smith said appreciatively. "I'll just have to get a shot. For Lizzie." He rolled to a stop and stood straddling the bike.

Taking out his camera, a new Leica 35mm, he followed the bird through the lens, waiting for the optimum time to snap a few pictures.

"Jack. I can see the steeple in St. Venant. Ever since we stopped there the name has been bothering me. Have you heard of it?"

"Sounds kind of familiar but I can't place it. Why?"

"Not certain. I know it from somewhere. A long time ago I think."

"I hate it when that happens."

When the bird swooped down with its long pointed bluish-gray wings, Hinton-Smith turned his bicycle to get a better view. It was then he made out an ancient Roman wall and a mound, on top of which looked to be, strangely, the topmost part of the parapet of a castle, crenellated for its defense. Strangely, in that even from this distance the castle walls then visible only appeared to be a little over a few yards in height.

The castle had been hidden from view by a succession of two smaller wooded hills, in addition to the many tall leafy poplars, oaks and elms lining the road when they were on level ground. The narrow tar road they were on led down from a squat hill, then crept between the two smaller hills, which were almost too trivial to deserve the title, and could only be considered hills at all on account of the flatness of the surrounding green countryside. The road then meandered through a hedgerow and skirted below the castle mound and into a medium-size town, St. Venant, home to two thousand or so persons.

Forgetting the peregrine, the lieutenant put the camera away, and scanned the remnants of the old walls with his binoculars.

"We have to go down there," Hinton-Smith said matter-of-factly, as he pointed down towards the mound.

"Michael. We have a mission to complete." Cawkins was serious. "I do recall a promise."

Hinton-Smith laughed heartily. "Jack. With all due respect for you and our superiors, this assignment will not add one iota of information to the general fund of intelligence. This area's been studied and restudied by the Staff College for centuries. They know all they're going to know, and you know it better than I."

With a look of consternation, Cawkins pulled out his map, locating their position.

"Michael. It's already late. By the time we're done with it, it'll be dusk. Most of our gear is back in St. Venant. We'll have to make our way back in the twilight, pick up the gear and continue on in the dark. We're supposed to get past Bethune tonight if we're to keep to the schedule. We don't have time."

"So we stay by the ruins. We have a tent, ground cloths and blankets don't we, mate. We'll make a shelter out of them. Besides, the knoll is the highest place around, next to the ground we're standing on. We should scout it. That's good ground, and it might prove necessary."

"I don't know. We'll have to do double-time tomorrow," Cawkins cautioned. "And I still don't think it's a good idea."

Cawkins had been promoted to captain and seconded to Palestine after seeing action in Mesopotamia in 1920, and on his off time had tinkered around many of the digs in the Holy Land. He fell in love with the early Roman era, studying the foot soldier on campaign, rather than the more popular analyses of the Caesars. Later, on duty in the Middle East, it seemed that every Roman wall or settlement had become the home of a more recent crusader castle. He felt himself drawn to this period as well. Notes were kept in a dog-eared, dull olive colored notebook, which he was determined to some day turn into a book. In fact, he lost his captain's bars for overstaying his leave on digs a few too many times. Naturally, the lieutenant had caught his bug.

It was in Cawkins's nature to become consumed in his passions, and normally, he would be eager to look at the ruins, but something was making him nervous, and it was not the mission. There was something he could not quite place. What his father used to call a bad feeling.

"Jack," Hinton-Smith said, relenting. "We'll just climb the mound to the castle, have a look around, and that's it. I won't even bother with the Romans. Okay? Of course, you can't either. Won't take but a couple of hours, will it? If you're worried about continuing in the dark, we'll just stay up there. Or, if you want we'll come down. I don't care. Of course, you are a soldier," he emphasized. "Used to the great outdoors. Right?" Laughing, he added, "Besides, you can teach me a few things. You'll like that, won't you? Come on then, Jack." He knew Cawkins could not indefinitely resist the urge to explore.

"I don't want to be caught out on the road after dark, and have to answer embarrassing questions," the sergeant protested, feeling the need to explain himself more clearly as if that would win the lieutenant to his way of thinking, but Hinton-Smith ignored him and started pedaling his way down the hill. He was sorely tempted to tell him the true nature of their assignment.

Unfortunately he had given his word. Michael was very sharp and Cawkins assumed he'd figure it out on his own soon enough. So far, he had not shown any sign that he had.

"We're not even in Belgium yet, so stop worrying," Hinton-Smith yelled back.

With a shrug of his shoulders, Cawkins ran with his bike to get a good start, jumped on, and pedaled to catch up.

Turning onto a dirt path, they soon reached the ancient stone walls and started the arduous climb up the steep mound, pushing their bicycles alongside them as they went.

"It looks like it's terraced, Jack. Like rice paddies."

"Those are trenches, Mikey. To make it harder on the enemy. They're probably from an earlier time than the castle. Maybe even earlier than the Romans. You realize, this is a *motte*, all man made...that we're strolling up. Don't you? An earthwork."

The lieutenant smiled enthusiastically at Cawkins. "Bloody well done, mate. See. I'm learning already."

Driblets of icy water trickled down pencil-thin paths to the bottom of the *motte*, occasionally crossing the switchback goat's trail they were following. The water and cold earth were all that was left of one of the fiercest winters on record. The snow was gone, soggy yellow grass was turning green, and the narrow path, though still dark from the remnants of water, was solid under their feet.

They were both breathing hard and sweating by the time they reached the first trench, even though the day had remained quite chilly. Now, as the sun dropped to the horizon, the air was becoming even cooler.

Each of them carried a small knapsack on his back, to underpin their disguise as tourists. The contents of the packs were simple camping gear, a blanket, a torch, a small hatchet, a folding shovel, and food for a snack—the rest of the gear was in St. Venant. As a safeguard, the sergeant had a knife strapped to his leg. As a further precaution in case they were stopped, that morning he left his pistol in their cottage in the village.

The last barrier to the top of the knoll, which was a lot larger than Hinton-Smith had estimated from the distance, was the greatest of the trenches, overgrown with tall scraggly weeds, and stretching along the whole length of the hill in each direction. It inclined to a depth of five yards, rising a good ten on the other side.

The lieutenant remounted his bicycle and glided down the near side, using the momentum to climb up the other, although he had to jump off mid-climb to keep going up the slope that had once been a steep vertical revetment, but now sloped into the scarp so easily that one could no longer tell where one started and the other left off. Cawkins could not help laughing at the youngster. Then he followed Hinton-Smith in the same manner.

"Jesus! Will you look at that," exclaimed Cawkins as he emerged from the one-time moat and caught up with Hinton-Smith, who was sitting astride his bicycle on the top and gazing open-mouthed at the tableland.

The grounds looked as if a giant hand had lifted them up and then hurled them downwards till they crashed to the earth. Only two walls of one corner of the castle still stood at any height, and those, only three yards. It was these crenellated walls they had seen from the road above, and they were far from intact.

The sergeant dismounted and walked over to the castle ruins.

"Do you think the damage happened during the Great War?" asked the lieutenant as he jogged to catch up.

"No," Cawkins answered, kneeling down to pick up an ancient brick shard. "Whatever upheaval occurred here, did so hundreds of years, centuries before." Pointing to the medieval wall, Cawkins continued. "This is the top part of a wall that was probably, say, twenty-five yards high. Now it's three yards. It looks like it was shoved into the ground." He stood back up. "That's odd," he said quietly, more to himself. The bad feeling was returning. "It's getting dark. Perhaps we should start down. I've seen enough of these to last a lifetime." There was something strange about this place. The air didn't feel right, even the ground beneath his boots did not sit well with him.

"Well it's one of my first," the lieutenant replied. "And you're the one who's wanted to inculcate in me the finer points in life...both ancient and modern. I'll help you put up the shelter. Then we'll explore. Come on, then."

Resigned, Cawkins waved him away. He let his bicycle fall to the ground, took off his knapsack, and held his hand out to the lieutenant for his, which contained the tent stakes.

"Let me have it. You go be Howard Carter."

Without even a feeble attempt to conceal his eagerness, Hinton-Smith tossed the pack over to Cawkins and turned back towards the ruins. Cawkins shook his head. "You're incorrigible," he said as he started to look around for a suitable spot to pitch the shelter: someplace level, with not too many rocks or depressions, and some grass for a minimum comfort.

Hinton-Smith's first objective was the part of the castle walls that remained standing. By now it was dusk and a wind was coming up. A heavy storm was imminent. He could almost smell the rain in the air. As he walked he pulled his coat closer to his body.

"Well, look at this," he said to himself as he reached the corner bastion. "Just like Jack said." It looked like the wall was driven into the earth by some enormous sledgehammer. Large stones that might have once been part of the castle walls were strewn about the grounds.

Dragging his fingers against the rough surface of the outer stone wall, he studiously made his way round. The top of the mound was sparsely covered with short brown grass and weeds, and some areas were a bit muddy. At the halfway point, he climbed a section of the wall that had deteriorated in such a way as to leave four uniform steps up to the top. From here, he could see all the ruins still extant, and was about to turn back to help the sergeant, when he felt a sudden urge to continue the exploration. As he walked near the inside of the wall, where two sides came together to make a corner, the ground gave way, and his left foot plunged into a small, jagged hole, leaving him in an awkward, twisted position. Luckily, he was not hurt, but his whole leg was caught fast. And curiously, as he felt around with his trapped foot, he could not feel any solid ground underneath. This was excellent! It was probably an opening to a tunnel. The lieutenant pulled and twisted, trying to ease his foot out, but nothing worked.

"Jack," he yelled. "Come here. Bring the shovels. And the torches. And the rope. Quickly now, Jack."

Cawkins was pounding the last of four tent stakes into the ground when he heard the call. The light was dimming. He jogged over to Hinton-Smith guided by his voice.

"You're not hurt, are you?" he asked as he spotted the boy.

"No, no. Just caught in a bit of a tight spot," Hinton-Smith answered. "Can you widen this hole a touch?"

With a wry grin on his face, the sergeant walked in a circle around Hinton-Smith. He sat down on a lower part of the wall. "Well now, Mikey old boy. If I just leave you there till morning, you won't be able to get into any more trouble."

"Jack. I am just now suffering from the greatest ennui. I humbly beg your assistance so I can carry on with my exploration."

"Hold on," Cawkins said as he got down on his hands and knees. "I'm weighing the options." He felt around the hole, trying to wedge his hand in between it and the lieutenant's leg. It was too tight, not even a finger's width of room. He next tried to push in the dirt around the hole but to no effect.

"Come on then, Jack," Hinton-Smith said. "I'll be old before you get me out."

"You're the one that wanted to come up here. Just had to explore."

Cawkins stood and jammed the shovel into the hard earth, starting a new hole a foot away, and laboriously worked it over to where Hinton-Smith's leg was imprisoned. After a few minutes exertion, he was able to push in the dirt around the lieutenant's leg, so Hinton-Smith could pull free. Without so much as a thank you, the lieutenant took the shovel and widened the hole till he could look down into the dark, gloomy space. He got down on his belly.

"What the hell are you doing now?" asked an exasperated Cawkins, as he wiped the sweat from his forehead.

"Torch, please," the lieutenant said to Cawkins as he held out his hand like a doctor expecting a scalpel. Accepting the flashlight, Hinton-Smith peered into the hole, shining the torch in every corner. Satisfied, he sat down on the edge of the hole, put his legs through, and started lowering himself down, bracing his arms and legs against the walls of the entrance.

"Brother," Cawkins said in exasperation.

Hinton-Smith let go of the top. It was only a short drop before his boots jarred onto the cave bottom.

"There's plenty of room. Come on, then. It's starting to rain. It'll be about four feet till you hit. Mind the slant."

"Good. Then we can drown like rats in your hole."

The lieutenant disappeared from sight, leaving Cawkins staring after him in consternation.

The pit was cold and so damp that precipitation immediately formed on Hinton-Smith's torch. For the first time since last winter, he could see his breath. The tunnel smelled of mildew, rancid water, and bat dung, and the lieutenant was certain no other human had stepped on this ground for centuries. He liked the feeling of walking on ancient untouched earth. It had the feeling of discovery.

"Are you coming?" Hinton-Smith called out.

"All right," Cawkins said, but he hesitated. "This is not what we're here for," he shouted into the hole. Maybe he should tell him. This was the second time when the boy had gone of and done something inadvisable. If he told him, he was certain Hinton-Smith would understand the importance of the mission and stop going off on tangents.

None too eager, he shined his torch into the darkness. Easing himself down into the opening, he strained to find the ground with his feet, then gave up and dropped, bending his knees slightly to absorb the shock. Cawkins reached solid footing with a resounding thud, and adjusted his eyes. To the sergeant, the darkness seemed tenebrous as Hades, black and foreboding, and that matched his earlier thoughts about the mound.

Following the hazy light from the lieutenant's flashlight, and testing the ground carefully with each step as he shone his own torch immediately in front, he slowly caught up with Hinton-Smith.

"I don't like this," he said. The sergeant felt a strange and illogical disquietude enveloping him. The very air was heavy, oppressive.

The passageway was only wide enough for one man at a time. Hinton-Smith, with his arms outstretched, and his hands braced against either side of the tunnel wall, proceeded with as much caution as he could bear. The incline was precipitous and slippery with dampness and they edged forward in small steps. After twenty minutes of bent knees and balancing their steps downward, their thighs were sore and starting to spasm. As the path made an abrupt turn to the left and down, it leveled out and widened ever so slightly. Directly in front of them and stretching from wall to wall was a black, gaping hole. There were two twelve-foot-long, roughly hewn lengths of wood lying over this rent in the passage. There was no other way across.

"Look, Jack. A bridge of sorts," Hinton-Smith said, shining his light on the spans of wood.

Cawkins squatted down to examine the logs. "They would take these up if they thought an enemy found the exit. This hole's an escape hatch,"

Cawkins explained as he blew and brushed aside a massive cobweb that tried to cling to his mouth and face. "They made it wider here to make it more difficult to cross." He spat to clear his lips. "I've seen this before. They'd sneak food in through here during a siege, or when the defense of the castle failed, this was the last chance to get out."

"If I see an old ham sandwich, I'll be discreet enough to ignore it," the lieutenant said sarcastically. He was more concerned with the grim, bottomless chasm that those two decrepit logs lay astride.

Cawkins also peered into it. "No doubt you want to cross over. Right? Luckily we have a lot of light and operating room and I sincerely doubt the logs are rotted after a few centuries."

Cawkins shined his torch to the edges and then into the pit to get a better look. He was worried. "Remind you of the bridge?"

"How could it not?" Hinton-Smith answered.

"I think we should turn around," Cawkins said.

Hinton-Smith warily stepped down on one of the spans to test it. The lieutenant pressed harder, then stepped back, thinking.

"Hold on to my belt," he said to the sergeant. Then he bent down to lift the log and tried to pull it over, the better to test it. No sooner had he swung the opposite edge into space when the span bent and crumbled, plunging into the abyss. "So much for that one." Both men stood quietly. Cawkins shone his torch on his watch. The log took a full minute to hit bottom.

Hinton-Smith hefted the other log. This one was sturdier. "Come on, help me." Hauling it across, they stood it up against the cavern wall at an angle and tried to push it in.

"I think this'll do," Hinton-Smith said as they edged the span back over the dark crevice, swinging it closer to the wall of the tunnel. "We'll have to move sideways, leaning against the wall as we cross. That'll help balance us."

Cawkins stood watching, hands on his hips. It was not the crossing of the log that bothered him. It was something else, less tangible, but all the same just as real. It was something evil. Something he had felt ever since they first spied the ruins. And if you had asked him to define that evil, he would have laughed in your face, because whatever awareness he had of it emanated from his subconscious.

"Give me the rope," Hinton-Smith said.

Cawkins looked at him incredulously. "This is ridiculous," he exclaimed. "We have a job to do, orders." He knew how stubborn Hinton-Smith could be. "You're not really going to cross over, are you?" For a fleeting instant, Cawkins again considered revealing the real import of their mission. The fact was, he was now almost as curious as the lieutenant.

"I'll go first. If it's going to break, it's surely going to break under you. I have a better shot."

After Cawkins reluctantly handed him the rope, the lieutenant tied his end securely around his waist. Then he pulled hard to test it. Satisfied, Hinton-Smith handed his torch to the sergeant.

"Shine it opposite, if you don't mind," he said.

Cawkins shook his head and braced himself as he belayed the rope. "You certainly are fond of rickety old bridges."

"I trust you old man," the lieutenant replied in earnest.

*    *    *

Hinton-Smith had spent the better part of his life trying to live up to the memory of his father, a man he'd never met, but whose legacy grew ever larger with each telling at the regimental mess.

When Hinton-Smith was twelve, quite blond, small and scrawny, he was sometimes allowed to accompany his father's regiment on maneuvers in the North Country. Nearby the camp was an ancient, rickety, worn out rope bridge, anchoring gnarled wooden slats that the soldiers assured him were left over from Hadrian's time. It stretched over a steep defile, with raging white water flowing over a rocky bottom. All that was missing in the lad's mind were the crocodiles, giant constrictors and jungle creepers. The top railing, made of a twisted hemp rope, at first glance seemed to be mostly intact: it was only frayed to the circumference of an inch in a few places, but some few of the slats were broken or missing. Others dangled down as if held by a thread, and some looked so decrepit, a sober man would have been afraid to place a two pound weight on it, lest the slat crumble. One had to cross at least two sections of four or more yards by holding on to the top rail and edging along the bottom rail, which was even more threadbare hemp. This bridge was known to everyone in the unit and had been off limits since two privates plunged to their deaths on a dare a year earlier.

Overhearing some of the soldiers challenging each other to cross the bridge, he was noticed and jokingly invited to join them. The young boy was very afraid of heights, could not swim a lick, and had seen the bridge a few times, each of which, when he thought about climbing across it, put a grapefruit size knot in his stomach. But he took the dare seriously: after all, he was the son of a Regimental hero. Greatly offended when they would not take him with, he snuck out of the barracks, followed them to the bridge, and willfully started out on it when they had got to the other side.

It was a moonless night, and the air was heavy with vapor—a hot, humid, muggy night when a plunge into the river might have been construed as refreshing.

Sweating profusely from the top of his head to the bottom of his feet, he grabbed the top rope firmly with both hands and gingerly stepped onto the bottom rail. Hand over hand and one foot shuffling after the other, he edged across. He made himself go. He was not fearless by any means, but he possessed the ability to force himself to do things that frightened him, purely through strength of will. When he arrived at the middle, he stood there, breathing heavily, and yelled to them. He forced himself to look down once or twice to face his fear, aided in this by the fact that it was so dark, he could not see the bottom anyway. He could only hear the distant crashing of the rapids.

It was here that he first met Cawkins, who had just transferred regiments after being busted to the ranks.

"What the bloody 'ell are you doin' out there. Get off the bridge, boy. We gotta come back over. You hear me?" yelled Harold Dobbins, one of the soldiers. "I told you not to come." He repeated to his mates, "I told him he couldn't come."

"I'm not budgin'. I swear it," Hinton-Smith yelled back, even though he was quite aware that the little breeze that had refreshed him seconds earlier was picking up steam.

"Who the hell is that?" Cawkins asked, and without waiting for an answer, bellowed out across the abyss. "And what do you think you're doing?"

"It's for you to find out, you bloody big twit," Hinton-Smith yelled back.

"You keep talking like that and you're going to wish you fell from this here bridge," Dobbins yelled back. "Now get the hell off!" Turning to Cawkins, he said, "It's the regiment's brat. Young Hinton-Smith."

"And who's that?" asked Cawkins.

"The regimental orphan," replied another soldier. "Both parents was killed right after the war. 'is father was a bleedin' 'ero, 'e was, Kenneth Smith. A real leader of men. The boy's Michael Hinton-Smith."

"Are you coming out here or not?" Hinton-Smith dared them through the darkness. Under his breath he said, "Kenneth Smith, I never knew you, but I'll jump off this bridge before I'll let them bully your son."

"Come now, lad. We're all mates here, ain't we?" Dobbins called out in a treacly, sarcasm-laced voice.

"I am not your bleedin' mate, Harold Dobbins. I do not need anybody or anything, especially you, Harold Dobbins," Hinton-Smith yelled back. "So come out on this bridge or bugger off. I don't need mates or sods or dimwits. I was born of Kenneth Smith and he did not bring forth any cowards."

Cawkins had heard of the boy's father. Cawkins had a great regard for heroes.

"Bloody old Harold dared the boy to come with us, thinking he'd be too scared," said the other soldier as he shoved Dobbins, who gave him a good shove in return. "Guess you were wrong, mate."

To the amazement of the others, Cawkins answered the boy in a much calmer tone. "Son, listen closely to me. All right?"

There was silence. So much adrenaline was pumping through the young lad's veins, he could have leapt to the other side by then.

Cawkins continued, "We need your help. We can't stay out here all night. Hell, if I get broken once more I'll end up being the damn stable boy. This little bridge can only hold one man at a time. You understand?" He paused but there was no answer.

"Now I know, and the rest of us know, you ain't afraid of no dare. It's just this idiot Dobbins that don't know shit."

"What?" protested Dobbins.

Cawkins firmly laid his large hand on Dobbins' shoulder. The grip left no room for further misunderstanding. "Apologize to the boy, Dobbins."

"Bugger all, Yank!" Dobbins protested, but a grimace appeared on his sallow features as the steel-like grip of Cawkins dug into his shoulder. "Right. Right," he whimpered. "Mike!"

"Mr. Hinton-Smith," Cawkins suggested.

"All right. All right. Mr. Hinton-Smith. Please accept my humble apology. I knew all along that you was a brave lad, I did."

Cawkins abruptly said, "That'll do" and released Dobbins, who simultaneously rubbed his aching shoulder and quickly put a good yard between himself and Cawkins.

"Michael. I want you to go back to the other side and wait for us. And next time we do something as silly as this, you'll be the first person I ask to be by my side. But hurry up, I'm a big man, the wind's starting to blow too strong for my taste, and my buddies and I would prefer to die at the hands of an enemy to breaking our necks on the rocks below."

\*　　\*　　\*

Stepping out onto the beam with his right foot, the lieutenant gingerly followed with his left, sliding it to join the first, his palms flesh out against the damp wall. One step at a time he told himself. Beads of sweat started to trickle down to his eyes and he carefully leaned his forehead to one shoulder then the other to wipe them clean. As he reached the middle, he could feel the board bending slightly and although every inclination in his being wanted to step it up and spring across, he controlled himself and moved slowly, only hurrying when there remained a single step to solid ground. Hinton-Smith ran his finger across his forehead, and flicked the sweat into the chasm.

"Are you ready?" he called over to Cawkins. Bracing to belay the sergeant his foot slipped on something, but he caught himself against the wall. Looking down, he saw a strip of blue cloth with dark black stains. He kicked it away and dug his feet in against the earthen trail. He had no idea that the stains were dried up blood, or the cloth, part of the uniform of a soldier, dead for many years.

"All right," Cawkins sighed. "Catch," he said, throwing the torch over.

Hinton-Smith plucked it out of the cool air with one hand and placed it on the ground so the light would cover the wooden beam.

Then, taking in a mighty breath, Cawkins leaned with both hands against the dirt wall, and started out, sidestepping one foot at time on the narrow plank. As he glided forward, Hinton-Smith reeled in the rope, hand over hand.

As Cawkins advanced to the middle, he felt the board bend under his weight. Then his heart stopped as he heard a loud crack.

Cawkins started to move faster. "Haul me in!" he yelled. "Now!"

Hinton-Smith pulled as hard as he could on the rope, and moved to the edge, leaning out over the chasm and extending his hand. The board splintered with Cawkins only four feet away.

"Jump!" Hinton-Smith cried out.

As Cawkins sprang toward him, Hinton-Smith dropped the rope and grabbed Cawkins's wrists with both hands. Then he fell backwards, using his own weight to haul Cawkins the last few feet.

Both men breathed hard for a few seconds, then Hinton-Smith bellowed, "Get off me then you big oaf! Bloody hell! You're crushing me!" and started to laugh merrily. Cawkins rolled over and got up, walking back to the edge of the hole. The lieutenant joined him on all fours and together they listened.

"How could this pit be so deep?" Hinton-Smith asked.

Cawkins looked at him. "Dammit Mikey. I burned our bridges."

"Nice way with words, Jack old boy," Hinton-Smith said as the clattering sound of the beam hurtling against the walls of the hole, finally echoed off into silence.

# CHAPTER 8

# AT ANOTHER TIME
# AND PLACE III

I t was all too easy, Sir Charles Whyntowne thought as they slowly
walked their horses along the rutted dirt road. How could
*L'Anguedoc* be tricked by a young boy?

Did he have his very own trickster, his Odysseus? Whyntowne
had come across the writings of Homer while in the Levant and had
learned Classical Greek to read them.

The boy was quick, using the scars received by brigands in Italy
when he was captured outside of Napoli. What luck to have happened upon such a boy and to have been able to free him. Sir Charles
had ransomed him with his own gold. Who would have thought
those scars would serve him so well. It had taken the boy months to
recover.

Why would *L'Anguedoc* be so quiet now he was captured? Certainly the charms had done their work, but this was a powerful man.
Whyntowne wondered if he was missing something? Something vital? What was *L'Anguedoc* up to? Could he simply have been done in
by the potion? Sometimes the simplest of answers are the truest. But
he did not believe it so with this man.

"Be alert," he said to Brockingham. "Pass the word."

The night seemed even darker if that was possible. As wind blew through the trees lining the road, some of the men would jump. Any sound out of the night could cause the same effect.

There were times one could barely see the man riding beside him let alone the men in front or further back.

Turning in his saddle to look to the northeast, Whyntowne saw the sky was just as black there, storm clouds shutting out light from the stars. Strange, he did not relish taking *L'Anguedoc* down into the burial chamber at night, even though it would be just as dark in there in the daytime.

They rode in columns of two. *L'Anguedoc* was in the middle of the line of horsemen. He had not moved since falling after downing the potion.

Brockingham rode down the line of knights, stretching some thirty yards along the road, and told them to be attentive. It was not yet over. After warning each man, he returned to the front.

Whyntowne had decided to go back for the slain knights once this was done. Many of the men were in mourning. He could see it in their eyes though none had voiced it. Two dead. They could not afford to lose many more. If they did they would not be able to finish.

At the rear of the column, Heidel slowed his horse, but barely. As he dropped behind Sebastian, he quietly withdrew his sword, placing it at his side.

"Sst," he whispered to Sebastian. When the knight turned, Heidel motioned for him to draw back. "I think my horse is lame."

"I'll look," Sebastian said. Dismounting, he walked back to Heidel. "Which?" he asked.

"Rear left," Heidel said, also dismounting, his sword still hidden.

When Sebastian bent over to look, Heidel brought down his sword, severing his head. It had been done neatly and quietly. Looking up, Heidel could just make out the last two riders receding in the distance.

Quickly he tied Sebastian's horse to a tree, mounted Heidel's horse and trotted to catch up. So, Sir Charles Whyntowne, *L'Anguedoc* thought, the odds become better for me.

Heidel was no more. His mind had been taken by *L'Anguedoc*.

In front, Sir Charles still mulled over the captive's passivity.

"Peter. Ride back and check on *L'Anguedoc*."

"How sir?"

"Poke him," Brockingham said.

"Sir?"

"He's mocking you, lad," Whyntowne said. "Check his bonds. See if he wakes."

"Yes," Dillon said, turning his horse and spurring it forward.

When he reached the horse bearing *L'Anguedoc* he was almost inclined to poke the man. The only movement was *L'Anguedoc's* body bouncing with each step of the mare. Not so fierce now, eh?

Dillon studied him as he walked his horse alongside. There was no movement. None at all. He might as well be dead. The potion should have worn off a bit by now. Did he give him too much? Did he kill him? Leaning in, he felt *L'Anguedoc's* neck searching for the vein. Nothing. No pulse. He sat in his saddle thinking as the horse bearing *L'Anguedoc* moved further away. Donnell and Quentin were closest. He would turn to them for help. As he started toward them something made him stop. He could barely see the two men as they rode together. But as they drew nearer, a third man rode up in between them. Dillon saw the third man bring down his sword on Donnell, almost cleaving his torso in two, then thrust his sword threw Quentin's belly.

The man governing Heidel's body looked ahead to his next victims and spotted Dillon. "You," he said. "Come here. I have something for you." Then spurring his horse and raising his sword above his head with two hands, Heidel charged forward.

Dillon did not have time to think, he could only react. Drawing his sword as he jerked on the reins, he yelled as loud as he could, "Dominic! Help!" and galloped toward Heidel.

As he closed the distance between them, he remembered Heidel's face, but the voice did not fit. Was it his imagination? *Oh My Lord!* Could it be?

They closed and Heidel struck the first blow. He was a huge man. Swinging down from over his head, his sword was met by the blade of Dillon, the impact driving the squire's arms in next to his shoulders.

Peter could feel a tremor go throughout his limbs. He quickly pulled his horse around and back. How many more of those could he take?

When Heidel came forward, Dillon now took the first swing and swiftly brought forth another, both aimed at Heidel's head. The sound of the clashing swords rang through the forest.

"Alarm!" Sir Dominic shouted. "Heidel's gone mad!"

"Hold on to *L'Anguedoc*," Whyntowne shouted back as he and Brockingham spurred their horses in Dillon's direction. "Don't lose him."

Heidel twirled his blade above his head to gain speed and brought it right at the young man's head.

As Dillon blocked the strike his sword broke in half, the blade catapulting through the air barely missing Dominic.

Before Heidel could swing again, Dillon charged. Ducking as he neared, he plunged the broken sword into Heidel's mount. The horse collapsed on top of the knight.

Whyntowne and Brockingham dismounted, ran to Heidel and held him down. Castillo readied his sword to slay him.

"Do we need the mask?" Turnbull yelled as he rushed up.

"Do we kill him?" Castillo asked.

"It is not Heidel's fault his mind was weak," Whyntowne said.

Peter Dillon ran to the side of the road and threw up. He had killed a beautiful animal and the thought made him sick.

"Can he recover?" Turnbull asked.

"No. We have lost him," Brockingham said. "Forever."

Whyntowne nodded to Castillo who brought his sword down hard and with precision. Heidel's head thudded on the cold earth.

"We take the head with us," Brockingham said, picking it up and holding it at arm's length to drain. He then took muslin out of a saddlebag, wrapped it around the head and tied it to his saddle.

"Peter," Sir Charles called out. "What is our cost?"

"Sir Quentin and Donnell for certain," Dillon said as he returned to the road. "But I have not seen Sebastian?"

"We must finish this. Come with me," Whyntowne said to Brockingham. They walked up to *L'Anguedoc's* still inert form.

Brockingham unfastened the mouthpiece of the mask and forced *L'Anguedoc's* mouth open. The knight tried to wrest his head away but Turnbull held him firmly in place. Castillo then grabbed the knight's tongue and Whyntowne cut it off. The mouthpiece was put back in place. "No more incantations, sir," Brockingham said.

Whyntowne blamed himself. He was well versed in *L'Anguedoc's* evil nature, but perhaps one could not really understand it until actually encountering it. This was not something you could learn out of a text or in a lecture. He now ordered all the men to close their minds to all thoughts. They had been trained thusly, but Heidel had been too casual about it.

"Bind the squire," Whyntowne ordered. "And place one of the masks on his head. He has not been trained."

This done, they quickened their pace back to the hill.

*       *       *

It was still dark when they started the arduous climb to the abandoned castle. A steady drizzle had dampened their cassocks by the time they reached the top and the weather was threatening to worsen. Streaks of lightning intermittently brightened the sky to the north and seemed to be moving their way.

By then *L'Anguedoc* had begun to struggle against his bonds but found them unyielding. What were their plans? Could they actually kill him? Why were his powers useless? He searched the caravan for minds he could reach, but there was only one and he could sense that the man Whyntowne had secured him. This knight was formidable, more so than any man he had yet encountered. Though he could not see through the lead mask, he knew Whyntowne was watching.

He vowed he would not go easily. There would come a time, even if only an instant, when another would let down his guard.

A group of eight men sat quietly near the walls of the castle under a hastily set up tarp, when Whyntowne's band reached the top of the hill. These men were dressed as knights. Chain mail covered them from head to toe. Over their armor flowed white robes, with large white Maltese crosses, bordered in black, on both the front and back. For long hours none had seemed to move or speak, as though they all were in deep contemplation. Now, they looked up and stared for a brief moment, then each began to don dark hooded cassocks over his armor. Each man's demeanor bespoke of sorrow, yet also of a fierce determination.

The sky had just began to lighten far to the east as Castillo and Turnbull untied *L'Anguedoc* from his mount and hoisted him on Sir Thomas Ward's shoulders, while Brockingham took Heidel's severed head and tied it to his belt.

Whyntowne walked over to his squire and helped him dismount. "Peter. You know why I do this?"

The boy nodded.

"It will be over soon and I shall free you myself. Now we must get on with it." He led the boy to the tarp. "Rest here, Peter. Know you have done well."

Castillo climbed down the entranceway to the passage first, then Turnbull and Whyntowne. Ward and Brockingham lowered *L'Anguedoc's* body into their hands. Other knights and a priest followed after them as they carried *L'Anguedoc* down through the tunnel and to the staunch wooden planks spanning the hole. In their absence, a thick rope had been strung across the gaping void.

"We should just drop him down here and be done with it," Sir Lucien said, breathing hard as he helped to carry the knight. He placed his arm around the rope so it lodged under his armpit and then backed up onto the boards. Sir Thomas followed holding *L'Anguedoc's* legs.

"As for me," Brockingham said, "I'd like to hear the thud when he hit bottom."

There was a brief, muffled laughter.

The descent continued to the graveyard where nine graves had been freshly dug, eight in a broad circle and one in the middle of the eight. Tombstones were lying to the side of each grave and all had names and dates already inscribed along with strange markings from the East. The center stone bore an inscription written in Aramaic.

The miscreant was roughly stripped, save for the mask, the two pieces now bolted together around his head, and thrown into the middle grave. A prayer and benediction were uttered by the priest. Holy water was splashed over *L'Anguedoc's* body. When he was done, the priest inscribed a parchment with an illustration of the burial site, adding pictures of demons at the corners of the center grave and Eastern symbols throughout. Folding it, he put it in his tunic and set about making a copy.

The eight men in hooded robes had ended their meditations and now appeared at the gravesite carrying stanchions with bright blue crystals on each end and placing one of them in each of the four corners of *L'Anguedoc's* grave.

Of these eight, many had tears in their eyes as together, they shook hands and embraced their fellows, saying fare thee wells and goodbyes. Swords drawn, they walked to the hole that they hoped would bear *L'Anguedoc* throughout eternity. One by one, each plunged his sword into *L'Anguedoc*. Hideous screams rent the still, musty air as Sir Charles and others stood by in silence. Golden amulets were placed around the hilt of each sword.

Loosing the head of Heidel from his belt, Brockingham placed it on top of *L'Anguedoc's* body. "Sir Heidel Morrstaed. May you guard him better in death than you did in life."

A marble slab with eastern markings was lowered into the hole where it fitted seamlessly on prepared ledges. Earth was shoveled on top. When it was done, these eight now walked to the fresh graves that surrounded the putrid hole. Each knight now descended into what was to be his own grave.

As Sir Charles Whyntowne, his face ashen, approached each grave, Sir Reginald Brockingham, also with tears in his eyes, handed him a stanchion and a vial containing a potion for sleep. These he passed to the knights within, saying kind words to each.

"*L'Anguedoc's* power has always been greater than ours, but you hallowed eight, together, can perhaps keep him interred. That is our hope, our prayer."

They waited for the potions to take hold.

With a command from Sir Charles Whyntowne, Brockingham, Castillo, Ward and Turnbull began to push marble slabs on top of the knight's graves, fitting them only inches above their still bodies, closing them in darkness. The tombstones with their names were now set erect.

"It is done," Sir Charles Whyntowne said, staring at the grave where they had disposed of *L'Anguedoc*. "I have never witnessed greater evil, and pray to never again."

He turned and with an effort, wiped the tears from his eyes as he walked around the circle of eight. He could only speak in a raspy choking voice. "These men have embarked upon the greatest sacrifice any man has ever made. I am humbled before them. We all are. There is no way to repay them."

Sir Charles Whyntowne bowed his head, brought up his hands before his chest and said a silent prayer.

He now opened his eyes, revealing an immense sadness.

"I would have the parchment," he said to the priest.

"But sir, we must have a record."

"I do not want this to become a shrine to evil," Sir Charles said, holding out his hand. The priest gave him the parchment and Sir Charles examined it then took one of the torches and burned out the middle bearing *L'Anguedoc's* name.

"There are still the two," Brockingham said.

"Yes," Sir Charles Whyntowne said. "The others."

"Something bothers me, Sir Charles," Brockingham said with much solemnity. He looked over the grounds and pointed at the tombs of their fellow knights. "Should we leave the names of our friends on the stones?"

"I know. This vexes me as well." This question bothered him in many ways. "They should be remembered. We owe them this. This crypt will never be seen." He scratched the names of the knights from the parchment and handed it back to the priest.

"But what if *L'Anguedoc* once more manages to live, to come back from the grave. Would their ancestors be in jeopardy? Would that we did not give him their names, sir."

It had been a long arduous trail, years. All Sir Charles wanted now was sleep, and dreams of his homeland. It did not take him long to decide.

"First let us unbind Squire Dillon. And strike the names from the stones. Then let us go from this place forever."

# CHAPTER 9

# THE D'JINN'S IN
# THE BOTTLE

Soon they were groping their way through a short, level passage, then down a decrepit, switch-back stairway, consisting of steps of mildewed and crudely-cut wood, both narrow and treacherous, even slippery. Eventually, the path angled down steeply, in line with the slant of the mound. Hinton-Smith led, focusing his beam on the steps immediately in front of him, with Cawkins following his silhouette, tensely holding his flashlight with a firm grip.

They each carried their torch with one hand and used the other as a balance against the rough tunnel wall, as they stepped gingerly along the slimy ground. Stopping abruptly, the lieutenant shone his light straight down, then bent over and picked up a bit of the gelatinous substance covering the steps. First rubbing it between his fingers, he brought it up to his nose to smell.

"Yuck! What is this stuff?" Hinton-Smith whispered.

"Bat dung, of course," answered Cawkins.

"Blimey! Of course," the lieutenant exclaimed, wiping his hand on the dirt wall.

"Just watch your feet. I don't want to have to carry you out of here if you fall," the sergeant warned. "I'd have to throw you over that damn pit." Briefly he wondered how they'd cross back anyway.

114

Were they trapped down here?

"I shall try hard not to be a maladroit," Hinton-Smith said with a requisite amount of sarcasm.

They could sense they were nearing ground level. It was a bit cooler. They both noticed a sickeningly sweet smell, like a dead, rotting animal. Neither man had ever smelled anything like it. The stench became unbearable as they proceeded, so strong it seemed to penetrate through the smallest pores of their skin.

"This is like a rendering plant mixed up with a country out-house," Cawkins said. He grimaced and instinctively moved his free hand up to cover his nose. Inadvertently, his hand hit the cave wall, coming upon something hard, and clearly man-made. Feeling blood come quickly to the surface of the wound, he ignored it and shone his light upward.

"Look," Cawkins said, as he pointed with his beam, illuminating an ancient torch holder. "Wonder if I can get this going?" Striking a match, Cawkins reached up and lit the remains of the oily, darkened cloth wrapped around the top of a wooden post. "Nothing like success, eh?"

"Right you are, Sergeant Major."

Under this new flickering light, ghastly shadows appeared. The walls seemed strange, as though coming alive with ancient faces cut into stone.

Neither man had looked at their surroundings before now, so intent were they on keeping their footing, but now they let their widened eyes roam over every extent of the wall within the range of their torch beams.

"Amazing," the lieutenant said. "It's like Westminster Abbey."

"This place is a burial chamber, Mike. A regular mausoleum. Will you look at these," he whispered in tones of reverence. Cawkins put his hand to his mouth and sucked the blood, then wiped it off on his shirt.

Hinton-Smith's jaw dropped as he slowly shone his light back and forth along the shaft, making a quick estimation.

"There must be over a hundred separate vaults hewn out of stone," Hinton-Smith said. "Just within our view. They cover the walls from top to bottom."

"Whoever lived here made the shaft out of their dead," Cawkins said. "The whole passage was their sepulcher, and chiseled in each stone is probably the likeness of the man buried there. Just like some of the Romans."

"My Lord! Incredible. Now aren't you glad you came?" exclaimed Hinton-Smith as he turned his torch to the path ahead.

"It's similar to the Lion's Mound at Waterloo," Cawkins said.

"What do you mean, Lion's Mound?"

"Well, it's man made just like this," Cawkins said. "And all those soldiers are buried there, just not in vaults."

"What soldiers are you talking about?" Hinton-Smith asked as his eyes scanned along the walls.

"The soldiers buried there, of course," Cawkins said, raising his voice. "From the battle, the casualties from Waterloo."

"That hill is made of dirt, nothing else."

"No. 40,000 dead made up the basis of the mound," Cawkins said.

"Can't be. I don't believe it." The lieutenant could feel his face and neck redden. Well aren't you the know-it-all, he thought, but his mind quickly returned to the tunnel. "I've never seen anything like this before. Not even in the catacombs in Mdina! Remember?" He could just make out the last corner where the stairs of the switchback ended. There, the trail became a straight shaft, still angling perversely downward, but widening.

"Of course I do. In Malta," Cawkins said. That's strange. He visited Waterloo. He knows that.

Another aspect of the cave wall caught the lieutenant's eye.

"Bloody hell," the lieutenant exclaimed, as he looked closer at one tomb, then another, and another. He saw what he thought were individual swastikas in the four corners of every tomb he looked at. "How the bloody hell did the Nazis get here?"

Cawkins looked closer at the engravings. They were very precise, as though the craftsmen had been quite meticulous and taken great care to get them just so. They looked like swastikas, but they were somehow askew. Cawkins studied them. Then he understood.

"They didn't. We'll most likely be seeing a lot of those swastikas in the near future, but these are different. Look closer," he told the young man as he shone his light directly on one of the signs. "A swastika is inverted. This ain't. It's an old Sanskrit symbol. Means good luck, or for these guys, maybe a protection for the next life. Hitler stole it, and like everything else he's touched, perverted it. But that's strange. Look at this other marking. It's a Vedic symbol, called *Pancha Ayudhaya.*"

"Sanskrit? Vedic? What're they doing here?" the lieutenant asked testily, as he continued to feel an urge to be contrary for no apparent reason. Hinton-Smith was surprised at his tone of voice. He heard it, but he could not associate it with himself. Where was this antagonism coming from?

Cawkins stared at the lieutenant for a minute, also surprised. With a great deal of patience, he continued. "When my sister was a child, perhaps two years old, she had this terrible rash. Nothing the doctors could do helped. They applied salves and herbs and other local remedies, even injections of something or other, and it would disappear for a couple of hours or a day at the most, and then return."

Normally, Hinton-Smith enjoyed Cawkins little "tales of the west," but this time he felt himself smoldering. A rage was building inside him. He could not understand why, and he was increasingly unable to control it.

The oily rag burned down to an ember then flickered out. As Cawkins moved on, the passage was so thick with the gloom of the dead that his own torches' light seemed to have diminished into a thin, pencil-like beam illuminating nothing. "An Indian girl, she was Osage, a friend, came one day with a holy man. The girl knew about the situation and went to the shaman and described it, and he thought he could help. I remember the shaman going into a trance, then telling us many things about our family's life, as though he *knew* he would not be believed by my mother unless he demonstrated this knowledge that he could not possibly know, or fake, unless he truly had the gift. Luckily my father wasn't home when they came, because he would have tossed the man out on his ear, regardless. As it was, my mother was more sympathetic, especially because she was at her wit's end, and by then, would've tried anything."

"Is there more?" the lieutenant asked impatiently. "Or can we continue the exploration?"

Cawkins turned and glared at the young man. "You asked for an explanation and I'm trying to give you one." Oddly enough, Cawkins was beginning to feel anger building up inside. "The holy man said that an evil spirit had attached itself to my sister, because it was jealous that she was a new being, and was having a happy life. He prepared a chain with a protection," Cawkins said. "And chanted over it for twelve hours." He stopped for emphasis, then spoke louder. "Twelve hours! Do you understand? An Osage holy man standing for twelve fricking hours chanting prayers over a charm. He then fastened it around her ankle. The rash vanished. It never came back."

"What's the bloody point to all this? Are you going to tell me your bloody holy man found his way to this cave?" the lieutenant could not help blurting out. "I thought you said this was Vedic?"

"You want to know how it got here or not?" the sergeant shouted back. "Everybody knows that Alexander made it to the East. Some say Christ did as well, and knights from the Crusades. Maybe some of them made it back. Schliemann found swastikas at Hissarlik for crying out loud. Now just shut up and listen. You're the SOB who wanted to come down here, aren't you? You had to explore, didn't you? Look. The *Pancha Ayudhaya*. See the signs?" he said, pointing at the markings on the tomb. "There are five of them, all weapons, arranged in a circle: the trident, bow and arrow, a discus-like saw, a sword, and a conch. The conch isn't really a weapon. It's for scaring evil spirits away. The sound scares them, when you blow it."

"So what? Are they the same as what your sister got?"

"Not the same protection. That was an American Indian shaman," Cawkins said loudly. "But maybe the same idea. That's the point."

"Blimey! Do I look like your bloomin' student?" the lieutenant yelled. "Bugger all," Hinton-Smith said.

"You know what else?" Cawkins yelled. "After we crossed that fricking bridge, I remembered where I heard of St. Venant."

"Where."

"That's where they found your father's plane. That's where he died."

The lieutenant felt as if a bolt of lightning had hit him. He knew his father's plane crashed on a hilltop. What if it was this one?

"Thanks for letting me know now," Hinton-Smith said angrily, then storming off to get away from the sergeant. He was perfectly capable of exploring the cave on his own.

Cawkins was too absorbed in his own thoughts to notice him leave. But what came to his mind was "stupid ingrate." He tried to focus on the cave walls but he was also confused at his growing irritation with the lieutenant.

He forced himself to return his attention to the vault directly in front of him. Why *would* Vedic symbols be in here? Were the signs a protection? He was finding it increasingly harder to concentrate. It seemed to be getting cooler. He hugged his arms to warm them.

"They put this sign on kids they thought were afflicted by the evil eye, probably adults as well. The weapons symbolized the power of the gods that wielded them."

"Here, look," he said as he pulled a small medallion from around his neck and turned around. "I got this when I was stationed in India..."

But Hinton-Smith was nowhere to be seen. The hell with him, the sergeant thought. He fingered the medallion. That was intriguing. What were the chances he'd have the same symbol? The same *Pancha Ayudhaya*. He looked for the lieutenant only briefly, then shone his torch down the remainder of the shaft and continued downward. As the path finally leveled off, Cawkins figured he had reached bottom and counted off twenty-one paces as he crossed a flat piece of ground. Noticing an absence of any form whatsoever, a minuscule black hole, he took that as evidence of an opening. Leaning against the void, almost as if trying to escape, was a skeleton bundled in a torn and stained red and blue uniform of a *Zouave* from the Napoleonic army. What *is* this place, Cawkins wondered? Then his light shaft caught the forms of more stones, that also looked to be man made, but these were more like normal headstones than the rest and formed half of a circle, with one standing apart as though a focal point and near the void he'd spotted. There were more symbols chiseled into this stone than the rest, and an inscription he could not decipher.

"Jesus," he exclaimed. "More graves."

In a far corner of the shaft, Hinton-Smith was becoming aware of strange thoughts entering his head. He thought he might like to kill every Kraut soldier; maybe the women and children as well; perhaps a few stupid Belgies and Frogs. *Why on earth was he thinking like this?*

Hinton-Smith stopped and listened, but all sound fell dead. His breathing stopped, as an unbelievable thought entered his mind.

*Is someone else in here with us?*

Then with his light, he wheeled around. But nothing could be seen in the claustrophobic darkness, save the accursed sepulchers of the ancient dead. *What is it?* He could feel something, as though a great malice had become corporeal and bore down on him. At first it seemed like an accidental shove, then he found himself inadvertently leaning forward as though an enormous wave was collapsing into him. And he could sense hatred unlike anything he had ever known before. His eyes began to bulge. Strange bumps and swellings appeared on his neck and back, moving from one spot to another. The lieutenant could feel his nose bleeding.

His hand opened, seemingly of its own will, and the torch fell to the hard floor, clattering amidst the silence, the light disappearing along with its echo and leaving the lieutenant in total blackness.

Then he heard a distant voice breaking the silence. "Mikey! What happened?" It seemed to come from the very ends of the earth.

The blackness weighed heavily upon him, dark as a tomb—the netherworld he now felt part of. Hinton-Smith felt his throat closing, as if in a vice. It was becoming hard to breathe. Something was inside him. There were thoughts in his head, but not his own.

A fierce, guttural voice whispered, "Spare this one. You can have the other."

Hinton-Smith's eyes returned to normal. The welts disappeared and he could once more breathe easily. But now the fierce hatred began to consume him, become his very own. It quickly mutated onto a more personal level. The very sound of Cawkins's voice now filled him with revulsion.

Hinton-Smith looked about for the only light in this never-ending darkness. He furtively began to close the distance between himself and the sergeant. What right did the bloody Yank have to talk to him like that? And him his superior officer. To his now twist-ed way of thinking he reasoned it might just do to teach his know-it-all mate a lesson of his own. It was almost too easy. Just follow the beam to the source. Not only did he feel a tremendous hatred for

Cawkins building up in him, but he was now certain that the sergeant had somehow tricked him into coming down in this hole to kill him. All these years, he had just befriended him in order to set this up, the bastard. He might have to do something about that. Perhaps more than just a lesson.

At the far end of the pathway, Cawkins dropped the focus of his beam to what appeared to be a small pile of sticks, neatly stacked, and a few feet to the side of the exit. He was cold, yet sweating profusely, and he could feel the veins tightening in his neck and forehead. His face was burning up. Somewhere from within came the thought, this isn't right. *Something is wrong here, in this hole. Something is trying to take over my mind.* If he didn't get out of here soon...

With a superhuman effort of will, he slapped himself hard across the face, raising a one inch crimson welt. Momentarily shrugging off the bizarre, almost narcotic state, he rushed to the wall where he'd seen what he took to be a small outlet, opening his shovel on the way. *I better be right.*

Cawkins now realized those were not sticks that were piled so neatly. They were bones. And they were not piled. It was more like one was reclining, and the other seemed to be leaning over and holding the first. It now struck him like a sledgehammer: had those two possibly murdered each other?

Laying his torch on the ground to illuminate the tiny opening, he started desperately striking at the dirt over and over with the sharp edge of the spade. He scraped the loose soil away, then jammed the shovel in again and again around the edges of the hole slowly enlarging it. He could feel the hatred creeping back into his consciousness, slowly, inexorably. He dropped the shovel and started digging and clawing at the dirt with his bare hands like some maddened beast. Stopping to wipe the sweat and dirt that had begun to drip down to his eyes, he remembered he had a friend down there.

"Mike," he yelled. "Where are you?" Then it hit him. What if Michael was struggling with this bizarre madness too?

Cawkins fought the eerie, inexplicable power, tensing his brow and neck as though trying to squeeze it out. He took a water flask from his belt, unscrewed the top and poured it on his face. Then he picked up the shovel and focused on the feverish exertion of his arms and the shovel. *Just dig. Focus on the digging. But what about Michael?* Finally, he broke through, into clear night air. There was still work to do if he was going to crawl through it.

"Mikey," he screamed. "Get over here. Bring your spade." But the sound of his voice only melted into an unanswered silence. Suddenly he felt the presence of someone else. Cawkins turned to look for the lieutenant again, just in time to see a shovel blade arcing down. He instinctively raised his right arm to absorb the full blow of the blade.

"I'm going to kill you, sergeant!" the lieutenant screamed with a savagery that seemed unrelated to anything human. His face was distorted with rage, like that of a furious gargoyle. Hinton-Smith raised the shovel over his head once more, his eyes horribly blank. But then, he hesitated for an instant, whether from his inherent goodness, or from some innate and ineradicable knowledge that this was his friend. The lieutenant shook as though he was waging a terrible battle for his own soul.

"KILL HIM! KILL HIM! KILL HIM!" raged a voice in Hinton-Smith's head.

Cawkins's right arm was slashed and bleeding profusely. The pain was excruciating, but he knew if he did not defend himself, he was dead. He quickly rose and grabbed Hinton-Smith in a dreadful bear hug, then brought his good arm up and hit the deranged youth so hard he knocked him unconscious.

"We gotta get out of here!" the sergeant bellowed. He dragged Hinton-Smith to the opening, and once more began clawing and hacking at the dirt to expand it enough to get through. He was too busy to notice the lieutenant had blacked out. Neither had he observed the small, recently disemboweled carcass lying close behind the upright bones: the source of the sickeningly sweet stench that they noticed earlier.

Cawkins shook the lieutenant awake and poured water on his face. "Move it," he yelled with all the authority he could muster and shoved him into the hole. Grabbing the sides of the opening, Hinton-Smith finally was aware enough to start pulling himself through.

Clenching his teeth in pain as he pushed the lieutenant's feet clear, Cawkins then grabbed his torch and squeezed himself into the opening. For tense seconds he wriggled through the hole, totally defenseless, his arms at his sides to make himself smaller, and driving with his feet until emerging into a cool, funereal rain. When he got out and stood, he saw the lieutenant hunched down on all fours, staring at the ground and retching violently.

Directly outside was another small muddy burial ground consisting of four more tombstones, making up another half-circle. The sergeant realized they must have originally been part of the circle inside. This part of the *motte* must have eroded. The four stones out here were inscribed with the same inverted swastikas as well as Sanskrit symbols.

As he got to his feet, he could feel something loathsome, demonic, trying to gain hold on him. It was happening again. Intuitively, he knew this patch of ground was almost as deadly as the cave. Grabbing Hinton-Smith's arm, he stood him up.

"Let's go," he yelled, hauling the lieutenant into a jog across the cemetery, till they reached a weed-infested field.

"What about our gear?" the lieutenant slurred somewhat dazedly when they had put some small distance between themselves and the cemetery.

"What about my arm, Mikey boy?" Cawkins shouted angrily. But Hinton-Smith did not answer, walking slowly away as if still under some kind of spell. The sergeant grimaced and rolled up his sleeve. He held his arm up in the rain till the wound was washed clean, then examined it. It was pared almost to the bone and would need a hell of a lot of stitches, but he didn't think it was broken. Unsheathing his knife, Cawkins cut a swath of material from his pants leg and wrapped his arm, all the while watching intently at the lieutenant's receding figure. At that moment, he had a pressing need to know if any vestige of whatever it was they had just encountered was left in the boy. He caught up to Hinton-Smith, turned him around and stared intensely into his eyes. He had no idea what to look for.

Now the full realization hit Cawkins. He grabbed the boy and shook him violently. "You tried to kill me!" he screamed. "What the hell were you doing?"

Hinton-Smith replied as if his mind was miles away. "Kill you?" the lieutenant echoed in a far off voice. "What? The gear."

"The gear? You want to talk about the gear?" Cawkins now real-ized the boy was lost. And he had no idea what to make of it. "We'll come back later," Cawkins said angrily. "Right now, I want to find a doctor."

What happened in there? What was that...that feeling of evil, of hatred? Was it only in his imagination? Or was it real? It sure seemed real enough. He honestly did not know. Did the same thing affect Mike? Something sure did. There was no doubt about that. What in blazes!

Cawkins knew he'd have to be careful from now on, have to watch his back.

*    *    *

They were only some fifty yards away from the deadly cave when they encountered the strangest site either of them had ever seen. So bewilderingly out of time and place in this farming area, or even on this continent, was an old antebellum three-story mansion, with dual white marble stairways curving up to the second floor, and six mas-sive white pillars supporting a second story balcony, that by all rights belonged on a Georgia plantation.

The manor, which took up at least an acre and a half by itself, was completely dark, except for one window on the upper floor, which showed a dim light, probably from a single candle.

Tired of hearing of Yanks like William Randolph Hearst buying an ancient Roman temple front and shipping it over to the New World to be part of his castle grounds or others modeling their mansions after Spanish cathedrals or Italian villas, the eccentric owner of this mansion decided to do the Yanks one better. He traveled to Hilton Head Island in the Twenties, and after visiting all the plantations on the island, bought the old mansion that best suited his taste, shipped it over piece by piece, and reassembled it, even going to the extent of hiring French-speaking Africans as servants to complete the picture.

Cawkins wasted only a glance on the manor, which was only a mi-nor curiosity in his mind. Though he could not help focusing on his throbbing arm, the better part of his attention kept going back to the cave. He kept asking himself what really happened in there? Did Hinton-Smith really attack him? How could he? What was that look in his eyes, almost...demonic? What was that feeling *he himself* had? That presence in his head. Hatred was the only word for it. He'd never felt anything like it before. Never. Not even in combat. Was it his imagination? Was it real? Nonsense. He did not believe in that kind of crap. Then what? Now his thoughts harkened back to his own story of his sister and the shaman. According to him there were evil spirits. What if he was right and where'd that leave them? Was the boy still affected? No, he could not believe in that rubbish. There must be some other explanation and that did not bode well for his mission.

Hinton-Smith followed docilely behind. His head began to clear as they moved further from that evil field, but he was in shock, overwhelmed with guilt and shame. He had no real idea of what had transpired. He had a knowledge of what he tried to do, but could not see that it was really him? How could this be?

He had always been certain he would be a hero, preferably in a far out of the way, exotic setting.

As an orphan, and one limited to the environs of the Regimental grounds, he had grown up with very few close friends. And so, except for untold hours on the sporting fields, he had lived his life in books.

In Kipling, H. Rider Haggard and A.E.W. Mason, in every dime novel he ever read, in every classic, or tale of the Raj, he identified with the hero, just as many young men and women do. With no parents at his side, Hinton-Smith made up grand lives for them and himself. In a different war, he knew he would have been in the desert with Lawrence, charging the heights at Balaclava, or fighting off the Zulus at Rorke's Drift: he had always been a sucker for long odds. From when he was a small boy, he was determined to be a hero and he was, for the most part, certain he was made of the right material. He had the occasional doubt, but does not anyone with intelligence have doubts? Now his infantile recklessness had led his closest friend into great danger, in which *he himself* had been the menace.

Hinton-Smith was not feeling very heroic at the present time.

# CHAPTER 10
# DEAD RECKONING

Cawkins rose before dawn the next morning, his arm aching dreadfully. Sitting up on the bed, he reached down and grabbed a clean pair of trousers, pulling them up with one hand, then slipped his other arm into a sling, gingerly anchoring it around his neck. The lieutenant was sleeping fitfully on the cot next to his. What must he be dreaming about? He took a pint bottle of Irish whiskey from his pack and took a long swig.

That's better. He took another drink, placed the bottle on a table and folded his blanket into a tight square. He stared at the slumbering boy for the better part of a minute then quietly exited the cottage and went out to a wide pasture of yellow grass and weeds. There were indistinct forms he could barely make out in the dim light, but as he drew near he could see they were sleeping cows and hay bales.

Cawkins placed the blanket on the soggy ground and sat down on it, resting his back against a freshly cut bale of hay. Now he had to think about the previous night's events and if his course of action should change: what it would even look like now.

He always liked this time of morning. It was quiet and harmonious, a far cry from last night, and he found himself to be more lucid. Today it seemed to take some of his anger at the boy away, but only to a small degree.

Every logical explanation for what had happened was deliberated on during the course of an hour. He dissected the event over and over again, until he felt like he was in a laboratory cutting up a white rat. It made no sense. Nothing made sense.

By then the sky was lightening, though it was still too hazy to make out the brown and white colors of the motionless bovines. He breathed the scent of the freshly mown hay and shook his head, half in desperation, half in disgust. His arm, in a crude, makeshift cast plastered on over forty stitches, and that he was certain was put on too hastily by an amateur, was causing him considerable pain. And try as he might to get rid of it, there was still a great deal of anger to go along with the injury. This was betrayal. Christ, it was attempted murder!

The same doctor had treated Hinton-Smith's jaw with ice. Hope he botched up the remedy on that one too.

He tried to stick to the facts. One thing for certain, Hinton-Smith was pretty eager to go down that hole and take him along. Had he lured him down there on purpose? Was this a premeditated act? Did Hinton-Smith temporarily go insane, leave his senses? Was it panic? Was he on some sort of drug? The one *logical* explanation that kept rearing its ugly head was that, if the lieutenant did indeed want him out of the way, then he knew the real purpose of the mission and was working for the French. Cawkins had to consider that possibility. He had to consider everything. The mission was basically one of espionage. As far fetched as it sounded, he could not rule it out. The lieutenant had spent time with the French. He seemed to like the French. He had friends among them. But even so, the French wouldn't kill a lowly sergeant to stop the mission. They'd probably just sign a non-aggression pact with the Germans, like the Soviets did. Hinton-Smith, a French spy. In a different circumstance, he would have chuckled over that one. Christ. But Hinton-Smith saved his life when the timber crumbled, didn't he?

"Jesus!" he said out loud. That's right. With that realization, he started to go over everything again. If that was really true, and Cawkins knew it was, then all his speculations before were wrong and left the one impossible explanation, the one he kept avoiding: that there was something else in that cave. But who, or what? And how it—he couldn't help thinking in terms of "it"—had imposed its thoughts or commands on the two of them. He was certain that something had affected his thoughts as well. Though now, with one night's distance from the incident, he had trouble believing some malevolent force had affected him. It was too illogical. He remembered having to force strange thoughts from his head, but there, in the blackness of the narrow tunnel, and amidst all those crypts, it was probably natural to have macabre ideas come into one's mind. Is that what happened to the boy? Just the terror of being in a crypt? No. He'd been in catacombs before and only showed fascination. If there was something, though, it had obviously had a greater affect on Hinton-Smith.

He kept coming up against a solid wall, beyond which he was certain lied the answer. But he could not get beyond that wall because, now, out of the cave, it all seemed so inconceivable. Could it have been a ghost? Some sort of infernal being? But he had never believed in ghosts. How could he think in such terms now? His was an Aristotelian worldview: it did not allow for this supernatural bullshit. But then there was the incontrovertible fact of his arm.

The other question was what to do about Hinton-Smith now? He had definitely changed. No doubt about that. But did he have anything to fear? He toyed with the idea of tying him up, but that would be the end of the assignment. Since the previous night, Hinton-Smith had been quite sullen, quiet. To Cawkins, it seemed as if he was ignoring the whole damned thing. The sergeant knew he'd have to put the best face on it, try hard to act normally and wait and see. There was the mission to complete and he was not one to quit on a mission. But from now on he would be damn careful. First thing back, he would try to transfer.

He went back to the cottage and poured some water in a pot and placed it on a burner. The lieutenant was still asleep, so he quietly removed his service revolver from the bottom of his pack and placed it in his belt next to the small of his back. If he had taken the revolver with him yesterday...Cawkins shook his head. He did not even want to think about it. Quickly, he packed the rest of his kit before waking Hinton-Smith.

The water boiled. Cawkins poured tea into the pot and let it steep for five minutes. "Get up," he said shaking Hinton-Smith's shoulder. "Time to go to work."

He put a steaming cup of tea into Hinton-Smith's hands, as soon as the latter groggily sat up on his bed.

"Here's some powdered milk," he said, tossing the package to Hinton-Smith.

The lieutenant reached up and caught it with one hand, pouring a bit into his mug and stirring it.

Cawkins lit a cigarette. He then handed the lieutenant a loaf of bread and a small piece of brown sugar. "We're going a long way today, so put this in your belly." He looked at the boy carefully, trying to see something, anything that would give him answers. Something that would either tell him to stay on guard or let his mind rest at ease. He corrected himself: there was no way he was going to be at ease.

Cawkins cleared his throat, as though the words he had to speak were painful. He looked at the lieutenant. "Mike. Yeah, something weird happened last night. I felt it. You felt it. Perhaps it had more of an effect on you. I don't know. But we still have work to do. I have one question for you." He stared intently in the lieutenant's eyes. "Do I have anything to worry about?"

"No!" Hinton-Smith blurted out, then he placed his hand on his jaw as if in pain. Turning away from the sergeant's gaze, he ripped off a small bit of bread as though he had contempt for it, and began slowly chewing, at the same time pulling on his pants, shirt and coat. He noticed the whiskey bottle standing on a table and walked over to it, opening it and taking a very long drink. The lieutenant coughed and tossed the bottle to the sergeant. Without another word, he lifted his pack, left the room, got on his bicycle and headed down the road.

All conversation stopped from that time. Over the next two days the two men toiled on their bicycles for seemingly endless hours as they rode along dusty country roads. They peddled through heavily forested areas, around gentle hills and flat farmland, crossing into Belgium south of Tournai a little after noon on the first day. The land now was very green and flat, although there were long stretches of inclines that stretched their legs to the limits of exertion.

They skirted the larger cities and kept to the village roads, finally passing south of Brussels near Waterloo, then following the Dyle River north to Louvain. Early on the afternoon on the second day, they stood astride their bikes on yet another forlorn dirt road, above Louvain. Still dressed as tourists, their military bearing was nevertheless unmistakable to the trained eye, and gave the lie to the masquerade.

Hinton-Smith gazed briefly through his binoculars and pointed in the direction of a great bridge spanning the Dyle River, which ran through the city. "We'll need that bridge."

"Shouldn't I mark it down to be destroyed?" asked Cawkins. These were the first words the two had spoken to each other in almost two days and nights, the lieutenant sullen and the sergeant wary and watchful. Hinton-Smith's words were a welcome relief, but was he back to normal or was he just putting on a show? What was normal now anyway?

Cawkins's anger seemed to rise and fall in direct proportion to the amount of soreness he felt in his arm. The whiskey was gone and the pain throbbed on and off. It had been easier to be magnanimous before a day of hard bicycling.

"No," said the lieutenant as they both looked through their binoculars. He looked again. "We'll need it when we advance."

"Well aren't you the optimist. I don't think we'll be moving forward as easily as we did with the French." Cawkins almost blurted out that he was marking it down to be destroyed, but caught himself. He already said too much. That could have given it away. He was still thinking of the boy as a possible spy. Well, he had to cover all bases didn't he?

The lieutenant looked at him and started to say something, but stopped before a word got out. He offered no more resistance than that. He could sense the sergeant's anger, and he could only blame himself. He had never felt so ashamed in his life. And he could see that he could easily become consumed by it. Awkwardly trying to change the subject, he indicating the sergeant's injured arm, and asked, "Are you sure you're up to handling the map?" Unfortunately, this was going from bad to worse.

"I'll manage," the sergeant coolly cut in, as he adjusted the slowly yellowing cast. He grimaced as a sharp bolt of pain coursed through his wound. "Don't worry yourself about it." His mind wandered back to that night. Then he steadied the notebook between the cast and his sling while he made more notations. His state of mind was in no way helped by the exhaustion from keeping a constant eye on the lieutenant.

Cawkins had never been sanguine about the coming contest, especially not now in his present mood. But then, an older man rarely is as ready for a fight, unless he has a great many younger men to do the dirty work for him. With a grim resignation, not satisfaction, he marked the bridge down to be destroyed. He used his left hand.

It was not helping his disposition that the lieutenant had kept silent on the real problem, kept silent period. Cawkins could not help thinking, *the sooner we finish with this, the sooner I get away from you, Mikey boy.* "Sir. With all due respect to our forces, we'll be lucky to make it to here," he said peremptorily, as he gestured with his good hand at the ground they were standing on and then out to the west bank of the Dyle. "There won't be any advance into Jerries' territory by the likes of us."

Both men knew their relationship had changed. Both were aware of the confusion, but neither was quite certain of the "how" or "why" of it. There had certainly been a bizarreness to the incident, like something out of the worst nightmare, and neither could stop thinking about it. All the same, neither man was able to put voice to the matter.

A fact's a fact, Cawkins thought. A couple of nights ago, Hinton-Smith tried to kill him, he was certain of that. By now he had played it over and over so much in his mind that he was sick of it. He just didn't want to believe it. That was the problem. He couldn't believe it. Why'd he do it? Why doesn't he say something about it? He had been like a son to Cawkins.

"I'm disappointed in you Jack." Hinton-Smith was relieved to talk, as long as it was about anything not related to the cave. Trying hard to block out the incident, he focused on the impending advance, and the sergeant's pessimistic attitude. He had heard enough defeatism in their recent interaction with the French, and he was still much caught up in the idea of the glory of war. Perhaps it was there he'd redeem himself. Perhaps the only place he could.

And he had other thoughts as well—thoughts that try as he might, he could not chase from his mind. He felt like a criminal. Someone caught in the act, something he shouldn't have done, ever. But there it was. He had almost committed murder. Against his best mate! He knew he was responsible. He could remember the action, but he could not put it together with himself, with either his conscious self or physical being. He knew he had not been in control, but how could he explain that to Cawkins without sounding like an idiot? Not in control? Then who was? Some sorcerer in a tree handling him like a puppet! Perhaps a demon, he chuckled in deprecation at himself. The more he thought about it, the more idiotic it sounded. Could he have been awake and blacked out at the same time? But then how did he even know what he did?

Hinton-Smith found relief as best he could from concentrating on the job at hand.

Periodically, and as innocuously as possible, Hinton-Smith raised his binoculars, took a quick look at the surrounding area, and then let them fall to his chest, suspended from their leather strap. In these brief surveys, he would ascertain another obstacle to be surmounted, bridge to be crossed, or road to be secured: roads the BEF would advance upon; where to place artillery; roads the Germans would use; the most important areas for defense; good ground; clear fields of fire; and optimistically, clear lines of advance.

Cawkins was occupied in the same way, painstakingly entering the information in his notebook and designating the locations on his corresponding map, though almost in complete disagreement with the lieutenant's outlook. And most importantly, designating the routes that would facilitate an escape to the coastal ports. This he did in code, and, continually, he watched the younger man to see if there was any change. No matter how preposterous the whole thing sounded, he could never again be absolutely, one hundred per cent certain of the lieutenant.

All in all, the game was rather academic by this time. This is where the Germans would attack. Everyone knew that. The lieutenant and the sergeant knew it. What was problematic for the Allies was tactical: how to deploy their forces in the best manner to stop them. What was problematic for the two men was the political situation. Since King Leopold of Belgium declared neutrality in 1936 and closed his borders to French military observers, no Allied soldiers were supposed to be there. They were out of uniform, spying on a neutral country. And now, on top of that, they also had to be concerned with a relationship strained to the extreme.

The lieutenant got off his bicycle and let it fall to the ground. "My arse is bloody sore," he complained as he briefly massaged the offending area.

"Less conspicuous, sir. The bikes, I mean."

The lieutenant scrupulously avoided looking at Cawkins. He was both confused and ashamed. How could this have happened? Did it happen? But there was the proof; the crude cast on Cawkins's right arm. He felt he was acting differently, more formal towards Cawkins, but he was trying to be the same as always, except for his inability to look the sergeant in the eyes. *He'd never called me sir before,* Hinton-Smith realized.

"I know. Anyway, what are we supposed to do? The Belgies are hiding their heads in the sand."

"Ain't that the truth," the sergeant major replied in his gruff voice. "They sure don't have a flair for the obvious."

"I don't want to seem naive. But I've studied my share of military history. Are they insane?" the lieutenant asked. "The Jerries came through them the last time, and they're going to do it again. Or am I missing something?"

A grim smile came to the sergeant's lips. He was tiring of a conversation which in normal circumstances would have been just that: normal. It occurred to him to ignore the small talk until the lieutenant brought up what was going too long unspoken. "No sir, you're not. I guess you might say hope springs eternal."

The Belgians were devoutly holding on to the idea that the Germans would never invade a neutral country, even to get at the French. They held onto the idea with the unrepentant fervor of a zealot, notwithstanding their recent experience of the last war and the Schlieffen Plan. In practical terms, this meant they would not exchange staff officers or have a joint staff with the Allies, have war games, or, most importantly, let the French and British march up to the Belgian-German border and construct fortifications to extend the Maginot Line. What it meant was the

Allies would have to fortify the Franco-Belgian border, then rush up to the Scheldt to form a new defensive line when, not if, the Germans attacked. And if there was time, up to the Meuse-Antwerp Line, some sixty miles distant, most likely while under fire from artillery and dive-bombing Stukas. Both of these positions were mostly unfortified, owing to the Belgians' neutrality. By now, most Englishmen held the view that a lot of men would die advancing into territory they would need nothing short of a miracle to hold.

It meant the Belgians would not officially allow the Allies into their country for reconnaissance, for fear of irritating the Germans. It meant that Hinton-Smith and Cawkins found themselves, illegally, sixty miles from the French frontier.

And it was not without risk for them. It would be quite embarrassing for the Allies and Belgians, and deadly for themselves, if they were caught. The Belgians would have to make a show of it or risk the Germans (who never considered that when they entered another country, they were invading it) inviting themselves in to protect them. Indeed, as recently as mid-November, German commandos kidnapped two English intelligence officers from Holland, smuggling them back to Berlin where they were implicated in a bombing in Munich, ostensibly an assassination attempt on Hitler, that in essence and fabrication of proof was not unlike the Reichstag fire.

Both men were executed by the Gestapo.

Hinton-Smith was still rather new to the game and retained his confidence, that is, as it pertained to the BEF. "The terrain's been fair the whole way in. I think we can advance easily, like we did to Brebach." He said this in the manner of a challenge.

Cawkins finally gave in to exasperation at the young man's naiveté. It was time for a lecture. "The Belgies won't let us in till the balloon goes up. I don't blame the ignorant bastards, though. Would you trust the English and French after Munich?"

Hinton-Smith hesitated, then replied simply, "Right." He could not help thinking, *could you trust me after the cave?*

"The key is how long they can hold their line. I'm sure we can advance to the Scheldt okay, but the French are more ambitious."

The lieutenant looked at him, questioningly.

"The French will want us to advance up to here," Cawkins said, pointing again to the expanse of the Dyle River.

"The lads can do it," the lieutenant interjected.

"Kind of depends on how much notice we get, and how fast the Jerries advance. Personally, if we have to go in, I wish we would stop at the Scheldt."

"D'Agapaeov told me if we get to the Dyle, we'll save twelve to fifteen divisions just by shortening the front."

"Sure." The sergeant laughed cynically. "If we get there, and if we can hold on to it long enough to fortify it." He raised his field glasses again, scanning both directions along the Dyle as far as the eye could see. He motioned for Hinton-Smith to do the same. He was going to make it simple. "What don't you see?" he asked.

"What do you mean?"

"Look. Look closely. What's missing?"

Hinton-Smith strained to see every little detail but did not quite understand. Scanning the whole frontier from north to south, it finally dawned on him.

"I don't see anybody. No work parties, no engineers. Nobody's working on the line."

"That's right. Very few anti-tank obstacles or wire. The defensive line itself is inadequate and even what they've got ain't finished. The Belgies are worried that if they seem too ambitious in building their defenses, they'll just end up irritating the Jerries." Cawkins looked through the viewfinder of his spy camera, a Minox sub-miniature. "We'll have to go down a lot closer for pictures. These stupid cameras are only good from close up."

"So we're going to look like bloody fools rushing up to the Dyle. The whole plan is really dependent upon the Belgians. They'll have to hold the Meuse and the Albert Canal long enough for us to dig in," the lieutenant said in realization. The Allies' "Plan D" for the Northern Armies was insane. Unfortunately, owing to the very small number making up the BEF (only one tenth the number of the French), it was going to be a French show.

"Look at it this way," Cawkins said, drawing in his breath and throwing out his chest in a very imperious manner as if he were tutoring a child and finally getting to the core of the matter. "Would you rather fight the Germans from behind the positions we've already fortified on the Franco-Belgian border, or from virtually naked positions on the Dyle or Scheldt?"

The lieutenant could only nod in agreement.

"So," said the sergeant, satisfied he'd made his point. "Do you think the Belgies can hold?"

"Not if the Jerries aren't swell blokes." He paused for a moment, thinking. "Staff already knows this, don't they? We're just the window dressing."

"You ought to know the answer to that," Cawkins said. "I guess we'll be able to tell them what they want to hear." The sergeant looked at him intently, trying to discern if he knew the real answer. "Well. That's enough of this, ain't it." Cawkins looked again at his map. "We can make the Albert Canal at Hassalt by evening if we hurry, then we'll head back to Brussels. Right now, let's take a closer look." Without waiting for an answer, the sergeant started down the hill. As Hinton-Smith followed after the sergeant, a voice inside his head screamed, *I don't know what happened! I don't know what happened!* And then, another, more inconsolable inner voice said, *I've failed you, Jack. I've failed you, father.*

# CHAPTER 11

# THE OATH

The journey back to British lines was more or less silent. There was the reconnaissance, of course—they returned by a different route, and notes on maps were duly recorded, but an uneasy lack of communication once more settled into place. When they reached British General Headquarters in Arras, Cawkins quickly dismounted his bicycle, and without a word, turned his back on the lieutenant and made his way to the red brick building that housed the General Staff.

Hinton-Smith stared sheepishly after him, tried to say something, but failed even in this simple task. Something greater than words was needed in any event. The lieutenant had to get his head clear, and the best way to do that, for him, was on the football field. It was turning into a hot day. He knew a good sweaty workout was the best thing for him.

Retrieving a soccer ball from his footlocker, he walked to the Regiment's field, one he had been instrumental in staking out. There, he dribbled the ball on his feet and knees, seeing how long he could keep it in the air. Tiring of this, he ran down the field, kicking the ball as if defenders were trying to wrest it from him. For thirty minutes, he practiced his shot from varying distances and angles, and lastly, he ran back to back hundreds till he was exhausted. Bending over and breathing deeply after one last sprint, his hands on his knees, the answer finally came to him.

He would go back there—the kits had to be retrieved anyway.

He would find out what was in that cave. He knew he was not insane. Something had forced him into that action and he was determined to find out what it was. And somehow, he would then prove to Cawkins the truth of what had happened. The sergeant was his big brother, father and friend rolled up into one; he would sooner do harm to himself than do anything to hurt Cawkins. He would make up for it. Hinton-Smith would do whatever it took to win back Cawkins's esteem and trust. He headed to the motor pool.

Cawkins was quickly ushered into the colonel's office. There was no time for niceties, or pretensions regarding the true nature of his mission. He laid out his maps and deciphered the codes for the colonel, the friend who had been promoted to Staff Intelligence from the Coldstreamers. Pointing to the Channel Ports of Dunkirk, Ostend and Zeebrugge, Cawkins said, "If worse comes to worse, the BEF should be able to make a straight line back to the beach. With due respect for the confusion of any battle, if we make sure we leave detachments at the crucial bridges, passes and crossroads, Ostend and Dunkirk would be the likely disembarkation points. Zeebrugge would be a backup."

The colonel's eyes glistened as he looked at the map. "We owe you a lot, and I hope we never have to make use of your work," he said. He gazed at Cawkins's arm for a second, then looked up at the sergeant. "Is there anything I can do for you?"

"Thank you, sir," Cawkins replied. The sergeant lowered his eyes and his voice, as if embarrassed. He would make his point quickly, and with as little notice as possible. "I would like a transfer. Do you still have the connections?"

"Just like that?" The colonel's eyebrows raised, both inquiringly and somehow, knowingly.

"I would like to be sent to a different regiment."

"Has this to do with the cast on your arm? The lieutenant?"

"No sir," Cawkins responded.

"What happened?" the colonel asked.

"Nothing, sir. Fell off my bike."

"Then why the transfer? You'd be separated from your mate, wouldn't you?"

"I respectfully submit that a change is sometimes good," Cawkins said.

"Fell off your bicycle you say. Right."

"Yes sir," Sergeant Cawkins said unhesitatingly. "Bad luck, sir. A three-inch piece of metal, just on the side of the road. I think it was shrapnel, from the last war. I tried to catch myself with my arm and sliced it open. That's what happened."

Cawkins felt the colonel's eyes boring into him, but he was sticking to his story.

The colonel exhaled a deep breath, looked to be thinking for a second, then turned his attention back to the map. "Right. The report's first rate and unfortunately, we may have need of it. Nothing's changed. We're still expected to advance to the Meuse-Antwerp Line. As for you, I want you to get to the infirmary and have one of our lads look at that, patch you up good and proper. Where is your lieutenant, by the way?"

"I'm not sure. We split up when I came in to report."

Once more, the colonel studied the big man. "I'm sorry. I'd like to help, Jack, but I'm afraid I don't have time just now. Things are moving too fast. Get your arm patched up, rest a bit and get back to the Coldstreamers. Maybe someone there can help you. They need good sergeant majors all around."

"Yes sir." Cawkins stood and saluted. He was more than apprehensive. As the incident receded in distance, or as a dream recedes from conscious memory, so too had the impression of some otherworldly presence triggering the mischief in the cave. What was left was the irrefutable fact that his mate had tried to kill him.

An army doctor re-stitched his arm, replacing the cast with a heavy gauze bandage, plunged a tetanus shot into his rear and pronounced him fit. And Cawkins made haste—he preferred to arrive back at Regiment before the lieutenant. He was able to catch a ride in the back of a two ton lorry heading toward Lille, and from there, he planned to travel the rest of the way on foot to 2ND Battalion Headquarters, now at Ferme d'Aigremont, an old Spanish farm that dated back to the Dutch resistance to the Duke of Alba.

Hinton-Smith also wasted no time. Still in the clothes he had worn for the last three days, and with a new determination, he started back to St. Venant, this time, on a BSA 500 cc. motorcycle. He

sped back along the winding dirt road, until he was once again looking down upon the castle ruins in the distance. He stopped for a
second, taking off his goggles, and coughing from his own dust. He
decided to have another look at the cemetery, and raised his binoculars to find it just southeast of the *motte*. Only one headstone was
visible from his present position and not surprisingly, the grounds
did not appear to be quite as ominous as they did the previous time,
especially looking so small and insignificant from where he stood. He
intended to pick up the gear from the ruins as planned—besides, the
quartermaster could make them pay for them—then he would see
about the cave.

Pulling the goggles back over his eyes, he took in a deep breath of
the pine-scented air, restarted the bike, and headed down the road,
following the same path he and Cawkins had taken a few days earlier
on bicycles. Before long, he was revving up the engine, and then racing it through the trenches to the top of the *motte*.

The gear was untouched, strewn on the ground where Cawkins
had left it. The shelter was still up. Hinton-Smith disassembled it and
rolled the blankets, tent and ground cloth up to manageable size.
Then he repacked everything into the bags they had left. All done, he
placed his hands on his hips and surveyed the area. He wondered
what had really happened. He had almost killed the sergeant at this
place. Let's see where it started.

He looked for the hole in the ground that had precipitated their
misadventure. Just looked like a harmless animal burrow now. His
heart quickened as he thought about going back down. He remembered the shattering of the wooden bridge, and how he had pulled
Cawkins across the abyss. That proves it right there, he thought.
Why would he save him, just to kill him later? He wished he had
been quick enough to use that argument with Cawkins.

He walked over to the other side of the mound, which faced St.
Venant. Focusing his binoculars downward, he could make out the
cemetery, which somehow, strangely, seemed to be only half. Not too
far away was the garish mansion, and beyond that, in the village, he
saw the pointed spires of a small, roughly built stone building, which
he took to be a very old church.

Could it have really happened, he wondered?

It would make more sense to go down and gain entry from the bottom of the hill.

"Hullo!" he said to himself. Even though the *motte* he stood on was of modest height, it was high enough, that the different perspective from above allowed him to see an outline, roughly encompassing the cemetery. He knew enough about archeology to know he would have never noticed this from ground level. Cawkins had described to him how from the top of Masada, he could make out the outlines of over eleven Roman camps surrounding the fortress at the bottom, whereas when he stood at the base of the plateau, he saw nothing except for rocks and dirt. It was now obvious. The perspective made all the difference. In medieval times, the cemetery must have been completely hidden inside the mound. The stones they saw inside were the other half of these. A lot of years of erosion to have done like this.

For whatever reason, somebody went to great pains to hide this place. The only things that came to mind were buried treasure or a desire to protect your loved one's final resting place.

He took another deep breath and walked the motorbike down the steep hill. Approaching the cemetery, he stopped, shoved down the kickstand to leave the bike and began a slow walk around the cemetery, which had a dismal appearance even in the bright sunlight. He felt no fear or rage—he was beginning to remember that now—but as he drew nearer, queasiness began to arise in his belly. Fighting it as best he could, he knelt down just outside of the circle and began to rub his hand over the ground that he estimated made up the outline of the hill before the many years of erosion. Looking at the stones, he could see there were no other markings other than those borrowed from the East. Every other marking, like dates or possibly names, looked as though they had purposely been effaced. He had forgotten about the markings.

He stood and walked closer to the hill. It took an effort of will, but he started searching for the entrance to that other world. Hinton-Smith stooped down and ran his hand along the grassy, weed-infested hillside. There was the hole, with dried blood encrusted in the dirt. It must be from Cawkins—blood he was responsible for shedding. It sent an immense wave of guilt down his spine.

The earth was moist and he ran it through his fingers, while trying to bolster his nerve. All at once, he turned on his torch and forced himself to get down on his belly. Just as he got down, a black viper slithered swiftly out of the hole, right at him. Dodging to his side, he saw the snake stop and coil. Before it could strike, the lieutenant smashed its head with the torch, then flung it away. Staring at the dead serpent for a second, he then got back down and crawled forward until his upper body was through the opening and into the blackness of the cave. Nothing was going to stop him from following this through.

Hinton-Smith's eyes tracked the beam of light as he strained to find anything that would make sense. It was then he spotted a large headstone so close to the inside wall of the mound as to lean against it. There were some Vedic signs on the side facing outward, but there were other characters he could not make out. By now, the dizziness and nausea began to overwhelm him, but still he inched forward. There were four other stones, but the largest dominated his attention. His shirt became soaked with sweat, and he closed his eyes to wipe his forehead. Something was drawing him inexorably further into the darkness, and he knew, in his gut, that if he went along, he was lost. His back wrenched upwards and he threw up. He spit and wiped his mouth.

He had to get out. It was as close to a feeling of panic as he'd ever known. Hinton-Smith began to wriggle backwards, pushing as hard and fast as he could. It was then that he heard a voice, other than his own, inner voice, entering his thoughts. Only one simple phrase rang in his ears: "Seek *de Belfort* in Highgate!" He knew a "Highgate." Cyrus and Lizzie lived there. *What was this? Why Highgate? Who is de Belfort?*

He emerged into the sunlight. Shakily rising, he found his limbs strangely enervated. He was dizzy. Backing up, he left the hillock as fast as he could get his feet to move. Hinton-Smith felt stronger with each step, and quickly distanced himself from the area. This couldn't be real. Maybe it was his nerves. How could a piece of earth cause this reaction? But why did he feel all right now? *Perhaps he was a coward.* He had panicked and attacked Cawkins, and it was that simple. But there *was* that voice. It said "Highgate." There must be a reason. *What was that voice? Could there actually be something in there? Was he losing his mind?*

Regaining his bike, he drove into the village and up and down the cobblestone streets until he spotted the old church. He knew he could never enter that cave again, but churches would have records; they love to make them. They love to keep them. He regained confidence with this thought. He *would* find an answer. As he reached the house of worship, he slammed on the brakes and briskly turned the bike out to stop. Jumping down, he had trouble turning off the ignition with either hand. Both were still shaking.

Hinton-Smith walked past a wooden cross, stuck in the ground of a well-kept lawn, and into the chapel. He briefly knelt at the first row of pews out of respect for other men's beliefs, and then walked up to the priest, a slender balding man, in an all-black habit, who was broken down from his many years. In French, Hinton-Smith asked, "Sir, while passing through the area, I saw the most interesting cemetery on the outskirts of your village, by the hill and mansion, and I wonder if you could tell me about it?"

The priest, who was lighting candles at a shrine for the Virgin, replied, "I would love to help you, but sadly, I cannot. My knowledge is little," he continued with humility. Pausing as if in thought, he then said, "This church dates back to 900 A.D. There are records, and they might include those of your cemetery, but I am not certain. Also, I'm afraid they are in Latin, and they must be very fragile from so many years. If you desire, I will show you to their resting place, but you must promise to be delicate with them."

"Of course I will," the lieutenant responded. "Thank you."

"Yours is only the second request I can remember," the priest said as he led the lieutenant to a bolted, wooden door. "A local scholar, as I recall, was also interested many years ago."

As soon as the priest left, Hinton-Smith began to look for manuscripts in the dark, windowless room that had once been a refectory, when the newly built church had its own small order of monks. The lieutenant painstakingly went over what records he found by candlelight, only stopping briefly for bread and strong coffee, which was proffered by the priest.

After hours of pouring over the old manuscripts, Hinton-Smith found a yellowing medieval scroll wedged inside one of the bindings, that appeared to diagram a layout of a small circular cemetery. Was this it? If so, it proved his earlier speculation correct: there had been eight graves in a circle, with one in the middle, and all had originally been buried inside the narrow, hidden passageway of the *motte*. Yes! He could just make out the partial remains of Eastern markings: the swastikas and the other signs Cawkins named. This had to be the same. There could not be two graveyards with these markings.

The scroll was bordered with colorful demons and engravings of strange, hideous creatures. His first thought was these were for ornamentation, but some intuition told him they might be some kind of admonition. A few diagonal lines covered most of the rest of the parchment, and where a line seemed to lead to a name, the whole text was scratched over. He wished he had Cawkins's expertise in these matters. The truth was, he missed his camaraderie with the old man.

To no avail, he held it up to the candlelight, straining to see any trace of the original ink. The printing under all eight diagrams of the tombs was severely damaged, and the center of the circle had been burned out. The only extant clue in evidence was a rose red cross.

Ecclesiastics love making records, the lieutenant once more reasoned, so there had to be some other record of the cemetery. The cemetery was well hidden so it made sense that any other records would also be hidden. Indeed, all information on the parchment he found was obliterated. Now he began a more detailed inspection. Hinton-Smith looked for loose stones in the floor; he looked behind old etchings; he searched all the desks and bookshelves for secret compartments or drawers. After another hour, the only things left were the four walls of the room, one side blocked by a gargantuan shelf full of dusty manuscripts covering most of the south wall, that he was certain he would not be able to budge. Just my luck. No doubt, if there was anything hidden, it would be behind that one. So now, he carefully went over all the stone walls. Two more hours went quickly as he searched, examining every square foot of masonry under candlelight held inches from the surface, painstakingly passing his fingers over every stone and the connecting plaster between, till his fingers were raw and blistered. But it was useless. There was nothing that implied anything hidden, and all that was left, was the shelf of manuscripts. That figured. He'd have to try to move it back.

Barely squeezing his fingers between the wall and the shelf, he tried to edge it forward. No luck. Standing back, he considered the problem. The shelf itself was heavy enough, but with the extra weight from the manuscripts, it was an impossible task for two men. And they would have to be careful not to tumble it over, and risk destroying all the knowledge in the old texts. There was only one way he could think of to move it away from the wall. Starting from the middle shelf, he took a stack of documents and placed them on the floor. Then he took another armful and placed it next to the first, endeavoring to keep them in order. Each shelf was some twenty feet in length. This was going to take forever. It was dawn when he finally lightened it enough that he could edge the shelf out from the wall. Soon after, he found what he was looking for.

Although the difference was very subtle under the dim light and narrow space, he noticed a rectangular area near the floor where the stones were all the same, but the mortar fixing some few, was a slightly different shade from the rest: it had to be from a later period than the rest of the wall. On his knees, he prodded the mortar carefully, and was able to loosen a stone, then another, which he then pried free with his knife. Behind this was a small hole. Hinton-Smith reached into the hole until his arm was extended up to his shoulder, at last feeling something hidden inside. Carefully drawing it backwards, he soon held in his hand an ornately carved box, which was sealed with the mark of what he reckoned to be a highly ranked church official. He was certain this seal had to belong to someone no less than a bishop. Eagerly carrying the box to the table, he set it down and lit another candle.

Slipping the knife's edge under the seal, Hinton-Smith carefully removed it and opened the box. Inside was a charred piece of parchment, but nothing on it was legible; it had purposely been defaced.

Not to be deterred, he lightly ran his hand over the blackened parchment. It was rough to the touch. He took one of the paper scraps he'd been making notes on and carefully flattened out the parchment, laying the paper flush on top. Then, holding his knife by the blade, he methodically rubbed the smooth part of the handle over the two pieces, and next carefully shaded it in with a pencil. It took him the better part of thirty minutes, but there, on the scrap of paper, appeared the rough outline of what was probably the original scroll. Whoever is in those graves must have broken a lot of vows. They did more than excommunicate them; they tried to erase all knowledge of them.

Cawkins would be proud of me, he thought, inadvertently. Then he remembered that the sergeant probably hated him.

The same outlines of the demons appeared on this etching, and that of the cross, and the names under the tombs had also been effectively destroyed. However, one curious bit of information had come to light: under four of the tombs in the outer circle, fragments of the dates of what he reckoned to be the span of their lives appeared. He could see enough to know that although their birth dates were all different, even if within a few years of each other, the dates of their deaths were all the same. Strangely, they had all lived a very long time—three into their eighties and one over ninety. For them to all die at the same time, one would think they must have died in battle or perhaps from a plague. How odd. They were pretty old to die in battle. Must have been disease. But in the same exact year, even to the month and day?

Hinton-Smith could not stop thinking about it. Could they have been put to death? Perhaps he was missing the simpler explanation, but he could not think of any other reason. Also, appearing in close proximity to two of the other tombs were fragments of an insignia which looked familiar but that he could not identify. This marking also appeared in conjunction with one of the dated tombs. Who were they? He looked over the dates again.

What, he thought? This can't be right. It couldn't be their life spans. He had missed a digit. That was dim, wasn't it? It was one hundred eighty and one hundred ninety, not eighty and ninety. Hinton-Smith stared at the numbers. He had to be sure. He had no idea what this meant or even if it meant anything. Why was so much care taken to hide this? To hide their very names?

There was no other information to be found in the church records. Hinton-Smith made notes of all the dates, carefully folding the etching and putting it in his pocket. Then he replaced the parchment, crudely resealing the box by using his lighter to re-melt the wax bottom of the bishop's seal.

By now he was more determined than ever to prove to Cawkins that something was in that cave, no matter how strange it sounded. He got down on his knees, and much like Sir Nigel Loring of the White Company, raised the box in front of his forehead and took an oath. Perhaps he should don an eye patch as well, he thought with much contempt for himself. Enough! He would unearth the truth and prove it to the sergeant. In the meantime, he would look after Cawkins and protect him as though he were the King himself. He would do whatever it took to regain Cawkins's trust.

Hinton-Smith then replaced the box, using water from his canteen to rewet the mortar and reseal the loose stone.

Carefully pushing the large shelf back flush against the wall, he then began to put the manuscripts back in place—another hour's work.

Finding the priest, he showed him the rose cross from the old scroll. "Do you have any idea what this signifies?" the lieutenant asked.

"Once more, I am at a loss to help," the Father replied. "But there is a man, a scholar. The historian I spoke of earlier. Perhaps he knows." Quickly writing on a piece of paper, the priest said, "This is his address. About six streets west of here. It will not be hard to find. The village is small. He is an old man, older even than I…I have not seen him in some time. And somewhat irascible. I am being kind with this choice of words. He might talk to you, he might not. One can never tell. His name is *Betancourt*."

Wonderful, the lieutenant thought. A choleric academic. "Thank you so much, Father," Hinton-Smith said, and he walked out of the chapel to his bike.

A warm breeze caught his face as he rode down the tree-lined streets. It was a sunny morning. Would the curmudgeon be home? Will he speak to me? Indeed, could he explain anything if he does?

Within minutes, he parked his motorbike in front of a small white wooden house, with boarded-up windows and a weed-infested lawn. Walking up an overgrown dirt path, he softly knocked on the door and waited. *If he is a scholar, he'll want to speak with me. I have information he's never seen.* The lieutenant knocked again, this time louder. He took the etching out of his pocket and unfolded it.

Soon, shuffling sounds emanated from within. The door edged open and a stale, sour air, rife with the scent of tobacco reached Hinton-Smith's nose.

"What is it you want?" a raspy, but mannerly voice asked.

Hinton-Smith held the paper up near the door in front of the man's squinting eyes.

There was a moment of quiet, then of recognition. The door opened wide. "Where did you find this? It is of the cemetery near the *motte*, no?" He reached for the etching and Hinton-Smith released it to his hand. "Come in. Come in," the man said as he turned and walked back inside, studying the parchment as he headed to a table, pulled a chair out and sat down.

"Sit, young man," he said. "Where did you come by this? I've seen another, but not with any dates under the tombs."

"In the chapel," Hinton-Smith replied. The lieutenant could see the man's liver-spotted hands and thin wrists protruding from the sleeves of a dark purple, moth-eaten sweater. His hair was greasy and flaked, but still black, though a two days growth of stubble on his chin was flecked with gray and white. The inside of his house was piled with musty-looking books and sheaves of papers, as unkempt as his appearance.

"I have been through all the manuscripts," the man said. "But I never saw this." He brought it closer to his eyes. "Hah!" he said as he quickly got up, went over to another desk, retrieved a magnifying glass and came briskly back to the lieutenant. "I have often wondered if there was something hidden in the church. An original. Where was it?" He moved a small lamp closer and began to pour over every inch of the etching.

The lieutenant smiled. *Irascible indeed.* "I am Lieutenant Michael Hinton-Smith, sir." He extended his hand to greet the old man, but found it left to dangle unwanted in the air. "I found it behind the shelving on the south wall. I have some questions."

"*Gilles Betancourt*," the man replied, not bothering to look up. "Professor. I have questions myself, but perhaps I can help you in some small way."

Hinton-Smith used his unshaken hand to point to the cross, now charcoal in color. "It was red on the original parchment."

"Ah, yes. This beauty," *Betancourt* said. "The rose red cross, the birthmark of the Merovingians. It later became the emblem of the Templars, an order of warrior-priests that had been formed to protect pilgrims on their way to Jerusalem. Unfortunately, they fell into disfavor with Philip IVth, the then King of France. This other symbol, in whole, it would look like this." He retrieved a pencil from the top drawer and quickly drew in the missing parts of an eight-pointed cross. "This is the Maltese Cross, the sign of the Hospitallers, another group of knights that went to the Holy Land. It was white to stand for purity, and bordered with black. It is interesting..."

Hospitallers, of course. I should have known that from Malta. They were Crusaders, knights. "Why?" Hinton-Smith asked.

"They were rivals," *Betancourt* answered. "Sometimes, enemies."

"Then why would they be buried together?" the lieutenant asked.

"And, young man," *Betancourt* said. "That is also one of my questions...These dates are somewhat, strange, troubling." His intense expression as he peered at the cross, showed Hinton-Smith that it was indeed more than "troubling" to him. Perhaps he had also misplaced that digit.

Professor *Betancourt* lit a pipe and reclined in his chair. "The date of death on these graves is 1397 A.D. That is fine for the Hospitallers...But the Templars, their Order ceased to exist some fifty years earlier. In reality, almost one hundred."

"Could it simply be a case of exulting, or boasting that their Order was the victor?" Hinton-Smith asked. "Outlasting the other?"

"Perhaps," *Betancourt* said, leaning forward over the parchment. "The crosses, both rose and white, seem to be on an equal footing and do not show any sign of ascendance." Excitedly, he grabbed the paper with both hands and brought it close to his eyes. "This makes no sense at all!"

He thrust the copy in front of Hinton-Smith.

"Did you see this?" *Betancourt* asked. "What is this?"

"I know," Hinton-Smith said. "Has to be a mistake."

"These people did not make mistakes," *Betancourt* said.

An uncomfortable silence pervaded the room.

Hinton-Smith left his chair and moved behind the professor to look over his shoulder. "Can you tell me anything about these Orders of knights?" the lieutenant asked.

"Do you have a good attention span, young man?" *Betancourt* asked abruptly.

"Sir?"

"To take notes, of course." He handed Hinton-Smith his pencil, then gestured to the other desk, where he had gotten the magnifying glass. "There. In the second drawer. Fetch paper."

Hinton-Smith retrieved the writing materials and once more sat across from *Betancourt*, his right elbow resting on the wooden table, his hand poised to write.

"Both Orders were formed to protect sojourners to the Holy Land," *Betancourt* said. "And both, later in their respective histories, became warriors. The Order of St. John of Jerusalem, which later became known as the Hospitallers, established a hospital for pilgrims some fifty years before the First Crusade. Italian merchants from Amalfi established the Order in 1048 and they were formally recognized by Pope Paschal II in 1113. I have seen the original Papal Bull in the Bibliotheca, the national library in Valletta. In the Third Crusade, they fought alongside Richard Coeur de Lion in taking Acre from the Turks, and then held it for a hundred years. With the demise of the Crusaders' fortunes, they fled to Rhodes, defending this island for another two hundred years before surrendering to Suleyman the Magnificent in 1522. They then roamed the Mediterranean for eight years seeking refuge, until Charles V of Spain offered Grand Master L'Isle Adam the strategic island of Malta as a bulwark against the Turk, for the price of one peregrine falcon a year, payable every year on All Saint's day."

"A peregrine, you say." That's what got me into this mess, the lieutenant thought.

"Yes. The Order held the island against the Turks, fending off a great siege as recently as 1565, but then, as the threat from Islam diminished, their power began to as well, until Malta was taken and plundered by Napoleon in 1798. Two years later, the French were tossed out, and Captain Alexander Ball, of His Majesty's Royal Navy, assumed responsibility for the government."

"The Hospitallers, knights from the Crusades, were around until the Nineteenth Century?" Hinton-Smith asked incredulously.

"There are those, who say they are still with us today," *Betancourt* answered.

"But why do you say this is troubling?" the lieutenant asked. What had all this to do with the cave? He was completely baffled by now. Facts and more facts that seemingly led nowhere.

"There is nothing troubling about the Hospitallers," *Betancourt* replied. The professor paused to stamp more tobacco into his pipe. He lit it and then puffed until smoke rose from the bowl. "*Pauperes commilitiones Christi templique Salomonici,* that was the original name of the Templars."

"The Order was established in 1119 by a group of eight knights led by Hugue de Payns and Godefried de St. Omer, to give escort to pilgrims on their way to Jerusalem. King Baldwin II gave them part of the royal palace which was Al-Aqsa Mosque to the Turks, and known as Solomon's Temple to the Crusaders. This gave the order its name."

"So, they were good men," the lieutenant stated, but there was a hint of a question in his tone. To this, *Betancourt* raised his eyebrows ever so slightly.

"They originally helped pilgrims, as I have said. They vowed to fight in God's name under their banner of the red cross, against the infidel, but never to strike a Christian; never to swear nor behave discourteously to any Christian man; to allow no woman to wait upon them, nor even to kiss their mother or sister; to attend divine service regularly; to be frugal at meals, and to become devout priests as well as sincere warriors. But later, they acquired great wealth and they made powerful enemies," *Betancourt* replied, now standing up and beginning to pace. "By 1291 the Templars had ceased to be primarily a fighting organization and had become the leading money handlers of Europe, owning vast estates and much treasure. Jealousy arose. In 1307, Philip IV of France, who needed money for his Flemish war and was unable to obtain it elsewhere, began a persecution of the Templars. On October 13th of that year, a Friday mind you, the king arrested all members of the Order in France and had their possessions confiscated."

"Is that why Friday the 13th is...?"

"You listen well my boy, and you catch on. Yes. By 1308 the persecutions were in full process. The knights were put on trial and were tortured to extract confessions of sacrilegious practices. The Pope, Clement V, at first opposed the trials but soon reversed his position, and at the Council of Vienne in 1312, he dissolved the Order by Papal Bull, *Vox in Excelso*. On March 19th, 1314, on the Isla de la Cite in the Seine River, the last grand master, Jacques de Molay, was burned at the stake along with Geoffroi de Charney, the Preceptor of Normandy. So much for the Templars. Though some were allowed to go into the monastery and devote themselves to prayer, they left no descendants. By 1350, their history was at an end."

"And that is who is buried in those graves?" Hinton-Smith asked, his head swimming with questions. Had he encountered the spirit of one of these knights? "Templars and Hospitallers?"

"Possibly," *Betancourt* said.

"But you're saying there were no Templars around to be buried at that time?" Hinton-Smith said.

"That is exactly what I am saying," *Betancourt* replied. "Not for some forty-seven years. Is it strange? I cannot say...honestly, I do not know what to make of it. And the other thing, the dates. These make no sense whatsoever. I have never encountered anything like this." Then he stared at the lieutenant, with an intensity that belied his frail features. "And if I might ask...What is your interest?"

Hinton-Smith felt uncomfortable under the glare that now fell over the scholar's soft features. Something was strange about that look. Something the professor had kept to himself, omitted.

Why hadn't the old man mentioned the signs from the East? Could he trust the man to not think he was crazy?

And what should he say? Hinton-Smith found it was more so that he could not yet bring himself to put words to his horrific experience. "Simple curiosity. I am in the BEF, seconded to the 11th Division, French 4th Army. I was assigned a simple reconnaissance and saw the cemetery. I'm a bit of an amateur medievalist." He inadvertently pursed his lips. "I could not resist exploring it." How easy it was to parley a half-truth into a lie. Too easy. He did not like himself for it. Enough of this. There was much to digest, to sort out.

Hinton-Smith stood up. "Thank you so much for your time, sir. I had better get back to Headquarters or they will count me as AWOL." He managed a slight smile.

"And the etching?" *Betancourt* asked abruptly, jolting up and moving between the lieutenant and the door. "Might I keep it? Or copy down the dates?"

"Certainly, sir."

Moments later, the lieutenant headed for Lille, camping out at the largest library in the city, until he was interrupted.

The next morning, May 10th, the Germans crossed into Belgium.

# CHAPTER 12
# THE HOSPITALLERS
## 1407 A.D.

The dark blue waters of the western Mediterranean crested and fell under cold swirling winds and gray autumnal skies. White-tipped waves raced to the shore, pummeled the sands and crashed upon the rocks, sending cascades of water hurtling skyward.

In a secluded cove, roiling waters buffeted a lateen-rigged felucca close in to shore. Sailors in drenched cloths struggled to gather in the sails and secure them to her masts.

To the south of the inlet was the fortress of Acre, finally wrested from the last Crusaders and now occupied by Egyptian Mamluks. To the north was Tyre and to the east, the Castle Montfort and the fields of Hattin, still a fountain of sorrow for the Crusaders though 200 years past.

Five men dressed in monk's garb, but noticeable for their knightly bearing, stood guard over two skiffs, beached on a small patch of russet sand under limestone bluffs. High above on those same bluffs stood two sentries staring out on the wind-swept waters for unfriendly sails.

Their last days on the Levantine coast were marked.

Further inland, and high above the bluffs, a burly man also in a monk's habiliment walked over the snow-covered grounds to the keep. His thick fingers and thicker forearms were more like those of a warrior than the appendages of a man of the cloth, and if one looked closely, a glint of something metallic appeared, though infrequently, at the end of his sleeves as he swung his arms in his walk. Keeping his head down as if staring at the ground or humble, all of Sir Reginald Brockingham's features except his thick red beard were hidden by the monk's hood. The air was blustery and melancholy. Still, he could hear the crunching sound of his boots as he walked across newly fallen snow. The man pulled his cassock closer to shield himself from the wind sweeping across the plateau.

Dark, cloud-covered skies seemed foreboding, stretching halfway down the promontory. This seemed providential to him, and suited their greater purpose. They would be invisible from the lowlands.

He now approached great poplars and evergreens and walked between other men, more noble in bearing but with a certain righteousness mingled with sadness in their eyes, and much to his surprise he now felt himself lacking in their presence. He raised his hand in acknowledgement of Sirs Dominic, Lucien and Argive, but inadvertently lowered his gaze as he passed them. Taking a quick glance backward before entering the keep, he saw young Peter Dillon and other men placing the last of the kindling and the cross completely upright. Almost relieved, he entered the gate. It would soon be over.

No one outside these men knew of the existence of the keep, high up on a plateau and shielded from errant eyes by a forest of trees.

Now inside, the monk walked in a straight line over the snow-dusted earth. He looked neither left nor right, preferring to keep his eyes on the ground in front of him. The severity of the affair, now so near in proximity, so close to its end, grew ever more real. Other men, also in sackcloth stood nearby and he realized he could not look any of them in the eye. He knew their fate. Why they had put themselves in this position, was beyond his discernment.

Would they really go through with it? Could he ever? And still, there was one more after this. Would it ever end?

Bounding up the steps into the tower, he found himself unintentionally slowing down as if he did not want to keep the assignation, as if his part, left undone, could postpone the whole horrible proceedings of this day to another.

And these thoughts made no sense to him. Why did he want it to end but dread the ending itself?

At the top of the roughly hewn stone steps, he came before a thick wooden door, flanked by Sirs Herve and Richard, also in coarse brown sackcloth. He nodded to them.

The place looks more like a monastery than a fortress, he thought as they pulled open the heavy door. This was for the better. If the Mohammedans found it and thought it was a fortress they would certainly explore or attack.

No words were spoken. The door closed swiftly behind him.

A spiral staircase led to the top of the keep. Brockingham rapidly ascended these last steps, now hurrying as if he wanted to get it over with.

Emerging out into the open, he saw another man, his back toward him, his arms braced against the parapet, his body seemingly slumped forward, and his right hand shuffling a golden neck chain between his fingers. A broadsword leaned against the stone wall.

"It is done my lord," Brockingham said.

Sir Charles Whyntowne stared out at the clouds. He knew the countryside of small rolling hills and fallow lowlands was still green, that the snow only reached the highlands. When the sky cleared he would be able to see Mt. Herman to the east, and to the west, the blue Mediterranean.

The keep had been purposely built in the center of a large tableland making it invisible to those below. The massif itself was on the highest ground for a great distance and its slopes were rent by a series of revetments stretching around its circumference.

Sir Charles Whyntowne turned as he pulled the cassock over his head, revealing a white robe with a large eight pointed cross, white bordered with black, on both front and back. Underneath the robe he was dressed from ankles to neck and wrists in the chain mail of a knight.

"Are the graves dug?" Sir Charles Whyntowne asked. "The stones in place?"

"Yes Sir Charles."

"Then let us finish it," Whyntowne said. "Convey my order."

Brockingham nodded and left.

Sir Charles took the sword and placed it through a loop on his belt. He fastened the golden chain, which bore an image nowhere seen in the European countries, around his neck and a silver helmet over his head. Then he started down the staircase.

It was with no relish he did this thing. As they pursued the second of their quarry, both he and the others had grown weary. It was hard to kill one of their own, hard to know their own must die to be successful.

They had learned much since encountering *L'Anguedoc*. They were not certain of the extent of his powers and to Whyntowne's mind, acted carelessly. This time they had moved precisely and they would continue to do so, keeping in accordance with the law.

As he emerged from the keep there were no longer monks to greet him, but fellow knights, all dressed similarly to him in their white robes, and six of their number wearing similar neckpieces and carrying giant metal stanchions with similar markings from the east.

Two more knights, Sir Baptiste and Sir Thomas, now emerged from the keep escorting a prisoner. This man was also of noble bearing, though arrogant in manner, unbroken. His chest was bare and bore signs of torture. His pants were coarse and soiled homespun cloth and his feet were unshod but in chains, as were his hands. His head was encased in a lead mask, much like a death mask from ancient tribes, with no openings for his eyes nor holes from which to take breath.

As the knights led him to the center of the gathering, a herald came forward and unrolled a document. With a brief look to Sir Charles Whyntowne the man began to read.

A scribe dipped his pen in ink in readiness to record the proceedings.

"You, *Cristobal De la Guzman* of the Order of the Templars are charged and found guilty of practicing the black arts."

"You, *Cristobal De la Guzman* of the Order of the Templars are charged and found guilty of apostasy: of leaving the church, consorting with infidels and giving allegiance to the religion of the Muslims."

"You, *Cristobal De la Guzman* of the Order of the Templars are charged and found guilty of suborning your fellow knights to evil."

"You, *Cristobal De la Guzman* of the Order of the Templars are charged and found guilty of stealing the wealth of your king."

"You, *Cristobal De la Guzman* of the Order of the Templars are charged and found guilty of abetting the death of over ten thousand innocents during the Children's Crusade, and sending many more into slavery among the infidels."

Rolling the parchment back up and neatly tying it with a leather cord, the herald stepped backward. Even in the cool air he was sweating profusely.

Sir Charles Whyntowne came to the foreground.

"In accordance with the law of Our Lord, our land and king you have been found guilty," Sir Charles Whyntowne said. "Our sentence is that thou shall be stripped of all titles and holdings. Your name shall no longer be heard in our kingdom and shall be stricken from all record. It will never again be known or spoken by our human race...You shall this day be burned at the stake."

Whyntowne's tone became less strident. "A priest is in attendance for you to make peace and be forgiven. If this is your desire, nod your head."

The prisoner nodded and a priest came forward, laying hands on *De la Guzman* and saying his benediction while the others watched. Grim looks were on every face, the mood somber, fearful. While the priest said quiet words of prayer, two knights tore the clothing from *De la Guzman* and unfastened his chains while others quickly painted him blue from neck to toe. Lastly, the mask on his head was also painted blue.

*De la Guzman* rubbed his wrists as if to sooth the pain from the irons. His haughtiness seemed gone. As quickly as they were loosed, the chains were refastened and he was escorted outside the walls to a clearing where the tall post with its crossbar, surrounded by a pyre made of twigs and branches at its base and top and larger logs below, towered above the ground. Some thirty knights made up his escort. Various servants and squires stood apart.

Eight lesser freshly dug graves surrounding a large open square were nearby. Headstones lie at the foot of each grave.

*De la Guzman* was led through the kindling to the stake. As they unbound his hands and feet, he groaned, bringing his hands up in front of his chest as if beseeching the gathered knights for the allowance to speak.

His tongue had been severed from his mouth.

Knights roughly forced his hands down and pushed his back up against the cross. With his hands forced behind the pole, they were once more chained together. Next were his ankles.

"Stop!" Sir Charles Whyntowne commanded. "Free his hands. And bring him parchment to write upon."

The scribe hurriedly approached with a clean scroll and pen, handing it to *De la Guzman's* outstretched hands.

*De la Guzman* wrote only two sentences, then held the parchment out to be read. The scribe handed it to Sir Charles Whyntowne, while the knights held him with firm constraint.

"I am innocent," Whyntowne read. "Let me bow down before my Lord one more time before I embark upon this last journey."

Sir Charles Whyntowne looked to his knights. His heart argued for this kind act, while his intellect said no. Why would a man practiced in heresy make this request? Would he pray to his own dark gods? Sir Charles would not do this with out the assent of his fellows.

As he looked from face to face he saw sympathy and knew that each of these men would have a similar request were they in *De la Guzman's* place. They were brave but compassionate men. There was no dissent.

"Let him kneel," Sir Charles Whyntowne said, but he motioned for the knights holding the stanchions to move closer to the edge of the pyre.

*Cristobal De la Guzman* knelt for only a few minutes, his hands folded in front of his black mask for the whole time. Standing, he glanced at the attending knights as if he could see through the mask and placed his hands out once more as if asking for the parchment.

Whyntowne nodded his assent and the parchment was handed back to *De la Guzman*, who quickly wrote one phrase.

Sir Charles read it silently. "You cannot kill me."

"Of this we shall see. Bind him to the stake," Sir Charles ordered. "Now!"

The knights pushed him back against the tall pole and chained his hands around it at his back. Servants approached and held lighted sticks above the kindling till smoke, then small flames began to appear and slowly grow in intensity. Soon the flames grew hot enough to ignite the larger logs below. A howl burst forth from the mask in a fiendish, shrill tone, still strong enough to echo throughout the grounds.

"The name *Cristobal De la Guzman* will be spoken no more," Sir Charles Whyntowne said. "From this day forth it will be lost to human memory."

As the fire began to rise, *De la Guzman's* legs began to smolder and the blue coloring turned black. Muffled screams were heard emanating from the mask. Black smoke rose from the pyre, melding into the mist and low clouds. The flames slowly crept up *De la Guzman's* loins, then his stomach and chest.

The crystal ended stanchions were placed in all nine graves, the honor reserved for eight of the knights in particular. Amulets were thrown into the middle tomb and those same eight knights, in their chain mail and robe of the Knights of St. John entered their own tombs. They were to a man as if in a serene state. Even the repulsive smell of burning human flesh no longer mattered to them. Some took a last look at the cloud-dusted sky, others waved or nodded to their comrades or took in the last deep breaths of their lives. Finally they all descended into their own holes in the ground.

Once more Sir Charles Whyntowne, pale and sorrowful, approached each grave and passed a vial to each man.

"Peter. We have changed our mind."

"Sir?"

"Have the names of these men, these eight, chiseled into their stones. They deserve to be remembered."

Brockingham frowned but Castillo nodded in approval. Dillon smiled.

By then, *De la Guzman's* cries had stilled. There was no motion but muscle and bone jerking as though prodded by tip of sword. The remains sizzled as air and grease were expelled and the fire smoldered: *De la Guzman's* flesh burned away, his bone and sinew completely black. The chains that once held his hands had fallen to the ground and glowed a dull red. What passed for a human body was lifted from the pyre and tossed into the square hole in the center. The stone slab placed over it.

Similar slabs were now placed on top of the tombs of the eight knights who would journey throughout time with *De la Guzman,* watching over him, constraining him. Tearful servants and retainers finished by shoveling dirt into the seams to make them fast.

"After the work is done," Whyntowne said, "soil will be piled over the stones and smoothed out. Seeds will be flung upon all the grounds. By the spring there will be no evidence of the gravesite."

"Once more we have said farewell to friends. And soon it will be our turn." Bowing down on one knee, Sir Charles once again offered a prayer.

Standing, he summoned Peter Dillon. "Peter, I think it is time you trained to be a knight." Putting his arm on the young man's shoulder, he whispered, "I myself will instruct you in the arcane arts."

CHAPTER 13

# A LIMITED ADVANCE

Hinton-Smith reached Ferme d'Aigremont late on the 10th of May, saw that the Coldstreamers had already decamped and headed north, catching up to the rear formations as they moved forward up the road some miles northeast of the castle. As he motored up the long double line of soldiers looking for the Coldstream Guards, he somehow heard his name called out over all the hubbub.

Stopping his bike on the side of the road, he looked up and down the line.

"Lieutenant! Sir!" Billy Graves yelled. "Over here! Lieutenant Hinton-Smith!"

The lieutenant turned in his seat, saw Graves and Parker waving. Graves was even jumping up and down like he was on a trampoline.

Well at least he was popular with his men, he thought as he walked his bike up to them.

"We didn't think you'd make it back in time, sir," Parker said.

"Good to see you, sir," Graves said smiling broadly. "We wanted to wait, but the sergeant major said we had to move out."

"Thanks, lads. Where is the good sergeant major?"

"Somewhere down the line," Parker said, pointing up the road. "You know. He said NCO type stuff."

"I'm warning you," Graves added. "He's in a nasty mood."

"Ain't we all."

Hinton-Smith revved the engine. "Keep your chins up, lads," he said as he turned and took off down the road.

Driving slowly now, he continued till he came to a crossroads where there was a large tent functioning as a command post.

Cawkins exited the tent just as the lieutenant pulled up.

"We have to speak," Hinton-Smith said excitedly.

Cawkins, a grim expression on his face, tried to answer in an even tone, but it was difficult and the words came out harshly.

"This ain't the time or place, mate."

"But, I found something..."

"Do you understand what's happening here?" the sergeant asked. "I have to get back to the platoon. You might want to join us." Then he abruptly turned away and jogged to rejoin the troops.

Hinton-Smith was the last person he wanted to see and he knew he was letting the matter interfere with his work. Couldn't have that. He was a professional from a long line of professionals. He had to act like one. Cawkins had put it out of his mind while the lieutenant was away but now he realized he had to face it one way or another. While he made his way back he decided he would treat the lieutenant the way he treated most officers—formally and distant, but with respect if due. The only difference was, in this case, he would be extremely careful.

Hinton-Smith watched him leave, then kick-started the bike and peeled off in the same direction, speeding by the sergeant on his way back to the motor pool.

*   *   *

The advance was fast. The misgivings Hinton-Smith and Cawkins felt a few weeks earlier, soon gave way to a mild euphoria as the Coldstreamers moved into Belgium. It was no more difficult than the Saar. There was no enemy to be seen, no screeching Stukas diving out of the hot sun: no Blitzkrieg. The only screeching at all was the music from the Regimental Band with their fife and drum and bagpipes and the motorized infantry sending up clouds of dust into their faces as they raced past. Instead, as they marched unopposed onto the flat plain of Flanders, Belgians of all sorts greeted them with cheers, flowers, cheese and wine.

The Coldstreamers reached the village of Leefdael, a few miles west of the Dyle around the thirteenth of May and immediately began to organize the defensive lines, clear fields of fire and dig foxholes.

Scattered bombing and artillery hit them the following day and claimed the first casualties, and soon the first stragglers of the retreating Belgian Army wandered in with tales of woe: rumors of poison gas nearly fomented a panic.

The BEF was soon in for it, but true to form, the Tommies held, and rumors reached Hinton-Smith's platoon that they were pushing the Germans back on most fronts for a great Allied victory. There were curious but minor hints of pressure on their right flank and to the south, and then occasional shelling from the latter sector, but the British retained the confidence they felt ever since the first move forward.

By the morning of the seventeenth, individual foxholes were joined together to form trench-works and artillery began to hit them with increasing intensity. Parker and Graves wanted to know the reason why.

"I'm going to find the lieutenant," Parker said. He took a quick sip of lukewarm tea. "I'm tired of being a clay pigeon."

Just then ten shells hit in quick succession, rocking the forward trenches; black dirt showered down on them as they dropped to the deck. On his belly, cup still in hand, Parker watched as particles of dirt sank to the bottom of the cup. With a resigned look, he dumped it out on the wooden planks covering the floor.

"I woulda still drank it, Mr. Pigeon."

"Right. See you," Parker said. From the air, the miles of trenchworks looked like a giant crenellated fortress wall, with jagged edges jutting forward and back rather than up and down. Holding his helmet firmly to his head, Parker sprinted down straight-aways and around many sharp corners, before coming upon the sergeant major.

"If we've had a great victory," Parker asked, "why ain't we moving forward?"

Looking through the periscope that extended over the trench wall, Cawkins said, "Damned if I know. There's nothing moving in front of us. It looks wide open. Maybe the lieutenant knows. He's further down." This bothered the sergeant as well.

"Let me know what he says."

Both of them ducked against the trench wall as they heard the whistle of more incoming shells. This grouping exploded to the rear but very close. With the last burst, Parker started out again, running in a crouch as he searched for Hinton-Smith. It took another five minutes, and fraught with more near misses.

As he ran up, he heard the lieutenant exclaim to a messenger: "You're balmy!"

"These are your orders sir," the messenger said.

"Can't be," Hinton-Smith said as he reread the command.

The messenger saluted. "Best of luck, sir," he said and then rode off on a bicycle down the middle of the trench seeking the next platoon. It was the sixteenth of May.

They were withdrawing.

Not one man among them could understand it. Now they fell back along roads made almost impassable, not from bombings (the Germans were saving the roads for their own use), but from thousands of tired, terrified, helpless refugees, carrying all they had on their backs, from fur coats to food to chairs to children, mixed with those few lucky enough to have bicycles or horse-drawn carts, piled to overflowing.

Hinton-Smith had never seen anything like it. All thoughts of the cave were gone. All conversation with Cawkins was purely military, dictated by the crisis of the moment, and there were certainly enough of those to go around.

The Germans strafed these gloomy columns, leaving wrecked carts, dead horses and bloated human bodies along the road to further hinder the retreat.

By late afternoon of the same day, it seemed as though the whole world had joined the flight, if only to make it more chaotic. One by one the retreating army crossed over bridges that Cawkins had earlier listed to be destroyed, and one by one they were blown up. The heat was sweltering. Sappers stripped to their bare-chests, sweating under the bridges they were preparing to demolish: some were almost pieces of art, hundreds of years old. The demolition of seven bridges was delayed for almost a day on account of the unending flow of refugees. Finally soldiers were ordered to chase people off the bridges and into the fields so the retreat would not be jeopardized.

The general's epiphany had come true with a vengeance. Soon, every day's order started with the word, "Withdraw."

Stukas were not so benevolent on the retreat. British soldiers spent more time diving into the fields to avoid strafing than they did fighting.

By the time one week passed, neither Hinton-Smith, Cawkins nor anyone else was really sure just how it happened, but they were being pushed back across the Scheldt.

Soon, the platoon completely lost contact with the rest of the Guards, and became an amalgam of any number of other units, and on the twenty third, they found themselves back at their original perimeter on the Franco-Belgian border, close to Lille. This boosted everyone's spirits, for at last they had good, strong, well-prepared defensive fortifications, even if they had been pushed back sixty miles in a matter of days. The question, "What went wrong?" resonated through the ranks and not a few of the soldiers blamed the French.

*　　*　　*

Not a few of the French took that same view of the English.

When Colonel *Maurice LeFevre*, a commander of a battalion in the French 1ST Army heard the BEF received the order to fall back to the coast he was enraged.

*LeFevre*, who was by no means an Anglophile, had indeed despised his allies from long contact and conflict with them during the last war and in the different colonies. He had no use for them. "They have no blood!" he would rail, and what most stuck in his craw was how few men they'd given to the fight. It was almost as if they were giving up before they started.

Colonel *LeFevre* got up from his map table and threw everything to the ground. Then for good measure he kicked over his aide's chair, picked up his own and threw it from under the awning.

He thundered at the attaché, "I will not retreat an inch!" with even more emphasis, if that's possible, than when he said it the first time in the Great War. "They are leaving us to fight *Le Boche* by ourselves. I knew it would come to this from the first! Well, so be it. They were little use to us in 1914, and we do not need them now." Holding up his fingers as if to portray a very small insect he said, "They are only a little gnat to *Le Boche* in any event. It is the French Army that shall prevail, or die in glory trying."

He was going through the same problems as his English counterparts: terrible communications; pressure from places where it could not possibly be; lack of ammunition, both small arms and artillery; lack of water and foodstuffs; antiquated guns and gear; horse-drawn transport; no air support; but all of his problems were to a much greater degree than those of his allies. He had a whole battalion under his command, but many of them would not fight. There was no morale, no discipline. Some were defeatist. Others wondered why they were asked to give their lives for a corrupt government and pusillanimous Ally. There were also brave men, willing to fight, but even these felt they had been let down.

Retreating was much easier than advancing, especially against tanks.

*LeFevre* was a tough and robust 44 year-old with energy that would be envied by any younger man. The Algerian desert and the austere life he was used to had kept him wiry and hard. His only luxury was a dark, pencil thin mustache that he meticulously rolled with wax every morning of his life, whether in the French outposts or the desert itself. And he was determined to fight.

"Get my driver!"

His aide saluted and ran out of the tent, soon returning with a convertible Peugeot. *LeFevre* jumped into the back seat while the aide rushed back to the tent and grabbed a Garand. The colonel never carried more than a revolver.

"To the Front," *Lefevre* ordered as the aide got in the car.

The driver peeled out of the command post and headed east.

Two miles from their position they crested a ridge that looked down upon an expansive low-lying plain.

"Here," the colonel said, tapping the driver's shoulder.

Slamming on the brakes, the driver brought the car to a jolting stop.

*LeFevre* stood up on the hood and looked through his binoculars. Dust was rising from the distance. It was just as he had feared: more

mechanized armor. But his first thought was not the tanks or the difficulty they presented, it was his Allies.

"And only nine divisions! They have obviously held back. And
leave the poor *poilus* to bear the brunt of the Germans again." He
jumped down into his seat and smashed his ancient riding crop
(some said it had one time belonged to Marshall Ney), against the car
door, causing the attaché to wince. "If they were serious, why only
half a million? The flower of French manhood was virtually wiped
out last time, yet we have fielded five millions."

The shrill sound of cannon shells began to pass overhead,
exploding just to their rear. Mounds of dirt flew in the air to the
front of the crest as the tanks began to find their range. They had
been spotted.

"Orders, *Mon Colonel?*" the aide asked nervously.

"Back to Headquarters."

Spinning the Peugeot around, the driver plunged his foot on the
gas, quickly shifting gears as they flew down hill.

*LeFevre* took a deep breath and looked at his subordinate. In a
calmer voice, he said, "We will fight. There will be another miracle.
Like the Marne. It will be gallant. For *La Gloire*."

# CHAPTER 14

# REAR GUARD

L ieutenant Hinton-Smith's eyes closed for a second, and his head briefly fell to the side. He jerked them back open and sat up. He was covered with oil and grime, he had not yet eaten today—they were on half-rations now—he had not slept in two days, and he had not washed in four. He let his eyes close again, and started to dream about taking a ride in a Spitfire with an open cockpit, and diving to strafe a German column, when he was startled awake by the arrival of a motorcycle: a runner from Headquarters.

The messenger screeched to a halt and was immediately surrounded by three soldiers, who leveled their rifles at his head. He pushed his goggles up so they rested on the front of his headgear and revealed circles of lily white skin where the goggles had been, in contrast to the mud and fine sand that covered the rest of his face. He could barely speak, so much of the same mud and fine sand had gotten into his mouth on the trip over from west of Arras, courtesy of two minor spills, both the result of marauding Stukas. Coughing to clear his throat, he said in a gravelly voice, "Give us some water, mates."

"Let's have your papers then, mate," demanded Corporal Parker, emphasizing the "mate," and keeping his rifle leveled at the man's head. He held out his hand for the identification.

"Bollocks!" the cyclist said then coughed again. "Give us a drink. Do I look like a bloody Hun?"

The corporal was insistent. "There have been reports of Fifth Columnists," he said forcefully. "Let's have them. Now."

With a look of profound irritation, the cyclist pulled out his papers and handed them over. While Parker checked them, Graves brought the cyclist a canteen.

Hinton-Smith took a sip of lukewarm coffee. It took a few seconds for him to realize where he was. Rolling the strong brew in his mouth, he saw the messenger take a drink and look with disdain at the corporal, the corporal returning the favor.

Then the lieutenant looked at the surrounding area, feeling he had slept so long that he needed to reacquaint himself to make certain everything was in order. There were three privates sleeping in various poses; two were spread out on the ground, one was sitting, leaning against a building. All were sleeping so soundly, even the roar of the artillery firing at the enemy from a mile west of them, or the shells exploding sporadically near their position, could not wake them. He saw the barricade his men had erected, made up of two burnt out vehicles rammed together, loaded and braced with furniture and railroad ties, and even cardboard boxes and a circa 1850's plow. Further out, past the barricade, he could just make out an irregular line of helmets sticking out of holes in the ground. He noticed that Parker and Graves, standing by the cyclist looked tired, but by no means beaten. Indeed, shirtless Billy Graves, a tall, gangly fair-skinned sort with a very noticeable farmer's tan and so many freckles he looked like he just stepped off a plowed field after completing his chores, stood there smiling at the cyclist as though he had just told him the funniest story ever.

"I'm lost. Is there an officer here?"

Hinton-Smith walked up as Graves pointed him out to the cyclist.

"We got another lost sheep, eh Billy?"

"All these trained soldiers getting lost," Graves replied. Then he laughed, scratching his head as though it helped him to think. "Those crazy Germans must sure love a fight."

The cyclist brushed his mouth with his arm sleeve, and tilted his head back to take another drink.

Hinton-Smith looked at him inquiringly as he politely waited for him to finish guzzling from the canteen.

"Sorry, Sir. Corporal John Stevens from 1ST Corps," the man said as he stood to a rather sloppy attention, saluted, and unshouldered a beaten leather dispatch bag.

"Is this from Arras?"

"We no longer hold Arras, sir. I'm coming from the Corps' Command, further back."

"I see."

"I got lost. I had to leave the road a few times...bloody Stukas. I need to find the forward command post for the 44TH Division. Where are we? I don't even know how to get back."

The lieutenant studied the messenger's weathered, wind-burned look, then motioned him at ease with a wave of his empty hand, saying, "You're not the only one. It was a pretty nice ride for you, eh?"

Stevens nodded.

"I can't even tell you if you're close. We're part of the 2ND Battalion, Coldstream Guards. The 44TH isn't even in the sector. As far as I can tell, we're one of the most forward units...None of my runners has made it back."

Hinton-Smith scratched at his new light brown beard.

"Quite honestly, I don't have the foggiest idea where our command post is."

"Well, you're an officer, sir," the messenger said to the lieutenant. "I guess I better give this to you."

Upon opening the bag, the messenger withdrew an official looking sealed envelope and handed it to the lieutenant, who, having one hand occupied with the coffee, ripped open a corner with his teeth, spitting out the residue. He put the envelope up to his mouth and blew it open, shook out a piece of paper, unfolded it and intently began reading. He looked it over for a full two minutes, then looked back at the Stevens, who had closed his eyes and was obviously breathing in the fumes of the coffee.

"Corporal Parker, get the man a mug, won't you," Hinton-Smith said. "Then find the sergeant major."

The corporal walked to a campfire over which some of the soldiers had rigged up some wire between two of the longer tent pegs to hold a teapot. They had somehow lost all their tea in the retreat, so had to settle for coffee instead.

"You're welcome to stay with us. Only sixteen of these are my men from the Guards," Hinton-Smith said. "Everyone else is a straggler from other units. They just keep wandering in. We were separated from the rest of our battalion some time ago." He pointed to the charred remains of a building that was serving as a makeshift field hospital. "You look hungry. You might find something to eat next to that burned out shed."

A huge khaki tarp had been thrown over the still standing corners and two adjacent walls of the building, to offer some shade to the wounded. The noise from thousands of flies was palpable as they swarmed over some amputated body parts that were discarded outside one of the windows, for want of a better place.

Hell of a location for the mess, Hinton-Smith thought as he watched Stevens walk over.

The flies were also attracted to the body of a dead horse that looked as though it was leaning against the building when it died, caught and disemboweled by shrapnel from an exploding artillery shell. Its grotesque pose was made even stranger by the cart still harnessed behind it, intact, although scavenged of everything valuable. Hinton-Smith offhandedly wondered how that bloody animal could stay upright, and like a mischievous child, toyed with the idea of pushing it over.

As the lieutenant stared at the carcass, Parker, a blond lanky boy from Yorkshire, walked back to the barricade. Seeing his officer looking at the long dead beast, he took his gas mask off his belt and pointing at the bloated animal, made a face and gestured as though he was going to put on the mask to protect himself from the stench. A crack of a smile formed on Hinton-Smith's lips. He gave Parker one of Winston's "V" for victory signs.

Parker delivered the coffee and went off to find Cawkins, who was on the other side of the horse cart hidden from view, helping one of the stragglers, a typist, clean and reassemble a Bren gun.

"The lieutenant needs you."

"In a sec," Cawkins said, then returned his attention to his raw trainee.

"What's next?" he asked the private. If this wasn't one hell of a snafu.

"Slide piston and breach block back in."

"Ok. Next?"

"Pull cocking handle to lock in place. Slide barrel in, secure body locking pin. Done," the boy said with more relief than pride.

"That's it, son. Good job. You're our new Bren gun operator."

The typist whined, "I have to carry this thing, by myself?"

"Quit complaining. It's a hell of a lot lighter than the old Lewis. And don't forget the ammo," Cawkins said.

Now he saw the lieutenant walking toward him. Cawkins was impressed with the lieutenant's newly found maturity in the last fortnight. He was witnessing the boy become a soldier, a veteran and a leader. In normal times he would have been proud. Now he did not know. Time alone would not heal the rift between them, it merely kept it the same—Cawkins was always aware of it.

"Sergeant," Hinton-Smith said handing him the papers. "They've ordered the 44TH to fight a rear guard action. They're supposed to be somewhere northeast of Hazebrouck."

"Well ain't they the queen of the fair. We've been fighting a rear guard action," Cawkins returned with a sarcastic tone.

"They're ordered to hold, but it looks like everybody else is pulling back to the Channel."

Cawkins's grim look was magnified as he read the orders. In disbelief, he exclaimed, "We're pulling out? Again? All the way to the beach? It's finally come to that?" *The scouting mission had been important after all.* "What are we doing with orders for the 44TH?"

"Another muddle...The whole BEF's pulling out. Everybody. The Germans have outflanked us. They're even bloody well behind us."

"And the Guards?" In all his pessimism, from the time with the French to the time of the advance, Cawkins never could have conceived of this—a complete rout. Not to the BEF.

"We don't have orders but I'm for staying."

"Well," Cawkins said, "I can tell you one thing for certain, if everybody packs up and leaves, it'll be a disaster. You're the only officer. It's your decision."

"You want to discuss it?"

"I'm in."

"Good show," Hinton-Smith said. "We'll hold them till dooms-day if need be."

"Yes sir."

"Right. So be it," Hinton-Smith said. Though he was putting a good face on it, to him, a hero did not retreat, and the whole British Army, of which he was a part, and which had been his life, was running from the enemy.

"The orders say to leave anything we can't carry," Cawkins said, holding the papers up. "All the ammunition, artillery, lorries, transport, even tanks."

"We'll need extra ammo and food, some medical supplies. Spread the word and let's start putting things together."

"You know there's no guarantee we'll get back," the sergeant said. In fact, there was no guarantee any of the BEF would escape, and that would mean a world full of Nazis.

For the last few days, Hinton-Smith could not separate the retreat from a notion of cowardice, especially the personal cowardice he was now certain he had experienced in the cave.

He had debts to pay, and so chose sacrifice. They would stay behind and fight so that the bulk of the BEF had a chance to escape. A brighter, clearer light shone in his eyes. Here, perhaps, was a chance for redemption. If they got lucky and made it back, so much the better, but if not, what worthier cause. He saw the sergeant's long face and slapped him on the back.

"Don't take it so hard, mate. It's about time for a good fight. Maybe I'll get my last stand. Like your Custer fellow."

Cawkins looked puzzled. This was more like the banter they used to have. More like the cocky Hinton-Smith he knew. He hadn't been this way in a long time. In the last few weeks, the boy had performed his duties with professionalism, but he was withdrawn, there was something missing. For the first time, he seemed, for want of a better term, normal. And it was welcome, regardless.

"Let's don't make that kind of stand. Custer was wiped out."

A smile crossed the lieutenant's face. "All right. Like Thermopy-lae," Hinton-Smith said his eyes twinkling with glee.

Cawkins groaned, then he could not help but laugh.

Hinton-Smith looked thoughtfully at the sergeant major. "They'll probably try to evacuate us from the channel ports. What's your guess?"

"Probably Dunkirk, Calais, Ostend. God damn it, eh?" Cawkins said. It seemed odd that he brought this up. "They don't have enough ships in the whole navy. I don't see many of us getting out."

"They're no guarantees in this life, right mate?"

"Now you know what war is, sir." Cawkins said. He shrugged his shoulders and walked away. He instructed a private to make a circuit of their defensive line and brief the soldiers, who were stationed over a two hundred-yard area, with two men dug in approximately every ten yards. Another private was sent to the makeshift hospital to tell the doctor to load up everybody, all the "useless mouths" who could be moved on one of the lorries. They would drain the rest of oil and water and leave them to run till they exploded. No gifts to the Germans.

Anyone too weak or wounded to be moved would have to be left to the mercy of *Le Boche*. The three men who had been sleeping were awakened and sent over to help the doctor and his assistants load the truck.

As the walking wounded began to move out, the lieutenant looked at the orders again and began pouring over his maps, hastily picked up from a small tourist shop in Tournai on the advance into Belgium.

*     *     *

A day later, on the twenty-fifth, Hinton-Smith watched as two lines of his weary Tommies jogged across the bridge at La Bassee—the last remaining bridge over the *Canal d'Aire a la Bassee*. Cawkins slipped off his pack and started gingerly pulling out sticks of dynamite as Hinton-Smith scanned the approaches through his binoculars. The Germans had to be quite close.

"Here," Cawkins said as he handed out six sticks of dynamite to Parker. He handed a detonator and spool of wire to Graves. "Run this to the other side, Graves, and tell Stevens and the rest to dig in. Site the Bren in on us."

"If you see any sign of Germans," Hinton-Smith said, "even if we're still out here, blow it. That's an order. Go!"

Graves sprinted down the length of the bridge unrolling the wire as he ran, with Parker anchoring the loose end. Cawkins handed six more sticks to Hinton-Smith, plus a roll of tape.

"Cut three twenty-foot pieces. It's the last of it." He tossed a roll of the tape to Parker. "You know the routine," he said. Both men quickly taped together three sticks of the dynamite then twined their fuses. Hinton-Smith gave them each a long piece of wire, which they hurriedly spliced to the fuses.

"Everybody ready?" Cawkins asked. Hinton-Smith and Parker nodded. "Then let's do the job. Lieutenant, when you've set the charge, run the wire back to me here."

Hinton-Smith leaned out over the rail. He looked lengthwise up and down the bridge for the best spot to place the charges. They had stopped over one of the main concrete girders. "Right here's as good a spot as any," he yelled back. The girders are pretty thick. You think three sticks will suffice?"

"It's what we've got."

"I'll take this one, then. Jack, you're going opposite, right?"

"Right."

"Parker, you take the next one down. Hurry. Splice it in to the main wire when you're done."

"Yes sir," Parker shouted as he ran down the track.

Hinton-Smith swung over the rail and climbed down. Cawkins ran to the other side and did the same. They both lodged the sticks in the "V" joint of the girder, one group at either end. Taping the dynamite to the joint, they ran a wire connecting the two groups and clambered back to the top. Hinton-Smith scanned the south entrance and beyond while Cawkins finished splicing the fuses to the wire.

They started to jog to the north side after collecting Parker, when they heard the unmistakable sound of treads. Hinton-Smith looked back. He could identify three light Krupp tanks—the PzKpfw 1s. He turned and yelled, "Blow her!"

But Cawkins bellowed even louder as he ran, "No! Don't touch that plunger! Lieutenant," he said, "We can catch the bastards on the bridge!"

"We'll never make it," Parker cried out. He was falling behind.

The first tank turned the corner before the bridge and started raking it with machine gun fire.

"Move it! Move it! Move it!" Hinton-Smith yelled. He slowed down, took hold of the corporal's sleeve and pulled him along.

"C'mon. Only fifty yards to go."

The first Panzer rumbled onto the bridge. Graves sat ready by the plunger, squeezing the handle. He was sweating profusely. "Please hurry," he mumbled. He had visions of bringing down the bridge on his mates. He could not do it. "Hurry lieutenant. Please."

Cawkins looked back. "One down. C'mon you sons o' bitches, get up here." He was breathing hard, his lungs heaving. Bullets were blistering the ground and rails all around them. Twenty yards left. By now two of the Panzers had alighted and all were firing at them. Luckily, they wanted the bridge intact, and so refrained from using their 37mm cannons. The second tank in line had to stop for fear of hitting the first.

Cawkins stopped running. He bent over and grabbed his pants near his knees. "Tell them to blow it, Mikey. I can't run no more."

"You're on your own, Parker," Hinton-Smith said. "Sprint!" then he grabbed Cawkins under the arm and started him forward, helping him run. "Blow it!" the lieutenant screamed out.

The third tank now made its way onto the causeway, firing as she came.

Graves pushed the plunger down as the fugitives took one last stride and jumped over the rail, falling a good ten feet onto the concrete. As they tumbled down the slope to the water, three great explosions convulsed the bridge. Graves jumped up and shouted "Bastards," as the Panzer crews tried to get out. Most were not fast enough. A few made it out and jumped off the bridge into the water far below, but most were trapped inside their machines as the concrete and steel structure moved up and down like a wreathing snake for some twenty-five seconds, then broke apart, falling with the Panzers into the canal like fragile pieces of china, exploding and shattering on impact.

As the three British soldiers scrambled back up the embankment, gray clad German foot soldiers reached the bridge: they had been outrun by the tanks. A patrol started down the cement bank and started firing.

"Take them out," Hinton-Smith shouted at Graves and Parker, two of best shots in the Regiment.

"Rifles only," Cawkins yelled. "Don't let's waste ammo."

Hinton-Smith made it topside first and pulled the sergeant up in time to hear six quick shots. Looking up he saw five German soldiers crumple, the last one scampering back up to safety.

"I got my three," Graves said.

"Bollocks," Parker said. "I bet I nicked that last one."

"Go check it out."

"No thank you."

The rest of the Germans offered up a few pot shots, but no one else tried to advance down the canal again.

"Scout party?" Hinton-Smith asked.

"Seems so," Cawkins said.

"They could be back tonight."

"We should move out before that. Say three hours rest. It'll be dark by then."

"Three hours," the lieutenant said. "I like it. By the way, mate, carrying you is like being under a grizzly."

Cawkins chuckled but there was no mirth in evidence.

*   *   *

That night, the water in the canal seemed motionless. There was no wind to cool the humid night or to blow away the sweet, fetid smell of the artificial riverbed, mixed with the oil and smoke from the three broken panzer hulks smoldering at the bottom.

By virtue of digging in on the north bank of the canal, Hinton-Smith's motley group of exhausted soldiers now held the southern-most point of the rear guard. No more Panzers appeared so for once the platoon had managed to put some distance between themselves and the mass of Germans. The lieutenant let three quarters of the men get some sleep. The remainder stood sentry in a staggered, cres-cent-shaped pattern on the edge of the canal, over a four hundred yard flank, with ten men as a reserve in case the Germans tried to test any part of the line. Though he was far enough away so that he could not hear the noise, Hinton-Smith could still see the bright, lightning-like flashes of enemy artillery punctuating the dark summer sky to the south. As one of the bright flashes crossed the sky, he saw Cawkins's large silhouette, evidently watching the same fireworks through his binoculars.

What better time to talk to him, Hinton-Smith thought. It was the first time in days he had the luxury to think and not simply react, and thinking led him to remember.

Immediately, he experienced an old, almost forgotten, but gut wrenching feeling of guilt. Every muscle in his body tightened up. He could feel the veins in his neck starting to stand out. Perhaps he was not yet ready. It had seemed so much easier, right after he had found the old parchment in the church. Maybe there would never be a good time. At least until he had figured it out for himself, or more importantly, felt like he had atoned for his sin. The guilt of what he'd done: trying to kill his best friend, weighed heavily on his shoulders. How could he have raised a hand against his mate? How could he not have controlled himself? The old questions came forward in a torrent. In truth, he almost felt too dishonored to even talk about the incident until once more deserving, and if that did not happen, he would be forever disgraced in his own eyes. Still, he knew what he had to do, and summoned that old force of will that had seen him through lesser trials and steeled himself for it. He walked up behind the sergeant, firmly putting his hand on Cawkins's shoulder.

"Jack," he said quietly. "We gotta talk. We gotta talk about the cave."

Cawkins pulled his arm away. "No. Not now. We don't have time."

"We're not going anywhere. We're stuck here at least an hour more. We need to talk about it now," the lieutenant said matter-of-factly, as he pressed down Cawkins's shoulder, forcing the surprised man to sit.

Hinton-Smith made himself look the sergeant directly in the eyes, something he had not been able to do since the incident. "Listen. I went back to get our gear right before the Jerries attacked. Then I went to the bottom of the *motte*. I found the hole we escaped from, and I tried to go back in, and got so sick, I threw up. Then, the strangest thing happened. A voice came into my head." Hinton-Smith inadvertently shook the sergeant.

"Do you understand what that means?" he asked. "There *was* something in there with us!"

Cawkins shook his head. He took the lieutenant's hand from his shoulder and stood up. "I'm not interested."

But now that Hinton-Smith had found the temerity to start, he was determined to finish. "I spotted an old church in St. Venant. It occurred to me that they might have records from the cemetery. I wanted to find out just who the hell was buried there."

Cawkins held up his hand to stop the story. He let out a sigh. "So, you're telling me there was some kind of hobgoblin in there, eh? Sorry. I'm not buying it. In fact, I'll tell you the truth, so you can stop thinking about it and concentrate on the matter at hand. When this campaign ends, I'm getting a transfer."

Hinton-Smith was stunned at these words.

"It doesn't matter to me what you found in there. Now, I want you to understand, I think you've done well in this, especially in all the holding actions, but I just don't know...maybe you cracked. And you could crack again in the future. Maybe you need to get help. As for me, I want to be far away from you, Mike." He took out his knife, slipped the blade under the filthy cast and slit through it. He gingerly straightened his arm and stretched his fingers, and looked at the scar, then tossed the bandage into the canal. "I'm happy to be through with this bullshit."

"But, I found information...you could at least listen."

"I'm sorry, lieutenant, but I have a few minutes, and I want to spend them figuring out our next move. To help us get the hell out of here, sir."

With that, Cawkins walked away.

Hinton-Smith looked at an oil slick oozing from the tanks over a stretch of muddy ground. "Right, be a bastard if you want. I deserve it," he said under his breath. "But I'll win your respect back, if nothing else." He knew he could not put the affair behind him until his oath was fulfilled.

*        *        *

*Betancourt* sat alone at the dust-covered desk in his musty study. It had been almost two weeks since the English lieutenant visited him, all but reawakening the terror of that night; a terror he had tried so desperately and so unsuccessfully to eradicate from his memory. There was a war on. Should he not be more concerned about a war? Since the visit, he had barely moved or slept. Bread, tobacco and strong coffee had been his sole nourishment, and the coffee was foresworn after the first few days for concern that he would never be able to sleep again. He considered drinking himself into oblivion, but realized the fear and guilt would only be exacerbated.

He was exhausted, only drifting in and out of sleep for half-hours at a time, but ultimately startling himself awake as if out of a nightmare.

The Englishman had seen something, of this he was sure. *Betancourt* could see it in his eyes, his manner. The professor was certain the lieutenant had been frightened by something as well, something he had not wanted to disclose.

Lying on the table in front of *Betancourt* lay the copy of the parchment. His life these last days had consisted almost entirely of staring at the paper, unmoving as if in a trance or paralyzed, barely breathing.

After the lieutenant had left, *Betancourt* had studied the drawing for hours, fixated on it unwaveringly. Then, slowly coming out of his reverie, he reached in his top drawer and thrashed through detritus accumulated over many years, moving scraps of notes on old paper, faded pictures, dry pens, ink bottles, a measuring stick, pencils, soiled handkerchiefs and a scissors, until he found a blank piece of thin white paper. Pulling it out of the drawer, he placed it over the copy, pressing it down flush until he could make out the outlines on the original etching. He traced the graveyard, but only in half, as it would have looked to him when he was last there some fifty years earlier. He had not known there was another half to the cemetery, but in an odd sort of way, this made sense to him.

*Betancourt's* hands trembled as he held the paper aloft, close to his eyes. Even with the passage of so many years, the vision of that horrible place was never far from his memory.

Hinton-Smith's visit had carried him back to that time: its smells of spring and sounds of night; the light breeze that carried the scents of pine and orange blossom. He could almost feel the wooden slats of the bridge under his feet and hear the rushing water of the creek.

She had met him there.

They had been good at keeping the secret of their romance. Indeed, when she disappeared, no one even bothered to question him. None even mentioned it except as in passing. For the others, there had been no connection at all between himself and Astrid. All these years, only his own guilt remained; his own knowledge of the event.

He could still imagine the lilt of her voice when she laughed, her smell of lilac, or feel the texture of her skin within his hands: all this for so many years.

He'd not done anything. What a vile coward he was.

Now the two etchings, the one from the church and the one in his own hand, lay side by side. That was where they had been. By the stones with the strange markings, at the time incomprehensible to either of them.

They met on the far side of the bridge late that night, and began to walk in the direction of that unholy place.

It all seemed so inevitable now.

He was familiar with the cemetery, many in the village were, but there seemed to be an evil character about it, an intangible...something for want of a better word—it was somehow indescribable. Can a place have an emotion attached to it, a mood? Of course, there is sentiment for those localities where something happened to us, whether for good or bad, and this one in particular was a cemetery; the place for our own end, an internment for the dead. There is naturally fear and revulsion for the certain eventuality of the end of our being, with volumes of dirt being poured upon our meager human remains. Is there one among us that can imagine no longer being? Without doubt, we view the burial as if we are still alive and the dirt clogs our nose and eyes and seeps into our mouth. But for this place there was something more than that common inexpressible foreboding.

No villagers ever went there. He and Astrid knew they would be alone.

As he sat there now, this night, involuntarily revisiting every memory, every impression, fear or horror, he found the thoughts ensuing from the lieutenant's visit were no less clear and no less confused.

A sudden urge seized him and he bolted up and rushed to his bedroom. Alabaster and deep blue chess pieces were scattered on the wooden floor from the previous times this mania had taken hold of him in the last two weeks. He picked up a knife from a teak wood stand and turned over the bare chessboard resting there. Now finding the slot in the corner, he carefully pried it open and withdrew a piece of blue cloth. It was from Astrid's dress.

*Betancourt* pressed it to his lips, feeling the cloth and breathing in the faint wisp of perfume that still remained of her. Then he kissed it and tears came to his eyes.

Lingering in this pose for only a moment, he carefully refolded the material, replaced it in the board, and fitted the rectangular piece of wood back in its slot, promising himself that if he ever succumbed to this sentimentality again, he would set the piece of cloth in flames, thus ending its existence as he should have ended his own mean life for failing her these many years.

*Betancourt* set the chessboard back in its place on the table, then began picking up the pieces on the floor. He meticulously started with the pawns, first blue then white, putting them all in place as if the game was about to start. Then he proceeded with the Bishops, Rooks, Kings and Queens. Last came the Knights.

Returning to his study, he sat, his elbows on the table and his hands propping up his head. Soon he was asleep and dreaming of approaching the cemetery with Astrid. She reached up and whispered in his ear, with a giggle in her voice. "We will make love here. No one will discover us in this place."

*Betancourt* saw himself in the dream, a mere boy of twenty years. He smiled in anticipation as Astrid, young and lithe and smelling of lilac, traipsed inside the half-circle of tombstones and began to dance as though waltzing with an imaginary partner, prancing up to the different stones, rubbing her hands over them and skipping around them as if they were her dance partners.

But now, in the dream, *Betancourt* realized where he was, and he jerked up straight in his chair, sweating profusely, but still asleep.

He saw himself join her inside the stones, embracing and kissing her. He could feel the softness of her mouth on his.

She drew him backward, near a dirt hillock, her back tight against a nearly vertical sheer wall. Then she pulled away. She had felt something, or better, the lack of something with her leg. Quickly getting down on her knees, Astrid brimmed with excitement as she felt around the edges of the small hole. "Look, Gilles, there is something here. A hole in the mound. Perhaps a cave."

She turned toward him, still on hands and knees, laughing like a seductress, tempting him. "We will go inside." She beckoned with her hand for him to follow. "Like Aeneas and Dido," she whispered. "Come."

He had bent down and grasped her hand, and now, he remembered how it felt; how warm and soft, small and sensual, but then suddenly her clasp turned painful as she began to squeeze and his hand involuntarily snapped back off the table as if he had touched a hot poker.

She was pulling him forward, but it was no longer about lust as he realized she was being dragged into that opening. He looked into her face, but it was not the face of his Astrid, but a face terrified and contorted out of all human semblance.

"Gilles!" she screamed.

There was a dark thick liquid, which he soon realized was blood, beginning to drip from her nose and ears. Her eyes began to bulge as if trying to escape from her head. Still she pulled him forward, as she in turn was being forced backward into the black hole.

As Astrid's legs disappeared, she fell to her belly, inexorably being drawn into the abyss. "Help me," she strained to cry out, but it only came in a hoarse whisper. She let go of his hand and spread out her arms in the form of a cross, to form a brace against the mound and the demon wrenching her away from the world of man.

Trying once more to speak, to scream, she could only manage spittle, as though her throat was being constricted.

*Betancourt* grabbed the sleeves of her dress, with each hand fastening on to the piece of cloth at the top of her arms. He put one foot up against the side of the hill to better pry her loose, then fell to his back and put up both legs as braces and pulled with every bit of strength. The cloth ripped off in his right hand. He could feel the bones in his left hand shatter, as her arm was wrenched away and she disappeared.

"Astrid," he whispered in a plaintive tone. He knew.

And he knew that the one thing that would happen if he followed her into that netherworld was his own destruction. Scrambling to his feet, he ran until he stood at the doorway of his parent's house, out of breath, awash with his own sweat and exhausted and weak from the distance covered.

He had never spoken a word of this to anyone.

He awoke, still sweating and wiped his forehead with a cloth. *Betancourt* had dreamed about that night many times since, but for the first time, the dream mirrored the events. It had happened exactly thus, even down to what they wore and the words they spoke. Why? Looking down at his soft hands he saw a scholar's hands, not those of a warrior, and one hand still useless from that night. He trembled at the knowledge of what he must do. Only once, in the last half century had he done anything remotely related to that night. Had he not gone to the church and inquired about the records, the lieutenant would never have come to him, and he could have remained secure in his cowardice, only reliving that night in dreams and undying thoughts. The Englishman certainly knew more than he admitted. Something very similar must have happened to him or he would not have gone to all the trouble to hunt down the diagram or bring it to him. Somehow it was comforting to the old man to know that someone else had gone through a similar harrowing journey.

But there it was.

Astrid had disappeared forever, and only her parents and a few relatives had raised any cry. The police and village elders concluded she had run away, that she would turn up someday with a new husband or child, and he had let them believe it. He should have led the whole village out there and razed the hill to the ground until they found out what happened, but he was too terrified.

*Betancourt* escaped his fears across the Pyrenees, settling in Valladolid, where he began to study, while as one year unfolded into another, memories in the village faded and only those few family members gave any thought to her. And as they died, only his memory remained extant.

He returned many years later, committed to exorcising this demon, but time passed by swiftly, and eventually, even he could not believe anything otherworldly happened, and he had rationalized it that way, easing his conscious mind into believing more mundane explanations. She had teased him and set up the whole knavery, terrifying him into thinking something snatched her, killed her. Then she ran off with another. Indeed, there are no demons or evil spirits, if you left out the existence of man of course. What if it was only a common criminal that pulled Astrid into the hole? Did not that make more sense after all? But it also made him all the greater a coward.

Until the day the English lieutenant came by. Then he knew. Something was still there, in the cave.

# CHAPTER 15
# THE RETREAT

The Panzer rotated on its axis as it turned to follow the bend in the narrow dirt road, leaving the dust from its treads hovering in a night air still hot and humid despite the sun having gone down three long hours ago. Before the dust could settle, Hinton-Smith, his back leaning tight up against the steep ditch bordering the road, and some fifteen yards away from the rest of the oversized platoon he now commanded, raised his arm to signal the sergeant major to send another man across. He stifled a cough from breathing in the dust.

Cawkins whispered, "Go!" and another soldier quickly darted cross the road and ducked down before the next German vehicle, another tank, could rumble into sight, slither down the route, pivot to make its turn, and disappear around the bend.

Private Hallow, who had somehow wandered in from the 5TH Gloucesters, who were supposed to be some ten miles away, was next. He had gotten separated in one of the tank battles, and had kept heading north, in the general direction of the flow of refugees and retreating soldiers, until he fell in with Hinton-Smith's group. "Bloody hell!" he whispered to the sergeant major. "The whole ruddy German Army must be using this road."

"Go!" Cawkins ordered.

Cawkins stared in amazement as the boy looked both ways down the dark road, then jumped up right before Cawkins would have pushed him, and ran across. He shook his head. This fellow is young. Then he tapped Parker on the arm to prepare him. Another vehicle, this time, a command car with what looked like three officers, roared past. They were so close he could see a gold wedding band on the left hand of the one who was a colonel. Cawkins also saw they were regular Army, and considering the rumors that had been afloat since the first days of the retreat, of SS men telling allied soldiers to throw down their arms and surrender, then slaughtering them, they were lucky. He would have liked nothing better than to throw a grenade into a car of SS officers. Hinton-Smith gave the all clear and the sergeant major ordered, "Go," after which Parker scrambled up to the road, partly running and partly crawling, as his upper body seemed to want to move faster than his legs, and he never quite got his balance. He dove head first down the slope on the other side and rolled a bit before Stevens caught him, and before the next tank appeared. By the time it was Graves' turn half the men were already across.

"Graves."

"Yes, sergeant major."

"Tell Parker to start moving the men out. Crawl a good hundred yards due north of the road and wait for us there. If we don't make it, head in the direction of the North Star. There," the sergeant pointed. "That'll take you to Dunkirk."

"Yes, Sergeant Major," he said, this time almost breathlessly, as the adrenaline welled up in his body. Cawkins could see it was hard for him to concentrate on the instructions. He was too absorbed with his impending run. Graves squinted as the headlights of an oncoming troop carrier glared in his eyes.

Cawkins wanted to be certain Graves understood. "Repeat what I said."

"Yes, Sergeant Major. Tell the corporal to move the men a hundred yards north. Assemble and wait. The North Star'll take us to Dunkirk. "

"Ok." Cawkins looked for Hinton-Smith's signal. "Go."

Hinton-Smith looked up, then made another notch in a ragged notebook, this one for a medium tank—he had already recorded twenty-nine medium tanks, forty-three light tanks, fifty troop trucks and eighteen armored cars. This went on from start to finish for a good two hours before Hinton-Smith and Cawkins were able to get all forty men across. The procession of German vehicles still went on unceasingly. Finally, the lieutenant and sergeant stole across the road themselves and ran to catch up to their men.

By now most of the British troops had already made it back through the small corridor Hinton-Smith and his motley group of men had helped keep open. Finally there were orders to fall back themselves—and the faintest glimmer of hope rose that they might reach Dunkirk. But now they were in open country and had to cover as much ground as possible every night before the Stukas could find them in the morning.

After forming up, two Coldstreamers on point wandered a few yards north.

"What's that up there so bright?" one soldier asked, as a red Very light streaked into the sky from fifty yards in front of him. Before the other man could answer, or dive for the ground, three rounds of machine gun fire hit him in the chest and hit the first man in the head. They were both dead instantly.

Hinton-Smith and Cawkins reached the column just as the light went up.

"Hit the dirt!" Cawkins bellowed, but many were hit in the opening fusillade.

Everyone scattered and dove into the grassy earth. Cawkins passed the word not to fire back, not wanting to betray their position any worse than it already was.

"Ambush," Cawkins said. "The Jerries are closer to the beach than us."

"They must have found a seam in the covering guard," Hinton-Smith said.

The Germans then started in with mortars. One of the first shells exploded near Cawkins, shrapnel catching him in both his left arm and left leg before he could respond.

"Dammit! In all my years of service, I've never even been scraped before," he said in a pained voice, as he tried to turn over to examine himself, and found that he could not quite manage. "Why now? This is frickin' stupid. You're on your own, kid."

"Corpsman! Corpsman!" Hinton-Smith screamed.

For Cawkins, first there was a burning sensation in both wounds, then a warm soft feeling in each, and finally a general sense of euphoria, as though he was on some type of drug. Everything appeared to be happening in slow motion, and he had the distinct impression that he was consciously watching the events from above, or out of his body. Finally, he struggled onto his back, cussing for all he was worth. Tearing off a piece of his shirt, he wrapped the arm, while the youngster, Hallow, who had crawled over to him, attended to his other wound.

"I was a corpsman in the Gloucesters," he shouted to the lieutenant, as the roar from the mortar explosions continued.

Cawkins was surprised that someone so young could have medical training, so he observed every one of his movements with a great deal of interest. He did not know Hallow very well as he had only joined them two days earlier. He hoped he knew what he was doing.

When the corpsman injected him with a needle, he wondered what it was for. He did not feel the injection, but was curious. It could not be morphine. It's just a goddamned flesh wound. Then for a few moments, he became totally disinterested in his own circumstances, and followed the battle's effect on the others as though he was viewing a newsreel in a theater back home.

Most of the men hurriedly began to dig holes, using their rifle butts or bayonets. Some huddled so low it looked like they were trying to hide behind an inch of earth or blade of grass. One man, who must have been a bookkeeper, or cook, or some other rear echelon type, especially caught Cawkins's attention, as he must have weighed over three hundred pounds. There he was, on his belly, trying to look invisible behind a three inch fence post that was knocked down in the barrage. His rear end was making a juicy target for any would be sniper. He saw another man, far afield, who was trying to crawl up to the main body of men; another was on his back, loading his rifle; yet another seemed to be feeling all over his body, as if checking to see if he was hit; and the typist, now a real veteran, was readying the Bren gun for action. By then Cawkins felt a complete calm overtake him and he wanted to sleep.

Hinton-Smith glanced over at the sergeant major and Hallow. The lieutenant was alarmed. He'd not been able to protect him. But then his training took hold—the situation had to be seen to first. Hallow looked competent so he briefly got up on one knee, oblivious to the tracers and rounds flying about his head and shoulders, and saw how the rest of the men were spread out over two hundred yards.

"Stevens," he shouted after getting back down. "Parker! Have the others crawl up. No standing and running. On their bellies only."

When he was certain enough time had elapsed that the men from the closest and on down had received the order, he crawled the few yards over to the sergeant, while all around the sky was lit up by tracers, red, and white, and gold, as though it was Guy Fawkes' Day back home. They were taking a terrific pounding.

"He's okay?" he yelled at the medic.

The medic nodded affirmatively, but shouted back, "I'm not certain about the leg."

Moving closer to make his own examination, he was relieved to see the sergeant major's wounds, even the leg, seemed minor. To the medic's horror, he shook the sergeant major to get him out of his stupor.

"Come on, Jack. This is nothing, for a guy like you," he yelled. "I've seen grannies playing football with worse injuries than these."

Cawkins groggily looked at the corpsman, "What'd ya have with a little kick to it?"

Hallow looked at the lieutenant. "I've already given him something."

Hinton-Smith nodded his head and said, "Humor him." So the corpsman reached in his bag, pulled out a bottle, labeled Scotch, which was actually filled with diluted kerosene. He handed it to the sergeant major, and simply said, "This."

Cawkins got up on an elbow and took a nice sized swig. "That hits the spot. Here. Now that's better. Try it. Damn good," he said, handing Hinton-Smith the bottle, which the lieutenant took a drink from, promptly coughed up and spit out all over them.

Coughing again, the lieutenant hacked out, "Even if I'm hit, don't give me any of that stuff...and if I ask for it, shoot me."

"Hmm!" Cawkins said, sitting up and putting out his hand.

Hinton-Smith looked at him.

The sergeant motioned with his fingers and the lieutenant returned the bottle.

Cawkins eyed the bottle for a bit and took another drink, this time swirling it around in his mouth, while both the lieutenant and the medic looked on from their prone positions.

"Tastes all right to me. I'll just keep this for you, if you don't mind."

"Sure," said the medic. "I've got another, but hadn't you better get down?"

Taking one more swig, Cawkins lay back down as though he was a child following orders.

"This is how I see it," Hinton-Smith said to the sergeant. "We have two choices: we sit here until they kill us all, or we bunch up what we have left and knock through, that way," and he pointed to a massive hedgerow, close in to the north. Cawkins, not altogether back to his senses, happened to glance back to where the fat man had huddled, and saw only a smoldering, smoking hole in the ground. He said to no one in particular, "That'll make for some real happy buzzards." Returning his mind to the present events, he weakly asked, "Bunch? What bunch?"

One of the other men crawled up. Neither Hinton-Smith nor Cawkins recognized him. Just another one of the lost Tommies, separated from his unit. "Sir, I only have a few rounds left," he yelled over the din of weapons fire. Hinton-Smith could see the boy was scared, maybe on the edge of just giving up.

Hinton-Smith motioned for the boy to come in closer.

"There's plenty of bodies around. Take some ammunition off those blokes," he said. "They won't be needing it. We're going to break out of here. We're going to snake up to that hedgerow and plow right through. See it?"

The private nodded. The hedgerow was about twenty yards north of them.

Just then Corporal Stevens scrambled up on his hands and knees. "The men are as assembled as they're going to get, sir."

"Right. We're going to break out through the hedgerow, Stevens. Take this man. You two have five minutes to pass the word and another seven for everyone to gather ammo from the dead and wounded. Set your watch. It should take us another five minutes to get close. Then we're lobbing..."

The lieutenant was cut off as another mortar shell came whistling in; he knew this one was going to be close. Pushing Cawkins's head down hard into the dirt, he covered the sergeant's body with his own. The explosion came from only four yards away and shook them as if a giant hand had pounded the ground in rage. The lieutenant looked up to see that no one was hurt. Then he grabbed Stevens by the arm.

"Listen to me. We're going to lob half of our grenades over that thicket. Corporal, make sure the men understand. Only half. We still have a long way to go. Then we're going to run over these bastards, and keep running till we hit the next canal."

"Sir?" Stevens asked.

"It's about two miles due north. We'll cross it and dig in. Husband your ammo. Make sure of your targets."

The sergeant, who was just now beginning to get his bearings back, although he was also just now starting to feel the pain from his wounds, spit some dirt out of his mouth and said in a gruff voice, "Right. Get going. You have seventeen minutes from now."

He looked over at Hinton-Smith. "Ok?" Cawkins said.

"Right. Let's go."

As soon as they crawled away and the sergeant and lieutenant were alone, Cawkins growled, "What in hell do you think you're doing? I'm already down. What are they going to do if you get hit?"

"Yeah, I guess that was rather dim."

"All right. Enough said. Remember, Mike," Cawkins said gruffly, "I'm one of the wounded. Leave me."

"You're not getting off that easily," Hinton-Smith said. "Start moving. Hallow, help the sergeant."

Stevens and the new man passed the word to others, who in turn passed it to others across the field—ammo was gathered, clips were checked and loaded, bayonets fastened. At the same time, they all started crawling toward the thicket.

As the soldiers edged forward, the machine gun fire now reached such a murderous crescendo, Hinton-Smith swore he could not hear his own thoughts. Two more men were hit by the rapid fire, and a third by a direct hit from a mortar as they moved. When they got within range of the hedgerow, Hinton-Smith got up on his elbows. He nodded approval as he saw his men pulling the pins from their grenades.

Looking at his watch, the lieutenant screamed, "Now!" and everyone lofted their grenades. As massive explosions hit in and around the hedgerow, it caught fire and soon was blazing.

Hinton-Smith helped the corpsman lift Cawkins, and the three of them rushed forward with the rest.

The conflagration of fire and wind directly in front of them brightened the whole field and threatened to cut off their escape, as the men bunched together and stopped advancing. Seeing the soldiers frightened and hesitating, the lieutenant left Cawkins's side and began to push and shove, and even bully the men around him.

"Move it! Move it!" Hinton-Smith screamed. "Move forward or I'll shoot you myself! Go!" So thick were the flames and gunfire from the other side of the hedge, only Hinton-Smith's insistence and prodding kept them going.

At the inner edge of the hedgerow, there were two Germans, both aflame, running the other way.

Once more helping the corpsman with Cawkins, the lieutenant burst through the first hedgerow. Standing in the middle, in a small area that was rimmed with fire, stood another German fighting with a luger. Hinton-Smith fired but only heard a click. He was empty. Ejecting the clip, he pulled out a new one. Just then he spotted the German take aim at Cawkins, who presented a closer target. Realizing he had no time to finish reloading, Hinton-Smith shoved Cawkins over and rushed at the German, hurrying desperately to push in the clip. The German looked completely surprised to see this madman running at him. Panicking, he fired too quickly, hitting the lieutenant in his left arm. He then compounded his error. He made the mistake of only firing once.

Hinton-Smith jammed in the new ammo, pulling back the slide to insert the first round, just as the bullet ripped into his upper arm.

The shock from the impact knocked him over, onto his back. No sooner than he hit the ground, he squeezed off a single round. The German, shot between the eyes, was dead on impact and fell into the thick fiery bushes.

"Jesus," Hallow exclaimed. "That looked like a bloody movie. Let me look at that arm," he said, rushing over to Hinton-Smith.

"I'm all right," answered the lieutenant, getting up with the medic's help. He rubbed his hand over the wounded arm, looked at Cawkins and managed a weak smile. If I can get the old man out of this muddle, I guess it's a start, he thought. "It'll wait. Let's get the bloody hell out of here."

The rest of the soldiers fired as they ran, no longer husbanding their ammunition. As they crossed the hedgerow, they shot at anything that moved. The Germans in and behind the hedgerow were wiped out—as many burned to death as were finished by shrapnel and small weapons fire.

When they reached the other side, the lieutenant yelled, "Run, and keep running! Don't stop!"

After some twenty minutes, they stopped, more out of necessity than safety. They all needed to rest. Hallow and Hinton-Smith propped up the wounded sergeant against a large, leafy elm tree. Then the corpsman ripped open the lieutenant's shirt to look at the wound.

"Dammit," Cawkins exclaimed in a whispered tone after looking around. "Stevens ain't anywhere. Did you see him?" he asked the medic.

"No. I don't know how any of us got out of there alive," Hallow said as he examined and poked around Hinton-Smith's arm.

"Only a handful of us did," said the lieutenant, now wincing in pain. "I saw Stevens off to my side right before I got hit. He disappeared. Why?" he asked, as if it seemed to be ridiculous to worry about one single life in this mess.

"His parents had a house directly across the street from my wife's in Aldershot. We had been comparing notes. We know some of the same folks."

"Sorry," Hinton-Smith said. "All right. That's enough work on me. Let's move."

"When is it going to be our turn?" Hallow asked.

"Don't worry," Hinton-Smith said. "Jerry's time will come. That I promise."

"You've lost some blood, sir," Hallow said. He started to wrap the lieutenant's arm. "There's no bullet, but you need some rest. You sure are the lucky one."

Hinton-Smith smiled grimly, gently nudging the sergeant. "See, Jack. What'd I tell ya?"

# CHAPTER 16

# THE KNIGHTS OF ST.JOHN
## 1422 A.D.

I n terms of history, Highgate and the surrounding area are young when juxtaposed to greater London, and not much heard of until William the Conqueror, though Roman Legions passed nearby on the way to their final campaign against Boadicea in 61 A.D. Legend has it that she was buried in a tumulus between Ken Wood and Parliament Hill, after embracing poison rather than being taken prisoner and made to shoulder the "yoke".

The hills of Highgate and Hampstead were too high and steep for the early Roman pioneers of Londinium, and they simply skirted the dense forests, with the wolves, stags, wild boar and oxen, when constructing roads to the north. Present day Watling Street ran west of the hills to the northwest, and Ermin Street wound north around the eastern slopes by way of Crouch End and Muswell Hill. Much later, after the invasion of 1066, the Norman barons used the woodlands as their private hunting domain, and these remained the royal hunting grounds for another four hundred years.

Sometime in the twelfth century, nobody knows exactly when, a small chapel was dedicated to St. Michael and attached to a hermitage built a hundred years earlier by a man named Faraldus, about whom nothing more is known. Pilgrims stopped to worship at the chapel on their way through the thick, dark woods, on the narrow meandering path which is now Southwood Lane, as they made their way to the shrine of Our Lady of Muswell to the east. In the thirteenth century, this area was given to the Knights Templar as an afterthought, along with land north of Kilburn Priory, in order that the knights might protect pilgrims from the many highwaymen and other black-browed scoundrels that haunted the midnight roads.

Early in the Fifteenth Century, not long after the Templars were persecuted, tortured and disbanded, a small cemetery was secretly laid out one black, somber night in a circle some ninety yards from the chapel, and a nine foot high wall, made of the darkest of stones, and entirely surrounded by thick jungle-like trees and vegetation, was raised to surround it. Knights stood guard as holes were dug in the solid earth. Holy words and incantations were chanted for most of the night as men were slain and buried—one poor soul still alive at his own internment. Only then, did eight brave knights descend to their graves. The priests and knights who officiated over the ceremony and the workmen who so hastily laid out the cemetery and erected the wall, were unceremoniously put to death before that same dawn. The executioners of these unhappy fellows were then put to death in turn. Many of these men were criminals and some already facing the hangman's noose: the priests and knights were volunteers and were buried with the requisite honors.

The chapel was put to the torch, the charred remains swept clean and buried under the original foundation. There it stopped, and as planned, the episode was lost to history, dying with the last memories of the mighty prelates who initiated the cruel burial. Only the wall remained, and before long, the chapel grounds were also overgrown with trees, bushes and high weeds, hidden from sight as well as memory, completing the task set so long ago. Curiously, there was an area, some two yards wide, that stretched around the whole circumference of the wall, in which nothing grew, not even weeds.

The razed chapel was discovered in 1824, by citizens interested in a place of worship located closer to their place of homestead. At some time previous, it had become part of the grounds of old Mansion House, built in 1694 by William Ashurst, and which stood empty, crumbling, and haunted for years. The chapel area was donated for a new St. Michaels; a large church designed for a congregation of fifteen hundred, with five hundred seats reserved for the poor. The church was consecrated in 1832. No mention was made of the neglected, melancholy ancient cemetery.

During the 1830's, many of London's older cemeteries became grossly overcrowded. To ease the congestion, larger cemeteries were planned on the city's outlying borders. Seventeen acres of steeply hilled and wooded ground, adjacent to St. Michaels and west of Swain's Lane, were set aside for Highgate Cemetery, and it was built during the second year of Queen Victoria's reign, 1839. The designer of Highgate, Stephen Geary, possibly discovered the existing cemetery alone on the hill, its black walls surrounded and hidden by great oaks and pines and jungle-like creepers by then, and decided those interred were in need of company. By the present time, this ancient cemetery had been all but forgotten.

Geary spared no expense or imagination on his project. A large Gothic entrance containing two chapels, one for Anglicans, and one for Dissenters, was crowned by turrets and buttresses, pinnacles and cupolas, the uppermost part of the wall crenellated to look like a fortress, with a bell tower looming over the Tudor-style gateway. A famous landscape gardener of the time created winding paths and flights of steps, following the contours of the sloping terrain. Trees, shrubbery, and flowers were purposely placed to give an almost mystical appearance when alongside the marble of doleful monuments.

So popular did Highgate Cemetery become, and so crowded, that seventeen years later, twenty more acres had to be laid out on the eastern side of Swain's Lane. This became New Highgate. An underground passage was built, complete with hydraulic lift to lower a coffin from the Anglican chapel on the west side in order to transport it to a grave on the east.

By 1940, the older of the two cemeteries, the west, was quite full—the only current and very rare burials were reserved for those with an ancestral plot, while the east side with its newer cemetery was nearing the same status. The tunnel was out of use and the hydraulic lift that had been considered quite the marvel of modern engineering in its time, was rusted and broken down, and both tunnel and lift were left to ruin.

By now, the cemeteries were quite bereft of the living, except for the caretakers, the occasional workmen, the occasional mourner, and local children who would sometimes sneak into the newer cemetery for play.

*   *   *

Unlike on the Continent, in England the cold weather would not let go. It snowed in Sheffield on the 23rd of May, and, although the snow melted by afternoon, most of the country remained cool even by English standards.

Jemmie Craven watched his breath form a funnel in the cool night air. He rubbed his hands together. It was much too cold for him. After tonight's work he would have a pair of better gloves than the fingerless, grimy red cloth gloves he was now wearing. And a hat and maybe even some new pants and a coat. After tonight his luck would change for the better. It would not hurt to have a few extra coins jingling in his torn pockets, a little meat to go in a stew, a few pints to wash it down.

Nobody was about at two in the morning. No lights shone in the vicinity on account of the blackout. Craven could barely see his hands in front of his face, but he had the streets to himself and was all the more confident in the darkness. Still, he was careful, more careful than usual for him. There would be patrols, either Bobbies or Home Guardsmen on the lookout for thieves, uncovered lights and vehicular accidents, of which there were many in the murkiness. There could even be...what did they call them? Oh right. Fifth Columnists. Would he love to run into one of them bastards. He'd throttle 'im to a pulp and then shove 'im up the arse of the local authorities just to prove he was as good a bloke as any of 'em.

Swain's Lane was an average size street at the bottom of the hill below the southern end of New Highgate Cemetery. There it melded

into Bromwich and Cheste Raydons. However, it narrowed apprecia-
bly if one followed it up the hill northward toward High Street. This
was the route Craven took as he contemplated the trappings of his
new life. Now his footsteps echoed loudly in his ears so he slowed
down and took each step with deliberation.

Not much to do. One simple rock. Maybe another tomorrow. Craven
felt the medium size stone in his pocket. He would have added a threatening note to it but he could not write. Well, let's have done with it.

As he got closer, nervousness became urgency. Now he wanted to
be finished and on his way. Craven began walking more briskly till he
was almost at the top of the street. There, he stopped just outside of
the north gate of the old cemetery.

Fumbling in his greasy pocket, he pulled out the rock that would
prove the foundation of his new lot in life. He spit on it for luck and
crossed the street. Drawing a bead on the uppermost window of Cyrus Wilson's house, he pulled back his arm and let fly. There was a
loud crash as the projectile shattered the glass of the window.

Seeing a dim light appear through the new hole in the window,
Craven turned and ran down Swain's Lane cackling like a banshee.
Finished and successful, his devil-may-care attitude returned. He was
certain with an arm like that he should have been a famous bowler. As
he ran he heard old Wilson cursing at the top of his voice, but had no
worry about being seen. In fact, this caused him to laugh once more.

It never occurred to him to ask why Bert Jones wanted him to
scare old Wilson. He just reckoned it would be a bit of fun. But he
was curious how Bert could pay him a whole pound. There must be
money in grave digging. Now all he had to do was collect what was
due him. Maybe it was worth more than a measly pound to the big
fat bloke. Craven always liked to have a little dirt on his friends. You
never knew when it might come in handy.

*     *     *

Matthew Boyden shifted uncomfortably in his chair. He arched his
back, cursed out loud, then settled back into a position of more or
less comfort, knowing it would only last for some fifteen minutes

before he would have to shift again. Wishing he could get up and run outdoors in the bright sunlit day, he sighed and resigned himself to the papers on his small, wooden desk.

"Lower back...again?" inquired Professor Littleton as he peeked into Boyden's office holding out a fresh folder containing research material to add to the pile on his assistant's desk. He walked in. "You're too young to have trouble with your back. Same old skiing accident, what?"

"Right. If I just stand for a moment, I'll be fine. It's really the bloody knee." Though Boyden was extremely tired of talking about the knee—he tried to act as though he was tired of it, although by now he really was—he was certain it was a good idea to keep drawing attention to his affliction. The professor was obviously too uncomfortable to even look at him while was he standing. After all, he belonged to an older, more polite school, and it was bad form to remind a man that he was crippled.

"Only another half-hour of slavery today, in any event," he joked. He heard a loud creak in his back as he stood, revealing the permanent bend of his left knee. A mere ten degree bend, it had kept him out of the service—another topic about which he readily joked—and was the result of an accident in the Tyrolian Alps, as he told anyone that asked. Racing down a glacier, he had reached speeds exceeding 70 miles per hour. It was the late spring, he was leaving the next morning and wanted to get in one last run. The snow was already melted at some of the lower levels, and it was so warm they were wearing nothing heavier than shirts and slacks.

Taking a shortcut to gain the lead, he hit glare ice and started slipping towards the edge of a two thousand-foot drop—a path that would land him just about perfectly on top of the chalet they had rented. As he seemed to regain control, he hit soggy turf, and bounded over and over again heading for the drop off. Yes, he had seen his entire life pass before his eyes, he told all who asked. Yes, he was lucky indeed, he resignedly responded to those who earnestly told him so, that he did not go over the edge. He remembered the trip to the hospital most vividly. Lucky indeed. He had finished the run, had he not? Even though it was in writhing agony on the back of a makeshift toboggan of tree limbs, branches, and cloth tied together by two blokes whose names he never discovered.

First putting a splint on to secure his leg, they lowered him down the mountain to the chalet, where they obtained a vehicle that took them to the nearest village with a doctor. With the knee both broken and dislocated at the joint, he had never experienced such excruciating pain in his life. The trek seemed endless. It took centuries.

Finally at the hospital, someone gave him enough shots of expensive brandy that the doctor could set the knee to the sound of his hysterical laughter—a nurse told him this later. The bad part of the story was, the doctor must have been last in his class—that always got a laugh. The knee, he would say, turned out like this.

When he got back in London, he checked with a number of specialists, some of the best. The consensus was they could break it again, then reset, but there were no guarantees it would turn out better. He couldn't go through that pain again, he would say. No indeed.

"Well," said the professor, "please use your last half-hour of servitude to look at these papers on the Near Middle East and tell me what you think of them. Tomorrow. Half past eight."

"Right, sir. I shall be here, papers read."

Littleton smiled an avuncular smile, and left the meager office located in an adjunct to the main building of the British Museum.

Only twenty minutes now, Boyden thought as he glanced at his pocket watch. The papers would have to go home with him tonight. He pushed his glass frames back onto the bridge of his nose, then reached under his desk to massage his knee. Straightening up, he had to push the wire frames up again. This caused a laugh. He could save more time if he changed the order of the process. He could not wait to get the damn brace off and was tempted to chuck it off right then and there and walk home without it, regardless of the cost.

Boyden had been at the top of his class throughout his "O" levels, "A" levels, and on to University at Cambridge, where he became one of the leading lights in his field: medieval archeology. After two years in central Italy, in the field, he had applied and been accepted to an internship at the British Museum. Definitely a plum for someone his age. Even had it not been for his knee, he would have been kept in

London, as he was considered too important by his government to be let back out in the field. It was not the British government that considered his presence in London important; it was the German government. And he was not actually German. His real name was Matthew O'Brien; his parents legally changed his name when they realized his academic abilities, thinking it would help him get into the better English schools. And he was not so much in favor of Germany, as he was loyal to Ireland. After all, the enemy of my enemy is my friend.

The pity was, he loved to walk, he loved to run, play football. It was bad enough being cooped up in an office all day, but career wise, as a scholar, it was a necessary evil. The story of the skiing accident was real enough, except for the last part. He had actually broken his leg, and it had been set perfectly. While recovering in Austria, for no particular reason other than feeling sorry for himself, he would from time to time rail out against whatever group or person came to mind. A doctor with Nazi sympathies happened to overhear a particularly nasty outburst directed against the British imperialists. Soon after, a fellow Irishman, a member of the IRA, coincidentally turned up at the same spa O'Brien had chosen for recovery. With a subtle nursing of all of O'Brien's anger, ego and idealism, the Irishman turned O'Brien into Boyden and an Irish patriot. The next thing he knew, he was in East Prussia for training.

Unfortunately, in his new guise, his only exercise now was more like limping to Tottenham Court Road, where he caught the Northern Line to Kentish Town. Then he hobbled—so he told himself in moments of self-pity—four hundred yards or so to Prince of Wales Road, turned right, and walked to his third story flat, more like a modest loft, where he would painfully climb the stairs.

Idiotic to keep that apartment, his neighbors would say. And he would agree and put it off to inertia, or say he would not give in one inch to the injury. The real reason was simple: it was convenient for his line of work, but only one other person in the country was aware of that.

Tonight, he had to change his routine, but this was another routine in itself. He took the Northern Line as usual, but changed at

Euston to the Victoria Line. This he took only one stop to King's Cross—St. Pancras, where he walked a short distance to his favorite fish and chips shop, the Barracuda. On Thursday nights, he would invariably go to the shop, and sit down and eat while he read the day's Times. It always took him one hour. Then he would go next door to the Cock's Crow, his pub, and tip a few pints of ale with the regulars, whom he'd got to know fairly well in the last three years, since leaving university. Then he would make his farewells, and leave, walking back to the King's Cross Station and heading home.

On the walk to the Barracuda, he always stopped at the same news kiosk to buy the Times, and about fifty feet later, he would casually glance to his left. Sometimes he would stop to look at the front page of the Times, and then look upwards to his left, but in any event, he only looked for a fraction of a second.

Tonight, the third shutter of the second story apartment was closed. He had to look twice, and did a regular double take any movie comedian would have been proud of. Trying hard to act natural, though adrenaline was now hurtling through his veins, he forced himself to continue walking. He would check it again on his way back. After three years of Thursdays, without variance, of seeing that same shutter open, he thought they had forgotten all about him. All the pain of his knee now seemed worth it. Finally there was a message for him. Of course, most of those three years had seen England and Germany at peace. His country had been at war with the Brits for centuries. Now a new worry entered his head. What if they simply wanted to tell him all bets were off? That his usefulness was ended before it had even begun. He laughed out loud. So, spies can be insecure. Bloody hell. They should be the most insecure.

He continued to the Barracuda, fighting with himself to proceed slowly, as if he could do it any other way with the bloody brace on. Now was not the time to do anything out of the ordinary. He pretended to read the paper though his mind was racing through every possible scenario, good or bad. The minutes dragged on endlessly before he felt it was all right to leave and go to the pub. There, he stayed for three half pints of ale, playing a half dozen games of darts to make sure he took a good enough while. After losing six straight games, he announced that he was leaving, and would never return until such time as his luck changed. This caused a great deal of laughter among his competitors, who dared him not to come on the next Thursday. He made a great show of condescending to accept the challenge, and left to a round of good-natured cheers.

It was now nearing dusk, and although there was no lighting from the street lamps, he was still able to make out the window. The shutter was still closed. Sighing with relief, he made his way to his tube station.

Arriving at the Kentish Town Station, he limped to his building and started walking up the wooden stairs. Halfway between the second floor, which had three flats, and the third, which only had his, he stopped as though to rest his knee. No one was around, but then, he did not expect there would be. He was virtually the only person to climb the stairway this far besides the landlord, who came up to get the month's rent, thirty shillings, only if Matthew Boyden did not bring it to him first, and he always made sure he did. He wondered about the wisdom of hiding the note in his very building. Someone had to put it there. What if they were seen? That could lead back to him. Sometimes he wondered if his handlers actually knew what they were doing.

He reached under the step he was sitting on, and quickly pried loose the board. Next, he took out a loose piece of paper, ripped out of "The Times" from March 10th, 1921. He got up and continued up the stairs to his door. When safely within, he bolted the door, and lit a small Bunsen burner, which was the building's equivalent to a stove. A metal stand, open in the middle to facilitate cooking with pots or heating a teakettle, was set over the burner, after which he adjusted the flame to the lowest intensity. He then carefully put the paper on the stand. He only had seconds. It would surely burn if left on too long, and though he had practiced it many times, this time was for real, and he was nervous. A single "X" appeared. There would be a meeting. There would be a mission. Placing the paper back on the stand after staring at the single letter for a bit, he let it burn. The "X" meant that he would have to go to a dead letter box and pick up the information. It was too dangerous to leave a real message in his building, but who would suspect a scrap of paper that was nineteen years old. The dead letter box signified by the "X" was in New Highgate Cemetery, behind a loose brick in the wall near the tombstone of Sir John Richard Robinson. He had taken to laying flowers upon the tomb, every other month. To the curious who sometimes asked, he said that Sir John was a great uncle on his mother's side.

Quickly, he rolled up his pants leg and ripped off the brace. He rubbed the leg to get the circulation going, then gingerly straightened it. Once they had reunited with the North and Ireland had got rid of the damn Limeys, he'd probably never bend it again.

*　　*　　*

It was amazing to *Betancourt* how life could change so much in such a few short days. There were no longer any lights in the village of St. Venant at night, and now, during what should have been the busiest moments of the workday, the streets outside his window were empty. Most of the townsfolk had left, joining the refugee columns fleeing the quickly receding front lines. Who was left, he had no way of knowing. If there were any, they were obviously keeping indoors or to themselves. Walking out his door and into the street on a warm, pleasant day, he stopped, closed his eyes and looked up toward the sun, breathing in the odors of spring. The sun felt good on his hands and face. Looking toward the marketplace, *Betancourt* could see no one. Not even a dog or cat was in evidence. He had not seen another person in a day-and-a-half. He liked this just fine. Most of the time he could not stand seeing other people.

Still, *Betancourt* knew he should join them. He was no warrior after all, just an old man who studied. He had never raised his fist in anger against any person or thing in all his seventy-three years: except for once. Did he have enough food to last a few more days, taking into account what he would need when he left? There were no longer any stores open where he could purchase goods. Could he leave without taking care of that infernal bond which held him in this place? No. He knew something would have to be done. Indeed, that was the only reason he was still there.

*Betancourt* had tried to leave. Only days after the onset of the German attack, he had hurriedly packed, intending to take just enough to see him through to Amiens. It would be hard enough for an old man pedaling a bicycle without a huge load, though he had never been one to need much. He could buy any necessities in Amiens.

This was a relief to him. He would get out and leave the nightmare behind. The Germans did not matter—they were simply a handy excuse. Since the visit of the lieutenant, he had gone back and forth as to what he should do: make an end to this memory or run from it. The Germans provided the justification. But again he vacillated. Finally, he realized he could not escape until the business was finished, or at least some semblance of knowledge or understanding was gained of what had happened. He could no longer live like this even if he was a thousand miles away.

On the desk in his study were the two drawings, still side by side, and on top of the one he had made, was the patch of blue fabric. He had not been able to destroy it, to cut his ties.

Even now, he could hear the rumblings of the artillery from the northeast. In the previous nights, he often saw swatches of lightning like flashes from the big guns.

What stygian being was in there? What had they encountered? The devil himself? It could not be. An otherworldly being. Nonsense. It must have been a simple criminal. Could it still exist sixty years later? What could the lieutenant have experienced? Why didn't he tell me? There must be something, or was he telling all he knew? Just an interest in history. He never said anything about an encounter. *Betancourt* was a scientist, a scholar. It was just too far beyond his reason that something like that existed. Like what? Impossible. It had been a man, a miscreant, a no good. And now he would prove it.

In the last few days, since he decided he must do something, must find out, his courage would often waver and he prayed for a Gypsy, a priest or spiritualist: someone who had experiences in these matters. Someone who could tell the future, or had knowledge of the duality of the world: someone who could see into that dark world where he could not. Over these many years, he had poured over books on myth and folklore, from Norse sagas to Gilgamesh to the Holy Bible:

anything he could get his hands on that might shed some light on his predicament.

What could he use? What would he take to do battle with whatever it was: a gun, a knife, an axe...a cross? He remembered never feeling so much hate and evil and fear in his entire life. His whole body had shaken for two days after that encounter. He had neither come out of his room nor eaten during that time. Three days after that, he had boarded a train and left for the Pyrenees.

It must have been a criminal. It simply could not have been anything else. Some sadistic bastard hiding out from the law in that cave. And he saw his opportunity. He must have been a very strong individual, but an individual, a man. They had been unlucky to have picked that time and that place.

So he would be gone by now, or, and then a weird chuckle emerged from *Betancourt's* lips. Or, he'd be ancient, shriveled up and frail just like himself.

More likely, the villain had been caught by authorities long ago and guillotined.

It was strange that it had taken this amount of time to see so clearly. His mind had been so clouded with fear. Of course, this must be true. He was certain the lieutenant had seen or heard something. Who knew what? The important part was the young man survived and this bolstered *Betancourt's* courage. He would finally make amends. It struck him as amusing that now, in his advanced years, when he was so less equipped to physically confront whatever devil lurked in the cave, that he could actually summon the courage to do so.

So it was. Even in the midst of this second great war, *Betancourt* would do battle. Now he scoffed at himself. What lofty terms he used.

He picked up the wisp of blue cloth and said, "I must do this thing now, before the Germans come. I resolve I shall end this tonight." He would find out the truth, then leave this place forever— leave this nightmare behind him.

There were many hours to pass before the light faded. Going back into his house, he put a pot of water over a burner. Then he went to the cellar and retrieved a bottle of Port.

He returned to his desk and, on a whim, took out a book at the bottom of a stack. Opening the leather cover, he laughed and began to sip a glass of the wine. *A Season In Hell*, he thought. Rimbaud. How very appropriate.

Everything he would need for his journey back to Spain was already packed in two small leather bags which fit in baskets he had fastened to his bicycle. The baguettes and cheeses, along with a change of clothes would hold him for the few days before he came to a major city. *Betancourt* hoped the trains would still be running to the south.

A new idea sprang into his mind: what if there was evidence in the cave! Why had he never considered this before? Evidence of the criminal and his act! This would indeed free him.

Yes. There would be evidence. This immediately made him feel better about the prospect of going out to the old cemetery. Thoughts of some otherworldly being disappeared from his mind. Still, he would take weapons.

He was startled by the whistling of the steam. Quickly, he removed the pot from the burner. Two spoonfuls of coffee grounds were thrown in a strainer and balanced inside a cup. He then poured the hot water over the strainer and let it sit.

*Betancourt* found his old navy blue waistcoat, filling the pockets with a knife, matches, candles and a heavy wrench. Should he take a cross? Just in case? It would do to cover all bets, he decided. Going to his bedroom, he opened a large chest which contained photographs, books and other articles left by his parents. There, wrapped in an oily cloth was his father's shotgun. Did it still work after all these years? He'd never even shot it. He dug deeper in the chest and found two boxes of cartridges. Opening a box, he cracked the shotgun open and put in two cartridges and closed the gun.

He raised it, much as he'd seen his father do and looked down the sights. He could feel the weightiness, especially in his left arm. Should he test it before going? This might arouse suspicion among those few still remaining in the village—better to wait until he was closer to the *motte*.

Finding himself strangely relaxed, he giggled. Finally it was going to be over, the decision was made. Within a matter of hours, he would be free. Fifty years of wrinkles near his eyes and the corners of his mouth seemed to smooth out and disappear as the tension and fear of all those years abated. He wished he had done this those many years ago, and forestalled a life of guilt and misery. What an impostor fear is, he thought. Why had he not had the courage to act on this before? Of course it was just a vile criminal and the evidence would prove it.

A handful of shells went into his pocket and he dumped the shells from the second box into a burlap sack. There was a slight smile on his face as he tore around the house to find a fold-up military shovel, an axe and a flashlight. What else? A lantern, he thought. Ah. Much better. It would free his hands. Finding a kerosene-burning lantern, he checked to see there was fuel, then stuffed it into the bag.

Now procrastinating, he went back to the bedroom and went through the books, clothes and food he'd packed for the journey, and questioned whether he'd taken the right things. Should he not take this book instead? What about this other suit? No! Enough of this! Now, it entered his mind to leave this very night, as soon as he'd gotten the proof.

The coffee was brewed strongly by the time he returned to his desk. Breaking open a loaf of bread, he sat with his book, sipping coffee and nibbling on the bread. From time to time, he would look toward the window, to see how much light was left of the day. Then, he would take a small bit of the port. He drank slowly. He wanted his mind clear for the task of the night.

# CHAPTER 17

# THE FIRST OF JUNE

Cyrus Wilson felt like a supplicant; a feeling he did not like one bit, and a situation he had mostly managed to avoid during his life, until now. He felt this way, a very helpless feeling indeed, as this would likely be his last chance, and it all devolved to the whim of one stupid bureaucrat, who would make his decision without even a token thought about Wilson's military experience, his knowledge, his competency, or his need to do something in this catastrophe. Cyrus Wilson had had a long time to think about it as he made his way from London, where he had already exhausted every avenue, and the patience of all he had sought out to help him. "All I want to do is help," he told Elizabeth Hammond. "Why won't they let me help?" Of course, her response was to ask if he should not at least give the Home Guard a chance, even if briefly. With anyone else, that would have been enough to earn a severe tongue-lashing. Instead, he remembered thinking how the Home Guard was for rickety old men and young misfits, sadly looked at her, said, "I thought you would understand," grabbed his old army kit, which had long been packed, and headed out the door. He thought about it now as he detrained in Dover, and looked across the bustle of faces for a likely person to give him directions to Dover Castle, which he had last visited almost sixty years earlier. This was rumored to be the "on the spot" center for the organization of the evacuation fleet. That is, of course, if it was ever needed: every last man in a position to know denied knowing anything. Once there he would try to make an appointment and kowtow to some twit bureaucrat, who would probably make the decision according to some out-of-date regulation that no longer had a bearing on anything. Perhaps the invention of bureaucracy had some stabilizing effect on the English speaking world, but Wilson figured it had squelched more good efforts, great projects, and much needed progress, than it had helped or fostered. It was less than an even bet that he would even get an audience.

When they heard the first rumors of the tragedy in Belgium, Wilson and the Hammond sisters immediately dismissed it as highly unlikely. The government was not exactly denying the possibility of disaster and evacuation, but it also was not admitting to anything dire. The average person on the street accepted the inevitable and began to seek solutions to bringing the lads home, while many in the highest realms of Government still sought solutions to the wrong question: how to win the battle. Nonetheless, as the rumors persisted and became couched in terms of near panic, Cyrus and Elizabeth had to lend it some credence. Elizabeth was completely helpless, absorbed in worry over her lieutenant, Kate volunteered to become a nurse and Cyrus decided to see if he could take more direct action.

First, he tried to rejoin his old unit in the Guards. Next he went to the Admiralty, to the Merchant Marine, and then to the Ministry of Shipping. All these offices were desperate for men, though they refused to say why, as if everybody did not already know, and they turned him down on account of his age. Strangely enough, he felt like a young man. He never thought of himself as old, even though he would sometimes jokingly refer to himself as an old man in order to make other people know he was comfortable with being old, so they would not be uncomfortable. His mind was sharp and he could still command, give advice, or think out reasonable solutions to problems. The main problem was that his body, no longer flexible or resilient, would tire easily or let him down some way or other. Unfortunately, any official who looked at him for the first time saw only the physical side, his shining

white head of hair, or the sagging skin and deep wrinkles of his face
and neck, not the clear thinking of his mind.

Receiving directions from a young Navy Chaplain, he stopped for
a while, breathing in and out deeply and thinking how clean and
brisk was the air by the sea. He had forgotten the difference.

Cyrus Wilson walked down the road leading to Dover Castle, carrying his kit in one hand, and then switching it to the other as the
first got tired. When his right hand was not occupied with the kit, he
absent mindedly stuck it in his pocket and rubbed a small piece of
paper—perhaps for luck, or out of nervousness—on which he had
written the name of a man (the bureaucrat), which he had gotten
from a friend in London, and which he kneaded so often since starting on this journey, the paper was almost worn through, and the
name almost rubbed out.

He was surprised to hear faint rumblings from explosions on the
other side of the Channel. Wandering out on the quay and peering
across the water, he could just make out the same black cloud of smoke
over Dunkirk that Hinton-Smith was using for a guide. The reality of
the war, even though he had already seen wrecked aircraft from his coach
window as the train drew closer to Dover, finally dawned on him (he
was an army man, and so needed evidence of a ground war, not an air
war, with which to relate), and gave him a greater sense of urgency.

Arriving at the Castle, and, pulling out the piece of paper on
which was now faintly written, John Willoughby, who was the secretary of some department or other, Wilson proceeded over the
drawbridge, showed the guard the name and received directions to
his office. As he walked into Dover Castle, he could not help admir-
ing the ramparts and massive keep where as a schoolboy of eleven, on
one of the school's field trips, he had gotten into trouble for slipping
away from the group with a few schoolmates, climbing to the top of
the ramparts and then hanging from them out over the sea.

He found the secretary's office, knocked on the door, peeked in
and saw a proper looking fellow in naval uniform, who did not
bother to look up, and decided right away that for all the trouble
this had been a bad idea. He hesitated, then figured he was already
here so he might as well make the best of it. Unfortunately, all the

arguments he had rehearsed on the train were gone, and all he remembered was the irritating feeling of being a petitioner at the
mercy of this little man.

Wilson walked to the front of the man's desk and was surprised to
find he was still being ignored. The man did not look at up him, but
continued to read a memo and make notes. Mustering all of his restraint, Wilson patiently waited to be acknowledged, though the
man, as far as he was concerned, was going out of his way to humili-
ate him. All in all, Cyrus Wilson figured he could take it for about
ten minutes maximum, and then he would haul off and hit the twit.
Luckily for the man, he finally addressed Wilson, though he still continued with his notations and did not look up.

"Do you have an appointment?" he asked, with as cool a reserve
as is humanly possible.

"No, I..."

"Who are you here to see?" the unsympathetic man cut in.

Wilson looked at the piece of paper again, even though he had
looked at it only seconds before, "Mr. Willoughby."

"That is Captain Willoughby," the secretary said icily. "I'd like to
help you, but the Captain is quite busy right now. If you do not have
an appointment..." He glared as if to say why are you wasting my
precious time. "I'm afraid there's nothing I can do."

Wilson felt his last chance slipping away, "I've spent my whole life
as a soldier. I want to volunteer to help evacuate the BEF. That's all.
My friend, here's his name," he said as he handed the secretary a different piece of paper.

The secretary looked at it and was surprised to see that it was the
name of an extremely high-placed army man. He now regarded Cyrus with some respect.

"He said the Captain could help me."

The secretary's features settled into a condescending smile. "We're
not evacuating the BEF. Where did you get that idea?"

Cyrus Wilson stared at the man in disbelief and could only disgustedly think, bureaucrat. "Look, sir," he snarled, with a particular
contempt settling on the word, sir, before he remembered his position
and instead, lied with what he considered was his last appeal. "My only

son is over there, and a lot of our boys. Please, *please*, sir. Let me man a boat, cook, carry supplies, pack ammunition, anything."

Now, his voice dripping with treacle, the man replied, "Sir. I'm telling you that there is no problem. I assure you. The BEF is doing fine and they'll be on the Continent for a long time. I'm sure your son is safe. He's probably giving the Jerries a worry or two, right now." He cleared his throat, looked down and resumed his paperwork. "Pardon me, but I must return to my work."

"Could I see the Captain?"

"Sorry. I told you. Captain Willoughby is too busy. Sorry."

Wilson stood over him for a full two minutes deciding whether or not it was worth popping him one. For all the arguments he had rehearsed, the one he never figured on, was that they would simply deny there was a problem. Even this late in the game. He had no argument for that.

As he walked out of the Castle, he wondered why anyone would lie to him. "Not evacuating," he said out loud. "Right! What a bunch of tommyrot. They're going to need all the help they can get. I guess that's so much for doing it above board." The hard part to figure out was what he was going to do and how he was going to do it. He had heard that some private citizens were tired of the Government and Army denials, and were looking for ways to help the soldiers, but he did not know any of these people.

It was almost dusk by the time he had supper and his evening tea, so Wilson decided to find a bed and breakfast and return to London in the morning. Besides, he figured, he might pick up more information in the informal setting of a person's house, and it made him feel closer to the action.

*     *     *

As *Betancourt* noticed it was becoming too dark to read, he glanced to the window and lit a candle. Much later, he walked to the window and stood, peering outside to the street. By now, everything was black. He could hardly make out the house on the other side.

It was time.

*Betancourt* slung the bag over his shoulder and picked up the heavy shotgun with both hands and started to the door. He hesitated. There was one more thing. He returned to the chest in the bedroom and took out a bible, wholly unused since the passing of his parents. He was not religious, had never been, but somehow, at this moment, the cross and bible seemed to give him strength.

The rumblings from the artillery had ceased and the night became very quiet. The air outside his house was sticky and he could feel his breathing become labored, as he trod out in the direction of a nearby wooden shed to find his bicycle.

There was a patch of roses, newly grown outside the storehouse. Stooping down, he took the knife from his pocket and carefully cut their stalks, put them in the bag and continued into the shed.

The bag was fastened to the front wheel basket and he balanced the gun on the handlebars as he slung his leg over the seat, mounting the bike. With one leg on the pedal, he shoved off with the other and began to pedal out to the empty street.

"Thou I walk through the valley of death, I shall fear no evil," inadvertently emerged from his lips as he passed by the chapel and headed out of the village.

As he neared the old mansion, now boarded up and empty, he could feel a quickening of his breath and heartbeat. Adrenaline surged in his arms and legs. An old man on such a mission appeared biblical to him: the eternal fight between good and evil.

Beyond the manor the paved road became dirt and uneven, and he tried to rein in his thoughts. It had been a criminal, nothing more. He would find the evidence and that would put an end to it. And what if there was a lack of evidence. No evidence at all. That would be even better. It would mean the rumors had been true and Astrid had left with another, never to return. This would not bother him in the least. Indeed, he hoped for it. Once more he smiled, though the adrenaline rush continued unabated.

Stars appeared and sparkled in their myriad numbers, stretching from the horizon and up, everywhere he looked, except from a large area directly in front of him where there was a void of blackness: the *motte*. What would he find? As though he had no power over his own legs, he began pedaling slower as he left the dirt road and cycled over a weed-infested field. He had not been anywhere near this proximity to the *motte* since that night. Would the entrance to the cave still be there? There must have been much erosion over the last fifty years. If not, he had resolved to fill it in himself as a fitting gesture to Astrid: a proper burial. Then he remembered the lieutenant. If he was right about him, the hole must still be there. He found himself hoping he was wrong.

To the southeast, the rumblings started once more. He could make out the outer half-circle of stones with each flash of light from the artillery. Gliding to a stop near the outer edge of the ring, he dismounted and lowered the handlebars of his bicycle to the ground. Sweating profusely, a sense of unease engulfed *Betancourt*, causing him to waver in his progress. Stopping, he shined his torch all along the lower portion of the grassy mound.

His hands were shaking as he took the lantern out of his bag and fumbled in his pocket for the matches. After lighting it, he felt a modicum of relief and it occurred to him to hold the lamp closely to his front, between himself and direction of the town, just in case anyone was still there. He inadvertently chuckled. He did not want anyone in the town thinking him stranger than they already did. Then he set his jaw firmly and started toward the sentinels of stone, the shotgun at the ready.

*Betancourt* stopped as he came abreast of the nearest tombstones. Holding the lantern out in front of his chest, he looked around and scoffed at his own nerves. He should have done this so long ago. What a fool he'd been to not come here before. There was nothing here. There is no *evil* here. Not in reality, not in sentiment, at least beyond the usual foreboding and dread that comes with a nocturnal visit to a cemetery. He felt nothing. What a fool he'd been. What a terrible coward and all for nothing. A life had been spent in fear and loathing for nothing.

He clutched the stems of his flowers tightly in his hand. "Astrid," he said. "I'll give you a proper burial if you are here, and if not, a blessing for you and your lover and your escape from our dismal village."

Kneeling down, tears came to his eyes. "I also beg you to forgive me for leaving you if it was some villain, or for cursing you if you ran away." Only now did he realize it was only his own fear that kept him from this place for so many years. He knelt for some time, and much of his guilt was purged as he once more relived that night. Finally, he knew it was time to end all the speculation and fears for good.

*Betancourt* put his hands on his thighs and stood. Picking up the lantern, he turned to the tomb nearest him, and held it close enough to see the out-of-place eastern symbols. How did they come to be engraved in these stones, he wondered? He traced his fingers along the lines of a swastika and felt the coarseness from years of exposure. How strange. All the dates and names had long ago been effaced, just as those had been on the parchment he had originally seen in the church archives. No memory of these men shall endure through history, he thought. What could they have done to deserve such treatment? He pondered his own record and who would remember him when he was gone. And if no one did, would it be as though he had never even existed, and what difference would it make in any event?

Now he went to each stone of the circle in turn, four in all, and explored their similar carvings and effacement: this, to see if any data had been left by mistake. There was nothing. The destruction had been meticulous.

His excitement grew as he would soon know the truth, but still there was something in the back of his mind that cautioned, "This is a very unusual place." Now, as he made his way toward the edge of the eroded hillside, he instinctively felt it might be best to proceed slowly in his search for the hole from which Astrid disappeared from him forever.

Shadows created by the fluctuating movement of the lantern, gave him a distinct feeling of uneasiness, and he noticed his heart was once more pounding. His imagination began to turn those shadows into great gargoyles, swaying to and fro, seemingly moving along with him, and then behind him, ready to assault him at any moment. Forcibly quelling his emotions, he continued forward.

He exhaled in a long breath, determined to get this over with now. *Betancourt* wished he had come in the daytime instead of night. Had it not been for nosy villagers he would have. For an old man who had experienced that long ago night with Astrid, this foray was quickly becoming too much to endure. Perhaps he should just leave. What difference did it make after all this time?

No, he thought. It is time. He would be a coward no more.

Sliding the lantern handle over his wrist, he held the shotgun with both hands, pointing the barrels forward toward the place where the vertical slope of the mound abruptly began. Then he moved a few feet forward, stopped and looked from left to right, following the light from the lantern along the intersection of the ground and the *motte*. Though he was certain he was in the exact place where he stood when Astrid was first pulled away from him, he could not see anything, no break in the earth, no hole. Perhaps his memory failed him. Turning around, he grasped the lantern handle with one hand and held it out in front at arm's length. He studied the positions of the four slabs. No, this is correct. Certain he was in the right place, he turned back and moved closer. Squinting in the dull light, he still could not see a thing. There was nothing to do but get down on his hands and knees and feel for the opening.

The weeds and dirt were cool and damp to the touch as he moved his hands along the earth, and upward along the wall of the *motte*. He felt the grime on his hands as he wiped sweat from his forehead. It is just too black tonight, he thought. He should go back and return in the morning. He could be here all night and never find a thing. The journey could be put off for one night. God knows he had already put it off for weeks.

Once more he had to still his nerves. "We will do this thing tonight and be done with it," he said out loud, annoyed with his vacillations. "I will no longer let fear orchestrate my life!"

Now he moved slowly along the wall to his left and closer to the middle of the half circle of tombs, pushing the lantern and shotgun ahead of him, then stopping and dragging his palm flush against the seam of ground and hill. He was determined to go over the whole mound, up and down, if need be. Moving another foot to the left, he jabbed his hand into the dirt, once, twice...*It went through! I found it! There! There it is. I knew it!*

*Betancourt* was exultant. His hands passed over the outline of the hole, examining its width and height, feeling the dirt, squeezing bits between his fingers. It would all pass this night. It would all be behind him. He would finally be rid of this curse, full of light and wonder, not darkness and fright. He would once more walk upright.

His hands firmly on the shotgun, he pushed it against the lantern base, edging it forward into the dark recess. *Betancourt's* heart beat rapidly now, and he felt he had the strength of a dozen young men. He breathed in deeply and blew it out in a slow stream, once again wiping grit and sweat off his brow and cheeks. The lantern now inside the hole, he pointed the barrel of the gun toward it and pushed the shotgun forward into the darkness. How obscene and dreadful this place had been to him for so many years. Now it was simply a hole in the earth, a rabbit warren, a nesting place; innocent parts of life.

Getting down on his belly, he began to crawl forward, moving the shotgun and lantern before him. He was relieved to see he would fit easily. It was much larger than he remembered. Images of Astrid being pulled away from him, now entered his mind and he fought to make them disappear. Feelings of panic arose in him, and his hands shot up to the walls of the hole. He would push himself backward. But the loam he felt was damp, almost fresh. So, the Englishman must have dug some of it out, enlarged it. Good! That meant he was inside and he survived the experience. *Excellent!*

*Betancourt* was now fully inside the earth. Still crawling forward, he alternately pushed the gun and lantern before him, into what he had previously conceived of as hell.

He felt a strange mixture of glee and trepidation as he edged forward. Now inside, he could see it was cavernous. He would be able to stand. Getting up, he brushed the dirt off his coat, and with eyes full of wonder, and his jaw dropped open, he looked around the cave. Now picking up the lantern and shotgun, he took a few slow steps further inside. So large was the place, even with the light from the lantern he could not make out the far side.

Four more stones, laid out in the same semi-circular pattern stood in front of him. There were the same markings, the same effacement. There was a center headstone. These stones were indeed part of the same grouping outside. Holding the lantern close to the center slab, he bent over to look at the strange writing. At first look, it seemed to be ancient Hebrew, a language he was acquainted with from his studies of the Holy Land, so he followed it from left to right, but he could not decipher it. It occurred to him that it might be Aramaic, a language he had never studied.

"This is quite strange," he said in a low voice. He could understand if the engraving was in Latin or even Hebrew or Aramaic. This made sense if they were Crusaders who had journeyed to the Holy Land. But coupled with the Eastern symbols, it was completely beyond his understanding.

All writing on the other tombs was effaced, as if someone marked them and then changed their mind. Of course that effacement might have come later. That made sense for the outer tombs.

His eyes now went to the ground at his feet. He turned around and scanned all the ground from the entrance to where he now stood. There were no bones. No blue dress or remnants of a blue dress. Nothing. She had run away. Lack of evidence is everything, better than all the proof in the world. He laughed out loud. If they had been married, he would have been a cuckold. How he loved being a cuckold at this moment.

There was a strange, clicking sound above his head, like two pieces of rock lightly banged together. Looking up, he saw only unfathomed blackness. He quickly lifted the lantern above his head and his heart stopped. Thin, soiled bones, a dirty gray and partly covered in the rags of a blue dress, hovered above him—the skull, with dark, mangled hair hanging downward, and face in a permanent grimace of terror and pain, staring accusingly at him. Suddenly, it dropped downward, stopping a few inches in front of his face.

"Aaiieehh!" he screamed until he had no more breath or voice.

"Aaiieehh! Aaiieehh!" echoed back from the void.

He tried to push the skeleton away, but the long hair, Astrid's hair he realized, wrapped around his neck and began to strangle him. She was murdered here and I did nothing to help. Now she takes her revenge upon me. But how? "Astrid," he struggled to say. "I tried to help you. To pull you away. I loved you. Don't do this to me."

As he struggled to draw air into his lungs, a voice came into his head.

"It is not your Astrid who kills you," the voice intoned.

The rope-like hair wrapped tighter around his throat. *Betancourt* could no longer speak. He knew he had only minutes to live. Why had he come back to this place? What is this voice? What was killing him? There was no sense to this. No logic.

"You have helped my sworn blood enemy. For this you shall die," the voice said.

What enemy, *Betancourt* tried to ask? He had no idea where the voice came from. He tried to speak but nothing passed forth. As the strands tightened, his eyes bulged and he gasped for air. At least tell me why, he thought to say. At least tell me what? To know was more important than to live.

The name *Sinestre L'Anguedoc* intruded into his last thoughts. *Betancourt* felt a great pain within his body, as though every part of him was blazing with fire. Then his consciousness came to an end.

*   *   *

The next morning, after eggs, beans, toast and tea, Cyrus Wilson went back to London. He was in an increasingly irritated state, his hosts and new friends having informed him of receiving the same runaround from the authorities.

"We must help the lads!" Wilson exclaimed. "I don't know why they are lying to us, but I know they are, aren't they?" Shaking the couples' hands forcefully in a show of common cause, he left for the station. In a few hours, he was back in Highgate and his favorite pub, the Hound's Tooth, which had occupied the northwest corner of Hampstead Lane and Bishopswood Road for one hundred and fifty years, beckoned with its camaraderie. There he was certain to find gents sympathetic to his cause, and though it was still early afternoon, Wilson settled down to what he was certain would be a very long session of drinking, indeed.

This particular day, he was even more demonstrative and cantankerous than usual. He raised his voice at both the barkeep and the barmaid, people he had known and been friendly with for years, and for this reason, and because they knew why he was upset, they took it in stride. The barkeep knew Cyrus Wilson better than most. Harry Kendall was a slight, but very fit man of 45, who was not able to enlist on account of a hearing problem, and so was used to people screaming at him. He told Cyrus his pint of bitters was on the house, while Polly Turner, his barmaid, a saucy and busty young lady who was not above letting her wares show in convenient places, even now during the cool London spring, told him of the latest rumors concerning a gathering of ships to help the lads: from Channel packets, pleasure steamers and destroyers, to fishing boats, yachts, and even row boats. She pointed over to a booth in a darkened corner of the pub, occupied by four rough and weathered men that Wilson took to be fishermen.

"Go talk to them," Polly advised him. "I told them about you."

Wilson looked over in their direction to see a lean, muscular man in a navy blue pea jacket waving his pipe in a good-natured manner that motioned for him to come over. Though two of the sailors exhibited indifference to anything other than their drink, he could see that some were eager to talk.

Cyrus Wilson finished his pint, walked over to the bar to get another (for which the barkeep would also not let him pay), and then headed over to the fishermen's booth and sat down at the single chair on the outside of the booth, after first turning it around so he could rest his arms on the backrest.

Ted Wadkins, the man who had waved him over, spoke to him quietly as though they were co-conspirators in some mischievous prank. The others leaned forward as if to block out any would be eavesdroppers.

"We heard tell about you," Wadkins said giving a nod in the direction of Kendall and the waitress. "We've been trying to find out what is goin' on over there ourselves. Nobody knows nothin'!" Wadkins raised the pipe to his mouth, inhaled then blew out a gray cloud of smoke. Then he leaned forward. "That is pure and simple rubbish, I says. What did you find out in Dover?"

"Not a bloody damn thing," Cyrus Wilson said.

Staring in Wilson's eyes, then briefly glancing around the pub as if to ensure no idle ears were listening, Wadkins said in a whisper, "We found a Dutch skoot, abandoned."

"We, the four of us, been watching it for three days now," a heavy-set, bearded man on his left intoned, after a quick gulp from his mug.

Wadkins gave him a look to get him to shut up and said, still eyeing him, "I figure some of the Dutch used it to escape, beached it up this estuary, and then couldn't get it free. They left it."

"Some bloody sailors," one of them said. The others stifled a laugh.

"So?" asked Cyrus Wilson, beginning to feel the beer, and not yet ready to make any new friends. "You're fishermen, ain't you? Don't you have a boat?"

"Some bloody minister..." exclaimed Bailey, the bearded man.

"That's ministry," explained Wadkins, with a little grin. "The Ministry of Shipping. They're requisitioning all sorts of boats. There's nothing we can do about it."

Cyrus Wilson shook his head, "Right. That's War Powers. I understand. What's your plan with the Dutch boat?"

The bearded man, younger than the rest, and not in the service because his was an essential job, could not contain himself any longer. Wadkins sighed and sat back for the ride.

Bailey managed to make a short story long, but the essential part boiled down to this: "We," the bearded man again gestured to include all his companions, "all of us here, we reckon to sail that skoot across the Channel, and pick us up some Tommies."

Wadkins nodded and said, "It's the least we can do. We have to help the lads. Right boys?"

All at the table echoed in a resounding, "Right!"

Cyrus Wilson was naturally suspicious, but he could not figure out what he should be suspicious about. For the last fortnight, he had been trying to find a way to help out as well, and, as it turned out, these were simply a group of true blooded Englishmen, who were going to do their utmost to be of service, and more importantly, they seemed to be inviting him to come along. Wilson was the only one among them who knew that if the rumors were true, it foretold of a crisis of immense proportions.

They sat around until dusk, drinking to each other's health, toasting King and Country, telling tales and jokes, and once in a while, patting each other on the back. At dusk, they got up—all except for Cyrus Wilson and Ted Wadkins were a bit wobbly—made their farewells and left. As they exited, Wadkins suggested that they watch the boat for a few more days. Nodding to Bailey, he said, "Maybe Bailey and I will see if we can find some way to hide that boat, disguise it."

"It's pretty big," Bailey said, laughing. He was pretty happy to be getting a real important job.

Ted Wadkins laughed himself. "I think we'll manage." He turned and patted Cyrus Wilson on the back in a good natured way, then motioned for his mates to follow him.

"We'll meet back here in two days."

"Why wait two days?" Wilson asked. "There's no sense in it."

"But I need time to disguise 'er," protested Bailey.

Wilson spoke simply and to the point. "Lads, if all I've been hearing is true, our boys might not have two days. We'll have the boat, but the Jerries will have the lads." He threw his hands palms up as if he had just defined an absolute answer to all questions. He cocked his eyebrows up to affirm the statement.

"From Dover, you can hear the explosions. There's black clouds of smoke all the way up the bleedin' coast. They're takin' it on the chin."

Bailey scratched his beard as if in deep thought.

Wilson could see he was trying to figure out some ingenious way of keeping his earlier mission. He also could tell that the others were puzzled. Perhaps they had thought of this adventure as a bit of a lark, because they had so much faith in the Royal Navy.

"You think it's that bad?" asked Wadkins, real concern on his face.

Cyrus Wilson pulled off his hat and slapped his knee with it for emphasis. "Bloody hell! I've been in the army my whole life! This is all I've been hearing, ain't it? The whole army's surrounded at Dunkirk with the bloody Nazis hurtling down on 'em. Could it be any worse?"

Each of the four sailors looked into the eyes of his mates, and something flashed in those eyes as they made up their minds. Cyrus watched this melding of minds with a fascination born of respect for these brave lads, and he was certain how it would turn out. A smile came to his wizened features as the sailors, as if with one mind, moved closer until they were in a small circle. They reached out and laid hand upon hand, like they were the four Musketeers—then Ted Wadkins broke the circle just to grab Cyrus by the arm and usher him in—and shouted, "Let's go! To the boat! To the rescue!" They then hugged each other in a warm sign of friendship and mission. Wadkins then gave Cyrus Wilson directions to a rendezvous.

"We'll meet in two hours," he said. 'Give the boys a bit o' time to sober up, and for me and Bailey, here, to round up some provisions."

Cyrus Wilson nodded his assent then stood, watching them leave. He wore the biggest smile he had had for days. Of course, though he would never admit it, in the back of his mind, he was coming to the rescue of the boy he considered his son, as he had done so many times. Like most parents, he could not get over the memory of raising a helpless little child, feeding them, cleaning them, providing them with all, and then not being able to give them their due as an adult because they still saw them as a child and still had to protect them.

And like any son or daughter, Wilson reckoned Hinton-Smith would be furious when he found out. At this he laughed.

It was now the evening of the first of June.

CHAPTER 18

# KEEP HEADING NORTH

ain pelted the ground and fell in ever thickening files. Even in the darkness, Hinton-Smith could make out thick columns of the downpour, pushed and buffeted by the wind and seemingly marching along with his every step. What a relief from the heat, he thought. He'd rather slog it out in this any day. The main roads were either still clogged with poor, miserable refugees or other retreating troops, and the lieutenant was well satisfied with the decision to keep to the fields. As the deluge eased up they happened onto a muddy pasture, so inundated with water, it took them a good three hours to cross, and he retracted his earlier affirmation. With each forward step, they sank into a foot or more of mud. They would painstakingly extricate the rear foot from the morass, shift it forward only to sink again. They plunged their feet in, then wrenched them out, over and over, and the lieutenant and the corpsman were carrying another man. It crossed Hinton-Smith's mind that the exertion alone would kill them. Like trying to traverse a patch of quicksand with an ox on your back. A good deal of time was spent stopping to help one another. Not one soldier managed to escape his turn at falling in the mud. The struggle to maintain balance and keep going assumed Herculean proportions, and by the time they reached the end of the field, everyone was exhausted, soaked and covered with muck.

With perfect timing the second wave of the storm hit, washing off a good deal of the filth, but when it stopped, the night cooled off and they cooled off as well. Their clothes were now soaked. All heavy coats and clothing had been abandoned at the front in Belgium, it had been so hot at the beginning of the campaign. There was no way to get warm except to keep slogging ahead.

In another brief lull in the storm, they spotted a deserted village, no lights, no people, no animals, carts or vehicles of any type. The few dirt roads had turned to mud, and steam rising from the still hot ground looked like vaporous ghosts out for a midnight stroll.

Carefully unfolding his worn out map, which had become soggier with each use, Hinton-Smith identified a small wood near Neuve Chapelle and placed them just north of it. No village appeared on the map and he realized the markings for it must have faded off from the moisture and use.

After passing through much of the village, the lieutenant saw an antebellum mansion rising specter-like out of the mist, with dual white marble stairways curving up to the second floor, and six massive white pillars supporting a second story balcony.

The torrents of rain began anew.

Hinton-Smith stared at the manor in disbelief. He once more looked at the empty space on his map, then up again at the foreboding edifice. *I've been here before. And with Jack. Holy Mother of God.* An involuntary shudder passed through his body. *We just came through St. Venant.* And he knew what was very close to that village.

The mansion was boarded up now. How could we come back to the very same area we explored in the spring? What are the chances of that happening?

He heard a faint voice. "Jesus Christ! Not this place. Mike. We ain't stopping here are we?" It was the sergeant. His voice sounded both pained and astounded. "You know what this place is?"

"I know. But the men are so bloody well exhausted. Everyone needs rest...That place, that...that cave. It wasn't that near the mansion, was it?"

"Close enough," the sergeant strained to say.

"Jesus! There's nothing for it," Hinton-Smith said. "We need shelter, and rest. Perhaps there's food inside."

Hinton-Smith shifted most of the sergeant's weight over to the medic and said, "Take him up to the porch, out of the rain. I'll see to the others."

"Right, sir," Hallow answered, pulling the sergeant's arm tightly over his own shoulder and starting up the steps.

"Wait," Cawkins said. Like an atheist caught in a foxhole, the sergeant, once more confronted with the cave, and in a much-distressed condition, was no longer so cocksure about the non-existence of ghosts or spirits or evil. He motioned for Hinton-Smith to come closer. "I don't like this," he whispered.

"Don't worry. We weren't even in the mansion before," Hinton-Smith said, looking down the thin line of men trudging up. "We'll be all right. That was a long time ago. No time to worry about it now. I have to post sentries."

"Me and the lieutenant visited this place before the war," Cawkins said to Hallow, as he helped him up the stairs. "It was after...well we didn't actually go inside."

"Take eight men," Hinton-Smith ordered Parker. "Fan out and reconnoiter the village. Leave one man on the outskirts on each side. I'll send others out to relieve them in an hour." He watched them leave, then followed the medic and Cawkins up the steps to the dry, covered porch. Graves and one other private followed close behind.

"Looks pretty cozy here," Hinton-Smith said. "It's retained some heat. What do you think?"

Hallow eased Cawkins down into an ornate deck chair, of which there were several. The sergeant closed his eyes and exhaled deeply with fatigue.

"At least it's dry," Hallow said, then stripped off his shirt and began to wring the water out.

"That's a good idea, isn't it?" Hinton-Smith said to Hallow.

"Let's try the door."

As Hallow fiddled with the lock, and then pushed against the door until it burst open, the lieutenant assisted the sergeant major out of his shirt and began to twist it. "I'm going to find us some towels, Jack."

Hallow turned on his torch and disappeared inside.

"Mike," Cawkins said in a curious whisper. "Don't bother. I think we should keep moving as long as it's dark."

"There's only a couple of hours before dawn. Tanks aren't going to cross those fields. We need the rest," Hinton-Smith replied as he draped the shirt over the sergeant's chest.

"Especially you."

Scratching his sore arm, then his leg, and shifting positions until he felt comfortable, the sergeant major managed a troubled laugh.

"Well, I ain't going to complain about the accommodations," Cawkins said, his last words trailing off as he fell asleep on the chair.

The medic came back onto the porch and mouthed the words, "Is he asleep?"

With Hinton-Smith's affirming nod, Hallow whispered, "Would you believe it? Not a single complaint."

"He's a master of the stiff upper lip. More English than we are."

"Right." Hallow said. "But I'm worried about the leg. Now, I'm no expert, but I'm out of sulfa and pretty much everything else as well. If we don't get him to at least a field hospital, he could lose it. I don't want to add to your problems, but that's my opinion."

He could *lose* his leg! Hinton-Smith had checked it and not thought the wound was that bad. "Are you certain?" he asked as he went over to Cawkins, opened the slit pants leg and stared at the bandaged leg. "How much time do we have?" the lieutenant asked, now more concerned.

"I covered the wound with the last of the sulfa. Three days at the maximum, I'd say. Maybe less."

"I'll let the men rest till dawn, then we're off. Jack will never forgive me if he loses the leg," the lieutenant said. But even before finishing the thought, he reconsidered. "Maybe we'll only rest for an hour then get moving."

The door swung wide as Private Graves excitedly ran out, something in his helmet. "Lieutenant! Lieutenant! Look! Eggs!" He brought a basket of about a dozen eggs and put it down on a chair in front of Hinton-Smith and Hallow. Both reached in simultaneously, grabbing an egg and then staring at it. Laughing, the lieutenant gently tossed his up in the air and carefully caught it. Hallow smelled his. "There's more," said Graves. "I found bacon, bread, coffee, and some sugar."

Hallow looked at the foragers with sincere respect. He turned to Hinton-Smith and said, "You Coldstreamers are the best."

"You ain't too bad a bloke yourself," Graves said. "I propose we make him an honorary Coldstreamer."

"Bloody hell, we'll make you an official Coldstreamer," the lieutenant responded.

Grinning from ear to ear, Graves added, "There's a wine cellar, sir. I found two cases of French champagne. I haven't had any of that since Paris."

"Cases? That'll cheer up the sergeant major," Hinton-Smith said. "But I remember you in Paris. We'd all be much better off if you stay far away from it."

"Sir," Graves said in a plaintive tone.

"Any whiskey? We might need an antiseptic. This place has everything else. Any medical supplies? Towels?"

"Didn't see any. Sorry, sir."

Parker came up the steps leading four of the men. Two of them lay out on the damp floor of the porch before he could deliver his report, while the other two sat with their knees up and their backs against the porch wall. All four were asleep in seconds.

"Sir. It's all clear. We found an old, beat-up truck parked in a warehouse on the east side of the village. I left one of the men. He thinks he can get it running, but its fuel tank is almost empty."

"We'll let them sleep a bit, then I'll send them out to see if we can scrounge up some petrol. There's a garage round back. Why don't you check on it after you eat something?"

"Right sir. How's this place, sir?"

Putting his arm around the corporal's shoulder, Hinton-Smith said, "I think it's got possibilities."

"Graves!" the lieutenant called out as he walked inside the mansion with Parker,

The private came to attention and yelled, "Sir!"

"Grab yourself something to eat, check with Parker on the location of the perimeter and spell the first watch in, say, twenty minutes."

"I ate, sir," said Graves.

"Sir. There's nothing more I can do for the sergeant major," Hallow said. "And I'd like to do my part, sir."

"Then both of you check the garage out back for petrol. Let me know. Then Hallow can take the watch. Somebody will relieve you in an hour."

"Yes sir!" Hallow saluted, and turned to leave.

"Hallow. Remember, when you're on watch, the whole company depends on you. If you close your eyes, you'll fall asleep...and if you fall asleep, I'll personally lead the firing squad."

"I'm not tired, sir." He turned and walked down the cellar steps.

Cawkins started awake and looked confused. It took him a minute to remember where he was, and another few seconds to realize he had just been dreaming about the very same place. He sputtered, "I don't like this place, Mike."

Hinton-Smith heard the voice and walked out to the porch.

"What's wrong? Do you want to go inside?"

"No, Mike. I'm all right. I just don't like it."

"Right. Well, we found some food. Let me know when you are hungry. I'm going to explore the rest of this place." Turning, the lieutenant headed for the door into the mansion.

Ten minutes later, Hallow and Graves returned, each lugging two five-gallon jerrycans, heavy with petrol, and headed inside. Cawkins stopped them from his chair. "Boys. Where do you think you're going with those? Are they full?"

"Yes sir," answered Hallow.

"What if they caught fire? It'd destroy the whole manor and us with it. Leave them out on the lawn. I'll let the lieutenant know about the petrol."

"Yes sir," Hallow said as he looked sheepishly at his mate. They turned around, went back down the steps and deposited the cans on the front lawn about forty yards from the porch. Then they split up to go spell the sentries.

Cawkins watched them as they left. "God almighty," he said softly. "You have to tell some of these boys everything."

Hallow walked through the deserted village unhurried by the still battering rain. Entering a tall barn-like structure he had been directed to, he looked around and saw a ladder up to a second floor. He would have a better vantage point from up there, so he climbed up and found a window facing the eastern approaches to the village, and pushed a heavy bale of hay over for a chair, by levering one corner forward, then the other, then repeating the process. He had stashed one of the bottles of champagne from the cellar in his kit, figuring to sneak a drink later. Removing it, he placed it between his legs and thought about taking a drink to warm up. His clothes were soaked through and the colder he got the warmer the bottle felt against his thigh. He lifted the bottle and looked at it. Very chilled and sorely tempted, Hallow knew if he took a drink now, he would fall asleep for sure.

"I guess you'll have to wait till we get to the beaches," he said, putting the bottle back in his bag.

The room lit up and seconds later he heard an enormous crack of thunder. Then, he promptly fell asleep anyway. Letting his eyes close just once, was all it took for him to drift off.

Hallow was still asleep, slumping down on the make-shift chair with his shoulder and head resting against the red wooden wall, and his legs balanced on the window sill, when Parker climbed up to the loft an hour later to take the next watch. Irritated as he was at seeing the sentry, who might be the only difference between life, death, or captivity, sleeping away, Parker decided right away he would not report it to the lieutenant—there was already enough disaster to go around. So he took out his anger by kicking Hallow's legs off the sill, causing the careless youth to fall off the bale of hay. It took awhile for Hallow to get his bearings. He coughed and scrambled to his feet. Parker went up to the window and looked out.

"Worried about that firing squad, eh lad?" Parker said grimly.

Neither man was aware of the silent gray shadows of the Wehrmacht skirmishers who were just then entering the village through the quiet, heavy mist.

The soldiers were fairly close when Parker first thought he saw movement.

"What is it?" Hallow asked, excitedly.

Parker squinted his eyes to see in the darkness. "Sshh!" he whispered. "Not sure. Could be more Tommies. Could be Germans. The rain's stopped again. Funny. Sky must have cleared. Moon's out." Keeping well back from the window opening, he strained to see any more movement.

"There," he said pointing down at the eastern approaches to the town. "Helmets are definitely German." There were two indistinct figures moving confidently down the road leading into the village. They were about two football fields away. "They look pretty careless. I guess they're not expecting to find any opposition. We better get back to warn the others," Parker whispered.

"What the hell are they doing out on a night like this when they don't have to be?" Hallow asked as he put one foot over the side of the loft, feeling around for the ladder. He quickly made his way down, and with Parker following, found an open window in the back, and hurried through it. Hallow was crouched with his gun at the ready, while Parker tumbled out.

"Okay, Hallow. You run back and tell them. I'll cover till I know you're away. Run fast, and try to be quiet. Keep to the north side of this street and don't worry about me. I'll be along. Go!"

Hallow tapped Parker's shoulder in a brotherly show of affection, then turned and ran off, staying gingerly on his toes like some maladroit gazelle, as though both trying to keep quiet and keep his feet dry from the standing puddles left by the storm. Parker shook his head as he watched him disappear, then he edged around the side of the huge, wooden barn to get a closer view of the enemy. Now there were four or five soldiers, only a hundred and fifty yards out, and slowly closing. Something faint was making noise and he could not quite discern its source, but he knew something else was out there. The metallic, whirring sound was somehow familiar. "Good Lord! Tanks!"

Parker quickly went back around the corner of the barn, stood with his back flush to the wall for an instant, considering a plan of action. Then he heard the first gunfire, and broke into a sprint. The firing grew louder as he neared the mansion. Turning a corner, he almost reversed directions mid-air, as he came within ten feet of running into the back of a German machine-gun team that must have gotten past their sleeping look out, and was now spraying the mansion with bullets and tracers.

Parker stared at the streaks of light coming toward him and heard numerous buzzing sounds pass him on either side, until he ducked, realizing those were bullets from his own mates. Angered, as though he could not divine any right the Germans had to be there, he didn't bother to duck down when he lofted a grenade. He watched as it exploded, destroying the German position and taking away that negligible right.

Searching his pockets for something white, he pulled out a handkerchief and, tying it to his rifle barrel, frantically waved it back and forth until his friends stopped firing. Then, after sprinting over the sixty yards or so of open ground, he took the steps up to the porch, two at a time, and yelled breathlessly, "Tanks! Tanks!" just as the first shell exploded on the ground outside the mansion, throwing up tons of earth onto the porch. Even as he yelled his warning, the lieutenant and the sergeant were rousing the men to action. Many were drunk or pretty close to it. Some men laughed as they ducked. One did not even bother to duck, and his head suddenly disappeared off his shoulders as another shell exploded nearby.

While the lieutenant looked for medicine on the upper floors of the mansion, some of the men had gotten into the champagne. One of the soldiers yelled out in greeting, "Prrarker me lad!! What's one bloody little old tank?"

Hinton-Smith and Parker pushed and nudged the befuddled soldiers to their feet. "Get the men out of here," he ordered. "If we get separated, same orders as usual. Keep heading north." Then the lieutenant motioned to Hallow to come over and help him gather up Cawkins. "Let's go!" he yelled.

The soldiers, though still a bit wobbly and not exactly jumping to the command, made ready to go. They had eaten and slept in their wet clothes. None had even taken his boots off. So they stumbled up, grabbing their weapons and ammo, and any foodstuffs within reach, and stumbled down the wooden stairs.

The men sprinted across open muddy ground as the explosions multiplied, tearing up the field with a Verdun-like frenzy, ripping huge furrows and creating moon-like craters. The rain had started anew and was coming down with a fury to match the shells from the

Panzers. Running as fast as they could on the boggy ground, Graves and Parker made for the first cover they could discern in the dim light: a small circular area that seemed to be partially surrounded by bits of wall, three to four feet high, and only 100 yards from the mansion. The other men hurriedly followed.

In the murky light, and pelted by heavy rain, they could not see they were heading for a small, ancient cemetery. The bits of wall were actually tombstones, four in all, set out in a semi-circle next to a tall grassy hill. Ten of the men made it to the tombstones and either dove over them or through the gaps to get to safety.

Hinton-Smith, bringing up the rear, was alarmed to see all of the men had hunkered down into this particular area. The semi-circle of headstones. Still, the current crisis was more in the forefront of his mind. What do they think they're going to do, make a stand against Panzers? They had used up the last of the anti-tank weapons days ago. Still shouldering Cawkins, he and Hallow hurried over to the edge of the circle of stones and crouched down. The lieutenant yelled, "Get out of there! It's a bloody trap. We have to run for it!"

No one stirred. To a man, they seemed to be paralyzed. As if some thing was holding them in the graveyard for its own sinister purpose. Hallow looked at one of the headstones and asked, "What is that? Is that a swastika?"

Cawkins's eyes were also drawn to the stone and he peered at it as if he was trying to make sense of an anachronism.

"Sanskrit," he muttered.

The bizarre spell was broken, as the mansion, looming behind the lieutenant, appeared to erupt. Hinton-Smith turned just as he heard an enormous crashing. A Panzer came rolling through the center of what had been a glorious manor, and was now just another shattered piece of rubble.

Hinton-Smith turned back and yelled, "Get out! Now!"

A puff of smoke left the muzzle of the Panzer's "88." The shell streaked to the cemetery sheltering the men as if it was on a guidance wire. It was a direct hit. The concussion knocked Hinton-Smith, Cawkins, and Hallow into what had become a gory, smoke filled hole. Another shell followed immediately on the heels of the first, hitting the mound directly above them and shearing off tons of dirt and rock to fall into the crater, now a smoking maelstrom of broken and smashed limbs. The Panzer moved on to wreak havoc elsewhere.

# CHAPTER 19

# THE CRATER

Colonel *LeFevre* winced from the memory as though with excruciating pain. His mouth twitched, sending the left half of his needle thin mustache jerking upward in a macabre salute. He trudged across a broad field, which lay plowed and ready for seed, but it would be a long time before any farmers began to harvest.

It was a dark night; the only light came from the stars, but it was not black enough to wipe out the vision in his mind's eye. The spasm, a recently acquired spasm, was not garnered from fear, but from anger and frustration. He remembered looking down from a hilltop position and seeing the long train of French prisoners. Try as he could, he could not forget the sight of the desolate, but insouciant, infinitely long columns stretching out in both directions over the horizon. He could not get them out of his mind. It was the worst feeling of helplessness he had ever experienced. He felt as though he wanted to grab every last one of them and shake them up and down and side to side until they would fight. He had never dreamed he would live to see the day when French prisoners would walk along with advancing Germans, with no coercion whatsoever; some still carrying their rifles which were periodically gathered up and crushed under the tanks; some wearing their kepis jauntily and joking and cavorting with their captors. It was more than a sin. Did they think it was 1870, when everybody just gave up? Or did they think the Germans were their Allies? What about their *real* Allies?

"It is all the fault of the British," he told the three young *poilus* who accompanied him as he slowly lowered his binoculars and returned them to a worn brown leather case.

If contempt for the British had been festering in the Frenchman for years, the debacle of the defense of Belgium, and the impending withdrawal of his English Allies from the Continent saw it rise to a boiling point.

He was one of the fighting commanders urging General Prioux to release part of the III Corps to join the British (after resigning himself to the first retreat), under the impression they were going to establish a beachhead at Dunkirk, keeping a presence near the Lowlands while the main fight went on in France, and thus offering a continuing threat to the right flank of the Germans. Also, and he begrudgingly admitted it, the Brits were the only ones putting up a fight, and he wanted a part of it.

Things went as well as one could hope, if you can extract any degree of consolation from being continually pushed backward until your only recourse is to jump into the sea, but it was better than not fighting. He happily tasted the acrid smell of battle and gave the English their due portion of respect for the competency and precision of the retreat. Then he heard that it was not simply a retreat to form the beachhead, but a total withdrawal from the Continent. First, he was astounded, then incensed, but too busy with fighting Germans to remonstrate with his British counterparts. Betrayal was the first and foremost word that came to his mind. Desertion the second.

His battalion finally made it to Furnes at 3 A.M. on the twenty ninth of May and was assigned a three thousand-yard front on the Bergues Furnes Canal line that helped form the Dunkirk perimeter. There, to his eternal humility, they were under orders to hold the line while His Majesty's Royal Navy evacuated as many of the BEF as possible. The idea was: "Let the French navy evacuate the French," and "the British evacuate the British," but, as per an earlier general agreement between the Allies, the better part of the French fleet was in the Mediterranean.

At 4 P.M. on May 31st, the order came down from Churchill himself that evacuation was to be equal, and *LeFevre's* battalion was ordered back to the beaches. It was not too big a difference in time, but up to then, before the orders for equality were literally forced on the British command, 150,000 British had been evacuated back to England; only 15,000 French soldiers had been taken out.

*LeFevre* immediately ordered his men to leave under the command of his attaché so he could stay. He made sure everyone, including the wounded (who he insisted were to be evacuated, over the harsh protestations of the British), left in time and in good military formation. Then, with the three young volunteers, who would not leave his side, he stayed and fought—although some of the Tommies who fought alongside him were not certain at whom he was really aiming his rifle.

When the last of the Coldstream Guards pulled out of Furnes (Hinton-Smith was still four miles south of the perimeter at this time), *LeFevre* made sure he and his men were the hindmost. He did it for *La Gloire*; like the Foreign Legion, or Hinton-Smith for that matter, he coveted the grandeur of the last stand. A day later, at La Panne, they were very close to the evacuation beaches, and, having felt he made his point, he decided he would save his three valiant followers, so they left with the last British defenders, but were separated and turned around during a ferocious assault by a squadron of Stukas. He and the three Frenchman were now like all other stragglers, alone, hungry, fatigued, and after desperate running from the bombing, further from the beach than they had been only a few days earlier. As with so many others, they would have been completely lost except for the gray, towering smoke surging out of Dunkirk, which, once the sky cleared, served as a beacon and guide, to what they thought was the haven of Dunkirk beach. The Germans were now closing in so fast, that it was quickly becoming an even bet whether or not *LeFevre* would even beat them to the beach, or if any ships would still be there when they arrived.

\*   \*   \*

When the lieutenant awoke, it was pitch black and very quiet. He tried to make out the time, but it was too dark to see his watch, and he did not realize he had been out for less than ten minutes. Hinton-Smith found himself in a sitting position, with his back reclining against the eastern wall of a newly formed crater. He noticed that the stones surrounding the crater were still standing, although one or two seemed to tilt at new angles. Instinctively looking around, he wondered where all his men had got to. A large fire had started and was slowly ascending the hillside. What was that? He could see a gaping hole in the *motte*, just about where he'd tried to enter a few weeks ago, and he could make out four more tombstones inside completing the circle. A larger stone was visible in the middle, cracked in two by the Panzer shell.

His attention now turned to what seemed to be a great weight on his legs, but his head ached and his mind wandered. He felt languorous, with a great need for sleep. The sky was very clear now, and he could make out a great many constellations that he had learned the names of long ago on campouts with Cyrus Wilson.

Next to him was Billy Graves looking as though he was asleep. Hinton-Smith strained to reach over and wake him. But as he grabbed Graves' arm, the private fell over. There was a huge gaping hole in his back. Billy Graves is already in his, ran through the lieutenant's head.

He wanted to find out what the weight was, so he put his arms back to prop himself up. Bodies, corpses were all he saw. Looking down, he screamed. There was a leg, still warm, and unattached to any body, lying on his legs. In revulsion, he reached down, grabbed the bloody appendage, and threw it away as he had thrown off a venomous snake.

Bullets whizzed by, then he heard shots. They must have heard my scream, he heard himself thinking, and chuckled in disbelief that he could be so rational when all his men, including Cawkins... "Jesus Christ, Jack!" he yelled out. All were lying there like so much useless rubbish. "I broke my vow, Jack. I'm sorry," he said in a low, anguished voice to the corpses in the hole. Feeling around, his hand grasped a gun. He stretched up as far as he could but could not get high enough to see. Then he extended his arms to put the rifle over the edge of the pit and emptied it in their general direction. At least six Germans opened up with all they had, exploding little pinpricks of dirt all around the perimeter of the hole, forcing him to bring the weapon down. The only articles of consequence any of the combatants managed to hit were three of the four jerrycans that had been left out on the front lawn of the mansion. They did not explode, but rather started leaking. This part of the lawn sloped downward towards the small cemetery.

Ducking back in the hole, Hinton-Smith gathered every weapon and all the ammunition he could reach, even though this meant going over his friend's bodies, and through their kits and pockets, just as he had coldly made them do a few days before. He found the Bren gun.

This is finally war, he said to himself. *Nothing could have prepared me for this. Nothing.*

The Germans now knew there was at least one soldier left alive, one who apparently wanted to fight it out. This caused some of their arrogance to fade, and caution to take over. They advanced slowly, staying low.

It was then that Hinton-Smith heard a faint whisper.

"Mike."

"Jack!" Hinton-Smith whispered back in disbelief. He would have recognized that voice anywhere, and he was never so delighted to hear it as the present moment. "Are you all right? Where are you?" He strained to see any movement in the crater.

Following the weak sound, Hinton-Smith finally spotted him on the opposite side of the large crater. He rolled over an unrecognizable corpse, to more easily reach the sergeant, but then realized he didn't have the time. Fighting back the tears that were welling up in his eyes, he swallowed and asked, "Jack. Can you hold out?"

"Sure, but I'm wedged in. I can't move," the sergeant groaned. He instinctively patted his arms, and then rubbed them as if he were cold. The stench from the burnt and torn bodies was overwhelming.

"Stay low, Jack."

"Lieutenant," called out Parker, from another corner of the crater. "I'm hit. I can't move my legs. Hallow's beside me. He's wounded in the jaw. He can't talk."

"Can you fire your weapons?"

"Yeah. I think both of us can."

"I'm going to bury myself over here and wait," he said, grimacing as he took hold of an unattached arm and placed it on his chest. "When the Jerries get curious and come over, we'll even the score a bit. Cawkins is over there, opposite me. Then I'm getting you all out of here."

"Just leave me," Cawkins said. "You can make it if you go right now."

"You should know me better than that, mate. Can't do it," Hinton-Smith said softly. "You know they're shooting prisoners, and that would make you quite unhappy. Now be quiet. We're about to have some visitors. Are you ready?" he whispered to Parker and Hallow.

"Check," Parker whispered back.

"Mike." Cawkins whispered, "Are you cold? Do you smell that smell?"

"What? Shsh. We have to be quiet. They're coming," Hinton-Smith whispered back. He put his finger to his lips to emphasize the point, checked his Bren gun, and then sat back to wait.

"Mikey," Cawkins repeated, trying hard to keep the fear out of his voice. "Don't you remember...the bottom of that cave? When it started to get cold?"

The last phrase stuck in Hinton-Smith's mind as he pressed his back to the crater wall, the automatic leveled at the ready across his chest. The phrase should have meant something to him, but right at the moment he was concerned with the Nazis. They were getting closer.

Cawkins saw it first. He blinked, two, three times, staring in disbelief, but there it was. About midway between the lieutenant and himself, something was moving among the dead and mangled bodies, pushing them up in some infinitesimally slow macabre dance as it moved under them. He wanted to believe it was another member of the platoon, still alive. But in his gut he knew it wasn't. Something was here with them and he was certain it wasn't human. He had to get out of there.

# CHAPTER 20

# THE D'JINN'S OUT

That same night, in one of those thick-as-pea soup fogs that has always characterized England, three other shadowy figures were taking their turns slipping and sliding down the banks of a river—actually more of an estuary—some fifteen miles east of London proper and just downstream of Gravesend.

Bailey slipped and started yelling as he tumbled downward.

"Blimey! Stop making all that racket!" Wadkins said. "You'll wake up every Home Guard twit in the country."

Cyrus Wilson looked at Ted with surprise and satisfaction. He had definitely found a man he could work with. Now he was certain their endeavor would succeed.

"Looks like your lads are still pissed," he said good-naturedly. Two of them had dozed off, nestled against the hull.

"They'll be all right once they get on the boat. They're used to it," he chuckled.

They heard a loud "thunk" as Albert Bailey found the skoot with his head. It was a fifty-foot, shallow draft barge, with an engine aft, and used to haul freight along the coast of Holland and up the rivers and canals, inland. Right now it was still partially grounded in mud: high tide was not due for another two hours.

Ted and Cyrus made it down the steep incline to the barge and waded out into the shallow water to where Bailey stood.

"Will this thing make it across the Channel?" Bailey asked, and then rubbed the bump on his head.

Cyrus laughed. Never had he felt better since he was a junior officer, full of strength and energy. "It had to get here somehow, didn't it?" But then he had second thoughts. He put his hand to his chin and rubbed it. "You lads did check it out, didn't you? It is seaworthy?"

"This is a good time to find out," Ted Wadkins said. "When the tide's out."

"Well, then, let's take a look," Cyrus said. "We ain't got nothing to do but wait anyways."

So the three of them slowly made their way around the barge, examining the hull of the ship with their hands and eyes.

It wasn't long before Wilson heard an exclamation from the opposite side of the skoot.

"Well lookee here," Bailey exclaimed, pleased to be the discoverer of the flaw. "Come here. There's an 'ole the size of a bicycle. Right here. Amidships."

Soon, the three men were examining the damage.

"What are we going to do?" Bailey whined. "We'll all drown if we take her out. Hell. She probably couldn't even make it to the Channel."

"Hm," Wilson said, as he felt the outline of the opening. "I wonder what caused this?" He wriggled out of his backpack. "I guess that doesn't really matter, does it. I brought some tools. Like Lord Baden-Powell said, "Be prepared. We'll just patch her up."

"But what can we use for a patch?" Bailey asked.

Wadkins playfully poked Bailey in the ribs. "I thought you wanted to be a sailor, Albert. What do you think we do when we have trouble at sea?"

"Damn right," Cyrus said. "Let's wake them other lads from their drunk and get to work. Most likely there are stores aboard, and if there ain't, we'll scrounge or rip up wood from the deck."

"Well let's get to it," Wadkins said. "Come Cyrus, I'll boost you up top."

As he helped Wilson get on board, he said, "Albert. You wake the lads."

By the time the others were on deck, Wilson had pried loose two benches and was separating the wooden slats from their metal fasteners.

"Check the hold for some sheet metal," Wadkins ordered. "Something solid and wide. See if there's a welding kit aboard and some nails."

"Aye aye, sir," Wilson said. Bailey smiled, repeated it and saluted, while the other two wiped the sleep from their eyes.

"You two help Cyrus carry the wood down to the hold," Wadkins said to the hung over, yawning lads.

After sealing the hole from the inside, the four of them climbed down and resealed it from the outside for insurance.

When they were finished, Ted once more gave Cyrus a boost up and onto the flat deck, then climbed up himself. Albert and one of the others passed up a couple of heavy boxes to Cyrus and Ted, and climbed up as well.

Opening one box, Albert started passing out bottles of stout. It was not long before the three younger men were drunk again, and then, asleep.

"I wonder if they should save a little of that courage for when they get across the Channel?" Wilson asked, wiping the sweat from his forehead. He had nothing against tipping a few, but they were presently going to need a different type of courage.

Ted simply nodded. "They'll be all right. I know 'em pretty well." Wadkins walked to the gunnels and looked over the side. Then he extended his view south toward the beach. By now, he could hear the waves lapping at the shore. "When we have a little more water under us...should be less than a couple of hours before we leave. I've already checked the engine. There's plenty of fuel."

He walked over to Wilson and put out his hand.

Curiously, Wilson extended his own. They shook.

"Funny," Wadkins said. "Me and the boys never thought to check the boat timbers. We might have all drowned if not for you. And me a sailor." Patting the old man on the back, he said, "Thank you, Captain Wilson."

"Ain't we all been at sixes and sevens for the last few weeks? Now we're going to do something about it. Right?" Cyrus Wilson walked over to the box of stout, bent over and reached in, taking out two bottles. Handing one to Ted, he made a toast.

"Here's to the Tommies...and blokes like you," he motioned to include the three sleepers, "who are man enough to bale 'em out of a rough spot."

"And to those dim Dutchies who had no idea of the tides hereabouts."

"Or how to fix a hole in a boat."

They clinked their bottles and settled down to tell stories and wait for the tide.

\*     \*     \*

Cawkins's mind flashed back to the cave. He never *had* made sense of the incident. No understanding, no rational explanation had presented itself. No matter how much he truly wanted to believe that something else had affected the lieutenant, doubts always remained, even to the extent of thinking Hinton-Smith wanted him dead. But now he confronted a very different truth, and realized how foolish he had been. He used every single bit of strength he possessed to try to move, and found every effort failing miserably. There was little power in his one leg and arm thanks to the wounds and he was wedged in like a cork in a bottle. The memory of a demonic presence that had tried to take over his mind came hurtling back into his consciousness, and was terrifyingly real. "Mike," he whispered loudly. "We gotta get out of here."

Hinton-Smith looked at him questioningly. "We can't," he whispered back. "The Krauts'll pick us off."

Cawkins looked back in the direction where he'd seen the movement. Everything was still. He hoped he was mistaken. He knew he was not.

"Mike. I'd rather be killed by the Krauts. You gotta help me. I can't move." Cawkins strained as hard as he could to extricate himself from the pile of bodies.

Parker and Hallow stared at the sergeant, then looked at each other questioningly, as if trying to divine the meaning of Cawkins's words.

"What are you going on about?" the lieutenant whispered, leaning forward to hear. The light in the crater flickered with the raging blaze. For brief moments he could see every part of the hole, but for others it was all in shadows.

Cawkins desperately tried to stand. He could move his upper body, but that was all. He used his arms to try to push himself free. "Mike," he whispered again, with urgency, pointing to where he had seen the last movement. "Look over there. Don't you remember where we are?"

Both men could by now hear the hushed voices and movements of the enemy. Hinton-Smith again pushed his back flush against the wall of the seven-foot-deep crater, and looked at the spot where the sergeant gestured. "Yes. I remember," he replied, but he had as yet made no connection. He was too absorbed with the imminent combat.

Parker and Hallow looked in the direction in which Cawkins's arm was pointing. "What is it?" Parker asked the corpsman. The depression, filled with the broken, tangled remains of the platoon was still. Then there was a movement, almost imperceptible, as though a part of one corpse jumped, but only just.

Cawkins tried twisting his upper body, as if it might free him. He was sweating profusely. The entanglement of dead bodies would not yield to his efforts.

"Mike," he whispered loudly. "You've got to help me. Please. I can't move." Cawkins desperately wanted to shout it out, but the Germans were too close.

Hinton-Smith looked to where the sergeant pointed. He saw nothing. He listened intently for the sound of the Germans, his finger tensing up on the trigger. Glancing back, there was something. Barely discernible. Something moved. Impossible! He stared at the spot for what seemed like an eternity. Nothing more. Wait! Now he saw it: the bodies on the other side of the hole, slowly began undulating up and down, as if something was burrowing a tunnel under them, driving them up, then letting them fall as it passed. But they were all dead. He was sure of it. They had to be. But then, when he first came to he had thought Cawkins, Parker and Hallow were dead as well. He strained to see, then he looked back at Cawkins.

"Maybe another one of the men is alive," he whispered back. "And buried under the muck." That is what he wanted to believe.

But Cawkins didn't buy it.

Parker had scarcely seen it—like something one catches out of the corner of an eye. He put it off to nervous palpitations of the dead men's muscles—the settling in of death. But neither he nor Hallow could ignore the look of sheer terror now on Cawkins's face. Then they saw that the undulation had started moving towards them.

Parker could not shift his legs either, try as he might. There was feeling in them, but they were wedged in too tightly by earth and other bodies.

"What are you talking about?" he whispered frantically to Cawkins. "What is it?" A sickening stench was making its way to his nostrils. His stomach felt ill. Hallow listened for the answer, but never took his eyes off the last place he saw the body parts rise. Both men now trained their weapons on that area.

The motion was drawing inexorably closer. It seemed to the soldiers to be an endless movement. A chill descended on the area immediately surrounding them.

The Germans were also edging closer. The Tommies could hear their guttural commands, and Hinton-Smith understood the command to flank their position.

"What is it?" Parker finally bellowed out. The Germans no longer mattered. He had to get out. He used every last bit of strength in his body to try to extricate his legs. He dropped his rifle and tried to haul himself out of the pit of corpses with his arms. Hallow, his face contorted with fear, followed the undulations with his rifle, as it neared Parker's feet.

"Don't shoot!" Hinton-Smith whispered. He still held to the hope it was one of his men.

But Hallow could hold back no longer and opened up, blasting the area with every last bullet, then continued pulling the trigger when he was empty—the clicking sound of the bolt filling the night air.

Still moving the forward, the Germans halted and crouched down, as they saw the flash of fire from Hallow's rifle muzzle.

Cawkins and Hinton-Smith waited helplessly. It would be their turn soon enough. They watched in terror as Parker drew his bayonet and frantically began digging into the dirt around his legs to loosen it. Hallow grabbed his own bayonet but started to saw through body parts holding him down. He cut through a torso and pushed the sides apart. This let him move about one foot upward, but no more. Both men now tore feverishly at the cadavers and dirt weighing them down, but to no avail. As the undulations drew nearer Hallow loosed a grenade from his ammunition belt. With tears born of desperation running down his cheeks, Hallow pulled the pin of the grenade and threw it at the last spot of movement. They saw Parker look dismally at them and then at Hallow, and then back to the cursed shifting carcasses. Parker crossed himself and started to pray as he pulled the pin from a grenade and cradled it close to his chest.

Cawkins and Hinton-Smith hugged the edge of the crater as the double explosion ripped apart the remaining corpses and detritus of the pit. When they opened their eyes, all was silent, and still. Hallow and Parker were gone, disintegrated, leaving no trace whatsoever. It was as though they had never existed.

The two men waited, breathlessly, as if the slightest sound might wake whatever was underneath the human debris. Even the Germans had stopped moving. They must have been thoroughly bewildered by the explosions.

Cawkins intently watched the area where Hallow had thrown his grenade. There was nothing. Minutes passed, interminably.

On the other side of the crater, Hinton-Smith could hear the Germans edging forward.

Cawkins still stared at the area. He thought he saw a movement, a twitch? But he was not certain. Maybe his eyes were playing tricks on him.

It started again. Now it shifted once more in Cawkins's direction. He had no idea how much more he could endure of this immutable and pitiless approach. The sergeant was nearing a state of panic. The oscillations were a scant six yards away, moving slowly, relentlessly toward him.

Hinton-Smith looked at him, then over at the moving burrow of cadavers, then back to where he expected the Germans to appear.

The Germans were getting close. He could hear them laughing. What would they be laughing about? Perhaps they were taunting them. And there was the unmistakable sound of jackboots hitting down on the wet, hard ground near the cemetery. He looked back helplessly to the sergeant, but he could not move. The Germans were too close. What was this thing? Then it hit him like a thunderbolt. It must be from the cave. How could he have not understood? It was so obvious. Come back to get the ones that got away. It was getting too close to Jack. He had to protect Jack. But what about the Krauts? *Bloody hell. Who will get us first?*

"Mike." Cawkins whispered. He was at the breaking point. Even though the thing was still five yards away, in its slow, measured advance, in his imagination he could feel it gnawing at his legs. It was a sickening feeling that any second something was going to reach up and grab on to his toes, or legs, or bowels. Like a nightmare where you try to use every ounce of strength, every bit of will, to even shift a fraction of an inch, but cannot. But this was real. He could not pull free. And there was certainly something coming straight for him.

The lieutenant heard the desperate plea. *What of his oath?* He had to do something. Now! He too would rather die at the hands of men. Slinging the Bren gun across his back, he tossed the shattered legs and arms off his chest and started crawling over the slimy, blood-drenched carcasses, the once-living bodies of comrades, toward Cawkins. He did not know if he could reach him first.

Hinton-Smith saw the trail of grisly body parts rising up and down, so glacially slow, but so inexorably towards the sergeant. It made him physically ill. It took him a very long time to reach Cawkins. Then he stood, hunched over, to get a better base for pulling Cawkins loose. He heard an order in German and knew he did not have much time left. Bending over and grasping Cawkins under the arms, he pulled as hard as he could. One of Cawkins's legs was stuck and would not budge. The deadly movement was only three yards away, and Cawkins was so panicked as to be no help at all. Like a drowning man, he grasped onto whatever was near, hindering the lieutenant's attempts to free him.

Hinton-Smith heard the Germans cocking their weapons. It sounded like they carried burp guns. They were almost to the edge of the shell crater, their torch beams crisscrossing the small area like search beams looking for airplanes. Through the thick haze, he could make out six beams of light. Probably SS with my luck, he thought. *With my luck?* He couldn't believe his own thought. What an idiotic idea that was? *I'll make my own luck.*

And with that thought, Hinton-Smith became more determined than ever. He got down on his knees and pushed one of the inert bodies off the sergeant. Then, ignoring all pity for the dead, he took hold of the unrecognizable form of what had been the bottom half of one of the men, withdrew his knife and began to saw through it. Every breath was labored. It felt like he was nearing the end of a marathon as he strained over every draw of the blade. Tears ran down his mud-covered cheeks, but there was nothing for it. Finally it gave way. He was certain it was the last obstacle pinning Cawkins in. Tossing aside the severed leg, he screamed as loud as he could, "Come on, man. You've got to help me. Use your arms. Push!" and with a final burst of adrenaline, he wrenched Cawkins free.

Edging to the hole, still steaming with smoke from the explosions, the Germans began to enfilade the far side of the crater with fire. They peered through the murk to see the resultant chaos, keeping their weapons raised in case there were any survivors.

Just then, another Panzer crashed through what remained of the manor. As they instinctively turned to look, Cawkins and Hinton-Smith saw a dark wraith emerge from the rubble of bodies in the crater. It seemed to be covered all in black and they were certain they could see right through it. Had this pushed up the corpses? It couldn't have, the lieutenant thought. It had no corporeal substance that he could make out, and he wondered how it could have moved the dead and mangled bodies in the hole. As Hinton-Smith climbed up the slanted side of the hole, struggling to pull the sergeant, he wondered what the bloody hell this thing could be. He had never in his whole life imagined anything like it.

But now he had to return to more mundane matters, such as when the German bullets would start exploding into his body.

Hinton-Smith realized he would never be able to pull Cawkins out, so quickly he ducked back into the crater and began to lift the big man's legs over the top, thinking to lever him, but then slipped back down himself. There was no solid foothold in the sticky, blood-soaked mire. And there were still six Germans and one Panzer to worry about.

Bullets started raking the crater, edging closer to the lieutenant. The dreadful phantom was moving closer. As Cawkins gazed on helplessly, Hinton-Smith pushed Cawkins's torso over the rim, then, with his last bit of strength pulled himself free.

The apparition seemed to tear something from its own head, revealing an almost human-like visage. Heaving the mask away it then turned its attentions toward the Germans, seemingly drawn by the flashes of light from their gun muzzles.

Amidst the furious gunfire, Hinton-Smith struggled to move the sergeant, finally rolling him behind one of the tombstones.

The German soldiers continued firing at the bodies inside the pit as the Panzer roared up, closing the distance. Some of the shells ignited the petrol that had slowly seeped into the crater, causing a fire to start in the hole. The Panzer stopped its advance, as a mist seemed to push forward and envelop the six soldiers in front of it.

The German soldiers were suddenly jerking in terrible paroxysms. Even in the murky light, Hinton-Smith could see their faces twisted in agony as though they were caught in the hands of some terrible fiend. He could hear their dreadful screams over the roar of the tank. Suddenly they began to turn their weapons on each other.

Hinton-Smith stood with his mouth agape while holding Cawkins, who was too weak to stand or move on his own.

The lieutenant stared incredulously. *How could this be happening?* He could only stare at the strange conflagration. He still did not believe his eyes. Some of the Germans turned their fire towards the tank. One shot—a million to one shot—pierced the glass of the tank driver's scope, following the tubing down to his eye, instantly killing him. He slumped forward on the gears and the Panzer started moving as his commander, who was watching the horrendous scene from his perch in the turret, yelled at him to stop. It was too late. The Panzer continued forward, moving across the gas-soaked ground.

As the soldiers in front of Hinton-Smith seemed to disintegrate the Panzer caught fire.

"Get out, men," the German commander screamed as the tank lurched ahead, then crashed down into the steaming crater. He was halfway out when there was a tremendous explosion, showering the area with shrapnel and detritus, and slaughtering the commander and the rest of his crew. A massive violent flow of fire hurtled upward and the entire crater was sealed in molten steel.

The stress of his wounds and their narrow escape caused the sergeant to pass out. Hinton-Smith lofted him up and swung him over his good shoulder. Quickly, he looked back to see if the apparition was still there, but saw nothing. Looking toward the rent hole in the mound, he saw the center stone, broken in two. There was strange lettering on the two half-stones and the lieutenant recognized it as Aramaic. He was able to translate the first words, but noticed more beams of light coming from the direction of the mansion. More Germans. Hinton-Smith briefly glanced into the hole once more then turned and trudged off, heading north. The scene of spectral devastation remained in his mind's eye for some time.

*   *   *

It was not an easy task, carrying a man who out weighed him by at least two stone, even though he had, at first, easily slung him over his shoulder like a large gunnysack of flour. He remembered thinking how strange it was, that carrying a dead weight, say a bag of flour or sugar, as he had done at a night time factory job in London for a little spending money, seemed much harder than carrying his live friend, even though Cawkins weighed more than twice as much. It did not take long for that idea to change.

The first night was the worst, when the wholesale destruction of his platoon was still fresh in his mind. Everything was still wet from the rain, and it was back to feeling like he had to pull his foot out of quicksand with every stride. In the first two hours, it seemed as though he made no distance at all, and after the first hour, his adrenaline had dissipated as the urgency to save Cawkins receded to the plodding reality of each step forward. He felt as tired as he had ever felt in his life, and his wounded arm began to ache and bleed afresh. It seemed that he was breathing so hard, that any German for miles around could hear him. His heart was pounding. The necessity of stopping for a rest hit him with every tug of his shoe from the soft earth, but he compromised by lowering his head and shifting Cawkins over to his left shoulder and carrying him there for awhile, managing the adroit movement without changing pace, though he heard a quiet groan from the sergeant.

It had taken a whole hour for his right shoulder to get tired. After shifting the sergeant, he moved his right shoulder around, forward and backward to loosen it up, but he was worried because it only took a half-hour before his left shoulder was begging for relief, and he had to do the whole movement in reverse. He tossed the Bren gun and ammo aside. If he ran into more Germans he'd have to make do with his revolver.

The first night he managed to make Hazebrouck, skirting it on the southeast, as he was not sure in whose hands the city now belonged. Right now, that first night seemed easy. Exhausted as he was at that time, it did not begin to compare with how wretchedly done in he was now. They had not eaten since the mansion, and what he took, he was parceling out to the sergeant. He was starving for food. Finally, concerned that he would not be able to keep going, Hinton-Smith ate half of a biscuit. He had managed a few hours of sleep during the last day, but was woken up by a scream—Cawkins yelling deliriously. It sounded as though he was having nightmares as well. The lieutenant was able to quiet him down, but then all thought of sleep was gone, so there was nothing for it but to start forward again, avoiding all major roads and villages, and only stopping once to forage from a deserted farm house.

The second night was clear and starry; there was no more rain, and the ground was firmer under his feet, the going easier. As he trudged along, Hinton-Smith kept hearing a strange, metallic, whirring sound that grew louder and louder till he realized it must be the sound of a whole armored division.

It was as good an excuse as any to stop and rest.

When it began to grow lighter, Hinton-Smith saw they had reached yet another canal, the Loo Canal. He eased Cawkins down, propping his head against a large, twisted, tree root that had managed to break free of the earth. Cawkins spoke his first clear words in two days. "Where are we?" he asked.

"Almost to Dunkirk. We're almost there."

"Do you have anything for my leg? It's pretty sore."

"I don't. I'm sorry, Jack. How bad is it?"

"I don't want to hobble about on one leg, Mike."

There was a quiet, yet strong resolution in the lieutenant's reply. He knew what Cawkins was getting at. "You won't. I promise."

"Leave me for the Germans, Mike."

"Okay," he said, waiting for the sergeant's reaction, then adding, "Just having you on, mate."

"Right," he groaned, but there was a hint of a smile. "Maybe you should just shoot me."

"No, old boy," Hinton-Smith said. "But if the Germans catch us, I'm relatively certain they'll oblige you. They're not going to take time to nurse the wounded."

He remembered there was one canal that flowed to the sea, but he could not remember the name. He took out his map and found the canal, hoping it was the right one and he could float the two of them down to the coast. Unfortunately, the Loo Canal angled away from Dunkirk, and he guessed that it came out behind German lines to the northeast. The outer lines of the BEF were hopefully not too far from the other side. Hinton-Smith wondered if it was worth the risk, bobbing up and down on the surface of the water. Almost sitting targets, but probably no riskier than any other course. And it would save what strength he had left. And it might bring them a bit closer.

He opened a tin of bully beef and gave it to Cawkins.

"Time for a bit of reconnaissance. I'll be right back," he said. He patted the sergeant on the shoulder, and then slid down the embankment on his behind, until he reached the water's edge. Taking off his boots and socks and stripping down to his skivvies, he wanting to keep his clothes dry, now that they finally were. Hiding the clothes under a downed tree, he entered the water.

The Germans had hastily thrown a low pontoon bridge across the canal to take the place of a noble old suspension bridge destroyed by the retreating Allies. Tanks, armored cars, troop carriers and motorcycles with sidecars, interspersed with a column of horse-drawn artillery were clanking and clattering across the pontoons in an endless stream. They were part of the 1st Panzer of Guderian's XIX Corps. The lieutenant made a mental note of various insignias.

Cursing himself for not having saved any explosives, Hinton-Smith searched for any other option, even swimming down to the old bridge to see if any loads had not gone off. Unsuccessful, he hurried back, realizing their present position would be discovered as soon as the sun was up: it was too easily seen from the pontoon bridge, though everywhere he looked was open ground, no cover. He had noticed what might make a good hiding place between the floats under the pontoons, but discounted that idea immediately. They would have to stay in the water and that would be worse for Cawkins's leg. Nearer to them was the debris from the original bridge. There were broken columns of concrete, some crumpled to the canal banks and above water. There had to be cover there.

The lieutenant helped Cawkins out of his clothes, then made a bag out of his own shirt into which he put both men's boots and clothes. Easing Cawkins into the water, and, using his left arm to cradle the sergeant and keep his head above water, Hinton-Smith carried the bag up high with his other hand, and slowly glided them downstream to the rubble.

Finding a sheltered nook under the two concrete pillars that had landed and somehow formed an inverted V, they hid underneath them for the whole next day, listening to the unending traverse of the armor across the pontoons, and praying they would not be spotted by the Germans, or crushed by the collapse of the V. Luckily, the water was shallow at this point and never rose to their hiding place. That whole day from morning until night, the Germans kept marching, unhindered, over their makeshift bridge, which rumbled and shook like a giant, unending earthquake.

Where in God's name is the RAF, Hinton-Smith wondered? What a bloody good target.

Cawkins's fever came and went, but his muffled screams could not be heard over the roar of the German armor, and Hinton-Smith managed to wake him when the fever broke.

It was during this time that Lieutenant Michael Hinton-Smith made a decision. During the whole time he carried the sergeant, he forced himself to only think of his oath, and of moving ahead—one more step, then another, then another. He had been afraid the burden, the pain in his shoulders and back, might weigh into any decision he made, but now, after a day of relative rest, he felt he could think over his alternatives objectively. Even though the vow weighed heavily on his mind, he knew the main consideration had to be the sergeant major's leg. Carrying the larger man, he knew it would take him at least two to three more days to travel the distance to the beach. He thought he could make it, but by that time, Cawkins's leg would be gangrenous at best; more likely, the poison would have spread by then to his whole body, and Jack Cawkins would be dead. If he left the sergeant to be found by the Germans, the best scenario was Cawkins would spend the rest of the war in a prisoner of war camp, and who knows if they would take the time to save his leg. Most likely, according to the rumors he heard was they would simply shoot the sergeant. Why waste time and energy on a wounded enemy? After all, we're talking about Germans, here. The blokes that coined the term "franc tireurs" during the First World War, for basically anyone who fought back, and then shot them as terrorists, and also shot hostages from any nearby villages as accomplices. Who was to say they would not be as nefarious this time around? The only solution that made any sense was for him to hide the sergeant in a safe spot, and make a mad dash for the beach— he figured he could reach Dunkirk, get some medicine and a couple of soldiers to help, perhaps even a vehicle, and be back before morning. The medicine was the important factor. He made the decision, but before telling Cawkins, he first wanted to make sure the sergeant was coherent. He wanted to give him the opportunity to weigh in. Hinton-Smith asked him a question that he knew Cawkins would respond to unless entirely disabled. Still a bit unsure about himself when it came to the subject of the cave, he said in a halting voice, "We need to talk, about the cave, don't we?"

Cawkins looked up at him and said gruffly, but in his usual straightforward manner, "Ok. Tell me your story."

For Hinton-Smith, those few simple words brought tears and a tightening of his throat. He could hardly speak, and took a few seconds to formulate his thoughts and words, and clear his voice. He had no way of knowing the sea change in the sergeant's thinking that had occurred in the graveyard. Finally, with a great exhalation, he began, building the story slowly, logically. "I went back for our gear, and I already told you about the church. That is where I went next. I wondered if they might have any records. I found a parchment with the insignia of the Templars. There were birth dates and burial dates, and another insignia, partially worn away, a Maltese Cross. These dates were laid out in a pattern, roughly matching the scheme of the cemetery we found. I realized the whole cemetery had originally been hidden in the hill, or *motte* as you called it. I found the parchment hidden in the walls of the church, by the way."

"What does that have to do with the cave?" Cawkins asked, turning and adjusting his back to the uneven ground.

"A local professor told me the history of the Hospitallers, a rival group of knights to the Templars, but he was as puzzled as I. I started to ask myself questions. Why hide the cemetery in that hill? Why destroy all memory of it and the persons interred? Even on the parchment, everything was defaced. Why were at least four of them buried on the same date? Later, in Lille, I tried to find out if dead crusaders were ever shipped home. That would make sense. They could all have died on the same date in a battle. But from what I could gather, only the highest of the nobility would have received that treatment. Do you know how long it would take to ship a dead body home from the Middle East? To England or France? In those days? At least five months on a ship, and that was the only way feasible. And there were so many of them." Now, he became excited. "It just dawned on me, like an epiphany—there was something in there with us. In the cave. Why? Because I felt it. And I felt it again when I tried to go back in there. Didn't you feel anything?"

"You tried to go back in there?" Cawkins asked, sitting up.

"Yes, and I can only describe the feeling as a sense of pure evil,"

Hinton-Smith said. "The most wicked, odious, foul hatred I've ever felt. And it was inside my head."

Cawkins breathed in deeply and let it out in a rush. "I saw it in your eyes," he said. "That night. When you tried to bash my head in, I saw something in your eyes...well there's a mouthful for you. You tried to bash my head in. Whew. What I saw wasn't human. I thought I was imagining things. I didn't know what it was then...I still have no idea."

Hinton-Smith looked at the sergeant incredulously.

"You felt it as well?"

"Yes, but I couldn't believe it. I began to feel hate in there, just hate for no reason. Then your actions, your attack. I couldn't make sense of it. You're the only person I'd even tell this to. I spent the rest of the mission trying to figure out what happened, and, get this," Cawkins managed a grim smile, "watching my back. I even tried to get a transfer when we returned."

"I would have," Hinton-Smith said honestly, and he could not help shuddering. "You felt hatred as well? Bollocks! But you didn't act on it. Why would it affect me that way, but not you?"

"I don't know," Cawkins said as his left hand automatically fingered the little silver vial that hung around his neck on a black, woven cord. "Maybe it was this. The *Pancha Ayudhaya* that I told you about. That I got from a holy man in India. These were also inscribed on those tombs. How's that for a coincidence?"

"I just don't know. Maybe I'm just a might more cynical than you Mike. Not as open."

"Perhaps that's what they call a ghost," Hinton-Smith said. "Some kind of infernal energy. Something that's hung around that cave for ages. I have a lot more investigating to do when this bloody war's over, and I'm going back there someday. I want to find out how four, and possibly eight Knights of St. John died, all on the same date, in the same place, at the same time."

"You're beginning to sound like me," Cawkins said. "I'm familiar with the Templars," the sergeant continued. "At the highest level of the order were guardians of occult knowledge. I've heard they received this knowledge from the East—the Himalayas, Tibet, and that fits in with the Vedic symbols we saw. But who knows for sure." He coughed. "They were supposed to have been the guardians of the Holy Grail. They took vows of poverty, chastity, and obedience, the same as monks, but as the order grew, rogues, robbers, and murderers were accepted, as long as they repented their acts. The funny thing is, that two centuries after the group's founding, the Templars owned nine thousand manors in France alone. Some poverty, eh." Cawkins chuckled, but this led into another spell of coughing. It took him a bit to clear his throat. "They were supposed to be subject to the Pope, but really answered only to their Grand Master." Cawkins stopped. He grimaced in pain and rubbed his leg.

"Take it easy, Jack. You need to rest."

"No. I'm ok. These guys were rumored to worship a Middle Eastern idol, Baphomet. That would've put them in good with both the Moslems and Christians. The Pope decided he'd had enough. He and Philip IV also decided they could use their wealth, so they seized most of their leaders, and made them admit to certain heretical practices under torture. Then they took their holdings."

"And we think we got it bad."

"Mike. Maybe our ghost was a Templar."

"A knight," the lieutenant echoed. "But how could he still be alive after all this time?"

The Templars were mentioned in the same breath with alchemy, the philosopher's stone. Do you know what that means?"

"Something about turning lead into gold?"

"That's right. But it was also supposed to give the knowledge to eternal life. What do you think about that?"

"I think we could both use a guarantee of that sort right about now," Hinton-Smith said, leading to a laughing fit that was so hard they had to stifle each other before they were heard by the Germans. It was the first time they had really laughed together since the "incident."

The lieutenant suddenly became very serious. "The professor said the tombs were dated fifty years after the last of the Templars. Whatever it was, it killed the Germans back there. But what's strange is, I think that it saved our lives. The thought came into my head back there, and I can't shake it."

Cawkins raised his eyebrows and looked up at him. "I think we should be happy we made it out of there, twice. You should let it go. As for me, I'm convinced."

"There was something else," Hinton-Smith said. "When I tried to go back into the cave, this voice came into my head. It said, "Highgate.""

"Like in London? In the north?" Cawkins asked with surprise.

"That's the only Highgate I know of."

When the sun went down, it left in its wake, glorious hues of orange, red, and purple. Smoke from the battles had functioned as a gigantic prism as it rose in the air, forming some of the most beautiful sunsets in the lieutenant's memory. When the last shades of crimson had faded, Hinton-Smith wakened Cawkins. He explained what he was going to do and why as he transferred the remaining biscuits and tins of bully beef from his pack. He took two biscuits for himself. Taking Cawkins's hand in his, Hinton-Smith stared at him. He squeezed Cawkins's hand tightly and said, "I'll come back for you, Jack. No matter what. I promise."

"This is the only way, Mikey," Cawkins said. "You go and Godspeed."

Hinton-Smith pulled a worn, soggy piece of paper from his shirt pocket, carefully unfolded it and handed it to Cawkins.

"Here. It's the rubbing from the parchment. Something to keep you busy."

And with those words spoken, he edged down to the water, waded in and pushed off to the other side.

Cawkins knew the lieutenant was doing the right thing, playing the percentages. He knew Hinton-Smith would do everything in the realm of possibility to return, and he also knew that he would be able to tough it out.

Straining to get up on his elbows, he watched the shadowy figure of Hinton-Smith disappear up the bank on the opposite side of the water, then resolutely leaned back against the broken shards that once formed the eastern part of the Loo Canal bridge to wait it out.

At least he was far away from that goddamned graveyard and whatever son of a bitch was in it, he thought, trying to pick up his spirits.

He felt the loneliest he had ever felt in his entire life.

# CHAPTER 21

# DENTAL WORK

That morning, Matthew Boyden woke up groggily to the sound of his alarm. He had not been able to get to sleep the previous night. Too excited. So he lay in bed, his mind racing, going over every possible scenario, until he knew the only way to slow it down was to open a well-read copy of Livy, which he perused until he could no longer keep his eyes open. That was around four in the morning. Now it was close to seven.

He put on a robe and slippers, lit the burner, and placed a teapot on the stand, dumping half a handful of tea leafs in the water. Slicing a thick piece of bread, he spread it with mango jam and sat down to wait for the water to boil. He drank the tea, with a spot of milk to give it a light brown color, then ate the bread and jam, and washed it all down with a pint of ale.

By half past seven, he was dressed, complete with knee brace and his Livy—he always carried a book with him, just in case he had to wait for somebody. He hated to waste time.

He boarded the Northern Line, sat down and read. Today it was Book XXII: Cannae.

It was quite a good cover wasn't it? Everybody had to have his teeth checked. A dentist. Quite clever. And not too far from his place of work or residence. Of course. He hoped they'd be clever. He didn't want to be shot as a spy on account of their carelessness. If he were responsible for getting himself caught, it would serve him right.

Saturdays were always to his liking, though he would've preferred to sleep late. But then, what was a little hardship for the good of King and Country.

There were only four stops to Warren Street, where he caught the train for Oxford Circus. Leaving the station, he only had to walk two blocks to the dentist's office, and conveniently, it was on the first floor.

Boyden knocked on the door, then entered. There was no receptionist, so he rang the little bell that sat on the front desk, and sat down and opened the book to his faded bookmark.

Within minutes, a heavy-set man, every bit the English gentleman, with ruddy cheeks, a jutting chin, and a thin, perfectly trimmed gray mustache to match his greased-back gray hair, and sporting a natty beige tweed jacket with elbow patches, came out and ushered Boyden into his office. So much the Englishman, that Boyden was a bit apprehensive to say anything incriminating as he was whisked along.

The dentist, who went by the name Ned Hoarsley, smiled thinly, exhibiting an attitude of superiority. He asked "Just a cleaning today, sir?" which served as the start of a recognition sequence, to put Boyden at ease.

"No, no. I have a terrible toothache today," Boyden said in response.

"Left or right?"

"Right"

"Bottom or top?"

"Top."

"Molar, wisdom, or incisor?"

"Wisdom."

"Right. Everything seems to be in order, sir. Come and sit down in the chair. I have only one other appointment today, and that is not for two hours. But it is a good idea to treat you as though you are a real patient." Hoarsley laughed. "Nervous, what? *Ja.* I'm German. Born in Cologne in 1895, I was asked to come here after the last war, went to school here, and stayed. I was contacted to begin work after the revival under der Fuhrer."

Boyden wasn't so nervous about the man's identity any more; he was wondering just how realistic the dental treatment was going to be. A German dentist is sure to be precise, but probably painful, as well. He sat down in the chair, anxiously noticing every detail of the doctor's equipment, but instead of prying in his mouth, Hoarsley cleared his throat as if to make way for a momentous announcement. He looked rather pleased with himself. It must be important.

Then, he rubbed his hands together, placed a towel around Boyden's neck, and said, "Open your mouth."

Boyden did.

"Wider." Hoarsley leaned over Boyden and looked in his mouth, with a dental mirror. "Not too bad," he said. He affixed a metal dental prop to Boyden's mouth to keep it open, and packed cotton between the upper and lower lips and the gums. "Don't worry. It will just be a cleaning." Then, he handed Boyden a sheet of paper on which was a single sentence:

Find out everything about *Guillaume de Belfort*. 12th Century A.D.

Boyden took the piece of paper and had to look twice at the message. He wasn't quite sure what to think. "You want me to do what?" he tried to ask, raising his voice a little in wonder, but garbling the words because of the device.

The doctor put his finger to his mouth in the manner of shushing the classicist. Very calmly, in a most congenial manner, he laughed, then cautioned, "Don't get excited, lad. What did you think you were going to do? Blow up Westminster Abbey? This is an intelligence gathering operation. If that's what they want, that's what they want. Do you know who this is?" Hoarsley asked, smiling in anticipation of the answer.

"No. I have no idea," Boyden answered. "What would a man who died eight hundred years ago have to do with us?" A slight bit of exasperation began to show in Boyden's tone.

Hoarsley raised his eyebrows in a condescending manner. "The name came to the *Ahnenerbe* through a séance. You know this, the *Ahnenerbe?* It serves as the SS Occult Bureau." Hoarsley chuckled. "Some explanation might not hurt. In those early days, just before the invasion of Poland, there were those among the leaders who were slightly nervous. They wanted to see where we were headed. *De Belfort* was, let's say, an accidental and welcome surprise."

"You want me to trace a name you found in a séance?" Boyden

asked incredulously. He pried out the cotton with his fingers, and took the dental prop out, spitting in a proffered cup. Raising his voice, he sputtered out, "What the bloody hell's this got to do with the war effort?"

"Quiet!" Hoarsley exclaimed, once more raising his forefinger to his lips. "Yours not to reason why, my dear chap." Hoarsley loved using Anglicisms, especially when the result was effectively hoisting an Englishman on his own petard, and an Irishman was close enough.

"Blimey O'Reilly! Hitler wants to invade, right? He needs information on beaches, tides, weather patterns, not to mention military information, troop dispositions and numbers, mines, gun emplacements, airfields, battleships..."

"Stop!" cried Hoarsley, standing tensely as if in any second the whole of MI5, the spycatchers of British Intelligence, would rush into his office. "Do you want to compromise me?" The top of his brow began to sweat profusely. "Why do they send me amateurs?" He leaned forward as if to run up and lock his hand over the reckless young man's mouth. In an angry loud whisper, he asked, "Do you have any idea how many of our agents have been lost due to carelessness, and lack of training? You've received no training, am I right?"

"I had two weeks of training..."

"Two weeks," Hoarsley sneered. "I've been in this country since the end of the last war. Do you know what my guiding light has been? Do you?" Before Boyden could respond, Hoarsley answered for him. "Caution is the order of the day." He waited to let it sink in. "We don't take risks, and that includes speaking loudly in my office. Do you understand? You put our very lives in jeopardy, inviting the hangman." Hoarsley reached into the front pocket of his jacket, pulled out a folded handkerchief, and nervously wiped his brow. Regaining his composure, he asked, "Do you have any idea how careful I've been? How thorough my cover?" Sitting down while waiting a response, he wiped his brow once more. Boyden could only shrug his shoulders.

"I'm a member of committees, organizations," Hoarsley continued. "I'm on the board of directors of banks and charities. I'm even in the bleeding Home Guard for Christ sake. I have taken nothing for granted."

Hoarsley had been made to deal with a few eccentrics in his day, but at least they followed orders, and he had always managed to keep his identity a secret. A look of dismay settled in on his fleshy features. "This is a good mission. Just a little academic research. What could be easier? Or safer? No risk of life and limb. I have an expert, ready at hand. Send him to the library to study." Even though he knew he was dealing with an Irishman, a member of an extremely independent and execrable race—to Hoarsley, every race that was not German was execrable, although the Irish just now seemed a wee touch more—he was used to people obeying orders with no questions asked. This reluctance, and questioning on the part of an underling was unconscionable, but he made a conscious effort to be politic. In a calmer tone, he asked, "It's your specialty, is it not? And they obviously thought it important enough that we meet in person. You are aware that isn't done very often? Indeed, it is quite the exception."

"All right. Just what is it I'm supposed to do?" Boyden asked with a sarcasm that was lost on the literally minded German.

"You are probably not aware," Hoarsley said, as a glint of satisfaction returned to his expression, "but we have succeeded in narrowing down the location of *de Belfort*'s final resting place. It is in England. In one of your old cemeteries. Our people have done this from Germany. Now we need you to find the exact spot."

"Certainly you will not mind my asking why?" said Boyden.

"No. No. Of course not," Hoarsley said, now warming to the subject. He leaned forward conspiratorially to continue. "You have heard of the spear of Longinus? Or Fulcanelli, the great alchemist?"

Boyden nodded in agreement. In reality, he had no idea who or what Hoarsley was talking about.

"The German people, through their Fuhrer, are now in possession of the spear. This is the same spear that pierced the ribs of Christ as he hung from the Cross. You know what this means?" he asked excitedly. "It is legend that whoever holds the spear will rule the world. And look at what we have accomplished in a few short months. I tell you this example, because der Fuhrer has realized that western science does not know all. Who in the west would believe such a tale of a spear? If nothing else, and I confide to you that I sometimes view it in this manner, after all, I am a trained scientist...You might call it 'covering all bets.' *De Belfort* was rumored to have lived for over one hundred fifty years. He learned much over those years, and the two most important things were alchemy and longevity. Fulcanelli, the greatest alchemist in living memory, was supposed to have found the key to transformation of base metals into gold, but how or from whom, no one has ever discovered. We think he learned from *de Belfort's* tomb. Now do you understand? Secrets were buried with him. Even testing the remains might bear important findings. Just think. Gold and Immortality. There really would be a thousand year old Reich." Hoarsley paused to catch his breath, staring intently at the Irishman. "This would be good enough in itself, yes? But there is more. We also learned of two other men, *de Belfort's* compatriots. *Sinestre L'Anguedoc,* buried in France, directly along our line of march. And *Cristobal De la Guzman* in Acre. Even now, special groups are stealing across Turkey's border to the Levant to find *De la Guzman.*"

Hoarsley counted on winning the young scoundrel over by flattering him if nothing else, letting on that he considered Boyden one of his inner circle. He picked his words carefully. "I should not tell you this," he said, making a great show of trust, "but there is a reason to seek all three. First, and I know you will find this hard to believe, we have been instructed on how to resuscitate them. Second, we have discovered that alone, they are powerful..." Hoarsley's eyes now gleamed. "But if we bring them together, their power will reign supreme. *De Belfort* was said to be the leader of these men. All Knights Templar."

Boyden sighed. "If their power is so great, what do they need you for?"

"That is the beauty of it my boy," Hoarsley answered, a wide look of excitement spreading over his face. "We have discovered how to control them, both individually and all together. Our researchers at the *Ahnenerbe* are of the best quality, first rate."

"I am aware," Boyden responded sarcastically, "that I'm in this to help secure independence for a united Ireland, not to satisfy the balmy whim of an amateur archeo-mythologist, or the like." Boyden laughed. "So the Fuhrer wants to set science on its head, and treat some ancient Aryan mythology as though it were real. That's for children. It's not going to win a war."

Hoarsley's face darkened. Imagine laughing at the Fuhrer! His voice turned shrill though he kept it at a whisper. He had tried to be reasonable, but that does not work with a spoiled child.

"This is your specialty, is it not? That is why you were chosen. Our leader wants this information, so it goes without saying, it is of the utmost importance. You have your orders, and you will obey them. Now leave my office. You will not come back here unless at my request. Procure the required information as quickly as possible. You will be contacted the usual way, presently. Good day."

As Boyden turned to go out the door, Hoarsley caught him by the arm. He held out his hand for the piece of paper, on which *de Belfort*'s name was written. "You remember the name, correct?" Boyden stared at him and said, "How could I forget, mate?"

"Then give me the paper." Hoarsley took the message, watched the young Irishman leave, then lit it on fire, and laid it to burn in an ashtray.

Hoarsley sat down in his work chair to try to soothe his nerves with a glass of Schnapps—the one exception to his rule of caution. He took out a piece of paper and started to write. This young hothead not only knew him, but could identify his place of work. The man was obviously too unstable for this mission. He questioned a direct order from the Fuhrer. When the information had been found, perhaps this association would have to end. It was a pity the Germanic race was reduced to employing non-Germans.

On the street outside, Boyden stood, staring into empty space, shaken. What a bunch of bloody idiots. Perhaps he was on the wrong side. Three years of this bloody limp so Hitler can look for his Holy Grail.

# CHAPTER 22

# JEMMIE'S GOLD

The smell of rain was in the air. A slight drizzle began to fall and dusk was not far off when Jemmie Craven, in his new green breeches and greasy shirt walked past the few customers sitting at the Flask's outdoor tables. He had already spent most of his newly gained money.

"Hi guv," he said in his jocular tenor to no one in particular. Then he sauntered up to the great oak doors of the pub, opening them as if he owned it, and entered.

The Flask had existed at its present location at 77 West Hill in Highgate since before 1715, and Craven's ancestors, stretching back at least one hundred years, had all managed, in one way or another, to bedevil the ownership.

No sooner had he entered, than the owner's wife rolled her eyes upwards, looked at her husband and said, "You 'andle 'im. I wants nothing to do wif 'im. Good day." She took off her apron, tossed it behind the bar and stomped out, unenthusiastically brushing by Craven in the narrow entranceway.

Craven turned to follow her exit with a bemused expression on his face. Then he turned back and headed to the bar.

"Hullo, Squire. The missus is in a bit of a mood today, eh? How about a nice ha'-pint o' ale?"

"Now you've gone and upset her again," the barman answered. "You have no credit hereabouts, Jemmie Craven. Why don't you give us all some peace and stay out. Why don't you go somewhere else? Go to the Hound's Tooth. It's close. A fine establishment."

Craven leaned forward across the bar. He had a silly grin on his unshaven face. "What's come of loyalty, eh squire?" His expression changed. He looked sad, even hurt. "I've been coming here for five years, I have. And for five years before that wif me poor departed father."

"Your poor departed father was here yesterday. He says he won't be paying your bill no more."

Craven broke back into his silly grin. "I could've swore I finished 'im off." Then he laughed uncontrollably. "Give us a drink, mate," he implored when he caught his breath.

Two elderly patrons, sensing the mood, got up quickly, laid half a crown on the bar and made for the exit.

Turning, Craven shouted, "Bollocks to you, old mossbacks. Jemmie has some coins for you lot, if you lay down and lift your skirts." Grinning once more, Craven reached into his pocket and pulled out some half-pence. He waved them in front of the pub owner's nose, and then stuck them back into his pocket.

"Yer costin' me business, Jemmie. Where'd you get them coins?" the barman asked.

Craven leaned forward again. "I got me some work." He held up his dirty hands. "See these blisters, squire. Bert Jones got me a job at the cemetery, diggin' graves for the high and mighty."

"I don't believe you. And I'll be sure to ask him. Why'd he give the likes of you a job anyway?"

"I did the man a favor. But that's between you and me Guv. I'm not supposed to talk about it."

The barkeep sighed. "I don't even want to know. Do you have any idea how much trouble you've got me into with the missus?"

Once more pulling out his money, and cupping it with his hand on the counter, Craven said, "I only want a ha'-pint, mate. Me money's good, ain't it."

"And then you'll leave?" asked the barman, relenting. Over the years, the Flask had served far more notorious characters than Jemmie Craven, and far more interesting. Dick Turpin himself had sat in one of the private alcoves and lifted a mug to the King. Of course, he was known to have tipped a few in most of the pubs in London, including Cyrus Wilson's favorite, the Hound's Tooth. A few days later, he had to hide in the Flask's cellars to escape that same King's men.

Grinning, Craven put his right hand over his heart. "You're a good man, Squire. You 'ave my word on it."

"All right, but just one," said the barman, shaking his head. He turned to pour the ale. "If my wife finds out I served you..."

While the pub owner's back was turned, Craven put the money back into his pocket, then innocently placed his cupped hand back on the bar, as if the coins were still under it. Soon after, the barman placed the mug of dark ale on the bar and slid it over to Craven.

\* \* \*

Turning the corner from Rookfield Park near the Holly Village homes, onto Swain's Lane, Kate and Elizabeth Hammond were amused to see two little hellions flying down the lane as if they were on wheels.

Both boys were wearing smaller versions of the steel helmets worn by the troops of the BEF. These were issued to many non-combatants for fear of possible air raids; and Nigel wore his ever present binocular case—a present from the lieutenant—hung from a strap around his neck. Kate laughed and brushed back her long, dark hair, while Elizabeth put on a serious expression and crossed her arms as she thought befitted an aunt when confronted by mischievous children. She even glared at Kate when she stooped down to gather in one of the boys.

Thomas Cochran ran straight at her and jumped into her arms.

"Hi honey," Kate said.

Elizabeth reproached them, "What are you two doing out so late? Your mum must be worried to death. And near the cemetery. Aren't you frightened?"

"No Aunt Elizabeth," Nigel answered.

Kate did not bother to try to pick him up. He was too "old" for that. "That's why we're running. The curfew, I mean. Not the cemetery. Mum won't worry. She knows we can take care of ourselves."

"Mum will be mad," countered Thomas Cochran. "And Lucy will catch us."

As Kate put him down he turned to Elizabeth and asked, "When will Lieutenant Michael be home?"

Though she tried to restrain herself, a smile now came to Elizabeth's face. "He said he'd try to get a pass home for Christmas. But he won't know for a bit." That was before the war started, but she did not want to mention the war to the boys. Now it was anyone's guess.

"Just who is this Lucy?" Kate asked.

"Just a girl," Nigel said, quickly turning and looking up the street. They had actually been running away from her.

"She's always pestering us to play," Thomas Cochran said.

"Is he going to bring home the sergeant?" Nigel Cochran asked excitedly. Hinton-Smith had told the boys he had a great hero for a friend, but neither the boys nor their aunts had ever met him.

"He didn't say," answered Elizabeth. "But in my next letter I'll be sure to ask."

Both boys were delighted. This meant late nights and exciting stories.

"Is the lieutenant a hero?" Thomas blurted out.

Now Elizabeth virtually beamed. "Yes. He most certainly is."

Kate added, "According to the Mayor, Michael and the sergeant captured a German city almost all by themselves. That was some time ago. We haven't heard anything of late."

"Boys, it's getting dark out. I think that Kate and I should walk you home," interrupted Elizabeth.

"Oh Lizzie," Kate said, laughing. "You're such a prig. They can make it home on their own. They're big boys now. Go boys. Shoo. Get home before Aunt Liz puts you in a buggy and wheels you home."

"Kate!" she moaned.

"Oh all right. You might relax. I'll see them home." Kate turned and walked away, calling back over her shoulder, "And make sure they're locked away for the night."

The two boys started running before Elizabeth could utter a word. Their laughter trailed down the narrow cobblestone street as the sisters heard other footsteps coming their way, and soon, a young blond girl came running down Swain's Lane, dodging around one and then the other, so close as to jostle each, yelling, "Sorry, mums," and kept going.

Kate giggled. "Perhaps I should try that tack."

*   *   *

Craven belched. He slid the mug back across the bar and said, "Yes my good man. That was fine." He wiped his mouth, leaving a dark streak of grease across his stubble. "Now be a sport, and give poor Jemmie another."

"You made a deal and you damn well better stick with it. Pay up and be off with you."

He put his hand out to accept the payment, but Craven slowly withdrew his own hand and started to snicker.

"Look," Craven said. "The money in me life disappears so fast. Just like me liquor."

The burley owner of the pub reached over the bar, grabbed Craven by the collar and pulled him so close he blanched from the odor of Craven's breath. "I want my money."

"You'll have it, Squire. I promise."

"And don't forget the rest you owe."

Lifting the mug by the handle, Craven smashed it against the barman's head. As he fell, clutching his wound, a small trickle of blood began oozing out between his fingers.

Craven stepped back, startled at his own violence. He had not intended this, but opportunity did not come his way every day, so he quickly ran behind the bar, found a wooden tray with the day's take, stuffed as much as he could in his pockets, and darted out of the pub, cutting across a small lawn to Highgate High Street.

A street cobbler sitting on a bench shook his head and asked, "What mischief you up to now, Jemmie?"

Craven slowed down, and spat on the ground. "Too much this time, mate."

"You better hurry, then. I saw the constable a short while back."

"Thanks, mate," Craven said as he started to walk at a brisk pace. As he approached Bisham Road, he heard the unmistakable sound of a Bobby's whistle. He turned to look just as Constable Nick Hensen came into view. Craven took off down Bisham and ran for all he was worth. Then he ran north, up the cobblestones of Swain's Lane. Hensen was only a hundred yards behind, and Hensen was a formidable runner.

With a leap, Craven grabbed the uppermost bar of the North Gate of the cemetery, clambered up and over, then jumped down and pressed his shoulders tight against the stone wall, breathing heavily. Highgate had served him well before. No one ever thought to look for him there.

Hensen stopped when he reached Swain's Lane. Looking up and down the street, there was no one in sight. He jogged up the lane to South Grove. No one that way either. Turning around, he paused as he passed the North Gate, took a cursory glance through the bars, thought better of it and continued back down Swain's Lane.

It was dark when Hensen was halfway to the bottom of the hill. He saw someone walking towards him and soon recognized Elizabeth Hammond. He slowed to a walk and approached her.

"Excuse me, miss. You didn't happen to see anyone running down Swain's Lane?" he politely asked.

"No sir," she answered.

Hensen rubbed his chin. "No one at all?" He looked up and down the street.

"No," Elizabeth said, concern coming into her tone. "Is there anything wrong constable?" Now she was fortified in her belief that she was right. The boys were too young to be out so late. The officer had probably been chasing some nefarious criminal down this very street.

"No. But thank you miss." Hensen put his right hand up to his forehead, tilting his hat up ever so slightly as he turned to look at the old stone wall.

"You're chasing someone. Is that it? Could he have jumped the cemetery wall?" Elizabeth asked. "But which one." Her gaze wondered from one side to the other. "East Highgate or the West?"

"They're both pretty high," he said. "The walls I mean." He grimaced as if thinking. "And lower on the east down here, but you didn't see anyone so I guess he didn't come this far. Sorry miss. Just thinking out loud, I am. I guess it doesn't really matter. He could have gone over the North Gate, but I'd never find him this late. He'll most likely be sleeping it off in his father's yard next morning. Thank you miss." Hensen turned and ran his hand against the rough stone wall. Could the likes of him get over that wall so fast? Then he cursed under his breath and walked back to see what damage Jemmie had caused this time.

Elizabeth continued up Swain's Lane. She quickened her usual pace. Something definitely was not on.

*   *   *

Craven stood flush against the wall and listened. As the footsteps receded, he moved further into the cemetery following the dirt path leading toward the Lebanon Circle. It was dark now, and he had never been this far into the old cemetery at this late an hour. Usually, after dark, he just lurked about the edges and gates. The North Gate in particular, had proved to be a profitable spot for his shenanigans.

Still, there's always a first time and the constable might come in looking for him, so he veered toward the Egyptian Avenue and kept going, now running fast up hill for a good fifteen minutes. Once there, he bent over, coughed and tried to catch his breath.

Glancing briefly down the Egyptian Avenue, his mouth dropped wide open. Heading up the narrow pathway, lined on both sides by broken-down tombs, was a bizarre-looking man, almost seven feet tall, and dressed all in black. Following the man was a troop of fifty knights in full regalia—chain mail, helmets, armor, white tunics with bright red crosses and armed with swords and lances. They were riding horses, caparisoned with similar white cloaks and red crosses, as if on parade and they were coming straight for him.

There was no sound as they marched. Craven was paralyzed in fear and wonder. Suddenly, they all disappeared save the man in black. He kept marching, up and through the entrance. He made an abrupt right turn in front of Craven, then motioned for him to follow.

Craven did not move. The man in black tossed gold coins over his shoulders from his white-gloved hands. As some of the coins hit the path, Craven smiled and ran forward, snatching them off the ground. The tall man dropped more coins as he walked into the darkness, leaving a shining trail.

CHAPTER 23

# DUNKIRK'S A DREAM, MATE

Hinton-Smith stopped and bent over, his hands sliding down to his knees. He knew he had to pace himself better. Breathing in deeply for a minute, his lungs felt close to bursting, his legs shaking, almost cramping. He thought he was in better condition than this, the wound and lack of food had obviously worn him down. Still he knew he had to persevere. Cawkins was depending on him. Straightening up, he wiped his forehead and started forward again, pacing himself at what he figured was a seven-minute mile—a stride he thought he could sustain for a long time. The land was fairly flat, with only small undulations. Grassy fields seemed solid under his feet, so did the ground as he entered a heavily forested area of pines and firs. He emerged from the trees and saw an open field, which he knew from the map stretched for miles ahead of him to the next canal, the last before the final leg to Dunkirk. As he ran, his mind was active. He made mental notes on roads, German dispositions he had seen and their direction of movement: what areas might be clear, which to avoid. He figured his best bet was to secure a motorcycle, hopefully he could find one with a sidecar. He was going to make it.

Awakened by one of his men who heard the faint sound of footsteps, Colonel *LeFevre* moved swiftly to the edge of the dense copse he had chosen for a short rest. It was now the dead of night, but the moon, shining through the combination of clouds and smoke, gave off just enough light to make forms visible, if indistinct through his field glasses. Something deep in the recesses of the colonel's mind identified the runner as an Englishman—the form and outline, the urgency and confidence of his step; all whispered Englishman to *LeFevre*. They were both moving in the direction of the withdrawal, but there were two differences, and to *LeFevre*, they were two crucial differences—he was walking, the other was running. He and his companions were fully armed, but no weapon was discernable on this fugitive. It was obvious to the colonel that this man was a coward, a deserter, who threw away his weapon. But he would not get away with it this night. He turned to one of his men, and without a second's thought, ordered, "Shoot him."

"But, *mon Colonel*," the man remonstrated. "He must be English, or French, no?"

"I said shoot him," the colonel shrieked out in his high-pitched voice. He was not used to having his orders questioned or disobeyed. "Shoot him. He is a deserter!"

Still the young soldier hesitated. He was exhausted and hungry. He stunk of dirt and oil and no chance to wash in two weeks. And he worshipped his colonel. He would have gladly laid down his own life for *LeFevre*, but he could not shoot this poor refugee. How could he shoot a brother at arms? A man who had no doubt gone through the same hell of the last week.

Colonel *LeFevre*, quickly descending into a paroxysm of rage, grabbed the man's gun, while yelling at him in such a sputtering fit that no one could understand a word, raised the rifle, drew a lead on the lieutenant, and dropped him with one shot to the head.

Lowering the gun, he looked sternly at his disobedient man, shoved the rifle back into his hands, and said calmly, "You are in very serious danger of a court martial."

"Yes, sir," he said while lowering his eyes. The colonel was perhaps a great man but also an arrogant, stupid, stuffed ass.

They walked over to where Hinton-Smith lay, and one of the privates checked his pulse. "He is still alive, *mon Colonel*."

"Then I shall administer the *coup de gras*," LeFevre said out loud to no one in particular, as he pulled out his service revolver and checked to see it was loaded.

The private stared in disbelief. This went against everything he had ever learned in the military, against honor itself. He put his hand on the older man's arm to restrain him.

Looking at the lowly private with as much contempt and condescension as he could muster, his face twitching, *LeFevre* slowly stroked his mustache for a full twenty seconds, but the private did not budge. *LeFevre* raised his pistol and pointed it at the private, but still the man refused to let go. Deliberately, *LeFevre* laid it hard across the man's face, knocking him down, then coolly cocked the pistol and aimed it point blank at the lieutenant.

"What's all this, then?" said a distinctly English voice, that might have belonged to an English Bobby, when out of the darkness stepped Captain Greer Riordan, an Eton schoolboy, Oxford and Sandhurst graduate, and up to approximately three weeks ago, a remarkably charming, intelligent, athletic and handsome fellow with incredibly piercing dark brown eyes. As he drew nearer, the colonel could only see what looked to be a broken down old man in clothes so ragged he appeared to be some skid row bum out to get a drink. He looked to be sixty at least (he was just short of thirty), but then there were those eyes, which still burned and belied the empty shell of his body. *LeFevre* wondered what this old man was doing in battle and figured he must be a rear echelon type that inadvertently got caught in the quagmire. He did not expect any trouble with him.

"Sir," the captain inquired with a very strong voice for one so haggard. "An enemy soldier? We should take him prisoner. Maybe he'll have information for Headquarters."

"No, he is mortally wounded. He will slow us down."

"Oh, you're French," Riordan said as he moved in closer to inspect the wounded soldier. For some unknown reason, perhaps because he harbored just as much enmity for the French, as *LeFevre* bore towards the British, he felt there was something amiss. Especially after they'd given no support at all during this whole campaign, at least that he was aware of. And the disheveled condition he and his men were in, was in no little part, owed to being let down by one French and one Belgian unit on their left flank three days ago, when the King of the Belgians surrendered out of the blue. Perhaps his hostility should have been directed more at the Belgians, but the captain, for all his education, could not now separate the two. Riordan was tired of running, and was just spoiling for a fight, any fight. And the French had taken the spot just below the Jerries on his list of candidates.

Riordan walked over to the fallen soldier to get a closer look.

"This man's English! A lieutenant," he exclaimed with a great deal of surprise. He looked up at the Frenchman, who he could now see was a colonel in the French Army, and motioned to his men. "Boys, come over here," he said in a mildly threatening manner.

Three rough looking Tommies appeared out of the gloom, rifles at the ready. Following them was a corpsman, who crouched down to explore the lieutenant for wounds.

"There's a crease of blood across his temple, but not very deep. I think he's just out cold. He's not lost much blood, sir. And there's a fairly recent wound to his arm, as well, sir."

Riordan stood and walked straight up to the Frenchman. "I beg your pardon for being blunt, sir, but what's this about?" he asked brusquely.

"This man is a traitor, a deserter. I caught him running away and I shot him. I am well within my rights, sir, and you, captain, have no right to question me."

"You shot him?" Riordan asked incredulously.

One of the Tommies spit out some tobacco on the ground. "The whole damn army's running away, mate." He spat on the ground again, this time in the direction of the colonel's feet.

The colonel could see only the rightness of his case, the discipline needed in battle, and his superior rank. He would permit no questioning of his logic or authority, and duly raised his pistol again. "I will finish it," he said imperiously.

Riordan calmly motioned to his Tommies to raise their guns and point them at *LeFevre*. He said, "With all due respect, sir, you even think about it, we shoot you." Riordan had recently shot one of his own men, when his company was panic stricken and on the verge of mutiny. It had worked and they held. He was certainly not going to hesitate to shoot this haughty Frenchman.

The Tommie with the tobacco said under his breath, "Probably be the first time you're under fire this war, Jack."

The other Tommies chuckled, though their captain glared dead ahead at the Frenchman.

"You have no right! The man is a coward!" *LeFevre* sputtered as the veins stood out on his neck and his face turned a deep crimson.

Still calm, but determined, Riordan replied, "God willing, if we get to England, we'll let a court martial decide."

"There will be two!" *LeFevre* shouted.

"So be it. Take the colonel's gun, private."

"Yes sir! With pleasure, sir!"

"Are these your men, Colonel?" he asked, pointing to the other two Frenchmen, standing, and one who was slowly rising to his feet.

"Oui," he said, summoning his most haughty posture and tone.

"I suggest you come with us. You'll receive your pistol back when we reach the British lines." He paused and nodded to his sergeant, who cleared his throat, winked at the Frenchman, and ordered in a gruff Scots' voice, "Corporal, take their weapons." Turning to a couple of privates, he said, "You two. Give us a hand with the lieutenant."

Two British soldiers picked up the still unconscious Hinton-Smith, put him between them, with one of his arms around each of their shoulders. The French private who had been struck by *LeFevre* insisted on helping, thus angering the colonel even more.

"What a bloody ignorant arse," Riordan said loudly making certain the colonel heard. He shouldered his machine gun and started walking north. "Let's go lads."

*　　*　　*

It was still dark as the Dutch skoot glided over the smooth waters of the estuary on a course for the channel. It was then, to Cyrus Wilson's great surprise and everlasting pride, that he and the others saw hundreds of boats, all heading out to sea, and they had no doubt where this motley group of scows, tugs, packets, trawlers, countless rowboats and even a small one-masted sloop, the America's Cup challenger *Endeavor*, were heading. All were piloted by private citizens, and Cyrus and his mates were joining them on the ship they had christened *HMS BEF*.

Cyrus Wilson's heart swelled, his eyes became teary. He had never felt so patriotic, so enamored of his fellow countrymen as at the present time. He was now certain the army would be rescued, would survive.

It was not long before they were out on the open sea. Wind came in from the northeast and men's clothing flapped vigorously in the bluster. The swells of the Channel rose and fell mightily, whitecaps shown in the moonlight and waves smashed over the slender, low gunnels of the Dutch skoot.

Three of the sailors were permanently hanging over the rails, vomiting, but Ted Wadkins steadily managed the steering wheel, while Wilson, the grizzled, white haired soldier stood next to him staring with binoculars toward the French coast. As the skoot occasionally dipped down into a swell, spray engulfed the little boat, drenching and chilling Wilson and Wadkins to the bone.

The sky to the east was lightening, and as the boat reached the top of a wave, hesitating there for only a moment, Cyrus could see the coast. It was going to be a clear day, except for one large factor. "Look at that black cloud of smoke," Wilson said. "It's gotten that bad, ain't it? Look at those little wasps flying in and around the smoke. Those are Stukas." He grabbed the wheel and handed the glasses to Wadkins.

"By God, it'll be lucky if we can help at all."

"We'll give it a go, we will," Wilson replied, smiling grimly. They would bring back the lads. "Got to. There ain't no other choice."

Cyrus Wilson was coming to the rescue.

*     *     *

Elizabeth Hammond was doing her part for the lads as well. Promoted to the map room in the underground War Office in December of 1939 after enlisting in the RAF, she was part of the group that kept the charts detailing troop movements, convoy movements and naval dispositions, as well as keeping track of the dispersal and availability of fighter and bomber squadrons, both at home and for the Continent.

Her first week at her new work had ended in cheers, congratulations and jubilation when the news came in of the Battle of the River Plate: still the only good news from the war effort. The Graf Spee had been cornered, forced into the neutral port of Montevideo and ultimately scuttled by her own crew. Elizabeth Hammond's shift usually started at 8 AM and consisted of accumulating intelligence for the next day's briefing, but during the hunt for the German battleship it seemed like they never left the map room for as much as a nap.

Almost every day she walked to the Archway Station at dawn hoping to catch one of the early trains into the city. It was an easy walk to the station, less than a half mile. But when she stayed overnight at Cyrus Wilson's she would go to Highgate Station, also a short walk. The difference was the trek down to the station platform: Highgate had been dug very deep indeed. For this reason Highgate station was designated one of the shelters in case the Germans bombed London. Every time Elizabeth used Highgate she promised herself she would count every last one of the steps down to see just how many there were, and every day she seemed to lose track.

The office she worked in was at Clive Steps, King Charles Street. If she made every change she could stay on the Northern line all the way to Leicester Square, change to the Piccadilly line to Green Park then go south on the Victoria line to Victoria Station where she could board either the Circle or District's line to Westminster where it was a short walk to King Charles Street.

In 1936 the Air Ministry believed that in the event of war, enemy aerial bombing of London could cause up to 200,000 casualties per week. Many key government offices were subsequently scheduled to disperse from central London to the suburbs, and some to the Midlands or Northwest. In the meantime, they decided to have a temporary government center for operations in London, underground and reinforced to protect from bombing: a bunker so to speak. This became the Cabinet War Rooms where in 1940 Churchill said: "This is the room from which I will direct the war."

It was another cool, gloomy day when she left home on a Monday morning and the sky looked like it was determined to stay gray.

At least it was not raining and there was no fog, Elizabeth thought as she walked to the station. Though she carried an umbrella under her arm, she hoped the weather would hold and decided to detrain early at Green Park and walk through St. James Park to enjoy the late spring air. If it rained so be it. She had her umbrella. There were just not enough chances to enjoy being outdoors these days. She breathed in deeply and sighed. Perhaps she'd see the King and wave when she passed Buckingham Palace. She had actually caught a glimpse of him once before his brother abdicated, when he was a mere prince. That caused a smile.

By the time she arrived at the platform and joined the bustle of people crowding through the doors of the waiting train it was 6 AM, and the cars were already full with people going to work. As she made her way down the walkway looking for a seat she realized they were all taken. Moving as far along the aisle as she could, she grasped one of the overhead hand straps on the train, said, "Morning," to her nearest neighbors, smiled at their return greetings and braced herself for the train to start.

Elizabeth looked at her watch. She was a bit obsessed with time and never wanted to be late. Accordingly, she always left for work or any assignation a good thirty minutes earlier than necessary. This morning, she realized she had outdone herself. Even if the trains were delayed at every stop she would be an hour early for her shift. No matter. There was always something to do.

Now, Elizabeth and other people standing throughout the center aisle of the train, hanging on to the loops and vertical grab poles began to sway and catch their balance as the cars started down the tracks. No one would fall over. They were packed in too tightly.

Her thoughts now turned to Michael. Worried as she was about him, she knew she was helpless. It was better to throw yourself into your work hoping your meager little bit in the war effort would do some good. As the news from the Continent began seeping across the Channel, it sounded so terrible she had resigned herself to losing him, to never seeing him again. At one point she thought they'd all either be killed or captured. How could you escape that Nazi juggernaut? That was a fear she kept to herself.

None of this meant she had fallen out of love. It simply meant that if she already gave him up for dead or missing, then she could not be hurt more when it turned out to be true. She was in effect preparing herself for the worst. And if he did return, it would be all the better. An ingenious bit of rationalization, her sister called it.

Every day in the map room as the personnel moved the troop markers across the board, she kept a special eye on the movement of the Coldstream Guards. Hope sprung anew with the news of the evacuation but there had been no news of the lieutenant. In the withdrawal there was such a mishmash of units it was almost impossible to keep track of any of their whereabouts.

It seemed incredibly strange to her that London was so untouched by the war. How could the lads be meeting such a catastrophe over there, not even two hundred miles away, while here it was so calm and peaceful? Two hundred miles! That was like taking the train to Birmingham or Bristol.

Getting down when the train eased to a stop at Green Park she squeezed back through the aisle as best she could, barely making her escape before the doors shut and walking up the steps to the surface and fresh air.

Cutting across the park she was moved by the smell of the grass and trees: how beautifully green it was in the park at this time of year. There were hundreds of what she imagined were like-minded people, some milling through the park, others hurrying here and there, some feeding the ducks: Churchill was often spotted feeding them. So many were in uniform, so many greeted her with cheer that she was incredibly proud of how they were holding up, what with the debacle on the Continent. What a stouthearted people are the English.

Big Ben loomed into view and she could see the Parliament buildings over the trees. This always brought forth a deep patriotic feeling. How smart it was of her to detrain.

There were many young soldiers among the throng and some of them were injured, probably fresh from Dunkirk. Looking intently at every face she hoped somehow Michael's would come into view. But every face just brought sadness and disappointment.

As she walked near the lake a soldier on crutches swung past her and smiled. He looked vaguely familiar, but she had other things on her mind and her curiosity slipped away as soon as he passed from sight.

The soldier took a few more steps then stopped. He had gone through a quite different thought process, straining to think where he'd seen such an attractive woman. Then he remembered. The girl from the train. That was months ago. It might be months before he ran into her again or more likely never. If he didn't say something now he'd regret it. They were at war. No one knew when things would be normal again. This present circumstance was just too lucky. It was definitely kismet. He had to do something about it. Roberts could feel his heart leaping into his throat as he bolstered the courage to get the words out.

"Miss! Miss!" Lieutenant Roberts shouted scant seconds later.

Elizabeth heard the call but assumed it had nothing to do with her. She stopped to watch some older people feeding breadcrumbs to a flock of pigeons strutting about the middle of the path when she felt a light tap on her arm.

"Miss," the man said.

Elizabeth turned. It was the lieutenant on crutches. She smiled faintly, then sympathetically. Poor boy. It could have been Michael in that situation.

He in turn smiled warmly. "Lieutenant Roberts. I don't expect you remember. I gave up my seat for you on the tube to King's Cross-St. Pancras. Before the war."

"I, I'm sorry," Elizabeth said. She scanned his face and eyes but she could not place him. A little embarrassed, she was also flattered that such a handsome young soldier would remember her. "I can't recall."

"You had dozed off. I woke you so you wouldn't miss your stop."

"Oh," Elizabeth said, brightening up a bit. "You have quite the memory. Even down to the stations."

"I see you're in uniform now. Very nice," Roberts said. "Um, I mean that you are part of the war effort."

Elizabeth laughed. "Of course. RAF. A WAAF."

"I hope it's not too forward of me, but could I interest you in a cup of tea?"

"Forward indeed," Elizabeth said. "I'm sorry but I'm off to work." Elizabeth felt badly turning him down, after all he was wounded, one of the brave lads. What had he been through? Her eyes could not help but gravitate to his wounded limb. Still she did have to be at work.

"You could walk with me. I'm going to the King Charles Street." He was handsome with golden blond hair, looked quite trim and martial in his army uniform even with the right pants leg split for the cast, and had a very pleasant voice, but she did this more out of sympathy for a wounded soldier than attraction.

"The War Room I presume? I'm impressed. Pardon my manners," Roberts said. "I don't even know your name."

"Shush. It's supposed to be secret, the War Room I mean. I'm Elizabeth Hammond."

"Splendid, Miss Hammond. I'll be discrete," Roberts said. "Are you in charge of the wool string or are you a push-pin girl?"

Elizabeth laughed. "Push-pins. No doubt you're familiar with the map room."

"I'd love to accompany you if you don't mind me lumbering along."

"Of course not," Elizabeth Hammond said, now feeling more at ease. "Were you hurt badly? I hope you don't mind me asking."

"Not bad. Flesh wound as they say. Should be able to discard the crutches in a few months. For now it's rehabilitation then back to war, isn't it."

They exited the park and headed down Horse Guards Road.

"It must have been terrible over there," Elizabeth said. "My boyfriend was in the thick of it. I haven't heard a word about him since the German's attacked. He was with the Coldstream Guards."

"They had a rough go," Roberts said. "The whole lot of us did."

"Were you one of the evacuees?"

"No," Roberts said. "I beat the rush. Caught shrapnel the first damn week. Bloody disappointing. Just got out of hospital."

"Oh. Sorry," Elizabeth said, but then her face lit up. "I know it's hardly possible, but one never knows. His name is Michael Hinton-Smith, my boyfriend I mean."

Roberts's face did the opposite. "A lieutenant?"

Elizabeth hesitated, fearing the worst as she saw the transformation in the officer's demeanor. "Yes."

"I do not like to bad mouth a fellow officer," Roberts said. "Especially when all I've heard are rumors."

Elizabeth stopped walking. Her heart sank. "What? Tell me. Do you know him?"

"It's said he ran away and left his men to die."

"That cannot be true! He's a hero."

"I'm sorry," Roberts said. "It's what I heard."

"I have to go now," Elizabeth Hammond said. "I'll be late." She hurried off, almost in a jog toward the steps leading to the bunker of the War Rooms.

Well played, Roberts, the lieutenant thought. He could not have made a bigger arse of himself. Really mucked it up. They were only rumors after all. He should have feigned ignorance or at least kept his big mouth shut. Now he had to figure out a way to repair a relationship that hadn't even begun. That was a first. Bad luck that bad news travels so quickly.

Indeed, the rumors made it back across the Channel before Hinton-Smith reached the French coast.

*   *   *

Corporal Stevens slowly worked his way along the bottom of the Loo canal embankment, followed by four other Tommies. One man crept along the top of the incline. They had a simple enough if audacious plan, and were now just waiting for the right time. They were already close enough to observe the insignias of the many German vehicles crossing the pontoon bridge. The corporal spotted some movement by the water's edge near a vast amount of rubble and quickly held up his hand to stop the other men. "Stay here," he commanded in a whisper. Rifle at the ready, he edged down closer, entering the water. Peering through the darkness, he spotted something again, but could not tell what it was. Stevens silently waded closer. There was a man, lying with his hand in the water. It looked like he'd come down to get a drink and died. Or conked out. Stevens had seen movement.

The corporal waded quietly toward him and upon reaching him, knelt down and turned him over. "Blimey, 'ow'd you get here." He motioned to three men crouching on the bank. "Come here and help me with this bloke. He's me mate."

The three Tommies scampered down the bank to the edge of the water and pulled Cawkins up the embankment.

"It's the end of 'em," a lookout called down to the corporal. "Last lorry in line. Let's move."

Two of the men sprinted to the south end of the bridge and entered the canal, while Stevens and another man helped the sergeant to his feet and started to carry him along the banks of the canal.

Hiding in the water, the two privates waited for the last truck to slow down as it edged onto the pontoons. When the front wheels hit the first pontoon, they would dip and the truck would have to slow down to almost zero.

Stevens and the others watched from the canal bank, ready to bring supporting fire. Then, as the truck slowed, both soldiers, one on either side of the pontoons, jumped up and out of the water, threw open the doors and tossed the surprised drivers into the canal. Putting the lorry in neutral till Stevens and the others could make it over, they then hoisted Cawkins into the back. It had taken less than a minute to commandeer the vehicle. They gunned the truck to high speed, catching up to the column in short order, then following it until Stevens recognized a shortcut and they veered off to the west.

Cruising unnoticed to within two-and-a-half miles of the city, they then had to show a white flag when they came under British fire. Cawkins beat the lieutenant to Dunkirk by a whole day.

\*     \*     \*

Though the sun had not yet risen, it was starting to grow lighter. Already Riordan could tell that it was going to be another beastly hot day.

"Well, at least we're getting close to the beach," Riordan said to his sergeant as he wiped the sweat from his grimy brow.

"Right."

"I wonder what's left of the army?" Riordan said.

Looking over at the proud Frenchman, marching under what amounted to a guard, the sergeant said, "What a bloody idiot. We're all running as fast as we can, ain't we?"

A few hours after the new dawn, Riordan was sure he could smell the burning oil from the fire they had been moving toward for the last couple of days, but he also noticed that it was suddenly cooler and there was the unmistakable freshness of sea air. Dropping back in line to where his men carried the lieutenant, he asked, "How's he doing?"

"He's still out, sir."

"Good show," he then said softly to the French private, so his colonel would not hear.

They slowly worked their way back to the beaches, across open fields, some of which were now flooded to stop the Panzers and where the water reached levels of up to three and four feet. The most remarkable sight was the unending profusion of wrecked tanks, lorries, armored cars, wagons, anti-aircraft guns, and other weapons and vehicles of all sizes and descriptions. It was the biggest junkyard they had ever seen—much of it sabotaged to keep the equipment from falling into the hands of the Germans. The rest had been destroyed by Heinkels and Stukas.

Hinton-Smith awakened as they wandered up to a beach just west of Bray-Dunes, but he had no idea where he was, why these soldiers were carrying him, or why he was hearing the pounding of waves hitting a beach. He knew he had been in a war. He had a faint recollection that he had forgotten something important, but the more he strained to remember, the less he could grasp it. The surroundings reminded him of some phantasmagoric scene out of a Poe horror novel, and he was frightened. It was an apocalyptic vision, a nightmare. Junked equipment was lying everywhere, some of it in flames, some smashed and only black and smoldering. Bombs from the Luftwaffe were falling sporadically. He could see that the soldiers carrying him were too numb to duck out of the way, although soldiers already on the beach ran for cover with every explosion or drone of the German planes. Luckily, the sand on the beaches muffled the explosions, and with rare exception, the only way a soldier could be killed was by a direct hit or if a Stuka came down to strafe them. Then a strange question occurred to him: he wondered who he was.

Clouds of sand hurled upwards when bombs exploded, and fireballs erupted when already disabled vehicles were hit again. There were jagged lines stretching way out into the sea, and it took him awhile to realize these were soldiers orderly queuing up to be picked up by little boats, some as small as row boats, to be taken further out to larger ships such as destroyers and cruise ships and delivered out of the chaos. There was also smoke on the horizon and explosions out to sea, and he could only guess that their rescuers were having a rough time of it as well. He turned to look at the strange soldiers surrounding him to see if he was imagining things, but one look at the open-mouth gape of what looked to be a French officer, whose once proud hauteur had degenerated into a feeble, slumped posture, told him it was all true.

*LeFevre* stumbled down to the water's edge, looking as if in a trance or final submission; there, other French soldiers were fighting over their place in the queue. In one of those rare visions, *LeFevre* saw the future: no beachhead, no France.

"All right, mates. Keep an order there, yes, you. Keep an order there. Jolly good," cried out a firm, bureaucrat's voice, a captain assigned to make sure the evacuation went off as smoothly as possible. He went from line to line in his area, accompanied by three of the biggest Tommies in the military police, keeping order in the queues, facilitating the order of embarkation, stopping fights, handing out cigarettes and whatever bits of food he could muster—keeping things moving along.

*LeFevre* heard this voice and roused himself. He had to make the best of a bad situation, and now hurled himself with his typical élan, into helping to organize the French troops.

When things had settled into an orderly process, the colonel's spirit was renewed. He spotted Riordan in a neighboring queue, and strode laboriously over the oil-soaked sand to berate him. "You!" he firmly declared, "I want your name and rank."

"Captain Greer Riordan, 6TH Durham Light Infantry. Want me to spell it out?"

The colonel knew enough English to consider this offensive, which was indeed the intent.

"I will see you and your friend at the court martial." *LeFevre* turned around and walked back to police the queues.

"Lookin' forward to it, mate," said Riordan's sergeant under his breath.

Just then, a minor riot began when a shallow draft Dutch skoot, manned by some drunken English sailors, motored almost all the way up to the beach, to stop in about six feet of water. Soldiers broke ranks trying to get a spot on the barge, swimming up from all directions. But two of the sailors, one, a much older man who seemed to have a lot of military training, restored order quickly, even rapping a few of the would-be interlopers on the arms with a long oar. Within minutes, they filled the deck to overflow with forty men, wedging them in, in order to take a greater number. Cyrus Wilson and Ted Wadkins made a show of shaking their fists at a marauding Stuka and then hoisted an over-sized Union Jack to the highest point of the skoot's mast. Soldiers from all over the beach cheered at the sight.

"We'll be back for you lot," Cyrus Wilson yelled over the din, as he returned to the rail and looked over the side. "I promise you."

Then, they used the long wooden sweeps to turn the ship's bow, and headed back out to sea.

For the next three hours, Hinton-Smith, Riordan, and his men stood patiently in the queues, which did not seem to be moving at all. Gradually they stood at the water's edge, then out into the surf, and then the deeper water, still in line, waiting for one of the small boats.

"So lieutenant," Riordan asked. "What happened back there?"

Hinton-Smith searched the captain's eyes as if to find the answer there. Haltingly, he said, "I don't know."

"The Frenchman...?"

"What Frenchman?" Hinton-Smith asked.

"Do you know your unit?" the sergeant asked.

All of the men's eyes turned suddenly to the east, as the faint drone of airplanes reached them. Some of the men tried to run back in the direction of the beach. Hinton-Smith followed the sound to try to spot the planes.

"Where's the goddamn RAF," asked Riordan as he peered up into the cloudy sky.

Other men tried to hurry to the boats and crowd on, but this was probably the least safe action. The Stukas screamed down at the larger ships, dropping bombs in the deep water, and then over the shallower depths where the soldiers queued. A small mail packet exploded in a brilliant shower of flames, and sank quickly. The men holding Hinton-Smith heard a bomb dropping directly at them, and shoved the lieutenant under the water at the last second before it hit. Both soldiers and Hinton-Smith were knocked unconscious, the lieutenant for the second time in twenty-four hours. Riordan waded over with his sergeant and pulled the men up and out of the water, dragging them all back to the beach. Then he sent the sergeant to look for his corpsman. The Stukas made another pass down the beach and dunes, strafing more helpless soldiers, then flew off to the south.

Further west, on the Eastern Mole in the Dunkirk harbor, from which the majority of the soldiers were being evacuated, stood Corporal Stevens and two other soldiers. On a cot next to them, being tended to by a regular army doctor and nurse, was Sergeant Major Cawkins, drifting in and out of consciousness. The contents from a bottle of plasma held by the nurse were flowing into his right arm. The soldiers held him while the doctor made a foot long slit up his leg to ease the pressure from the wound.

Suddenly Cawkins awakened. "You've got to find the lieutenant. He was coming back for me," the sergeant cried out.

"There, there," said the nurse. "Nothing to worry about now."

"But he's going back..."

"Calm down, soldier," the doctor said as he motioned for the nurse to ready a hypodermic. "Everything is all right. We'll take care of your friend."

She slipped the needle into his arm and he drifted off.

"He keeps yelling about his lieutenant," Stevens said. "I saw him get wounded. I think he was killed." He shook his head. "I can't make any sense of it."

*     *     *

Cyrus Wilson and the skoot made three more round trips before the Germans closed in and ended the evacuation. During all the return trips to England, he asked every soldier, whether English or French, if they had seen or heard of Hinton-Smith, or even if they knew anything about the Coldstream Guards. Nobody had heard a thing.

After his final return to Dover, Cyrus and the others had tea with the thankful soldiers, then Wadkins and his fellows made teary farewells, and took the train up to London. As an old soldier, Cyrus felt like mingling with the Tommies and exchanging stories. They were his kind, and he ended up staying for a whole week, making himself useful, as a nurse, a courier and just plain good listener, before taking the evening train back to Victoria Station and London. Again, no one had information about Hinton-Smith, although he ran into a few members of the Guards, who could only advise him that many soldiers had been separated from their units, and that the units themselves were all mixed up. He did overhear a few soldiers joking about how, "Some soldiers seemed to be a bit more eager than others to get to the beaches," but this meant little to him.

# CHAPTER 24

# WELCOME HOME, MIKEYBOY

It was early on a dull, brisk morning when Will Baker and Bert Jones approached the tool shed for the older cemetery.

"I hate 'avin' to dig this early," Bert Jones groused, his breath visible in the cold air. "Ground'll be hard as ice."

Baker patted his arms with his gloved hands, shivering as well. "See, I told you we shouda done it last night, I did. But you was too busy." He hunched his shoulders as if it would help.

"I hope it's a hot summer," Jones said. He took the keys out of his frayed pocket. "Well, we better get to it," he said as he fumbled with the lock to the tool shed. "See. I can't feel nothin' with these gloves on and me hands is still freezin'."

They walked into the shed and procured two shovels. Jones also took an old pick that they used in the winter months when the ground was rock hard.

"I thought you hired that good-for-nothing, Jemmie Craven, to help us?" Will Baker said. Then he stopped walking, bent his head and blew his nose. His particular method was to tilt his head, plug one of his nostrils with his thumb, hold the other wide open and blow, creating a faucet-like effect. Then he would do the same with the other.

"Fine work, says I," Bert said, then he snarled. "I did hire that no good, soes you could 'ave more time to blow your snout. He'll be along if he knows what's good for 'im."

"Did I tell you what that stupid sod Craven did anyways?" Bert asked. "I told him to put a little fear into me mate Cyrus Wilson and what does he do? He goes and throws a rock at his window after midnight! And that's supposed to scare 'im? I ask you?"

Will grunted in acknowledgement. "He ain't the cleverest bloke, eh?"

"He better be clever enough to show up this fine mornin' says I."

Neither of them liked getting to the cemetery this early, and it had been a cold early summer in London. And, it seemed to both of them, there was of late, a strange uneasiness in Old Highgate: it felt as if the very earth was spiritually unclean. Curiously enough, this presentiment was felt only in one certain part of the grounds. And if neither of them could understand this vague feeling, they could at least stay away from that area of the cemetery—particularly at night, when their imaginations reached their uttermost limits, and every shadow conjured forth images fraught with mystery and horror.

Today's job was to dig a trench to check on old sewer pipes extending to Fitzroy Park, and very close to the black, decrepit walls of that ancient, unknown cemetery.

A thick mist still covered the ground, some places reaching up to shoulder height. Bert and Will walked past Comfort Corner, so named because so many people named Comfort happened to be buried there, and headed toward the Egyptian Avenue. Neither man talked. Bert Jones' demeanor bespoke of a fowl mood, and Will Baker was a bit queasy in the stomach. It was too early, too cold, and with the fog-covered dawn, things seemed out of place, almost eerie.

Bert Jones pulled a weathered piece of paper out of his pocket. It was a map of the borough's sewer lines.

"Here's where we start the bloody trench," he said to Baker, pointing to a spot circled on the map, and then indicating a spot on the ground.

The sun was just beginning to melt through the haze, and there, on the opposite side, the thick, jungle-like foliage dissolved as if in a dream. Now, directly in Baker's line of sight, rose the spikes of a wrought iron gate. As Baker squinted, trying to find the location of the dig, his eyes were drawn up to those dreadfully sharp points. He'd never seen any kind of construct there before. There was something hanging on them. As a flash of heat ran through his empty stomach, he realized what it was. Will Baker started screaming.

There, impaled upon the spikes of the gate, was the withered body of Jemmie Craven. Three of the thick nail-like projections had pierced his chest clean through, emerging from his back, another through his right eye.

"My Lord Jesus!" Bert Jones exclaimed. "Will you look at that!" He put his thick hand on Baker's shoulder. "Calm down, Will. Calm down." Then he moved closer to examine the body. "There's another blinkin' graveyard yonder," he said as he peered through the bars of the gate. "I'll be damned. I never knew…"

"Don't go over there," Baker importuned. He was backing up, never taking his eyes off the gruesome sight. "Stay clear," he shouted. Now, all the warnings, the apprehensions of the last few weeks seemed to point to this one ineluctable fact. It was too much for Baker.

"When it comes down to it, it's just another stiff," Bert Jones said. "See. He must have tried to climb over and slipped. I guess Jemmie showed up for work after all. And lookee here. Look at all this money lyin' on the ground. Ol' Jemmie musta struck it rich. Maybe he found it inside this old place."

"Or robbed a bank," Will Baker added. A great fortune could not have quelled the rumblings in his stomach.

Bert Jones bent down to gather up the gold. He motioned over to Baker. "You better go find a constable. You'll make no mention of the coin of the realm, will you now? To the good constable, I mean."

"I'm off. I hope you like being here abouts alone," said Baker as he left to find an officer, and to get as far away from that ghastly sight as possible.

*     *     *

War of a different sort, war games in fact, were played out on other fields in London itself. These were games on a much smaller scale, and involved some few of the neighborhood children, who would oftentimes divide into sides representing English or German soldiers, emulating their heroism or villainy in exaggerated style. The children, of whom ten year old Nigel Cochran was one of the leaders, took their parts quite seriously in these games, although those taking the role of the Germans might once in a great while exhibit a slight degree of half-heartedness.

Whether they felt an empathy from playing war in a place where real soldiers had come to rest is a matter for conjecture, but of all the places within a short time's walk or run: Hampstead Heath, Waterlow, Dartmouth, or Alexandra Parks; or Highgate or Queen's Woods, and the Crouch End playing fields—none had the mystery, enchantment, or adventurousness the children associated with the old and new cemeteries.

As far as the children were concerned, the older section of Highgate was much too hard for them to gain entrance. Visiting hours had been truncated and admittance limited to guided tours, due to rumors and strange goings-on: ghost sightings, witchcraft ceremonies, vampire sightings, and general hooliganism. Presently, the guided tours had been suspended for what was hoped to be the short duration of war. In addition, they would have to climb some fairly high and smooth stone walls, and go over barbed wire fences to gain access to the older cemetery. This seemed too daunting a task even for the older boys, when all they had to do to enter the newer section, was to wait for the caretaker—really only a volunteer docent who was too old to run after the likes of them—to take a nap or go to the WC, then run in and lose themselves among the monuments. Though every lad of them would be loath to admit it, there was also the slightest bit of apprehension when it came to contemplating the older cemetery, and it was a relief to them all that its entrance was so difficult.

The Cochran brothers got an early start on the fourth day of June, partly to avoid being caught out late, and partly to avoid a certain little blond-haired girl. Lucy Simmons had been trying to tag along with them, ever since most of her friends were dispersed around the countryside in anticipation of a German onslaught.

The Cochrans, both dressed in heavy sweaters and long pants, met the rest of their mates at Waterlow Park, near the hospital, and quickly started for Swain's Lane.

It was a cool morning, the sky was just beginning to lighten, and mist rose to at least four feet for the entire length of the street. It was then they heard Baker's scream.

*    *    *

Cyrus Wilson headed over to the Hound's Tooth as soon as he arrived back in Highgate, some seven days after his adventure. He was going to act humble, he told himself, but he was very proud of his effort and he certainly expected to be lauded—a triumphant return. He could not wait to see Elizabeth and Kate and hoped they might wander into the pub after work. And what about Michael? Would he be surprised when he returned and found out.

Entering through the swinging doors, he went straight up to the bar, fully expecting Harry Kendall to treat him to a round. Instead, he felt a coolness. Everyone seemed to be staring at him, but no sooner than he tried to catch someone's glance, it was averted, their eyes quickly downcast. These stares were not by any means, in adulation. Indeed, their aspect was more that of pity.

Harry Kendall was not in sight, neither were Cyrus's compatriots from the rescue. For some odd reason everyone evidently found it hard to look him in the face. He stood for a few minutes with both hands on the bar, a foot up on the footrest, and a helpless, confused look on his face. Polly came out of the back, saw him and tried to turn around before she was spotted in turn, but she was too slow. Perhaps it was better to get it over with and so, she went up to him. Like the others, she seemed to feel badly, and, instinctively, looked away as she spoke.

Wilson managed a smile. He looked very old just then.

"What is it, lass? Tell me." Then the thought first entered his mind. "Polly. What is it? Oh Lord. Not Michael? Dear, tell me."

She turned her face as she started to cry, wiping away a tear when she yelled to the back room, "Harry Kendall! Come out here. It's Cyrus. He's back."

As their paths crossed she whispered, "I don't think he knows."

Cyrus watched as Kendall walked slowly out of the back room where he kept the supplies. He seemed to be gearing himself up for a miserable task as he approached, but Cyrus eyed him hopefully, like a beggar, even though he could feel a thousand butterflies in his stomach, and an utter fecklessness in every limb.

"He's not dead?" Cyrus asked in a trembling voice.

"No, no, nothing like that. He's in hospital."

Cyrus collapsed on the barstool, exhausted in his relief. Sighing heavily, he said, "Give us a pint."

"Sure. It's on the house." Kendall poured him a mug of ale, put it down in front of him and waited for him to take a sip. Cyrus drained the mug in one long swallow, wiped his mouth with his coat sleeve, then looked back at Harry Kendall with steely eyes. He could sense there was more.

"Give me another."

The bartender poured another half-pint into a mug and slid it across the bar to Cyrus's hands.

Cyrus Wilson could see that the barkeep was having trouble speaking. Was Michael maimed? Did he lose a limb? Was he not going to make it? What was it? "Out with it, then," Wilson said impatiently.

"Mike's been called a coward...a deserter."

Cyrus's jaw dropped a full mile. Of all the terrible things he could have imagined in the last few minutes, this one caught him totally off guard. Barely comprehending this information and its implications, he could have asked what happened or how or where. Instead, his dumbfounded look quickly turning both grim and resolute as he challenged his friend. "Do you believe it?" Then he gestured around the pub. "Do they?"

Kendall, eyes looking down at the bar, shrugged his shoulders as if he really did not know.

Cyrus did not argue. He did not change expression. On this point, he could only accept blind faith. He glared at Kendall for awhile as he tried to digest the information. Finally, he erupted, "Is that what this is all about? I thought I had a lot of friends in this room!" As he gazed around, he saw many of them, all either making believe he was not there, or trying to avoid his look. "I guess I was bleedin' wrong."

Reaching coolly in his pocket, he pulled out money for two pints, slammed it on the counter hard enough to shake liquid out of two nearby mugs that had been filled to the brim, gave Harry Kendall a very rancorous look, turned and marched out.

A nasty scowl took form on his features as he stamped down the dark, deserted street. They were so eager to accept him as a hero, and now they're just as eager to crucify him as a coward. He headed in the direction of Elizabeth Hammond's flat, instead of his own house, intuitively knowing he would find sympathy at her door.

He was wrong, and he knew it the minute he saw her eyes. Just like the others. She could not look at him, and was disconcerted and ashen-faced, not even extending the courtesy to invite him in.

Cyrus Wilson could not be mad at her, instead he could only feel an immense sadness. He could not bear to ask her why. "Did you go to see him?" he asked slowly.

"No, I couldn't," she responded icily.

Cyrus could not believe the cool tenor of her reply. "You haven't seen him!?" How could she be like those others?

"No."

He stared at her dully and could not think of anything else to ask or say. He tried to think if there could be any reason why, but was unsuccessful. Finally giving up, and feeling, almost against his will, a bit of anger creeping into his once-fond thoughts of her, he turned and walked down the two flights of steps to the building entrance and the street.

Elizabeth closed the door, leaned up against it and cried, sunken deep in her wretchedness.

She took herself very seriously, especially with regard to her ideals, and it had now led to this. After hearing of the rumors from Lieutenant Roberts, she first tried to ignore them, not telling anyone, even Kate, but doubts soon began to creep in. Her curiosity got the best of her and she started asking questions of people at work. The news had spread quickly to London, and before Cyrus returned, she had made up her mind. Kate argued with her but to no avail.

She had been in love with a hero, an ideal, not an ordinary man. The mere thought of accompanying him to a ball, with her in a splendid gown, and he in his regimental dress red uniform, made her heart swell. Perhaps, at one time, another chap in the same uniform would have had the same effect on her, but upon hearing the news of Hinton-Smith's heroic participation in the Saar offensive, she had almost burst with pride, and had fought a monumental battle within herself, to keep from heading to the nearest street corner to proclaim the news. It was almost as though she was doing something more for her country, because of her relationship with him.

Elizabeth might as well have told Hinton-Smith, "Come back to me a hero, or come back on your shield," as a Spartan mother might have told her son, twenty-five-hundred years earlier. "Do not disgrace the uniform!" Even coming back with a few trivial honors would have been enough, but coming back in full disgrace for all to see, had produced a shame in her that was unbearable.

Elizabeth Hammond was an idealist. She had sought perfection in a man in uniform, and now that uniform was immutably tainted. The insinuation had been enough. Everyone she knew or encountered, with the exception of Cyrus and Kate, ironically the two people closest to her, thought he was guilty. Elizabeth was a woman who, from an early age when she had lost both parents, needed and eagerly sought the acceptance and approval of those in authority, whether it was from the adults who ran the orphanage she and her sisters had been sent to, or her teachers in school or superiors at work. For her, his innocence or guilt did not matter: their disapproval of Hinton-Smith was irrevocable. Had he at least the decency to come back dead, either as a hero or a coward, she might have been able to go on with her life after a suitable period of mourning, so, two days after she heard the news, when the rumor was pronounced fact, she pronounced him dead, and from then on, considered him as such. It had not been an easy resolution for her—she felt an immense amount of guilt, especially when she thought of Cyrus Wilson. She felt she was deserting both of them in their hour of need, but she did not see any other way.

Elizabeth even considered quitting London, moving up country or immigrating to the States. It was all too much for her.

She had prayed for Cyrus's return so she could ask for guidance, and even sought out a local minister for counseling, but the fact was, unconsciously or not, she had made up her mind when she first heard the rumors confirmed: Michael Hinton-Smith was a deserter. She could not think of him, speak of him, or acknowledge any reference to him. He was dead to her, plain and simple. And now, the decision made, she had an aching in her heart, a vast emptiness for a lost ideal, and she was in mourning.

"Who is it?" Kate asked as she came into the front hall.

"Cyrus."

"Well, where is he?"

"He knows. He probably hates me." She once more started to sob.

Kate was by now exasperated. "What do you expect? You're being a bloody idiot. It was only a few months ago you were celebrating him as a hero, wasn't it?"

"Kate! Stop! I can't help it." Then she said in a low, almost inaudible voice, "He betrayed me, us...I feel badly enough."

"And well you should. It's the bloodiest stupid thing I've ever heard. He didn't betray anybody. You don't even know his side of the story, do you? And he's lying in a coma in hospital. He needs you."

"We've already had this argument. It's over. Period. Now leave me alone. I cannot speak about it anymore."

Grabbing Elizabeth's arm and gripping it tightly, Kate said, "Well I'm not deserting the lieutenant or Cyrus when they need me. You can take your holier-than-thou attitude and chuck it for all I care." Kate rushed out the door and slammed it shut, hurried down the stairs and ran after Cyrus Wilson.

When Wilson heard the small, dainty footsteps running after him, he was certain Elizabeth had come to her senses. He smiled and turned, but was surprised to see Kate running up and tearfully hugging him.

"He's innocent," she cried. "I know it. It's a mistake." She kissed Cyrus on the cheek. "Don't think harshly of Lizzie. She's confused. Lizzie's talking like some crazy person. She'll get over it. She'll return to her senses. I'm certain of it." She put her arms around Cyrus and hugged him.

Cyrus stared at her, considering her words, but now there were other issues, more important. "What do you know?" he asked.

Unlike her sister, Kate had gotten to know Hinton-Smith as a person, not an icon. She was now eighteen, working as a nurse for the Royal Air Force. Some people do not realize the value of what they have, until it is put in jeopardy, and upon hearing the bad news, Kate realized that she might actually be in love with the lieutenant, and knew immediately that she would do everything possible to see him through this crisis. She rushed to the Royal Northern Hospital on Holloway Road, and had continued going every time she was off duty, even though the lieutenant was under guard and no one was allowed admittance beyond the lobby. She was even the smallest bit exhilarated, and she had no problem admitting this little secret to herself, that Elizabeth had forsaken him if only for the time being. Until she had met the lieutenant, Elizabeth had always seemed to monopolize any of the lads that came around, even if they had been originally interested in Kate. Now the field was open for the only person that mattered to her, and Kate did not care if he was labeled a coward or a traitor. She was certain he was still the same good heart-ed, gentle, upright lad he'd always been.

"He's under military guard. They won't let anyone see him. The only thing they'll tell me, is he is still unconscious, and they heard he had amnesia when he was brought to Dunkirk," she said breathlessly, as she tried to keep up with Cyrus, who was briskly heading for the Archway tube station.

"They'll let me see him, or I'll know the reason why," Cyrus Wilson shouted. "And somebody'll bloody well pay for this rot, goddamn it!"

They arrived at the hospital at a little past eleven, and were surprised to find the admittance desk empty.

Not bothering to question their good luck, Kate leaned over the desk to find a roster. Nothing there, so she went around the desk and found it on a brown bulletin board on the rear wall of the admittance room.

"He's in Fourteen B, second floor," she whispered. She could not help smiling at the way they proceeded, like two spies penetrating the secrets of empire.

They tip-toed down the hallway to the stairs leading to the second floor, carefully listening with every step for the sound of any enemy sentry, doctor, nurse, or guard. They sneaked up the stairs, mindful of every creak of the wooden steps, hesitating at every half-way turning point.

Cyrus Wilson stealthily looked up and round the corner, then gingerly proceeded to the top. Once there, he looked up and down the hallway.

"It's clear. Let's go."

He found a sign with directions to the various rooms, found Fourteen B, and motioned for Kate to follow. Kate's heart was pounding, as it had every time she visited. This was the first time she had actually gained admittance. Little beads of perspiration formed on her brow, and her hands grew just a bit damp. Would he recognize her? Perhaps she would be the only one he recognized. But what if Hinton-Smith only saw the little girl she once was. She worried that she could never supplant Elizabeth in his heart, and in every comparison she made between herself and her sister, she came out the loser. She fortified herself by remembering that Elizabeth had renounced her love for the lieutenant, then tormented herself with the thought: how could he ever stop loving my sister? The realization hit her that she must really be in love with Michael Hinton-Smith, and she would stand by him forever, regardless what happened, thus proving the pureness of her feelings.

Then she caught herself. These thoughts set her up to ridicule: she sounded every bit as lame as her sister but in the opposite direction. She needed to simmer. Lizzie would come to her senses and most likely soon.

They peeked around a corner and saw a guard posted at the door, but he was sleeping in his chair, which leaned back against the wall. His head was limply dangling from his neck as though he was a rag doll with no spine for a prop, and it appeared to Kate and Cyrus that they could not have woken him if they had wanted. Wilson quietly opened the door and they went in. They saw two cots (there was a severe shortage of hospital beds at this time, as the government was husbanding all beds for the expected onslaught of the Luftwaffe), one occupied by a desolate RAF flight sergeant, who was so badly burned when he bailed from his Hurricane, that he was in a white gauze wrapping from head to toe, and the lieutenant in the other.

Hinton-Smith looked serene in his sleep. A large white bandage covered the majority of his head from the forehead up, extending down the right side, and stopping just short of his neck. Various small bandages covered other wounds where small pieces of shrapnel had been extracted. One arm was also bandaged. The only reminder that he was still with the living was a drip bottle connected to his other arm, feeding a glucose solution to him intravenously, and the small movement of his chest as he breathed. The pilot would moan from time to time, but nothing he did raised any response from Hinton-Smith.

"He's sleeping," Cyrus said.

"No," answered Kate, sadly, as she felt Hinton-Smith's neck for a pulse. "His breathing is shallow. And his pulse is rather faint. He's unconscious, in a coma."

"I've heard of that. It ain't no good, is it?" Cyrus kicked the wall of the room so hard in his anger, he punched a small hole.

Kate put her arms around Cyrus and hugged him tightly. Sobbing, she said, "He'll come out of it, and he'll be normal. I know it."

They stayed till almost dawn watching over him, trying to detect any subtle movement, then decided to leave before light broke. Kate waited for Cyrus to turn away as he walked to the door, then went over to the lieutenant, kissed the first two fingers of her right hand, and silently pressed them on Hinton-Smith's quiet lips.

The guard was still asleep, but they hurried down the hall and steps, and rushed to the entrance. A dowdy old nurse was now at admittance.

"Where are you going? You can't be in here at this hour."

Kate yelled back, "It's okay. We're feeling much better now. Wonderful care at your hospital. Cheers."

"Come back! I'll call the guard!"

"Make up your mind, you twit," shouted Cyrus as they pushed open the door and left. As soon as they were out of the hospital, they broke into a run, feeling like little children that had just put one over on the schoolmaster, then started laughing until they both ran out of breath.

The underground was for the most part empty as they boarded one of the trains and Cyrus Wilson became more serious as they sat for the long ride to Highgate. "I'm never going to talk to your sister again as long as I live."

"But Cyrus, she's..." Kate started to protest.

"No. I'm sorry. Loyalty. Nothing's more important. Without it, there ain't nothing, is there. Even your lowest dog is loyal."

"Cyrus, you mean so much to her."

"I thought Michael did as well," Wilson said. "I'm sorry, but that's final." His stern look said that any further argument was futile, and the long way home was painfully silent, only broken up as they left Highgate station when two society people out on the town, and driving with their headlights out due to the regulations of the blackout, screeched to a halt, almost running them down as they tried to cross the street on Tottenham Lane on the way to Kate's flat.

"You stupid sods!" Wilson roared at them as they sped away.

Upon reaching Kate's flat, Cyrus kissed her on the cheek, then turned and walked silently toward his home.

\*     \*     \*

The next morning saw Cyrus down at the Coldstream Guards' Regimental Headquarters in Aldershot at eleven in the morning. He was duly informed of the charges against the lieutenant and the circumstances as known: the claims of *LeFevre* and the intervention of Riordan. So far, none of the men who had served with Hinton-Smith in Belgium had been located, or had come forward. No one knew of the whereabouts of Sergeant Major Cawkins. As the adjutant said, "The whole mess of the evacuation still needed a bit of sorting out." By the late afternoon, Cyrus heard a rumor that was circulating among the soldiers that Hinton-Smith had run out on his men, none of whom survived.

# CHAPTER 25
# SHELL SHOCK

By late August 1940, it was clear to the English, if not the Germans, that the RAF was being slowly attrited into oblivion. Replacements for both pilots and airplanes could not keep up with losses, and the British had been outnumbered from the outset: in some actions, as much as ten to one. Aerodromes and their fields were hit with such frequency that squadrons often times had nowhere to take off or land, or fields that usually handled three or four squadrons could manage only one or two. The attacks on radar stations were knocking out communications and the ability of Fighter Command to direct their squadrons efficiently. Few doubted that elimination of the RAF meant invasion and the end of freedom, perhaps plunging the entire world into an age of darkness.

Then began one of those strange concatenations of events that started out from an unintentional bombing, due either to navigational error or jettisoning bombs out of fear, possibly eagerness to get home, or even embarrassment of returning with a full bomb load, and resulted in an incredible strategic turning point. Bombs fell on London, inundating Finsbury Park, Islington, and the East End, and within twenty-four hours, Churchill had eighty Wellingtons and Hampdens dropping bombs on Berlin. In the next act in this chain, Hitler screamed, "Since they attack our cities, we shall extirpate theirs," and he changed the main emphasis of the attack to the English cities, thus giving the RAF a desperately needed chance to rest, regroup, and replenish. Londoners would bear the brunt of the onslaught from now on.

*    *    *

From almost the first moment they learned of Hinton-Smith's return, Cyrus or Kate or both, depending on Kate's hours on duty, went to the hospital and camped out in the waiting room, asking all and sundry for information regarding the lieutenant. Finally worn down by Kate's gentle persistence and Cyrus's dogged determination, the two doctors in charge of Hinton-Smith's recovery, an army physician, who was in charge of the day-to-day supervision, and an army psychiatrist who consulted when needed, decided to supersede protocol and speak with them.

The physician, a portly, middle-aged man, with two lone, dark brown hairs sticking out at the crown of his head which was otherwise bereft of hair, was dressed in a typical white doctor's smock, with a stethoscope wrapped round his neck when he walked into the meeting. He was a kind man in his own condescending way, and politely waited for them to sit, then sat down himself.

"As you know, we're quite busy here, so I'll get right to what you want to know," Penrose said. "Then Captain Hardin and I will answer any questions you might have. Is that all right?"

Both supplicants nodded their assent.

"As you know, Lieutenant Hinton-Smith was wounded in the evacuation'" Penrose said. "We believe he suffered three types of wound, two of which can be serious: a contusion of the brain from a bullet wound, and a concussion from some type of explosion. The reason I am being somewhat obscure, is because we don't know exactly what is causing what." He hesitated for a second to see if they were following him. "We do know that he was caught in a bombing attack on the beaches of Dunkirk, and there, he sustained the injury which, I think, left him in this coma-type state. Earlier, perhaps only twenty-four hours earlier, he was hit a glancing blow in the head, on the right temple, from a rifle shot." Seeing their worried expressions, he hastily added, "This bullet wound was physically little more than a scratch, but apparently accounts for his amnesia, which he had when he arrived at the beach." Dr. Penrose kept his explanation relatively simple for these non-medical types. "A bullet to the arm suffered even earlier is already starting to heal."

Captain Hardin, lean and garrulous in his officer's uniform, had no similar code of simplicity. He unctuously rubbed his hands together as he readied himself to display his knowledge. "First off, I must caution you that the length of time a victim is unconscious can usually be correlated to the severity of the brain damage, and the lieutenant's injury is no longer acute, but chronic." He looked up over his spectacles. "Let me explain: a concussion can result in widespread paralysis of brain function, but does not necessarily result in brain damage. Usually there is a better than average chance of reversal. On the other hand, a contusion is far more dangerous." He glanced around to make sure everyone present was aware of the gravity of his words. "It also involves head trauma, with the addition of edema and possibly multiple intracerebral hemorrhages. Cerebrospinal fluid pressure has probably been raised, and this can cause severe demyelination, and/or often result in a coma, the latter which is presently the condition of the patient."

Dr. Penrose, hands behind his back and listening intently, stopped to interject, "He is basically saying that the lieutenant has suffered a bruised brain." He raised his eyebrows as if to emphasize the point.

"Is he in danger?" asked Kate.

The psychiatrist signaled the doctor that he would like to handle the question. "The problem is, he has both these conditions simultaneously. Physically, I'd say no. Would you agree, Doctor?"

"Yes. On the positive side, we find no incidence of a hematoma, or brain swelling. This most likely indicates that permanent damage is unlikely. He isn't in any great danger, as far as physical brain damage is concerned. Mentally, I'm not sure."

Cyrus said, "I don't understand."

"The wounds are minor, on a physical level," said Dr. Penrose.

"Yes," added Hardin. "It's been reported he already had amnesia when he arrived at the beach at Dunkirk. Then he received another tremendous shock to his system. If and when he comes out of the coma, you can expect to see cognitive impairment. This means: defects in memory; problems with personal orientation; reduced ability to use logic, think in the abstract, or even compute numbers. His show of emotion might range from being flat, a monotone, to constant giggling or crying, hysteria or even extreme anger…and, one might say, there may be mental changes."

Throughout the lecture, Kate had been able to keep calm, but now, in empathy for the lieutenant, she could no longer control her emotions, and burst out sobbing.

"I'm sorry to be so blunt," Hardin said to her. "But I feel it's important you know the worst scenario now." He hesitated and looked at Penrose. "There is also a best scenario," he added to leave some sliver of hope for the distraught young lady.

"But even at best," Hardin frowned as he went on. "He could have persistent symptoms, such as headaches, dizziness, uncontrollable shaking, an inability to concentrate, and some anxiety. You might want to call it, "shell shock." This is a relatively new concept from the last war."

Kate had not heard of this. "Shell shock," she asked? Now Hardin was really in his element. He leapt into his explanation. "When a patient comes out of a coma, such as in the lieutenant's case, he might relive the trauma, perhaps over and over—in dreams, recollections or flashbacks, or some stimulus might cue a recreation of the event. He might be doing this even now. Does he try to avoid all recollection of the event, or black it out? What happens subconsciously? Psychologically speaking, Michael has been under great stress. Case in point: we don't know why he was running away."

"Doctor," Cyrus said quietly, but forcefully. "He was not running away."

Hardin cleared his throat and nervously fingered his spotted bowtie. A small bead of sweat appeared on his forehead. He hemmed and hawed for a second, then rephrased his statement.

"Something traumatized him…whether it was the wound to his head, the loss of a best friend, suffering through a horrendous bombardment, or even the odium of a constant retreat…to the extent that he could no longer accept this condition, and withdrew into himself. This often follows a physical injury." He wiped his brow.

Cyrus had wanted them to be blunt, but now, forgetting that Kate was a nurse, and probably had at least an idea what to expect, he also wanted to give her some hope. "What's the good news?"

Penrose smiled and walked up close to Wilson, leaning toward the older man.

"If he comes out of the coma, and I'm reasonably sure he will, recovery can be spontaneous and rapid. In all honesty, we can't really offer a complete prognosis until he comes out of the coma, and we can start testing him and treating him. You will have to be both supportive and patient."

"Complicating matters," Hardin said in a petulant manner, as though someone was trying to take away a favorite toy. "Some pigheaded French colonel is pressing hard for a court martial." Then, eyeing Cyrus, added hastily, "For God knows what reason."

"But I and Captain Hardin assure you, we will not release him from our care until if and when he is completely recovered," the doctor said, as if that statement would ease every care and worry which those attendant could possibly have. Again, showing kindness, though Cyrus Wilson felt it was somehow in contradiction with his patronizing attitude, Hardin said he and Penrose would arrange for them to sit in the lieutenant's room a few times a week.

Hoping to stimulate something within him to stir, for the next few weeks Kate went to the hospital on her rare off time, sat between the two cots and read from selections of Kipling and Conrad, both Hinton-Smith's and Cyrus Wilson's favorites, much to the appreciation of the pilot.

Not long after, with the consent of the two doctors, Wilson succeeded in getting the lieutenant transferred to Whittington Hospital, which was at least very near South Grove, in Highgate.

*   *   *

On September 7th, starting in the early evening and lasting through the night, some 1700 Londoners were killed and injured from the nonstop bombing of the Luftwaffe. Now the shrill sound of the sirens was for real. London's East End and docklands were devastated.

Slum land property collapsed, with scarcely a house escaping destruction in some areas. Smoke from burning houses and buildings filled the air, blackening it till daytime turned to night.

The bombing continued for fifty-eight straight nights. For most of these, the Luftwaffe targeted South and East London, coming in over the south coast between Beachy Head and Foreness, leaving the people of North London, including Highgate, living relatively normal lives.

Dispersion of children, non-combatants, and non-essential persons to the safer countryside had begun much earlier in preparation for the bombing and threatened invasion. Much of this dispersal had been voluntary, and even now, especially with so many bodies to evacuate, no one was forced to leave. Thus, Nigel Cochran and his friends and younger brother were still living at their homes. There was no school nor organized activities for the children, and except for the air raid drills, when they huddled together far below the surface in Highgate Station, they had the run of the city, and the most freedom they had ever experienced.

Some days, the Cochran brothers and company hiked over to Islington to see the damage. Other days saw them as far afield as White Chapel or the docks. One morning, they found the remnants of a bombshell casing by Leicester Square, and spent the rest of the day looking for other souvenirs. Another day, they sneaked aboard an abandoned double-decker bus that had crashed headfirst into a deep bomb crater and had yet to be towed out. These excursions seemed to give their war games more impetus, and they played at them daily, but most of the time the games were played closer to home.

Meeting at the entrance to Waterlow Park on a cool, dreary overcast day towards the end of September, the boys, with Nigel Cochran in the lead, walked through the park and nonchalantly up to the gates of New Highgate. Nigel went ahead to scout while the others hung back. No attendant was in sight.

"Come on, then," Nigel Cochran said as he returned. "But keep it quiet." The six of them furtively walked in and headed down the Serpentine path to Cundey's Corner without stopping until they had put some high bushes between themselves and the line of sight from the attendant's usual post. Then they split up.

The eastern, or new, cemetery was completely different from the older of the two cemeteries. It was flat, resting on a level area that sloped gently down off Swain's Lane, and easy to find one's way around in, with little if any natural cover for the war games. Tombstones and monuments were in abundance, of course, and these provided various hiding places, but it was commonplace and dull when compared with the old cemetery's ostentatiousness and magic.

None of the children had ever done more than look at the old cemetery through the North Gate, and that view was limited, so they could not readily compare. To them, the new cemetery was the best of all possible worlds, and due to its ordinary appearance, there was not much to scare them, other than it being a cemetery. They all had doubts about playing across the road.

Nigel Cochran's team had only run about a hundred yards down Top Road when he stopped abruptly in his tracks, exclaiming, "Oh no!" and motioned his mates to stop, by sticking his arms out to his sides. It was too late. Only twenty yards away, in mid-jump off Karl Marx's monument, knees bent and arms out for balance, was Lucy Simmons, and there was nothing for it: she'd already seen them and was all smiles.

"Where have you lot been?" she asked. "Why didn't you have to go to the country? Can I play with you today? All of my friends went to the country."

Simultaneously, the boys shouted, "No!"

Everyone turned as they heard shouting coming from the direction of Cundey's corner. Suddenly, three boys came sprinting into view.

"Bloody hell," Nigel Cochran said. "You're supposed to give us a full count. Right?"

"Never mind that," Simon Street shouted, through heavy breathing. "The caretaker's on the warpath. And he's a bloke this time and quick. He's right behind us, he is. Run!"

They could hear a man's gravelly voice shouting from the distance. "If I catch you bloody nippers, you'll know what for!"

Lucy stepped directly in front of the boys. "I know a shortcut out of here," she said.

"I know who you brats are," the man screamed, as he drew closer.

"And I'll know your parents soon enough. We have the goal for the likes o' you."

Thomas Cochran yelled, "Bloody, bloody, bloody! Now we're done for."

"Will you let me play with you?" asked Lucy with the utmost calm.

"There ain't no bleedin' girls in the bleedin' army!" Simon yelled.

"I can be a nurse," Lucy countered.

"Can you get us back to the entrance without him seeing us?" Nigel Cochran asked.

"Dammit. Here he comes. Let's go," shouted Simon Street.

"Not only that, but I know a way into the old cemetery," Lucy smugly replied as they started to run.

"Right. Follow Lucy," commanded Nigel Cochran. And they all ran off, leaving the path and running through the trees and across the horsetail, shrubbery, dense grass, nettles, and even various tombstones set in the ground. Under Lucy Simmons' direction, they let the attendant see them dart down Back Road, then doubled back across Burma Road, around the circle, staying close to the outer wall, until they made it to a hidden spiral staircase. The boys were surprised and hung back.

"Come on, then," urged Lucy Simmons. "This goes to a tunnel under Swain's, and comes out in the old cemetery. Hurry before that old geezer finds what we're about."

One by one, they descended the stairs, only to find themselves in a cold, damp, completely black tunnel. By the time their eyes adjusted, they were so far into the darkness they could not see a thing. There were puddles of water on the ground, it reeked of sewage and oil and the tunnel was too wide for them to straddle it with their arms. They were blind, and gingerly reached out with their hands to feel for something solid. Normally, the boys would put on a solid front and act tough, especially with a girl around, but here, it was as if they each were alone in a universe of darkness. Hearing each other's voices did not seem to ease the fear.

The last one down the steps no sooner touched the bottom, then abruptly said, "Bugger all! I'm off." He turned around and went back up the iron stairs.

The others, relieved that they would not be the first to back out, turned and rushed up the stairs after him. After the "scream," which had become somewhat legendary to them, no one really wanted to go into the old cemetery.

Emerging from the stair well back out in the daylight, Nigel Cochran was surprised to see that his whole gang, with the exception of Lucy and Tommy, had left. The caretaker was nowhere to be seen.

"Maybe we'll come back here some other time," Nigel Cochran said, putting on a brave face.

"And I don't even mind being a nurse," Lucy said, smiling.

# CHAPTER 26

# THE MATES REJOIN
# THE LIVING

Just outside the port of Bournemouth, at a hastily built field hospital made up entirely of large gray and khaki field tents sporting large red crosses on a border of white, Sergeant Major Cawkins had almost finished his rehabilitation. During the course of two months, he had gone from delirium, fever, and complete bed rest, to sitting up and joking with the nurses and doctors, to exercising his upper body, to exercising his legs while in the bed, to crutches, and finally a cane. Everyone on staff was excited by his progress, but he wanted more, and he wanted it faster, so he worked harder than anyone, tiring out the nurses until they started exercising him in shifts.

From the moment he could talk, the sergeant asked everybody he saw if they had heard what happened to Hinton-Smith, but nobody seemed to know or was able to find out. In actuality, the doctors were at first so concerned for Cawkins's health, they did not let any information which might have an adverse effect reach him. Later, as the sergeant recovered, information was still not forthcoming.

Cawkins spent much of his waking time encumbering his attendants with some rather peculiar requests: all dealt with medieval studies, the Crusades, in particular the exploits of the Templars and Hospitallers, and medieval Continental cemeteries. He wanted every

319

volume he could find on these subjects, and eventually persuaded one of the nurses to go to the British Library on her leave in London, when he had exhausted all local resources.

For a long time, he ignored or, at least, put off the central question. Had Hinton-Smith tried to come back for him? Did he go back, only to find him gone already? He had no idea.

He did not know if Hinton-Smith was dead, wounded, or in a prisoner of war camp. What else could account for him not coming back? Did he even have enough time? That there was a strange, otherworldly being in that graveyard—of that he had no doubt, and with the living memory of that nightmare seared in his mind forever, all doubts about Hinton-Smith had vanished entirely. Still, what had happened to the lieutenant?

This was made more compelling by a pointed remark on the first visit from his wife Maggie, a smallish, golden-haired woman who looked almost like a child next to her tall and broad-shouldered husband, even when he was lying in bed. It was the second week he had been back, but only the first he had actually had his wits about him. One of his oldest friends, a sergeant from the 7th Guards Brigade, First Sergeant Simon Topham, whom he had known since serving together in Simla after the Great War, had also stopped by with a few mates when he heard Cawkins was wounded.

They had been visiting for some time when Maggie Cawkins, becoming more and more perturbed and vexed about what sooner or later must be said, finally interrupted the soldiers. "I still cannot believe he left you like that."

Cawkins looked at her, and then at the others, as if to say he did not understand.

"He ran away. He left you to die. Michael, your lieutenant," Maggie finally said. "How could he?"

Topham signaled his friends and got up, not wanting to reopen any old wound, but Cawkins motioned for him to sit back down in a manner that brooked no right of refusal. "I don't get what you mean." His face had already started to redden and he was beginning to feel agitated, as though he would not lend the least credence to what she said.

One of Topham's friends, a tall, thin soldier with a pencil-thin mustache, said, "If he ran away, mate, I don't blame 'im. It's not as though it's the bloody Four Feathers."

"Was that your lieutenant, mate?" the other asked with genuine surprise. "The whole army's heard about him. Coldstreamers aren't known for running backwards."

"Some stupid Frenchie stopped 'im. That's the funny part. They should have been kept busy enough, stopping their own," said the first. "And what about old Riordan—starin' down that Frenchie." The two soldiers had a good laugh between them.

"Toppy. What's going on?" Cawkins asked his friend.

Topham put a friendly hand on Cawkins's shoulder, while Maggie turned away and wept. "Jack," he said, trying to make light of the matter like it was an almost common occurrence. "He wasn't the only one. Some lieutenant from the 2nd Grenadiers had to shoot three blokes that started to panic, or two whole brigades might 'ave turned and run."

"I heard some others had to be stopped by the bayonet," added the tall, thin soldier, with the mustache.

The other man, short and feisty, grumbled, "They should shoot the lot of 'em, as well as that lieutenant. A blot on the reputation of the Guards. That's what, ain't it?"

The tall soldier laughed. "They were so eager to get out of Dunkirk, they crammed themselves into boats like bloomin' sardines in a tin."

"Toppy. Maggie. I don't understand. Is Michael dead? What?"

Maggie Cawkins spoke first, through her tears. "You haven't heard? Nothing?"

"No, nothing."

"He's in a hospital in north London, in a coma, under guard. He's been branded a coward and a deserter."

"He left you to die, mate," said the tall soldier.

"And all his men," the short soldier said angrily.

"The hell he did! Who told you these frickin' fantasies? A god-damned fairy?" Cawkins shouted as he got up on his elbows. "I know you," he said to the feisty one. "You were back here, wet nursing trainees, when we were getting our asses blown apart." Cawkins strained to sit up, and for a moment, the small man backed up a few feet, concerned for his wellbeing. Topham positioned himself between the two, pushing gently on Cawkins's shoulders to ease him back down onto the bed.

Maggie Cawkins was concerned that he would weaken himself and set back his recovery. "Stay still, Jack. Please. The nurse said you should stay calm."

"And you," Jack yelled even louder at the thin mustache. "What action did you see? Were you under fire? Or were you with your buddy here?"

A nurse ran in, cautioning the visitors. "Shame on you. You'll have to leave, if you keep working him up. And you, ma'am, ain't he your husband? Shame on you getting him all agitated like that. You soldiers! Do you twits think `e's been away on `oliday?"

"Shut up," Jack shouted at the nurse, her jaw dropping in surprise as she decided discretion and a quick exit were the better part of valor.

"And Toppy, you better get that tiny prick and his pal out of here before I whack `em." He need not have said the last, for they were already edging toward the door. "Hey you two. Just so you get your damn stories straight. Hinton-Smith didn't run away, he saved my life. And you," he scowled as he looked at his wife. "How could you ever listen to such rubbish? You know the boy. C'mere."

Maggie moved forward hesitantly and before she realized what was happening, Cawkins pulled up his blanket, grabbed her hand and put it on a long row of stitches running down his left leg. "Feel this? Without Mikey I would have lost it. No leg! A cripple, a gimp, if I even made it back."

Maggie pulled her hand away like the wound was a red-hot poker and sobbed. "Now just get out of here. All of you!" He lowered his voice, although his glare remained fixed on the two soldiers. "Toppy, stay awhile. Let's talk about old times."

"Whatever you say, Jack, but what about...?" he asked, gesturing after Maggie, who tearfully hurried out of the tent.

Cawkins merely shrugged his shoulders. He was mad at her.

When the two soldiers and his wife left, Cawkins spoke quietly to his friend. "In the first days of the war, we were seconded to the

French Army. Damned if Mike didn't capture a 200 man garrison almost by himself, staring down a sniper and shooting him. Something right out of a movie."

"Well," Topham said. "You never know when it just becomes too much, do you?"

"Maybe. But it was the boy who chose to fight as a rear guard," Cawkins said. "We had no orders. Could've retreated with everybody else." Cawkins stared at Topham to emphasize the point. "He saved my ass again in a hedgerow. We were down to maybe twenty men. The damn Krauts had gotten in front of us. We were ambushed. I was hit by shrapnel early on, helpless. You should have seen him." Cawkins became very animated, sitting up and gesturing with his good arm. "Mike led a charge that wiped out the Germans. He got hit stepping in front of a Kraut that had me in his sights. Mike fell to the ground from the impact but still managed to fire off a round. Hit the bastard right between the eyes. Then he helped carry me till we found an old house for shelter from a rainstorm. I must have told him a hundred times to leave me behind but he said the Jerries were shooting prisoners."

"Do you get it?" Cawkins cried out. "He was going to take a bullet for me. That's a coward?"

"Sounds like he deserves a bloomin' medal," Topham conceded, though he seemed to squirm in his chair, trying to adjust to the strange turnabout.

"There was a sudden attack—Panzers—and we all rushed out of the house. There was a great explosion. Everyone was killed in the explosion, except for me and the boy."

There was no way in hell he was going to mention anything about the graveyard. "Again I told him to leave me and save himself but he wouldn't have any of it."

Cawkins took a long breath and squirmed a bit in the bed trying to find a more comfortable position. "I was in and out of delirium by then. I remember being carried, then set down by this blown up bridge. Now, if it wasn't Mike who carried me, who was it? He was the only one left."

"Mike was wounded, exhausted and giving me most of what food was left." Cawkins sat up again on his elbows looking at the tent canvas, thinking. "Here's what happened. We reckoned he could make it back to our lines in half a day, but if he carried me, at least three. Mikey found a place where I could hide. The Nazis were everywhere. He was going to find a vehicle and come back for me. You know what his main concern was? Do you? He wasn't going to let me lose my leg to gangrene."

"So you think these rumors are all rubbish?" asked Topham, genuinely surprised.

"Think? I don't have to think! They are! He could've left me a dozen times. I told him to, I swear," Cawkins said in earnest. "But he said he'd come back. I don't know what happened to him after he left, but I knew...I was certain, he'd return."

As he related these tales, Cawkins felt his own guilt physically welling up in his throat. He coughed and took a drink of water. How could he have ever doubted the boy? What a fool he had been.

"Well he couldn't, you know. Least ways, after the Frenchie shot him."

"What? A Frenchman shot him? How in God's name did that happen?" Now he sat up all the way. "Well," he said, clearing his throat. "At least I know he's alive." Suddenly feeling very fatigued, Cawkins lay back down and closed his eyes. He raised his arm to shake hands with Topham, who shook it, said, "All the best," and left.

Before Cawkins fell asleep, he realized that a great weight had been taken off his shoulders: Hinton-Smith was alive. There was a reason he didn't come back. He now had someone to share the burden of his story: the demon or whatever the hell it was. And more importantly, he had his best mate back. Michael would emerge from his coma. Of that he was certain. Mikey was too stubborn to sit out the war like that. Way too stubborn. Cawkins smiled and drifted off to sleep.

After Topham's visit, Cawkins redoubled his efforts both in research and rehabilitation. Whatever Hinton-Smith had done back in the cave, he was no coward and certainly not a deserter. He'd clear Michael's name if it were the last thing he did. He owed him his life. He spent the rest of his confinement writing letters to whomever he thought could help. For some reason, none of the letters were answered, and none of those he tried to contact responded. Cyrus

Wilson, who was one of the people he wrote, later said he never received any such letter.

Cawkins did hear that a French colonel was agitating very strongly against Hinton-Smith.

He also wanted to get back in the fight, to get even. Cawkins had heard rumors that the next fighting would be in North Africa, and he wanted to be ready.

\*　　\*　　\*

The Junkers 88 bomber was specially equipped, pared down to achieve a greater speed and range. It did not carry the usual payload of 4000 lbs. of bombs; the little bit of armor she had, had been stripped off, and the Daimler-Benz engines had been replaced with two suped-up Jumo 1200 hp engines. With the newfound speed, the pilot was pretty certain he could outrun any British Hurricane, and maybe even give a Spitfire a run for its money. About the only concession to convention and safety were the three 7.9 mm machine guns.

All of the three crewmen were handpicked, one of the few crews of its kind: all were SS. Taken from the rolls of the Waffen SS, they had gone through commando school, been specially trained as bomber pilots and crew, and participated in actual missions. Thereafter, because they had proven to be exceptional "party" men, they were utilized to fly Nazi bigwigs, sometimes even Goebbels and Himmler, to party rallies, staff meetings, or far afield to headquarters in Poland or Norway—most of the time they were glorified chauffeurs. Whenever a mission of this type came up, they fell all over themselves to participate.

Fifty other Dorniers and Junkers were waiting in line, four abreast on the tarmac, their twin engines roaring, to take off into the night on their journey to England. Some were already aloft and easing into formation or circling over Cherbourg, waiting for their comrades to join them on this night's assault on Britain. After all the bombers were in the air, they would rendezvous with a fighter escort of Messerschmidt 109's over Ghent, then proceed over the channel. All of the regular crews were happy they were flying at night. It was a dark and overcast and they hoped it would be the same across the channel—less chance of search-lights, ack-ack or Spitfires finding them.

A sleek, black, unmarked Mercedes pulled up to the side of the Ju 88, and a man of medium height, slender and almost delicate look-ing, stepped out. His face was smooth, he only shaved every third day, and his short blond hair, combed back and held in place with hair cream, gave him the appearance of a youngster. He was in full aviator's gear, from his waist-length, black leather jacket with sheep-skin lining and collar, to his aviator's headgear. The only things one might have noticed to be out of place were the black walking shoes that looked like they would be fitting attire for an English schoolboy.

He walked casually to the bomber, carrying only a small suitcase of English make and an army brown haversack, also made in Eng-land. He reached the port on the underbelly of the bomber, lofted both case and pack through the hole and, grabbing the sides with both hands like an accomplished gymnast, swung his feet up into the entrance, then pulled the rest of his body up and inside.

As soon as the man was aboard, one of the crew gave the pilot a signal, and they were off, taxiing down the runway. A second crew-member directed the youngest *Obersturmbannfuhrer* in the entire German army to sit down on what amounted to a folded blanket placed on the inner metallic hull of the fuselage. When the aircraft reached a cruising altitude of 12,000 feet, another crewman came over to the stranger and offered a hot mug of coffee.

Stripped of even the barest insulation, the Junkers rapidly became cold. Eber took the mug and cradled it in both hands to draw heat off the cup. To the crewman, a hardened Nazi himself, it looked like Canaris, the Head of Intelligence, wanted to infiltrate Eton.

Normally, Heinrich Eber would be acquainted with the crew. They would be part of his unit, this craft would be a glider, and they would land together and fight together. He preferred gliders. Tonight was going to be different.

The plan was to accompany the bombers on their route to Lon-don, and while the other Dorniers and Junkers saturated the blacked-out city with bombs and incendiaries, this plane would break off and head toward Scotland. Over Scotland, Eber would bail out.

When Eber finished the coffee, he pealed off his aviator's uniform, underneath which was a gray tweed suit and a heavy cardigan sweater. Under this, he had the warmest underwear the Third Reich could afford.

He unpacked a black parachute from his haversack, and laid it out end-to-end for inspection. Eber never relied on someone else's prudence. Carefully refolding it, he placed it on the floor for when he would need it. Next, he checked one of his two weapons, a semi-automatic colt pistol. It was his favorite after the luger, and if he was inadvertently caught, it would be easier to explain away an American gun than a German. The other was a custom-made stiletto which he had taped to his right leg.

Heinrich Eber's look belied his true nature. He was one of those pseudo-intellectual gangsters that felt so much at home in the SS and Gestapo. He studied history and philosophy and came to the conclusion that might made right, and he could get away with whatever he was strong enough to get away with. He would leave it to others to clean up the mess.

He had a personal stake in the war. After all, he had done quite a lot to start it. He was second in command when his German commandos dressed in Polish uniforms and attacked the German radio station at Gleiwitz, and he also participated in the kidnapping of the two English officers, Stevens and Best, from Holland before the war had become hot. The first mission gave Hitler an excuse to attack Poland; the second, after the English officers were blamed for an assassination attempt on Hitler, allowed the Fuhrer to inflame the German people against the Allies.

Since then, he had participated in operations behind enemy lines in Poland and Norway, and had organized English and French-speaking commandos to drop behind enemy lines to disrupt communications and cause various other forms of havoc during the route of the Allies in France and Belgium.

And now, he was fresh from a meeting with his Fuhrer, and suffused with his own importance. Indeed, for this singular honor, he had been pulled out of his commando unit in northern France, where he was involved in planning his usual form of behind-the-lines mischief for the invasion of England.

It obviously was an important assignment, but there were questions that kept raising their heads, and he was concerned. He had no real idea of the mission and would not find out the exact details until he met his contact in England. And it was obvious he would be acting as a spy— and perhaps, he was the wrong man for the assignment. What puzzled him the most, was that his orders originated from a little-known section of the *Ahnenerbe*—a branch also known as the Nazi Occult Bureau, a branch of the government that had provided him with one of the oddest of experiences. The Fuhrer's last words were striking: "Yours is the mission that will win the war for us."

He was not a man to harbor doubts for long, and it had the personal stamp of the Fuhrer, so he let it go at that. It must be important. His Fuhrer was never wrong. His was a true belief.

A lieutenant walked back from the cockpit, balancing himself with his hands. He shouted to Eber over the loud drone of the airplane. "The captain thinks you might enjoy the view of London. You can come forward."

"Ja," Eber answered. He quickly changed it to "Yes," and got up.

In the cockpit, Eber could see that the clouds had disappeared, and what looked like a huge circle of many raging campfires loomed off in the distance.

"That is London," said the pilot. "You can see what our Luftwaffe has done to it."

As they approached the burning city, the plane started jumping up and down, buffeted by the anti-aircraft fire. Eber's knuckles turned white as he clenched the rail of the pilot's seat for support. Then it felt like he was being turned upside down as the captain peeled the Junkers off to the north. He decided he really preferred gliders.

Eber went back to the rear of the aircraft. Sitting down cross-legged, he placed the haversack between his legs. He found a pair of gloves and a thick, black scarf. He wrapped the scarf around his neck, tucking the ends under his jacket, put on the parachute, making sure it was secure, then the gloves, then sat back to think, to mentally prepare himself for the jump. The biggest problem was going to be the cold. He had no worry of a bad landing, or being caught.

Locating radar stations, and destroying them, had been a priority from the start of the Luftwaffe's offensive. The previous few nights, the Luftwaffe had attacked up and down the coast and inland in what might have seemed a random attack if one looked at the various targets. Eber would have been even more mystified about his assignment, had he known that this feint was to hide the fact that radar stations, in almost a straight line to Dundee, including Bedford, Leeds, and Douglas Wood, had been viciously inundated with explosives, thus making a radar-free path into Scotland: all this just for him.

This also accounted for the flight plan to accompany the bomber groups to London, instead of taking the shorter route from Stavanger, Norway. A lone bomber might have slipped through, but why take a chance?

A crewman came up to *Obersturmbannführer* Eber and told him they were approaching the drop zone. Eber got up, made one last check of his equipment, and headed for the hatch, which the airman then opened. The man held up his right arm, looked at his watch and counted. "*Funf, vier, drei, zwei, eins*," and brought his arm down. The plane was at fourteen thousand feet, about forty miles due west of Aberdeen, Scotland. Eber jumped. He had a long way to go to reach London.

\*     \*     \*

The early morning of September 17th, saw Cyrus Wilson exhausted from being up until midnight, and surly from fatigue, after sorting people in and out of tube stations used for bomb shelters during air raid training exercises, and Kate equally exhausted from working double shifts to help with all the RAF pilot casualties.

Upon his arrival at home the evening before, Wilson had found a letter from one of his old commanders of the Coldstream Guards, questioning why one of his best soldiers was idle, and asking him to volunteer in whatever capacity. For a long time he had been convinced of the dire necessity of the struggle they were in, and now he swallowed his pride and decided he would do whatever job was deemed necessary, even if he had to be part of the Home Guard. At least he would be doing something. First thing the next day, he went down to one of the volunteer depots and signed up.

Consequently he was tired but exhilarated as he flopped down on his living room sofa. He smiled. It was a good thing to take part.

At three that same morning, Michael Hinton-Smith opened his eyes for first time in over two months. There was a hint of a smile on his gaunt face, as though he had just woken from the most pleasant of dreams. And indeed, he had. He had been walking down the long, narrow corridor in a musty-smelling museum, viewing a medieval tapestry that hung for the entire length of the wall, and detailed colorful scenes from history. As he progressed down the hall, often tracing the various figures with an outstretched finger, it was almost as if he could feel the living flesh, so real were the images. Examining a section that seemed to be from the Crusades, he came to the picture of a young warrior, a red cross running the length of his white tunic, over glistening silver armor, and even for a dream, he felt himself mesmerized by the very handsome lad, with long brown hair and beard, and piercing blue eyes. As Hinton-Smith stared at the picture, the knight began to move. To the lieutenant, it seemed only natural as the knight stepped down and out of the fabric and became three-dimensional, alive. It was if they were lifelong friends, brothers, and the man promised to take Hinton-Smith with him to the East. He would show him things unknown to even the brightest, well-traveled of men, wonders and knowledge the likes of which were known only to the few, the initiates, because he, the lieutenant, was rightfully one of them. But the lieutenant had difficulties, things he had to make right, and he was not sure if he could accompany the knight. The young man smiled at Hinton-Smith and pledged that this journey would be the most important undertaking of his life. And, as for his troubles, the knight promised to find solutions to all of them before they left, thus reassuring Hinton-Smith that he was indeed free to leave. Next, they were flying, as if on their own power, over seas and land. Hinton-Smith recognized the Parthenon, St. Sophia in Istanbul, Susa, the ruins of Persepolis and the acropolis of Babylon, as though he was being led along the Royal Road. From Bamian, they headed northeast to Gilgit and Hunza and were soon viewing a monastery near Mt. Kailash. It was as though the lieutenant's guide had discerned his most ardent desires for adventure and knowledge.

When he woke up, he felt as if the journey had actually taken place, and at first thought he was still in the Himalayas.

More corporeal wants arose soon after. He was hungry, but not overpoweringly so. He surmised he was in a hospital and wondered why he was there, spending a good ten minutes or so examining the bottle of clear liquid suspended above his arm. The first thing he remembered was he had been in a war, but not how he had got out of it and into this place. He vaguely knew who he was, and this knowledge became stronger in him with each passing moment. None of these few memories were, however, clear or precise; all were hazy like the nebulous characters of a dream, within a few minutes of waking. Something or someone seemed to be missing, but he could not put his finger on it. He did have a fairly clear memory of a soft, mellifluous voice, almost but not quite recognizable, whispering in his ear, drawing him back to this life. If he ever saw the owner of that voice, he thought he might fall in love with her. And that was strange, in that he was certain he already had a love.

A particularly pleasing quatrain had somehow entered his head, and kept repeating itself over and over:

> Oh ye who tread the Narrow Way
> By Tophet flare to Judgement Day,
> Be gentle when the heathen pray
> To Buddha at Kamakura!

It made him think of a friend: a very good friend, but which friend, he could not say. Did he know anyone from India, or a Buddhist? Kamakura was in Japan. Strange, the things one remembers. Then he realized it was from Kipling, from Kim. Why would he know that? He also felt as though he had gotten the best, most restful sleep he'd ever had, and lived a whole different life within his dreams; one that almost made up for all the sleep he had missed over there, on the Continent. Yes. That was where he had been. He automatically tried to raise his arms to stretch, was surprised to find very little strength, so, out of curiosity, he tried to raise his legs. They felt like lead weights. Not panicking—his mind was not yet clear enough to panic—he bemusedly wondered how long he had been asleep. He sat like that for two whole hours, pondering these questions, along with the age old questions that one only finds time for after a near death experience: why am I here? Where did I come from? Where will I go from here? And, why did I come back?

Few answers came to mind and those that did were discouragingly obscure. He found he did not have the capacity to perceive, or focus; at least he was not sure which one it was.

A nurse came in, turned on the main light, and out of habit began performing all her duties, including turning the patient, without even noticing he was awake. Trying to speak was also difficult for Hinton-Smith, and when he managed to hoarsely say, "Ma'am," it looked as though she jumped about five feet. As she regained her composure, he was certain that she was quite deliberately cool to him. When he tried to talk to her or ask questions, or even ask what day it was, she simply responded, "I don't know," and continued with her work, nervously scurrying through her tasks, like a little field mouse gathering fodder. She ignored him to the best of her ability. Finally, he summoned all his strength, sat halfway up and with a raspy voice yelled, "Well at least get me a bloody newspaper, if you won't answer me," and was surprised to find he could still shout.

"Sir," she muttered in surprise.

"Get the hell out of here and don't return till you have a bloody newspaper!" He was indeed angry.

Again, "Sir!"

"You heard me!" he bellowed. "Go! Now!"

Never did he remember having such a hair trigger temper.

She scampered out of the room in embarrassment, while he fell back, exhausted, onto his pillow, breathing heavily and sweating. The nurse ran to look for the guard who was supposed to be on duty, but was loitering near one of the other nurses, because his charge had not changed position in over two months.

Finding him, she half lectured, half castigated him. "You better go check on your prisoner. The bloody maniac's woke up. He screamed bloody hell at me, he did!" and then she ran off to try finding the newspaper that she had seen earlier on one of the doctor's desks. When she returned, she had a pile of newspapers under her arms, ranging from old to new. Still, she was relieved to see the guard at his post.

"You come in there with me when I give him the papers," she insisted to the guard, who had already looked in on the lieutenant, more out of curiosity than concern. Only eighteen, fresh out of school, new to the army, and still wanting much experience, the guard had been told not to speak to Hinton-Smith as well.

"Are you sure we should give him those? We're not supposed to talk to him," he asked, somewhat confused.

But the nurse had made up her mind, taking the line of least resistance. "He's a human being, ain't he? We don't have to say a word. And I'll not be having him yelling the high heavens at me."

The nurse reared up her shoulders, put her head down and marched into the room. To keep up appearances, she looked disapprovingly at Hinton-Smith, then dropped a half-dozen newspapers on his lap. Clearing her throat, she huffed, "You're quite welcome indeed," turned and marched back out of the room.

Hinton-Smith watched her leave. He stared at the pile of papers and felt the weight on his legs. His hands shook from weakness as he lifted the first one, a morning edition of the "Times." Then his eyes and mind began to devour them.

Amongst all the headlines, certain were of particular interest to the lieutenant, as he started out with the most current headlines and stories: in the Daily News of September 16th, 1940: "HEAVY ITALIAN LOSSES ON LIBYAN BORDER," and "THE PALACE BOMBED FOR THIRD TIME." In the London Times of August 12th: "AIR BATTLES OVER THE COAST;" followed by, "FOURTEEN RAIDERS SHOT DOWN," and "RAIDS OVER FRANCE." And in the Daily Telegraph on August 15th: "144 RAIDERS DOWN FOR LOSS OF ONLY 27 PLANES," and "DIVE BOMBERS SWOOP ON CROYDEN." He read that RAF bombers had attacked military objectives in France and the Low Countries, concentrating on aerodromes and long rows of barges being assembled for Hitler's projected invasion of England; that the Luftwaffe had turned Rotterdam into a city of ruins, with 30,000 dead, and was now intent on doing the same to London; that battles over England were now starting in earnest; that bombers were now inflicting real damage on English cities. But the RAF was shooting down Messerschmitts, Junkers, and Heinkels by the dozens, and causing a lot of Weltschmerz for Herr Goering. Then the papers redundantly noted, as they had noted in almost every article about the Home Front for the last six months, that hospital beds had been cleared of all occupants not deemed in desperate condition, as they expected 140,000 casualties from the first onslaught of the *Luftwaffe*. Gas masks had been distributed. Women and children from the threatened urban areas were evacuated to the country and resettled. His Majesty's Government, now under Churchill, had assumed control over every aspect of life, whether military, civil, or economic.

Each of these simple sentences took him three or four times to read through. He could not seem to focus his concentration any better than that, but fought the frustration as best he could, certain that it had to end.

The next time the guard came in to check up on him, Hinton-Smith begged him for more information about the war, and out of sympathy and youth, the young private complied. He brought him up to date on the military and domestic situations as he knew them: the fall of France, the onset of the Battle of Britain, and the threat of invasion, but was discrete enough not to mention anything of the lieutenant's house arrest. Because of this discretion, the last bit he mentioned, trying to make it as casual as possible, was the miracle at Dunkirk. Hinton-Smith's expression immediately went from one of great interest, to one of exceeding horror, and the scant color he had vanished, leaving a ghostly pallor.

"Jack," whispered Hinton-Smith, his eyes downcast. "I didn't go back for you. I let you down." His feeling of remorse was overwhelming.

Uneasy, the guard slowly backed up. Speaking rapidly as he withdrew, he told the lieutenant that an old man and a pretty young lady had regularly come by to sit and watch over him throughout this period of his unconsciousness. However, he was uncertain of their names.

When the private left the room, Hinton-Smith wept.

\*     \*     \*

If asked, Colonel *LeFevre* would assuredly tell anyone who would listen that if Riordan would have obeyed orders, "The situation would be over and done with." Evacuated from Dunkirk, he went back and fought in the Battle of France, but was once more evacuated at the request of *De Gaulle* to help organize the Free French from England.

For some unknown reason, and this is no exaggeration, all the wrongs of the campaign had by now been summed up for *LeFevre*, in the person of one lowly lieutenant: the failure of the majority of the French to fight; the lack of air support; the lack of support from the British; the crushing defeat of the French. Anything and everything could be laid at Hinton-Smith's doorstep. He even managed to obtain a pass to view Hinton-Smith while he earlier lay in coma at the Royal Northern Hospital and his anger mounted with each passing minute.

*LeFevre* became active with the Free French and *De Gaulle* while in exile in London, but no matter how busy his schedule, he never lost sight of the poor, broken Englishman, lying in his hospital bed. Taking a flat in Highgate, when Hinton-Smith was transferred, it was almost as though he was worried that the British authorities would subvert his designs, and he must keep a close watch on his quarry. He truly meant to see him hang, and until that time, his monomaniacal quest would not let him put his full attention on anything as insignificant as the war.

Unknown to the few that were the lieutenant's supporters, the situation had become quite political. Many members in the British government felt guilty about how they had treated the French: in the lack of a substantial expeditionary force; the holding back of RAF squadrons when the French were begging for them, both during the evacuation to Dunkirk, and later during the Battle for France; the egregious contempt and disregard shown an Ally by having a British-first embarkation policy at Dunkirk, only put right by direct orders from Churchill; and finally, the destruction or disablement of the available French Fleet at Mers-el-Kébir along with any French soldiers that happened to be defending them, to keep the warships from falling into the hands of the Germans. Perhaps they thought the prosecution of one small lieutenant would make up for all their misdeeds and lack of foresight. Even Captain Riordan, with all his connections, was finding himself in a bit of a hot spot right now. They transferred him out to North Africa before he could even catch his breath from Dunkirk.

But Cawkins, being in a hospital near an army base with the coming and going of many veterans, became privy to much talk of the lieutenant's situation. He was also on a list to be transferred out as soon as he was fit, but he would have none of that. He planned to go to Highgate to see Hinton-Smith the minute he was able. Figuring he had at least a couple of days leave coming, he would sneak out before the doctors pronounced him fit, if need be.

During one of his early morning rehabilitation sessions, the air raid sirens went off and all the patients that could go on their own were rushed out to a slit trench, a few yards beyond the tent camp—soldiers and nurses carrying those who were too seriously wounded. Cawkins only managed to stand it in the trench for a few minutes, then he was out, crutches and all, rushing to join a Bofor's crew, who let him take a few shots at the enemy planes. He did not hit anything, but felt a great rush of adrenaline and some satisfaction that he was able to strike back. When the raid was over, he was surprised to see a middle-aged WAAF walking out over the fields defusing unexploded bombs, as nonchalantly as though she was picking tulips on holiday in Holland.

Cawkins shook his head in amazement and looked down at his crutches. He slowly extended his arms, then let go, letting the crutches fall to the ground. Unaided, he walked gingerly back to his quarters.

It was time. He made plans to head for London to see Hinton-Smith, and perhaps, just perhaps, he'd pay a little visit to a certain Frenchman.

## CHAPTER 27

# LOST IN THE MAGIC JUNGLE

I t was early afternoon, on another gray, overcast London day when the Cochran boys and their gang finally got up the gumption to sneak back into New Highgate and explore the tunnel reaching to the old cemetery. Though it was still dark and musty in the tunnel, Nigel had secured a torch before going and that eased the fear and apprehension they felt the first time down below. The passageway was navigated without incident and a new game started soon after the children emerged on the other side. Simon's team took the part of the Germans, and stood at the bottom of the steps, in front of the Colonnade, hands over their eyes, and turned facing the Tudor Gate. The cemetery was completely empty, and silent save for the occasional sound of small animals rustling among the fallen leaves of autumn. Nigel Cochran looked at his team of English warriors, turned to start up the stairs, and with his right arm, gave the signal to advance. They all proceeded to run up the pathway of stairs, Lucy Simmons following Nigel's band out of a sense of gratitude and loyalty, for being allowed to join in. Knowing his foes rather well, Nigel motioned for his team to continue up the stairs, while he stopped short, turned and looked through his binoculars just in time to see Simon sneaking a peak. After giving the scamp a good chastisement, he bounded up the remaining stairs to find his friends all frozen, dead in

337

their tracks. None of them had ever seen anything like this: great sycamores and ash trees abounded, and ivy clung to both walls and
mausoleums, overgrowing the place like a tropical jungle. Further in they
could see giant elm trees and yews. A winding, loose gravel path curved
upward into the cemetery and mysteriously disappeared. And if one
strayed off the paths, one could become hopelessly lost among the tall
grasses, shrubbery, nettles and tombs. Ivy grew on the first crumbling
tombs that came into sight, and looked like jungle vines to the children.
Everywhere they looked was green, green, and more green: a dreary, dull
green on this cloudy day. One might as well expect Robin Goodfellow to
rear out among the briars, a mythical Sinbad chasing a sword-wielding
skeleton, or a great white hunter slashing his way through the undergrowth with his machete. It was a mystical, phantasmagoric place where
anyone or anything might happen upon them.

Nigel Cochran realized that if they stuck to the path, they would
find a good enough place for an ambush. It would be foolish to head
into the dense interior. There was so much of it, they would most
certainly get lost. The grounds inside were immense.

They jogged near the triangular-shaped tomb of Sir Loftus Otway, designed in this fashion to commemorate his service during the
Peninsular War against Napoleon, and stole a peak through the skylights. Then, Nigel had to make a decision when they reached
Comfort Corner. There were three paths, and he had no idea where
any of them led. Being a cautious lad, he chose the middle. They
proceeded more slowly now, both to look for a likely place to hide for
their ambush, and because they were winded from the steady ascent
into the netherworld of the cemetery as well. Though no one would
admit it, a certain amount of uneasiness added to their sluggishness.
They were only in here on account of a dare.

Halfway up the route Nigel Cochran had chosen was a massive
gateway, flanked by huge, stone obelisks, which at one time had been
painted in garish reds, greens and yellows. What paint was left was
now faded, and the rest of the surface of the obelisks had gone back
to its original dull light brown. This was the entrance to the Egyptian
Avenue, a hundred feet of pathway flanked on both sides by iron
bound stone sepulchers, and leading to a lone cedar of Lebanon.

"We'll keep going down this path," said Nigel, as he looked up the Avenue, which was built into the steepest part of the hill. "This other one's too obvious. Simon would think we're in there. I want to surprise him."

"Well," Lucy said. "Your plan is fine, but I want to go in there and look. I've never seen anything like this."

"Right," said Nigel. "When you come back, be careful they don't see you."

"Maybe you can sneak up behind them and we'll catch them between us," added Thomas Cochran.

Thus, they parted: the boys, unknowingly headed for the very North Gate that had always appeared so ominous when viewed from the outside, and Lucy, slowly proceeding up what was sometimes known as the "Street of the Dead," exploring each tomb with its names, and dates, and epitaphs as she went.

At the end of the Egyptian Avenue, Lucy found a curved road, also flanked with iron bound, stone sepulchers, but this time, comprising a perfect circle. When she peered into one of the more decrepit tombs, that had lost a door from years of neglect, she saw seven intact coffins laid out on stone shelves. There were two more that had deteriorated, but she did not get close enough to see if there were any remains. As she was looking, she heard a noise, and hastily, if uneasily, ducked inside. Nigel was right. Here they come. Her face contorted with disgust as she saw a skeleton, brown with decay, and long, dusty, gray hair still protruding from the skull, ensconced in a partially open coffin.

Sure enough, with Simon in the lead, the "Germans" crept forward in single file down the narrow path of the Egyptian Avenue. Simon could not resist the foreign-looking surroundings.

When they approached the circle, he motioned for his companions to start up one side, and he would take the other, thus catching the "Brits" in the middle. He had only just gotten out of sight of his mates, when Lucy, arms stretched out over her head, and screaming savagely, jumped out at him. Simon jumped so high, Lucy insisted to the others, later, that he hadn't yet come down as the others came running into view.

"I thought you were only going to be a nurse," Simon complained, as he tried hard to regain his composure, and act as if nothing happened.

"I'm an English nurse," Lucy tersely replied, and then she ran off, back down the "Street of the Dead" to the main path.

During the day's play, many Germans were killed many times over, and many British soldiers had their wounds tended to. Some RAF pilots were even given a mock burial. As they crossed over the grounds that day, they saw the statue of a mournful woman being comforted by her mother and a contemplative angel deep in meditation; another youthful angel sat on a tomb holding a swaddling cloth. A fifty-foot long, triangularly shaped tomb was pranced upon; a gigantic mausoleum, modeled after a tomb of a king of Halicarnassus was scaled with great effort, and the multi-storied catacombs below St. Michael's Church were peered into with a mixture of wide-eyed awe and respect.

Never having been on the western grounds before, the children had not heretofore realized there was an even older section to the cemetery. Perhaps their intuition or innocence had guided them away from that ancient, doleful place until now. Somehow, the play drifted over to the decrepit bricks and stones of the old cemetery, which was less than one twentieth the size of the more recent burial ground, and dated back to the early Fifteenth Century.

None of them had been this far into the cemetery, or this far off the path, all day, and none of them had ever heard of these old grounds. They knew instinctively that this area was much, much older than the rest, perhaps going back to the very beginning of time.

At this point, Nigel Cochran signaled the rest of the children to come together to rest under a lonely, mournful oak that was splintered in two, having been recently struck by lightning. They had filled used milk bottles with water to use as canteens, and Mrs. Cochran had given the boys enough sweet bread for everyone to share for rations.

The time passed as they joked and teased and told stories of what they considered to be of great merit, and the sun slowly slipped to the horizon. Simon's "Terror" they christened the incident in the Egyptian Avenue, and all of them, even Simon, although begrudgingly, laughed heartily whenever somebody brought it up. The night would soon be upon them, and none of them, intrepid warriors that they were, wanted to be in this place after dark.

Nigel Cochran got up. Everyone took this for a sign that it was time to leave. But Simon, in a moment of inspiration, crowed, "I dare you Limeys to go over the old stone wall."

Everyone thought that was one of the best dares anyone had come up with yet and a proud expression came across Simon's face, until Nigel countered the dare. "Why don't you Krauts go?"

For the next few minutes, a silence prevailed, as obviously no one wanted to take up the challenge. Nigel stared defiantly at Simon. In effect, it was a double dare.

To everyone's surprise, the first person to speak up was Lucy.

"I'll do it," she said. "I'll prove I'm brave enough to play war with you lot, and I'm brave enough to play in the Old Cemetery." Then, she walked over to the ancient wall, turned, and looked at the boys. "Well? Aren't any of you courageous lads going to give a lady a hand at climbing this wall?"

The others looked to Nigel for direction. Shrugging his shoulders, he took a long swig at his bottle of water, like it was something much stronger and he needed the courage it would bring, and walked over to where Lucy was standing. He cupped his hands together and said, "Put your foot here and I'll boost you up."

Lucy put her right foot up on the homemade stirrup, and said, "Close your eyes. I don't want you looking up my knickers."

"All right," he said. "They're closed." He soon felt the slight shoe in his hand, then the weight of her body as she balanced on the wall and pulled herself up. Then nothing as her foot left his hands. True to his word, he did not open his eyes. Only the other boys saw her climb to the top of the wall. She looked down at Nigel to see that he kept his promise, then waved to the others and disappeared.

Simon quickly motioned for his companions to gather around. When Nigel returned from the wall, Simon said, "I've got a great idea. Let's leave her."

The other boys laughed, nodded in agreement and started to quietly edge away. Thomas Cochran looked to his big brother for direction.

"I'm not sure," Nigel said.

The others looked at him in exasperation and rolled their eyes. Simon said brusquely, "Come on, then. Don't be a twit. She's just a girl." All then turned and ran.

Thomas Cochran looked at his brother again. A tear was running down his soft, white cheek.

Finally, Nigel Cochran said, "Don't worry. It's only a game. It'll teach her a lesson." He was feeling a little guilty as well, but his main concern was irritation that his gang had not even bothered to consult with him, and had just run away.

As Nigel grabbed his brother by the arm to leave, the little boy looked back with an immense feeling of guilt. It could not be right, but he did not want to be left behind, alone, and so followed with no more protest.

*    *    *

No sooner had they left, than a young academic type limped over to the damaged oak tree. Boyden had found it very peaceful to walk around the cemetery before his fake injury. Lately, he would find a spot under a tree and read, or write up his notes and research for the library. Picking out a different spot each time he came, he used both cemeteries so as to not draw any undue suspicion to his dead letter box.

In two years of visiting the Highgate cemeteries, he thought he had seen all of the grounds. Rarely did he see other people visiting the old graveyard. Every plot of land had been sold years before and any newcomers had to prove ancestral rights. Only the occasional groundskeeper or gravedigger made an appearance, and explaining his desire for peace and quiet, Boyden flipped these people a few bob, the gates were opened and no questions asked.

Thus the noise from the children had piqued his curiosity. Now he was doubly glad he had followed the sound to this place. He had no idea there was a cemetery within a cemetery in Old Highgate, and, a glance at the stonework, told him that it most likely dated from the Crusades. What luck! A medieval site right in his own back yard. He hobbled up to the wall, rubbing his hand over the dark moist stone. With this discovery, his day was made. This would make his spy friend happy—too bad he would never see him again.

Unfortunately, it was getting near five-thirty, and with his handicap, he would need a good half-hour to make it back to the entrance before the groundskeeper left. Next time he would get here earlier.

He had not taken thirty labored paces, when he thought he heard something coming from the opposite direction, that of the cemetery: almost like the voice of a little girl. He stopped to listen, but heard nothing more. "It's your imagination, old boy," he said out loud. "You better stop imagining things and get back to the entrance before you get locked in. Then your imagination could really run wild."

*     *     *

Lucy Simmons' feet hit the ground only minutes earlier, and she stumbled as she tried to keep her balance. Her knee scraped the wall on the way down, and she rubbed it to take the pain away. Excited to be in this undiscovered place, Lucy looked in every direction. The day was rapidly losing its light and she wanted to look at everything before it got too dark to see. She suddenly realized there was silence. Where were the others? They should be over the wall by now. She turned and looked to the top of the wall, expecting to see little hands and then heads, followed by whole bodies appearing over the top. Why were they so quiet? Leaning closer to the wall, she placed her ear against it to hear them climbing on the other side, and unconsciously folded her arms across each other as though she was suddenly cold.

"Nigel?" she softly called out. "Simon? Hurry up. It's going to be dark, soon." Then she laughed and called out in a taunting tone of voice, "You're afraid aren't you? Come on, then. There's nothing to worry about. You lot get over here right now."

Nothing happened. No sound, no movement. A practical lass, and now becoming just a bit apprehensive, she marked a "cross" into the ground by the section of wall she had climbed over, so she could find it again, then glanced around the cemetery wall to see if there was an easier way to get out: perhaps a broken-down section of wall, a tree's branch extending to her side of the wall, or a vine clinging to the stone. Now, she walked around the wall. Had she looked more carefully when she and the boys first approached this forlorn site, she would have been surprised to discover that there was a wide swath of ground, extending for two yards, and completely surrounding the cemetery wall, in which there existed no living thing other than mildew-producing fungi. It was certainly a place of death. And inside the ancient walls, it was completely barren except for dirt, weeds and the tombstones.

It took her some twenty minutes to circumnavigate one-half of the grounds, then she decided to make her way directly across to where she had climbed over. She reached in her pocket and pulled out her last bit of sweet bread and began to nibble uneasily.

Coming to the center of this ancient ground and decrepit, mildew covered walls, she found a circle of sleepy, crumbling sentinels of stone with strange foreign engravings that reminded her of a library book with pictures from Easter Island. These tombstones, whose sculpted gargoyle-like features glowered out upon the world, looked as though at one time they had a sacred obligation to thoroughly unnerve anyone, such as grave robbers, foolhardy enough to come anywhere near. And indeed, they had that effect on the poor little girl. She was no longer the brave lass that volunteered. As she gazed around the burial ground, her eyes became larger and larger. This was completely beyond her experience.

Inside of those baleful, threatening visages was another circle of more mundane, normal looking stones, and one large gray tombstone in the middle, on which was also engraved odd, foreign writing. It looked as though the strangely sculpted stones were guarding the one set alone in the middle, so she took that one to be the resting place of a very important person, perhaps even a king. All of the stones had peculiar markings, most of which she had never seen before. The exceptions were the swastikas that, to her mind, somehow seemed askew.

Unknowingly, she then walked over a barely discernable pattern, that of a skeleton, just breaking the surface of the dirt.

The light was fading. Already everything was a hazy gray and black. Objects were becoming indistinct at best.

She started looking around for a piece of wood or a large stone, perhaps a tombstone that she could edge over and lean against the wall. She moved with more of a sense of urgency now. If she could only find something she could step up on so she could reach the top of the wall with her hands. There didn't seem to be any easy way out of there, and she inadvertently started walking on her tiptoes, as though she was afraid she might wake up the inhabitants. Looking very carefully as she walked, Lucy strained to see something to use for a stair.

As she strayed further and further from the wall, she found herself getting colder. Her search for a lever brought her closer to the circle of gargoyles. Lucy heard a sound, not any clearer than the hazy images she could still discern, but a sound nonetheless. Backing up, she kept going until stumbling into the black stone of the wall. She could feel tears welling up inside, but she refused to give in, to cry like a little girl. Maybe it's just a stupid rat, she tried to convince herself. Keeping her back against the wall, she slowly lowered herself down to her haunches as though that would make her smaller and less likely to be found. She was certain something else was in here with her. Now she panicked. Now she screamed Nigel's name out.

Lucy had no idea what caused her to look to her right at that particular time, but she did, and what she saw caused her hair to stand on end and her face to flush bright crimson. Cool sweat formed under her arms, running down her sides to her small waist.

Right in front of her face, a leg came through the ancient wall as smoothly as a knife cutting through a gloomy, mold-covered jam. A whole body followed, dressed completely in black, with a bright, white shirt, covered by a black formal dinner jacket and cape. A tall, black, stovepipe hat made the figure look seven feet tall. Completely materializing through the wall, he turned to Lucy as though he had been looking for her. Lucy Simmons froze in fear as she saw his grotesque face, frozen in an unholy, half-smiling half-grimacing expression. It seemed that the left side of his face was permanently sunk lower than the right, but still leaving a horrendous smile, which flashed dull, white teeth, matching the dolorous pigmentation of his face. Standing straight in front of her, arms akimbo, he leaned back to let forth an earth-shaking scream. His whole body shook with the effort, but no sound reached Lucy's ears. Indeed, no sound came out of those rueful lips, but tears seemed to be falling off his cheeks.

He raised his right hand with a flourish, bringing the white, gloved appendage up towards his chest. He then turned away, but his hand, now floating in the air by itself, disembodied, continued to motion for her to follow. He started walking. Lucy could feel the presence of something hateful drawing near. A malignity so powerful, she did not yet have the resources to comprehend. She could not see a thing, but she began to smell a sour, acrid odor, that was starting to make her stomach feel nauseated. There were invisible hands closing tightly around her throat, and blood began to seep from her ears and eyes. She tried to scream.

\*    \*    \*

Two persons who had not seen Cyrus Wilson since well before his escapade in Dunkirk were the two gravediggers, Will Baker and Bert Jones. They decided to pay him a visit coincidentally on the one night that Kate Hammond insisted he take a rest from his new work and their hospital vigil.

Wilson ate very lightly, only a few biscuits, put on a dressing gown and lied down on his sofa, thinking to catch up on his Dickens, but his eyes grew tired and he soon fell asleep. All of the commotion and anguish of the last few weeks had exhausted him and he was finding that he needed a lot more sleep than usual.

It was close to midnight when Wilson was startled awake by a knock at the door. He cursed as he got up. "I'm coming. Don't break the bloody door down," he yelled. Feeling around his bed table for his torch, he turned it on, careful to keep the beam focused to the floor. "It better be a bloody emergency," he said as he straightened his robe, pulled on his trousers and went downstairs to open the door, only to find the two reprobates.

"Jesus. To what do I owe this bloody great honor," Wilson said with the maximum amount of derision he could muster. He stayed in the doorway as if to block it and lifted his light to shine directly in Bert Jones' eyes.

Jones brought up his hand and squinted but did not waste time. "Now you have to sell the house to me. You can't give it to that traitor, that runaway."

"I can give it to anyone I damn well please." Wilson knew he was speaking of Hinton-Smith and that made him even angrier than he already was from being woken by these two twits.

"Look here, you old geezer. I offered you a fair price, and that little bastard of yours is most like to spend the rest of his days in stockade, or maybe one early morning in front of a firing squad." Bert paused to let this last bit sink in. "So what's it going to be?"

"You don't understand something," Wilson said very deliberately to Jones. "Just so you know, it's got nothing to do with the boy. I don't like you." He paused to look at them. "I've never liked you. Plain and simple. And I'll be damned if I'd ever sell to you. Understand? Hell could freeze over before I'd sell to you." Cyrus Wilson was working himself up into a fine lather and yelled, "I'd burn the damn place to the ground, before I'd sell it to you. Hell, I'd put a beacon for the Nazis on it and let them bomb away with my blessing!"

"Looks like being a traitor runs in the family, don't it," Will Baker, the joker of the two sneered.

But Bert was no longer in the mood to talk. He pushed Wilson back into the house, and followed, with Will Baker close behind. Grabbing Wilson by the arm, Bert slammed the door shut and swung the old man over to Baker, who grabbed his other arm and pushed him back. "Where's your hero, now, mate?"

Jones shoved him back over to Baker. Now Will Baker kicked Cyrus Wilson's legs out from under him.

Baker spit on his back as he lay on the floor. Wilson cringed as the moist wad hit his back.

"You don't feel so almighty now, eh."

Wilson was on his hands and knees, trying to rise, when Baker got down on him as though he was riding a horse, slapping him hard on his sides. Baker then grabbed Wilson's head by the hair. "I think me mate's boots are a bit dirty. Maybe you want to clean them off," he taunted as he forced the old man's face closer to Bert Jones' muddy boots.

"Never," whispered Wilson, right before Baker rubbed his face back and forth on the boots.

"I'm spent," Baker said, breathing heavily. "I'll check the kitchen. All this work's brought up a powerful thirst." He pulled Wilson's head off the floor. "That all right wif you, mate?" He chuckled and then sauntered off to the other room, opening drawers and cabinets, till he found a pantry with a few bottles of ale.

Jones picked Wilson up off the floor, held him in the air for a few seconds and then threw him down unto the sofa like he might throw a bag of soiled clothes. "Remember, mate" Jones said, wiping his hands together. "You 'ave a decision to make. Right?"

"Bollocks to you!" Wilson said in a much-weakened voice.

Baker returned with an open a bottle of ale, gave his mate a swig, guzzled down half of it himself and poured the rest of it over Wilson's head. Picking up a corner of the old man's robe, he wiped his mouth on it, belched, and threw the bottle against the wall to break into a hundred pieces. "Thanks for the drink, mate. Cheers." He took his pants down and urinated on the floor, pulled them back up and walked to the door. "Toodle do," mate."

Standing over Wilson's limp body on the sofa, Bert Jones spoke once more, "I want this here house, mate. And I'll have it, I will. I guarantee it."

CHAPTER 28

# THE SMALLEST
# HERO

By nine that evening, townsfolk from all over Highgate borough were searching from Queen's Wood to the north to Hampstead Heath in the west, from Crouch End and Hornsey Rise in the east and St. Albans to the south for a missing little girl. No one had seen her since she left by herself after lunchtime to go play.

No one had thought to ask any of the local children and none of them offered up any information when they heard of the search.

Simon Street thought it was one of his best pranks ever. It would teach her a lesson. It never occurred to any of the boys that she might be in danger, though they were certain she was pretty scared by then.

Torchlight beams crisscrossed the night air looking ever so much like the lights that crisscrossed the night skies in search of German warplanes, just lower to the ground. They even searched New Highgate Cemetery where it was rumored Lucy liked to play, though no one thought to look in the older cemetery.

A brief fight ensued when a local Home Guardsman, one Bert Jones, insisted that all lights were forbidden at night, and could have been tragic if Nick Hensen had not heard the ruckus, separated Jones and Stanford Simmons and promised to bring as many Bobbies from the station as possible to continue the search until the Simmons girl was found.

Thomas Cochran was very quiet at dinner that evening. So quiet, that he appeared to be ill. He would not eat, would not talk or laugh at any of his mother's attempted jokes, and he had lost what little color an English boy has at this time of year. Finally, his mother sent him up to bed. "Should I blame you or call a doctor?" she asked Nigel when she came back downstairs.

After eating, Nigel Cochran excused himself and went upstairs to their shared bedroom. His brother was lying on his bed, which was more like a glorified cot with a thin foam mattress. He was curled up and on top of the quilted wool cover. Thomas had been softly crying, but now he had stopped. He had come to a decision.

Nigel walked up and sat on the bed. "Tommy, can you picture Lucy? She's probably home with her mum right now. Mad as hell at us." He chuckled at the image.

"Should we tell mum?" Thomas asked.

"Bloody hell no!" Nigel answered. "Ain't we in enough trouble?"

Nigel Cochran then saw a sight he'd never seen before. His little brother sat up, wiping the tears from his eyes with the back of his hands. The whiny little boy's expression was gone, replaced with a look of quiet resolution.

He made it plain and simple. "We have to go back."

Nigel was surprised. Before he could respond, his brother added, "Now."

Incredulously, Nigel Cochran asked, "You want to go back to the cemetery? Now? In the dark?"

Thomas Cochran started putting on his long pants. It was cool after dark at this time of year. "Yes. Now. Are you coming?" he asked with a forcefulness that belied his age.

"After our mum just screamed bloody hell at us? And that was for not coming in before dark. And you want to go back to the cemetery?"

"Now?" he repeated. "We have to go. We left her," he said with determination.

Nigel Cochran gave forth with every argument he could muster: sneaking past mum; sneaking out of the house; sneaking back in; cemetery after dark; coldness of the night; Bobbies on patrol; the curfew; ghosts.

And Thomas Cochran won the argument with one question, "If we didn't go, what would the lieutenant think?"

With a look of abject resignation, as though he was facing a firing squad at dawn, Nigel Cochran sighed, went to the closet and looked for some rags. He then wrapped his shoes in the rags for quiet, then looked for candles and some matches, while Thomas Cochran went downstairs and assured their mother that he was fine. He gobbled down some pudding and a glass of milk to prove the point, said he was very tired, kissed her goodnight, and went back upstairs.

While Nigel Cochran wrapped his brother's shoes, they decided they had better wait under the covers for a bit, until their mum came up to tuck them in, a part of life that Nigel definitely felt he was too old for, but that he would not complain about tonight.

Ten minutes after the tucking in, they opened a rear window, and with Nigel Cochran going first, shimmied down the drainpipe to the fire escape. Stepping quietly to the ground, they took the wrappings off their feet and stowed them on the last step of the fire escape for easy recovery. It was the darkest night they'd ever seen: the sky was overcast with storm clouds black with rain, blocking out any light from the stars or moon. Plus, there was the blackout. Nigel Cochran was extremely cautious when leading his brother across the narrow streets, listening for cars they could not see in the darkness.

They kept to the smaller streets to avoid any Bobbies or other people who might ask them questions, heading up Hargrave Park to Balmore Street, then over to Cheste Raydon, where they could see the wall of the new cemetery.

Nigel's hands were trembling and his stomach was jumpy. It was a lot easier to say let's go to the blinkin' cemetery when you were in your own well-lit room. And this wasn't even the blinkin' old cemetery yet.

If Thomas Cochran had second thoughts, he did not show them. They headed up Swain's Lane to the Gothic Entrance of Old Highgate. It was locked, and looked much taller and more imposing in the dark.

"Well," said Nigel Cochran, immediately regretting that he opened his big mouth. "The easiest way to get in is probably the North Gate."

Thomas Cochran did not look at him, he simply headed up Swain's Lane as though going through the North Gate was the most obvious solution in the world. By the time they arrived, both were breathing hard from the climb up the steep hill. Nigel Cochran was thinking about the North Gate the whole walk up Swain's Lane, and all the stories he had heard—ghosts, vampires, black magic, dead people rising from their graves—came back to haunt him. He remembered how he had to make a force of will just to look inside, and that was during the day. And now he had to take his little brother inside. "Jesus," he exclaimed. It was the first time Thomas Cochran had ever heard his brother take the Lord's name in vain.

"We'll have to climb over," Nigel said.

"I think it's too high for me," answered his brother, but with a child's eye for scale, he looked down to the bottom of the iron spikes, and sure enough, there was room for him to squeeze under, while Nigel scaled the black, wrought iron gate.

Thomas Cochran was about half way under when he chanced to glance up, into the dark forest of the cemetery—his brother was already petrified on top of the fence. Try as they might, they could not move. Coming out of the trees towards them, was an extremely tall man, dressed all in black from head to toe, except for a white dress shirt. The man was so tall, Nigel was sure he would knock his head on a large overlying oak branch, and he would have to duck. But the man kept coming, and did not duck. His head passed right through the branch, and as if to gloat, he purposely walked through another fully-grown oak.

All Nigel Cochran could think, was come on, Nigel, jump, jump, jump, but he couldn't get himself to move an inch, and the shadowy wraith was drawing nearer. Then he heard himself yell, "Run, Tommy. Run," but Thomas Cochran had got his jacket caught on a bottom rung of the fence.

"I'm stuck," Thomas Cochran yelled. "Help me. Hurry."

The phantom stopped some five yards away, letting both boys see his gruesome smile, then he raised his right, gloved hand and slowly shook his finger at them, as if to admonish them, "No, no, no. You don't want to come in here." Then, to their disbelief, he abruptly vanished.

Thomas Cochran felt a large hand grab hold of his right leg. He started screaming, "Nigel, Nigel," and then just screaming—as it appeared the ghost had come around and grabbed him from behind.

Nigel Cochran's paralysis was finally broken by the screaming, and he jumped down. As soon as he hit the ground, he heard an adult voice trying to reason with his little brother and stop him from screaming.

"Quiet, lad. It's all right. There's nothing there," he said as he unloosed Thomas Cochran's jacket and pulled him back through the fence. Nick Hensen stood him up and patted his head. "Are you all right?" he asked.

The tall Bobby in the dark blue suit took hold of Nigel with his other hand. "Hullo," the constable said. "I've got meself two live ones. What's all this, then?"

Surprisingly, Thomas Cochran started struggling. He was determined to go back in. He squirmed against the Bobby's grip. "We have to go in there!" he yelled.

Hensen chuckled. This showed great restraint, because he was in danger of bursting out laughing until he buckled over. "Hush there, lad. You'll wake the dead," he said. "And some o' the living. You two are the youngest grave robbers in the city. What are you about? Going to stake some vampires?" Then he laughed.

Thomas Cochran tried to twist out of the large man's grip. He writhed, he contorted, he tried to kick the Bobby in the shin, screaming, "We have to go! We have to go in!"

With the first kick, Hensen lost his sense of humor. "I think you lads better tell me where you live," he sternly suggested, while taking the little boy's arm in a firm grip and twisting it just enough that the little boy could not move without feeling a great deal of pain. With the answer from Nigel, he hauled them home, dragging Thomas Cochran, more or less.

From that time on, the boys were under virtual house arrest.

## CHAPTER 29

# BAD DREAMS ALL AROUND

**E**ber easily landed within his drop zone. Though he did not care much for parachuting, he had previously made over fifteen practice jumps, and four combat jumps. The four combat jumps had been behind enemy lines, at night, in the early stages of the war.

The first thing he did upon landing was gather his parachute and dig a hole. Then he took out his compass, took an easterly bearing, tossed the chute and compass into the hole, covering it with dirt and patches of grass, and started walking towards Aberdeen. If asked, he had left school and was on his way to London to join the RAF, and he had first-rate papers to prove it. He knew he was too young, he would say, but he would lie about his age and hope they would take him. No doubt, the Germans would be in trouble very soon, and he didn't want to risk missing the whole affair. A natural mimic, with a good ear for languages, he could sound Scottish, or Welsh, or like an upper class Londoner, if need be. The strange thing was, he was never stopped, never questioned, and only rarely looked at on his way to London, and that was by schoolgirls who took an immediate fancy to him—the young lad who they supposed was going off to war.

He made Aberdeen by the next morning, and caught an early train to Glasgow, by way of Dundee and Perth. He arrived in mid-afternoon, detrained to eat, and noticed there were plenty of young soldiers in the city of Glascow—at least near the station—and quite a few on the train. He was surprised there were so many, and that they were in such good cheer after their countrymen's debacle on the continent and chalked it up to their misguided sense of superiority. They would be losing that quite soon. After eating he caught a new train and slept most of the way south to London.

In less than two days from his departure, he reached his destination. Detraining at Euston, he brushed past the crowd, which mainly seemed to consist of women of all ages, many in uniform, and soldiers, and caught the tube to Oxford Circus, where he got down. He had time to kill before his rendezvous with Hoarsley, so he walked around looking at shops, and then down to the East End, where he viewed the destruction and smoldering fires from the recent bombing with pleasure.

Eber had not been trained in tradecraft, but he was smart enough to not just walk in on the dentist. Instead, he planned to arrive an hour early and make certain everything was safe, that he was not heading into a trap.

He walked up and down the street looking for a place with a good view of Hoarsley's building. Settling on a small cafe that had two tables in an outside patio, he purchased a Times from the nearest stand, sat down and ordered a cup of tea and scones. It did not seem as though anyone was watching Hoarsley's building. Nonetheless, he patiently read his paper and kept an eye on things, especially anyone who might linger on his or her stroll down the street. At half past five, now reassured, he paid his bill and walked across the street to Hoarsley's office.

"You're here. Finally," Hoarsley said after they had exchanged passwords and he had ushered the young man into his inner office. "You are quite young," Hoarsley observed, raising his eyebrows in question.

"You needn't worry yourself," Eber calmly replied.

Hoarsley nervously clapped his hands then rubbed them together. Something in the young man's eyes was dangerous.

"Let's get down to business." If he'd learned anything in his meeting with Boyden, it was to be even more cautious. "I'll make this brief. Our uncle (this was his new code name for Hitler) wants some information. I have a student here in London who is in a good position to get that information, and he is one of us. In any event, he is supposed to be. The problem is, and this is the reason you've been sent here, the chap doesn't seem to want to complete his studies or show us his work. That is, if he's done any work at all. His actions imply that he wants to drop out. He thinks our concerns are absurd."

"Are you at liberty to tell me what is this information?" Eber asked.

"No," Hoarsley replied. "Not yet. I'm sorry, but I must be cautious at this time." Hoarsley cleared his throat and looked at the agent. "That's it."

"That's it?" asked Eber, surprised. "You had me flown over here and thrown out of a plane so you can use me for muscle?" Eber had watched his share of American gangster movies. He usually identified with the mobsters.

"Dear Uncle puts great store in his and his nephew's education. Especially in these trying times. Need I say more?"

Eber shook his head.

"I would've done it myself, but…"

"Of course you would have," Eber said without a hint of sarcasm, having long been used to office types who had no fear as long as someone else did their dirty work. "Please continue."

"I have requested the young man to meet me here in half an hour. If he comes, you will do your best to persuade him to get on with his studies. Uncle does not like to be kept waiting. Now, can you handle this sort of thing?" Hoarsley asked.

Eber nodded his head contemptuously, "If I cannot, I'll at least be discreet enough when I kill him."

Hoarsley smiled thinly. This *was* a very dangerous man. "Come, sit down in my chair. I'll look at your teeth," Hoarsley said, as he clasped Eber's elbow and led him to the dental chair. "We mustn't think that way this early. He may yet come around." He laughed, "In fact, young master Matthew should be here any moment."

The time passed slowly and Boyden failed to appear. Finally Eber looked at the doctor as if to ask, what now? An hour had passed since the time of the scheduled meeting.

"My guess is he's dropped out," was Hoarsley's terse response. He disappeared into the reception room for a second, and re-entered wearing a long beige topcoat. "I don't like to do this, but it appears we have no choice. I'll show you where he lives. You can take care of the rest."

"That's fine with me." The sooner he was back in the war zone, any war zone, the better. "Any limitations?" Eber asked before they left the office.

"Only one," the dentist replied. "Don't kill him...yet. Remember, we need him for the research." He paused as if going through a mental checklist. He checked a patient's file, switched off a burner that was warming a pot of tea, and turned off the lights. "Right."

Eber nodded affirmatively.

Twenty minutes later, they walked down Prince of Wales Road, passing Boyden's flat. There was no noticeable light coming from his third story window, but that was easily explained by the blackout order. He might still be in. They kept walking, Hoarsley keeping up a conversation of small talk, Eber contributing little or nothing. After walking a several blocks past the apartment, they turned and started back. "You didn't see anything, did you?"

"No," replied Eber.

"I'll wait for you here," advised Hoarsley, when they reached Boyden's flat. "Don't be too messy, too loud, or too long. Right?"

"I'll be persuasive," Eber said softly as he started across the street, raising his hand to signify that all was understood. He believed a few words went a long way.

Boyden was a young man, and though very bright in an academic sense, and very idealistic when it came to the hope for Irish union, he had a young man's naiveté when it came to worldly issues. Being a citizen of Great Britain, he was habituated to the liberty, freedom of speech, and freedom of action associated with a democracy, regardless of the subjugation of his countrymen. After his first and only meeting with Hoarsley, it had only taken one day for him to make a decision. He would quit spying, the same as he would quit any occupation he didn't like. This Pan-Germanic medieval mysticism was too strange. Perhaps he would find other ways to help Ireland. The next day he told Professor Littleton that he had learned of an American surgeon, and he

wanted to take a leave of absence to go to America to have the operation on his knee. If successful, he would come back and join in the
fight. Going home, he took off the brace, forever, he hoped, and threw
it in the garbage. With the brace went all pretensions and cautions of
being an agent. It never occurred to him that someone else might not
let him quit so easily. After all, they were in England. He had already
paid the month's rent; no one knew his residence, not even Littleton.
Naturally, he was startled when he heard the knock on the door. He
threw on a shirt, hurried to the entrance affecting his limp just in case,
and opened his door a crack. It was flung back in his face so violently,
he flew backwards almost five yards, sustaining a bloody nose and severely bruised forehead in the process.

Bright red drops of blood trickled onto his hand as he cupped his
nose. When he managed to look up, he saw his young assailant going
over his flat as if he was a Scotland Yard detective.

"What the bloody hell?" Boyden said with a nasal quality. He
tried to get up, but his legs proved too wobbly and he fell back down
against the lime colored wall of the flat. "I don't have any money,"
Boyden pleaded. "You're tapping the wrong bloke."

Eber laughed and threw the shaken academic a towel from the
bath. "You can't guess why I'm here, mate?" he asked, quite surprised.

"I didn't pay my bar bill?" Boyden replied sarcastically as he grimaced in pain, holding the towel to his nose.

Eber replied very coolly. "My colleague, Dr. Hoarsley, asked you
for some information. You've displeased him. The point is, get him
his information." Eber looked down at him. "I want to be unequivo-
cal about this. Get the information and you can go back to your
pitiful life and I can get back to the Continent. Are we clear?" Taking
a torch from Boyden's table, Eber walked up, stuck the flashlight under Boyden's chin and lifted his head with it. "Don't and our next
discussion will be quite nasty."

Boyden stared at him. Both of his hands were now holding the
towel to his face. He could not believe he'd let this slight youth petri-
fy him, decided it was the shock of the blow, and quickly tried to
figure if he should even the score. But fear showed its trembling face
as he realized the young man was German, and if they could get to

him now, here in England, they could find him anywhere. It did not matter whether or not he could fend off this bloke. He knew in that instant, that he was a great coward, and that he had been an even greater fool. "Yes," he said resignedly, "I'll do it."

"Good," replied Eber. "Yes, this is good." He stood up, a contemptuous look on his face. He despised weakness. "I guess you don't know everything, eh, sport?" he said, after staring at his victim for a moment. "You have two days. Only that. I will be your guest until the end of that time. Understood?"

Boyden abjectly nodded his head.

"Good day. I will return presently," Eber said as he turned and went out the door.

In disgust, Boyden muttered, "Germans." Hoarsley knew his residence. He went to the wastebasket and humbly retrieved the knee brace. At that moment, Matthew Boyden had an epiphany: his life was up. These people would not let him live. Feeling a bit queasy in his legs and stomach, he rushed to the bathroom and threw up.

*　　*　　*

Hinton-Smith's recovery seemed to proceed rapidly from his first waking moment. He was young and had been fit, so it was no surprise to his doctors that he regained his physical strength quickly. In fact, Dr. Penrose remarked that the lieutenant "seemed to grow stronger by the hour." His memory, with the exception of his recollection of the events between his encounter with *LeFevre* and his awakening at the hospital, improved as well, if not as quickly.

One morning, after reading the war news in the Times, he came upon a one paragraph article, hidden among the pages of the domestic news.

The headline was much smaller than the headlines from the war, and probably deservedly so, due to its unfortunate insignificance when compared with the magnitude of the former. Hinton-Smith found it interesting for the same reason most people find it interesting to read about their hometown or an area of which they are familiar. It read: "PARENTS OF LOST LUCY SEEK HELP." The article went on to explain that nine-year-old Lucy Simmons, of 18 South Holloway Road, Highgate, N.6, had been missing since the previous night. Rachel and Stanford Simmons prayed for their little girl's return, and begged anyone with information to come forward. The local Anglican Church offered a reward of 100 pounds for information leading to her recovery. To this, he thought, "I must have been by that house a hundred times," and then remarked out loud, "I remembered, by God! I remembered."

His recovery pace was set back temporarily when he had recovered enough of his memory to wonder why Kate kept coming to visit, and why it was her voice he recognized instead of Elizabeth's. And again, when his curiosity finally had to be satisfied as to why his visitors were always ushered in by a soldier who seemed to always be at the door, and who accompanied him everywhere from the bomb shelters during air raid drills, to the mess hall and the w.c.

The end of his relationship with Elizabeth would have been grievous for him if he had not retained this somewhat dazed state of mind. He understood, but he did not have the concentration to dwell on the loss. She was one of the strongest memories he had of those halcyon pre-war days in Highgate, and at first, whenever he looked at Kate, the constant subtle reminders of Elizabeth's features, her similar gestures, and affectations: all he could see in the younger sister, and the similarities were enough to make him not want to see Kate at all. The more he observed her dedication to him, the more he relented, although at first, he felt a remorse and even a little guilt at liking that attention, for he still felt bound in some way to Elizabeth, and sometimes had reveries that she would change her mind.

One day he said, "Kate. I don't think you should come so often. I know you're busy and your hospital needs you." Then he watched helplessly as her eyes turned downcast and she cried, and abruptly turned and left. He was certain it was for the best.

But after a few days without her, he was surprised to find that he missed hearing her voice, and having her near, and begged Cyrus Wilson to deliver an apology.

Upon returning, she was hesitant and quiet, and he could not quite figure out the right words to say. After a few minutes she turned to leave, and Hinton-Smith cried out, "Forgive me, Kate. I was a bloody idiot. Please forgive me."

Kate walked slowly to his side and took up his hands in her own. She smiled. "I forgive you, but you really should not be so cruel to one who only wants to help you."

He squeezed her hands and said softly, "I'm a stupid twit and I'm sorry. Promise me you'll come by and read to me every day. Even if it's only for a few minutes, but come. You must. I need you to come."

He found her voice very soothing, and found solace in the fact that he could retain focus on its soft timbre and rhythm though not necessarily the meaning. It was especially calming after he began to have a second dream, a recurring nightmare, soon after his transfer to Whittington Hospital. Cyrus was also pleased with his renewed willingness to listen to her, and joked to Kate, "See how he's forgotten your sister already. The doctor said that he might be a bit off." Kate took this occasion to punch him.

When Cyrus finally broke the news of *LeFevre* and the impending court martial, Hinton-Smith could only laugh.

"So much for the hero of Highgate," he said.

Being ever so logical, he reasoned to Cyrus and Kate, "I suppose I could have run out on my men, or just turned tail and run away, but I'm not sure. It's not that I don't remember anything, rather, that the memories are a bit confused. I'd rather not think I would do something like that, but I don't know. I just come up to this bit, that I can't see through, can't remember beyond." He did not mention the three things that he remembered with infinite detail: the incidents at the cave and crater, and his abandonment of Cawkins. Was there justice in any of this, he did not know? Perhaps the fates were punishing him for the initial offense, trying to kill his friend. No news of Cawkins was forthcoming. Wilson could not find a word about him, not even from friends at Aldershot. Hinton-Smith was resigned to the fact that he probably died near the Loos Canal.

Wilson, with a rare show of affection for one of his stamp, put his hand on the lieutenant's shoulder, "You didn't do anything wrong. It's not in your nature. That Froggie's a bloody fool, whatever his problem, and we'll prove it."

Hinton-Smith was not afraid of the court martial, but the attempts to remember had began to strain him. He had a childlike naiveté when it came to faith in the English system of justice, but he was afraid of the nightmares, though he'd never mentioned them to anyone.

Every night they started the same innocent way: he was walking down the narrow corridors of a primitive museum. The only light was from the burning torch he held in his hand. He assumed it was night for there was no other light at hand, and there were no other people about. There was no fear at this time in the dream, but by now, he could tell he had been here, in this very situation, before. He even pinched himself to see if he was really dreaming. As he reached the end of the dark passageway, he began noticing the strange moving shadows on starkly barren, old oak walls, and realized it was his own shadow, multiplied in number and moving in relationship to the rising and falling of the torch's flames. He noted that he had dreamed this before as well, but was certain that this time it was not a dream. At the end, the passageway narrowed to slightly wider than a door, and he instinctively knew that he should turn back. As he turned, he heard odd, rasping sounds over the crackle of his torch, and now he remembered and there was fear. This must be a dream, he thought, but no, it isn't. He had somehow dreamt the future and now it was really unfolding.

He had to go through the small doorway. He must not, could not face those sounds. "Why can't this be a dream? I want it to be a dream," he ardently pleaded to himself.

Edging through the door, the sounds receded as they always did, so he was somewhat relieved, but now he had to look at the walls, and he hated looking at those stone walls, punctuated every few feet with stern, medieval, wooden, gargoyle-like figures, that seemed to be alive and moving in some weird, macabre dance to the flickering light. The somber, grotesque visages, which must have sprung from some hidden antediluvian existence, would suddenly stretch forth from the walls as if to ensnare him with their evil, hideous grimaces, but would stop inches short of touching him.

Then he would see Jack Cawkins sitting in a comfortable, cushioned chair. Cawkins was in uniform, and he looked up at the lieutenant, giving him a big, friendly smile. Hinton-Smith did not want to move, but some strange force propelled him forward. A voice, from some place inside his head, began to whisper, "Kill him, kill him, kill him." The voice grew in strength. It was implacable, unrelenting, adamant in its blood lust. Hinton-Smith continued moving towards the sergeant. The voice continued, "Kill him. He knows our secret. Kill him." Now there was a knife in the lieutenant's hands. He was standing over Cawkins, the blade raised over Cawkins's head, and the sergeant sat there, smiling at him as though they were the best friends in the world, and no matter what he did, Jack Cawkins would still forgive him. But the voice was unyielding. He could not fight it anymore, he could only close his eyes and bring the blade down and make the voice stop. Then in a miraculous transformation, perhaps common to any dream that becomes too threatening, he found himself watching from afar, as if it were the cinema, and there was another young man, who looked a lot like him, but not exactly alike, and was not him, in some sense, but was him, in another. And the young man he was watching turned back into himself. He summoned all his strength, and yelled "No!" at the top of his lungs, while still preparing to plunge the knife, but now, into Cawkins and then his own black heart. Before he brought the knife down, Hinton-Smith's sleep state changed from deep to light, and approaching consciousness, his mind would somehow alter the facts to make them more palatable, and less harmful to himself and Cawkins, but this rationalizing became less easy to do with each succeeding nightmare. The first few minutes of wakefulness would usually be spent in continuing the rationalization.

At first these images alternated, but recently, the third transformation seemed to have taken ascendance, leaving no room for its inverse.

When he was fully awake, he'd realize that Cawkins was most likely dead already, and he would feel that much worse, knowing his broken oath, and broken promise to return.

The ghastly figures never hurt him, or the other "him," and the duration he had to endure their approaches seemed to vary with each dream. The last time was very long, indeed, and he had woken in a cold sweat before the strange transformation had time to occur. As before, he was certain it was all real, and was even wishing it was a dream when he awoke.

Reflecting on that most recent nightmare, Hinton-Smith was certain that if he had not either woken up, or transformed into the other "him," he would have killed Cawkins and not awoken again.

He knew that if he were to stop the nightmares, he would have to solve the mystery of the cave, and now began to pester Cyrus and Kate and even the nurses to bring him certain materials from the different local museums and churches. The most illustrious of them, the British Museum, would not oblige them, however, as they required any researchers to be accredited academics, and though frustrated in thinking this might hurt his efforts, Hinton-Smith swore to make do with what he had.

He started out looking at every Knight Templar that went on the final crusade. And every Hospitaller. Then he tracked their histories after the Crusades, if they had survived, up to their deaths. He made a list of every Hospitaller and Templar who died in 1397, the date on the tombs in France. He made lists of those who went, whether they came back to Europe or stayed in the Middle East, but had no recorded funerals. The lists of names still ran into the thousands. And he was astounded that the memory of so many people existed, and how even more must have simply disappeared with the passage of time.

It was becoming very difficult for Hinton-Smith to maintain his focus. This was hopeless. Not thinking he could narrow it down anymore, his mind became restless and he started to read about the other crusades, starting with the First. That is when it got interesting.

He noticed there was a duplication of names. Some few of the Templars who defended Acre during the last major crusade in 1291, had the same names as some of the first Templars in 1120. That was not so extraordinary. They could have kept the same names as part of a tradition, or maybe they passed them down: father to son, to grandson. But three of them were only mentioned in very rare Moslem chronicles. There was no mention of them at all in the Christian chronicles from those times. The descriptions of these men were eerily similar. They were mentioned in the Moslem records for every crusade, starting with the First Crusade in 1147 where they were captured and turned to that religion but escaped, then continuing on to the fall of Acre in 1297. One would think at least one of their names would have made it into the Christian records. At least one. But there was no mention of them anywhere. Had their memory been erased just like the names of the men from the parchment and cemetery in St. Venant?

Their histories read like something out of H. Rider Haggard. Their names were *Cristobal De la Guzman, Sinestre L'Anguedoc* and *Guillaume de Belfort. De Belfort.* Somehow, he knew that name.

# CHAPTER 30

# THE HOUND'S TOOTH

From the very moment the Cochran brothers were left at their house on Pemberton Gardens, Thomas Cochran was scheming to go back to the cemetery. As for Nigel Cochran, he had little taste for going back to Highgate for Lucy, even though it had by now become a crusade for his younger brother.

Nigel had now discovered just what it meant to be a big brother— and one who was hero-worshipped by his younger brother. It was a responsibility he could not escape, nor would he want to. He was surprised to find he rather liked it. The hard part was to live up to it.

The evening they were caught at the cemetery, neither of the boys could sleep. Most of the night was spent talking in hushed tones of what they called the "dark man." Thomas Cochran thought he was good and was warning them away from something bad. "He's a ghost," Nigel argued. "How could he be good? He was trying to keep us from finding Lucy." He did not tell his brother that he suspected foul play on the part of the "dark man." He wanted to protect him from that possibility if he could.

"We'll go back and find Lieutenant Michael," Nigel whispered in the still of their shared bed. "Aunt Kate said he's in the Whittington. He's sick, but he'll know what to do. And he'll help us."

Elizabeth and Kate had agreed to keep the scandalous part about the lieutenant's confinement from the boys. It would not have mattered. Hinton-Smith was the boy's hero, and that was that: they were as loyal as Cyrus Wilson.

So, after Thomas Cochran finally fell into a troubled sleep, dreaming of cemeteries, tall "dark men," and lost little girls, Nigel, though still concerned of the awful fate that might await them at the cemetery, made plans to sneak into the Whittington Hospital to find the lieutenant. He'd help them somehow.

It was by now the evening of the 26th of September. He would let his brother sleep a few more hours then wake him up at ten.

\*    \*    \*

Later that same evening, on a very humid yet cool fall night, a young WAAF corporal, studying her tube at the Dover radar station, picked up a large build-up of aircraft over Pas de Calais, which unfortunately broke up, then reformed, then headed in different directions, then broke up again and so on, as the German bombers tried to confuse the warning systems. A track plotter at Bentley Priory placed markers on the large map table, following the build-up as best he could according to the directions given him. More reports came in from the other coastal radar stations and visuals from the Observer Corps started reaching the Maidstone center.

Squadrons from Group 11 headquarters were scrambled to meet the invaders. Telephones rang at the dispersal centers, red Very lights shot into the air, pilots ran to their Spitfires and Hurricanes, climbing up and in. Blue smoke rose up from the Merlin exhausts as they started the engines, bringing them to a roar. They hurriedly clipped in their straps, slid shut their planes' canopies, taxied down the runways and took off, gaining the required height. Then a controller on the ground gave them a compass bearing, which they would follow to look for the enemy bombers, and hopefully intercept.

On three consecutive nights, starting on the 26th of September, Feldmarschall Kesselring, commander of *Luftflotte* 2, ordered a full half of his attacking bombers to come down from the north, crossing into England at low altitude near West Beckham, in the hope of catching the RAF by surprise.

In the southern sector, the Dorniers crossed the coast at Beachy Head heading north, but Spitfires from Biggin Hill tore into them before they had gone five miles inland. Other squadrons of Spitfires and Hurricanes soon joined the fray.

In the north, the Heinkels managed to skirt the Observer Posts at Norwich and Bury St. Edmunds, and flew too low for the radar stations. Luckily, a Czech pilot, flying reconnaissance in a large radius out of Duxford, spotted them as he turned north to head back to base. The Czech called in to sector headquarters, which in turn called Group headquarters, which in turn called Bentley Priory, the center of Fighter Command. Plots were added to the huge map in the operations room, then orders were sent out in the opposite direction, but along the same chain. In the space of twenty minutes, squadrons from Duxford, Debden, and North Weald were scrambled, and in another five to ten minutes, when the Heinkels reached North London, the Spitfires and Hurricanes attacked.

The idea was to stop the Germans before they reached London. Unfortunately, no matter how efficient the system of defense, many of the German bombers got through, even when they were first intercepted far out of London. There were simply too many of them. The RAF pilots would have to land, refuel, and re-arm, and try to catch up and have another go. At a certain point, it would be up to the barrage balloons (balloons anchored to cables which forced the German pilots to stay high, thus making their accuracy more difficult) and light anti-aircraft guns, of which there were precious few in the relatively undefended area of North London.

The new strategy worked for a time, until the Germans were over Hampstead Heath, Waterlow, Alexandra Parks, Highgate and the Queen's Woods, when the full fury of the RAF fell upon them, causing some of the bombers to drop their loads before they could reach their intended targets.

\*   \*   \*

The rhythmic sway of the car lessened as the train slowed down to ease into the next station. Cawkins pressed his face against the window and looked out: the sign said Southfields, bringing on pleasant memories of athletics and sunshine. Looking at his wife and thinking to wake her, he decided against it. Let her sleep rather than listen to one of his tales. Cawkins had been to Wimbledon only once, but it was amazing: not just the setting, which was incredible in itself, but the match he saw that one time.

Recently back from Spain where he and Hinton-Smith had gone to observe the British component of the International Brigade, and where they had been sucked into the fighting around the Jarama River, he was ready for a good rest. That's the kind of world it was: from one war to the next. The lieutenant had gone back to Sandhurst and he went back to train at Guards' Headquarters.

Though quite the novice when it came to sports other than riding and shooting, he still played most of them. Cawkins appreciated all sportsmen and loved, when at all possible, seeing the greatest athletes in the most important games, whether a Test Match, World Cup Game or World Series, and he counted himself very lucky to be at Aldershot when the United States Davis Cup team came to London to play Germany in the semi-finals at Wimbledon in 1937. He couldn't resist going up to London to watch.

The smell of the freshly cut grass, the mixture of sweat with the hot tingly feel of the sun beating down on your arms, the incredibly long queues, a pint or two, the oily smell of chips, heavily perfumed women and cigarettes, the excitement in the crowded grounds in a world inexorably drifting off to another war: it was more than a tennis match. Gottfried von Cramm against Don Budge: the top two amateur tennis players in the world. Cawkins had never seen anything like it.

The stadium was sold out. Cawkins only managed to enter because one of the soldiers on leave who served as an usher snuck him in.

Von Cramm played like his life depended on it, and knowing Hitler, it very well might have been. He remembered the German winning the first two sets in very tight play with Budge taking the third and fourth. Cawkins was tired just watching them. It seemed like each man had already sprinted a few miles back and forth. Two hours had elapsed by then and he had been standing the whole time.

Throughout the match the crowd had roared after every point as though their national honor was at stake, but it wasn't the American they cheered. Ironically, the crowd was unabashedly in the German's corner as he had lost the last three Wimbledon finals but in defeat had proven himself to be the best of gentlemen. Stranger yet, Von Cramm's coach was the living legend, the American, Big Bill Tilden.

By the fifth set, the crowd simply roared for the most remarkable tennis they had ever seen.

Even Queen Mary sat in the Royal Box along with English and German dignitaries.

Budge went down an early break in the fifth, but fought back to tie it up. From then on the battle seesawed with no one able to take advantage. At 6-7 in the fifth, Budge had match point but couldn't convert.

Then there came long rallies and many deuces but no one could prevail. Finally at another match point, Von Cramm hit a crosscourt all but unreturnable and charged the net. Budge sprinted to his forehand side, dove outside the sideline and blasted a passing shot down the line before tumbling to the ground near the stands. Before he could see the result, the crowd rose and cheered in unison: Budge and the United States had won. Many said it was the match of the century and Cawkins, though never having seen tennis anywhere near this quality had to go along with them. He took up the game the next day.

Then there were the political and national implications. Budge later said that Von Cramm received a phone call from Hitler right before the match and he emerged from that call completely ashen.

When he thought about it now, Cawkins would not be surprised if the Nazi bastards bombed Centre Court to get even.

It was not a long ride from there to Highgate Station: two more changes of trains if he remembered correctly.

Cawkins dozed off as the train began to pull out of the station, and in his sleep he dreamed he was playing Von Cramm. He served and the German returned it to his backhand and charged the net.

Cawkins dipped the ball crosscourt and Von Cramm lunged, barely getting his racquet on the ball and sending it at an angle inside the service line. Sprinting up, Cawkins threw up a middling lob and looked over to see the German ready to smash one down his throat. Right when Von Cramm struck the overhead, Cawkins ducked. The ball hurtled past him and he ran to retrieve it as it rolled into a hole in the lower stands. Diving into the hole, he could hear it caroming off the black walls. They looked familiar. He was back in the cave! Starting to sweat profusely, he was absolutely terrified, but this soon turned into anger. His racquet now metamorphosed into a sword. He'd slice the SOB into oblivion. Where is the bastard? Now hearing a noise, like metal on metal, he saw it: a rat-faced skeleton in a ragged cowl. Cawkins ran at it, bringing the blade down on its head and cleaving it in two. The thing fell to the ground and shook in frenzied spasms. It was then that Cawkins started awake. He was still on the train. That bastard's lucky.

Cawkins got up and stretched. They were just pulling into another station. He looked out the window for a sign. Cawkins always liked the relaxed feel of a train: you get on and they take care of everything. There's no pounding on the back of a horse or riding over bumpy dirt roads in a car or truck. What a life of ease. This was how the nobility must live. And the oil and diesel smell of a station was a part of it that always conjured up memories.

He looked at his wife, curled up on the seat next to his, and reached over to gently wake her.

"We're here," Cawkins said. "Victoria Station. Time to switch lines."

The day before, a Guards officer came to the hospital outside of Dover, found the sergeant and presented him with his orders. He only had three more days to complete his rehabilitation. Then he was to report to Guards' Headquarters at Aldershot. If they realized he was sufficiently recovered, they would have probably shipped him out right then.

The strange thing about his stay in hospital, was that it was somewhat similar to that of Hinton-Smith's. The similarity came in the form of guards. They were much less conspicuous than those at the Whittington, numbered only a few and kept their distance. But the sergeant knew they were about nonetheless.

They appeared some three weeks into his recovery and made every effort to appear as though they had nothing to do with him.

At first Cawkins figured it had something to do with his former exploits until one of the nurses commented on how nice of the young soldier to mail Cawkins's letters for her. All right. The soldier had taken letters for her three times. Once was courtesy, twice was downright suspicious and the third left no doubt in his mind. Something was going on. Then he remembered his nurse remarking on how concerned this same guard was with the state of his recuperation.

Why would these same soldiers come by so many times unless they were checking up on him? He did not know any of these men beforehand.

Did North Africa need men this desperately? Did they think he was malingering?

One letter had gone to his friend in Intelligence and another to Cyrus Wilson: he still had received no answer. Obviously these were desperate times, but this was ridiculous.

So of course Cawkins started to monitor their movements: when the so-called soldiers changed shifts; when they ate; when they were not in obvious proximity.

The only thing he could reckon was that it had something to do with the railroading of Hinton-Smith. Toss a bone to your Allies to patch up a rough spot. From all he'd been able to put together, that was what he figured the army was doing. Why else? Made no sense at all in any other context. The French colonel? Perhaps he initiated the whole thing, but now his own army was carrying it through. Cawkins trusted the army explicitly in some ways, and not at all in others. He counted this among the latter. Throw in politicians and a war and you're really screwed.

Cawkins decided to once more risk going AWOL. He had Maggie sneak a uniform into the hospital, told the duty nurse he had a two-day pass, waited for a break in the guard and simply walked out. He later met Maggie at the train station where she had tickets in hand.

He had to make one more attempt to help Hinton-Smith before leaving for North Africa. Cawkins had no idea what he'd do. He was not even certain how to find the boy, or who would listen to him. The one thing he remembered was that Cyrus Wilson had been a regular at a pub called the Hound's Tooth and it was located on Hampstead Lane in London. He had no idea if Wilson still frequented the pub but it was close enough to the underground that it would not hurt to inquire there first. If he was not there, they would next try the address on South Grove. To further complicate matters, he did not know if Wilson was in touch with Hinton-Smith.

Maggie shifted her position and rubbed her eyes. "Already?" She slowly rose. "Are you certain you want to do this?" she asked. She could still not get her mind around what she considered a gross betrayal, no matter what her husband said. "This could land you in serious difficulty, couldn't it?"

"I have to," he answered. "I owe him."

Cawkins gathered two bags of luggage from the overhead bin and started toward the door. He felt good, determined. The strength had returned to his legs and arms, his spirit: he was ready for anything.

"What's the good?" she asked as she followed him down the steps of the train to the platform. "He's in a coma, isn't he then?"

"I don't know. I don't even know if he's in London." The sergeant's face and neck started to turn crimson. He knew he had make a mistake bringing her along but he had needed her cooperation.

"I know you're not happy with this, and I'm sorry about it, but he's in trouble and I aim to help."

Maggie Cawkins threw up her arms in resignation.

"Come on honey," Cawkins said, in a more amicable tone, and picking up his pace. "We have to catch the tube north." He had to at least try to find him, to see him. He had to do something.

"Besides. We'll have a pint, maybe even see Cyrus Wilson. You've heard a lot about him but never met him. One of my favorite people. I'm sure you'll love him."

*   *   *

It was dark. Time to go. Banished to their room for the next week, they were only allowed out for supper. Nigel Cochran knew his mum would soften up earlier than that, except if she found out what they were about now. He waited with his ear to the door to hear when his mother retired to her room. She was so mad with them she did not even come up to tuck them in.

He knew she always read for a bit before falling asleep. When he heard her door close he started counting off the minutes.

A half hour passed. Nigel nudged his brother awake.

"She should be half asleep by now," he whispered. "Let's go find the lieutenant."

And quiet they were. They had their routine down by now. Within minutes, they were walking up Junction Road, almost to Archway, when Nigel Cochran spotted Constable Hensen, only fifty yards down the street.

"Quick, Tommy," he whispered, grabbing his brother by the hand and pulling him into Archway Station before being seen.

Running down a flight of stairs, Nigel headed for the turnstile, put two coins in the slot and passed through, his brother close behind.

They boarded the tube to Highgate, the next stop on the Northern Line. They would have to double back.

The only times they had been on the subway before, were with either their mother or father, but Nigel Cochran was undaunted. As soon as the train stopped, he read the signs and led his brother up the long escalator leading to the station's exit booth. He understood that if he looked like he knew where he was going, most adults, even those in uniform and even this late at night would not bother him. At the exit, he sped through the turnstile without breaking pace, handing his and his brother's tickets to the surprised attendant on the fly. He found another sign with an arrow pointing to Old Shepherd's Road, which he judged to be the nearest exit to the hospital. Nigel Cochran was now in a hurry. He had a mission, and the prospect of seeing the lieutenant had already bolstered his courage.

After they climbed two different sets of stairs to reach the surface, they emerged into the dark night.

They were both breathing hard as they finished walking up the incline to Old Shepherd's Road. Taking his brother by the hand to cross Archway to Jackson Street, Nigel Cochran was very disoriented in the darkness. Even though he had played in this area all his life, things did not look familiar in the blackout. The memory of the last time they had gone out in the dark came back like a shot, and he looked at his brother and inadvertently shivered. Purposely putting that experience out of his mind, he forced himself back to the present.

"If you're puffing after the short walk up to Shepherd's, Jackson's going to kill you," he said to his brother. They both laughed, but Nigel immediately regretted the comparison.

They walked down Southwood Lane, turned east for fifty yards on Highgate High St. past a village bakery and pub, then cut across South Grove to the narrow, descending alley that was Swain's lane. Unfortunately, they would have to walk past the infamous North Gate, and when they reached South Grove, they started running as fast as they could, not stopping until they were half past the towering brick walls of the old cemetery and through the gate of Waterlow Park. Now things looked more familiar. Once inside they followed a dirt path to the hospital. It had taken them more than thirty minutes to reach the Whittington.

Thomas Cochran gazed up in awe at the immensity of the hospital complex. When you are a child, everything appears much larger, and even though the boys had played in the nearby park, and talked to the soldiers coming and going from the Whittington, somehow they had never appreciated its great size until this night, when they had no choice but to go in and find the hero, Hinton-Smith.

"We'll never find him, Nigel, then we'll have to go by ourselves again," Thomas Cochran said, almost whining. It was the first time since this all began, that Nigel detected a hint of fear in his little brother's voice.

"Don't worry. We'll find our way around. I promise you." This was more the way it should be. He was taking care of his little brother, not just coming along because he was ashamed. A smile appeared on his face. "We'll go around to where we used to watch the soldiers coming and going. That should be the front entrance."

No sooner than they had started around the building, the air raid sirens blared overhead. With a rare intuition that this was for real, Nigel grabbed his brother's arm and started running back the way they had come. "Come on," he yelled fearlessly over the din. "The highest place around is St. Michael's. It ought to be a real bloody good show."

\* \* \*

In the Whittington, Hinton-Smith took the screeching sound of the air raid siren in stride, and took it as a sign of improvement that he did not jump. By now, his physical wounds were healed, while his mental state was still somewhat disoriented, and in fact, almost possessed since coming across that name, *de Belfort*, and remembering where he first heard it. Every waking moment was consumed with finding out more about this knight, but with every night's sleep, the dreams grew worse. His routine of mental and physical rehabilitation as supervised by Hardin and Penrose was just something to get through. The research had become preeminent, but soon he had exhausted all the archives collected for him. When an army attorney, whom Cyrus considered the equivalent of a wet-behind-the-ears, junior public attorney, complete with a certified guarantee to lose the case, came once a week to inform him of his rights, and any progress, Hinton-Smith was unconcerned. He did not care what happened to him legally, but was eager to leave the hospital and start visiting the local church annals himself and looking around Highgate for clues.

That night it hit him: what if *de Belfort* is like that thing from the Continent? And here in Highgate. How could he have not put that together before? *My God! I have to find out. I have to get out of here.*

While he contemplated this new idea he began to get out of his hospital clothes and put on his uniform. This was something he had not done since coming back. Dressed like a soldier he could walk right out and no one would be the wiser. The siren was as good an excuse as any. He was about to fold up some clothes and pillows to put them under the covers and fool the guard but then the guard burst in.

"It's the real thing! I'm taking you to the shelter. Let's get out of here!"

Hinton-Smith hurriedly finished dressing. As they rushed out the door, another young soldier came up and grabbed Hinton-Smith's arm, and the two of them escorted the lieutenant down the stairs to the basement, where they were promptly turned away by an old maintenance man, now a volunteer.

"This here shelter's closed. It was okay for drills, lads, but this ain't no drill, so off wif you to the nearest tube station. Go to Highgate."

The guard asked, "Ain't Archway closer?"

"I'm supposed to direct you to Highgate. The hospital's the cut off. Too many going to Archway, I reckon."

The volunteer looked Hinton-Smith up and down. "This lad doesn't have a helmet, does he then? What's the matter wif you soldiers. You are taking him outside aren't you?"

"Right," the guard said. "But it's not that far."

"Bugger all," the old man said. "It's far enough. You don't want him hurt again. Wait here."

"But sir..."

"Wait. I'll be right back."

In less than a minute he returned with a helmet, strapping it on Hinton-Smith's head himself. "Now, hurry up."

Hinton-Smith observed the guards closely as they escorted him back up the stairs and out the front entrance of the hospital. The aired smelled of smoke but it felt good to him. He took in a deep breath and wished he could stay outside for the whole night. Perhaps there would come a time when he could desert these guards and get free. Then he could do whatever he wanted. He wondered if he could pull rank but quickly remembered those lot were under quite different orders. Still, it felt good to be in uniform, as though he was returning to a normal state of affairs.

His mind was a jumble of ideas: there was *de Belfort*, the dreams, the war, Kate and Lizzy. It did not occur to him that he might get in worse trouble for breaking free, only that he could perhaps escape the dreams if he was back on South Grove staying with Cyrus Wilson. He needed to study, to find out. He had to regain his condition, get back to the fight. And lastly he knew he had to make his peace with the loss of Elizabeth.

Hinton-Smith even considered going back to the Coldstream Guards' barracks right then. That's where he remembered much happier times.

*      *      *

The Free French were ensconced in a building near Piccadilly Circus, in the center of London as a temporary headquarters: how temporary depended upon the duration of the war.

In a display that could almost be described as routine during these early days of the war, *LeFevre* sprung up from his chair and began to pace about the office. His pacing was more like a forced march on campaign in the desert.

"You cannot trust the English!" *LeFevre* sputtered, his face flushing redder by the moment.

"I will go to Dakar," *De Gaulle* answered patiently, which was somewhat out of character. *LeFevre* was now famous, or perhaps infamous among the French for his temper. The two men would frequently seem to be at each other's throats and could often be heard arguing and yelling from the outer offices. At least three aides had bets as to when the first fist would be thrown, or, at least in *LeFevre's* case, the first challenge to a duel would be issued. For *De Gaulle's* part, he found it better to let the colonel rant on until he was spent. He had decided early on that the colonel, despite his various and sometimes petty idiosyncrasies, was a valuable part of his government. Besides, his mind was made up.

"This Operation Menace," *LeFevre* carried on to little avail. "They will only kill Frenchmen."

"*Vichy* French" *De Gaulle* corrected.

"Still, Frenchmen," *LeFevre* shouted.

"You must calm down, please," *De Gaulle* said. "And sit. You make me nervous."

*LeFevre* hesitated. He stared at the general. Perhaps he'd gone a bit too far. He sat in the uncomfortable wooden chair and spoke less passionately, but only just.

"The Governor General. I know him. *Pierre Francois Boissom*. He lost a leg proving his worth. At Verdun. He will fight."

"I go to prevent this."

"*Boissom* is loyal to a fault. The government in France is now *Vichy*. He will side with *Vichy*. The English will bomb our fleet."

"I go to mediate, to bring them to our side," *De Gaulle* said, sighing with exasperation. "This is possible, no? A better outcome, no?" How many times would he have to repeat this? His patience would inevitably reach an end.

"They use you," *LeFevre* said. "To say they have the blessing of the Free French. That is all. The gold reserves of the Bank of France are in Dakar. The English want our gold and our fleet. It is a fool's errand, harmful for us whatever the outcome."

*De Gaulle* stood up from his desk, a small modest wooden desk in a small modest room. Though *LeFevre* was not a little man, he was dwarfed by the tall general.

Not looking at the colonel, *De Gaulle* walked to the door and opened it, leaving no doubt as to his intent.

"We have to start fighting somewhere." *De Gaulle* said, turning and staring coolly into *LeFevre's* eyes. "If it is against *Vichy* so be it. I will brief you when I return."

*LeFevre* did not move.

*De Gaulle* respected the colonel: not only had he fought in the initial invasion, but after being safely evacuated to England, he had gone back for the Battle of France. But enough was enough.

"Dismissed."

*LeFevre* frowned, got up and stiffly saluted, then walked out the door.

It was late when Colonel *LeFevre* exited the Free French offices at 4 Carlton Gardens. It will be another *Mirs el Kabir*, he thought with certainty as he headed briskly past the Royal Academy of Engineering. He continued his fast pace up Pall Mall to Haymarket and then to Piccadilly where he caught the Northern Line. Many days he would walk all the way to Highgate, eschewing any mode of transportation that did not keep him fit. There would come a time when the Allies went back to the Continent and he would be ready both in mind and body. The years in the desert had taught him discipline if nothing else. Tonight he would take the subway on account of a friendly little barmaid who worked at a local pub, The Hound's Tooth. He would have hated to admit it, but after these continuous set-tos with *De Gaulle*, he needed Polly Turner to calm him down.

It was a cool, overcast night. It seemed it always was in this city. He much preferred the desert and hoped that *De Gaulle* would succeed in securing the Free French a part in any North African campaign. That was something they could agree on. Then they would fight the true enemies of France, though he only wanted to do so as an independent unit, not intermixed with the English and having no control over their own men.

Except for Polly Turner, he did not care much for the English and never had. It was always a matter of trust. For the most part, when he visited her at the pub, he kept to himself, picking her up at the rear entrance. He rarely went in.

Like small animals that begin to act strangely, hours before any human can discern an approaching storm, fire, or other natural disaster, people from all over North London, whether regular sojourners at their local pub or not, seemed to congregate to overflowing that evening in the many taverns in the area. It was as though they intuitively felt they needed an extra bit of cheer and camaraderie, although some certainly needed an extra bit of courage, and hoped to get it from a bottle or mug.

This night, *Maurice LeFevre* decided to go in. He felt a need to be around other people, even if they were English. Perhaps after his little dalliance he would sneak off to the hospital to see that swine of a deserter. He had the suspicion that he was not being told everything about the lieutenant's condition. How could a coma last this long? He was either never going to come out of it or he already had. He had no trust for them. The ignominious English might be trying to backtrack on their obligation. He would be outraged if this were so. Colonel *LeFevre* was unaware of the lieutenant's recent recovery but was aware that the Hound's Tooth had formerly been his godfather's usual haunt. On his rare visits inside he had asked Polly to point out Cyrus Wilson, but the old man had never made an appearance.

Polly Turner quickly ushered him to a stool at a small table in a dimly lit corner, where *LeFevre* lit a cigar and ordered a brandy.

Cyrus Wilson and Kate Hammond had not been in the Hound's Tooth since the day Cyrus returned from Dover and found out about Hinton-Smith and the disloyalty of his friends. Kate subtly encouraged him to rethink his anger, to try to understand why his friends might believe the ugly rumors. She knew how much the stubborn old man missed his mates and the fellowship of the pub on Hampstead Lane. This was the night she finally convinced him to go back in. It had been a strenuous task, but she counted on the added inducement of going straight to the hospital from there. Even if he only stayed for the time it took to drink one pint of ale, she promised she would be satisfied. Then, if he was still irritated, she agreed that they would leave and go see the lieutenant.

The bar reunion was hard at first, but soon, with Harry Kendall's good humor, Wilson fit right back in, as though he had never been gone. All the bar's patrons seemed obliged by a general understanding that certain topics were off limits, especially Dunkirk, and all were discrete enough to keep this understanding intact.

Polly took a basket of chips and another brandy to *LeFevre* soon after they arrived. "That's Cyrus Wilson," she whispered as she pointed out the old veteran.

"Perhaps I should question him about the traitor," *LeFevre* said. He started to stand, but the barmaid pushed him down.

"Not if you want to go home with me!" Polly Turner exclaimed.

*LeFevre* raised his eyebrows. How insubordinate. Perhaps that is why he had remained a bachelor for these many years. There would be another chance to talk to Wilson. He counted on it.

Even Elizabeth Hammond, who had only been in a tavern a dozen times in her adult life, wandered in this same evening, accompanied by two soldiers in uniform, both junior grade lieutenants—one of whom looked very much like a spoiled rich boy, definitely out of the ordinary for her, and the other Lieutenant Kenneth Roberts, fresh off his crutches—and actually sat down and drank a full mug of ale. When she saw her sister, she nodded, but was still feeling too guilty to come over and attempt a reconciliation with Cyrus.

Everyone seemed to be handling this heightened atmosphere with calm, even though some antediluvian instinct inside them was churning about. Then Bert Jones and Will Baker strutted in, went up to the bar and made room for themselves by shoving two men aside as though they were parting the waters.

Grudgingly, but not wanting any trouble with the two rowdy be-hemoths, the two men moved down a few feet and pretended to be indifferent.

Jones and Baker immediately downed two pints apiece, called for two more and began harassing anyone within reach.

The first two men decided to find a different pub.

Will Baker turned around and leaned back with his elbows resting on the bar, so he could better scan the environs to see who he could next offend. It was only seconds until his eyes lighted upon the best of all prospects, and he used his elbow to nudge his friend. "Look who's here?"

Bert Jones smiled, nudged him back although a wee bit harder, then followed the direction of Baker's glance until his eyes rested up-on Cyrus Wilson.

Bert Jones had been biding his time with an uncharacteristic pa-tience, since the night he and Baker had bullied the old man. Remembering back to the old days and old habits, which, after all, were heavily ingrained in his psyche, he knew he had gone a bit too far and actually worried that any knock on the door was going to be a Bobby or barrister, come to make him pay. After a few days, and no repercussions, his aggressiveness returned, and his confidence and arrogance in his newfound powers and position grew apace.

Ordered down to South London for the past week, he helped with digging out victims, shoring up shelters and buildings, and re-pairing defenses. Not initially wanting to go, he felt that his prestige and position in Highgate were at stake, and so it was necessary. As luck would have it, he was in the right place at the right time to cap-ture a shaken German crewmember who survived the crash of his Dornier. Earning a three day break, and a much welcomed bit of no-toriety, he headed back to Highgate ready for a new showdown for the house, and gathered up Baker to go to the Hound's Tooth. He figured to have a few pints so he would not feel any remorse if they went over to browbeat the old man again. As they headed to the pub, he wondered why he would ever feel any remorse, and put it down to what he considered a newfound sensitivity from witnessing the de-struction in the south. And this, he determined to rid himself of as soon as possible. He better not tell this to Will, he thought, though he might save it for the ladies.

"Well knock me over," Bert Jones chortled. "Our best mate."

"Cyrus, old man," Will Baker called out across the pub in a high-pitched voice, imitating what he took to be an upper class Englishman. "Where have you been, old sport?"

As Jones turned to join him, Harry Kendall grabbed his arm.

"Bert, take it easy on the old guy, okay?"

Bert Jones stared coolly at the barkeeper and said, "Would you like to take his place then, mate?"

Kendall said nothing, but he released Jones' arm, under the pressure of his glare.

"I didn't hear your answer."

"No," Harry said quietly.

"What? I think you ought to speak up," Jones said in a louder tone. "Let everybody hear."

"Don't do this to me, Bert. I've always been fair with you."

"Then shut your gob and don't bother me."

"Right," Kendall said ashamedly. Harry Kendall wanted to sink into the floor as Jones turned to leave. He had never felt so impotent or spineless in his entire life. He turned from the bar and began to wash some dirty mugs his barmaid had collected.

Jones and Baker swaggered like two ill-bred fops over to Wilson's table. By now, the ale was beginning to make itself felt.

"Hello luv," Jones blurted out to Kate Hammond, putting his hand familiarly on her shoulder as he sat down.

"Stand up," said Baker in a playful voice, with little trace of menace, as he grabbed Wilson and hoisted him up out of his chair and carried him over to Jones, plopping him down on the big man's lap. The two louts laughed heartily. Someone standing outside and overhearing them would have thought they were playing. Jones jumped up as though something foul had been put on him, heaving the old soldier to the floor.

"Sit down in your own chair!" Jones shouted, then picked Wilson up and carried him back over to his chair, shoving him down. "Us lot don't sit on the floor in a fine establishment like this." Wilson tried to struggle free and took an ineffectual swing at Jones, but his tired and frail old bones were no match for the two toughs, and none of his former friends seemed to be interested in taking on the brutes.

They played their game, or different variations of it for a few more minutes, until Cyrus Wilson crossed his arms and decided he might as well suffer the humiliation stoically. Kate, so aghast, and so surprised these two would have the audacity to bully Cyrus in such a public place that she stood still, completely dumbfounded, finally got up and screamed, "Leave him be you bloody bastards!"

Wilson motioned for her to leave it alone, as he knew she was not safe from these two, even in this place, simply on account of her being a woman.

English hooligans, *LeFevre* thought as he watched. The British are either bullies or cowards or a combination. We should never have had to rely upon them. The old man is punished for the misdeeds of his son. A pity.

Laying a pound on the table, he got up and left. At this point in time, he did not even care to see Polly. Perhaps he would rise early and see *De Gaulle* off.

Now, Elizabeth Hammond and the two young officers marched over in the direction of the embattled table.

Unfortunately, the charge of Elizabeth and the two officers was not like cavalry to the rescue. Elizabeth rushed up, shouting, "Leave that old man alone. You're not worth the sweat on his brow."

Unfortunately, by then the two ruffians were drunk enough to have even less control over their actions than usual. It was a bad time to pick a fight with them.

Jones patted Cyrus Wilson on the head. "You've been a good lad," he said. He then waltzed up to Elizabeth. "I've been wanting to punch your snobbish, know-it-all mug for some time," and he cocked his arm and threw a punch that would have floored the young lady, had not Roberts managed to get between them at the last second and suffer the blow. He began to bleed from his upper lip and nose as he stumbled backward.

Will Baker took the other soldier and threw him head first through a plate glass window at the front of the pub.

"Just like Dodge City," Baker exclaimed, smiling gleefully.

Then Bert Jones turned his attention back to Elizabeth and Kate, while Baker gathered up Cyrus Wilson in a bear hug.

Roberts ran toward Jones, who managed to side step, grab the lieutenant's shoulders and toss him threw the same broken window. Roberts landed on the pavement close to his friend.

"Bloody Hell!" Nick Hensen exclaimed, making his rounds as the second officer crashed through the window. He rushed inside the Hound's Tooth in time to see Bert Jones roughly grab Kate by her arm.

What's all this then?" the constable asked. "Picking on women? You blokes are so tough we should use you against the Jerries."

Jones, startled, turned to see the policeman, and dropped Kate's arm as if it was a hot iron.

"Don't you two have anything better to do?" Hensen asked.

Baker stood Wilson up, patted him off as though he were a child dirty from play and went over to stand by his friend, saying with as much deference as he could muster, "We was just playin' around."

"Right. I can see that," Hensen said with the requisite sarcasm.

"They've been bullying Cyrus Wilson," Elizabeth exclaimed.

"I think you and your mate better come with me down to the Stationhouse," Hensen said, looking sternly at the two.

"See," Will Baker said. "You shouldn't drink so much."

"Oh shut your bloody gob." Jones replied.

A bully's stripes just don't change, Hensen thought. Both of these blokes are larger than me but they know I can have them thrown in gaol and leave them there. Hensen had nothing but contempt for the two.

As they exited the pub, the three of them stopped and looked up simultaneously, as they heard the irregular beating of a Heinkel's unsynchronized engines.

"What in bloody hell is that doing up here, in the north?" Hensen asked.

# CHAPTER 31

# TO THE SHELTERS

Nigel and Thomas Cochran raced up the walkway to the church. Pulling the huge wooden doors open, they carefully felt their way down the aisle to the egress leading to the outside balcony. It was completely dark in the interior.

"What about Lucy," Thomas Cochran asked. "Ain't that what we came here for?"

Nigel stopped for a moment. He had never broached the subject of Lucy's welfare with his brother. He figured at best, she was home with her parents by now, thinking daggers into him and his group of friends. But then there was that "dark man." What if there was something really evil in Highgate? Perhaps in that really old bit. Then she was dead. He did not even know if his brother understood death, but that was something their parents should explain, not him.

"Are you having me on?" he asked. "Lucy's probably waiting for the fireworks right now. If she was with us, she'd be dragging us up the steeple. And you probably wouldn't be able to keep up with her. Me either."

The inside of the church had a musty smell, and was hot and stifling, especially after their run, and it felt good as the fresh air on the stone balcony cooled their faces. There was a time, before Julius

Beer's tomb was erected out of spite to purposely block the Sunday view of the London gentry, when hundreds of Londoners would gather on St. Michael's balcony on a pleasant Sunday afternoon for a view of all of South London. Now remembering the view was blocked, Nigel said, "We'll go up the steeple. We can see everything from up there."

They went back into the church, stumbling around until Nigel found the steps leading up to the steeple.

"Should have brought a torch, shouldn't we?" Nigel Cochran said, trying to make a joke of it.

"Hold my hand," Tommy Cochran said. "I can't see anything."

Nigel took his brother's hand and led him slowly, step by step, up the winding staircase.

When they got to the top they were some seventy-five feet above ground. Both boys squinted as they looked around to find any windows. They'd never been up there before but Nigel remembered seeing the sun glinting off what he thought must be glass windows when he occasionally glanced at the steeple from the street far below. He just hoped they were on all sides. The show would most likely take place in the south, so that was the side he explored first. A faint light came in from that side but all the windows were high above their reach and they were stained glass so they would not be able to get a clear view. Nigel reckoned it was better than nothing. "Stay here," he told his brother, then he went back down to see if he could find a chair or something to climb so they could watch the coming conflagration out of the steeple's windows.

\*     \*     \*

There were three people who were not interested in being in the pubs or later, the shelters. Two had more important, world-shaking schemes on their minds. The third had self-preservation on his. He figured he'd be safer out in the bombing, playing the odds, then he would be if he disappointed his two new friends.

Earlier, the most difficult part for Boyden had been convincing Eber that he would have to get his old position back at the Museum.

He would need their vast resources in his new research. Regaining his position would also give him more clout at the British Library. Most of the works he would need to see were quite ancient and only available for short periods of time to scholars. It was all he could manage to just convince Eber that he would have to see Professor Littleton by himself. It would be bad form, not to mention, peculiar, to have the young man accompany him.

Boyden was certain that Eber counted him as a dilettante and coward, and thought he had nothing to worry about. Still, he only agreed with the stipulation that he convince the professor to meet him at an outdoor café where Eber could find a nearby table and listen in on their conversation. He would not take the chance that Boyden might develop some backbone. They had headed off together and split up just before reaching the café.

Eber waited a few minutes, letting the Irishman get situated at a table before finding one of his own, ordering a coffee and nestling behind a *London Times*.

The professor showed up on time and Boyden half-stood to wave him over.

"I don't want to seem as though I'm running away," Boyden told the professor, as Littleton sat down at the street café in Soho. "I decided it was better to put off the operation until the end of the war. I want to help with the war effort. We have to stay together in these times."

"Good show," Littleton had said. He bought it. The senior professor was big on patriotism. "Lucky for you, young man. The Board has not found a replacement. I think I can arrange a favorable decision." He paused to think. "I know someone over at MI5, counterintelligence. With your background, that would be perfect. I'll make a call. I'm sure you'll be hearing from them."

"Thank you, sir," Boyden said. Bet the Nazi youth liked that one. It was all he could do to keep his expression upbeat.

"Jolly good show indeed, lad," Littleton said as he sipped his tea. "It will be fine if you return to your research immediately."

"Thank you, sir. I will," Boyden said. They continued to talk of the war, of their research and other niceties until Littleton had to leave.

Alternately downcast, Boyden fought the urge to laugh at this new bad luck. Good Lord. From the fire into the frying pan. That particular background check would be pretty interesting.

And the Nazi had heard the whole conversation.

For the next few days, Boyden spent every waking hour trying to track down any mention of *Guillaume de Belfort*, but there was nothing to be found. There had been no mention of a *Guillaume de Belfort* in any of those precious books, or records, or lists of crusaders. Nothing in cemetery lists, or enrollment lists. As far as Boyden could see, if *de Belfort* had existed, all knowledge of him had been wiped clean from the slate of history. Ironically, some scant information did exist, as Hinton-Smith had discovered, but in a few small, local church archives.

And throughout those days, there in the shadows, had lurked his cool, efficient keeper: never curious, never asking questions, not even talking. But making sure Boyden kept his nose pouring over the research.

Boyden made copious notes to throw Eber off, but the day of reckoning had fast approached when they would meet again with the spymaster dentist. He had considered approaching the authorities but Eber had given him not an inch of breathing room in which to do so. And even if he had been successful, telling Littleton for instance, he would probably spend the rest of his life in gaol, unless they hung him first: that's what he assumed they did with spies. Early on he realized his only chance was to outwit them. A plan of action was formulated. It was simple and it was the only plan he had.

Near the end of what he thought might be his last night on earth, he excused himself to go to the loo. Eber laughed. "Nervous?" he asked. It was the first thing he had said that day.

Boyden managed to laugh as well. "Actually excited," Boyden said. "I think I've made some headway." Then he walked off. Couldn't hurt to have him think there's progress. He headed out of the stacks and painfully made his way upstairs. He could hear Eber's precise footsteps behind him. The German was still not taking any chances. He was pretty certain Eber would stop at the entrance—that's what he'd done before, probably didn't have bodily functions himself—so once inside, he listened, and sure enough, Eber's habits were like clockwork. Quite the German.

Boyden had the intuition, that whether or not he delivered the goods tonight, he was a dead man. If not tonight, soon. If not by them, certainly when MI5 began to check his background. He wondered if they indeed did still hang spies.

In any event, he had not been able to find anything about the knight. What was with these stupid, bleeding, occultist idiots— goons running bloody séances? He had about one minute. He quickly pulled down his pants and unwrapped the brace as speedily and as quietly as possible. Pulling his trousers back up, he grimaced as he straightened his leg and started kneading it to regain some circulation. He could fake the limp for one night. God knows he should be able do it in his sleep. If they had read the files on him, and after all, they were Germans, they would know that the brace forced him to limp. They'd seen him limp the whole time they'd been in contact. With that bloody brace on, he might as well have been crippled. They wouldn't be on their guard for a cripple. He just hoped they didn't kill him before the hook was baited.

He had concocted a story with just enough mystery, truth and occult nonsense to entice Hoarsley. And there just happened to be the perfect place to try to shake them.

They rendezvoused at Hoarsley's office, just before dusk. Hoarsley was reclining in the only chair in the flat other than his work chair. A sweet smell wafted up from his ever-present pipe.

"Well lad," Hoarsley said in an almost kind avuncular tone. "What do you have?"

Boyden took a deep breath. This was it.

"There's no record of a *Guilluame de Belfort*." He looked into Eber's cold eyes to see the effect. There was no emotion, unless it was that of anger. But he always looked angry. That was odd. Eber's complexion was now reddening. It was almost as though he recognized the name and disapproved. He was indeed surprised and angry. Bloody well great, Boyden thought. Nothing like your executioner being upset with you.

Hoarsley sat up. He was already on edge. After all the years of preparation and waiting, this was his first major task, and he wanted results.

"I checked all the chronicles. From the well known such as de Join-ville and Villehardouin to the obscure such as Ibn al-Athir. I checked lists of knights from France, England, Germany, and Flanders. I checked enlistment rolls of the ascetic Orders of Knights such as the Templars, Hospitallers, and Teutonic Knights. I looked at abstracts from Belfort, France and Belfort, Flanders, and also under different variations of the spelling. I checked records of supplies, from horses to provisions, and from armor to weapons. Nobody ever sold anything to a *Guillaume de Belfort*. As far as I can determine from the record," he said, first letting out another deep breath. "This man did not exist."

"Impossible!" Hoarsley cried out.

Boyden held up his right arm, as if to quiet a child. "But I found something strange. I found a record of eight knights who simply dis-appeared around the time frame you're looking at. Strangely, or coincidentally, they all belonged to the same order, the Hospitallers. They had come back alive and well from the defense of Acre. That was in 1291. They seemed to have the ear and friendship of Philip IV, the King of France. There is even a fervent panegyric from the King himself, as though they had done him a great favor. But in spite of this, all eight cease to exist in the records. No burial site is accord-ed them. They're just...gone."

"So. This is what you have for us?" Hoarsley fumed. He fidgeted in his chair, and looked at Eber, who was sitting in the dentist's work chair. Eber stood up, threateningly.

"Well, in my field, there are always speculations, rumors... guess work," Boyden hastily continued. "We weren't there. So how can we know what really happened?"

"And we are not interested in a history lecture," said the cool Nazi commando, his voice quite loud for him.

"Sometimes we get lucky, and we are geniuses. Other times new evidence is found and we look like fools," Boyden said with urgency. His time was running out. He could see Eber was getting restless, but Boyden had to make this as credible as possible. If he just gave it to them straight out, it would not seem so enticing.

"Bear with me, sir," he begged. "If only for a little longer. You have to hear it all to understand."

"Continue," the dentist said. "But give me something."

Boyden could feel his heart racing. "There have long been rumors of knights who went to the East, India and Tibet, and came back with great secrets…"

Hoarsley now leaned forward the slightest bit, his curiosity aroused. Himmler himself had sent expeditions to Tibet. With his left hand he motioned for Eber to sit back down.

They must have heard that one in the séance, Boyden thought. "Even Hindu chronicles tell of white men who wore red crosses on their clothing, and came much after Alexander. The legends say some who managed to return used that knowledge for good. Some for evil. Almost the whole of the Knights Templars were caught, then tortured, and then put to death. All their fortune was taken by the King. They were buried under unmarked stones. Most knowledge of them was erased, as punishment for their misdeeds, but also so no one could follow in their footsteps. There are rumors that one of these burials took place in the north, on a heavily wooded hill, overlooking London. Mind, these are rumors, legends."

Hoarsley's pipe came out of his mouth. He laid it on an ornately decorated desk, and unctuously rubbed his hands together.

Eber's expression did not change. He sat with his arms folded.

"About a hundred years ago, a new cemetery was built in Highgate Borough in the north. Sometimes I sit in there, and relax, go over my research…all to help my cover. I keep a dead letter box there. I've just discovered an ancient walled area. It's a burial place, quite old. I think this is what we've been looking for. You did say this *de Belfort* was in England?"

"Yes," Hoarsley said, his eyes wide, his mouth almost salivating.

"The modern cemetery surrounding the old walls is so overgrown, it looks like a jungle. I've been in there over a dozen times, and never knew the old place existed before this week. I just stumbled upon it. Fate, I guess." He chuckled, but there was very little mirth in his laugh. "I doubt if anyone's been in there for ages." Boyden could see from Hoarsley's expression, that his story had taken hold. Hopefully he was calling the shots. He slowly breathed a sigh of relief. "Besides the fact of these walls, I don't know if any of the rest of this is true, and even if it is, I don't know if *de Belfort* is buried there. But the cemetery is called Highgate. It's actually quite well known. And it's only a short distance from here." And now for the clincher. "Three days ago, when I happened upon this old place, I looked through the gate. I'm not one hundred per cent certain, it was dusk, but I thought I saw the insignia of the Hospitallers, the knights who legend has it, captured and executed the evil ones. That could mean that they are guarding the resting place of your knight." He let this sink in. "Had I not seen that insignia, I would have had no idea that Crusaders were buried there."

Boyden had no idea how close he'd come to the truth in his fabrication: his jaw almost dropped into his pocket when Hoarsley spoke.

"Good show," Hoarsley said. "I've only received a communication this morning from the *Ahnenerbe* to find a Highgate something. That is all they said. I had no idea of the cemetery. Jolly good show."

Boyden's jaw was not the only one to drop. Eber was completely dumfounded.

Hoarsley went out to the waiting room, bidding Eber and Boyden to follow. Hoarsley put on a charcoal topcoat and a black derby, and unaccustomed for him, slipped a small revolver into his pocket. Lastly, he went back into his office, alone, opened the safe and withdrew an old plain notebook. He opened it and read the strange hand-written scrawling silently. Placing it in his hip pocket, he went back out.

"Let's go then, me boys," he said jauntily.

They left Hoarsley's office and headed for the Oxford Circus station.

\*    \*    \*

Inside the Hound's Tooth, things had just begun to settle back down with the exit of Baker and Jones, when the blaring Banshee wail of the air raid sirens began. No one in the pub actually panicked, as everyone was by now quite used to the sound and quite aware that they never seemed to signal anything, for bombs had never yet dropped anywhere near. People quite naturally took their time.

*LeFevre* was halfway to Whittington Hospital when the sirens went off. On his way to see if the lieutenant was, indeed, still under arrest and in a coma, he hesitated, then decided it could wait till the all clear. He then hurried off to the Archway Station shelter; he'd head to his office after the raid, having had enough of all Brits, including his barmaid, for one night.

No one will ever know how one lone Heinkel managed to get so far into London, without at least sending off the sirens, and giving ample warning time, but the Heinkel's bombs started exploding only a few minutes after the start of the sirens, and so near as to rock the Hound's Tooth for a good thirty seconds. Then the panic began. People rushed to the only exit, crowding each other until it became a crush, and only a few could exit at a time. Outside they all blended into a horde of people rushing tumultuously for Highgate Tube Station.

Parents gathered their young and rushed outside, heading for the nearest shelter. Loiterers, and people trying to save as many of their belongings as possible, before heading for safety, were nudged along by the wardens. Fire brigades got ready for action. Home Guardsmen checked their weapons and rushed to assembly points. Bobbies helped usher and direct people along.

High above the barrage balloons, and out of reach of the anti-aircraft flak, more bomb bay doors were opening, as the main groups of Heinkels and Dorniers arrived.

As the first bombs exploded, Hensen pushed his two charges up against the Hound's Tooth's brick wall for safety. "I guess this is your lucky day, blokes. You have jobs with civil defense, right? I'm letting you go. So get to it."

"Thanks, guv. You won't regret this," said Jones, quite relieved.

"We just had a might too much of them spirits, constable," Baker added. "We didn't mean that lot no harm."

"Don't be so thankful," Hensen said. "You're on your own pledge, and I'll expect you at the Stationhouse early tomorrow." Hensen turned to hurry away to his post. "Don't forget," he called back over his shoulder. "Early. Or it'll be that much the worse for you."

Jones waited for him to disappear around a corner building, then said angrily to his mate, "What're you waiting for you bloody twit! We have to get to the shelter!"

"But what about our job? The constable?"

"This is war, mate. Bombs are falling! He'll never know."

"I thought we had to help out," Baker said. "Besides, we might find some goods if we stay out."

This made Bert Jones angrier, because now he had to weigh the advantages of loot against the disadvantage of being a target for the bombs. It did not take him long to decide.

"Get to the shelter. We'll 'ave plenty of time to do our jobs after they sound the all-clear."

Bombs seemed to be exploding everywhere. People from all over Highgate were streaming out of the pubs, houses, business establishments and apartments and heading for the shelters.

As they got into the flow of people, Jones spotted Hinton-Smith being escorted from the opposite direction by his guards.

"This might end up a pretty good night, after all," he said as a gleeful look returned to his eyes.

Nearby, another person had also spotted the lieutenant.

"Will," Bert Jones whispered, drawing his mate in close, and pointing out their target. "We're going to separate him from his guards. Bump into the one on the left...accidental-like, and make sure you do it hard." He winked as if to convey his meaning more forcefully.

"Ain't we in enough trouble?" Baker asked.

"Don't worry, this'll be worth it," Jones said.

Baker nodded, resignedly. He did not like being in trouble with the law. Still, this would be bloody good fun. Waiting for the right moment, he walked up and slammed into the unsuspecting soldier, knocking him out cold, while Jones sucker-punched the other guard. This done, they grabbed the lieutenant and wrestled him into the nearest alley.

"What right 'ave you to me mate's 'ouse?" Baker said, slapping him hard across his face then shoving him forcefully at Bert.

They shoved the lieutenant back and forth, sometimes to each other and sometimes against the brick walls surrounding them.

"You're a bloomin' coward," Jones screamed. "And a traitor to boot."

But just as Baker started to push the lieutenant back toward his mate, Hinton-Smith, purely from instinct, dropped down. Baker pushed empty air and lost balance, and Hinton-Smith tried to sweep his legs out from under him, but was not quick enough, still too weak. Slowly standing back up, the lieutenant raised his hands, prepared for more difficulty.

"Why you dirty little bastard," Jones screamed as he reared back his fist to deliver a blow. Surprisingly, he felt his arm get caught up in mid-swing, and he could not, try as he might, bring it forward. He was a strong man and he had never felt such an iron-like grip take hold of him before. He turned to see an unfamiliar man holding his arm, just before he saw a big fist come towards his face. The punch smashed into him, and the big brute fell back, his large hands practically covering his face. "You broke my nose!" he whined.

Will Baker quickly got up, made a step towards Jack Cawkins, thought better of it, and went over to help his friend, saying in a low subservient tone, "I don't want no trouble."

"You don't eh," Cawkins said. "Then you better take your friend and get out of here, now."

Will Baker meekly complied, slung Jones' arm over his shoulder, and half-carried, half-walked his mate out of the alley.

The sergeant watched the two slink away.

"Are you all right?" Cawkins asked, laying his great hand on the lieutenant's shoulder, but Hinton-Smith did not even hear him, he was so transfixed on the amazing sight before him.

*It's Jack*, he thought as he looked up into the eyes of Jack Cawkins. *I left him over there and I never went back. He's alive. Thank God.* And now for the second time in this personal nightmare, he cried. The first time for Cawkins's seeming death. Now it was for his resurrection.

"Jack, I'm so very sorry..."

*       *       *

There was no one else on the street as Bert Jones and Will Baker made their way to the Highgate Station shelter and down the stairs, almost seventy feet underground. They found a corner in which to huddle, next to the barkeep from the Hound's Tooth. Looking at them suspiciously, Kendall asked, "Gettin' 'ere a might late, eh, chaps? Bloody Hell! What happened to your face?"

"And it ain't none o' yer damn business, is it?" Jones retorted. The barkeep, now finding a bit of his lost courage, disgustedly waved them away.

"Bloody twit," Baker sneered at him. He pulled out a flask of whiskey that he kept in his jacket pocket for hard times. He took a sip and passed it to Bert Jones.

# CHAPTER 32
# REUNION

In Highgate, at the surface, bombs continued to fall; buildings crumbled or disintegrated, killing people, burying people alive. Incendiary bombs caused horrendous fires, but most of these bombs ignited a good half-mile southeast of the station. And in a part of the city that was usually quiet—the cemetery—a number of great explosions occurred, one after another, cutting a huge path straight through the melancholy grounds.

Before the first bombs had fallen, Nigel and Thomas Cochran managed to lever one of the smaller wooden pews up the stairs to the steeple, and then lug it up the last section, which was a spiral staircase. Looking up at the stained glass artwork, Nigel found a section that was plain clear glass, tipped the pew on its end and leaned it against the wall, so that the upper portion, which was the siding of the pew, made a three-foot-long platform, about four-and-a-half feet below the frame of the window.

"There's room for both of us, I think. Want to go first?" he asked.

"No. You can go," Thomas Cochran answered.

Shrugging his shoulders, Nigel shinnied up the seat of the pew as though it was a small sapling. Using his arms to pull himself to the top, he got to his knees then carefully stood up, leaning his face against the wall to keep his balance. The first bomb exploded just as he raised his face to the window. It was marvelous, and he had a front row seat. "Tommy. You have to come up," he whispered in wonder. "This is incredible!"

"All right," Thomas Cochran said begrudgingly. It was one thing to go to the cemetery to save a damsel in distress, especially when he was in part responsible. It was another to climb up the steeple of St. Michael's, and then up to the window to balance precariously over such an immense conflagration, when somewhere in the back of his mind, was the fear that he might see a little, forlorn shape, lying motionless on the cemetery grounds.

Reaching his brother's side, he had to be boosted up a little more to see over the top of the window frame, but even he was impressed, though he deliberately did not look down into the cemetery.

Searchlights crisscrossed the evening sky like giant shimmering spider webs. Nigel followed them upward with his binoculars and was sure he saw the underside of a German bomber. Anti-aircraft fire peppered the sky with thousands of little clouds, sounding like thousands of little firecrackers snapping. Barrage balloons hung high over the city, but were well below the brothers' vantage point. And the city, even with all of its lights out, was lit up from the many fires dotting the landscape. Though less than a minute ago they could hardly see a thing, now they could make out landmarks all over the city. There was Big Ben and Trafalgar Square. The dome of St Paul's Cathedral stood out like a giant egg, ready to hatch if unlucky enough to be hit.

Both boys heard the shrill whining of a five hundred pound bomb, as it plummeted earthward.

Nigel grabbed his brother's head, tucking it into his own stomach and then, bending over the small boy to protect him, shouted, "This one's going to be close." One second later, with a better intuition of just how close, he straightened up. "Jump," he yelled, just as the bomb exploded, rocking the church and shattering the glass of the window into thousands of shards. As they hit the cement floor, Nigel, though having his breath knocked out of him, managed to cover the younger boy's body to protect him from the flying bits of glass. The platform they had been standing on toppled over, crashing onto the floor a few feet from Nigel Cochran's head.

*        *        *

Hinton-Smith was strangely lucid, considering all he had been through. Apparently, the brief fight had only succeeded in angering him, and the anger, as it grew, went a long way towards ridding his head of the cobwebs. He was now quite clear about whom he was, and he understood why the two gravediggers disliked him, tried to beat him. He wondered if they were up to their old tricks, picking on Cyrus, and a flash of intense heat permeated his whole body. If they were, he thought, and before the thought was even completed, he felt a rage building inside him. This, he was certain, had never happened before. *Except when he was in the cave!*

He was startled. Another epiphany. The voice in France had said Highgate. And here he was, back in Highgate. *The cave. The crater. Highgate. Had the voice somehow shepherded him back here? And Cawkins. Here was Cawkins.* Hinton-Smith stared at him. "I don't understand. How...?" the lieutenant asked.

"Remember Stevens? He found me, not long after you left. He commandeered a truck and we rode to the beach in style. If that stupid Frenchman hadn't shot you, I know you would have brought me out."

Explosions were so near they were deafening. They ducked as clouds of dust from a direct hit of a brick flat hurtled skyward and dirt and rubble filled the air. Another brace of sirens went off as another group of bombers approached.

"Jesus!" Cawkins said. "I left Maggie to find the nearest shelter when I saw you. We better get to a shelter."

"Right. This is like the war, and we had better get out of it," Hinton-Smith said to Cawkins with the straight-forwardness of a child. "I'll show you the way to Highgate Station."

Cyrus and Kate, already in the shelter, spotted Hinton-Smith and Cawkins coming down the last flight of stairs minutes later, and started to jostle through the crowd to join them. Cawkins stayed on the stairs for a better vantage point. He soon spotted Maggie and brought her over.

"Maggs and I arrived just in time for the fireworks," Cawkins said as introductions went all around. "Then Mike and I had a little altercation with two large scoundrels, who seemed to want to push the boy here around."

"Will Baker and Bert Jones," Cyrus Wilson said with a mixture of disgust and contempt. Then he wished he'd kept his mouth shut.

"They were jostling Cyrus around at the pub earlier," Kate said. "They've been harassing us..."

"Shush, lass," Cyrus Wilson hastily said. "We don't want to upset the lad." Hinton-Smith had lost at least ten pounds since his injuries. He had spent over two months bedridden and no matter how much strength he had regained, was in no condition to do anything about Baker and Jones. And Wilson knew just how stubborn the lieutenant could be. Then he smiled to think the lad had taken after him. He probably learned it from me, Wilson thought.

Kate Hammond had already rolled up her sleeve. "But look what that brute did to my arm," she said.

Wilson put his finger to his mouth and shook his head. It was too late.

Hinton-Smith's ears peaked like a startled animal's; a whole new look came into eyes. His anger returned. Anger had never stayed with him for any length of time, but somehow, this time, he felt himself relish it. He looked around the platform to see if he could spot the two bastards. If he had his service revolver he would put an end to them right now.

He had to caution himself. What kind of insane thought was that? It would be out and out murder. His next thought was they deserved it, and then, that we live by the rule of law. Why was this succession of contradictory thoughts pestering him? Now he was more furtive as he looked around for the two gravediggers.

Soon after the reunion, the all clear sounded and the warden gave permission for everyone to leave. Bert Jones and Will Baker, on the far side of the tracks and close to an exit, wasted no time in being the first ones out. They needed to report to duty, while trying to make it look as though they had been on duty the whole time. They were also eager to look at the cemetery, to see if any damage had brought new valuables to the surface.

"I think we should take you back to the hospital," Wilson said to the lieutenant. "I don't think you're supposed to be out, are you.

Where's your guards, anyway?"

"One night away won't hurt anyone," Hinton-Smith said. As they moved to the stairway and the crowd of the refugees began to thin out, he was taken aback when he saw Elizabeth and two soldiers staring at him from the other side of the subway tracks. She looked away and made no move to come closer and speak. It did not matter. A plan was forming in his feverish mind. He needed Kate and not Lizzie. He took her by the hand. "Kate, would you mind taking care of an invalid for a night?"

She blushed and said, "Of course."

"Don't worry. I won't ravish you," he said, managing to force a grin. After all, there were other things on his mind. Quite like the cunning of a peasant, he thought. Or a wolf. And Kate would provide the least resistance of all concerned.

"I agree with Cyrus. You should be in the hospital," Cawkins said. "You're not going to do anything foolish, are you?" The sergeant knew him as well as anybody, and he had noticed a strange glimmer in Hinton-Smith's face, and it definitely did not bode well for the louts that had pushed him around.

"You think I would leave this lovely lass...and me in my condition. I'm just going to sleep, if that doesn't upset milady, here." Now he smiled.

"Sergeant Major," interrupted Maggie. This is what she called him whenever she either wanted to be sure she had his attention, or when she was mad at him. Presently, it was a little of both. "Let the two be alone for awhile. You don't have to be the mother hen."

"All right, all right," he said against his better judgment. "Cyrus offered us a room at his house. We'll be there. If you need anything at all..."

"We'll be fine, mate," Hinton-Smith replied.

With that said, they started up the stairs and out of the shelter. At the top, Cawkins was amazed that the lieutenant seemed even stronger. A new look of resolution began to show in his eyes. The recovery had grown apace when he found out those blokes hurt Cyrus and Kate. This is what adrenaline can do for you, Cawkins thought as he stared at the lieutenant. Or hate.

"Mikey?" Cawkins asked once more. "Are you thinking to do anything about those two SOBs?"

Hinton-Smith looked at Kate and pulled her close. "That's me mate. Always looking after me."

"That's not an answer. You are, aren't you? Look me in the eye and tell me you ain't." The sergeant stared at the lieutenant.

"I'll take care of it, Jack. It's my business," he said. "But don't worry. In due time."

"Right. Enough of this. I'm off. You can follow me or not," Cyrus Wilson said. He was exhausted from all the fighting, bickering, bombing and worrying and just wanted to fall into his bed and sleep. Bombs had fallen near to the south of the station and he wondered if he still had a house to go to. He needed to see. Reckoning the clean-up squads could make do without an old man for one night, he used this excuse for not helping. Motioning for the sergeant and his wife to follow him toward Southwood Lane, he started walking.

Cawkins did not want to let the lieutenant out of his sight, but with Maggie glaring at him, his options were quickly slipping away.

Taking hold of Hinton-Smith's shoulder, he looked him square in the face and said, "Well, don't tell me, then. I might just see to their ugly mugs myself." Cawkins was still trying to figure out what ideas were hatching in the lieutenant's brain. There was something off about him, but he was not sure what. Cawkins was worried. "You keep an eye on him, miss."

"Kate," Maggie said in exasperation with her husband. "Just take good care of him." And she firmly grabbed the sergeant's arm and led him off after the old veteran, while Kate and the lieutenant started down empty Archway Road in a circular path back to her flat, partly to be alone and partly to avoid the destruction and fires.

*   *   *

It was the first time Elizabeth Hammond had seen him, and somehow, the lieutenant seemed diminished from how she remembered him. Of course he'd lost weight on account of his condition and injuries but it was more that that. Perhaps he was just not so much larger than life now she was out of love with him.

Not wanting to have an uncomfortable situation, Elizabeth persuaded her two escorts to wait underground until the last people had cleared out. Only then would she let them escort her out of the station.

"So that's the coward, eh lass," said Roberts, still holding a cloth to his nose and immediately realizing he'd stuck his foot in his mouth again. Damn. Too bad the bloke hadn't punched him in the mouth so he'd keep it closed.

Elizabeth Hammond looked down at the ground. "Don't say that," she said. "Please."

"Sorry," Roberts said. "Really."

The other officer added, "You know him, eh? Bit of a rum chap. He looks terrible, like he didn't eat for a month. Hell, he look's worse than we did after our set-to at the pub."

The two of them laughed, although Elizabeth could not bring herself to join in.

As for Lieutenant Roberts, he was preoccupied by other matters. The one thought on his mind was to figure out how to get rid of his mate. He had only three days before he shipped out to the Middle East; and the present might be the only time he had. Thoughts of mortality had entered his mind and thoughts of loneliness as he prepared to re-enter the fray. What in bloody hell *had* that chap Hinton-Smith been through? Would he come out like him, or at all? He desperately wanted someone to think about when he went into action. Someone to fight for beyond King and Country. Someone to think of him. With the clean up and rescue work impending and needing volunteers, every moment was precious. He wanted to tell her he loved her and then he'd opened his big mouth again. Great timing. He had to find a way.

As they exited Highgate Station, he got between Elizabeth and the other officer. "Which way, lass?" he asked. Elizabeth Hammond gestured towards St. Albans Road and started walking.

Squeezing his mate's shoulder, Lieutenant Roberts stated rhetorically, "They must need volunteers for this mess," and his mate, getting the idea, agreed, said his good-byes, and left.

"I'll meet you at the fire station in an hour," Lieutenant Roberts yelled after him.

The other officer yelled back, "See you then," but did not expect that it was a good bet.

The closer they got to St. Albans Road, the greater was the damage: bombed out buildings and houses; fires burning out of control. They could feel the heat from the flames, even though the fires were burning a good half-mile to the east. Flakes of ash settled on both their uniforms. Sensing something else was different, Elizabeth realized that it was not pitch-black outside, but instead there was brightness akin to the light of a full moon, eerily swathing everything in hues of reddish browns and yellows, on account of the burgeoning fires and smoke. They were about halfway there, when Elizabeth began worrying about her own flat, which had been part of a government public housing projects—hers in particular was a large house turned into a number of medium size apartments. Would everything she and her sister possessed be gone, up in flames? Truthfully there was not much, but the important things, the pictures of their youth, their parents: these were precious and irreplaceable.

Near Dartmouth Park Hill, there were two houses on Denton Street completely turned to rubble, and being sifted through by Home Guardsmen and firemen for any survivors. She could not help stopping and staring, as tears formed in her eyes, and she found herself leaning on the officer. Lieutenant Roberts comforted her as best he could, putting off his own agenda for a better time and place.

More destruction was evident as they neared St. Albans, but Elizabeth's building had not been touched at all, and she felt a strange sense of guilt for being so lucky.

"Why weren't we hit, Kenneth? Why are we so special," she asked? But he could only shrug his shoulders in ignorance, as he walked her up the stairs to her door.

"I want to see you again," he said in a soft, almost shy voice.

"I'm sure we will..."

Both of them stood uneasily still at the entrance to her flat, hesitating, avoiding each other's glance, and feeling that it was not the right time for even a kiss on the cheek. So, they parted with a brief shake of the hands. Lieutenant Roberts went back to the fire brigade station, while Elizabeth Hammond went in, and nervously shuffled through important papers she had to study to get a higher security clearance. She now wanted to help with the war effort more than ever and realized she could start this instant. Grabbing her coat, she ran downstairs and headed in the direction of the nearest relief station. She had to help her more unfortunate neighbors.

# CHAPTER 33
# TREASURE HUNTING

Will Baker and Bert Jones made their way to headquarters, and, be-coming the very souls of obsequiousness, reported directing people to shelters, keeping order, digging out survivors and getting them to aid stations, clearing rubble and lending aid to the fire fighting auxiliaries. Earlier, they had smeared themselves with dirt and oil to lend credence to the lie. They also managed to receive permission to attend to their other job, after helping in the general clean-up, and then, true to form, headed directly for New Highgate Cemetery, leaving their supervisor thinking that if he only had more like those two, his job would be easy.

They went straight for the maintenance shed to get torches and digging implements, then headed for the gate.

A cursory inspection of the ground evoked a curse from Will, "Blimey. There's no goods for us here. Nothin'. This bit ain't even been touched."

"It's no matter," said Bert Jones. "Ain't we been through this part a hundred times. Most of the recent burials been right here, so there ain't nothin' new anyways. We already nicked whatever's worth bein' nicked. Let's go over to the other place."

"Right. We'll visit the old fellers," Will Baker chortled. By now, they were at the southernmost point in the cemetery, so instead of walking back to the gate, they saved time by climbing the low wall near Cheste Raydon.

Bert Jones locked his gloved fingers together, forming a step for his mate who swung his left foot into the sling and stepped up, grabbed the top of the wall, and pulled himself up. Straddling the wall with his legs, he reached down so Jones could hand him the tools, which he dropped to the ground on the other side, and then the torches, which he turned off (he didn't need someone to spot them and get curious) and balanced a yard away on the flat top of the cemetery wall, so he would have room to help hoist Jones up.

They jumped down to the street with no incident, although both were breathing hard and perspiring. Retrieving their tools and torches and crossing to the other side, they headed up Swain's Lane to the North Gate, unlocked it and entered.

No one could see them from outside of the high walls now so it was safe to turn on their flashlights. They were immediately struck with the enormous amount of damage and stood still in open-mouthed wonder for the better part of a minute as greed and anticipation grew in their minds. Slowly they started picking their way through tons of debris: uprooted monuments, piles of torn up earth, crumbled mausoleums and exposed bodies and skeletons.

Many of the corpses were better preserved than one might think: some blackened and shriveled up, others still with muscles and tendons with the skin stripped off, almost like Egyptian mummies. Other skeletons looked like they had only dark, sticky twine attached to the bones: some were simply darkened bones. Many had been in the ground for the better part of one hundred years.

The stench blossoming up from all the open graves was overpowering. Coughing, Baker pulled out a greasy handkerchief and held it over his nose, then tied it around his face. Bert Jones did the same.

Baker bent over and, pushing a steaming heap of remains to one side, started sifting through the first open grave he came upon. Fishing out an old, golden pocket watch, complete with gold chain, he held it up for Bert Jones to see and clucked, "Mine," as he dangled it in front of Jones' widening eyes.

Bert Jones chuckled. "I think this is going to be a good night."

Will Baker stood up and started jumping around. Then he grabbed his partner and did an impromptu jig, laughing all the time.

"We're gonna be rich," Baker said. "We're gonna be rich."

Given the setting, the two of them looked like two drunken, crazy ghouls, doing a midnight dance macabre to raise demons from Hell.

"Ha, ha! We're gonna wake these folks up," laughed Jones.

"It's okay by me as long as they pay for the favor," Baker said as he grabbed his mate and spun him around.

Jones shook himself free and stopped. "We better get busy. There's a lot of ground, and we should do some fixin' up as well."

"Right. Let's go."

"Bloody hell, how could they miss the other cemetery...and this?"

"What do you mean?" asked Baker.

"Did you see any damage on the other side of the fence?" Jones asked as he walked through the churned up earth to another of the open graves.

"There weren't none."

Jones patted him on the shoulder and said, good-naturedly, "Just our luck, eh, matey." He jumped down into a large open hole.

The bombs had made a great corridor through the center of the old cemetery, starting from the north wall near Southwood Lane and just east of St. Michaels. After climbing up on one of the memorial tombs, Baker shined his torch over the grounds and could see that the corridor was about fifty yards across, and stretched in a southwesterly direction to the Holley Lodge side, barely missing an old chapel.

"It hit those old gents, Bert." He felt his mouth getting dry.

"That ain't no nevermind. Get down here," Bert Jones yelled as he shone his light all over the hole. "This be one o' them graves where folks are buried one on top o' the other."

Will Baker scrambled down and said in a hurt tone, "All right. All right. We never had a gander inside them ones."

"There must be ten o' them down here," Jones said. Then he raised his voice again. "You bloody twit. I think I'll turn in your bloody, thievin', graverobbin' hide to the Bobbies." Then he laughed uncontrollably, slapping Baker hard on his back.

Baker joined in the laughter with an impish sparkle in his eye. He'd get the sod back.

They proceeded through the demolished areas, picking through the ruins and holes in the ground, stopping here and there to explore for trinkets and baubles, and occasionally shoving and jostling each other as though they were little kids at play. The atmosphere was gruesome. Many corpses were exposed to the night air for the first time since death overtook them in their youth, or old age, or sickness, or bad luck. Body parts were strewn about, along with the bones of the long time dead.

Some families had no money for a large sepulcher, so they bought one plot of land, 3X6 feet, and buried each member in turn, as their respective times came, one on top of the other. In one case, the depth of the grave extended downward to hold thirteen bodies.

"Nasty, ain't it," remarked Bert Jones, in as philosophical a tone as he was capable.

"We'll 'ave work here for a good month," Baker said, looking in all directions. He suddenly remembered something else. "Bert."

"What?" Jones asked.

"I was just thinkin', let's just see what these graves hold, then get out o' here," Baker said nervously. "All these bodies 'n such, they're makin' me feel a little out o' sorts."

"I guess it wouldn't hurt none to start the cleanup tomorrow. You know, it ain't that long ago we found poor old Jemmie..."

Will Baker shivered, involuntarily. "God damn it. Did you have to mention 'im? What do you think I'm on about? Let's get on wif it and get out o' here."

*     *     *

By the time they had reached Cyrus's house, Jack Cawkins's irritation had reached a boiling point. He was ever so careful to hide it from his wife, and knowing she usually was quick to fall asleep, he settled her down in Hinton-Smith's old upstairs room.

"I need a cup of coffee, dear," he said. "I'll join you soon as I'm done. Good night." He closed her door and went back downstairs.

"Cyrus, now don't give me any malarkey," Cawkins said. "I want you to tell me what's with those two sons o' bitches."

Cyrus Wilson was ashamed and feeling quite spent. For the first time in his life, he had begun to realize his own frailty: he was old.

"Them two been bothering me for years, but Michael put a stop to it as soon as he grew big."

"Why didn't you go to the police?"

"Oh, it was just little things, trifles," Wilson said. "I gave as good as I got. I told Michael to leave it alone, I did. But it started gettin' worse when he went off to war...When I got old." It was hard for him to say those words.

That was all the sergeant needed to hear. If Hinton-Smith was going to do what he reckoned he was, he had to 'head him off at the pass.'

"Where do they live?" Cawkins asked. It was not that he was worried about the welfare of the two bullies. He was worried about Hinton-Smith in such a weakened state.

Wilson did not need any persuading. "Right. They're over in the projects, off Holloways Road," and he went over to a front closet and pulled out a rifle that had been there since the Great War.

"Where do you think you're going?"

"I'm coming with you, of course."

"No, no, no. Things might get nasty."

"That's why I'm bringing old Betsy, here," he said, gesturing with his rifle.

"Look, Cyrus. I shouldn't even be doing this. I don't want to get you in trouble."

"I aim to get those two bastards in trouble," Wilson said with feistiness. "It was me they were toying with at the pub, now wasn't it? Pushing me around and hurting Kate. I'll show 'em what for." He was wide-awake now.

"You're a soldier, right?"

Cyrus Wilson was taken aback, both surprised and pleased that this tough, front line sergeant major would honor him by calling him a soldier. "Right," he said proudly.

"Coldstream Guards?"

"Right," he beamed, but then he wondered where this was going.

"Now, I know you're retired from active duty. Is that correct?"

"Yes it is." Now he was getting concerned. He remembered how officers and sergeant's minds worked.

"But you have accepted a job as an air raid warden, under the auspices of your former regiment."

"Yes," he said with a sinking feeling.

"And you know, as a sergeant in the Coldstream Guards, I can give you a direct order, which you had better obey."

"Right, but..."

"I order you to stay here, and guard these premises against those two frickin' assholes, and if they show up, blow their heads off."

Cyrus Wilson frowned for a second, then a slow smile crept up on his face. He optimistically clenched his rifle. "Do you really think they'll come?" he asked hopefully.

"I overheard them in the shelter." Cawkins had no problem with lying. It would be hard enough to go up against those two without having to look after the old man. "That's why I need you here. Now, give me more specific directions, and look sharp."

Seconds later Cawkins left the house and turned down Southwood Lane. Wilson told him they could be at the cemetery if they were not at home or tending to their volunteer duties.

Then Cyrus Wilson barricaded the windows of the house. He left the front door untouched, but locked, satisfied that he'd given the bastards only one way to enter, and he and Betsy would be waiting. Finished with the work, he moved his easy chair right in front of the door, sat down, rifle across his lap, and nodded off to sleep.

*   *   *

Kate Hammond and Hinton-Smith made much slower progress on their way to her apartment, and he was quickly winded—it was the most he had walked in months, and he was much weaker than he thought. His calves were aching and his thighs felt heavy. And strangely, he was ambivalent. He had his plan, but here was Kate. He now realized that Elizabeth no longer mattered; he could even bring himself to forgive her. But Kate—her voice, her kindness and compassion, the way she laughed— how she had cared for him, looked over him. How could he have been blind for so long? He took her hand in his. But then there was Cyrus. Cyrus and those two bastards—they had even hurt Kate. Hinton-Smith felt the rage once more building inside. He would have to find a way.

"This is taking too much time, Kate. Don't you have to report? They'll need all the nurses."

Kate stopped and hugged him. "Don't say that. The only nursing I'm going to do tonight is to take care of you."

Hinton-Smith wondered if he could change his plans for this night, and considered this as they walked along Archway. The smell of smoke permeated even through this relatively untouched area. He realized that this was a woman who would give herself completely, and if he had not still been just a wee bit off, he might have been content to forget everything, and settle down with her—after the war, of course. But, unfortunately, he was a bit off, and once more, he was intent upon doing his dirty work.

Figuring he had a long night ahead of him, there was no reason not to let both Kate and himself be happy for a few hours. He would walk her home and stay and talk, and let her nurse him.

Though he had made a remarkable recovery, he was nowhere near his old self, and worse, he was blind to his real condition. Hinton-Smith really felt he was in good enough shape for those two blokes. After Kate fell asleep he would go about the vile business. He would teach that lot a lesson they'd remember, now, tonight.

In actuality, he had lost more than just weight in the hospital. Almost skeletal now, he was haggard and weak and in need of a good, few months of fresh air, healthy food, and lots of exercise. He was not much of a threat to anybody.

They walked on to Archway Station, cut across on MacDonald down to Dartmouth Park Hill, south for almost a quarter of a mile, then over to Croftdown Road, and back north to St. Albans.

Kate stopped abruptly and started to laugh. "I guess I should have got you a wheelchair. You didn't know you were going on a marathon," she said as she opened the outer door to her building.

"Now we need a rope and a pulley," he joked as they went up the stairs to her flat, which he had seen so many times before when visiting Elizabeth. "Will Lizzie be home?"

Kate was startled. "I...I don't know," she stammered. "Will that bother you?"

"I reckon it might have," Hinton-Smith said. "A few months ago, perhaps. But I've met someone else." The lieutenant stopped and turned toward her, placing his hands on her waist. "Perhaps you know her. She's about, let's see...yes. About your height."

He looked her up and down as she smiled. "Your pretty color of hair. Yes. About your hundred stone..."

She laughed and pushed him back.

"I think she dresses a lot like you." Then he pulled her close and kissed her cheek. "To answer your question, I think Lizzie will have to find someone else."

They continued up the stairs, both of them giggling like school children, entered the flat and found it empty.

"Let me light a candle," Kate Hammond said.

"How romantic," Hinton-Smith replied.

"It's just the war," Kate said, giggling. "The blackout."

"All right, then," Hinton-Smith said. He cleared a place for himself on their sofa, by removing two pillows and a pile of old books and placing them on a table.

Kate returned with a candle and a book, Lord Jim.

"Sit down, and I'll read to you."

"I'd like that," Hinton-Smith said as he leaned back on the soft cushions.

Kate sat down beside him.

Shuffling his shoulders to find a more comfortable position on the old chesterfield, he closed his eyes as she started to read. He was prepared to make chit-chat for a time, make his excuses and leave, but there was that angelic voice, the voice that had seen him back from the dead, and before he knew what he was doing, he leaned over and kissed her affectionately. This was not what he planned, but he could not help himself and leaned forward again, this time kissing her passionately. He said in a low voice, "I want to stay together tonight."

"You must know how I feel about you, but I don't know..."

He kissed her again, whispering softly, "It will be all right."

"What if Lizzie...?"

"I told you. She had her chance."

Standing up, Hinton-Smith pulled her to her feet, and embraced her fully. Kissing her again, Hinton-Smith whispered in her ear, "I love you," and tenderly picked her up in his arms and carried her to her room. He was both perplexed and pleased with his own audacity. Perhaps it was the uncertainty of war, the uncertainty of what might happen later this very night.

Putting her down on the bed, he lay down beside her and drew her to him, kissing her neck and beginning to feel her body with his hands. Her smell and touch were intoxicating. And as she began to breathe more heavily, her sounds raised his level of desire. Now, he got up on his knees, took her hands in his and pulled her up and next to him. As they embraced, he slid his hands under her dress and began to slide it upwards, never once losing touch with her soft skin. He lifted the dress over her head as she shyly lowered her eyes and smiled. Hinton-Smith unbuttoned his bulky shirt and slid down his pants.

They pressed together, gently caressing each other and then he began exploring her body with hands and lips and soft bites. He lay back down and pulled her on top of his body, kissing her tenderly for a long time, before rolling her over on her back. They began to make love. It was the first time for both of them, and it was love. And, if not for the other matter, he would have been content to lie in her arms forever.

When they were done the lieutenant rolled back over on his back, while continuing to kiss her. Then Kate brought her head down to his chest and fell asleep.

Hinton-Smith lay there on his back for a half-hour listening to her breath, feeling her heart beat, and considering his plans. One part of him wanted to stay, but there was another part of him, somewhat new and not wholly evil by any means, but certainly ready for mischief and mayhem. And this part of him knew he had to leave.

After he was sure she was soundly sleeping, he carefully extricated himself from her arms, and got up, dressed, and quietly left the flat. Silently descending the staircase, a new thought came into his mind. Perhaps he need not go to the extreme of killing the bastards. Could he not simply throw a scare into them? Perhaps then he could return to Kate, and perhaps even clear his name and rejoin the Coldstreamers.

# CHAPTER 34

# TREASURE HUNTING WITH THE ANCIENT ONES

Immediately upon leaving Wilson's house, Cawkins saw the great black wall of Old Highgate. It was a lot closer than he thought and it made sense to check for the bastards there first. He looked up at the walls. They were much too high to scale without a rope. He'd have to find an entrance.

Reaching the northeast corner of the cemetery wall, he turned down Swain's Lane and saw the North Gate on his right. Cawkins walked up to the iron gate, resting his hands on the bars while he peered inside. Even in the hazy light he could see the grounds looked immense, and overgrown with large trees, tall grass and weeds and brush. The path from the North Gate meandered to the west and uphill, disappearing into the darkness. Staring through the bars for a long while, he began to appreciate how hard it would be to find someone in this place, and he had no idea how it was laid out. Cawkins would not be able to see much. He'd have to move quietly and rely on his hearing.

He also began to remember the last time he was in a graveyard and it sent a shiver throughout his body. Let's get on with it, he thought. If he didn't move soon he might lose his nerve. He pushed on the gate and was surprised it opened as easily as it did. Cautiously he began to walk down the path.

As he went deeper into the cemetery his senses were assaulted by noxious fumes rising from gruesome, newly unearthed remains. He pulled a handkerchief out of his pocket and covered his nose. Straining to see in the hazy light, he inadvertently stumbled over a concrete tombstone in the shape of a cross, tumbled over in the bombing. The clatter from the breaking statuary seemed to echo for a long time. Great! A cemetery is hardly the place you want to make a lot of noise. If those bastards were in here, they could have heard that.

And indeed they did.

"What was that?" Jones asked in a hushed tone.

"Someone up to no good," Baker answered. "Reckon it's a grave robber?" Then he started to giggle at his joke.

"Shsh," Jones said, putting his finger up to his mouth and listening. "This is our place, ain't it," Jones whispered sanctimoniously. "We best put 'im straight, eh?"

"Sounds like 'es over toward the North Gate."

Jones nodded and crept forward, motioning his mate to follow to a nearby large painted obelisk next to the trail the intruder appeared to be on. Hiding on the far side of the monolith, he raised his pickaxe behind his head like a baseball bat. It did not occur to Jones to kill, but he was intent on doing a lot of harm. Baker stood on the other side of the path crouched behind a headstone covered with thick vines, his shovel ready.

Cawkins froze for a minute to listen and let his eyes adjust. He considered going off the path, but it was too thick with fallen leaves and thickets; he'd make even more noise. There was nothing but silence, so he gingerly got up and moved forward into the grounds. How big is this place, he wondered?

Long minutes passed as he traveled further along the trail.

A thick fog, rising some two feet above the surface, covered the ground ahead, making the trail all but invisible. Cawkins moved ahead carefully. He could not see his feet below him as he entered the foggy area. It felt like being blind. Shuffling his feet against the tarred path in case there were bomb craters or more toppled headstones, he started forward again, walking slowly.

Suddenly, Bert Jones stepped out from his cover.

"Hello mate," he said coolly. Before Cawkins could react, Baker stepped out and brought the blunt side of his shovel down on the back of the sergeant's head. Cawkins crumpled to the ground.

"Who'd I whack?" Baker asked as Jones crouched down to see.

"Bloody hell!" Jones exclaimed as he turned him over to see. "Lookee who it is. We'll never have a night as good as this, will we?"

Bert Jones laid his heavy boot into the sergeant's ribs.

"How's that for your fist in me chops, mate?" he said loudly.

Jones studied the inert body and fingered his chin as if in deep thought. "C'mon Will," he said. "I've got me an idea." He reached down to grab Cawkins's arms. "Grab his legs, boyo."

They carried the sergeant over to one of the empty graves and dumped him in.

"Give us your spade," Jones said, snickering. He then began shoveling loose body parts into the grave, on top of Cawkins, while Will Baker took the pickaxe and hooked and pulled more bloody detritus into the hole. Jones could hardly contain himself. "He'll have one hell of a good wake come mornin'."

"I almost feel like stayin' till he wakes up, that I do," Baker said.

"We 'ave work we best get to," Jones said. "Let's go."

"Might we stop by on the way out?" Baker said with glee.

"Why Will, me mate. Yer surely sentimental, ain't you?"

\*   \*   \*

Hinton-Smith could not help but think how steeped with irony was the new hope attendant on his gruesome mission, as he made his way up Swain's Lane, between the two cemeteries, to the house on South Grove where he had spent so many happy times. He wanted to kill the two blackguards for how they had treated Cyrus. He knew they had bullied Cyrus before. Hinton-Smith knew this for a fact, even though Wilson had tried to keep it secret. The lieutenant had been stronger then, soon after leaving Sandhurst, and thought he had settled the matter. He heard rumors anew in the hospital (even a pariah is privy to gossip) and now the rumors were confirmed. His own set-to with the bastards did not matter, but Cyrus Wilson, that was a different story.

Cyrus was his father as far as he was concerned. And Kate. You cannot let someone threaten your woman, or your father. But now, everything was up in the air.

He was rational enough to know that if he committed murder, he would protect his loved ones, but spend the rest of his life in prison. How would he then keep his oath regarding Cawkins? How could he help his country in its greatest hour of need? No, he had to settle the matter with the gravediggers in a less irrevocable manner.

The streets in the neighborhood were empty by this time, the smell of smoke still permeated the night air, but many of the fires were down to their embers, and only the passing sounds of ambulance and police sirens were heard off in the distance. Furtively trying to enter the house, as though he was a thief, he eschewed the front door, as he did not want to wake or alert Wilson or the sergeant, and knew that Cyrus sometimes fell asleep in the chair opposite that door. All the other entrances on the first floor were blocked by Wilson's barricade. Although it would not have taken a great effort to get through one of the windows, he figured that would definitely wake everybody up, and at least Cawkins, if nobody else, would undoubtedly see through his plans.

Wilson kept his rifle in the house, so it looked like he would have to find a different weapon, and that was all right. Now that he had amended his plans, and only sought to throw the fear of God into those two, he figured a gun might make it too tempting to go through with the original plan. Better to have done with that. Then he remembered the workshop behind the house, and quietly went around and entered the old brick shed. Searching the dusty shelves, he found a vintage bolt-action service rifle, a bit rusted out. Hinton-Smith stared at it then put it down.

Exploring around in the dark a bit longer, he played with a knife, feeling its rusty edge for a few seconds, then found an old hatchet, which Wilson must have sharpened recently. He raised it up and down a few times to feel its heft. A bloody hatchet he thought. Like one of Cawkins's Indians. Perhaps he should scalp them. That would surely be a lesson learned. He wondered if you could live after being scalped. Probably better to use the blunt bit, he thought as he left

Wilson's home for the projects. Those two were huge and he knew he was not at his best: it was important he got in the first knock.

Reckoning on taking the shortcut across Waterlow Park and behind Whittington Hospital, he noticed the wrought-iron gate of the north entrance to the old cemetery was wide open, and swinging just enough to make it appear as though it was beckoning him inside. Indeed, he felt some odd force compelling him to move through the gate. A force he tried to fight off. *I have work to do. I don't have time for this.* But he found himself going through the gate regardless, almost as though he was being pulled.

*   *   *

"Lookee there," Baker said in hushed, almost awed tones. The swath of destruction had led them all the way to the ancient cemetery, a place scrupulously avoided since finding Cravens earlier that summer. Baker wiped the sweat from his brow. The recent fires and smoke added up to an uncomfortable heat and humidity, making this a strangely hot fall night, and Baker felt dirt and grease between his arm and forehead and grinned. Looked like they done quite the job to fool the supervisor.

Pulling his sleeve further down to where it covered his forearm, he wiped his face again, this time getting a better job from the cloth. Then, standing his shovel on end, he leaned on it and said, "That's enough for one night. I'm about dead."

Bert Jones sat down on a heap of bones the two of them had shoveled into a macabre pile, as though he was at Sunday dinner sitting on his aunt's best sofa. He let out a great sigh of fatigue.

"You're a funny bloke," Jones said. "I'm damn near spent too but I ain't leavin' till we check on them old geezers. The Kraut bastards hit there too."

"Tonight," Will Baker grumbled? "We've already been out here a couple of hours. What's wrong wif tomorrow? They ain't goin' nowhere."

"You know, boyo, hardly nobody knows about that place. We've never been in there, and I bet there's gold. This might be our best chance. Maybe our only chance. Maybe the Krauts did us a favor. Besides, everybody's busy tonight diggin' through the wreckage. They ain't going to bother us. What if someone else gets the bright idea to do a little treasure huntin'? We already had to stop one such, didn't we?"

Baker grudgingly nodded in assent, but did not stand up until Jones moved, and still waited a few seconds before following. He would have been loath to admit that his procrastination was fueled by fear, more than any fatigue.

Deep inside the cemetery, most of the hazy light, from the fires and smoke in the city, was cut off by the tall ash and sycamore trees. Although a mere six feet apart, neither man could make out his mate as more than a ghoulish silhouette—a shadow with only blacks, grays, and whites for color, and only an indistinct boundary for the outline of his body. Both took their time as they walked over to the ancient cemetery. Even before they discovered Jemmie Craven impaled upon its gate, this place had engendered in them an eerie feeling of dread. Coming up to the old decrepit stone wall this night in particular, with all the exposed corpses, caused both men to hesitate, trying to work up their courage.

Bert Jones took off his right-hand glove and reached up approximately eight feet to run his fingers slowly along the top. He brought his hand down and looked at the dirt and mildew on it, rubbed it between his fingers, and smelled it. It was counter to his nature to let Will Baker see he was scared.

"Are we going in or not?" Baker asked impatiently.

"Hold yer horses, mate. Look at this," Jones said, showing the mold.

"Mold! We're violatin' God's own place and yer worried about stupid, bloody mold? Jesus!" Baker said loudly, betraying his anxiety.

Disregarding him, Jones said, "We better clean this up. If the superintendent saw this…"

"Balls to the superintendent! Bloody balls! I'll look over those geezers to see what they was buried wif, but then I'm off and you can do what you want."

"Don't get testy wif me, mate," Jones said. "Or I'll knock you out and throw you in wif 'em."

"Bloody hell," Baker said, nervously rubbing his hands together. "Let's just go and get it over wif, and then go home."

"Right. Sorry. Maybe I'm a bit cranky. Must be me nerves from the bombing."

"Yeah? Well keep it to yerself. I went through the same goddamn bombing in case you forgot."

"Right. Right," Jones said. "Let's get on wif it."

Walking around the aged, weather-beaten wall, they found the ancient gate, with the wrought metallic spears, points aiming straight up to the sky, held together with three solid oak beams, one a foot from the top, one in the middle, and one a foot from the bottom—the same spears that still had traces of Craven's dried blood. With a great deal of effort, they tried to pry open the gate, which had not swung free for six hundred years. Sweating and cursing, they used their tools as levers, then as hammers. Forgetting their worry about attracting attention and the uneasy feeling they shared of entering this antediluvian place, they pried and they pummeled. They shook it and tried digging under the foundation, until the veins stood out on their necks and the sweat poured forth till it burned their eyes. But the gate would not budge. They dug under the gate, but the spears were sharply pointed on both ends, and both men had a healthy girth. A lot of men would have given up by this time and hour, but Bert Jones and Will Baker were now extremely worked up and nothing was going to keep them out. Angrily throwing his pick and shovel over the wall, Jones looked at Baker as he handed him his torch.

"Well?" Jones asked.

Baker, with a look of defiance, lofted his tools over the wall.

"Well?" Jones asked.

Will Baker moved close to the wall and formed a step with his hands. Bert Jones stepped into it, hoisting himself up using the wall for support. As soon as the better part of Jones' body was leaning on the old dilapidated wall, it collapsed, and he went with it, falling to the other side. This caused a great release of nervous laughter from his friend.

"Get over 'ere you sod," cried Bert Jones as he got up, brushed himself off and started into the interior.

"I'm coming," Will Baker said, doing his best to stifle the laughter.

He hurriedly clambered over the new opening in the wall. "You hurt?" he asked, actually worried. He started to jog to catch up.

Jones just cursed. "Bollocks! Move it!" He was already twenty feet into the accursed place, and he had no desire to savor it alone. Strangely, he could only see three tombstones in his immediate area, and wondered why they deserved their own private burial grounds.

There was not much damage, only one bomb crater was in evidence, and that explosion had missed all but one of the three. There was some rubble from one stone that must have suffered a direct hit. The burial chamber was open, and the light from their torches, reflected off something metallic, which on closer inspection proved to be a complete, if thoroughly rusted and deteriorated, chain mail tunic, covering some very old bones.

"'E must 'ave been a bloomin' knight, 'e must," whispered Baker in a tone of wonderment.

"Right. And look at his sword, would you," said Bert, flashing his light into the hole.

The sword was just an ordinary sword, but they could see the hilt was something rare and special, even when covered with centuries of dirt and mold. Jones brushed off a few maggots and looked more closely. It was made of silver and gold, and was inlaid with two of the largest rubies either of them had ever seen, and numbers of smaller sapphires and emeralds. Baker started another impromptu dance, until Jones stopped him.

"Let's save the celebratin' for tomorrow. If this here's a samplin', we might want to dig up some of these other fellows before morning, and some nosey fool wanders in here and sees what we're up to. You realize, mate," Bert Jones said quietly. "This night could make both of us gentlemen and millionaires."

"Millionaires...maybe," Baker snorted, patting his mate on the back.

Suddenly, both of them almost jumped out of their skins as they heard a scream from the further side of the cemetery. When his adrenaline settled down, Jones shoved his partner and chuckled, "That'd be 'is nibs, wakin' up."

Baker looked at his friend for a moment, puzzled, until it sank in, then he broke out in laughter.

In another part of the cemetery, very near the monument to Tom Sayers, the last of the bare-fisted prizefighters, Hinton-Smith heard the same bloodcurdling scream, recognized the voice in spite of the distorted, tormented sound, and rushed off in that direction. As he drew closer, the lieutenant heard another anguished cry the likes of which he had never heard before and hoped he would never hear again. And before him, a ghastly pile of limbs began to eerily move as if coming back to life, as Jack Cawkins struggled to escape his gruesome prison.

"Bloody hell!" the lieutenant exclaimed, as he peered through the murky light, not sure his eyes were telling the truth. Hinton-Smith froze. Something just like this had happened when they were in the crater.

Then he realized this moving pile had been the source of his friend's cry.

Some of the corpses were still possessed of blood, which they had generously shared with Cawkins, buried as he was in a human abattoir. Rushing over, Hinton-Smith started tossing aside the body parts, using the axe as an aid. Carefully, he uncovered the sergeant major. Helping the groggy man to his feet, he was smeared with almost as much blood and gore as the sergeant.

Cawkins was dazed and shaking. He could barely lift his hands up to his aching head. Neither could he stand on his own, his legs were too rubbery. Standing only a second, he then collapsed to the ground.

Having a pretty good notion of the hooligans responsible, Hinton-Smith angrily thought to leave him and get on with his task, but he could not tell if the sergeant's wounds were dangerous, he was so fully drenched with blood. He once again hoisted him on his shoulders, determined this time, to finish the job of taking him to safety.

It took Hinton-Smith a long time to carry Cawkins out of the cemetery and up Swain's Lane: he was a lot weaker than he thought. Breathing heavily by the time he reached the house on South Grove, he set the sergeant down and propped him up against Cyrus Wilson's door. Looking him over once more to ascertain how bad he was, he found he could no longer wait. He made a noise loud enough to wake up the household, then headed back to the cemetery, more resolute than ever.

*I'm going to put a very big scare into those two. The likes of which they'll never forget.*

*      *      *

Two others heard the wretched scream from their position at the uppermost floor of St. Michael's steeple. Neither lad had been seriously hurt during the explosion of glass, but Tommy was in a state of nervous exhaustion and fear from such a long day and night, so Nigel put his arm around him and they had hunkered down in a corner of the steeple. Both boys jerked up at the first scream, and Nigel got up and balanced the pew back up against the wall so he could return to his vantage point. Before he could ascend the pew, Cawkins's second and more piercing wail reached their ears.

"Nigel," said his little brother in a plaintive tone. "Don't leave me. Please." The little boy, who had been so unwavering for so long, was now terrified.

Nigel Cochran hesitated. His curiosity almost got the better of him, but staring at his brother, he relented, walked back to sit down next to him, and put his arm around him.

Thomas Cochran started to cry. "How will we find Lucy? Or the lieutenant? I'm scared to go in there."

"I don't know, Tommy. But I promise you. We'll find her, somehow," Nigel Cochran said. "I'm scared as well."

Thomas Cochran drew his knees up to his chest, then circled them with his arms, and clasped his hands. He glumly looked at his brother and shook his head.

*      *      *

Greed had impelled Bert and Will to pursue their nefarious robbery. By now, both were loaded down with swag: each wore helmets made of silver and gold, and together, they carried a silver chest, set with red rubies and star sapphires, and filled with gold weapons inlaid with jade and chalcedony, silver rosaries, jeweled girdle clasps, and armlets set with topazes and amethysts. Caution and fear were gone, completely replaced by insatiable avarice. They emptied the grave that had been opened by the bombing, and then had proceeded to dig up the other two graves.

Carrying their loot to the damaged part of the cemetery wall, and leaving it, thus freeing their arms for new goods, they continued their exploration.

A sense of wonder arose, and fear once more made itself known as they felt their way through a cordon of fierce marble sentinels, streams of light from their torches illuminating the stern visages now overgrown with moss and noxious weeds. Bert Jones clenched his torch so tightly, he almost crushed it in two.

In what for him would pass as a tone of reverence, Jones whispered, "I never seen nothin' like this before. Just take a gander at those stones."

"This place is unnatural, ain't it?" Baker said. "I told you we ought to call it a night. I think we got enough."

Jones agreed whole-heartedly, but he would lose respect if he did not stick with the task. And he would never admit fear to anyone, let alone Will Baker. His mate would ridicule him for the rest of his days if he showed any sort of weakness in this place. Not without a genuine affection, Jones chuckled and said under his breath, "It's a tough business being a bloody hero to a twit."

"What?" Baker exclaimed. "It's gonna take us at least two trips just to carry that lot home."

"Just a wee bit more, laddie." He could see himself living in Wilson's house. He could give him twice the amount. He could buy a mansion if he wanted with these goods. The hell with Wilson's house. Jones laughed to himself as he pictured the old fossil coming to visit. He'd certainly invite him. That would show him.

Shafts of light looked like swordplay in the darkness as they explored the outer circle with their torches, both of them stalling for time, or a good excuse to finish with it. But they could not stall forever. Soon, they came to the place of a large toppled headstone, the centerpiece of the unholy ground. They slowly made their way through a group of eight tombstones in a wide circle, surrounding a large and ominous smoldering hole, rank with the fetid odor of the long dead, and where the stone slab had once stood.

*    *    *

Cyrus Wilson's eyes shot open. Feeling the weight of the rifle still in his lap, he jumped up, grasping it with both hands. He fumbled around in the darkness, searching for his torch and found it on the kitchen table, then turned his attention toward the front door. "What in bleedin' hell is it now?" he asked about the noise that had woken him from a deep, if fitful sleep. He switched on the torch. "Michael? Is that you?"

He went to the front door and tried to open it, forgetting that he had locked it earlier. "Bloody nuisance!" Now he searched his pockets for his key. Pulling it out, he inserted it and opened the door.

"God Almighty!" he said as Cawkins's upper body slumped forward and fell into his doorway. "God! What happened to you? You smell to high hell. How'd you come here?" When Cawkins did not move, he checked for a pulse, and sighed in relief when Cawkins finally groaned. "How in bloody hell am I going to get you into the house?" Wilson stepped back to think on it. It would not be easy. Cyrus spit in his hands and rubbed them together. Then, cradling the sergeant's shoulders, he levered the big man back and forth a few inches at a time, making progress in fits and starts as his hands kept slipping from the blood and guts covering the sergeant from head to toe. When he had Cawkins halfway through the door, he had to stop and stretch his back. Taking a deep breath, he went to the loo and secured a dry towel to clean off some of the muck. Then he'd be easier to move.

It was not until he had Cawkins inside and propped against his old, beige rattan chair, that he stopped to consider how this happened. It made him boil. "I certainly know who done this fine bit 'o work," he snarled. "Me lads need some help."

He washed the dark red muck from Cawkins's face, then washed his own hands and went to the closet where he kept his Sunday best. His uniform from the Great War, pressed and crisp as though he intended to use it in the present war, hung inside. He was very proud that it still fit, although it was a bit tight around the middle. He went back to the rocking chair, and found old Betsy right where he'd put her down, minutes ago. Wilson had kept his Lee Enfield in perfect working order for all these years. He took it apart and cleaned and oiled it every day, just as he had done in the field. Then he went upstairs to the attic and retrieved an old shotgun that he used for hunting grouse in the North Country.

"The gloves are off," he exclaimed as he left the house and headed down Swain's Lane.

*   *   *

By now, Hinton-Smith was reentering Highgate through the North Gate, and as he walked briskly along the gruesome trail carved out by the bombing, he was certain he saw a beam of light reflect off a tree or something shiny, and fade off into the night sky. He followed the beam back the other way to the ground, and saw another beam of light emanating from the same place. There's your origin, mate. Not a hundred yards away. Be calm. Be quiet. Don't give them a warning. Just like war games, we want a good surprise, don't we? Now caressing the blade of his ax, Hinton-Smith headed stealthily in that direction, toward the high black walls of the ancient cemetery. "You've pretty much mucked this up, haven't you," he chided himself in a moment of lucidity. But he couldn't help it. The more he thought of what Jones and Baker did to the sergeant, the more his anger welled up, the more his thoughts left Kate and normalcy, and returned to retribution and mayhem.

*   *   *

Shifting her position in the small bed, and a faint smile on her lips, Kate Hammond opened her eyes. The bed felt warm and comfortable, but it was pitch-black in the small room. Stretching her hand above her head, she could barely see her fingers, and wiggled them just to see the movement. What a strange turn of events. Only days earlier she would never have dreamed this would actually happen. Herself and Michael. There had been only wishful thinking, fancies.

She listened, wanting to hear his breathing. Now on her back, she reached out to touch Hinton-Smith's chest just to make certain it was not all her imagination: she wanted to rest in his arms and be reassured of his presence. Kate felt only an empty sheet and blanket. There was no one else in the bed. She turned toward the side where he'd slept and felt a slight declination. It did not even feel warm, as if he had just got up. Now she felt all over the bed in almost a panic. The bed was empty. She stopped moving and listened. Perhaps he was getting something to eat. The flat was not all that large and the room was silent except for the sound of her breathing. The whole flat seemed silent. That's odd.

"Michael," she whispered.

She sat up and peered into the darkness.

"Michael."

Hastily grabbing her robe off a small end table, she put it on and stood up.

The lack of an answer made her nervous. She felt a chill right through to her bones, and a fear like nothing she had ever felt before.

"Michael. Don't joke like this. You're frightening me."

Pulling the robe tightly around herself as if to fight her apprehension, she lit a single candle and looked around the small flat, and then started to cry. Strange shadows from the flickering candle ebbed and flowed about the walls. The shadows themselves were frightening. Where was he? Searching about the small flat Kate found no one—not Michael, not even Elizabeth.

Returning to her bed, Kate sat down, folding her arms as if hugging herself. She tried to think rationally. Obviously he had left. Was it because of her? He had thought better of it and still loved Elizabeth. That made sense. But he had come there and said he wanted to be with her, not Lizzie. He had kissed her. They made love. They had fallen asleep in each other's arms.

Kate realized she knew so little of men.

Suddenly she began to shake: a tremor worked its way from her shoulders to her feet. There was another explanation, much worse.

She had an overwhelming intuition, or worse, dread that Hinton-Smith had left to find Baker and Jones. To get revenge. Michael had lost so much weight. He had been in total bed rest. He could not possibly be strong or fit. How could he take on those two? And she was just as alarmed he was going to get beaten up, perhaps killed. And what might be worse. What if he killed those two? He'd be a murderer! He'd be locked up forever. Either way she would lose him. Kate had no idea what she should do.

CHAPTER 35

# THE TOMB

With Bert Jones in the lead, the two gravediggers slowly edged closer to the circle of tombs. As Jones put a hand on one of the outer stones, feeling its eroded surface, he saw a large, smoldering crater in the ground near the center, wisps of steam and smoke still ushering forth from it into the hot night air.

"Bloody hell will ye look at that?" Bert whispered. "'Ere's where one o' them bombs took a direct hit."

Will Baker narrowed his eyes as he strained to focus on the destruction. He was trembling, though not noticeably enough for his mate to see. Minutes passed before either of the men got the nerve to move forward, but after awhile their greed won out and they cautiously walked through the outer circle and up to the dark pit. Both stood at the edge as though peering over a great height, with their heads stretched as far as possible out over the hazy abyss in order to see, their weight on their heels, and their bums sticking out behind them for balance, to keep them from plunging in. Thus they stood gaping upon the strange, disquieting rent in the earth. It was terribly quiet.

"Well what's this?" said Baker as he espied the recumbent tombstone, knocked off its rightful place and resting on a newly formed mound of dirt and debris to the side of the hole. It was lying at an inclined angle.

"Uh huh," answered his mate, focusing his attention on the hole. "God Almighty!" he exclaimed. "Something in there stinks to high heaven."

"Look," whispered Jones, now in a state of awe. He pointed out the stone to Will Baker with the beam of his light. "I never seen writing like that."

Baker glanced up and looked at the stone. He scratched his unshaven chin.

"Biblical, maybe," Baker said. "I reckon we ought to try them in the circle first." This open gash in the earth was just too much for him: he imagined demons sprouting forth, evil beings, devils, Vampires. And in a ghastly image, he saw beastly hands picking up Jemmie Craven and hurtling him down on the iron stakes where they found him. Then those same gnarled, grizzly paws grabbing him and pulling him down into the abyss. It was time to leave. He'd had enough. "I'm off!"

"Are you balmy? I bet there's more goods in there than all the others put together," Bert Jones said, pointing down into the hole. "And it's open and ready for the pluckin'!"

With a chuckle and a quick shift of his weight, Jones pushed Baker over the edge of the hole.

"Why don't you go have a spot o' tea wif old Johnny and find out, boyo?" He doubled over with laughter as Will Baker screamed and went tumbling down, into the fissure.

Baker's torch went out and he disappeared. There was no noise, no cursing, no light, only dead silence. Jones kept laughing as he leaned far out over the hole, straining to see. Interminable seconds went by.

Hinton-Smith heard the laughter as he approached the wall that separated the two cemeteries. That must be them. Now to business. "Strange," he said, running his hand over the rough edges of the wall. This wall seemed much older than the other walls. Wonder why Cyrus never told me about this? Did he even know? It looked old enough to be from crusader times. Finding a thin tombstone, he levered it over and propped it up against the stones, stepped up on it, and pulled himself to the top to peer over to the other side.

The lieutenant felt a breeze at his back. There was a clearing of smoke as the wind rushed through the grounds, and just barely revealed the circle of sentinels, but he was too far away to tell whether two of them were his quarry or just thick headstones. They all looked alike.

There was also one indistinct dark shape that appeared to be partially bent over and moving, and he was certain he recognized that laugh and girth to belong to Bert Jones.

None of the other figures were moving.

Jones stopped laughing as an indescribable loathing came over him. "Stop muckin' about you twit!"

Suddenly Bert Jones felt something on his right foot. "Aaahh! Aaahh! Aaahh!" he screamed before he could focus the torch on his boot. He saw a human hand and screamed again before he recognized the glove, with the bare fingers sticking out. Damn twit! He could not let Baker get away with this.

It was Baker's turn to laugh, and in true flattery to his mate, he too doubled over, down inside the grave.

"There ain't nothin' more down 'ere than you got in your brain! Now 'elp me out," he said, laughing. Suddenly, Baker's expression changed. His crowing stopped. Fear took its place.

*　　*　　*

Hoarsley was losing patience. The three of them had left his office a good half-hour before the bombing, caught the last train out of Oxford Circus, and made it past Tufnell Park, and most of the way to Archway, when the train abruptly stopped, and all the cabin lights went out.

"It must be an air raid warning," said Hoarsley, turning on his flashlight. There was no one else in their car. "They sometimes stop the trains as a training procedure."

"How long?" Eber inquired.

"I don't know. Boyden?"

"No. I've never been caught on a train before. During a drill that is," Boyden answered.

They waited in the total blackness for ten minutes. "Could be hours," Hoarsley said. "We're not far from Archway. We'll walk."

Eber found the emergency release with the beam from his light, pushed it, and the door slid open. They got down, only Boyden having difficulty, as he meticulously feigned how he would move if he was still wearing his brace.

They walked for another ten minutes, when they heard voices coming through the tunnel ahead. "There are people down here," Hoarsley whispered, quickly turning his beam the other way, then off. "It must be the real thing."

A faint smile came to Eber's lips.

"We have to turn around. If we go to the shelter, we'll be stuck there until the all clear. Of course, we would be safe from the bombs," Hoarsley said.

"Could be all night," Boyden added.

"Be men," Eber said disdainfully. "We have a mission. Boyden. Take off the brace" he ordered, shining his torch beam on Boyden's offending leg. "Or it'll take us till morning to get there."

Boyden was sweating. His brow felt on fire. How was he going to explain the absence of the brace? Jesus Christ, it's been nice living. He looked blankly at Eber who was coming in his direction as if to take off the brace himself.

His rescue came from an unexpected quarter. Hoarsley grabbed Eber by the arm. "Turn off your torch," he whispered. "Do you want to be seen? And leave the brace. We cannot risk it. There might be others down here, police or soldiers. Perhaps someone he knows. We cannot compromise our cover."

"What now?" Boyden asked, trying hard to hide his relief. "We have to get to the surface if we're going to get to Highgate."

Hoarsley frowned. "Back to Tufnell Park. I hazard it's too shallow for a shelter. Hopefully empty due to the raid. We'll surface there and head north. We have time."

\*   \*   \*

As Bert Jones shined his light into the black chasm directly on his mate, he saw a confused, then strange grimace come over Will Baker's face. Nothing like he'd ever seen before. Something was wrong. This was no prank.

Baker urgently extended his hand, and Jones, noting the change in his mate's demeanor, got down on his belly and reached over to grab it. Before he could, Baker seemed to be slowly pulled back out of reach by some unseen force.

"Stop muckin' about! We 'ave work," Bert Jones yelled, stretching his hand out as far as he could reach, and angry that Baker would try this stupid joke twice in a row, but there was a hint of dread in his voice. Baker vanished from sight and there was again total silence. Then Bert Jones heard a terrible scream that left nothing to the imagination. Something was dreadfully wrong.

Baker screamed again as his eyes popped to the size of eggs and he was drawn backward into the hole. His body was being crushed as if it were no more than a paper airplane after a child has become bored. His bones were being broken, his body shredded, and his life force taken away.

Bert Jones lay on the ground, too stunned to move. Getting to his knees, he flashed his beam in every direction, but try as he might, he could not see anything in the ominous nothingness of the pit. Baker had seemingly disappeared. "Will. Come out o' there. Enough's enough," Jones pleaded.

Still, there was no answer. Without seeing or hearing anything more, Jones ultimately knew. Both terrified and bewildered, he stood and began to slowly back up. With the sound of a giant thunder crack, Baker's body exploded out of the hole in shards of crimson, torn into small pieces that rose fifty feet in the air, then floated down like bits of red snowflakes.

Jones turned and ran, stumbling and lurching like a drunken man. As he tripped over one of the monstrous figures of the circle, he cursed loudly as if hoping that in waking them, the dead might come to his aid. He sprinted to the ancient wall, running his hands over the cold stones to find the place where the wall had crumbled earlier. Jones was too panicked. He went to the wrong place. He could not see. Reflexively, Jones reached to his belt for his torch, tracing the belt along his whole girth, but realized he must have dropped it. Now in a frenzy he scrambled along the wall desperately feeling for the opening. It was too tall for him to climb without aid. His lungs felt like they were about to explode and he had to stop, if only for a second. Stooping over, as he grabbed his pants' legs just above the knees and breathed in deeply, he felt an odd chill creeping slowly onto his heels and ankles, then moving forward to his toes as though a temperature lowering mist had enveloped them. Then he smelled something so noxious, so perverse and evil, that he fell to his knees and threw up three times in quick succession, until he had only dry heave. Regaining his breath, he heard a chinking metallic sound, together with the sound of something dragging along the ground. With the great surge of energy, Jones jumped as high as he could, seizing the top of the wall with both hands and pulling himself up. He was going to escape, and shouted back in defiance and relief. "You won't get me you bloody bastard." In reality, he had not seen a living thing. In his confusion, and hope that he had imagined the whole phantasmagoric incident, he cried out to his late friend. "Will. Come on then. Yer right. Let's go. We'll finish tomorrow." He sat on the wall for an instant, awaiting a reply even though he knew there would be none. "G'bye, boyo," he finally called, then he jumped.

On landing, his foot came down on a piece of the wall that had previously been knocked loose, and he heard his ankle crack even before he felt the excruciating pain. Panic once again set in, and he half ran, half crawled away from the ancient stone walls, before stumbling amongst some of the corpses exposed by the bombing. Absolute terror now enveloped him. He could not move without touching those once-living remains. He tried to get back on his feet, looking around for something to use as a crutch, and grabbing at one of the tombstones for support. It toppled down onto his wounded limb, trapping him. Struggling frantically to push the two hundred pound stone off his leg, he then tried to pull his foot out from under it, but could not do either. He felt a cold chill slowly surrounding him, turned, and saw something horrible beyond imagination, slowly, inexorably moving toward him. He began screaming, incessantly, until his end.

Hinton-Smith, still balanced atop the wall, stared open-mouthed as the whole ghastly drama unfolded. An inner struggle for his own sanity had been going on for months, and though he looked somewhat normal on the surface, this fight had been simmering internally ever since the cave. The struggle had gone back and forth with each new trauma, each new set-back, but every time, his drive to get back into the fight, his friendship with Cyrus Wilson and Jack Cawkins, his warm memories of the earlier days with Elizabeth, and recently, his budding love for Kate, had brought him back from the brink. Now, seeing these brutes die in such a horrendous, unbelievable manner; men who needed punishing, and who he had come so close to killing himself, put him back on the brink, leaning heavily to the other side.

Just as abruptly, another realization brought him back. *I have to warn Kate and Cyrus, and Jack. Nothing else matters.* There was nothing he could do to help the wretched gravediggers. It had happened too quickly. The immediate problem was how to get by that thing. As he lowered himself very gingerly, he wondered what it was. Jesus! It couldn't be some kind of weapon dropped by the Germans? He chuckled thinking that was the most idiotic notion he'd ever had. No. This looked like it had been here for centuries, and it seemed to have the shape of a man. Whatever it was, he had seen it rise out of that hole, after launching bits of human flesh before it, and then he had seen it tear apart the other one. Both of those blokes were big men. It had to be them. They were always together. What could have done that? Not another human. Now it appeared to be heading towards him, and it was between him and the North Gate.

He inadvertently turned back to take one more look inside the ancient cemetery. Something else had caught his eye. Just enough light from the fires was flickering over a tombstone lying at the center of the circle. The same strange writing he'd seen someplace before was now glowing in the surrounding darkness. Remarkably, the circle of tombstones was almost the same. It now dawned on him, as if centuries of cobwebs had just been melted away from his consciousness.

"My God," he said in a whisper. "I've seen this before. In the cemetery on the Continent."

It was then that he heard the voice, as if it had been patiently waiting for that recognition. Incredibly, it was in his mind. It said, "It is time you have come."

Hinton-Smith now felt himself immobilized as if in a mesmerist's trance. He strained to move his arms and feet, then, to wiggle his small fingers or toes, anything, hoping that if he could break free from his paralysis for only a second, he would regain full movement and be able to escape. But he could not. He had grave doubts about whether or not he was breathing or his heart was beating.

The sheer hideous terror he felt when the red cloud burst forth from the tomb, had quickly transformed into curiosity. What is this voice, this thing? Instead of wishing to flee, Hinton-Smith found himself strangely compelled to know everything about this horrifying, primeval wraith, so like the creature they had seen on the Continent. Within seconds, he had an inexplicable intimacy with the apparition.

An image formed in the lieutenant's mind of a young man in armor, a brilliant red cross emblazoned on his chest that extended most of the length of his white tunic, and covering the chain mail beneath. A very pleasant looking man, with long blond hair and beard, and bright blue eyes—almost beatific in appearance, heroic and a warrior, and Hinton-Smith thought he had seen such a likeness on the Bayeux tapestry on a visit to Normandy during the lull on the front— and *in his dream!* Strangely, he was drawn to this being and had a feeling, almost a certainty, that he knew him. Of course, that was impossible, but now, the uncanny figure in the middle of the dark grounds, in slow stages, began to appear corporeal, taking on the features of that very knight from the tapestry. *I dreamed this!* That was where he had encountered this knight! He realized he had never seen the actual tapestry, but only in his dream. And all that now enfolded, seemed familiar. As the warrior drew nearer to the lieutenant, he held out his hands extended before him, palms up in a beckoning, welcoming manner, and Hinton-Smith knew without a doubt, that this was *Guillaume de Belfort*, the same name that had been scorched into his consciousness, there, on the Continent.

*De Belfort* was a Knight of the Order of the Temple. Promising he would reveal all to Hinton-Smith, his recollections were instantly in the lieutenant's mind as though the two of them were now one. Hinton-Smith felt the whole history of the being, melding with his own. No words actually ushered forth from the black shape the lieutenant saw approaching him, but he began to know everything that had ever happened to this man, as though he had lived the experiences himself: his early life in the monastery, his training as a knight, his time in the

Crusades, his travels to the Eastern lands, indeed, all his successes and failures.

At the same time, *de Belfort* divined everything that made up Hinton-Smith, including all of his strengths and weaknesses.

Words and visions, laid out as if in a mural in the British Museum or recited by an ancient Greek rhapsode, quickly formed in Hinton-Smith's mind.

*De Belfort* was a knight. He and two of his friends had been trained to the knighthood since early childhood. They were taught the noble virtues, bravery, obedience, humility, charity, piety, and reverence. Coming of age when the Pope, Urban the Second, began preaching of a Crusade to the Holy Land, he and his friends paid serious heed.

He was an idealist. He would not go to the Crusades to purge his soul of past and future sins. He had striven throughout his life to cleanse his soul, to make it pure, to avoid all mortal sins and evil, using the Holy Bible and his own conscience as a guide. Indeed, his order refrained from taking part in the many wars of the time, simply because the Commandment says, "Though Shalt Not Kill." Still, he was trained from youth to be a warrior, though raised in a monastery, as his parents were taken from him at an early age.

"Much like you," he communicated to Hinton-Smith.

"You can imagine my happiness, when I learned of the Templars: an order of warrior monks formed to protect pilgrims trekking from the port of Jaffa to the Holy Sites. I was trained as a warrior, and in my youthful hubris, I had a great desire to put myself to the trial. In the Holy Land, not only would I walk in the footsteps of Abraham, Moses, and Christ, but I would test myself in defense of fellow pilgrims. I would use my skills in the service of humble mendicants, not join in the slaughter of Moslems."

"Thus I and my friends joined the Order of the Temple to protect pilgrims on their journey to Jerusalem. We three were as brothers. Not of the blood, but of the Temple: warrior knights who took the vow of monks as well. We had grown up together, studied together, trained and worshipped together. Now we would embark on this greatest and holiest of all adventures."

"I will not blame myself for being disingenuous, for it was certainly going off to war. But I had lived my entire life cloistered with the best of men, and to a man, we took the road to Byzantium. I can now see my greatest sin was that of pride."

"I went in the footsteps of Bohemund and Tancred, but even more incredible, we walked the same land as Solomon and David, the Messiah, the Prophets! Can you even begin to imagine what this meant to three such as us? Every hour I could feel the smile on my lips, the wonder in my mind. I saw astonishing sites, the likes of which few men ever are entitled to see: splinters of the true Cross that had been found buried under the shrines of the Holy Sepulcher; water from the stream that had sprung from the rod of Moses. In a colored vial, there was a bit of darkness that had been one of the seven plagues of Egypt; and, I held in my own hand, the spear which had pierced the side of Christ."

"But I became disillusioned. The first problem arose with my conscience. We were asked to participate in the siege of cities. Even though I was trained as a warrior, this did not correspond with my conception of our duties, for this was offensive war. Then I saw my own people, the Crusaders, pillaging villages of innocent people, even Christian villages. As the Crusaders approached one hamlet north of Tyre, a throng of people emerged waving Christian banners. All were Christians, though Semitic. The Crusaders slaughtered them to a man as we three stood back and bore witness. I had ventured forth to protect such people from other men. Was it not sufficient villainy to harm women and children of the Turks? But now to do the same to our fellow Christians? I began to wonder who were the barbarians, indeed? But what did it matter to them? When Pope Urban II called for the liberation of Jerusalem at the Council of Clermont in the Year Of Our Lord, 1085, he proclaimed that God would absolve all sins, past or future, of any knight who would join a crusade to the Holy Land. What did men care of their rape or butchery or savagery when they were guaranteed entry to the Kingdom of Heaven regardless of their acts?"

"Then there were the jealousies and finally open warfare amongst the different crusading factions. To a more worldly man, this would have come as no surprise—they had always fought each other in the lands of Europe. But even the Templars came to blows with the other orders of warrior monks, such as the Hospitallers. It was this group that was later sent to the East to learn our secrets, and eventually proved to be the undoing of my brothers and me."

This was no mere panorama of images passing through the lieutenant's mind. He also felt emotions stronger than any he had ever remembered feeling before: he could see these events, feel them, even experience the taste of foods and sweets from Arab bazaars in Jerusalem or the smell of incense from the Church of the Holy Sepulchre. He felt the excitement of *de Belfort's* journeys and unheard of experiences, the arrogance of one with great power, the depth of his disgust with himself and his fellow knights, and finally the sorrow and humility of one who realizes his own failings.

"It progressively became worse. After conquering the city of Antioch, Christian men, knights included, were drinking and stealing, then raping and butchering innocents. Indeed, they cut open the bellies of helpless Turks, and led them around by the entrails."

"Later, Christian soldiers became starving rabble, salting the bodies of dead Turks to preserve the meat, and barbecuing live Turkish children on the spit. They became cannibals."

"My brothers and I could no longer continue with this charade, for we three would as soon revenge the pathetic Turks with the blood of Crusaders. Make note, this was only the First Crusade. Horror piled on horror over the course of seven crusades, and to our undying shame, we participated in this first before realizing the evil of them."

"At this point, we decided to return to Flanders to our monastery. There had to be a certain nobility to the sacrifice of our youth. Were we not defending pilgrims? Were we not now holding Jerusalem, the city of Holies, of Christ? We had conquered, now we must be merciful. We now agreed that there was nothing noble in the actions of these Crusaders. We would seek out the Pope's representative on our journey home, and give our apprehensions. Unfortunately, our new quest was soon ended. We were captured by the Turks."

"Ordinary soldiers were executed or sold into slavery if captured, but we were knights, and according to the rights of our rank, we were entitled to be held for ransom, so we assumed we would soon be home. But as we were also monks, part of a religious order, the Moslems decided to break us on the sword of apostasy. They wanted us to betray our faith, to turn us to Islam."

"We three made a pact to submit, in the realization that this might lead to our only hope for escape and salvation. What was a word of submission to Allah, when our true beliefs remained securely in our hearts? Besides, were we not all People of the Book? We would acquiesce only until our first chance. It was long months before the time came, but we made good our vow, escaping from the walled prison of Edessa. Unfortunately it was not meant for us to go home."

"Disguising ourselves as Bedouin mendicants, we traveled west, but all roads were blocked by the Turkish armies of Malik al-Zahir Baybars. Of necessity, we turned east, toward the Euphrates, through Persia to the Oxus River of Alexander. Further on, we crossed the vast Karakoram Range into Ladakh. Then, in our youthful zest for knowledge, our overriding hubris, and, to our eternal damnation, we traveled further east to the Himalayas and Tibet and sought out the men who knew everything."

"We studied from these men for twenty-five years, in which time we learned the ancient laws and secrets. We became all knowing, all-powerful and immortal, but we had not lost our pride. We made our way home, and were sought out by Bernard of Clairvaux himself, the founder of our Order, to help in the campaign against Damascus and to protect Jerusalem. Even though we were disgusted by the actions of our fellows, we succumbed to the promise of riches."

"In spite of our vast knowledge were we not still men?"

"By then the Templars had accumulated great wealth and they would share it with us for our allegiance. And so it went. Whether we had lost our moral compass in the East, I cannot tell you. What I can say, is that all knowledge is not for the better. We fought in the latter crusades until situations arose that even we could not condone."

Hinton-Smith could now feel the great amount of contempt *de Belfort* had for himself.

"There was an inkling of humanity still residing within us, and it was brought forth when we learned of the misuse of the children, inspired to have their own crusade, but iniquitously led into slavery in what became known as the Children's Crusade. We three, finally recovering our ethos, our very decency, objected strenuously to this subterfuge, and for our trouble, brought down the wrath of Kings and the Pope upon our heads."

"We had reaped the envy of these kings for having the knowledge to produce wealth and eternal life, and had now given them a reason to terminate our brotherhood. The King of France struck at all Templars to get at us, but to no avail. We were much too powerful by this time."

"The other Templars fought back, and because they were against the monarchy, they were maligned and considered evil but it was not true. Do not the victors proclaim that which is true? Those not slain in battle were put to the stake."

"Making a truce with the Moslems, the King bartered for safe passage to the East for fifty of his knights, of the rival sect called Hospitallers. These knights would seek out our knowledge so they could return and destroy us three remaining Templars."

"Some seventy years after the last mortal Templar was tortured and killed, in 1380, these Hospitallers returned from the East. For our part, the arrogance had stayed, even grown. We thought they would never be able to touch us."

"We were wrong."

"When we realized our error, we separated, fleeing to different countries in the idea we would dissipate their numbers and strength. The greatest sorrow then dawned on me, as I mourned the separation from my comrades. These Hospitallers now hunted us down with impunity over a period of decades. They no longer feared us, for their knowledge was as great as ours. We were seized, but could not be killed, so, labeling all of us heretics, the King condemned us to eternal damnation and eternal life in our tombs, imprisoned until time is no more. I had no contact with the others, had no idea what happened to them for centuries. There, in the Eastern lands, we had learned the ability of communion through our minds. In my wrath and anguish, I could not succeed in this for many years, indeed, centuries. I cannot tell you why. Then, as one day I wept for my many sins, I thought of my brother, *Sinestre L'Anguedoc*. The sorrow was so intense, it somehow passed onto him and we discovered we could once more communicate in this manner."

The entire tale had only taken seconds to convey, though Hinton-Smith felt as though he had lived through a second lifetime. It ended on an anguished, sorrowful note. "As you can see from my humble surroundings, and my ghostly form, I was punished for my arrogance, in the same manner as any wretched, classical warrior in antiquity."

Hinton-Smith was astounded. He found himself more interested in this bizarre creature than he was in his own fate.

Almost immediately as questions formed in Hinton-Smith's mind, there were answers to those questions, also in his mind. He began to ask, "Why are you telling me this? What does it have to do with me? Why didn't you just kill me like the others?"

*De Belfort* somehow thrust the answers into the young man's consciousness. "I need you," the voice said. "My brother, *Sinestre L'Anguedoc*, in France tested you to see if you were pure—a true stalwart, worthy of our Order. He tried vainly to turn you against your friend. To see if he could make you kill him, but he could not."

Hinton-Smith was at first startled, then he felt an enormous unburdening of the weight he had born for all these days, and strangely, a genuine sentiment for the bearer of such glad news. With these words, *de Belfort* had lifted the immense guilt that had hung over him since the spring. *I had been forced to try to kill Jack.* It was not a moral failing on his part. In fact, he had been able to overcome an extremely virulent compulsion. He would not have been able to kill Cawkins after all. A great relief filled his soul and a flood of strength returned to his body. During this whole time, these were the only thoughts that were actually his, emanating from his own mind and not planted there by *de Belfort,* who now lifted his control.

With this newfound gratitude, and in spite of all he had witnessed, the lieutenant's curiosity began to approach fascination. "You have lived all this time. Why don't you give your knowledge to us?" he thought.

"What do you see before you? Is it a wise man? Or an illusion. An empty, shriveled up form, neither alive nor dead?" No sooner than this thought entered the lieutenant's mind, than *de Belfort's* handsome figure dissolved into the almost transparent, hideous form that had initially greeted him.

"Look upon this ugly, withered corpse," *de Belfort* commanded. "This is what I really am. This knowledge is not worth anything to anyone. It is worse than useless. It has kept me alive and in limbo these many centuries. I cannot live. I cannot die."

*De Belfort* once more assumed the corporeal form of the knight.

Hinton-Smith could feel a mixture of anger and great sorrow enter his being. He saw he could find the wraith beastly and repugnant, but when *de Belfort* assumed the guise of the young knight he found him strangely compelling, even charismatic. The lieutenant was beguiled; he could not help himself from asking questions. "Why do you kill?"

"I make no excuse. We were trained to fight. Weren't you? We became inured to it. We reveled in our martial skills. I am imprisoned in this forlorn crypt for eternity, and when I sense the presence of any living being, whether it be rat, fox, bird, or human...even insect, I have the implacable desire to kill it. Anything that has the blessing of life. My envy of their ability to smell a flower, kiss a woman, taste a sweet wine—all the things that have to do with life. Even a lowly rat can do these things after its own nature. I cannot. So I kill. I take from them what I will never again have. You have witnessed how I kill. And it's not something I can be reasoned out of."

"But would not wisdom come from your many years?" the lieutenant asked.

"What of wisdom? Men live and men die. This we cannot change. I sought knowledge of all. I sought eternal life. What you see before you is the price of that vanity. Death would now be a blessing for me. Think now on this, truly."

De Belfort now vanished, leaving Hinton-Smith with his thoughts.

His mind was filled to bursting with images of Jack and Cyrus and Kate and his lost love for Elizabeth. He journeyed back to the cave, to its horror, to the campaign and its horror. In his mind's eye he saw the whole futile operation in Flanders and its waste. He saw his men perish on the battlefield and in the crater, but he also revisited those times he loved: of training, of travel and research, of his desire for knowledge, of his sometime wish to live forever, to learn all there was to know, from languages and history to science and building. Did they really have all that in common? Then his thoughts turned to what he'd seen through *de Belfort's* eyes, and the handsome visage of the Knight Templar reappeared.

"I know many things, but only one of importance," *de Belfort* said. "And that is something I learned years ago in the Eastern Land. To leave this netherworld of neither life nor death, I need aid. The answer to leaving this existence lies there, in the East."

"If I can blend my essence into a corporeal frame, a tangible, incarnate body, I could travel back to Tibet and seek the arcane knowledge once more, but this time, not for self-aggrandizement, but to end my existence. I need someone who is pure in heart, or he would not stand up to the rigors of the transference—that of my essence melding into his. There is a way. I know this, for I came across this science before, when my friends and I studied there, though, in our ignorance and arrogance we paid little attention. We were young. Why would we consider ending our existence? This also I know, *and promise*, that when I have accomplished my task, I would stop killing, out of gratitude. Perhaps give my knowledge to people true of heart, to you, through you, and then die peacefully."

"I need you for this work. This is the reason my brother of the Temple sought you out. And I."

Hinton-Smith was dumbfounded. He was the one this thing wanted. Try as he might, he could neither break the spell, nor argue logically against *de Belfort*. Where would he be during this odyssey? Yet, he still felt this strange gratitude.

The sad, dolorous voice again made itself heard in his mind. "Your consciousness will still be with you, though in what I can only describe as in limbo. I will only make use of your flesh and blood. I cannot make the journey in this form." The voice in Hinton-Smith's head maintained a deep, resonant, though even tenor, that of a pedagogue to a student, a mentor to a youth. "And when my spirit lies in peace, your mind would reawake from what would seem a deep slumber and rejoin your body."

"Is this so much to ask? A poor wanderer only seeking to come to a final rest, the eternal rest of death."

"You must consider this. You are already in debt to me," the voice imparted, leaving no room for doubt as to its meaning.

Hinton-Smith gasped in horror. "You killed those two on my account?" he asked incredulously.

"Yes." But *de Belfort* lied. That he lied did not in the least enter the equation. His blood lust was impetus enough for any of his depredations, but now he had other reasons.

"So you do not think me unkind, I shall give up one life to you when you agree to my proposal. A life I will not hesitate to take if you do not accede to my wishes."

"Think about this debt you owe me. Do not leave others to pay it." The admonition, with its resoundingly implied threat to everyone he held dear, thundered in the lieutenant's ears.

\* \* \*

Up in the church, Nigel could no longer restrain his curiosity.

"Tommy. Stay here. I have to see what's happening out there. Don't worry. We're safe. Nobody even knows we're here."

Quickly, Nigel ran to the broken window and clambered up the side of the bench. He carefully brushed away loose bits of glass that had fallen on the narrow windowsill so he could rest his hands on it without cutting them. Then he put his face between the still hanging shards and stared into the dark, trying to find the origins of the screams.

"There!" he said excitedly as he peered through his binoculars.

"Tommy," Nigel said in a loud whisper from the church window, as he pointing to the ancient cemetery. There was a thin figure, quite some distance away, but recognizable to the youngster, though it took him a few seconds to put it together.

"Tommy, get up here. I think it's the lieutenant."

Thomas Cochran looked up from his corner.

There were new flashes of light. The fires from the bombing seemed to restart themselves as the winds picked up. During a brief burst of light, Nigel saw all the way to the walls of the ancient cemetery, and the figure balanced on the section nearest St. Michael's, became clearer.

"It's the lieutenant. In the cemetery. I'm sure it's him."

Thomas Cochran's fears immediately evaporated. Now they could surely save Lucy. This was all he needed to regain his earlier courage. Jumping up from the cool floor, he shinnied up the bench with the agility of a monkey, and, without Nigel's help, pulled himself up over the sill to look out. Nigel handed him the spyglasses.

"That's the place we left Lucy, ain't it?" he said excitedly to Nigel. "Lieutenant!" he yelled as loud as he could. He kept yelling.

Nigel Cochran joined in, both of them yelling, "Hinton-Smith! Hinton-Smith!" like it was a cheer at the local game.

In the cemetery, the lieutenant heard these fervent voices calling his name. Somehow the spell was broken. Hinton-Smith could not quite recognize the voices, but he suddenly knew he better get out of this place. Anybody, man or ghost or knight, who could kill so easily, could not be telling the truth. The only thing he believed of *de Belfort's* tale was that he had been forced to attack Cawkins in the cave. Then he cracked a grim smile as he realized that was the only fact in the whole story that was to his benefit. He quickly glanced up at the steeple of St. Michael's, but could not see the faces that belonged to the voices he heard, though they continued to call his name. Nonetheless, he was thankful. Salvation from the church, he thought. How ironic. This is the last time I visit a cemetery. From now on, it's churches, and churches alone. He turned from *de Belfort*, jumped down from the wall and began to sprint for the North Gate.

Behind him, the façade of the seeming knight began to melt away, leaving in its place an angry but weakened, fuliginous shadow needing the comfort of its hole. Assuming human form had greatly enervated the ghastly being, but given rise to a greater urgency. He had been close this time, so close. But he was pleased as well, that he could so patiently wind out his story to this mortal enemy, this descendant of the Hospitallers. The last of his kind. There had been an almost overwhelming desire to destroy him right then. *De Belfort* had waited an eternity for one such as he to come to this place. How many were the years? Never once did he believe it could ever come to pass. He was certain their numbers had dwindled: had not the Templars been reduced to only three. Indeed, what were the chances that the only descendant of those that imprisoned him would happen upon *Sinestre L'Anguedoc* on the Continent, and at a time when their powers were bolstered by such evil upon the land?

Much of the story related to the lieutenant was true, with suitable enhancements and shadings, except for the one great omission. *De Belfort* would save telling him until the very last moment before he melded with Hinton-Smith's body, for he would certainly accomplish this, and, at that point, the process would be too far along to halt. Then he would exult and his enemies would be no more.

At the same time the lieutenant jumped, Nigel jumped down to the floor of the church loft.

"C'mon, then," he shouted to his brother. Together, the boys ran down the stairs and through the aisle, and into the smoky evening air.

Running past Sayers' dog's statue, Hinton-Smith was sure he caught a glimpse of someone or something running alongside. He looked in both directions, but at first saw nothing. This only inspired him to quicken his pace. Then, out in front, as he turned right along the path, he saw a giant black figure, lurching down the path in front of him. The figure reached the now-shut North Gate, and turned to reveal a hideous grimace, under a black, stovepipe hat. Hinton-Smith figured this thing could not be worse than the one he'd left behind, and charged right up to the gate. He could not budge it, try as he might.

The dark man jumped up to the top of the gate, resting with his haunches on the tips of the spears that formed the uppermost part. He motioned for the lieutenant to join him. Hinton-Smith ran twenty feet back along the path, turned and sprinted to the gate. Jumping when he was about four feet away, he wondered if there would be room, but managed to grab the top bar with his hands. He then pulled himself to the top and over. On the other side, he looked for the weird guide, but he had disappeared, and the gate, seemingly of its own power, now creaked open, and swung back and forth.

As he reached the street, he saw two little figures running down Swain's Lane towards him. He crouched down as soon as he recognized them, and they threw themselves into his arms.

"We can't stay here. We have to move!" Hinton-Smith yelled.

Grabbing each boy by the hand, he stood up. "Let's go, then. Be quick about it."

The lieutenant and the boys started jogging down Swain's Lane past the harrowing gauntlet of the dark, stone walls of both cemeteries. As they ran, Hinton-Smith could not keep his mind from drifting back to the knight. Had *de Belfort* really killed those two for him? He now remembered both dreams, both too real and both hard for him to differentiate from reality. And the knight: was he the good man from the first dream? No. He must be the evil voice from the second.

*   *   *

Hinton-Smith and the boys did not stop running until they reached the narrow sidewalk to the door of Kate Hammond's flat. Thomas Cochran looked at the lieutenant, and grimacing, pointed at him. Hinton-Smith looked down at his uniform. It was mired with bits of hair and skin, and blood, some still fresh and wet. He smelled awful.

"Yucch!" Nigel Cochran said.

The lieutenant put his hand on one of the wet parts of his uniform and squeezed it. Somberly, he said, "Thou shalt take a lamb without blemish and thou shalt kill it at dusk, and thou shalt take of the blood and put it on the two side posts and lintels upon the houses where they eat it." He then rubbed the blood on the middle of the door, making a crude X. He realized this might seem a bit odd to the children, so he winked at them, saying lightly, "Read your Bible. A little of God's own protection from the bombs." Then he opened the door and led the two boys upstairs. On the second floor, as Hinton-Smith reached for the door handle, the boys pulled on his hand. "Lucy's still in there," Thomas Cochran said and then the boys relayed their tale. "That's why we came to find you."

"We knew you were the only one who'd believe us," Nigel Cochran added solemnly.

Hinton-Smith was going to say, you don't have to worry, she's dead, but he thought better of it. He had not seen any evidence of the girl in the cemetery, but he saw an uncanny determination, especially in the little one, to go and bring her out. The boys had absolutely no idea what was in there and he did not want them to go anywhere near Highgate. Even Cyrus Wilson's house was too close. And returning to the cemetery was not the heroism he was looking for. That was supposed to be against other men. Unfortunately, he could see these staunch little warriors would go back if he didn't do something. "I'll make you a deal. If you promise to go home, and stay there," he said emphatically. "I'll go back to the cemetery and try to find her." Quickly, they both nodded in agreement.

"But part of our pact is, you cannot leave your house until I return. And if I don't return before morning...this is important." He looked sternly at them. "If I do not return, you must never go into the cemetery again. Agreed?"

"I agree," Nigel Cochran said, greatly relieved.

"Why?" asked Thomas Cochran.

"I'll answer that question when I come back. Well?" he asked. "I won't go back for Lucy if you don't agree. Tommy? I want your solemn promise."

"Yes," the little boy responded.

"Now, not a word of this to Aunt Lizzie or Aunt Kate. We wouldn't want to frighten them, would we?" Hinton-Smith cautioned. The boys gave him their word. What choice was there, he thought? Let two small boys go in my stead? *How strange. They saved me, now they would send me back.*

But perhaps it's about time, he thought, now becoming angry with himself. Here he'd been lollygagging in hospital for God knows how long, when there was a war on. And this thing waiting for him in the cemetery. Obviously, one *Guilluame de Belfort* was somehow related to that bloody ghost back on the Continent—the bastard that started all his troubles. It was about time to square accounts. But he would need help, and there was only one person that could help him. Bloody hell! There was only one person in the world who wouldn't think he was a bloody loony and out of his mind, and he was out cold. He knocked on the door.

## CHAPTER 36

# BACK IN ACTION

The lieutenant was greeted by a tearful woman dressed only in a light flannel robe and carrying a dish with a lit candle. Her eyes were red from crying, and there were deep shadows under her eyes from lack of sleep.

"You're safe. Thank God," she said as she rushed out to greet Hinton-Smith. She hugged him tightly and started crying anew. Standing back to look at the lieutenant, she saw her nephews.

"What are you boys doing here?" she asked, bewildered, and bending down to gather them in her arms. "You're supposed to be home in bed. How late is it? You're mother will have a fit. She must be worried to death!"

"Kate," the lieutenant said, grabbing her by the shoulders. "There's trouble. I don't have time to explain. I have to leave."

"Oh my baby," she said softly through her tears, as she tried to hide her surprise and sadness at the way he looked. The dirt and blood and candlelight made the lieutenant appear ghoulish, far worse than he actually was. "I don't understand. Do you mean to the shelter? Are the bombers coming back?"

"Don't worry about the bloody Germans," he said excitedly. "They're the least of our problems. I want you to dress and be ready to leave at a moment's notice. I have to get Cyrus and Jack. Then I'll be back for you and the boys."

"Wait here," Kate said. She left and quickly returned with a wetted cloth and gently began to wipe the grime and blood from his face and hands.

He pushed her back. "You don't understand. I have to leave."

"No, you don't understand. I'm not letting you go anywhere, with you looking like this," Kate insisted. "Are those cuts? What happened to you? What is all this blood?"

Suddenly she turned ashen faced. She leaned back and fell to sitting on the couch, her hands covering her cheeks. She looked up at him, accusingly. "What have you done? You went after those two, didn't you? Did you murder them? Is that why you're in such a hurry to leave? The police would arrest you in a moment with all this blood. Oh my God!"

The two boys could only stare in wonder.

"Blast all! It wasn't like that. I went to get even," he said rapidly, raising his voice so that he was almost shouting. This was no time to nit-pick. "But I didn't touch them. That... that thing did. But that doesn't matter, does it. Everything's changed. We're all in danger."

"What?" Kate asked, completely confused. "How do you explain this?" she asked as she held up the incriminating washcloth, now covered with blood. She waited for an answer that did not come. Then she quickly changed tack.

She turned to a cabinet and brought out a bottle of wine and a glass.

"This will calm you," she said, opening the bottle and pouring the glass to the brim. "Sit. Drink it."

"You have to get out of those ghastly clothes," she said. Next, she took out some men's clothing from the closet. "Put these on. They're Cyrus's," she said to Hinton-Smith.

He looked at her doubtfully. Perhaps the best course was to humor her. There was no way in hell he could explain this. The lieutenant started to change out of his clothes. "I'll do anything you want, but you have to get dressed and be ready to leave when I get back."

"Of course," she said, but as he finished putting on the clean clothes, Kate wrapped him in her arms. She kissed his cheek. "Do you have to go?" she said seductively.

Turning to the boys, she affected a stern look and said, "Don't look."

The lieutenant felt himself yielding to the wine and her soothing presence. Maybe it was a dream after all. How could any of the last half-hour be true? He felt so incredibly exhausted, almost too tired to argue. Could that thing really exist? Was it just another one of his dreams? The picture of Jones being torn asunder arose in his mind. No. It was real.

"I don't have time," he said less resolutely. "You don't understand. I have to go."

"Not yet." She stroked his forehead. "Tell me what happened, baby."

He took a deep breath before answering. "They're dead, those two. Ripped apart. But I didn't touch them. I swear I didn't. I went to teach them a lesson but I didn't have to. Somebody else beat me to the punch."

"The bombing?" Kate asked, putting both hands to her mouth as if afraid to hear the answer.

"No, it wasn't the bombing," he answered matter-of-factly. Then he looked at the young brothers, who were now both staring at him wide-eyed, with the little one seemingly on the verge of tears. "I think you should take the boys upstairs, Kate. And let them rest. This is going to be a bloody long night."

Kate looked at him uncertainly, considering everything she had heard. She still stared at the lieutenant as she took the boys' hands in hers. "Don't go anywhere," she said to Hinton-Smith. "I'll be right back." Then she led the boys up the stairs to her loft.

"You lot should be ashamed," she said, crossing her arms as they reached the top. "I just hope your mum slept through all your shenanigans."

"I'm sorry," Thomas Cochran said.

"Me too," said Nigel.

"Well, I'd like to believe you," Kate said. "But for now, I'm angry with you. Aunt Elizabeth was right. You must show more responsibility to your mum. Just get undressed, get into bed, and I'll see to it you get home bright and early tomorrow morning. Then your mum can decide what to do with you."

The boys silently stripped down to their underwear and got into bed.

Satisfied, Kate went over to the window, drew it shut and bolted it. "Good night," she said, and went out of the room and down the stairs.

"Well," she asked, as soon as she entered the room.

"Do you really think I murdered them? Is that it?" Hinton-Smith growled. He was once more growing restless.

Kate folded her arms in tightly, against herself, and looked at the floor. "I don't know what I think."

Hinton-Smith felt as if he was in a play with lines that had long ago been written for him, and which he had to recite, regardless of the consequences. "Well, you're partly right," he said. "I went down to the projects to kill them. And intent is almost as good as the deed. I took an ax from Cyrus's work shed. But on the way I thought of you, and our future...that I'd rejoin the Guards, and come back and we'd be together."

"I just don't want you to get hurt again," Kate said and then began to cry. "I thought they'd beat you."

He could not wait any longer. So many lives might depend on how fast he moved. "Kate. Please forgive me, but I have to leave," the lieutenant said. "Lock the door and all the windows. Don't go near them until I come back." Realizing what a paltry defense that was, he wondered if she should take the boys to the police station, but that was closer to the cemetery. Cawkins and Wilson were on South Grove, much nearer *de Belfort*. They have to be warned. "I have to leave now." He went to her and tried to kiss her, but she turned away. Looking at her sadly, he then walked to the door, exited the room and rushed down the creaky steps.

Kate was still weeping as she watched him leave. She confusedly walked to the door, latched it, and secured the chain. Then she walked over to the bed and sat down with her head in her hands and sobbed. "Please Michael, don't hate me."

Only minutes before the lieutenant showed up with her nephews, she had rung the police station. She had no idea what to do now. She could not believe how terrible he looked. But worse, would she be the impetus behind his arrest?

It was another ten minutes before Kate discovered her nephews were gone.

\*  \*  \*

"Nick. Take Wingate and go down to Highgate. They hit us pretty hard down there," said the police superintendent. Unlike the streets near and around Highgate's cemeteries, the local station house was tumultuous with activity. "There was a strange call that came in. Something about those two lads you had a run in with earlier. Seems someone wants a settling of scores."

"Right. I'm off, sir," Hensen said.

Much of the operation of civil defense for the area was coordinated from there, a small brick, two story building with only four barred holding rooms or cells, a mess area and changing room. The Bobbies could be called on for any chore and found themselves filling in for anybody or anything that had been overlooked in the initial planning, as well as being responsible for their ordinary duties: they worked as firemen, air raid wardens, guards, and lookouts; they operated searchlights, A.A. batteries, and some were now busy clearing fire lines and digging people out of the rubble. If anyone was sick or injured, whatever the task, the Bobbies would fill in.

\*  \*  \*

Hinton-Smith ran most of the way. Unfortunately, he had to pass between the old and new cemeteries to get to South Grove, and as he drew near Oakeshott Avenue, the last street before the old cemetery, he felt his determination start to waver, ever so slightly. *That won't happen this time,* he determined, summoning up his old force of will. He broke out running in a dead sprint. Whatever was in there, he was not going to give it a lot of time.

When he reached Wilson's house, he threw open the door and burst inside.

Cawkins sat up, startled. He was holding a slab of red meat to his forehead and was in a foul mood. Immediately observing the blood smears still on the boy's neck and hands, he got up and seized him sternly by the shoulder. "What in God's name have you been up to?" he yelled. "And where the hell is Cyrus!"

"It's here!" the lieutenant said excitedly. "That thing! Whatever it is. Just like the one in the cave. But here, in Highgate!"

In an agitated blur, Hinton-Smith went on to describe his encounter with *de Belfort,* word falling upon word so fast, they oftentimes blended together. Cawkins could barely keep up with the deluge.

The sergeant was stunned. His eyes opened wide, and he could barely utter a single word. He fell back in his chair.

"Are you all right?" Hinton-Smith asked, catching his breath.

Seconds passed as Cawkins stared at the lieutenant. Finally, he cleared his throat. "Yeah. I've got a pretty nasty bump on my head, but I'm all right."

"Where's Cyrus? I thought he was here with you."

"I don't know. When I came to, he was gone...You better back up just a mite. The thing from the cave...?"

"He talked to me, Jack. I don't know how. Somehow he was in my head," Hinton-Smith said. He tried to slow down, but the words continued apace. "It was one of his brothers we encountered in the cave. He called him *L'Anguedoc.* There was a larger tombstone inside the cave. With an inscription. I saw it when I went back there to get our gear. I saw the same thing here. I'm pretty sure it looked the same."

Cawkins looked at him with a mixture of confusion and horror.

"'He who resides within is damned for all eternity,'" Hinton-Smith said with deliberation. "My knowledge of Aramaic is pretty meager, but loosely translated that's it.

"You're going way to fast," Cawkins said. "The same thing we saw in that cave is here?"

"Not the same, actually," Hinton-Smith said. "I don't think so. But the same kind of thing."

"I need a drink," Cawkins said, and he got up from the rattan chair, headed for the kitchen, where Wilson had shown him a small cooler, filled with fruit and vegetables (Kate and Elizabeth had made him keep these, though he only ate them when they were around). He opened a cabinet next to it and spotted a beer, but before removing it, he noticed a half-filled bottle of whiskey hiding innocuously behind a bottle of vinegar and an unopened jar of baking soda. After so many years in England he still could not figure out how the Brits could drink warm beer. It made him shudder. He poured himself a glass of whiskey, downed it in one quick gulp, then took a long swallow out of the bottle, and brought it back with him.

*   *   *

Kate had barely left the room, when the Cochran brothers quietly got out of bed and got dressed. They were not about to stay put. The window was locked, but the bolt was on the inside. The boys were now quite expert in stealing away from their relatives unseen.

Upon hearing the argument and the mention of murder, Nigel was at first surprised, then agitated, and finally angry.

"See, Tommy," Nigel said, walking over to the covered glass window, unbolting it and pushing it open. By now, regardless of his fears, he was as committed to finding Lucy as his brother. "You can't trust anyone over fifteen. Even the lieutenant. He was never going to go back to Highgate. He lied. He was there to murder somebody. He won't go back."

There was a one-foot-wide ledge directly beneath the window. Nigel crawled out onto it and from there, he spied a fire escape with stairs that looked to reach within a few feet of the ground. He motioned for his brother to follow. It was hard to see, but they crept down the steps, not caring about the danger. When they got to the bottom, Nigel saw that they still had a good eight feet to go, and he could not figure out how to release the bottom ladder. Nigel knelt down on the last step, then grabbed the metal with his hands and slowly lowered himself down until he was hanging full out from the ladder. Then he jumped. Thomas followed, and was caught by his brother.

The sky was eerily dark and hazy brown from the combination of smoke and moonlight. Searchlights once more crisscrossed the night air.

"I think you're wrong about the lieutenant," Thomas Cochran said as they started down St. Albans Road toward Swain's Lane. "Can't you see there's something wrong with him."

"I guess he's still wounded," Nigel said, unconvinced.

"He was fighting with Aunt Kate and yelling and swearing. He'd never do that."

"Maybe you're right. But I doubt he'll keep his promise to us."

"I don't know," the little boy murmured after a moment's thought. "He's a hero, isn't he?"

"Let's get on with it, then," Nigel said as they started running. I know a place right behind Oakeshott. The wall's pretty low there, and it's warped a bit in one spot. We can crawl over it and we'll be right in the cemetery. I went there once with Simon but we didn't go in. We heard a big dog barking."

"Great," Thomas Cochran said.

Ten minutes later, they approached the leaf-covered, grassy incline that led up to the wall, and both boys were thinking of the dreadfully grotesque "Man in Black" who had appeared the last time they tried to break into the old cemetery.

The slope was only twenty feet long, but it was so steep and slippery, they had to crawl on their hands and knees. At the top, Nigel walked along the stone wall, using his hand to feel for the section that was damaged. Thomas Cochran followed close behind, holding on to his brother's shirt.

*       *       *

A single candle, melted by half, burned on the small dining room table. Shadows and light from the flame flickered on and around the faces of the two grim men seated at the table.

"So what do you suggest we do?" Cawkins asked uneasily. Now it was here. He felt like he had been run over by a tank.

"We have to fight it," Hinton-Smith said.

"I think we stay as far away from that place as possible."

"He wants my soul, Jack," the lieutenant said, looking Cawkins in the eyes.

"I think that's a pretty good reason to stay away from there. Besides, why put stock in anything he would say? Trust that thing? That's insane." Cawkins stared intently into the lieutenant's face and knew there was no arguing. He couldn't let him do this by himself. And he did not want him to do anything at all. He slammed the whiskey glass down on the armrest of his chair. "Look. We can't go off half-cocked. We have to figure this out. You said he left his grave?" Cawkins asked. "That's different. The one on the Continent never followed us. And we only felt his presence when we were in the cave, or the vicinity of the graveyard. We didn't see anything or feel anything when we were out of that range. Right? He might have been somehow held to that place. This son-of-a-bitch sounds like he can move around."

"Perhaps," Hinton-Smith said. "I remember, when that Panzer shell exploded in the cemetery, it knocked over the tombstone. I didn't see the bloody thing until after the explosion. And when we were in the cave, we never saw him. Of course, the tombstone was intact," the lieutenant added, trying to puzzle it out. "And you know what else? When the second Panzer plowed into the crater and erupted, the hole became a molten inferno. It was so hot and bright, I could barely look. I had to back away. I didn't see it after that. And you couldn't. You were unconscious. Of course, I didn't stick around to ask questions. But *de Belfort* went outside the circle of tombstones, and out of the grounds of the cemetery here, if only for a few yards. He obviously has power within the range of the cemetery, but I don't know how far it extends. It could reach anywhere. Even here."

Cawkins did some quick figuring. "Are you connecting the presence of that stone over the grave with keeping the bastard locked in?"

"Something like that. But now he's out, and he says he needs me for this journey," Hinton-Smith said. "If he can leave the graveyard, then nobody's safe. If I don't go back, he's promised to kill everyone that's dear to me. Everyone! I know this for a fact. I've seen what he can do."

"Well, I know this for a fact," Cawkins said. "I'm not letting you go back there, period."

The door to the house burst open and Kate ran in, excitedly.

"Michael," she cried, rushing up to the lieutenant. "The kids ran away. I didn't know what to do. I'm frightened."

"My God!" the lieutenant exclaimed. He put his hands on Kate's shoulders. "They think I broke my promise." Suddenly, he released his grip on her. "They went back to Highgate Cemetery," he blurted out. "That's where they went. I have to go."

The sergeant major looked calmly but forcefully into the blue eyes of the lieutenant, so recently almost vacant, now seemingly alive. The old spark was returning. "I can't let you go," he said. "We have to think this out. It must have to do with the actual stone. Some kind of talisman or power embedded in it. We saw those in the head-stones in the cave. You say it's toppled over right now?"

"Yes," said Hinton-Smith quietly, but it made no more difference to him than one lonely blade of yellow grass did to the whole cemetery. As he wavered in his weakened physical and mental state so many times this night, he wavered once more. How could he involve Cawkins in this mess? How could he make Jack help him? It was a bad idea that brought him back here. There was no way to beat this thing. He had to find a way to leave Cawkins behind.

"Probably a direct hit from the bombing. Maybe we could put the stone back in place. Seal him in forever," Cawkins said, thinking out loud. "Maybe that's what the Hospitallers did."

"For Christ's sake, Jack. His mate in the cave controlled us when he was still entombed. You can't do anything against *de Belfort*. Only I can. You think I haven't explored every angle? Everything? It's hopeless. I'll give him what he wants. My life for the children. My life for my friends."

Kate stood by, her hands covering her mouth and her eyes wide with horror as she tried to understand.

"Ok. That would be a good move. You want to be a martyr? That thing is pure evil. It'll be in your body and freed of its prison, and you want to believe him? What if he just keeps your body for good?"

Hinton-Smith looked questioningly at the sergeant.

"There were other things on the parchment you gave me. Sanskrit that I couldn't get translated till I got back to England. The translation left no doubt about one thing. The other Templars were wronged. Tortured and made to confess to crimes they never committed. But *de Belfort* and the other two, they were villainous, first-rate sons-a-bitches. Now it starts to make a little sense. The Hospitallers imprisoned them and then wiped out all memory to protect the rest of us. But more importantly, not only did they put them in their graves, they figured out how to keep them there. They can't die, but they can't leave."

"His jailers must've had a great sense of humor."

"Yes. Imprisoned forever."

"Perhaps not forever."

The sergeant looked at him grimly. "It must be some kind of talisman, in the grave or in the stone. Maybe the surrounding graves also have some part in it. Maybe they were Hospitallers, maybe the surrounding tombs in France too. The stone's toppled right now, and that's why he's out. That's my guess," Cawkins said. "We have to get him back in. How the hell did they do it?"

"You want to risk all our lives on a guess?"

Kate looked back and forth in horror, trying to follow what were to her, cryptic utterances. Approaching hysterics, she screamed, "What are you talking about? What does it have to do with my nephews? Your life for the children's? Why?"

"Michael. There was one thing I didn't tell you," Cawkins said in a soft voice. "I was pretty bored in the hospital, so besides the research, I started doing genealogies..."

"Do we have time for this?" Hinton-Smith said, raising his voice in exasperation.

"I think so," Cawkins said intensely. "Listen. Obviously, trying to follow the line of a Smith would take forever, but Hinton, that's a different story. I was able to trace it back, all the way to Rhodes, to the Hospitallers. To the Fifteenth Century, a man named Whyntowne. A knight."

Hinton-Smith stared into the sergeant's eyes. "So?" he said skeptically. "I can't risk the children."

"This knight was sent by the king of France to destroy three Knights Templar. I couldn't follow it further. This man was your ancestor. He knew the evil of these men. And did something about it. What if that's why he wants you? To undo the work of your ancestor? To get revenge."

"Then he has a great sense of irony, doesn't he?" How could he discover something so far back in time? *How could this thing know my ancestry?*

A raw look of determination started to grow on Hinton-Smith's face. They were wasting precious time. He turned and went up to

Kate, placing his hands on her shoulders, then hugging her. "Kate. I'm going to go get the children now."

"Did you forget that we're a team?" Cawkins asked, standing up to his full height. "Cyrus has lamps. He must keep paraffin around here somewhere—maybe combustibles for a Molotov cocktail."

"In the work shed. Out back. Why?"

"I have a few grenades in my kit. We'll burn the bastard's home. Like you said that panzer did. We'll push the tombstone into the grave and destroy everything in that hole. Fire. Fire destroys every- thing. We'll burn him to a crisp. That's what we'll do."

"First rate plan. Why don't we just shove the stone up his arse? What if he's no longer there?"

"I don't think he can exist for long without the grave. If he could, his buddy on the Continent would've left when the tank shell freed him. You said so yourself. Come on. We ain't got all night."

"Jack," Hinton-Smith said very deliberately. "I said he disap- peared. I never said he went back into the tomb. He might be free."

"Sweet Jesus!" Cawkins exclaimed.

Kate pulled herself away from Hinton-Smith and sat down, her head in her hands, sobbing.

The lieutenant kissed her on the forehead. "I have to go," he said softly. "I love you." Then he turned away and walked out the door with Cawkins.

"I need to do this by myself," Hinton-Smith said as they walked down the dirt path to the workshop.

"No," Cawkins said.

"You should stay here," Hinton-Smith said. He opened the door to the shed. They went into the cool, darkened room.

"No," Cawkins said, shining his torch around the dark shack.

"But someone has to stay with Kate and Maggie," the lieutenant argued. "Somebody has to keep them safe."

"No," Cawkins said, forcefully. "I'm coming with you whether you like it or not." The sergeant raised the torch and shined it on the young man's face. "I know," Cawkins said. "I know about your oath."

"What!" Hinton-Smith exclaimed, shading his eyes from the

light, then turning away. "What are you going on about now," he said in a much quieter tone.

"I know you almost as well as I know myself," Cawkins said. "Do you think I didn't see what you were doing? Playing the mother hen with me. On the campaign. It's a guess, sure, but an educated guess."

Hinton-Smith fidgeted with a lamp from the workbench and did not answer.

"Well," Cawkins said. "I'm right, ain't I? And you think you need to keep me away from this thing, to fulfill this idiotic knight errantry." He took the boy by his shoulder and turned him around so they were facing each other. "You don't owe me anything. How many times have you saved my life? Besides, that bastard in the cave, and his brother or whatever he called him. They're responsible for a good share of our troubles. I hereby release you from your oath. Well?"

Hinton-Smith breathed in deeply and slowly let it out. This was a lot of new information to digest with very little time in which to do it. He would have to figure out how to protect Cawkins on the fly. "Right. Let's get on with it. I reckon it's about time we paid the bloody bastard back."

CHAPTER 37

# EVERYBODY WHO'S ANYBODY GOES TO HIGHGATE

Hinton-Smith prayed they would not be too late. He had his doubts about whether Cawkins was right, and was not at all certain what they could do, but he could not just leave the boys to their fate. Could he bargain with *de Belfort*? Could they trick him, or stall him? Could they destroy him? He did not know the answer to any of these questions. *De Belfort* said he would give up one life if he agreed. Did that mean the boys? Could *de Belfort* read the future? Did he know they were coming? Would he only yield one of them? Which one would he free? If only he was at full strength, could see the problem clearly. It was almost too much. Truth be told, he was glad he had the big man at his side once more. Still, only one thing was for certain, he would trade his life for the lives of the children, if it came to that.

As they reached the North Gate, they saw the strangely grotesque "Dark Man" perched on top of the gate and motioning them to join him. Cawkins stared open-mouthed as the gate swung open and Hinton-Smith went inside. He was certain that the Dark Man's hideous grimace bore a trace of melancholy.

The tall man in black jumped down and sadly motioned for them to follow.

It was almost one hundred and eight years ago that the Man in Black had been one Thadeus Reason, a recent widower who came one night to proclaim his undying devotion for his treasured lost love. He wept tears for long hours over her freshly dug grave, then meandered around the west cemetery in his anguish.

He came upon the ancient cemetery, and for some reason, an interest for the site grew forth in him, and allowed him to bathe in forgetfulness for the first time since his sweet wife's death.

He found himself compelled to climb over the wall, and once inside, encountered a voice, speaking in his head, not unlike the experience of the lieutenant, except it was a very angry voice. *De Belfort*, reading Reason's mind and history, had found him unacceptable for his purposes, and like a woman scorned, had decided to make him pay a foul retribution.

The misshapen scowl Reason wore all these subsequent years was from the enormous fear that *de Belfort* had inflicted upon him. The punishment for not being suitable was an eternity in this nether world of neither life nor death. The crowning debasement was to be the servant of his tormentor, luring new victims to *de Belfort*.

Directing them to the ancient cemetery, the Dark Man led them up to the rusted black gate, which now creakily swung open for the first time in six hundred years. The two soldiers walked through, shining their torches before them, and finally setting their beams in the direction of the ghastly hole, still smoldering from the explosions.

Cawkins laid down the paraffin, a lamp, rags, cardboard and wood shavings near the pit.

The lieutenant, dubious at best, placed a jerrycan of kerosene and more combustibles next to the other materials, then stood up and scanned the rest of the grounds.

Off to his left, he spotted three meek little figures laying face up, motionless, their heads to the north. His heart sank as he viewed the tiny bodies. He ran over to them, knelt down and felt the younger boy's wrist for a pulse. Cawkins came to his side.

"The boys are breathing," Hinton-Smith whispered. "But what is this little girl doing here?" There was dried blood caked near her eyes and nose. He felt her small neck, then stood up slowly, shaking his head. *This is the life he promised me. He kept his word. Perhaps he was telling the truth.*

"She barely has a pulse." Hinton-Smith took off his coat and placed it over the poor disheveled body. "We have to take them out of here. Jack, this is strange. *De Belfort*, I don't think he's here."

"That means he can leave the cemetery," Cawkins said.

\*   \*   \*

At the main entrance to the West Cemetery, Eber finished picking the padlock to the gate. It was a stubborn lock. In the end, he had had to use his stiletto. The lock mechanism sprang after a few minutes.

As soon as they had passed through the gate, Eber shut it and put the lock back in place. The gate would appear locked except on close inspection.

They headed up the steep flight of steps through the Colonnade, Boyden leading the way. Hoarsley stopped to stare in amazement. "I've never seen anything like this," he said.

"Right out of some Arthurian legend, right," Boyden said.

"Let's get on with it," Eber said impatiently. He shook his head. He was tired of hearing this occult drivel. As they neared the site of the ancient cemetery, he seriously considered whether he should just kill them both and be done with it. Ever since learning this was about *de Belfort*, the name he'd heard uttered at Wewelsburg Castle, his notion of the mission had soured. This was absurd, even if Hitler ordained it.

He wanted back on the Continent. Then he could get back to the fight that mattered.

\*   \*   \*

Cawkins stood, his hand on his chin, looking downward as if into the abyss of Hell itself. Now that the problem was directly in front of him, it did not seem so easily disposed.

"I'm sorry, Mike. For the life of me, I'm not sure what to do. If we destroy his grave, we'll never trap him inside. What if I'm wrong, and he can survive outside? What if in blowing up his tomb, we destroy whatever kept him in? We free him!"

"I told you it's complicated, didn't I? Perhaps he is down there. Perhaps not," Hinton-Smith said. "I think your first idea was right. We destroy it, fill it in, but my guess is we need him in there when we do it."

"And how in hell do we do that?" Cawkins asked.

Close by, Boyden saw the entrance. "This is it," he said, and pointed to the wrought iron spears of the ancient cemetery's gate. Then all three were startled as they glimpsed a tall, dark figure, with white gloves and a whiter complexion, appear in front of them, waving the three of them inside the gate. Now, even Eber was gape-mouthed.

The Dark Man led them forward until they could just make out two indistinct figures standing motionless inside a circle of tombstones, then he vanished.

Eber, interested in more mundane forms of life, slowly drew his revolver. "Shsh," he said, feeling relief in spite of himself, that he could utter the following words. "They're men. Perhaps they're stealing your discovery," he said sarcastically. Eber held out his hand, motioning for the others to stay back. Then he silently moved closer to the gravesite.

"Gentlemen," he quietly greeted the two soldiers. He moved the pistol up and down, to signal them to put up their hands.

Boyden did not care one way or another for these new interlopers. This would be his best opportunity to escape and he meant to play it to the maximum. He ignored them and walked quickly up to the gravesite. Hoarsley rushed close behind, quite beside himself with excitement.

"This is it. This is the grave," Boyden shouted. "See the tombstone with the Biblical markings. It has to be *de Belfort's.*"

"Who the hell are you?" asked Cawkins. "How do you know about *de Belfort?*"

"The men with the guns generally ask the questions," Hoarsley said, as he drew his pistol and pointed it at them. "What do you know about *de Belfort?* Where is he?"

Eber looked into the empty, steaming hole and laughed. "There's nobody here. This is a bloody joke. Look. Go ahead. There's nothing there. And if there were, it would be an old corpse shredded by a bomb. Nothing more, nothing less."

Hinton-Smith looked curiously at them, wondering how anybody else could possibly know about *de Belfort*. Perhaps there was a way to find out. "He's here all right. In fact, I visited with him not more than an hour ago."

Now, Hoarsley was delirious with joy. "You spoke with him? He's alive? The thousand-year Reich is at our fingertips. I'll be a hero when I return to the Fatherland."

"Shut up, Hoarsley," Eber screamed in a high-pitched squeal. "These are Englishmen, the enemy! You," he said, shouting at Hinton-Smith. "If *de Belfort's* here, you go down into the grave and bring him out."

This was not the result the lieutenant expected. "You want me to go...down there?" Whoever these blokes were, their secret was out. Hinton-Smith knew immediately they could not afford to let Cawkins or himself live. He looked down into the hole. He was not going to let this be his final resting place.

"If you don't," Eber snarled, "I'll shoot your mate, here. Now go!"

*     *     *

Elizabeth Hammond helped dole out bandages to doctors and nurses to wrap the injured, and when the bandages had given out, she tore strips of cloth from hospital bed sheets and towels to make up the difference. After all the pre-war preparation, she and the other volunteers were surprised that the supplies ran out so quickly, but guessed that most had been hoarded for the soldiers. She smiled and was attentive to the poor victims, and more importantly, managed to show a stiff upper lip in spite of the seriousness of some of their wounds: after all, her sister was the nurse, not her.

When most of their patients were asleep, either drug-induced, or from fatigue, one of the doctors, who had spent two years in Ceylon and fancied himself a connoisseur, found a large pot and brewed tea, scrounged up some milk, sugar, and cups, and poured a hot cup of the light brown liquid for all the staff and volunteers.

Elizabeth Hammond felt good about the effort she was making. A newfound empathy had arisen in her and that good feeling led to a stir of sentiment for Hinton-Smith. Not that she could ever love him again, she told herself. At the shelter, she had seen the look on her sister's face, and she would never do anything that might ruin her happiness. But now she fully realized the wrong she had done the lieutenant and how childishly she had handled the whole affair. She wanted to make amends.

Many of the people lingered over their cups of tea, exchanging both funny and stirring anecdotes, and comparing notes and techniques, then went back to caring for the injured until the head doctor decided that things were under control, and he could send most of the volunteers home.

Now wide-awake from the exertion and stimulus of good works, Elizabeth had no thought of sleep. She was full of energy and thought it would be fun to surprise her friend, Lieutenant Roberts, who had gone to the Fire Station on High Street, another main coordinating point for North London's Highgate section, just across from Waterlow Park.

Lieutenant Roberts and his mate Lieutenant Malcolm had spent the better part of the evening helping to dig survivors and corpses out of the rubble from bombed-out buildings.

Elizabeth arrived close to 4 A.M., just as the greater number of volunteers decided to call it a night.

There was an entire block of apartments off Cholmeley Street that had been hit hard, but had not yet been searched. Out of a sense of duty and necessity, the two lieutenants agreed to continue their work in this section of the city. Elizabeth agreed to volunteer as well.

The only other volunteer was surprisingly a white-haired, aged soldier, fat around the middle, sloppy and smelling of fetidness and alcohol.

"He doesn't really fit my image of the volunteer," Lieutenant Roberts whispered to his friend.

"Maybe his name is Falstaff," Malcolm said. "At this point, my boy, you're getting a little gamy as well."

"Thanks," Roberts answered. "Not in front of my lady, if you please. If you had worked as hard as me and Falstaff, we'd have freed all those poor chaps by now."

*   *   *

Hinton-Smith eased himself down into what seemed like nothingness. Even the dirt had a sickening feel to it. It was completely dark, the only light emanating from Eber's single torch beam. His heart was pounding. Whatever fleeting hopes he earlier entertained of de Belfort's benevolence had disappeared entirely. He knew he was in the home of pure evil. So far, it seemed empty, and that was his best prospect.

As his eyes began to adjust, he could see the grave was cavernous in size. He could stand up, walk around and not even be seen from above. "My God!" he said, and his heart began to race as he saw a man looking at him out of the darkness. It's de Belfort.

"I've come back," Hinton-Smith said haltingly. "Like you requested." But there was no answer, not verbally nor in his head. Curious, he slowly moved forward, then stumbled as his foot hit something hard. The lieutenant caught his balance and reached down. There were small metallic swastikas embedded in the ground. All over the place. Are they part of the solution? Quickly he jerked his head up in the direction of the knight. Still there was no movement from him. What is this? As he drew nearer, now shuffling his feat to avoid tripping again, he could see it was a life-size likeness of a knight. Complete with Maltese Cross on his breast! The lieutenant could see that the statue was sculpted out of a marble-like pillar, stretching down from the surface. He discovered seven more of them, roughly in a circle, and then he realized these steles, with their stern visages of Knights Hospitallers, extended down from the positions of the tombstones surrounding de Belfort's grave up above. Rubbing his hands along the surface of one of them, he felt indentations—more Vedic symbols. He wondered if these were more of the constraints keeping de Belfort locked in, and if these were the likenesses of actual knights buried at the same time—each one had his own distinctive features—but there was no time for speculation: there were other, more corporeal problems at hand. He got down on his hands and knees to see if he could pry up one of the swastikas.

Wrenching one free, he felt its heft and put it in his back pocket. This ought to do, he thought, in more ways than one. Let's just hope it isn't the one key piece keeping the arsehole in here.

Then he went back to one of the knight-like pillars. He had seen writing etched in the stone and now moved his head close and felt along the indentations. Rubbing his fingers along the pillar he discerned a name: Sir Reginald Brockingham. This was incredible. It must be one of the men who put *de Belfort* away. He moved to another statue and read Sir Peter Dillon, then Sir Lucien Castillo and Sir Argive Turnbull. He stopped at the fifth name and gazed on in wonder. Sir Charles Whyntowne! *My God! This was the name Cawkins spoke of. Was this my ancestor? Cawkins was right!*

Hinton-Smith got down on his knees before the knight and put his hands together as if in prayer. "Sir Charles. Please help us destroy *de Belfort.*"

"All right," Eber called out. "Enough of this. Come back up," he ordered.

"Looks like there will be three more additions to the cemetery," Eber said. "I never trusted you for a minute, Boyden. You with your last minute find. I have a hunch. You seem to be walking a bit differently of late. Roll up your leg."

Boyden looked at Eber, then pleadingly looked at Hoarsley.

"Help me up," Hinton-Smith called out from the grave. Eber nodded to the sergeant, who went to the edge and crouched down. As the lieutenant jumped, Cawkins caught him by the arm and pulled him up.

"Well?" Eber asked.

"Nothing," the lieutenant answered.

"Well?" he asked Boyden.

"Better do it, lad," Hoarsley said.

"No! No! No!" Boyden pleaded, dropping to his knees. "I swear *de Belfort* is here. All the research proves it. And the séance. This is Highgate Cemetery. There must be something down there. That bastard's lying. He's English. He doesn't want Germans to find out *de Belfort's* secrets. And he's admitted he's here. Please. I've done all you asked. Don't kill me."

Hinton-Smith quickly exchanged a questioning glance with Cawkins, who shrugged his shoulders. His expression suggested it was better to let them play it out.

Hinton-Smith thought he could go him one better. He could see the older, professional-looking type was torn between wanting to believe the sniveling academic, but leaning toward the schoolboy. Now, which one of these arseholes is the most dangerous? Coolly he spoke. "He's telling the truth. I saw him. I spoke with him."

The light returned to Hoarsley's eyes, and an anticipatory smile came to his lips.

"No matter," Eber said, and suddenly pointed his revolver at Boyden, firing a shot that caught him between the eyes, then quickly trained the muzzle back on Hinton-Smith and Cawkins, even while Boyden fell to the ground, dead, his eyes wide open in shock and surprise. "I never much liked you anyway, mate," Eber sneered.

"Good show, Mr. Boyden," Hoarsley said. "You fulfilled your duty." He turned his attention to the lieutenant. "Let's hear what you have to say about *de Belfort*."

"Why?" the lieutenant asked. Looks like it's the schoolboy.

"Are you hombres spies? Here in London?" Cawkins asked incredulously.

"Shut up," Eber said, motioning with his gun. "Move closer to your friend. Over by the grave."

Cawkins slowly edged over toward Hinton-Smith.

"Now, answer the man," Eber said. "Or, as I've said before, I'll shoot your mate." Eber pointed his revolver at Cawkins and pulled back the hammer. "Be quick about it, or I might just shoot him anyway, for sport."

It's now or never, Hinton-Smith said to himself. He could shoot Cawkins just as fast as he shot the other poor bastard.

"Your dead friend was right," the lieutenant said. "But I don't think you understand. This thing, *de Belfort*, is extremely dangerous. We came here to destroy him." Hinton-Smith gestured at the flammable materials they had brought. "You have to help us."

"That's nonsense," scoffed Eber.

"*De Belfort* might present a threat to you," Hoarsley said, patting on the notebook sticking out of his pocket. "But I can control him."

"I think you're both wrong, mate. But, this man," Hinton-Smith said, pointing at the sergeant and carefully watching Eber's eyes. "He's the expert on *de Belfort*. He knows more than I do."

And in the quarter-second interval that Eber shifted his focus to the sergeant, Hinton-Smith threw the swastika in the pitching style that Cawkins had taught him, slamming the SS man on the side of the head, slashing his ear and temple open in a wide gash. Eber, on reflex, fired one shot into the air as he stumbled backward, grasping his head, but Cawkins was on him in a flash, grabbing his gun hand at the wrist and shoulder, and throwing the straightened arm down, across his own knee. There was a sudden audible "pop," as Eber's arm cracked like a dry twig. The pistol fell to the ground as Eber bent over in pain.

At the same time, Hinton-Smith body-tackled Hoarsley, driving him to the ground. Hinton-Smith grabbed his pistol and slapped him across the face with it.

"No more! No more!" Hoarsley cried.

"Funny thing is, mate," Hinton-Smith said to Hoarsley. "Your boy was right. *De Belfort* was here, but I don't think you'd find him too congenial."

"All right," Cawkins said, after picking up the revolver, checking the clip and pointing it at the two Germans. "Get up."

Hinton-Smith got up off the dentist and stared at the grave.

"You saved my life," Cawkins said softly.

"Right. I know," said the lieutenant, scanning the ground for the swastika. "And it's getting to be a full time job, ain't it." Finding it, he walked over and picked it up.

Cawkins's expression remained grim. He sensed the night was far from over.

Hoarsley stood up and brushed himself off, then went over to help Eber, but the young man pushed his hand away.

"Jack, he's gone," the lieutenant said. "I swear *de Belfort* was here." By now, Hinton-Smith was crouching on the edge of the pit, looking inside.

"I believe you, Mikey," Cawkins said. "I believe you."

"But that means he can leave," said the lieutenant.

"I know," replied the sergeant. He blew air through his mouth in a long exhalation. "Cyrus and Kate are in danger."

"Everyone," Hinton-Smith said, pointedly, then he showed Cawkins the swastika. "But there's something else."

"What?"

"Down there, in the hole, there are eight statues of knights with their names engraved on them. One of the names was Sir Charles Whyntowne. You were right."

"But that still doesn't tell us how to destroy it."

"I know." He held up the swastika. "I better replace this. It's what I threw at the bloke." Who knew what it did in the scheme of things, but he did not want to take a chance. If this prison held up this long, Sir Charles probably knew what he was doing. Hinton-Smith took Hoarsley's torch, jumped back down into the hole and did his work. Within seconds, the sergeant was once more helping him up.

The lieutenant walked over to the children, gently nudging them.

"Move," Cawkins said to Eber and Hoarsley, prodding them in the back, to head them down the path to the North Gate.

"What are we going to do with these blokes?" the lieutenant whispered. Even while forming the question in his mind, he was peering in every direction, expecting to see *de Belfort* or the tall man at any moment. "We don't have time to deal with them."

"Right," Cawkins agreed. "But we can't tie 'em up and leave 'em, can we. They'd be dead before we got back. We'll have to split up to save time."

"We're only saving them for the hangman."

That was pretty cold, Cawkins thought. Odd. Not like the boy.

"You take them to the police station." Cawkins knelt down beside the three children. "Wake up, kids." He began to rub the arms of the larger boy, and then moved his legs up and down to get his heart pumping. After a few minutes, Nigel Cochran's eyes opened. Cawkins sat him up, got him to his feet and then helped the other two.

"I'll take the kids and get my wife and Kate," the sergeant said as he lifted Thomas and Lucy up. "We'll meet you there in ten to fifteen minutes. We'll have to find Cyrus, then I want us all to get the hell out of here."

Hinton-Smith looked questioningly at the big man, then averted his eyes. "I better carry Nigel till we separate," Hinton-Smith said. "He's still a bit wobbly."

They hurried to the North Gate, turned up Swain's Lane, till they reached Bisham Gardens, then Hinton-Smith put Nigel down.

"Can you walk?" he asked the boy.

"Yes," the bleary-eyed Nigel answered. "I think so."

"Is this Lucy?" he asked, pointing to the little girl held by Cawkins.

"Yes," Nigel said. "You kept your promise. I didn't think you would."

"It was a hard one to keep. Right," Hinton-Smith said and turned off on the street leading to the police station on Highgate Hill.

Carrying the children, one in each of his arms and Nigel Cochran by his side, Cawkins jogged the rest of the way up Swain's Lane to Cyrus Wilson's house.

*   *   *

It had taken Wilson a long time to walk to the projects, where Baker and Jones shared a ramshackle, one room-flat on the first floor of a seedy, broken down building.

For the second time in this longest of nights, Cyrus Wilson realized that he was, indeed, old. He was sweating from the walk and out of breath, though it was mostly downhill. His calves were stiffening up, and the top of his right knee ached. He toyed with the idea of shooting them then and there, bedding down for the night and turning himself in to the police in the morning and be done with it. He was so tired he did not care if he had to sleep with their sodding corpses.

But they were not home. He banged on the door, peered in through the single front window, then knocked on the glass. If they're not here, that means they must be at the cemetery. He did not trust them to abide by their responsibilities and help with the clean up. No. For a long time he had suspected them of grave robbing. Wilson had never actually caught them at it or seen them stealing, though he had seen them in the cemetery much past their normal working hours. But he certainly did not put it past them lot. Perhaps this was the night when he'd catch them with their hands in the stew. He would bet his life they would go to Highgate and see what they could steal. He walked back to the street and started the long way back. Now mostly uphill.

Damnation, he thought. It'll feel good to kill them after all this work. He deserved a reward. He would have thought to look in the bloody cemetery in the first place, except for some reason, the idea of going into that place this particular night, just didn't sit well with him.

*     *     *

No sooner had Hinton-Smith and his prisoners entered the station-house, when Hoarsley rushed forward to the front desk in defiance.

"Call your superintendent," he yelled at the man on duty, and then continued non-stop with abuse and invective until a tall, thin man, with a modest gray and white mustache, came out into the reception area. Before the new entrant could muster a word, Hoarsley screamed in full bluster, "What murky road has our country taken, when some young hoodlum like this can point a revolver at its citizens? First he interrupts my work, shoots one of my assistants, then his accomplice breaks my other assistant's arm."

Hoarsley had kept quiet on the walk to the station house and he had used his time well. He concocted a story that would utilize every facet of the encounter to his advantage. "Do you know who I am?" he shouted.

"No, but..." said the intrigued superintendent.

"Mr. Ned Hoarsley, doctor, 74 Oxford Circus. I'm a British citizen, a well-known dentist, and upstanding member of this society, a member of the Home Guard..."

"Then what were you doing in the cemetery?" Hinton-Smith asked.

"We'll ask the questions, if you don't mind," Superintendent Kendricks said, frowning at the lieutenant and sticking out his hand. "If you please. The revolver, sir."

Hinton-Smith placed it in the superintendent's hand. The chief turned his attention back to Hoarsley. "Now, what were you doing there?"

"I'm a part-time archeologist. My assistant, the one he murdered right before our eyes," he said, pointing at Hinton-Smith. "A Mr. Boyden. He works, I should say worked, at the British Museum. You can call them tomorrow morning."

"He's lying," said Hinton-Smith, but he already did not like the way this was going. "If I'm a murderer, what the bloody hell am I doing escorting my victims and accusers to you? Am I daft?" How could he tell them what the spies were looking for? Even that they were spies. They'd think he *was* daft. Where was Cawkins? He'd better get there soon. "I'm a lieutenant in the BEF, Michael Hinton-Smith, fresh out of hospital after Dunkirk. You can check that out."

"Sir," called a voice from the front doorway. It was Nick Hensen. He was with Wingate. "This is important."

Hensen moved briskly to the front desk, sizing up the three visitors on his way, and whispered in the superintendent's ear.

"Wingate was down in Highgate when he heard a gunshot."

"That I did, sir," Wingate said. "Sounded like it came from inside Old Highgate."

"Did you find anything, a body?"

Wingate blushed. "I wasn't goin' in there on this night."

"I understand," the superintendent said. "I'd consider meself balmy if I went in there."

"So, what have we here?" Kendricks said, looking the three suspects over: a tall, gaunt, sickly looking youth in outsize clothes, a schoolboy with a broken arm and a smell of wickedness, and one pompous, red-faced, overbearing holier-than-thou dentist, and a corpse.

"Why don't you fetch some biscuits and tea," the superintendent said to Hensen. "We're all a bit out of sorts. I'm peckish meself. A spot of tea might settle us."

Hensen nodded and disappeared through a door to the back.

Superintendent Kendricks, a man proud of his ability to suss out a suspect's guilt or innocence with a simple glance at his demeanor, turned to face the three, a neutral look on his face. "I think it's best if all three of you stay here for the night. We need to get to the bottom of this. George," he said, motioning toward Eber. "Would you be so kind as to fetch a doctor for this one?"

"Right" Wingate answered. He turned and walked out of the building.

Hinton-Smith had no time for this. There were people he had to warn, to remove to safety. He was certain that many would die this night if he did not move with alacrity. "I brought these people to you in good faith. They are spies. Look at this one," he said, speaking rapidly and pointing at the scowling boy. "Look at his face. Hitler Youth all over it. He shot the other man. And this one," he said, pointing at Hoarsley. "Obviously the mastermind, if you want to be generous with the term." He looked around the room, searching for an opening. Should he wait for Cawkins? Would even Cawkins be able to convince these twits?

"As well as that may be" said the superintendent. "I'd feel better if all three of you kept us company for the night." He called out to the rear of the station, "Hensen!"

Well, that's it then, the lieutenant thought. They're going to lock us up. It's now or never. He looked around the main room of the station, measuring the distance to the door. Best to put a little knock on them. Something he learned in soccer.

Hensen returned, a teacup in hand and chewing on a biscuit.

"Right, sir," he said, after swirling the tea in his mouth and swallowing.

"We're going to have three guests for the night, Nick."

"I thought as much," Hensen said. "There are three more cups steeping."

As soon as Hensen walked up and stopped in front of the chief constable, Hinton-Smith plowed into him, hurling Hensen into the superintendent, and bowling them over as if it was a game of ten pins, and they were the seven-ten split. The superintendent howled as hot tea scalded his chest and legs.

Hinton-Smith raced out of the station and turned south as though he was heading down the hill to Archway. By the time Hensen and another officer got out the door, he had ducked behind a building on Hornsey Lane to go back toward Wilson's house.

*     *     *

The four volunteers had moved off in different directions, Elizabeth Hammond and the officers towards Cholmeley Park, and the old man toward Winchester Winch.

They kept at it, shoveling dirt and debris, moving small and large bits of concrete rubble, and picking through the wreckage, until they had to sit down for a breather.

"You're out of condition, mate," Lieutenant Roberts said and laughed. The three were in good spirits. So far, there were no victims to be found in this vicinity, and that meant that many of the people in the neighborhood had made it to the shelters. The houses and buildings could be rebuilt or repaired, not so any victims.

"Just keep it up," the other lieutenant replied. "I don't think I'm at all appreciated here. Perhaps I should join our Shakespearean friend?"

"Please do," Lieutenant Roberts replied.

All three of them were almost gray from the dust and grime, and when Elizabeth wiped Lieutenant Roberts' forehead with the sleeve of her uniform, it left a bright white swathe running across.

Malcolm shrugged his shoulders, and headed back down Cholmeley. It did not take long before he came to the intersection where it converged with Winchester Winch.

The old volunteer was finally tiring as well. Sitting down on what was left of a retaining wall, he inadvertently stopped to pat and rub his arms from a chill. He reached under his tunic and pulled out a small flask of cheap rum, which he proceeded to guzzle, and finishing it off, threw it away. It crashed and broke on the street.

Lieutenant Malcolm turned toward the sound. It was eerie being out here in the ruin and destruction all alone, and at first startled by the sound, he was relieved to trace it to the old man. Smiling, he watched as the geezer wiped sweat from his forehead and then picked his nose and flung it with a finger snap. But then he saw the old man sit up straight.

Suddenly, the man's ears pricked up, like a fox sensing the dogs, and like smelled something putrid. Lifting one arm, then the other, he sniffed under each, made a face as though he had an audience, and then snickered. Within seconds his smirking turned to a hideous scream as his eyes popped from their sockets and his body was squeezed dry of blood.

Lieutenant Malcolm ran toward him. What in high hell could have done that? Kneeling down by the body, he saw a corpse that was deflated like a popped balloon.

There was no one about as Malcolm scanned the street in every direction. There were only the strange brown air and the searchlights still hunting for Nazi planes. Now he felt something on his shoulder. A strong nausea enveloped him as he turned to look and in horror saw the fingers of a skeleton resting there. It began to squeeze till the bony grip penetrated his shoulder and the claws of the fingers came together. Malcolm felt his collarbone snap as he tried to pry the skeleton away. Another icy hand now pierced his other shoulder and the lieutenant could no longer move or struggle. Malcolm's end came soon after and was not pleasant.

# CHAPTER 38

# DE BELFORT

And what of *de Belfort*? Where was he, Hinton-Smith wondered? Had he been there in Highgate watching everything or was he free for good, out of the cemetery? If only he understood more. He searched his mind. Was there anything that *de Belfort* let slip that might be a clue? But first things first. Where was Cyrus? He would have undoubtedly gone to the projects to look for Jones and Baker otherwise he would have seen him. Cyrus would not have found them, so he probably headed back to Highgate to see if they were working. That's where he had to go to find Cyrus and get him to safety. He knew he had to hurry. What worried the lieutenant was if Cyrus searched for them among the work parties and volunteers. He might be safer for the moment but how would he find him?

As the lieutenant cut through Cromwell Place, the destruction left him weak in the legs, with nausea in his stomach, and a fierce hatred of the Germans. He saw what appeared to be an English version of a lunar landscape, only partially mitigated by the haziness from the half light: whole walls were gone from apartment buildings and houses; wires and steel reinforcing rods protruded from walls that had been severed on the diagonal or only half destroyed. Piles of concrete lay everywhere, and the acrid smell of cordite pervaded the air. He remembered his time on the

Continent and how Belgium, Holland and Poland had ended up.

There was a line of six bodies lying in a neat row; all covered with what looked like a dark green bed sheet, so he knew the work crews had already been through the place. But why just leave them? Strange. At least only six in this area. Then we were pretty lucky, considering. He was tempted to sift through the rubble, but there was no time. It was almost mesmerizing in its destruction. How could anyone survive this?

How bloody stupid to worry about a man from another age, when his country was fighting for its very existence. Then he shuddered. Something in his gut told him that *de Belfort* might even be worse.

*     *     *

Elizabeth Hammond and Lieutenant Roberts drifted closer to Winchester Winch in their search for survivors. They walked slowly, peering through the smoke and dim light using Roberts' flashlight.

"Shsh," Elizabeth Hammond whispered as she reached out her hand to grasp the lieutenant's arm. "I hear something." Both the lieutenant and Elizabeth stopped moving and listened. There was a faint sound, someone groaning.

"I think it's coming from over there," Roberts said, pointing toward the remains of an apartment building—all that was left standing was a metal-reinforced door frame, cluttered with debris. Particles of dust hovered in the air.

Roberts took Elizabeth's hand and they hurried over to the spot. With emotions bordering on elation, both of them felt as if saving this one person would make up for all the others lost over this terrible night. Roberts listened carefully for the direction. The man groaned again, and they let the intermittent moaning lead them on. But ten yards from the doorway, Roberts suddenly stopped and bent over. There was an officer's uniform that seemed to be partially filled with something. Somehow it seemed vaguely familiar. Examining it closer, he abruptly dropped it with an extreme revulsion.

"What is it?" Elizabeth asked.

"Nothing," Roberts said. He was certain it had been human, a soldier at one time judging by the uniform. But from these remains, that speculation was quite a leap. But why saddle her with that? There was no head, and the rest of the body had been shriveled up. There was no skin, just soft flesh. Some muscle tissue, and some still identifiable organs: a heart, one lung, and what he took to be a liver. Must have been a direct hit. What else could have done this? He urgently tried to rub the feeling of touching "that" from his hands, but the sensation stayed. Nearby, about ten feet away, there appeared to be another lump of clothes. The last thing he wanted to do at that moment was to find and handle another one of those.

"Come on," Roberts said, and he rushed in the direction of the sound. Both of them began to toss wreckage and trash aside.

\*     \*     \*

Hinton-Smith was not the only fugitive on the streets this night. Two other men could not believe their luck. The bloody imbecile of a superintendent had even returned his handgun. Although he should have been reasonably secure after the good mayor of Highgate himself had come down to the station to vouch for him, Hoarsley figured the possibility was very great that the superintendent might change his mind and rescind the offer. Their time was up. The mission would have to be aborted. His end of the spy ring closed. So, instead of predictably heading to the nearest tube station, Archway, he led his young compatriot up the hill to Crouch End. They would try to go as far north as possible, then head for Liverpool, where they could catch a ferry to the Isle of Man, then to Ireland. Unfortunately, they got turned around in the now unfamiliar, bombed-out surroundings. They had just done another about face, which brought them onto the rubble-strewn street of Winchester Winch. There, Hoarsley spotted a lone figure that somehow seemed less than human. As it drew nearer, it appeared more to be a dark black, formless mass, and Hoarsley instinctively knew.

"It's *de Belfort*," he said excitedly. "He is alive! This is better than I hoped." So zealously had he yearned for this success, he was too entranced to feel any fear. He smiled warmly at Eber. "We've done well, my boy."

Eber stood open-mouthed, in shock. "This all has to be some imbecilic hoax, made up," he said. "This *de Belfort* of yours cannot really exist. It's a trap. We need to leave."

But for Hoarsley, this was a culmination of all his work. All those years of surreptitiously building his network: the close calls and setbacks, the time his whole nascent operation was rolled up by MI5—he still did not know how he escaped. And his success after his superiors hit upon the idea to recruit Irish discontents. How he loved Matthew Boyden at this moment. It was too bad Eber was so trigger-happy.

Once more, the thousand-year Reich was at his fingertips. Once more he had visions of how he would be greeted when he returned to the Fatherland, when the war was over and Germany ruled all. He walked up to the apparition as though he was some kind of idiot savant, who had prepared thoroughly for his one unique mission in life. "Monsieur *de Belfort*, sir," he said. "I am Heinz Muller, an ambassador from the great German Reich." Reaching into his pocket, he pulled out the notebook and began to read the Aramaic incantation, written down phonetically for him in English characters, and garnered from a séance.

Meanwhile, Eber slowly pulled out his stiletto. An enormous rage was building within his head. He generally liked this feeling, and had used it to good benefit on previous missions that demanded a high degree of ruthlessness. But this time he was somehow not the one in command. "You're going to bring a ghost into the Third Reich?" he screamed. "Are you stark raving mad, Hoarsley? You will control this thing! You could not even control Boyden!"

Hoarsley was a much bigger, if older man, and he was not going to let some young ignorant goon destroy his enterprise, just as he was about to triumph. He surprised Eber, by pulling out his revolver and whipping the barrel across the stunned boy's face. Eber angrily got up to face off, his stiletto in hand.

If one could discern the form of *Guilluame de Belfort's* face, one would have seen a great, wicked smile. With the certainty he would soon be in possession of a body, he no longer needed the Germans. How fitting that Germans would summon *L'Anguedoc* forth through this strange process of séance, and start this sequence of events. They give us new life and think they can control us. How arrogant.

Once melded with Hinton-Smith, he could travel to his fellow Templars' graves and free them himself. No one would control them.

It filled a particular whim of his to force two who were allies to fight to the death. Before this night, it had been a long time since he had killed. He would make this slaughter last, savoring every moment; reveling in it. Before this night, it had been a long time since he had mutilated human flesh. This too he would savor. And there were two of them, so more the pleasure for *de Belfort*. Killing was his sole passion— he cared for little else. In his many years of captivity in that foul, dark hell, he fantasized of death and murder and pain. He hated the living with all that was left of him. Of this he had told the truth to Hinton-Smith. There were two, and he would play them off as a torturer might torment the flesh of his victim before snuffing out his existence. Time had become eternity for him and he would draw it out.

In the dark, smoke-shrouded street, Hoarsley could not get off a single shot before Eber rushed him, knife raised in his good hand. Soon they were on the ground, and even with his broken arm, Eber's youth and greater dexterity won out. In a rage that was great for even him, Eber stabbed the dentist some forty times and then dug in and cut out his heart. He got up but found that the anger in him was still growing. He hated everything: Hitler, Himmler, his brother, his parents, his few friends. He hated himself with a passion he never knew existed. There was only one way to end this abomination that he called himself. He went to Hoarsley's body as if in a trance, picked up the revolver, put the barrel in his mouth, and fired.

Not far away, Roberts and Elizabeth both started at the sound of the shot. A few minutes later, he drew her attention to an indeterminate figure that he assumed was a man, moving slowly toward them, and not more than fifty yards away.

"Hello, was that you?" he shouted. "No? Then be a good chap and give us a hand."

The strange form kept moving in and out of the rubble and crumbled buildings.

"What's all this, then," Roberts yelled, in his most commanding tone. "Stop mucking about." This had become a bad enough night without being snubbed by some twit. Roberts stood up.

"Stop," Elizabeth said. "Let it go. Don't forget the poor man buried under here."

"What are you?" Roberts shouted. He handed Elizabeth the torch. "A bloody thief. I'll bloody well bet you are." The lieutenant stood up and walked in the direction of the figure, towards one of the larger piles of rubble in the center of a shelled-out apartment building.

"Don't leave me," Elizabeth pleaded.

"That was a gun shot, Liz. Someone needs help."

Roberts rushed away, but the figure continued to ignore him, and then seemed to disappear into the ruins.

If Roberts had been zealous to get at this criminal, now he had second thoughts. He felt fear, and a vicious loathing, and he knew intuitively that this was not your average person. He slowed down his pursuit, became more circumspect, and very quietly edged forward. Something inside him told him to stop, forget about it, but his vanity would not let him. His heart was beating so loudly he was certain it could be heard in the next borough. He could not see anything and there was no sound other than his heart and heavy breathing, so he kept moving in the direction from which he had last seen the man's shadow.

Roberts came to a simple white picket fence that must have been put up by one of the tenants, for it was quite amateurish, though it was the only thing left standing vertical. Unlatching the gate, he entered and walked forward towards another doorframe still standing. Part of the brick wall attached to the doorframe still clung to it, sticking out like carbuncles on an old vessel, as though too obstinate to fall. There was a dinner table, still set, food untouched except by dust and ash. On the floor nearby were two small dolls and a pillow. Roberts walked down the five steps to the back entrance, and in surveying the crumbled down relic of a once resilient habitation, saw a man's arm, and then one leg.

"Another survivor," he called out to Elizabeth. He rushed over and tried to pull him clear. Then when he could not budge him, he began tossing the debris off of the body, hoping the man was still alive. He got down on his knees and again tried to pull him out, and when this failed he tore at the other rubble and dug with his hands like a dog after a buried bone. Finally succeeding in his efforts, Roberts was disheartened that he was too late, but seeing the man's body was intact, he murmured, "At least you died a normal death." Then he caught himself up for implying that the others died of something less than normal, though being caught in a rain of bombs was hardly normal. "Bloody hell, what are you thinking about," he asked out loud. "What do you think bombing victims have to look like?"

At least the exertion from the digging had calmed his nerves a bit. He was thinking more clearly now. Then he heard another noise, coming from further in the wreckage, where the walls still stood intact. He went in to investigate, moving slowly, trying to not make much noise. Every sound of his feet stepping down reverberated like the explosions from cannons. Even though sirens and bells from ambulances and fire wagons could now be heard in the distance, he was oblivious to all but his own movements. He took to putting his feet down gingerly, feeling for the gravel underfoot, even lightly crushing it with a rubbing movement before actually placing all his weight down. So concerned with being quiet, he failed to notice a half-inch twirled reinforcing bar extending out of a nearby wall, and walked right into it, receiving a two-inch gash across the cheek that only just missed poking out his right eye. Patting the wound with his hand, and then pressing it for a second, he cursed. "You stupid twit," he said as he took out a cloth and pressed the wound again to flush it and wipe up some of the blood. He searched for interminable minutes, before turning around and starting back to the entrance. The bloke couldn't disappear. He must have found another exit, probably a hole blown out in the bombing.

Returning to the victim, he bent over to grab his arms, and began dragging him out of the building where he could be easily found in the morning. He had pulled him about ten feet when he suddenly felt very fatigued. The man was heavier than he'd thought. Letting go, and straightening out to stretch his back, he saw the figure again, standing in the shadows.

\* \* \*

Cyrus Wilson found the night air around the cemetery to be dark and foreboding as he approached the main entrance gate. It was locked so he searched for the caretaker's shed to wake him and take the keys.

"Hullo, Ned," he said to the old man, bent over in his chair and looking quite cadaverous in the torches' light. "Strange times, eh?"

"Just because all hell broke loose when the Kraut bombers dumped their load on us?" Ned mumbled sarcastically. He was not one bit happy about being woken up for a second time that night. The first time was when the sirens blared and the bombs exploded.

"What are you doing here this late, Cyrus?" he asked, squinting, and noticing the rifle and shotgun.

"Looking for the boy," Wilson said.

"Here? At this hour?"

"I think he had a little disagreement with your mates."

"I saw nary a one all night."

I reckoned that, Wilson thought.

The caretaker handed Cyrus Wilson the keys and said, "If you see 'em, shoot 'em for me, will ya."

"Right. Thanks," Cyrus said as he took the keys and left. He heard Ned curse behind his back, and the door to the wooden shed slam shut. "Thanks for the great help you old sod," he said under his breath.

Reaching the main entrance, he found the lock already open on the imposing metallic gate, and shuddered as the iron pole noisily dragged along the ground when he pushed it. Looks like the blighters are in. He took a deep breath, squared his shoulders, hiked up his pants, and went in.

Carrying his two guns, old Betsy slung over his shoulder and the shotgun at the ready, Cyrus Wilson was certain he would find Jones and Baker busy robbing graves, or worse. He had no illusions about the pair, and proceeded very quietly up the narrow dirt path to Comfort Corner. Once more up hill.

Soon, he began to softly whistle an old Irish folk song to calm his nerves. He could not figure out why he should be so nervous. Nothing ever frightened him, especially those two louts, but here in this place, with so many bodies, some fresh, most decomposed to some degree or other, and remains scattered around, he felt a revulsion that was most unsettling. What devastation. Wilson looked up at the night sky, raised his arm with fist closed and cursed the Nazis. At that moment he knew he would do anything to help with the war effort.

But first, the bloody blackguards.

When he shone his torch on some of the fresher carcasses, he espied maggots and worms crawling about as if at home. If he stopped whistling, and he did a couple of times to cover his nose with a handkerchief—the human offal gave off such an offensive smell—it became so quiet, that any noise at all, a rat scurrying out of his way, for instance, sent shivers down his spine or made him jump. He would rather have the constant noise of his whistling.

"Hullo," he yelled out. He would give the sods fair warning, he would. Then he'd blast them to Hell. "Where are you bastards?" he said into the darkness.

"I'm not going to spend the whole night lookin' for the likes of you. Show yer cowardly mugs if you dare!"

No answer was forthcoming. Cyrus could not find any trace of the gravediggers or Hinton-Smith. Exhausted from the long night, uphill hike and longer travails, he picked out a low standing monument and stopped to sit down and catch his breath.

*     *     *

Near Winchester Winch, in a small cul-de-sac, Lieutenant Roberts was still trying to corral the mysterious figure that had so far managed to elude him. But he was getting close. He could see it only a few yards away. Why did he feel that now it was waiting for him?

"So, you decided to come back, laddie," Roberts said. "Maybe you'd like a bit of this," he said as pounded his fist into his hand. He was no longer apprehensive, just angry—the same overwhelming anger he had felt earlier. Something here was different. He just had not figured out what as yet. Shaking his head quickly back and forth, as if to get rid of a pesky fly, he felt the rage abruptly disappear. It was then when he noticed the smell: an indescribable filth, an evil filth if there could be such a thing.

The apparition remained motionless and speechless as Roberts strained to see.

"Come on out then, laddie, before I get nasty. Maybe I'll bring you in for a bath."

The figure seemed to hover over the ground. It started to float in his direction.

"All right, mate," Roberts called out. "Stop mucking about." He felt his confidence returning when he realized it must be a joke. "Malcolm, is that you?"

As it moved closer, Roberts realized he was seeing right through the thing. When he squinted, he could make out a broken wall of red brick directly behind it. No joke. His emotion changed from irritation and reprisal to abject fear. He began to move backwards, but the thing stayed with him. He walked faster, but it was catching up. Turning to run, he began to feel an intense pressure on his limbs. Roberts could no longer move. He felt like he was being torn asunder, but how? Then his torso was being compressed from all sides as though he was in a giant vice. His eyes bulged out. He heard the question, "What are you, you bloody bastard?" forming in his mind and he tried to shout it out, but the force on his windpipe was too great. He could not scream though his mouth was strained open in an awful grimace. As the vice tightened on his throat, he could not move or breathe. Next, he was certain he heard his own death rattle, but he was not dead. He felt himself being carried for what seemed to be a long time.

"Mark. Mark Roberts!" Elizabeth yelled. "Where are you?"

The sky was now an eerie dark yellowish-brown color and the air was heavy with smoke.

Elizabeth Hammond was scared. She stood up and listened intently, but there was only a dark and ominous silence.

"Lieutenant Mark Roberts!" she cried out again. "You leave off and come right back over here. Do you hear me? Right now!"

Elizabeth knelt back down and returned to her digging, now frenetically. Anything, to forget the silence. The moaning had become less and less intermittent, and soon, stopped all together. Though resigned to the victim's death, she did not know what to do other than continue to dig him out. At least he could have a proper burial. She had just begun to sob when she felt something touch her shoulder, and she heard a soft, familiar voice.

"Elizabeth," Hinton-Smith said. "Are you all right?"

Her heart stopped. He helped her to her feet and brushed the dirt from her sleeves. She wept softly and put her arms around him, hugging him tightly.

"Michael. Can you ever find it in your heart to forgive me," she said through her sobs. "I'm so sorry for all the misery I've caused you. I'm so sorry that I didn't believe in you. That I didn't have faith in you. I'm so very, very sorry. Please forgive me." She pulled back to look at him. "I'm so frightened," she said, then hugged him once more.

Hinton-Smith closed his eyes and thought how different things might have been, and then he once more heard *de Belfort's* voice thundering inside his head, as though his own brain was rebelling and screaming bloody epithets at him. It said: "Have you made a decision. I grow tired of waiting."

\*   \*   \*

After changing into a clean shirt—his last one was soaked through with sweat from his unsuccessful chase, tea stains and a whole day and night without rest—Hensen returned to the front desk of the station, prepared to go out again wherever he was needed, but preferably to give it another go at finding the fugitive. The station house was quiet. Some officers had gone home to finally catch a few hours sleep, while others were still out in the areas hardest hit by the bombs.

"Most of the fires are either smoldering or completely out by now," the duty officer said. But some curious reports have started filtering in from the Cholmeley area. Nothing too out of the ordinary, considering. Just more bombing victims. Right? Anyway," he qualified his last remark, "More than we had initially estimated."

"Why did you say curious?" Hensen asked.

"Well, I guess some of them were pretty well torn up."

"Bombs will do that," Hensen noted sarcastically.

"Right. And they probably did," said the officer. "Have you had any luck with the Simmons kid?" he asked. Then he turned back to his newspaper, yesterday's edition of the Times, as if signaling that the conversation was now at an end.

Oh Lord, Hensen thought. How could I have forgot the little girl? Even with all this turmoil. He sighed. The night was getting longer.

But as if in an answer to a prayer, the door to the station opened, and in walked Cawkins, his wife, Kate, and the three children, now all wide awake.

"Where's Hinton-Smith?" Cawkins asked the duty officer.

"Hinton-Smith?" the officer responded, puzzled. Then he saw the girl. "What's this!" he exclaimed. "Hensen! Look here. It's Lucy Simmons! How in God's name..."

"I'd stop swearing and bring her parents in, if I were you," Cawkins said wryly.

"Right, sir. Sorry. Sorry," the constable said. "We've been looking for her. I'll ring them."

While the constable picked up the phone, Hensen stepped up quickly. "I'll handle this," he said. "Sir," he addressed the sergeant. "We've been looking for that young lad. Pardon my asking, but what do you know about him?"

"Looking for him?" Cawkins answered with surprise. "He was supposed to meet us here." He looked at his watch. "About ten minutes ago. It took us longer than expected on account of the kids." Lucy and the two brothers had finally woken out of what could only be described as a deep, trance-like sleep, remembering nothing. Cawkins wanted to carry them to make haste, but in their state, he decided they would benefit more from the walk.

"Well," Hensen said, measuring his words carefully. "He came to the station, but then he ran away. Knocked over me and the superintendent on his escape, he did."

"Escape!" Cawkins exclaimed.

Now, Kate burst into tears. She did not want to be suspicious of Hinton-Smith, unfaithful like her sister, but she could not help it. There were just too many questions: the blood on his uniform, why he was so secretive, the murder of those two louts, the prospect of his life for the children's and what that could possibly mean, and now, his running from the police. It went on and on. Now she did not know what to think.

Hensen sized up the girl's outburst and seized the moment. This could be one of the easiest convictions on record. "My partner and I, we heard about a disturbance in Highgate Cemetery, the old cemetery." He paused dramatically. "We found a body." He looked intently at the girl to let it sink in.

Cawkins was not amused. "The lieutenant brought in two people, spies. Germans! Where are they?" he demanded.

"We sent them home," Hensen said. "The boy running out...that pretty much proved his guilt, says I. And spies? Germans?" he said with as much condescension as possible. "Are you mad? This is London. We took addresses. One of those men was a respected dentist. The other was a mere boy. A doctor patched up the lad's arm and we let them lot go. We know where to find them."

"You damn idiot!" Cawkins yelled. "I was there with him. Those two you let go...They *are* Krauts. Searching for some kind of relic in the cemetery. That skinny young one...he killed the guy you found. They're probably out of the city by now."

"Right, sir," Hensen said. That would make him look like a bloody fool. He was reddening about the neck and face, and took an immediate disliking to the sergeant. "You might keep your tone down now. We're all civilized here, ain't we? Your lad obviously was up to mischief. The bloomin' mayor himself come down and vouched for the other two. And I'd appreciate it if you would let me talk to the young miss."

Cawkins was not about to let some non-military person denigrate a member of the Guards. The lieutenant was a hero. And he could personally attest to that fact.

Standing up, jutting out his chin and stretching his neck, he said forcefully, "I'm a sergeant major in his regiment, the Coldstream Guards. Heard of 'em?" he asked sarcastically. "I was with him on the retreat to Dunkirk. He led a rear guard action. Hell, he saved my life. Carried me for miles on his shoulders, and he was wounded at the time. If it wasn't for him I'd be crow bait or in a Nazi prisoner-of-war camp. I'd stake my life on the boy."

Hensen had staked out his position and his ego would not let him budge. He stood right up to Cawkins and growled, "You might lose, says I."

"With all due respect, officer," Cawkins said as coolly as possible. "I'd put my life in his hands sooner than I'd trust you with five bob." He banged his fist on the desk. "I'll find him for you, bring him in myself and clear this up."

"Maggie," Cawkins said, turning his back on the Bobby. "You stay here. Kate, you too. Don't leave." Then, as he turned again and started to leave the station, Hensen rushed over in front of him, barring the way, his hand tightening around the grip of his billy club.

"I can't let you go, sir," Hensen said. "You're a potential witness." He now spoke very deliberately. "Perhaps even a suspect. Look at you. What's all this, then," he said pointing to the dried blood and muck on Cawkins's uniform. "I don't suppose that's from Dunkirk as well," he said with a sneer. "What was a Yank doing at Dunkirk anyway, eh? I'd have to talk to the superintendent before I let you go. And he's gone home for the night. You'll have to stay here."

"You stupid son of a bitch!" the sergeant exclaimed, marching up and standing nose to nose with the constable. "You're wasting valuable time."

Hensen motioned for two officers to come over. Each locked an arm around one of Cawkins's arms. "Now, sir," Hensen said. "You're not going to make me lock you up, are you now?"

Cawkins stared at him, but he was thinking. He had to find a way to convince them, or at least get the stubborn ass of a constable moving. He knew he could lay them out flat right there, but realized there was a better way, one where they could prove useful. So he stopped struggling, trying to ratchet down the tension. "Ok, ok. Let's work together. Go ahead," he said. "Talk to her if it'll make you happy."

"Right," Hensen said, squaring his shoulders and strutting over to Kate Hammond, who was now sitting on a bench, her head in her hands, next to Maggie Cawkins and the wide-eyed children.

"Do you know anything about this, miss?" Hensen asked.

Kate, sobbing, looked up guiltily at Cawkins, then the constable. "I, I don't know," she muttered. "Those two, they bullied Cyrus Wilson, his foster father. He was just going to pay them back. But I don't know what he did."

"What two is that, miss?"

"You know them," Kate answered. "Those two were at the Hound's Tooth."

"Oh, right," Hensen said disingenuously. "Them two. If he was just defending his father, nobody's going to blame him. Least of all me. Did he kill them?"

Kate, try as she might, could not bring herself to lie. "He told me he set out to murder them. But then he said he didn't."

Maggie Cawkins put her hands over Thomas Cochran's ears, but Nigel had been listening intently.

"Then," Kate said. "I just don't know."

"The lieutenant rescued Lucy," Nigel said. "He and the sergeant."

"Hush lad," Hensen said. "That was part of the cover-up." By now he would not have been surprised if the lieutenant had kidnapped the Simmons girl in the first place.

"Well, well, well," he said, putting his hands on his hips. "We've got a pretty busy lad on our hands, haven't we? He almost put one over on us, and did a clever job of it. What a nice plan." He raised his eyebrows in the direction of Cawkins, as if to say I told you so. "Murder a couple of blokes and put 'em in the path of the German bomb run. That'll leave a lot of evidence, won't it?"

Just then, the doors to the station were flung open by a thin man with two day's worth of stubble on his face, dirty clothes and smelling of alcohol. Behind him rushed a frail looking woman, her brown hat askew on her head and tears streaking down her face. Immediately, Lucy stood up and ran towards them. "Mum! Dad!" she yelled excitedly. Rachel Simmons, now bawling out loud, crouched down to receive her daughter. A broad smile appeared on Stanford Simmons' face as they both smothered Lucy with kisses.

"Mr. Hensen," Simmons asked, standing up and putting his hand forth to shake the constable's. "Where on earth did you find her? How?"

Hensen pursed his lips as though he was loath to admit it. He gestured toward the sergeant. "The Yank brought 'er in."

Both parents now approached Cawkins with profuse thank yous.

"Me and Lieutenant Hinton-Smith, of the Coldstream Guards," Cawkins said, pausing to let the words sink into Hensen's thick skull. "The lieutenant found her in the cemetery. Highgate. I was just along for the ride."

\* \* \*

The lieutenant's eyes jolted wide open. *De Belfort's* unearthly form was moving towards them. Hinton-Smith quickly shoved Elizabeth to the side. "Run," he shouted at her, but she fell to the corner, astonished, her hands covering her open mouth. He now faced *de Belfort*. "Here I am. Take my soul or whatever it is you want."

Suddenly, Hinton-Smith found himself being lifted and hurled into the middle of the street. He hit the pavement and tumbled over. As he struggled to regain his bearings, he heard a familiar voice in his head.

"I will take it," *de Belfort* said. "My conscience lo these long years weighs heavily upon me, and I prefer to have your consent. But make no mistake in thinking me kind. I do not believe you have yet attained a point of willingness, such as I desire." Now, his voice sounded like the hissing of a viper. "If you don't readily acquiesce, I will take it anyway and it will be all the worse for your friends. Do not be so foolish as to think you can save them. A lesson must be taught, that you do not delay a second time. Behold."

Hinton-Smith's head was violently jerked upward. There, suspended above him at the top of the doorframe, was Elizabeth. She was different somehow, but he could not quite understand why. Everything about her seemed a dark crimson. Her arms were outstretched as if she was coming to hug him once more, but she was not moving. Her dark brown eyes were vacant: there was no life in them. It hit him forcefully. She was dead, the redness, her own blood.

Hinton-Smith was mesmerized as he stared up at her. He could only watch as a newly formed scowl formed on her once beautiful features. Her face was an infernal death mask glaring down at him, serving to remind him that he had failed her. He could not take his eyes off her wretched, accusing glare.

Elizabeth's body, which *de Belfort* had suspended next to the door as if hanging her out to dry on a gruesome hook, finally acted as if it was dead, and subject to the laws of gravity. It fell down, but then tumbled over itself, moving across the street and hurtling directly at him.

Hinton-Smith tried to shuffle backward, crab-like and out of the way, but Elizabeth's body fell into him, collapsing his arms and legs and settling to a stop right on top of him, her face to his. He could feel her warm, red blood washing over him, soaking his shirt, when the voice once more rang in his ears: "Now, my patience is at an end. Consider this. You must meet me in the cemetery by the tomb. It is there that we will become one. If you fail me, I will not kill you, but you might very well wish I had. For if you do not come by the time of the dawn, you will have no one left in this world that is dear to you, and you alone will be responsible for their deaths! I've taken Elizabeth from you. Others will follow. It is your decision. The sooner you appear, the better it will be for them. You must be willing. Adieu."

Hinton-Smith slowly sat up, cradling Elizabeth in his arms. He lifted her head onto his lap, and started to caress her hair.

"Lizzie, my Lizzie. Of course I forgive you," he said sorrowfully. "And please, please, forgive me as well."

## CHAPTER 39

# FILLING IN THE HOLES

While the Bobby questioned Kate, Cawkins used the time to figure out a plan. Wilson, if Hinton-Smith figured it right, had left to help them. If he went to the cemetery to find the gravediggers, he should have been there roughly the same time they had run into the Germans. So, he probably tried to find them at their flat, first off. They wouldn't be there because they were killed. Cyrus wouldn't know that, so he would reckon they went to their posts with the emergency teams, in which case there wouldn't be anything to worry about. But what if Wilson thought they went back to the cemetery? If Cyrus went there, then there was a lot to worry about. Where was *de Belfort?* His best guess was the bastard would have to return to his hole. Hinton-Smith must have gone to the cemetery. The other doesn't matter. Now, how could he convince these lame-brained Bobbies to take him there?

*     *     *

Not long after his most recent depredation, a now delicate, brooding figure slowly and surreptitiously crossed the grounds of Old Highgate on his way back to the ancient cemetery. With what remained of a mind that was once luminous in its brilliance, he thought about what had brought him to this turning point—a last chance at freedom. Like an eighty-year-old man, who still feels like a youth in his own mind, he still felt that he was a man, though the remnants of his humanity had disappeared long, long ago. Though his senses were much diminished, he could smell the smoke from the fires, and the stink of his own foul odor; he could feel the cold that seemed to follow him everywhere; and taste the warm blood that had sometimes splattered from his hapless victims to his lips, even hear their helpless screams. But he now had the intuition that his thought processes and physical means were declining, and seemingly in direct proportion with the time he was away from his prison.

He was aware that he had once more taken other human life, but he was not certain why he hated so intensely. And although that had never quite mattered to him before, he wondered about it, and whether all the so-called power he had accumulated was worth his captivity or his depravity. It was very hard for him to think. He could ask questions, but could not find the concentration to focus long enough to consider any answers. He now was sure he had been out far too long. He could feel his energy dissipating by the minute. Had he used up so much force in killing the woman? The others?

*De Belfort* would have taken Hinton-Smith right then if not for this weakness. He knew he could kill no more until he was restored.

Why did he feel this total enervation? Was it really because he was out of the tomb? That made no sense to him. Whyntowne had constructed the vault to keep him in, not to give him more power. Perhaps this Whyntowne had learned more than he after all. If the tomb could restore him, then he would keep returning to it.

This made it even more important to meld his body with that of the lieutenant.

Before the discovery of Hinton-Smith and this night's taste of freedom—the first for him since he was entombed—finding an end to his existence would have been far preferable to remaining a prisoner in the grave. Now, there was an alternative much more to his liking.

He was curious: would the grave restore his powers? He had no idea, but he anticipated it was so. He was certain he must regain strength for his own safety and to accomplish the transference with Hinton-Smith. He must hurry. The vigor he felt this night, the omnipotence he felt for the first time in what must be so many hundreds of years, had been exhilarating and he was eager to return and see, for there were always some certainties.

If this age was similar to most other ages, there would be those who would want him to pay for his malevolence, and that small bit of humanity that remained, told him he should rest in a safe place until once more whole. His nighttime activities had left him weakened, and after so many years in the same place, even though it was in essence his prison, the foul tomb served also as his only sanctuary. How ironic that he would share it with his persecutors.

He was very impressed with how the methods of destruction had improved over the many years, and wished, with whatever human sentiments still existed in his worn-out shell and worn-out mind, whose sentience by now was more animal than man, he understood and could command such powers. It amused him to think that mankind had little matured or civilized itself over the centuries. It was obvious that some new crusade was presently occupying men's attention, probably not much different than the wars he had experienced, but at a more cataclysmic rate of destruction. What he could have accomplished with powers such as these.

*Guillaume de Belfort* was by now not much better than a depraved, rabid beast, albeit with an innate facility for cunning and deceit still functioning. He felt quite at home with the immense devastation the modern day humans were able to perpetrate. Ironically, with all his centuries-old wisdom in a state of great diminution, he misunderstood and underestimated the power and frequency with which this devastation could occur.

*   *   *

Cyrus Wilson was weak and stiff from fatigue, but he was resolved to even the score. Slowly getting up, he stretched his arms skyward, coughed to clear his throat and headed toward the Lebanon Circle, from whence, he had decided, to resume his search.

As he reached the Egyptian Avenue, he suddenly changed his mind about the Circle. No one would be there. If those bastards were even in the cemetery, they would probably go looking at the parts that were hit by the bombing. They should be cleaning if they were working. But he figured they were grave robbing, or body snatching, them lot, and that would take them to the same area. That's what Hinton-Smith would reckon. That's where he'd go. Perhaps he's even here.

Wilson had never noticed how deathly quiet this place was at night, and he did not want to overstay his welcome. It was a lot different than looking out at it from his upstairs window. For the first time he understood that Elizabeth's fears were no joke. He looked up at the lonesome cedar tree. The western cemetery was just too large for one man to search. He knew this. He could see the bloody place from his house. He should have tried to rouse Cawkins.

Looking up to the north, he could just see the rooftop of his own house, and he wished he was there right now and out of this muck. At least it helped him get his bearings.

As he thought of all the work he was going through to get to those twits, it made him angrier and even more desirous of revenge.

After the briefest of deliberations, he decided to follow the great swath of destruction and torn up earth, with its overturned monuments and upended trees. It formed a relatively straight if grizzly trail through the darkness.

His heart was beating fast, and he was relieved to not have to pass the Terrace Catacombs, with all of those dreadful cadavers entombed above ground. That was no place for a corpse. A man should be buried six feet under. He wanted no part of that lot this time of night.

Wilson soon came upon a yew-lined dirt path, paralleling the mutilated ground, and much easier to walk upon. But as soon as he reached the trail and started forward, a slight movement to the right caught his eye. Wilson raised his shotgun and directed his beam as he left the path, squinting and walking through knee-high vegetation in the direction of the wall that bordered the Holly Lodge Estate. There it was, the wall, only twenty feet from the path. Cyrus turned his light on what looked like a clump of clothes. Maybe a man's jacket, he supposed. It looked familiar.

"Dammit," he said out loud. "Where are they?" Wilson had to stop. Moving a few yards past the soiled jacket, he felt something, but had no idea what it was. Shining his torch all around, he shivered and his palms went clammy. There was a sense of evil there. No. It was an overwhelming power, and evil did not do it justice. It made him want to *do* evil. There was a powerful hatred that hated with so much fervor, it could kill with only the emotion, nothing else needed. It was the first time in his life that he realized how close humans were to the beasts of the forest; the first time he realized that he could kill in cold blood, and any human could as well.

The reverie lasted only seconds, and as he backed up, he found himself sweating profusely, but he seemed to have moved out of range of this diabolic field. The venomous thoughts diminished as he retreated. His shirt, trousers, and even jacket were soaked through with sweat, and he felt that a great battle for his soul had been won this night.

Wilson had to sit. This was it. He had enough for one night and the bastards could wait until morning. I'm old, Wilson thought. I cannot keep this up all night. Wilson needed some tea, something to eat. He sat down on a bench, reckoning a few minutes would do. Looking to the north he tried to see his house but he was now too far into the cemetery. Everything was blocked from view by the surrounding trees.

Right. Time to go. Wilson stood up and began to walk back.

But there was something. Another glimmer of movement. The second sign of life he had seen since entering the cemetery, but only a faint glimmer. Were those bastards playing him for the fool?

Strange though, he had not heard a thing.

"Bert Jones, you twit. Is that you?" Wilson yelled.

He squinted his eyes to peer through hazy darkness and focused his torch in that direction. "Will Baker!"

Probably a bloody rat.

There was the motion again. It was much closer than he had thought, and he could now see it was much larger, the size and shape of a man, but in the dim light and smoke, the boundaries of the shape were indefinite. Wilson walked in its direction. It seemed to be beckoning to him. The figure was slight. Perhaps it was Hinton-Smith.

"Michael?" Cyrus called out questioningly. He felt queasiness in his stomach and without even realizing he was doing it, he instinctively began to raise his shotgun.

\*    \*    \*

Cawkins realized there was only one thing he could do. He had to get moving. This moron was wasting too much time, disappearing for God knows what reason.

"Officer," he called to Hensen, who, satisfied with his interrogation, had gone into the superintendent's office to brew more tea. "Officer Hensen."

"Yes, yes," Hensen said from the other room. He soon emerged, carrying a tray with five cups of steaming tea. By now, Nigel and Tommy had been bedded down in one of the cells, and Maggie and Kate were quickly fading. The ladies were handed two of the cups, Cawkins, the duty officer, and Hensen himself, took the other three.

He went out to brew tea? Cawkins could not believe it, but he knew he had to remain agreeable. If somehow this bloke ever gets in my unit...

"Constable," Cawkins said, taking a brief sip. "I've been weighing all the boy's options, and I think I've figured out where he is...Highgate Cemetery." He would never convince Hensen of what was really behind the murders, but what he could do was lead him to the cemetery and Hinton-Smith. If nothing more, there would be one more man to help with the dirty work.

Hensen made up his mind quickly, sipping the last of his tea while walking to the door. "Humph," he said, as though it were a hollow victory. "I should've known that. Returning to the scene, eh? They all do. Just remember," he said, focusing a stern eye on the sergeant. "You may not be under arrest, but I'll be watching you."

"That's fair warning," Cawkins said grimly, as he followed the officer. Too bad he couldn't give the Bobby the same fair warning about what they were about to encounter.

They had barely walked one city block when they met up with two very distraught officers. George Wingate had found what was left of two victims. Both constables, though veterans on the force, looked completely unnerved. Wingate said, "There's a blood trail. Awful it is."

"So," asked Hensen, expecting the worst. "What did it lead to?"

"We didn't have the nerve, Nick," said the other Bobby, graven-faced and almost ashamed.

"What? What do you mean?"

"We didn't follow it, damn it!" snapped Wingate. "You didn't see what we saw, so don't be so fast in making judgments."

"I'm not making anything. Have you seen a young lad?" Hensen asked.

"I haven't seen anybody, livin' anyway, for the last hour. Why?" asked Wingate.

"We'll see," answered Hensen. "I have a bad feeling about this."

"Bad feeling!" the other Bobby exclaimed. "Are you serious? I just saw enough to give anybody an 'orrible feeling."

"Something tells me this ain't anything to do with the bombing," Hensen said. He was just now beginning to wonder how many this madman managed to do away with. It made no sense. Was he another Jack the Ripper? "Show me the way. We're following that trail." He looked at Cawkins. "I want you all backing me up."

"I told you," Cawkins said with exasperation. "He went to the cemetery. We don't have time to go off on a god damn goose chase."

Hensen looked him over contemptuously. "I'll make the decisions here, and you'll do what I say," he said. "Maybe this will lead us to your lad."

Cawkins stopped arguing. It could be that *de Belfort* was out of the cemetery. For the first time he hoped Hensen was right.

The four of them hurried down Highgate Hill Street, remarkably untouched and stark in its quiet and normalcy, toward Cromwell Avenue, and into the wreckage, a very nervous Wingate leading the way.

*     *     *

The strange figure moved toward Cyrus Wilson, in slow, almost human steps. "What are you?" Cyrus cried out as it drew closer. "Bloody hell," he yelled. "You're a bloody corpse! Stop! Stop right there!" he ordered. Cyrus stared with wide eyes, as he leveled his gun at the risen corpse. He inadvertently backed up as though he had no control of his legs. Approaching him was the most god-awful thing he had ever seen. It was a corpse. Just bones, covered with some skin, some muscle tissue, and a horrific stench. It was not as if he had not seen more deteriorated bodies, in either war, or just now in the cemetery. It was a matter of this dead thing coming towards him. It could not be real. It had to be some bloody illusion. But the dead body seemed to hang motionless in the air, and to his horror, now hurtled over the ten feet separating them. Cyrus Wilson fired the shotgun, but the blast had no effect as the creature crashed into him. He could feel the dirt and grime and sticky flesh rub against his face and mouth, smothering him. He spat out as he fell under the weight, trying to keep any of that revolting flesh from entering his mouth. Hitting the ground was painless, or at least the adrenaline coursing through his body helped him ignore it. Grunting and growling with every effort, he shoved his shotgun against it for all he was worth, and was surprised to see the corpse was light, just as he would have suspected a half-disintegrated body to be. So how the hell was it able to force him down? And what in the world was it doing, ripping through the air, anyway? It flew away from him, and broke up in the doing, but he felt something else. Now there was tremendous pressure on his back. Had he broken it, or at least injured it in the fall? But it was increasing. All the blood seemed to be flowing to his head. It felt tremendously heavy, and bloated, like it was full to bursting. What was doing this to him?

\* \* \*

Hinton-Smith gently rolled Elizabeth's body to the ground, placing her head down last. He stood up and took off his jacket and gently covered Elizabeth's silent form.

Suddenly, the lieutenant froze. His eyes slammed shut and he became completely motionless. Then he went into a paroxysm of pain and anguish, screaming at the top of his lungs, "No! No! Please don't. I beg you!" His body seemed to shrivel up, and he squeezed himself about the shoulders with greater and greater intensity. As he fell to the dirty street, his eyes closed so tightly, the sockets ceased to exist. Hinton-Smith now viewed the death of Cyrus Wilson. He was seeing it through the eyes of *de Belfort*. The lieutenant felt as though he was going into a seizure.

As abruptly as it had begun, the struggle ended. He sat up and pulled his legs to his chest. He sat still, his head buried between his knees. Then, thundering in his ears, the startling admonition: "Jack Cawkins is next!" The lieutenant jumped up and started to sprint toward the cemetery. There was no choice.

He hurried past an officer sitting on a bench who seemed totally unaware of the nightmare.

"Get out of here!" Hinton-Smith yelled as he ran by, but the soldier didn't move.

\*  \*  \*

Wingate showed them the first body. It was the older, fat man the young lieutenants had nicknamed Falstaff. This one was not so bad. But the next, Lieutenant Malcolm's, was hardly anything identifiable as human remains. Aside from the BEF uniform, what was left of him just seemed to be foul meat and broken bones. A pack of wild animals could not have done a better job. It was then they heard Hinton-Smith's dismal scream. They rushed down the street to the corner, then cut through a bombed out pharmacy and across the ruins of an apartment building.

As they ran onto Cholmeley Park, they saw even worse devastation, and there, fifty yards down, on the side of the street, next to a doorframe standing amidst all the rubble and broken-up bricks and concrete, was a lonely figure under a blanket.

Hensen crouched down to look. He lifted the edge of the cloth, and Cawkins bent over to look. "My God," the sergeant exclaimed. "This is terrible. Oh God."

"What?" Hensen asked. "Who is it?"

"Elizabeth Hammond. She's the sister of the girl in the station. The one I came in with." He stood up and shook his head, sorrowfully. "She was Hinton-Smith's fiancée."

Hensen bent over to look. "Right. I've seen her. What do you mean was?"

"She left him."

"We'll send somebody to pick her up," Hensen said, now almost sick to his stomach. "What a waste. She shouldn't just lie here." He put his hand on Cawkins's shoulder, but this time, almost sympathetically.

"Think, man. Could this be another revenge killing?" He stared at the sergeant, but no answer was forthcoming. Cawkins could not wait any longer. He started heading southwest down Cholmeley Park. Quickly the officers started after him. He had not moved thirty yards when he stopped abruptly, holding up his hand to signal Hensen and the other officers to stop.

"What now?" Hensen asked plaintively.

There was a man on a park bench facing away from them. Dressed in an army officer's khaki uniform, he sat as though oblivious to the horrendous murders, or even to the bombing; having a quiet night relaxing, smoking a cigar, perhaps a few more pleasant reminiscences on the bench.

As they approached, Cawkins noticed that the man was shaking, almost imperceptibly.

"Jesus," Cawkins cried as he reached the front of the bench. "What's wrong with him?"

"Lieutenant," Cawkins asked. "Are you all right?"

There were strange reverberating sounds, issuing forth in a tortured staccato as the man tried to speak. Roberts sputtered, shaking a bit more than before, and stared, terrified, straight at them. A spot of blood appeared at the top of his forehead. As they gawked, other spots appeared in a straight line down the front of Roberts' face, as if on a seam. His fear seemed to become greater, and the shaking, more violent, as the thin cigar dropped from his hand. But it was not a cigar. It was a strip of dead, hardened flesh. Roberts started to split apart on his own seam, his flesh and bones coming apart, as though a man with an axe was cutting a block of wood for the fire.

Cawkins grabbed the boy by the shoulders, trying to hold him together. He felt nausea welling up in his belly as his eye glanced past the poor soldier, and caught sight of the dark red blood trail continuing in the same direction, back toward Highgate cemetery. Even in the dim light, he could follow it fifty yards down the street. "Look," he said, taking off his jacket and pointing at the blood on the street. He handed the jacket to the third constable. "I don't know if it'll do any good," he said. "But bind him in this, until we can send help."

Hensen felt a hot streak running down his back, as he looked at the telltale trail. He would have bet his life that the lieutenant was on his way to the cemetery to cover the last of his tracks.

"Come on," Cawkins shouted, grabbing Hensen and Wingate by the arms. "We gotta move it!"

*    *    *

Hinton-Smith ran like he'd never run before. No race, no track meet or soccer game had ever seen him move like this. He cleared the five-foot fence surrounding Waterlow Park, hardly breaking stride, and he glided over the soft, browning grass of the park as if on wings. The farthest gate on the west was open and he streaked through it to the North Gate. Only then did he pause.

There, impaled upon the wrought-iron spears of the North Gate, was the tall man in black. The wry smile gone, blood seeping from his wounds, his eyes frozen wide open. How can you impale a ghost, Hinton-Smith wondered. And he could not help himself, moving closer and putting his hand forward to feel the strange creature. His hand hit solid flesh, but then the body started to rapidly deteriorate, right before his eyes, going from warm flesh to cool bones and finally dust in only seconds. Another betrayal paid. Nothing was left save ragged clothing and the top hat.

Hinton-Smith climbed the gate, clambering over the jutting spikes, and jumped down to the other side. Then he sprinted up the path for a hundred yards, before diverging off into the tall grasses, shrubbery, nettles, ivy and tombs, towered over by great sycamores, ash and yews. Any thoughts of revenge, of outwitting *de Belfort* or of trapping him back in the tomb were gone. There was only the hope to save Jack and Kate. Nothing else mattered. He would give himself up.

There was no trail through this part of Highgate and the only light came from the few stars peaking through the clouds of smoke, but the lieutenant continued on at breakneck speed, jumping over monuments and fallen trees, and veering toward every opening in the jungle-like thickness along the way.

His sense of direction was unerring and he soon came to the old wall of the ancient cemetery. As he scaled the black stone, he heard *de Belfort's* voice in his ears: "It is well you have come. But look yonder and see the price of your irresolution, and waver no more!"

As Hinton-Smith peered through the darkness, he heard a rustling sound. Looking in that direction, he saw a small mound. It began to move. A collapsed shape, quite vague in the dim light, rose slowly from the dirt. The semi-round silhouette was connected to a trunk that seemed to be dark red and khaki. Soon it was held up by two trembling sticks—its arms, and still rising. The lieutenant could see the thing had been a man. Now on legs, and at its full height, it reached down and picked up a round object, the size of a soccer ball and affixed it to the top of its form. In horror, the lieutenant recognized the ball as the battered head of Cyrus Wilson, dead, bloody, crushed and twisted into contortions of pain. Now the figure lurched toward him. When only a few feet from the lieutenant, the pathetic corpse dropped to the ground, thrown off, lifeless. *Guillaume de Belfort's* ghostly black form, replete in rusted chain mail, stood in its place.

"Thus to the friend of one who betrays *de Belfort*," rang in Hinton-Smith's ears.

An unmitigated rage welled up in the lieutenant. In a paroxysm of fury and energy, Hinton-Smith lunged at the evil shroud-like apparition, his arms flailing as he tried to hit or find some physical part to grasp, to destroy his tormentor. "You bastard!" he screamed. "You SOB!" But it was all for naught. His enraged fists passed right through the ghostly knight. Again and again he swung until he collapsed with fatigue.

*Guillaume De Belfort* laughed mournfully. "I'm sorry. Alas, I cannot thus die. Would that it were possible." His tone once more became strident as he said, "Now join me."

*De Belfort* started to move directly to his grave, but hesitated for a fraction of a second in his progress, shifting more in a circle, as if avoiding the tombstone, and entering from the far side. He performed this brief detour without drawing too near the stone. "I believe you now understand your course. I wait upon you, sir." Even after all those years, he had not figured out how his contemporaries had held him in, though now, his suspicion that it was simply the stone, seemed to be proven, and so he was respectfully circumspect and vigilant.

It was as if an epiphany to Hinton-Smith. *De Belfort* avoided the headstone. That was it. It all made sense now. If *de Belfort* needed his body, he must not be able to stay long out of the tomb in this present form. He had no intention of returning to India. *Jack!* Good old Jack was right. *De Belfort needed his body to return to life.* Hinton-Smith intently watched the malefic spirit's departure, now certain that the stone must keep him in, but he knew intuitively he must not think about it. He could not give away his plans. The lieutenant forced himself to visualize the deaths of Elizabeth and Cyrus, no matter how painful, as *de Belfort* descended into the grave. Hinton-Smith wondered how much more of this nightmare he could take. He fought back the numerous thoughts and speculations about *de Belfort*, and concentrated on the villainous deaths. If he was going to defeat this thing, he had to hide his thoughts. Perhaps there was a way. He had to convince *de Belfort* he had given up.

*   *   *

In this he was wrong. *De Belfort* felt some of his strength returning, gradually but certainly entering his limbs as he went deeper and deeper into the hole. He wasted no time in trying to divine the lieutenant's thoughts. They were meaningless to him, for he knew Hinton-Smith was powerless to stop him. All humankind was, and there were none left of the Hospitallers who possessed the secret knowledge equivalent to his own.

*De Belfort* laughed at those same knights who foolishly buried themselves along with him. Why had they not arisen to stop him? Was not that why they were buried? What a waste of their lives!

Now *de Belfort* had more important things to deliberate. He continued to question his prison and his relation to it. Did this loathsome vault indeed replenish his strength? Did the Hospitallers intend it that the same power that imprisoned him, was at the same time, the source of his strength. Had the knights figured out how to, in effect, tether him to this hole in the ground? What if he took the lieutenant's body and still grew weak away from the tomb? At the very least he would have his vengeance.

He had done good work this night. He had achieved a measure of revenge. He wondered if his hate had not kept him alive as much or more than his vaunted powers, or those which seemed to be vested in his prison.

Michael Hinton-Smith, he thought with some satisfaction. It had worked out well with him. He should understand how little choice he has. He will now yield to save the last of his friends.

"The sins of the fathers shall be visited upon the sons, Michael Hinton-Smith." How implausible that the last living ancestor of the Hospitaller who imprisoned him, would chance upon their graves. Thus does fate work. And he would reveal this last to Hinton-Smith at the exact moment of transference. It would be the lieutenant's final thought. *De Belfort* would live in his body, and his revenge would live for eternity.

And what made it better yet was he would make the transference right over Sir Charles Whyntowne's grave. How fitting.

*   *   *

As soon as *de Belfort* disappeared, Hinton-Smith rushed up to the stone and tried to push it toward the pit, but it was too heavy. He strained to lift the corner of the tombstone in order to topple it end over end or lever it to the hole, but he could not budge it. Looking around the piles of dirt, wrenched from the earth during the bombing, the lieutenant found the combustibles, grenades and the can of kerosene he and Cawkins left earlier. Should he dump them in the hole or place the grenades under the slab to try to move it? No. It might destroy it and then there'd be no way to keep *de Belfort* in. Damn it! He needed help to lever the stone.

As he picked them up, the light from a torch hit his eyes.

"Hinton-Smith," Hensen shouted out. "Stand down, you bastard. Hands above yer head. It's over."

With a quick glance at the new interlopers, Hinton-Smith ran over to the tombstone, threw the cardboard and paper into the hole, and started to pour the kerosene onto it. "Good. C'mon, then. I need help. We have to move the slab."

Hensen sprinted over the grounds and tackled the lieutenant, knocking the kerosene can to the ground and spilling most of the contents into the hole.

Cawkins now hurried over to the two men on the ground.

"What have you done, man?" Hensen shouted. Hinton-Smith feverishly tried to wrestle free, but he was too weak. "You need to help me!" he yelled as he struggled. "We have to destroy this grave!" But Hensen had his arms pinned fast to his sides.

"Oh no," said Wingate, only a few feet away. "Look here. Another one. My God! Just his head!" Wingate crouched down over what remained of Wilson. "I know 'im," he said. "Wilson! Cyrus Wilson."

Cawkins pried the constable away from Hinton-Smith and pulled him up, as another Bobby rushed up to help Hensen.

Angrily wrenching his arms away from Cawkins, Hensen marched over to Wilson's corpse. "Look at this!" he screamed. "Bring your boy here, sergeant! Let 'im see 'is work!"

The two soldiers could only stand and stare. Then before Cawkins could stop him, Hensen walked up to Hinton-Smith and slapped him across the face. The Bobby grabbed him by both arms and shook him violently. "How could you do it? I don't give a damn about those bullies, but how could you murder your girlfriend and the others, for God's sakes? This Cyrus Wilson, he was a harmless old man!"

Cawkins separated them again, this time keeping a firm grip on the Bobby.

The lieutenant looked back toward the still smoldering hole, as if the fiend would reappear at any moment. How far were they away from it? Did it even matter? He had to get Cawkins out of here, fast. *De Belfort* could kill every man of them in seconds and he'd go for Cawkins first. *Why hasn't he come back? Is he too weak? Is he toying with me?*

"Let me go," Hensen growled at the sergeant, struggling feebly against his grasp. "I'm all right. I won't touch him."

"I'd say you better not, pal," said Cawkins threateningly.

"Right. Don't worry," he shouted back at Cawkins. "But he's under arrest. George," he called to the other officer. "Take this bloody bastard to the station."

Wingate roughly put his hand on the lieutenant's shoulder, and the third Bobby took hold of the lieutenant's opposite arm. All three policemen now looked at Cawkins as if daring the sergeant to stop them.

"Hold on!" Cawkins bellowed, stepping directly in front of the constables. "You're not taking him anywhere!"

The lieutenant looked sadly at the ground where Wilson lay, shaking his head. "You just don't get it, do you?" he said. But he was trying to think. He could not let Jack fight with them. He had to get him moving.

"Be careful with him, George," Hensen ordered. "I'll seal off the area for the investigation,"

"Don't you understand anything? The boy didn't murder anybody," Cawkins yelled as Wingate and the others roughly prodded the lieutenant forward. "No human could do that! Cyrus was his stepfather for Christ sakes!"

"And you," Hensen said, addressing Cawkins. "You'd best mind your own business or we'll throw you in with him."

"Why you dimwitted SOB," Cawkins shouted. But before he could take his wrath out on the officer, Hinton-Smith had figured out his plan.

"Don't get yourself in trouble, mate," he said calmly as the officers started pushing him forward. "You don't have time. Take Kate. Take the children. Take your wife and yourself as far away as possible. It is imperative. Go! Now! I know what I have to do." There was only one possible solution.

"I can handle these twits," Cawkins said, fists clenched. "I'll thrash the lot of them with pleasure."

"No, Jack, please," Hinton-Smith said. "Think of the others. Their safety."

"You're sure that's what you want?" Cawkins asked, not sure it was the right move. He was ready to thrash somebody.

"Bollocks to you both," Hensen screamed. Their conversation meant nothing to him. "Keep moving!"

"No time to talk, Jack," Hinton-Smith said quietly. "*De Belfort* said you're next. Don't just walk, run!"

Cawkins still hesitated, though it did not take much to understand the implications. One of them had to get everybody out. He started backing away, his eyes still on Hinton-Smith.

"Are you sure?"

"Go! Now!"

All the Bobbies stared intently at the lieutenant, ready for anything. Each one of them wondered if he might try to murder them. What indeed was he capable of?

The lieutenant saw their fear. Perhaps he could use it. "I won't resist," Hinton-Smith said to Hensen, as the sergeant turned and started running out of the cemetery.

"I can control myself. But I have two conditions."

"You have nothing!" Hensen bellowed.

"You say I've done these things," the lieutenant said calmly. "If you don't want me to continue, perhaps with you and your lads, you better listen."

"Listen to him," Wingate said, visibly trembling.

"Right," said the other constable. He was tensed up, on his guard.

This was taking too long, Hinton-Smith thought. At least Jack was out of there.

"Just help me move this headstone back in place. And let me cover the old man up. That's it. Quickly now."

Hensen looked at him quizzically, then took off his jacket and started to put it over Cyrus Wilson.

"No," the lieutenant said. "Hand it to me. I'll do it. He was my father."

"And you'll come peaceably?" Hensen asked, confusion in his voice. Why the tombstone? What was his angle? Now he wondered why the boy wanted Cawkins to take everyone out of there. Hensen nervously glanced at the fallen tombstones.

"Right," Hinton-Smith said. "On my word. As an officer and gentleman."

Hensen picked up Wilson's shotgun and held it on the boy.

"Just don't try anything," he said, while nodding to the others to move the headstone. "I won't hesitate to blow your bloomin' head off."

The lieutenant took the coat, kneeled down and gently placed it over Cyrus Wilson's remains.

"Cyrus," he said, tears starting to run down his cheeks. "You were a good man, the best. I'll never forget you."

Hinton-Smith said it quickly and stood. He looked with concern at the officers as they struggled with the tombstone. "If they cannot move it they better come with us."

Grabbing the lieutenant by the arm, Hensen walked away quickly with his quarry.

Wingate and the other Bobbie tried everything from levering, to pushing to lifting, but in the end they could not budge the stone slab. They were lucky. They left before *Guillaume De Belfort* had regained enough strength to bother with them.

*       *       *

Not much later, Hensen and the other Bobbies finished their oral reports to the superintendent.

In a holding area of solitary confinement, consisting of an eight-by-ten barren cell, with only a toilet, sink, an uncomfortable looking bunk bed, all attached to the walls, so the prisoner could not throw them around if he decided to have a fit, and padded all the way around with four inches of soft cushioning, in case he decided to end it all by bashing his brains out, was Hinton-Smith, in a straitjacket, and still in his oversized clothes. The boy had a blank expression on his face.

This was all done at the request of the lieutenant, with the additional provision that everyone stay as far away as possible. Food was to be lowered from a ceiling grate. No one was to come near. No visitors allowed. In exchange for these "favors," Hinton-Smith would confess to the murders. There would be no trial, no appeal. He would be transferred within the hour to a hospital for the criminally insane, far out of London, where he would be similarly sequestered till the end of his days.

The lieutenant reckoned there had to be a reason *de Belfort* wanted him and him alone. Why else would he have gone to all this trouble? There must have been any number of bodies he could have used on this night alone. Perhaps it was his ancestry, that *de Belfort* was still fighting battles of centuries ago. But if he was the only one suitable for this "transference," he could use that against him. If *de Belfort* could indeed take over his body without consent, he would find himself similarly contained, this time in a corporeal body that hopefully would not be able to break constraints, and probably then viewed as the madman the authorities figured Hinton-Smith already was. He prayed no one got too close, and fell under his power. If *de Belfort* could wander this far and still have his strength, then all bets were off anyway. He must get far away.

\*    \*    \*

Cawkins ran all of the way back to the police station, beating the officers by a good ten minutes. There was a great fear in his heart, and not a little anger as well. He would follow Hinton-Smith's exhortations, but only to a point. He was going to destroy that bastard in the grave or die failing. Bursting into the station, he found Kate and Maggie. "There's going to be another bombing. Get ready to leave. Wake the children!" He did not allow them time for questions. It was the first story he came up with, it was somewhat logical, and it was a hell of a lot easier to explain than the real thing. "Kate," he said. "Michael's all right. He asked me to take everyone to the country. Now." With the children dressed and ready to go, he persuaded them to go on ahead of him. It was not easy, but it was the rare civilian who could resist a sergeant major's orders. It had been harder yet to find one of the few cabs operating after curfew, but the duty officer managed it for him.

They would gather up the boy's mother on the way. There was to be no dissent.

As soon as they had driven out of sight, he started toward the cemetery. Approaching the North Gate, he looked at his timepiece. They should be well on their way out of Highgate by now, and on the road to Bridgwater.

The sky to the east was starting to lighten. He hurried through the North Gate and down the path leading to the Egyptian Avenue. But now, the distinct, shrill sound of the air raid sirens again filled the air. Cawkins looked up. The steeple of St. Michael's towered over the mausoleum to his right. In back of the steeple, searchlights were once more tracing through the dawning sky. German planes were returning. The probability of them hitting the same area was small, but he made haste.

Sweating profusely as he came to the wall that had earlier crumbled under Bert Jones' weight, he scrambled over the rubble, into the unholy place. His hands trembled fiercely, as he surveyed the grounds. The drone of the Dorniers and Heinkels was soon heard, then the rhythmic *pom pom pom* of the anti-aircraft guns, then the black puffs in the sky as the shells exploded, searching for the bellies of the bombers. Soon new explosions erupted in the city.

In the vast catacomb beneath the graveyard, *de Belfort* was only now feeling the whole of his strength returned to his being. He had his answer: if he stayed out too long in his present form, he might disintegrate altogether, but if he stayed near the grave, he could replenish. This place kept him captive, but kept him alive and strong. The why no longer mattered. It would not be long before Hinton-Smith joined him and he would finally be free. It was time to collect his soul. And time to take another of his friends.

Cawkins found everything near the fallen tombstone: the lamps, the paraffin, the flammables and the two grenades. The can of kerosene was three-quarters empty, but the cardboard still stank of it. He hurriedly poured the paraffin into the lamps and lit the incendiaries, all the while thinking it was nowhere near enough. A faint whistling came from high above and Cawkins knew this bomb was going to be close. He gathered the materials and ran the few feet to the open grave. Crouching down beside *de Belfort's* underground chamber, his hands still shaking, he dropped the combustibles into the hole, then drenched them with the rest of the kerosene.

The whistling was quickly becoming louder. It *would be* close.

Cawkins ran back to get the lamps and the other kindling. He returned and dumped everything into the grave, pulled the pins from the grenades and dropped them in as well. "I hope you enjoy this, pal," he said, and kicked the empty kerosene can in for good measure.

Now Cawkins sprinted as fast as he could and dove behind the rubble of the wall, just as he heard two muffled explosions. The grenades, he thought. He covered his head with his hands just as a thousand pound bomb exploded with tremendous force, rocking the grounds of the entire cemetery with the force of an earthquake, and toppling the inscribed stone back over the still smoldering hole. In what must have been a mathematical improbability, the stone fell in the exact same position it had occupied for all those earlier centuries.

Cawkins peered over the fallen wall, and his jaw dropped as he saw the very ground near each of the surrounding graves began to tremble. Gaunt fingers burst through the soil, first from one of the graves, then another. Soon, whole skeletal arms appeared, then skulls, and shriveled torsos, until eight withered skeletons in rusted chain mail and armor emerged from the earth and shakily stood in a circle around *Guillaume de Belfort's* tomb. Each of the skeletal remains held a long stanchion, topped by a crystal. Through the haze Cawkins saw a blinding laser of blue light, travel from one of the crystals to the next and the next, until all eight were connected by the shimmering rays, making a prison of light around the central tombstone. Within an instant, Whyntowne and the others regained the form and knightly uniform of their youth: the skeletons were once more Knights of St. John. Now another beam of sheer white light traveled from one of the eight tombstones to the next until all the stones and the knights were connected. From the center of each of the eight knights and each of the eight tombstones, shot forth another beam of light, now bright crimson, directly at *de Belfort's* stone. With a blinding flash and the sound of an eerie, horrendous howl, which was later reported to be heard over the whole of Highgate, and reaching as far as Muswell Hill, Finchley and Hampstead Heath, tons of dirt and debris from every direction around the burial site, hurtled into the hole, effectively slamming shut and stopping up the tomb.

Cawkins grimaced and plugged his ears. The beams stayed focused on the central stone for a long time, seemingly bolstering the impediments to escape, as the stone heated up and the inscriptions glowed a fiery red that reflected off all the cemetery walls and beyond. The strange shriek lasted this entire time. Then slowly, the light faded into nothingness and disappeared, along with the long wailing cry. The knights seemed to greet each other as long lost friends, before slowly returning to their skeletal forms and into the earth, until no sign of them remained except their tombs.

When the smoke cleared from the cemetery, Cawkins stood up stiffly and stepped inside the ancient walls. The hole was once more filled and the stone again in place on top, looking uncannily similar to other quiet resting places, except for a few new abrasions in the medieval granite.

There was one thing Cawkins could not get out of his mind as he stared incredulously at the gruesome sentinels of stone, still intact, and guarding *de Belfort*. It was a question that has bothered almost every man who has gone to war, and under the circumstances, it bothered him greatly right now. How many bodies had they found? Had he not been over the same ground where many of them were murdered? Why the other fellow and not me? Why his time, and not mine? Why had *de Belfort* not fulfilled his threat and come out to claim him?

As a young soldier, he had heard many stories about the man-eaters of Northern India. Pilgrims might be sleeping in a secured area, or at least, what they thought and hoped was secure. A leopard, either too old to catch game, or wounded, or maybe even used to eating humans during a time of plague, might come into that place and grab the first person he came upon.

Once it was reported that a leopard actually crept over thirty pilgrims, who were sleeping overnight in a bungalow on the road between the holy shrines of Badrinath and Kedarnath, near a tributary of the Ganges River. The great cat selected one, and crept back over the others while carrying its victim, not even waking any of those at rest.

Cawkins exhaled deeply. "Maybe it's just luck. Plain and simple. Good luck, bad luck. That's all, and we've used up a major portion of ours, Mike and me."

He knew he had to somehow prove Hinton-Smith's innocence, but he had no idea how. Nevertheless, there was one more thing he could do. Sergeant Cawkins was not an uncomplicated man, but he did have a habit of tracing straight lines, and moving quite readily from cause to effect. It seemed to him, that of all the connecting circumstances, or dots, if you will, there was one that never should have taken place. And to his mind, if you eliminated that one occurrence, most of this would not have happened. Of course, he was wrong, in the sense that Hinton-Smith's own ancestry proved his undoing. But Cawkins could not have known that.

As he turned to climb back over the broken wall, he lowered his head to wipe his brow of sweat. "Holy Mother of God!" he exclaimed.

Laid out near the rubble in front of him was a treasure worthy of King Solomon's Mines.

*   *   *

In the jail's shelter, most of the Bobbies and criminals and bureaucrats huddled for shelter during these new explosions. Some were frightened, some were unconcerned, others just wanted it to be over so they could get on with what would be another very long day's work. But in one corner of an armored car making its way toward Sheffield in the north, a welcome serenity had come to the eyes of a frail-looking man in a straitjacket. He had no idea that Cawkins had gone back to the cemetery, and he would have been terrified to know that he did, for he cared to know only one thing. He had left Jack Cawkins alive. He had fulfilled his vow.

*   *   *

Late the next morning, Colonel *LeFevre* rolled over in bed, kissed an English barmaid, sat up and stretched his arms over his head, eager to start his day. He got up and dressed in his uniform and went outside to buy the Times at a local kiosk.

*LeFevre* approved of the carnage, not because he wanted the English to be beaten, he just wanted them to know some semblance of the suffering of the French and their cities.

Sitting down at an outdoor tavern, he ordered his usual strong black coffee, then buried his head in the paper and studied the war news. It was a warm, fall day, but hazed over by the still gray smoke of the fires.

His habit was to first read any article concerning France, whether about Vichy, the colonies, or the Free French of which he was a prominent part, then articles concerned with Britain's overseas adventures, particularly in North Africa, and finally, news about the Home Front in England: the possible invasion, the bombings, the air defense, etc.

The coffee arrived. No watered down English tea for him. Going back to the paper, while munching on a piece of white bread and a chunk of hard brown sugar, he came across an article concerning Highgate: an eyewitness account of last night's bombing. As he read on, a strange intensity came over him, one that he usually associated with war games or the actual battlefield. The twitch that he'd been burdened with ever since the fall of France, but that had abated somewhat since his work in England, now came back full force, sending his mustache up and down like a piston. As he became more engrossed, he could not help but read out loud: "And horrible it was, so we takes him in," said Constable Hensen. "Cleaning up this morning, we found the rest. And God help us! I've never seen anything like it. Even the old descriptions of the Ripper. There were seventeen dead in all and one we still 'aven't found. More like mangled beyond recognition, I says. All the same way. All in one night. God help us. And no more reports of deaths, or murders since his arrest, not even from the last bombing. You might say the proof's in the pudding. I didn't think a man could do that to another man. It was inhuman. Like an animal." A cooler voice added, "We've put the bloke in an institution for the criminally insane, and you can bet we'll be throwing away the key."

Hinton-Smith's name was never mentioned, but with the description of his alleged desertion, of his being shot in France, his amnesia and the subsequent concussion at Dunkirk, the colonel immediately knew who they were talking about. He jumped up from the table and shouted triumphantly, "Ah, see! *Voila!* I could have saved you the trouble."

Just as he raised his hand to slap it down on the table and punctuate his victory, he noticed, peculiarly, that standing in front of him was a thickset sergeant major in uniform.

"Are you Colonel *Maurice LeFevre?*" the stranger asked.

"*Oui,*" said the puzzled Frenchman.

Cawkins pulled back his right arm and fist and released the full force of it into the colonel's face, leaving *LeFevre* sprawled on the ground and soaking in scalding hot coffee and a bit of his own blood.

It was certainly not enough but it would have to do for now.

"Compliments of Sergeant Major Jack Cawkins, Lieutenant Michael Hinton-Smith and the Coldstream Guards," Cawkins said. Then he turned and walked away.

THE END

17783128R00293

Printed in Great Britain
by Amazon